The Janus Co

By Graeme Gibson

Published by Kilbryde Press 2014

First published on Kindle August 2103

Cover design by Flipside Creative

www.flipsidecreative.co.uk

For my wife

Acknowledgements

Thanks go to Kim and Sinclair Macleod of Indie Authors Scotland for all the help, guidance and inspiration given to me over recent months. The enthusiasm they imparted and the guidance they provided is beyond thanks. Also, to my friend J.W. (you know who you are) for the encouragement, pointers and constructive comments which brought this novel to final fruition. I don't think I would have made it without you. Thanks, too, to Louise of Flipside Creative for the design of the book cover...as I said, you're the professional! And finally, to my wife who has put up with many, many months of sighs and frustration as I wrote and re-wrote chapter after chapter

Prologue

Tuesday 31 October 1967 – Glasgow

It was a great day for a funeral, but words like "great" and "funeral" don't sit well together in the same sentence, Jamie Raeburn reflected gloomily. A dense pall of smoke and dust rose from the demolition works at the old Saracen Foundry and hung in the damp morning air, clinging to clothes and staining buildings. When absorbed into the moist autumn air it became almost viscous, filling nostrils and coating tongues. It was so thick you could taste it! And it was raining...again! *But when does it ever do anything else in this God forsaken city,* Jamie asked himself? He was disconsolate and miserable and wished he could be somewhere else, *anywhere* else, with the events of the last year completely erased from his memory, like chalk marks on a pavement washed away by the rain.

The early morning mist that had surrounded him like a protective ghost and penetrated into every nook and cranny of the city was lifting at last and he could now see the entire length of Saracen Street to its junction with Keppochhill Road. St. Gregory's, the first stop for the hearse and the two limousines waiting outside the close mouth, was hidden from sight behind the tenement buildings lining the roadway but the melancholy toll of its funeral bell could still be heard, reverberating off the surrounding factory chimneys and the old tenement walls.

A small crowd had gathered, shuffling about on the pavement outside the close, and Jamie felt uncomfortable with the eyes of this throng on him. He still blamed himself for Jack Connolly's death, even though doing so was irrational, and he still saw accusation in every sideways glance. *I'm just being paranoid* he told himself again for the umpteenth time.

Taking a final drag of his cigarette he braced himself to join Jack's family for his friend's final journey. He dropped the cigarette to the pavement and ground it angrily into the concrete with the sole of his shoe. Reluctantly, he allowed his eyes to wander to the hearse. The coffin was already installed, in full view, surrounded by gleaming brass fittings and by a mass of floral tributes.

He heard the family descend the stairs from the flat on the second floor. There was no conversation, just the heavy slap of soles and the click clack of heels on the cold, stone stairs. Jamie made his way into the close and waited, stepping aside into the passageway leading to the back court. Jack's mother led the family and greeted Jamie with a sad, stoical smile. She said nothing. Everything that needed to be said had been covered in the three weeks since her son's murder, the three weeks of Jamie's downward spiral into Hell.

Jack's father followed. A big man, straight backed and grave faced, looking strangely out of place in his charcoal grey Sunday suit and black coat, his lugubrious expression deepened by dark, heavy, rings around his eyes. The sisters came behind; Bernadette and Colette with Anne-Marie, the youngest, trailing them. Anne-Marie forced a smile and took hold of Jamie's arm as she passed. 'Stay with me, Jamie,' she pleaded quietly, her eyes filling with tears. He slipped his arm around her waist and fell into step with her, just ahead of Teresa O'Brien, Jack's fiancée of only a few weeks. Bringing up the rear were Jack's brothers - Liam, Gerard and Vincent - all of them grey faced, solemn.

Outside in the street, the crowd had swelled and people stood to both sides of the close like a guard of honour. Jack's mother, as usual, took charge. Apart from his own mother, Jamie had never known a woman with such fortitude and strength of character. She pointed the family to the waiting cars, directing Jamie to the second limousine where he was to accompany Jack's sisters, Teresa O'Brien and Jack's brother, Liam.

Jamie waited on the pavement as the four girls climbed into the car. A fresh fall of rain started and beat down on his bare head. Behind the cars, at the western end of Saracen Street, a loud boom resonated through the morning air, shaking windows and doors, and another part of the old Saracen Foundry came crashing to the ground. A new column of smoke and dust rose inexorably into the rain filled sky.

Fine particles of brick and mortar from the former steel works now covered the whole of Possilpark in a film of filth and clinging dirt. As Jamie looked around he realised just how desolate Glasgow had become. *Maybe one day Glasgow will be "the dear green place" again but right now it's the dear grim place*, he ruminated, *an enormous shit hole, a giant demolition site.*

With the girls settled, Jamie clambered into the car and eased himself into the space between Teresa O'Brien and Anne-Marie. The door was closed by the chauffeur and then they were off, driving slowly down Saracen Street towards St Gregory's. On both sides of the road people stopped what they were doing and watched with bowed heads and sober, unsmiling faces. Jack had been one of theirs.

As the sad procession approached Keppochhill Road the hearse slowed and pulled in through the gates leading to the chapel with the limousines following in close attendance. Jamie sat unmoving, staring forward through the glass partition behind the driver, his eyes fixed unwaveringly on the silver Flying B crest set on the apex of the big car's bonnet. He listened to the crunching of the tyres on the wet gravel and heard the swishing sound that accompanied the car's passage through the puddles that are a permanent feature of Glasgow at this time of year.

The chapel appeared before them now, its red brick façade standing out gaudily against the drab, grey background of tenements. The cars stopped in front of the big double doors and the family spilled out onto the gravel. Jamie looked at the ashen faces of his fellow passengers as they descended, one by one, from the limousine and his courage began to wane. Anne-Marie took hold of him again and he felt a shiver pass through her. Her control was going and her grief, subdued in the car, was resurfacing. Jamie put his arm protectively around her and felt her lean against him, sobbing gently. Following Jack's mother and father, the party filed into the chapel and out of the rain.

The sight that awaited them took Jamie's breath away. Every pew was filled with mourners and more people stood at the back, near the doors, and filled the aisles on each side. The numbers were staggering and Jamie immediately grasped the magnitude of the people's sense of loss. He had been here the night before, at the Vigil for the Deceased, and the number then had been staggering. He hadn't expected the same today but it appeared as if the whole of Possilpark had taken the time to be here. He felt overwhelmed. The family proceeded down the centre aisle under the solemn gaze of the mourners and filed into the front pew, set to the right of the altar. Jamie left Anne-Marie with her sisters and made his way along the front to his place at the far end. As he looked along the line of bowed heads he caught sight of Anne-Marie's eyes gazing forlornly back at him. He forced a smile but somehow it seemed out of place.

Outside, the weather was threatening again. The sky had turned a dismal slate grey, like molten lead, and heavy black clouds were stepped up in layers along the horizon. The strengthening wind was bringing clouds scudding in from the west, a portent of what was to come. The main tower of the chapel with its dull, metal clad spire was now almost indistinguishable from the grey sky around it. Continuing its solitary, melancholy chime, the funeral bell echoed off the walls of the ageing buildings around the site and filled the air with infinitesimal shockwaves. The haunting notes of Bach's Prelude No. 1 in C Major filled the nave and drifted outside into the grey, early afternoon light, intensifying the oppressive feeling of gloom which seemed to pervade the place.

The coffin was brought to the altar and placed reverently before the assembled mourners. Father Daly, whom Jamie had met briefly the night before, made his way down the centre aisle between the rows of standing mourners. The men, old and young, in uniform dark suits and all with white shirts and black ties, some with black armbands; and the women, all in dull, drab colourless dresses and coats, their heads covered, wept openly and clung to friends and family. The quickly failing light filtering through the stained glass windows bathed the entire nave in an eerie glow. It gleamed on the veneered oak of the coffin and glinted dully on the brass fittings while the flames of a multitude of candles danced in the gentle draught wafting in from the still open doors. The air was heavy with the scent of lilies and incense.

As the priest drew level with the front pew Jamie saw him turn his head and run his dark eyes along the bowed heads of the family to lock, finally, on his. Jamie tried to imagine the man's thoughts. They had spoken the night before, after the Vigil, and the Priest, a kindly man, had said then that he would pray for him. Jamie sincerely hoped that he would because right now he could use all the help he could get. He returned the prelate's sympathetic look and held the man's gaze for an instant before the priest turned away to commence the Mass, but the man's contemplative gaze had given Jamie the strength to face the remainder of the day.

Jamie Raeburn was not particularly religious but he believed in God...and in fate. He closed his eyes and said a silent prayer, not for himself, but for Jack Connolly. Jack hadn't deserved what had happened to him. He, Jamie, had been the target of the attack. Jack had been an innocent victim caught up in Jamie's troubles. Jack was the quiet one of the two, avoiding trouble where possible, always ready to compromise and walk away. Jamie, on the other hand, attracted trouble. It followed him like a shadow, some might say like an old friend, ensnaring him and involving him in its fateful projects. Unlike Jack, Jamie *never* walked away. On the contrary; when trouble presented itself he usually met it head on without a thought for the consequences. But, inexplicably, he usually managed to extricate himself with his skin intact. He would say, if you asked him, that it was fate...it wasn't his time. Unlike Jack. Suddenly, the thought of praying made him feel like a hypocrite. How could God possibly listen to him? He had already killed one man and, chances were, he would kill again soon. But, wasn't it true that you sometimes had to fight evil with evil...fire with fire? He shrugged mentally and tried to concentrate on the service.

He listened as Father Daly began his priestly duties; running through the Funeral Mass by rote. Jamie, a Protestant, struggled with the alien liturgy of the Catholic Mass and his thoughts began to drift away under the hypnotic tone of the priest's voice. His mind flitted from one memory to another, mostly painful, and the faces of

Jack and Lucie materialised before him; Jack, the closest of his friends, the guy who had saved his life months earlier, and Lucie, the girl who had filled a void in his life with love, tears and laughter. The image of Max Kelman intruded into his thoughts. Max Kelman; supercilious, egotistical, violent and, above all, evil! It was Kelman's greed, his violent threats, and his coercion and moral blackmail that was keeping Lucie from him. And it was Kelman who had been behind the attack that had led to Jack's untimely death. These thoughts gnawed at him and he could feel a cold fury build in him again. But this wasn't the time or the place for fury, that time would come when he returned to England to get Lucie back...and to avenge Jack's death. Revenge is a dish best served cold, he remembered from somewhere, and now he understood why.

His mind continued to wander and the memory of another crept into his thoughts, accompanied by an unexpected feeling of guilt. Kate Maxwell's face appeared in his mind's eye, serene, sad, almost angelic...but then, he had always regarded Kate as his guardian angel. But why now, he wondered absently? On reflection, it was the pain of his break up with Kate all those months earlier that had brought him to this low point in his life. Kate was a part of all this...and, though he tried to deny it, she was still a part of him. Jamie dragged his thoughts back to Lucie. She needed him now, more than anyone, and he couldn't fail her. He couldn't lose Lucie as he had lost Kate, so he would do what he had to do...meet the problem head on, as always, and to hell with the consequences. The mellifluous voice of Father Daly delivering the Benediction cut into his thoughts and brought him back to the reality of the present.

The mourners filed out of the church and waited silently as the coffin was carried from the chapel and placed in the hearse. Some of the congregation drifted away, a few returning to their homes or to work while others made their way to waiting cars, ready to follow the cortege to the cemetery.

Jamie took his seat in the second limousine as before, between Teresa and Anne-Marie, and tried to hold himself together. This was worse than anything he had ever experienced in his young life but breaking down now wasn't an option. The hearse pulled slowly away from the chapel doors and the limousines followed sedately behind, swinging down the curving driveway towards Saracen Street and past the ranks of solemn mourners who lined the sides of the road, their eyes averted as though unable to look.

As they drove away from the chapel Anne-Marie clutched tightly to Jamie's hand, sobbing uncontrollably, and Teresa, a ghostly white, fidgeted nervously with the diamond ring adorning the third finger of her left hand and the single red rose lying on her lap. Jamie stared, unseeing, at the sad drawn faces of the others with a lump in his throat and a twisted knot in his stomach.

The cortege and the convoy of cars turned onto Saracen Street towards the dark pall of polluted air hanging over the old foundry and the cemetery of St. Kentigern's beyond. The greyness of the firmament and the claustrophobic effect of the tall, dismal, smog stained tenements towering oppressively over them filled Jamie with a growing sense of futility and hopelessness.

But life goes on, he realised. People were going about their business as usual in the shops along Saracen Street and a woman, raincoat belted tight around her waist, was pushing an old pram piled high with washing en route to the "steamie". This was normality. At the junction of Balmore Road and Hawthorn Street a gang of Irish navvies, hard at work on the roadway, ceased their labours and turned to face the procession, bowing their heads and placing their hands over their hearts in a gesture of reverence which brought a lump to Jamie's throat. As they passed the Art Deco fronted Vogue Cinema on Balmore Road happier memories flooded into Jamie's mind; memories of nights spent there with Jack and with numerous girlfriends in the back row, and he smiled in spite of himself.

Finally, the Cortege reached the gates of St. Kentigern's and swung into the cemetery. Jamie gazed out from the limousine, taking in the serried rows of gravestones and the leafless trees. A blanket of gold, yellow and brown leaves covered the ground and gave some modest colour to the otherwise drab, grey landscape.

Some mourners had already gathered around the open grave and were being joined rapidly by others as Jamie emerged from the limousine and joined the other pallbearers at the rear of the hearse. He waited anxiously, following the undertaker's instructions, and lined up alongside Jack's brother Liam. Jack's father and his uncle Dermott took their places at the front, his two elder brothers, Vincent and Gerard were at the rear with Liam and Jamie in the middle. The coffin was lifted onto their waiting shoulders and, slowly and carefully, they made their way over the wet, leaf strewn, slippery grass towards the grave and the assembled crowd.

Father Daly stood beside the roughly hewn hole, his Bible clutched tightly in both hands and his knuckles white with the strain. Jamie glanced at the man and their eyes connected for another micro-moment. Once again, Jamie drew strength from the Priest's look.

Gently, the coffin was placed on the wooden slats placed over the open grave and webbing straps were passed beneath the casket and given to Jamie and the other pallbearers. With each man taking the strain, Jack Connolly was lowered into his final resting place. Jamie bit his lip, tasted the strange metallic flavour of his own blood, and struggled to retain his composure. The sound of unbridled grief filled his ears and just as the coffin settled, the heavens opened and rain fell in an unrelenting downpour. A bright flash of lightning lit up the western sky, followed seconds later by the crashing, angry rumble of thunder. Jamie looked up into the heavens; the bright, white flash of the lightning still imprinted on his retina, and smiled bleakly. '*You're going out with a bang, big guy,*' he said quietly to himself.

The Committal was over quickly and the mourners began to leave, some remaining for a few moments of silent contemplation around the grave. The rain which had been falling for days with little respite had turned the ground into a quagmire, the soil waterlogged and heavy and churned up by the shuffling feet of the mourners. As the people finally drifted away Jamie remained at the graveside with Vincent and Liam Connolly. They huddled together at the edge of the roughly cut hole, looking on silently as the remainder of the family headed for the Wake. Elderly members of Jack's extended family, old aunts and uncles, were helped to waiting cars by other family members and family friends. Young and old alike, all of them united in their grief, hurried to the waiting cars to escape the torrential downpour.

'Why don't you come with us now, Jamie?' Vincent suggested quietly, putting his arm around Jamie's shoulder. 'Ma and Da want you to come...and Anne-Marie will be upset if you're not there.'

'I'll be there, Vince,' Jamie promised. 'But I want to spend some time here with Jack first.' As he spoke he was aware of his voice shaking with emotion.

Jack's brothers nodded in unison. They understood Jamie's anguish and the pain he was suffering. They had listened to him tear himself apart since their brother's death and they had tried, without success, to ease his troubled conscience. Jack's death wasn't his fault, they told him; *they* knew it, the *family* knew it, *everyone* knew it…everyone, that is, except Jamie himself. But they understood too his need to be alone with his thoughts now so they shook his hand solemnly, pulled their heavy, black coats tight against the cold and the rain and trudged away towards the roadway and the waiting cars, kicking through the fallen leaves and slipping and sliding on the wet, muddy grass.

'We'll send the car back for you,' Vincent called back, halting his progress until Jamie had nodded in acknowledgement.

Jamie watched them go, ambling down the gently sloping track like two great, lumbering, black bears, to the waiting limousine which sat about thirty yards away, its engine idling. The two men turned as one on reaching the car and waved, their hands and faces picked out like white flags against the now obsidian sky. Jamie saluted them with a wave of his own and turned back to the grave. He heard the engine pitch of the limousine increase and then the car pulled away, the growl of its motor gradually fading in the distance. Silence returned, broken only by the scornful cawing of crows in the surrounding trees. They had seen it all before.

Alone at last, Jamie let his feelings show. Oblivious to the rain which had saturated his clothes, run down his face and neck and trickled coldly down his back, he looked up into the darkness and let the fat raindrops crash against his face, cleansing him. He didn't mind the rain, not now. It hid the tears that were stinging his eyes and coursing down his cheeks. *What is it they say, big boys don't cry? Bollocks!* He murmured softly.

His attention was centred on the gleaming brass plaque fixed to the coffin lid, its words partly obscured by the grit and earth thrown by mourners and by the single red rose dropped in by Teresa. Jamie knew the words by heart but he read them aloud again anyway; John Francis Connolly, Born 23 September 1946, Departed from Us 16 October 1967, R.I.P. He felt the words glare resentfully back at him and was filled with an almost overpowering feeling of misery and desolation.

'I'm sorry Jack; it should have been me,' he sobbed quietly. 'Christ, why did all this have to happen?' he asked, louder now, repeating that question for the thousandth time but, as on every other occasion, the answer eluded him. The intensity of the rain increased, battering the sodden earth, splashing in the puddle at the bottom of the grave and banging on the coffin top like a corps of drums in an Orange Parade. *For fuck sake*, he reflected morosely, *a typical Glasgow funeral…black sky, pishin' rain and a wind that could cut you in two.*

This wasn't his first funeral. When you reached his age older members of your extended family start to drop off but, try as he might, he couldn't remember one occasion when the sun had shone. *Why do you Tims prefer to bury your dead, especially on days like today, rather than say your farewells in a civilised manner…in a nice, dry, warm crematorium?* he asked his departed friend. It was one of those questions that he didn't have an answer for and he suspected Jack wouldn't have the answer either. He felt vaguely guilty thinking about it and pushed it away, turning his attention back to the grave.

He sensed movement behind him and turned, wiping tears from his eyes with the back of his hand. Teresa O'Brien stood a few feet from him, her head was down and her small body shuddered with the violence of her sobbing. Jamie looked around but there was no one else there, only Teresa and he realised that she too had stayed behind to have a moment of peace with Jack. He stepped towards her and held out his hand, willing her to take hold of it and join him. The girl reached out with her small, glove encased fingers and took short, unsteady steps towards him. He squeezed her tiny hand reassuringly and guided her to the edge of the rudely dug grave, wrapping his arm around her. Teresa's sobbing abated a little as they stood there in silence. The minutes passed as they grieved together, each of them engrossed in their own personal thoughts of the young man lying in the veneered wooden box below them.

'You *didn't* let him down, Jamie,' Teresa said suddenly. 'There was nothing you could've done.' Her voice was low and Jamie realised she must have been standing behind him for a while, listening. 'What are you going to do now?' she asked after another pause, turning her face towards him.

Jamie looked down at her small, pale face, her eyes red rimmed with endless crying over the weeks since Jack's death. Devoid of makeup, her face drawn and her eyes sunken and dark with lack of sleep, she looked almost beatific, and his heart was filled with sadness. He thought about her question. What *was* he going to do now? In the course of only a few weeks his world had been turned upside down; the girl he loved taken from him, his best friend murdered in front of his eyes and another man lay in the morgue, killed by Jamie himself. *What the fuck am I going to do now*, he asked himself? What *could* he do? Only one thing was clear; he had to get Lucie away from Max Kelman. His "work" trip to Belfast the weekend before had provided him with the means to do it…but could he?

'I don't know, Teresa. I really *don't* know where I go from here,' he answered her truthfully. 'What about you?'

Teresa's tears erupted again, flooding down her pretty, grief filled face and he could almost feel the pain radiating from her. 'I'm p-pregnant Jamie,' she stuttered, her voice filled with anguish. 'I d-don't know what I'm going to do either. I'm lost without him.' The unexpected reply and the abject misery in her voice hit him like a slap in the face and he struggled to find words to respond. 'What did Jack say when you told him?' he asked eventually.

'Jack didn't know,' she whispered sadly. 'I only found out myself last week.'

Jamie tightened his hold on her and she turned her head into his chest, pressing it against his sodden coat and sobbing uncontrollably now. He tried to calm her, whispered soothingly, but words of solace were hard to find. For the first time in his life Jamie Raeburn felt totally inadequate.

'Jack told me about Lucie,' Teresa continued quietly when her sobbing had eased. 'You have to go back for her Jamie.'

'Aye, I know,' Jamie replied. 'And I will,' he said, trying to sound confident, but struggling.

'Jack said you would,' she continued quietly. 'He knew you better than anyone, I think, and he said you would sort it out.' It was said with a degree of certainty that only Jack could have instilled in her.

Sort it out? Jamie repeated to himself. *Aye, I'll sort it out alright, but how, that's the question?* Max Kelman wasn't a man who would bow easily to pressure and to "sort it", as Teresa put it, would take a lot of nerve and an even bigger slice of luck. 'And what else did Jack tell you?' he asked, veering away from those disturbing thoughts.

'He told me that you and Lucie were happy together,' she said, smiling wanly. 'He never thought you'd get over Kate, you know.' She paused, as though the very mention of Kate's name would raise a spectre, and then continued, softly. 'He said that he once thought you and Lucie were worlds apart and that it wouldn't work out for you both…but you proved him wrong.' The words were tumbling out of her now and her smile was warmer. 'I think that's what brought Jack back to me,' she finished wistfully.

Get over Kate? I don't think I'll ever get over her, Jamie thought to himself, and his conversation with Roisin Kelly only days before came back to him then. But getting over Kate and getting on with his life were two entirely different things. He felt his eyes fill up again and turned his face to the sky once more to let the rain wash down on him. 'Who else knows about the baby?' he asked gently.

'Nobody else knows…you're the first,' Teresa replied quietly, her words stunning him.

'Jesus Christ, Teresa!' Jamie blurted, his eyes widening in dismay. 'You're dealin' with this all on your own? You haven't even told your mother?'

'I can't Jamie,' she whimpered. 'She'll never forgive me an' my Dad will kill me. They'll be so ashamed…*I'm* so ashamed.' Her sobbing started again, with a vengeance.

'Ashamed? Why?' he retorted angrily. 'For Christ's sake Teresa, Jack loved you. I know that for a fact because he told me…the night he was stabbed. Did you know he asked me to be his Best Man for your weddin'? You two were in love and you're havin' his baby, what is there to be ashamed of in that?'

'I'm scared, Jamie. I don't want people to think badly of me.'

'Oh, come on Teresa love, nobody's going to think badly of you,' he whispered reassuringly, pulling her closer. He felt his protective instincts kicking in and he knew, instinctively, that he had to help her through this crisis…she was going to struggle on her own. 'Come on, let's go to the wake. We'll tell Jack's Ma and Da the news. They've got a right to know,' he suggested gently. 'They'll give you all the love they would have if Jack had still been here…and I'll be with you,' he added, hugging her tightly. 'I'll be there when you need me, I promise.' When he said that he meant it but, on later reflection, he wondered if it might be a promise that would be hard to keep.

Jamie released her from his arms and hunkered down at the edge of Jack's grave, his coat-tails trailing behind him in the mud. He still held tightly onto Teresa's hand. 'You're going to be a dad, Jack,' he whispered, breaking down again. 'Christ Jack, I'm sorry. *You* should be here with Teresa, not me.' A wave of wretchedness broke over him and his sobbing turned to full-scale tears, but he felt no shame in that. Teresa squeezed his hand, helping him to regain control, and he straightened up with a cough to clear the lump in his throat. 'I'll look out for Teresa, Jack…*Lucie* an' I will look after her,' he continued. 'I'm goin' back,' he whispered. 'An' I know you'll be with me, watchin' my back.'

His voice broke again as a tearful Teresa squeezed his hand tightly and tried to smile

Part I

Glasgow Kisses

Chapter 1

Friday, 25 November 1966, Glasgow
The Waldorf Bar in Cambridge Street was, as usual for a Friday night, full to bursting with the same crowd of regular week-end drinkers standing three deep to the bar counter. All of the tables were occupied by semi-inebriates and the barmaids were rushed off their feet but soon the bar would empty as the younger drinkers drifted off to the dance halls and the nearby clubs. Friday nights were always the same; everyone had cash, the girls were dressed in their shortest skirts and the guys were done up like tailors' dummies in flash, made to measure suits, collars and ties.

Jamie Raeburn was champing at the bit. Time was moving on and the lure of the Locarno, the City's main dance hall, was strong, but if he and his mates didn't get their fingers out and get there soon the queue would stretch right down Sauchiehall Street and the pick of the talent, namely the birds with the shortest skirts and the biggest tits, would have been snaffled up. Friday and Saturday nights were only for one thing, Jamie reminded himself...then reflected that wasn't strictly true and revised his thoughts instantly. Friday and Saturday nights were for *two* things...first, getting a few pints down his throat and, second, and much more important, getting his tongue down some willing little bird's throat and his hand, at the very least, into her knickers. But tonight, as usual, the rest of his mates were spending too much time concentrating on the former and not paying nearly enough attention to the latter.

Jamie's problem, if you could call it a problem, was that he had been "out of circulation" for eight months and now he was trying to make up for lost time. Being "out of circulation" in Glasgow usually meant that you were enjoying an all-expenses paid stay in Barlinnie, the big, grey, desolate building out at Riddrie, that holds the city's miscreants at Her Majesty's Pleasure. In Jamie's case, however, the sentence he had served was of a different sort. He had been involved...in common parlance "going steady", with a girl who had taken him for a ride, mentally as well as physically, and it was an experience he was now putting behind him. The young lady in question, one Carol Whyte, had spread her affections a bit wider than Jamie and had played the field behind his back. Catching her *in flagrante delicto*, "at it" in other words, had been a bit of a shock for both of them but probably more of a shock for the poor guy lying on top of her, given Jamie's size and his reputation. As it happened, Jamie had taken it reasonably well and had moved on, but his pride had taken a bit of a knock. He wouldn't get into that situation again, he told himself regularly, and a series of one night stands was the inevitable result.

He tugged up the left sleeve of his immaculate wool worsted, brown herring bone Hector Powe suit and looked impatiently at his watch, hoping the others would get the message. 'Come on you lot!' He sighed loudly. 'If we don't get to the Locarno soon nookie will be off the menu for tonight,' he moaned, giving voice to his frustration.

'Then you'll just need to shag that big lassie you shagged last week,' one of his pals sniggered. 'Big Bertha, wasn't it?' the lad added, sarcasm oozing. Jamie quickly identified the culprit, Gerry Carroll, and decided he'd get his own back on the bold Gerry later.

'Loretta,' Jamie retorted, with feigned annoyance, to a background of laughter. 'Her name was Loretta, an' she wasn't that big, she was...she was just well built,' he added, finding what he thought was an appropriate response. But derision was the name of the game and his mates piled it on.

'Aye, right!' Jack Connolly, his best pal, retorted with a snort. 'Ye could've tied up the Queen Mary with yon bra she wis wearin'...an' her dress was straight out o' Black's of Greenock,' he laughed. Black's, being manufacturers of tents, painted an unfair but vivid picture of the delightful, if admittedly somewhat large, Loretta. 'But ah'm impressed, Jamie boy,' he continued, 'She must've been somethin' special, right enough, 'cos ye've actually remembered her name this time.' The rest of the lads were enjoying the banter...Jamie wasn't.

'Aye, she was *"well built"* right enough,' another pal, Tony Boyle, chipped in, repeating Jamie's earlier retort. 'Built like a fuckin' Russian Shot-putter.' The laughter was growing louder and even Jamie was finding it hard not to join in. But he wasn't about to throw in the towel, not yet anyway.

'Alright, alright,' he conceded, 'She might have been a bit on the big side, but she had a really pretty face...and, as you've already pointed out, she had tits to die for,' he fired back dreamily. He looked around their faces and smirked, content in the knowledge that he had scored with Loretta while the rest of them, those of them who had actually managed to *get* a lumber, hadn't got past a quick snog. He paused, just enough to emphasise his next shot. 'How many of you got a leg over last weekend, remind me?' he sniped cockily and waited, grinning. 'Ah, that's right, I remember now...none of you,' he chortled, raised his eyebrows, and waited for the inevitable riposte.

Jack Connolly provided it, just as Jamie had known he would. 'Nah, we didae,' he agreed with an exaggerated sigh. 'But ye dae realise that wis only because we were worried about *you*, big man. We were scared shitless that ye might need handers.' Jack was struggling to keep a serious expression on his face and Jamie waited for the follow up. 'That Loretta of yours wis so big we thought we might huv tae come team handed tae get ye away fae her...an' that reinforced concrete gusset she wis wearin' to haud up thae tits o' hers, wis awesome!' he grinned, paused and pulled a face.

'You had a good look at them then,' Jamie laughed.

'Oh aye,' Jack snickered and the rest joined in. 'But jist remember we aw sacrificed our chances o' nookie tae make sure ye escaped yon lassie's clutches with yer baws in one piece...or two pieces, tae be precise,' he finished, creasing himself with laughter. 'On the positive side, she wis a bit more wholesome than that tall stick insect ye took hame the week before...an' Quasimodo's sister the week before that.' General uproar followed.

Jamie scowled. 'Aye, very funny!' he retorted, pretending disgust.

Jack grinned and patted him on the shoulder, pointing to Jamie's empty glass. 'Dae ye want another?' he asked, the banter already forgotten.

Jamie shook his head in refusal. He had already downed six pints and the last thing he needed on a Friday night was brewer's droop. 'Nah Jack, I've had enough, thanks. I'm just goin' outside for some fresh air.' He scraped his chair back on the wooden floor and stood up. 'I'll wait for you lot outside,' he called back loudly as he headed for the door.

The others watched him go, despairing a little, and Gerry Carroll shook his head slowly. Jack was watching Jamie shrewdly and Jamie could guess at the content of the conversation that was about to take place; he'd heard most of it before. Gerry, Tony, Jim and Vinnie would all be moaning that he was taking life too seriously these days and that he needed to lighten up, and Jack would jump to his defence. That's why Jack is my best mate, he reflected, he sticks with me through thick and thin.

As he forced his way through the crowd of drinkers at the bar he turned and looked back at the group. The discussion had already started and he saw Jack let out a sigh and turn towards him. Their eyes met and Jack smiled guiltily. Jamie smiled back. He pushed open the pub door and stepped out into a curtain of snow. Big white flakes drifted down from the sky, picked out in the haloed light of the street lamps, and were already lying thick on the ground. 'It's snowin',' he called back, unheard over the din of laughter and music.

He let the door swing shut behind him and dug out his cigarettes. Sticking one between his lips he flicked the wheel of his lighter with quickly numbing fingers and brought the flame up to the tip of the ciggy. Cambridge Street was deserted, the snow undisturbed, virgin. It was falling more heavily now; enormous white flakes formed a sheer, white drape and settled on his suit and his hair. Jamie cursed under his breath, berating himself for ignoring his mother's advice and refusing to wear a coat as she had suggested. He should have known better, his mother was usually right, and now his best suit was going to get soaked…and all for the sake of looking good in front of the talent. *Vanity, vanity, all is vanity*, he thought, trying in vain to remember where he'd heard the quote before.

Jamie drew in a lungful of smoke, coughed a couple of times, and gazed along the deserted road. Circular pools of pale yellow, phosphorescent light formed beneath the streetlamps and reflected brightly off the snow. He looked up into the sky and the heavy white mass above him. *It will get worse before it gets better*, he thought, *and a knee trembler up a close or in a bus shelter tonight really will have to be a "quickie"*.

A crunching of gears and a squeal of brakes announced the arrival of a green, white and gold Glasgow Corporation bus as it careered round the corner from Renfrew Street. If the snow kept up the buses would probably stop running and that really would put a damper on the night. He watched as the bus trundled slowly past him in low gear, its wheels leaving two broad, black lines, like scars, in the virgin snow and its interior lights dancing over snow covered bins and discarded rubbish at the roadside.

As the bus disappeared from sight a semblance of quiet returned to the street and only the din of the music, rowdy voices and laughter coming from the pub disturbed the peace. But mingled with the noise Jamie imagined he heard a cry for help. He peered keenly into the curtain of snow but could see nothing. Cambridge Street was completely deserted but he could make out ghostly shapes moving beneath the Christmas lights in Sauchiehall Street, about 150 yards away.

There was another cry, louder this time, clearer and more distressed, and he could hear other voices cursing and swearing. Someone was in trouble. On the far side of the road there were only derelict buildings but about twenty yards away to his left an alley cut a gap through the tenement walls and disappeared into darkness. Whatever was going down was happening in the alley, Jamie realised instantly. He considered going back into the pub for Jack and the boys but discounted it. That would take too long. Without thinking, he set off for the alley, slipping and sliding on the slick carpet of snow. He never had been one for thinking too long in situations like this.

As he reached the opening leading into the alley his shadow was thrown against the stone wall by the streetlights, appearing like an apparition through the curtain of snow. He stopped and squinted into the shadowy alleyway, his eyes finally picking out the source of the commotion. About twenty yards deeper into the lane four vague figures were swarming around a solitary form lying curled up on the ground, like flies round shite, he thought, kicking and stamping their victim mercilessly. They saw Jamie the instant he entered the alley and two of them broke off from their assault on the hapless victim to face him, fists up and snarling.

Jamie came to an abrupt halt and tried to assess the situation. His head was telling him to run like fuck, but his heart wouldn't let him.

'Fuck off!' one of the thugs shouted as he approached Jamie recklessly. 'This has got fuck all tae dae wi' you,' he added in a broad, guttural, Glaswegian accent.

Jamie smiled grimly. The guy was right, it did have fuck all to do with him, but he knew that if he left them to it, the man on the ground was as good as dead. Jamie had this thing about helping underdogs and the guy lying there in front of him, an American sailor by the look of him, was certainly one of those. The Yank was sprawled, defenceless, with his back now propped against the wall of the building behind him and his head lolling to the side with each blow that landed on him. He appeared to be bleeding heavily and was still being kicked ruthlessly by the two remaining hoodlums. Blood had spattered the snow around him in a circular, windmill like pattern and his clothes were stained with the gore streaming from his mouth and nose. 'I can't do that,' Jamie fired back, surprising himself as much as the thug. His voice sounded cold and measured when, in reality, he really should have been shitting himself. He slipped his hand into his jacket pocket and felt the comforting little strip of folded newspaper he always kept there for emergencies. Surreptitiously, he tucked it into his right palm. Slowly, and out of sight of the approaching men, he took three pennies from his trouser pocket and fitted them snugly between his fingers, nestling against the folded paper.

The villain who had given the warning grinned and gave a careless shrug. 'Fuck you then ya wanker, ye'll get whit he's gettin',' he said, baring his teeth in a malicious grin and swaggering confidently towards Jamie, with his pal in close support. Jamie didn't wait. Rising slightly onto his toes, he launched his attack. The guy, about 25 or 26 years old Jamie reckoned, having expected Jamie to back off, was taken completely by surprise. Before he could recover, Jamie was on top of him, smashing his coin reinforced right fist into the man's throat. The thug recoiled in shock and Jamie followed up quickly, smashing his forehead into the thug's nose with a sickening crack, breaking bone and cartilage, before the second man could react.

There was a scream and a gurgling noise from the injured man before his buddy caught Jamie with a deflected blow to the side of the head. Jamie turned towards the man as another punch caught him, this time above the right eye. Blood trickled down into his eye, temporarily blinding him, and he moved back out of range. Shaking his head to clear his vision he watched the second man close in again. Confident now, the thug charged at him, and the signet ring on the man's right hand that had already caused damage to Jamie's eye, glinted in the half light. Jamie brushed the man's arm aside and threw out his right fist, the three pennies tearing viciously into the man's cheek and impacting violently on his jaw bone. The hoodlum came to a shuddering halt, a look of disbelief on his face. Jamie struck again. This time his fist crashed into the man's lower ribs and a mouthful of foul breath was expelled from the villain's lungs, accompanied by an agonised cry. The man backed off, shocked by the ferocity of Jamie's attack, screaming for help.

The two thugs still mugging the sailor broke off their assault and quickly turned their attention to Jamie. He now only had seconds to finish off the second man. Stepping in close to the man he feinted left then sidestepped and pirouetted past the ned with a movement that Scottish Ballet would have been proud of, smashing his elbow into the man's jaw. There was a satisfying jolt and a horrible cracking sound, like snapping wood, as the guy's jaw fractured. *So far so good*, Jamie thought fleetingly, *I might, just might, get out of this in one piece.*

His hopes were quickly dashed. The two remaining gangsters came at him simultaneously in a concerted attack and he felt a heavy kick land on his right thigh and a fierce punch caught him on the ribs. He lost balance and staggered away but the men followed up quickly and a second punch landed on his ribs while a third sank deep into his abdomen, winding him badly.

Jamie fell backwards, crashing into the wall behind him and coming to a shuddering halt. Unsteadily, he managed to regain his feet and draw himself up. Wary now, he turned to face the men again. Time was running out for him. They came at him again, attacking simultaneously from both sides and with his back against the wall Jamie had no way out. Punches rained in on him from left and right. His head was being pummelled and he lashed out instinctively, catching the man to his right with a stinging punch to the mouth. The pennies nestling in his fist did their work again, smashing teeth and splitting the thug's gums and lip. There was a muttered curse. The man spat out a tooth, shook his head to clear it, and then both men launched a fresh attack.

Jamie knew it was time to get out but he couldn't leave the sailor. He screamed at the stricken man, urging him to get up, willing him to move. The American, still groggy, managed to struggle unsteadily to his feet and lean against the wall for support as his blood dripped onto the snow. His once white shirt was now stained a deep red and his right eye was badly cut and swollen and closing rapidly, but he appeared to be functioning...just.

The two thugs began to circle Jamie again, their half closed, predatory eyes searching for an opening, and Jamie prepared for the onslaught. They attacked from both sides again, their timing perfectly orchestrated, and Jamie was forced back under a flurry of punches. He felt knuckles tear the skin above his left eye and another vicious blow caught him on the ribs. Pain racked him. Another fist landed on his mouth splitting his lip yet again and the salty, metallic flavour of his own blood filled his throat.

Trapped, he threw punches at random and felt one connect on an attacker's mouth, the skin of his knuckles tearing on the man's teeth. A kick caught him on the back of his left calf and he buckled. His ribs ached with the effects of two punches near his heart and everything was slipping away from him.

The Yank was up on his feet but was still leaning heavily against the wall. The two thugs were between Jamie and the sailor but the Yank was now staggering towards them, yelling. The men turned and that moment's distraction gave Jamie the opportunity to escape from the entrapment of the wall. His spirit lifted but soon came crashing back to earth. From the deeper gloom of the alley two more men appeared at the run, and instinctively Jamie knew it wasn't the 7th Cavalry coming to the rescue. *It's Time to go*, he told himself. The odds, stacked against him from the outset, were now impossible.

He reacted quickly and grabbed the American by the arm. 'Run,' he screamed, 'Run like fuck!' Pushing the sailor ahead of him he started to run towards the perceived safety of Cambridge Street.

The American, though groggy and seriously weakened, was still *compos mentis* and aware of the danger. His legs pumped into action and he started to run but he was staggering and swaying wildly, like a drunk, on the slippery surface. He wasn't going to make it, Jamie realised.

Bravely, he turned to face the four men behind them in a heroic effort to give the American time. The men spread out, trying to cut him off from escape and he knew he was in serious trouble. If the men succeeded, he was in line for a serious kicking. One of the two new men grinned malevolently. 'You're gonnae get a right fuckin' doin', pal,' he spat out brutishly as they started to move in on him.

Jamie ran. One of the men tried to cut him off but Jamie's momentum and a wild punch thrown with his makeshift knuckle duster forced the hoodlum back. Scrabbling for purchase on the snow covered surface he slithered along the alley towards Cambridge Street. As he ran into the light a feeling of euphoria flooded him but it was short lived. Two hard blows, one after the other in rapid succession, struck him low on the back. Pain seared through him; pain like nothing he had felt before. He staggered on but his legs began to buckle and give way. Just ahead of him he saw the American crash face down on the roadway in front of the Waldorf.

Jamie too was falling now. He couldn't understand why everything around him was turning black, as if the street lights were turning off…one after another. He lost focus momentarily but was vaguely aware of light flooding out from the open door of the pub and of people running. Angry voices were shouting and someone called out his name but for some reason the lights were extinguishing faster now… and he was falling into a deep black, bottomless chasm.

Through it all, one voice penetrated the veil of darkness; Jack Connolly's voice, screaming from close by. Jamie felt himself being lifted from the cold, wet ground and his body cradled in someone's arms. 'Jamie! Aw naw, Jamie, for fuck sake, naaaaw!' were the last words he heard before the lights went out completely.

Chapter 2

Kate Maxwell rubbed her eyes and yawned. She had started her night shift in Glasgow's Royal Infirmary at eight o' clock that night, just over three hours earlier, and already she was feeling the strain. Weekends were always the same; a constant stream of patients flowed into Accident & Emergency and the Intensive Care Unit, where Kate worked, grew correspondingly busier. Already tonight, two young men had been wheeled into the unit, one from surgery with multiple stab wounds and the other in a coma after taking an overdose of drugs. Neither of them was likely to make it through the night, she thought sadly.

Three and a half hours into the shift and she had been on the go all the time without a break. She joined her colleague, Barbara Laing, at the Nurses' Station and lifted her hand to her mouth mimicking drinking a cup of tea, breaking into a tired smile as Barbara nodded enthusiastically. As she headed for the little kitchen that served the ward the telephone on the desk started to ring, its shrill repetitive brrr, brrr...brrr, brrr, reverberating through the ward. Kate stopped dead in her tracks and looked back expectantly as Barbara picked up the handset and spoke. Abruptly, Barbara pushed back her chair and rose to her feet, beckoning urgently. 'Another one coming in,' she whispered loudly.

Seconds later a trolley crashed through the swing doors, the body of a young man prone on top with his upper head and his lower body swathed in bandages. Kate and Barbara quickly took command, manoeuvring the trolley into the room newly prepared for the patient and, with the help of the porters, transferring the young man's body onto the bed. Sachets of saline and drugs were quickly attached to their supports and wires from the monitors were deftly attached to the young man's torso. As the electronic displays sprang to life Kate Maxwell stared down into the young man's face and an unexpected frisson of excitement ran through her. Something she couldn't rationalise or explain was drawing her to him in a way she had never experienced before.

'Not what I expected,' Barbara Laing whispered across the bed as they made him comfortable. 'I expected the usual spotty little ned, the usual weekend detritus...but this one looks different somehow.' She looked at Kate and saw the faraway look in her friend's eyes.

Kate smiled. She was still shocked by her inexplicable attraction to the man and shrugged, trying to deny the feelings that were crowding in on her. *I'm married*, she told herself, though she knew that even that part of her life was a sham. She saw Barbara watching her strangely, as though seeing something in her expression that shouldn't be there. She finished tucking the sheet below the mattress and hurried from the room, eager to get away. 'I'll make the tea now,' she called back over her shoulder.

Later, as they sat together sipping the hot, sweet tea, hypnotised by the somnolent silence of the settled ward and the rhythmic sounds of the monitors, Barbara finally raised the subject that had been bothering her for some time now.

'What's wrong, Kate?' she asked softly. They were both Charge Nurses and had worked together for almost a year now and they were friends, of a sort. Barbara too was married, but for her it was the second time around. At thirty five, ten years older than Kate, she had seen most things and could read the signs.

Kate returned her look with sad, tired eyes. 'Is it that obvious?' she asked.

Barbara laughed softly. 'To someone like me, someone who has already been there? Yes, it's that obvious.'

'I don't know what to do Babs,' Kate started before breaking down. 'I don't think I can go on much longer. My whole life is a sham,' she continued, her eyes filling up.

'Is he playing around?' Barbara asked bluntly, a little more than she had intended. She had suspected for some time that Kate's husband was the root of the problem and Kate's bitter snort in response to her question surprised her.

'No, it's not that,' she countered sadly. 'If it was it would be easier, I'd just walk away...leave him,' she continued. 'It's not some*one* else he's in love with, it's some *thing*... he's an alcoholic.' A tear rolled slowly down her cheek and she wiped it away with the back of her hand.

There was a moment's silence before Barbara continued. 'How long has he been drinking?' she asked, gentler now.

Kate shuddered, her mind drifting back over the years of her marriage. 'God knows,' she sighed at last. But it's been a long time,' she confessed. 'He always was a drinker and I suppose I thought it was normal at first. But he started drinking heavily soon after we were married. He stopped for a while when we moved up here to Glasgow and I thought...I prayed, that he'd beaten it, but he hadn't. The last year has been hell.'

'Is he still working?' Barbara asked.

'No, he lost his job months ago and I'm struggling to pay the bills,' Kate sobbed. 'He disappears for days on end and then, when he does come home, he's always looking for money to buy more drink. We argue constantly.'

Barbara nodded slowly as she digested the facts. She truly felt for Kate because she knew exactly what Kate was going through. She had been in the situation Kate was now and had faced the same dilemma. 'What about his family...your family, do they know?' she asked.

'God, no!' Kate replied. 'Though I'm pretty sure my mother suspects something. His family wouldn't believe it anyway...they'd probably blame me,' she added with a sad little smile.

It was time to lighten the mood, Barbara decided, she could return to this subject later. 'So, what is it with that lad who came in earlier...James Raeburn?' she asked with a smile. 'I saw that look you gave him. Do you know him?'

Kate smiled again, tears forgotten for the moment. 'No,' she giggled guiltily. 'I've never set eyes on him before...but I sort of wish I had. There's something about him...I can't explain it,' she heard herself say. 'I wish I did know him.'

'Well, when he regains consciousness you'll have plenty of time to get to know him then,' Barbara laughed.

'Am I being stupid?' Kate asked.

'Stupid?' Barbara laughed again. 'Don't be silly. He's a good looking guy. He might just spice up your life a little, who knows?

'Have you ever been tempted?' Kate continued.

'Whoa,' Barbara chuckled. 'You're getting personal, Kate Maxwell.' Kate immediately looked contrite and Barbara softened. 'I'm joking, Kate, I'm joking. Yes, I've been there too, but never with a patient...but that's not to say I wouldn't have been interested if the right one had been wheeled in,' she added with another giggle. She leaned across the desk and picked up the Nursing Notes for Jamie Raeburn. 'Let's see,' she murmured quietly. 'What do we know about the mystery man?' She scanned down the page, nodding occasionally. 'Okay,' she started. 'He's twenty one...twenty two next May, and he lives in Knightswood.' She watched Kate's eyebrows furrow.

Kate Maxwell lived with her husband in Ibrox, on the South side of the River Clyde...at least, that had been the original scenario, but, mainly because of her husband's drink problem, she hadn't managed to get to know the city. Her life was now just a vicious circle of eating, sleeping and working. She had never heard of the Glasgow suburb of Knightswood...it could have been on the dark side of the Moon for all she knew. 'Knightswood?' she echoed.

Barbara laughed again. 'I'd forgotten you're a foreigner, Katie dear,' she said. 'It's out to the west of the city, on the other side of the river from you. You've heard of Drumchapel?' she questioned and waited for Kate's nod of acknowledgement. 'Well, Knightswood is out towards Drumchapel but it's not nearly as "wild west" as the Drum, it's bit more pretentious,' she said with a laugh. 'And...yes, he works as a welder.'

Kate laughed now, her mood lightening. 'It doesn't say *anything* about that in the notes,' she giggled. 'I've read them...so how do you work that out my Nurse Holmes?

'Elementary, my dear Nurse Watson,' Barbara snickered in return. 'Did you notice those little burn marks on his forearms?' she asked, and again Kate nodded. 'My first husband was a welder and his arms had little burn marks on them, exactly like those on young Mr Raeburn.' Barbara grew serious again. Kate needed a man in her life, she thought, and she was too young to stay tied to a drunk. She looked at Kate penetratingly and placed her hand on top of Kate's. 'I think you need some fun in your life, Kate Maxwell,' she said eventually. 'And James Raeburn might be that fun...just don't get burned again.'

*

Four days later, Intensive Care Unit.
A dull red glow filled Jamie Raeburn's eyelids and he felt hot, burning hot. His body was slick with sweat and he thought for one horrible moment that he had died and gone to hell...and "Auld Nick" might appear at any moment. But if he was thinking then he must be alive, mustn't he, he reasoned logically. A phrase by French philosopher, Descartes, came to him but where he had picked it up God alone knew. "*I think, therefore I am*", he recalled. Who said Glaswegians don't do culture, he mused groggily. *Right, if I'm not in hell, then where on earth am I*, he wondered? His last recollection was of Jack Connolly's voice screaming out his name, telling him everything would be alright and then hearing Jack shout for someone to call an ambulance. If everything was going to be alright then why the fuck had he needed an ambulance?

The harsh red light that had been permeating Jamie's brain softened into a soft pink as he tried to open his eyes. A strange, throat catching smell hung in the air and it took him a moment to identify it as disinfectant. Another wave of relief swept over him. His senses appeared to be working so he had to be in the land of the living.

Something, or someone, was moving close to him. He turned his head towards the sound while attempting to prise open his eyes at the same time and was rewarded for his efforts with a searing pain that started in his back and radiated out through his entire body. His eyes were fully open now but they were refusing to focus. Wraith like shapes in blue and white drifted around him then faded from view. A door banged shut and then there was only silence. The ghosts had departed.

Slowly, the mist before his eyes began to clear…quadruple vision became double vision and then normal sight returned. He found himself in a small, green painted room which was, in effect, little more than a cubicle. He was lying, face up, on a hard bed and tubes and electrical wires were attached to his arms and his chest. He started to panic, feeling a bit like Lemuel Gulliver shipwrecked on Lilliput and tied to the ground by the island's tiny inhabitants. When he tried to move again the pain returned, worse now, and he sank back onto the bed with a gasp, his body once again soaked with sweat. He groaned loudly and closed his eyes.

The door opened with a bang and he heard the rapid patter of feet rushing towards him. He opened his eyes and allowed them to swivel towards the noise but he was afraid to move his head for fear of the pain that would inevitably follow. A solitary figure in blue was coming towards him, concern wreathing her face, and panic engulfed him again. He identified her as a nurse as she walked over to a large monitor which sat next to his bed and it was only then that he recognised the unbroken, high pitched tone of an alarm. The nurse scanned the monitor before turning to him and running her fingers deftly over the wires connected to his chest. He felt the light pressure of her fingers on his body as she refastened one of the links disconnected by his movements and the unremitting tone of the alarm ceased immediately, replaced by a regular beeping sound which emulated the steady beating of his heart.

Jamie looked up at the nurse and a shy, tentative smile spread across her face, replacing the concern. When she spoke her voice had an almost soporific effect. 'You're back with us, then,' she said happily, her smile widening, and Jamie saw then how pretty she was.

He felt like shit but this girl's smile was lifting his spirit. *Change of venue*, he told himself, *I'm in heaven…or somewhere very close to it*. 'Where am I?' he mumbled, his mouth dry and his tongue swollen and coated with fur. He was having difficulty forming the words.

'You're in The Royal Infirmary, the Intensive Care Unit,' the nurse replied, taking hold of his wrist and placing the first two fingers of her right hand firmly on his pulse.

'How long have I been here?' Jamie asked, his speech still laboured.

The nurse was checking the watch pinned upside down on the left breast of her uniform and paused for a moment before replying. 'Four days,' she said eventually.

Fuck me, Jamie thought, *four days! What the hell happened to me?* He turned his head carefully, trying to catch the eye of the nurse once again but had moved back to the monitor and her back was turned to him. Jamie took in the blue dress uniform with its white bib front and apron, its short sleeves piped with white, the white collar and the belt which accentuated her attractive shape…and her sheer nylon stockings. Well, he hoped they were stockings and not the panty hose that girls were wearing nowadays. Whatever they were, stockings or tights, they certainly made her legs look good. Suddenly, and unexpectedly, he felt himself harden…despite whatever drugs had been pumped into him. What a body, he thought appreciatively. And those legs…Wow!

He tried to attract her attention but didn't have much luck. She was engrossed in whatever it was she was doing at the monitor and seemed lost in concentration. He tried a cough and was surprised when it worked. The nurse came out of her reverie and turned to him. With his vision now fully restored he saw that his first impression of her had been spot on. She was beautiful…stunning! His heart was beating faster now though more in hope than expectation, he suspected. She had a lovely, oval shaped face framed by long, lustrous, dark auburn hair which was swept up behind her white uniform cap. Her eyes, almond shaped, were set beneath finely shaped eyebrows and were a deep translucent green, like bottomless pools in a tropical rain forest. Flawless skin, a finely sculpted nose and full, red Cupid's bow lips completed the picture. When she smiled, Jamie caught sight of a slightly bent front tooth which, instead of detracting from her beauty, seemed, perversely, to enhance it. He was smitten.

He wanted to keep her there talking but an uncharacteristic bout of shyness gripped him. Perhaps the drugs gave him Dutch courage but somehow he managed to banish his shyness and pose the question now uppermost in his thoughts. 'When I get out of here is there any chance that I could...?' he managed to blurt out before being stopped dead in his tracks by the sight of the girl's left hand being waved in front of his face and the thin gold band on her third finger. Jamie was crestfallen.

'I'm married,' she said, stating the obvious, but Jamie thought he detected something in her look that told him she wished she wasn't. Or was that the drugs playing tricks on him, he wondered?

'That's a pity,' he replied with a sigh. 'You're really beautiful and I would have loved to take you out.' He tried to lift his head from the pillow again but forgot the consequences of doing that and his pain returned with a vengeance.

The blushing smile which had appeared momentarily on the nurse's face was replaced immediately by anxiety. 'Don't move,' she said gently, applying pressure to his shoulders to push him softly back onto the bed. Her right hand moved to his wrist again as she checked his pulse again. It was racing now.

Jamie looked up at her. She was probably a few years older than he was, maybe 24 or 25 and around 5'3" or 5'4" tall, he guessed. There was a subtle hint of perfume surrounding her and he breathed it in ostentatiously, cheered by another smile that spread across her face. A wisp of hair escaped from behind her cap and fell forward over her eyes, forcing her to release his wrist to tuck it back into place. To Jamie, even that innocent action was sensual, erotic almost.

She held his look, her green eyes twinkling, and her fingers reached for his wrist again. Unconsciously, she began to stroke his skin and felt a tremor of excitement ran through him. Suddenly, she realised what she was doing and pulled her hand away quickly, eliciting a soft moan from Jamie's lips.

'I'm sorry,' she murmured apologetically, embarrassed. 'I shouldn't have done that.'

'Hey, don't apologise,' Jamie responded quickly, trying to smile. 'I was enjoying it.' He hoped he was breaking down her defences. 'Where are you from?' he asked, trying to keep her there with him for as long as possible. 'You're not from around here.' She laughed softly. It was a deep, sonorous, sexy laugh that set his pulse racing again.

'Ten out of ten,' she replied. 'I'm English, from The Midlands…a little mining town called Calverton, just outside Nottingham. Have you heard of it?'

'No, can't say I have…but I *have* heard of Nottingham,' he replied seriously. 'Nottingham Forrest…good football team.'

'You like football, then?' she asked, keeping the conversation going.

'Oh aye, I like it a lot,' Jamie responded enthusiastically. 'I play a bit.'

'Really? So did my Dad,' she replied getting caught up in it. 'He's a miner but he played for Mansfield Town when he was younger. Have you heard of them?'

'Yeah, I have actually,' Jamie replied and laughed at the look of disbelief which spread across her face. 'I do Littlewoods Pools every week,' he explained. 'Mansfield Town, English Third Division. Am I right?' he continued, grinning as her expression changed.

'Yes,' she confirmed with a grin. 'You are. My Dad played for them about fifteen years ago,' she threw in. She seemed impressed by Jamie's knowledge of the lower reaches of English football. Jamie, on the other hand, was impressed by her.

They were gazing at each other again and the look Jamie had seen earlier was back in the girl's eyes. He prayed he wasn't misreading things. There was only one way to find out. 'Listen,' he started in a low voice. 'I know you're married, but if there's a chance...I mean...I really would like to see you again.' She didn't respond right away, taken aback by the directness of Jamie's approach, and he waited for the expected negative response.

She surprised him and, to a lesser extent, herself. 'Do you really mean that?' she asked, her voice no louder than a whisper. Jamie thought she was wrestling with a dilemma...a line in the sand that she was now thinking of crossing.

'That's a silly question,' he replied, keeping his voice low to match hers. 'You already know the answer,' he continued, persuasively.

She blushed and took hold of his hand again. Her eyes seemed to be searching his face again, looking for a reason to go forward with this or to retreat. There was a moment's silence and her face grew serious. 'Yes,' she said finally. 'I'd like to see you again too.' Jamie couldn't believe what he was hearing. 'I'll come to see you when you're moved into the recovery ward,' she continued.

'And later? When I get out of here?' he pushed.

'We'll see,' she laughed softly. There was a pause as Jamie digested this piece of news. 'Maybe you won't want to,' she added.

Am I dreaming, Jamie asked himself? The silky touch of her fingers on his wrist convinced him otherwise...he was fully awake. 'No chance,' he whispered, taking hold of her fingers. He still half expected her to pull away but, to his delight, she didn't. *I'm winning,* he told himself, and was about to move on to the next stage of his conquest when the door swung inwards and their nascent love affair was interrupted by a dishevelled looking young man in a white coat. The man, a doctor Jamie assumed, swept hurriedly into the room with an older, more senior, nurse in his wake, like a pilot fish following a shark.

Jamie let go of the nurse's fingers and she moved quickly to the foot of his bed, picking up his notes and updating them. Jamie turned his attention to the doctor and waited.

The man made his way to Jamie's bedside and gave him a professional smile, exhibiting nicotine stained teeth in the process. 'Hello Mr Raeburn,' he started. 'I'm Dr McLean and this,' he continued, turning to the older nurse, 'is Sister Maguire. You're looking better,' he announced.

Jamie kept his body still and swivelled his eyes to look at the man. 'Am I?' he asked stiffly. 'I hate to think what I looked like before, then,' he continued. 'To be honest, I still feel bloody awful.'

The doctor smiled and the effect softened his features. Jamie examined him more closely. He was probably in his late twenties or early thirties, Jamie guessed. His white coat was crushed and the shock of dirty blonde hair above his sallow face was unkempt and straggly. He was scarecrow-esque and his hair looked as if it hadn't been intimately acquainted with a brush or comb for weeks rather than days. His eyes were dark rimmed, probably from lack of sleep and, as Jamie watched, amused, he tried to stifle a yawn. The stethoscope dangling precariously around his neck risked being snagged on a row of pens which filled the breast pocket of his coat.

'That's only to be expected after what you've been through,' Dr McLean advised.

'What exactly *have* I been through, doctor?' Jamie asked quietly.

'You don't remember?' the doctor queried, leaning over Jamie as he stuck the ends of the stethoscope into his ears and pressed the cold metal of it against Jamie's chest.

'Not a lot...bits, that's all,' Jamie replied as the doctor moved the stethoscope across his body.

'You were in the wars,' the doctor replied as he rose up. 'Stabbed in the back a couple of times, not to mention being kicked and punched about the head and body,' he explained in a matter of fact, almost bored tone. 'Fortunately, you're still with us...but it was touch and go for a while. Your liver was damaged and you lost quite a bit of blood. You've got three cracked ribs and a lot of bruising.'

Jamie lay still and digested the information. Suddenly he remembered the American and wondered if the man had made it. 'How long will I be in here doctor?' he asked, his eyes moving back to the younger nurse who was still hovering at the foot of the bed.

'In here, the ICU,' the doctor said quietly and paused, considering the timescale. 'Maybe another couple of days,' he continued. 'Then we'll move you into the recovery ward and after that you're probably looking at another 6 or 7 days, maybe a little longer.'

'And what about the Yank sailor? Did he make it?' Jamie enquired.

The young doctor's haggard face split into a wide grin. Suddenly he looked more his age. 'Oh aye, our American friend is very much alive...and telling everyone about the mysterious stranger who saved his life.'

'Who was that?' Jamie asked, surprised.

The doctor looked down on him, his tired eyes opening wide in amazement. 'You really *don't* remember, do you?' he said, shaking his head. 'Apparently, it was you...you saved his life...or so he says. Quite the hero, eh?' he smiled.

Jamie's eyes registered shock and he was conscious of the young nurse's eyes on him. He wondered what she was thinking. For Jamie, the news was *under*whelming. He could do this...in Glasgow being a hero was simply a guarantee of more trouble; hero = hard man = target to take down. *Shit, shit, shit* he repeated over and over in his mind. Please God, make this go away, he prayed. He tried to move but the pain ripped through him. The wires, tubes and needles pulled at him and he groaned involuntarily.

'Try and lie still,' the doctor said solicitously as the young nurse came to Jamie's side again and eased him gently back down onto the bed. 'I know it's uncomfortable,' the doctor continued. 'But all of this stuff is necessary.' He waved his arm around encompassing the equipment.

'Uncomfortable!' Jamie retorted through gritted teeth. 'That's an understatement.'

'We'll get you something for that,' the doctor continued. He turned to the young nurse, holding out his hand for Jamie's notes. Already prepared, she handed them to him and the doctor scanned them quickly. 'Give him another 10mg of Morphine and repeat it every four hours,' he instructed, scribbling an addition to the notes and returning them. 'The Morphine will ease the pain and help you rest,' he said and nodded in the direction of the young nurse. 'Nurse Maxwell here will be keeping a close eye on you,' he finished off with a smile then turned away quickly and left the room, the Sister Maguire following dutifully behind him.

'So, it's Nurse Maxwell,' Jamie said, grinning, as the door closed. 'What's your first name?'

'Katherine...Kate,' she replied with a shy smile.

'Nice name,' he said. 'I'm Jamie.'

'Yes, I know,' she responded huskily. 'And I *will* be keeping a close eye on you.'

She left him then and Jamie returned to the thoughts of his unwanted hero status. That was just the sort of thing that brought challenges...of the physical sort. In this city a hero was somebody every wee psycho wanted to chib and he could get into enough trouble without that. *Christ, what a mess,* he thought. Kate Maxwell returned at that moment and provided him with welcome distraction.

He watched as she busied herself with a small phial of morphine and a hypodermic syringe, carefully removing the seals on both. Deftly, she inserted the tip of the needle into the tiny bottle and drew some of the fluid into the hypodermic. She came to him then, smiling, and lifted his arm, examining it carefully. Seemingly satisfied, she laid his arm back down and then tapped the syringe lightly with her fingers before expelling a minute amount of fluid through the needle.

'What are you doing?' Jamie asked anxiously, having developed a sudden aversion to needles.

She smiled down at him and temporarily eased his fear. 'I'm going to give you a shot of morphine and I'm just making sure there aren't any bubbles in the syringe,' she explained. 'We don't want bubbles...that would be *bad* medicine,' she laughed and her face split into a grin as Jamie's complexion changed colour to a ghastly white. Kate took hold of his wrist again and lifted his arm. 'I'm just looking for a good vein,' she continued with another smile, anticipating Jamie's unspoken question.

Her smile lit up the whole room and Jamie instantly felt better. He looked into her eyes and was struck again by the depth of colour in them. They sparkled, like emeralds caught in the rays of the sun, and her hair was darker than he had first imagined, almost black in fact. When the light hit the burnished copper strands in the dark chestnut they glowed like neon strips. *And* she had a lovely figure and a magnificent bum! He was love-struck and he wanted her.

Kate was still smiling as her fingers held his arm firmly.

'Will I live?' Jamie asked, jokingly.

'Oh yes, you'll live,' she laughed. 'Your pulse is racing just now...but it'll settle down soon.' She could have added the words "when I leave you" because it was obvious what was causing his heart to pound but there was no need...they both knew why his heart was pounding. She laughed quietly as Jamie's cheeks reddened.

'Will this hurt?' he asked nervously. 'I'm not fond of needles.'

'Hush,' she whispered. 'I'm sure it won't hurt a big boy like you,' she said, holding his eyes with hers and the look in those deep, green pools settled him. Suitably distracted, he hardly felt the sharp prick of the needle as it entered his arm.

'There you go. You'll feel better soon,' Kate promised as she withdrew the needle from his arm and pressed a piece of cotton wool to the tiny incision. 'You'll sleep now and I'll be around, don't worry.'

'Thanks,' Jamie replied dreamily as the morphine kicked in. He was already feeling better but that, he suspected, had little to do with the morphine. Just being close to Kate Maxwell was calming but the morphine too worked its magic and the pain began to ease. His eyes drooped and he slipped back into unconsciousness. The last thing he saw was Kate's smile and then he was drifting away on a cloud of cotton wool.

Chapter 3

Jamie was moved into Ward 2, the Recovery Ward, two days later. Still heavily bandaged he presented as a passable Egyptian Mummy. He still felt pain when he moved too much but, on the plus side, the dark bruising around his ribs and eyes had faded to a pale yellow. The move took place late in the afternoon, just before meal time, and as a result he felt neglected and a bit sorry for himself. The ward was busy with all of the beds occupied and the nurses were rushed off their feet. He hadn't realised how demanding a nurse's work was and he was full of admiration for them. Being a welder really wasn't so bad, he realised!

But Jamie quickly discovered that he wasn't an ideal patient. The nurses scolded him constantly for doing things that he shouldn't and a feeling of helplessness enveloped him. He wanted to move about on his own, he was gasping for a cigarette and he was embarrassed by having to piss and crap into a cardboard container.

There was a big man in the bed next to Jamie's and he, like Jamie, was heavily bandaged around the head and body. He lay quietly, completely still, and Jamie thought at first that he could be dead. When the evening meal was served Jamie picked disinterestedly at his food. Home cooking it wasn't but it didn't matter much; he had other things on his mind, things of a carnal rather than of a carnivorous nature. He looked at the nurses, appraising them and comparing them to Kate Maxwell. A few of them were around his age but the majority were in their thirties, or older. The younger ones were, in the main, attractive but there was something about Kate that they didn't have and he spent a lot of time trying to figure out what that something was.

Visiting hour that first night, from 7pm until 8pm, turned out to be an hour of unmitigated suffering. His mother and father arrived at seven pm prompt as part of a crowd of visitors and swept into the ward like a tsunami as the doors opened. Jamie spotted his father's sour look immediately, a clear indication that he was here under protest. To be fair, his father had to get up for work at four o'clock every morning and visiting Jamie meant he wouldn't be home until late tonight. Jamie's mother, however, was a force to be reckoned with. If she insisted that he come then he came. Anything for a peaceful life!

Doctor McLean joined them at Jamie's bed shortly after their arrival and closed the curtains to afford them a semblance of privacy. Jamie shook his head. How curtains gave discussions privacy he still couldn't work out. The doctor started into his spiel immediately. 'There's no need to tell you that James is lucky to be alive,' he started. That's it doc, Jamie thought sarcastically, break it to them gently. 'One of the stab wounds was particularly serious. It cut his liver and he bled internally from that.' Jamie now found himself listening intently, starting to take in things he hadn't listened to before. 'As I say, he was lucky...he was brought in here quickly and we were able to stop the bleeding...but a few minutes later and the result could have been different.'

He was going over old ground but there had to be good news, Jamie hoped. There was. 'Thankfully, James is progressing well and there shouldn't be any long term damage,' the doctor continued and his professional, plastic smile was back. 'He will need to stay with us a bit longer but he'll be allowed home soon.'

Jamie felt a wave of relief flood over him but he detected a hint of anxiety in his mother's voice when she spoke next. 'Will he need someone with him all the time, doctor?' she asked. Jamie's initial thought was that she was probably worried about her job, but that was unkind and he immediately chastised himself. His mother worked because she had to, not because she liked to, and without her wages coming into the house they would struggle. More guilt, he sighed silently. Maybe if he gave her more each week his mother could stop working. Nice thought but impractical, he realised.

Fortunately the doctor put his mother's mind at rest. 'No, not at all,' he assured her. 'James just needs to rest and build up his strength,' he continued. 'And a District Nurse will call in to see him. He's a strong lad so nothing special is required.'

'Thank you, doctor,' Mary Raeburn replied, clearly relieved.

There was an awkward silence, broken finally by Dr. McLean. 'Well, unless there are any other questions, I'll leave you in peace,' he said, casting a quick look around their faces and waiting for a moment just in case one of them thought of something to ask. Then, when met with silence, he thrust out his hand and shook hands with Jamie's father and mother, pulled back the curtain and left.

Jamie looked around the ward. Men of all ages were propped up on pillows, surrounded by visitors, and all of them appeared to be searching for something meaningful to say. All of them other than the big man in the next bed who lay alone, still apparently asleep.

The remainder of the visit was mental torture for Jamie. His mother nagged him relentlessly, berating him for his stupidity in getting involved in the fight in the first place and his father simply brooded in silence with his face like thunder. He was probably desperate for a pint of Newcastle Brown, Jamie thought sympathetically, and, come to think of it, I could kill a Guinness myself. He said little, nodding with resigned acceptance at his mother's little speech, and allowed her loving chastisement to wash over him. He experienced blessed relief when the bell rang to bring the visit to an end. Finishing it with a bell was appropriate; Jamie felt as if he'd just gone ten rounds with Henry Cooper. He smiled ruefully.

His mother returned his smile, blissfully unaware of what was behind it. 'We'll be back tomorrow, love,' she said and leant over the bed to kiss him before pushing herself to her feet. Jamie looked over to his father who smiled back at him and raised his eyebrows to the ceiling. The anticipation of another ten rounds tomorrow was almost too much for Jamie and as they passed through the doors he let out an enormous sigh.

As the last of the visitors departed, the ward returned to normal and the big man in the next bed turned painfully towards Jamie, his screwed up eyes reflecting his discomfort. 'Hey buddy,' he wheezed. 'Are you the kid who was stabbed in Cowcaddens on Friday night?' Jamie heard the words and turned towards the man, annoyed.

Who are you calling "kid", was Jamie's first angry reaction before he recognised the accent and the face behind the bandages. 'You're still here then,' he replied, stating the obvious.

'Yeah kid, I'm still here… thanks to you,' the big American responded gratefully. 'I thought I was a goner until you turned up.' The man was speaking slowly and steadily as though he wanted to be sure he could be understood. 'Listen kid,' he continued. 'I really want to thank you for saving my hide. I'm being moved back down to the USS Simon Lake at Holy Loch tomorrow.' The man's voice was charged with emotion and Jamie felt embarrassed. 'I heard your Mom talking there...she thinks you were crazy for getting involved,' he continued. 'And she's right...but if you hadn't, those guys would have kicked me to death.'

Jamie smiled grimly as memories of that night flashed back . 'Aye, they probably would,' he laughed morosely. 'Kickin' folk to death is a National Sport in this city, second only to football.' He coughed, grimacing with pain as the hack caught his cracked ribs.

'My name's Conor, by the way, Conor Whelan,' the American continued.

'And you're a sailor,' Jamie added.

'Yeah, I am. Lieutenant Conor Whelan, Conor with one "n", U.S. Navy...at your service,' the American said proudly, sounding just a little pretentious. 'What's your name kid?' he asked.

'Jamie Raeburn, Welder, 1st Class, John Brown & Company...best shipyard in the world, by the way...and stop callin' me kid!' Jamie fired back cheekily, grinning from ear to ear as the Yank started to laugh. The laugh was short lived and a scowl of pain appeared on his face. 'Conor?' Jamie continued, repeating the name. 'Unusual,' he remarked.

'It's Irish,' the American replied. 'It means "lover of hounds", according to my old man.'

Jamie looked at him dubiously. 'Oh aye?' he fired back sarcastically, his eyes taking in what they could of the American's handsome face beneath the bandages. 'Hounds...as in dogs? Makes a change from sheep,' Jamie sniggered. You don't look like the sort of guy who would have to settle for dogs.' He laughed louder and carried on quickly before the American could respond. 'Right enough, it's hard to tell,' he conceded. 'Look at me, for example. I know it's hard to believe, but I've been out with a few dogs myself recently,' he added, keeping a straight face with difficulty. A puzzled look appeared on Conor Whelan's face. Lost in translation, Jamie thought, and laughed again.

Jamie's laughter was infectious and the American soon joined in but stopped sharply as pain kicked in. 'Jesus, I won't forget those guys in a hurry,' he drawled. 'Listen Jamie, like I said, I want to thank you properly,' Conor Whelan repeated. 'If I leave you a telephone number will you call me when you get outa here?'

'It's alright,' Jamie replied genuinely. 'You don't need to thank me. You're alive, that's enough,' he told the man but his thoughts were already back on the events of Friday night. 'What the fuck were you doin' there anyway?' he asked eventually. 'It's a bit off the beaten track for you guys, especially an officer. There's no prossies down that way,' he added. 'Unless you know somethin' I don't,' he finished with a smile.

Jamie didn't get an answer. Their conversation was interrupted by the arrival of Kate Maxwell at Jamie's bedside but the anxious expression that had passed, albeit fleetingly, across Conor Whelan's face made Jamie wonder...just what *was* Lieutenant Conor Whelan doing there on Friday?

But now Jamie had more important things on his mind. Even with his senses deadened by the drugs he felt a surge of arousal as Kate appeared beside him. She really was beautiful, he noted again. Her dark hair was swept back and her big green eyes, full mouth and sensuous lips set his pulse racing. And when she smiled, two big dimples appeared on her cheeks. *Remember, she's married*, he told himself.

'How are you?' she started, looking shyly towards Conor Whelan as she spoke.

Jamie followed the direction of her look and caught his new friend's eye, smiling as Conor winked surreptitiously, and then he turned his attention back to Kate. 'I feel better every time I see you,' he said as his eyes settled on her.

Kate blushed nervously and smoothed down the front of her uniform dress which only enhanced the fullness of her breasts and aroused Jamie even more. He looked down the bed, a little self-consciously, noticing the tell-tale mound at his groin. Ah well, he thought sheepishly, at least she can see the effect she has on me and she'll know I want her. Are you flattered, Kate Maxwell, he wondered?

'I'm glad you're feeling better,' Kate stammered shyly, which Jamie took to be because of Conor Whelan's attention. 'I'd better get back to work,' she continued. 'I'll come back when I finish my shift in the morning,' she said, almost whispering.

'Yes please,' Jamie replied. 'I'd like that.' He smiled at her and held her wonderful green eyes with his big brown ones for a wonderful moment...like the positive and negative poles of a magnet.

Kate gave him another nervous smile. 'I'd better go,' she repeated quickly. 'I'll see you in the morning.' She was smiling but Jamie got the impression that she was still a little nervous about where this was going. He watched her longingly as she left the ward and willed her to turn around as she reached the door. She did, smiled back at him and then she was gone.

'Well, well,' Conor smiled knowingly. 'That little lady seems to have the hots for you, kid,' he observed. 'And she aint no dog!'

'Aye, she's quite somethin', isn't she?' Jamie agreed with a wan smile. 'But she's married, mate...and knowin' my luck, her man's probably a big bastard,' he laughed sardonically. 'Yeah, I want her...but who knows?'

'Why the doubt?' Conor continued. 'What's up?'

Jamie lay back and examined a spot on the ceiling above his bed. 'Well, last time I got involved with a good looking bird like her she started playin' around behind my back,' he said quietly, almost to himself. 'Maybe I'm just feelin' guilty.'

'*You're* feeling guilty?' Conor repeated, bewildered. 'I don't get it kid...oops, sorry, Jamie,' he corrected himself with a laugh. '*She's* coming on to *you*...what is there to feel guilty about?' he asked.

Good question, Jamie thought, what *is* there to feel guilty about? He found himself explaining and realised, quite suddenly, that he was explaining the situation to himself rather than to Conor Whelan. 'When I found out I felt like shit,' he said quietly. 'I'm just feeling sorry for what it'll do to the guy when he finds out.'

Conor Whelan looked at him in amusement. 'Shee-it, Jamie,' he laughed. 'That's way too deep for me. Okay, I hear what you're sayin' kid, but I still can't believe you'd give up that little piece of tail because some other dame did the dirty on you,' he argued, shaking his head in disbelief. 'Simple truth...that little lady wants to get laid...by you, end of,' he continued. 'And what her old man don't know won't hurt him,' he rationalised. 'Hell kid, if I didn't lay married broads I probably wouldn't get laid at all,' he finished with a laugh.

Jamie looked at him. The twinkle in his new friend's eyes said it all. The big American was right, what harm could it do? And Kate Maxwell was a hell ova lot better looking than some of the girls he'd shagged recently, he reminded himself. He started to laugh. 'You're right, fuck it,' he grinned. 'What her old man don't know won't hurt him,' he laughed, mimicking Conor, accent and all.

They spent the next hour or so chatting about anything and everything, but mostly about women. Conor Whelan had been born and brought up in the Roxbury suburb of Boston. He was fourth generation Irish-American and fiercely proud of it. His great granddaddy, as he referred to him, had gone over to the States from Ireland back in the 1800's and Conor's grandfather and father had both been cops in Boston. His father still was but he spent his days behind a desk nowadays. Conor had been expected to follow in the tradition but he had other ideas. One fine afternoon, when he had finished school, he had gone into the city and paid a visit to the U.S. Navy Recruitment Office and had signed up there and then. His father had taken it badly at the time but he had been forgiven now.

Conor wanted to see the world and, in the words of the song, had joined the navy to do just that. Jamie had been impressed with his descriptions of Hawaii and Japan and his stories about the Japanese girls gave, as Jamie had put it, a different slant on sex. But he had been to some shit holes as well and Hue and Da Nang in South Vietnam and Dunoon didn't tick the boxes of "exotic" as far as Jamie was concerned.

Americans, in general, tended to turn Jamie off; his experience of them at the Locarno most weekends saw to that...the old wartime phrase "over paid, over sexed and over here" hit the spot. But he found himself liking Conor Whelan and he was glad he'd gone to help the American...even though he had come out of it badly. When he broached the subject of why Conor had been in Cowcaddens that fateful night there was an awkward pause and Jamie got the impression that the American was avoiding the question. He implied it had something to do with a woman which, given that he was a Yank, probably had more money than sense, was lonely, and was away from home, might be fair enough but Jamie felt there was something else. But if there was some other reason, did it really matter, Jamie asked himself?

They talked until late and their raucous, bawdy laughter drew the wrath of the nurses. Eventually, with the ward lights extinguished they fell silent and tried to sleep.

For Jamie, sleep was difficult. First of all, he was uncomfortable. His bandages were rough and itchy and he found the heat in the ward oppressive. He thought of home. There, the central heating was rarely used and his mother relied on a coal fire in the living room to provide heat for the whole house. As a result, Jamie was used to sleeping in a cool bedroom and no matter what he tried here, even throwing the bedcovers aside, the heat was too much for him. Secondly, he couldn't get Kate Maxwell out of his mind. Carnal thoughts kept him awake. He did doze off from time to time but tossed and turned incessantly until exhaustion finally won.

Chapter 4

Conor Whelan couldn't sleep either, but he had other things on his mind. Jamie Raeburn's question as to why he had been at that particular spot in Cowcaddens on Friday night had unsettled him and he was sure Jamie had picked up on it. That wasn't a question Conor could answer. At least, it wasn't one he could answer honestly. He would probably be dead now but for Jamie Raeburn's arrival on the scene that night and for that he owed him...big time, but he was worried about Jamie's suspicion. He liked Jamie a lot but the kid was one sharp cookie. His evasion when Jamie asked him outright why he had been there would have been picked up and he knew he'd need to watch his step from now on.

His mind drifted back to Friday night. His rendezvous with Brendan Kelly had been arranged at short notice. The phone call earlier in the day had taken him by surprise and, without back-up and against his better judgement, he had gone along with Brendan's request. He had taken a taxi from Central Station, getting the cab to drop him near St. George's Cross to the north of the city centre. He was about a hundred, maybe a hundred and fifty yards from the address for the rendezvous...and he was early. He had played that bit by the book and watched the building from the shadow of a close entrance further down the street for about thirty minutes before going in. He felt uncomfortable; this wasn't his usual role, he was an analyst, not a spook and being alone and unarmed had unsettled him. But everything appeared to be perfectly normal. It was a typical Glasgow tenement in a typical Glasgow street and, as far as he could see, there was nothing out of the ordinary and the street was deserted. Lights were on behind curtains and blinds in most of the apartments and he could hear faint music coming from a radio. He'd been in worse places in his life; he remembered thinking at the time. The snow had started to fall as he waited and he stamped his feet to keep warm. He felt out of his depth, exposed, and was keen to get the meeting over with and back to the U.S.S. Simon Lake as quickly as possible. Deciding that the area was clear he had made his way along the road towards the address.

Stepping into the close mouth he had been startled by the sudden appearance of two young men who appeared from the back of the building. He had backed up against the close wall, allowing them to pass, and they had walked out into the darkened street, laughing and joking. They had paid him little attention but there was something about them that had worried him at the time. Some sixth sense sent a warning tingle down his spine. When the noise of their footsteps and voices had faded into the distance he had climbed warily to the second floor. He recalled that the door had been opened quickly to his knock, revealing the face of Brendan Kelly, and relief had flooded him. Brendan had stepped aside and ushered him in and had then waited by the open door, listening for a moment, before following him through to a basic, poorly furnished, room and kitchen.

The meeting had been brief, but necessary. Discussions such as they were having weren't advisable on unsecure telephone lines and Brendan Kelly was nothing if not paranoid about security. And that was when Brendan had dropped his bombshell.

'We're bein' watched,' Brendan said easily in his soft Irish brogue. 'So watch yer back.'

Conor remembered the cold sweat that had broken out on him then. 'Who's watching? How do you know, he had asked? His voice had been an octave higher than normal and Brendan's cold smile in response would stay with him forever.

'As to who,' Brendan responded. 'I don't know. It might be the Brits...or it might be Loyalists from the North,' he shrugged. 'But whoever it is, they're out there. My boys have spotted them.'

'But why?' Conor had persisted. 'How can they know?'

Brendan had simply given a cold laugh. 'Brit security's paranoid, they watch everybody...an' it's me they're watchin' sonny, not you.'

Conor distinctly remembered Brendan watching him with an amused look as he had fretted. 'As long as they don't see us together you'll be fine, Yank, don't worry,' Brendan said with a laugh.

A comforting thought, Conor remembered saying, but he thought it prudent to mention the two young men in the close mouth. Brendan had laughed aloud. 'They were mine,' he said. 'We saw you in that close down the road an' I sent them out to make sure you didn't have a tail.'

'If they don't know about me why would I have a tail?' he had asked, but Brendan deigned not to reply, which simply strung Conor's nerves even tighter.

When he left the flat later, stepping tentatively out into the deserted street, he had looked up and down the road in both directions searching for anything or anyone out of place. But, as before, there was nothing to arouse suspicion and there was nobody about. The snow was lying thick by then, pristine and unmarked by the passage of feet or vehicles. He had walked down past St Georges Cross and then took the fateful decision to return to the city centre via Cowcaddens. His eyes had darted from shadow to shadow. He could see no one but he had the feeling that he was being watched and that had unnerved him.

Lying here now with the benefit of hindsight, Conor realised he had made a big mistake. The route up through Cowcaddens was quiet and there was a lot of derelict property. He had tried to find a taxi but the snow had cut the traffic down. He knew now that he should have headed down towards Charing Cross which was always busy on a Friday night...and the Shore Patrol would have been there in force too. Yeah, big mistake, he told himself.

Walking in the shadows his nerves had been constantly on edge and the feeling of being watched had been pervasive. He turned frequently to look over his shoulder, sometimes stepping into close mouths to listen for the sound of running feet, but still there had been nothing out of the ordinary. He had been in situations like this before, he had reminded himself, and in far more dangerous places. He put his feeling of unease down to a sense of paranoia instilled in him by Brendan and had trudged on through the snow, eventually reaching Cambridge Street. The tension in him had started to ease then. Soon he would be in Sauchiehall Street, mingling with the crowds, and that would provide relative safety. Looking back, he realised that the perceived proximity to safety had resulted in him dropping his guard. That had been his second big mistake. Field work clearly wasn't his forte.

The snow, falling lightly until then, had started to fall from the heavens in giant flakes which quickly obliterated the road and pavement. He remembered seeing the derelict buildings on his left and the "KEEP OUT" signs warning the public that they were dangerous and about to be demolished. He had noticed too the broken windows and heard the sound of water running from a burst pipes inside the properties. The lights of a pub had appeared in front of him through the curtain of snow and he began to relax even more. Soon he would be in the crowds in the centre of the city. He was happily anticipating the train journey back to Gourock and the ferry across to Dunoon when they came for him.

The attack had taken him completely by surprise and that worried him. He remembered passing a gap between two derelict buildings on his left, an alley, when two men had appeared out of the darkness. He had sensed danger and pressed his back against the stone wall behind him, wishing he had brought a weapon. The men were young and they were laughing and joking easily. One of them was buttoning up his fly and Conor presumed what he now knew he had been expected to presume; two young guys, too much to drink, down the alley for a piss. He had relaxed again but as he eased himself away from the wall and started to walk on he was grabbed from behind. Something blunt and heavy, he didn't know what, hit him hard on the back of the head. The pain had been excruciating but it was only the hors d'oeuvres. His arms were pinioned tightly behind him and he was frog marched into the lane. He felt the stickiness of his blood matting the hair at the back of his head and a warm trickle ran down his back. He knew he was in serious trouble. Two more men waited in the darkness deeper in the alley and he could remember one of them laughing harshly and the words "we've got some questions for ye, Yank" spoken in a guttural, Ulster accent. These two men were older than the two behind him and the one who spoke was obviously in charge.

He was still held tightly, his arms locked behind his back, and he was unable to move. All four men were so close now he could smell the sweat on them. The two older, harder faced men were his interrogators and their questions had started immediately.

"*Who are you?*" They asked. "Just an American sailor out looking for a woman", he had told them. "*Wrong answer Yank*" came the reply, accompanied by a back handed slap across the face.

"*Why were you meeting Brendan Kelly?*" "Who's Brendan Kelly?"

"*What is that cunt Brendan planning?*" "I told you, I don't know anybody called Brendan Kelly."

And so it had gone on. They weren't getting the answers they wanted and the man in charge had laughed harshly and nodded to his companion. A punch had landed hard on Conor's cheek loosening two of his teeth and before he could recover the man's knee hit him viciously in the groin. He had wanted to buckle with the pain then but the two men behind him held him upright, their grip unyielding. There had been a gurgling laugh from one of them and then another backhanded blow had landed on his right cheek. More pain and more blood. A ring on his assailant's finger ripped the skin over Conor's eye.

"Don't fuck with us, Yank," his questioner had said softly and that softness racked up Conor's fear. "I'll ask you again…who are you, and what is that Republican cunt Kelly planning?"

Conor remembered repeating his earlier denials, pleading ignorance, and then the roof had fallen in. The violence of the attack was like nothing he had ever experienced before. Punches and kicks had rained in on him from every angle. His ribs took a pounding and punch after punch landed on his stomach, his head and his groin. Held tightly from behind, unable to avoid the blows, he quickly started to lose consciousness.

He could remember the men behind him letting go of him and the cold, wet, snow covered ground coming up to meet him as he crumpled like a rag doll. All four men had started on him then. He had curled up foetally in the snow, his arms wrapped around his head for protection, but it was futile. He remembered expecting to die then. He remembered too screaming and shouting for help but expecting none. Hanging on by the skin of his teeth, all he could hear was the heavy, laboured breathing of his attackers, their curses and their cruel laughter as they hit him again and again.

And then Jamie Raeburn arrived. The kicks and punches had lessened immediately as the two younger guys had pulled away from him but apart from that he could remember little else until Jamie had screamed at him to run. After that, he remembered bursting into the light of the main road and people swarming around him, more shouting, more swearing. He had passed out then and his next memory was of waking up here in the hospital. He shuddered and felt the sweat grow cold on his body.

As he looked over at Jamie lying in the adjacent bed he could see the price the kid had paid for playing the "Good Samaritan". Conor Whelan closed his eyes and offered up a silent prayer thanking God for sending him to help. Sleep, when it eventually came to him, was troubled.

Chapter 5

As Conor Whelan lay in his bed tormenting himself with the events of that Friday night, Kate Maxwell sat with Barbara Laing at the Nurses' Station in the I.C.U. She was troubled and it was showing. Going to see Jamie Raeburn earlier had been a fateful step, maybe even a mistake. "Don't get burned" she remembered Barbara saying but that, Kate sensed, was what might happen.

Talking to Jamie Raeburn was easy. He was good fun. He made her laugh…and that was something she hadn't done for a long, long time. He fancied her, she could see it in his eyes, and she felt the same about him. Their mutual flirting had made her feel good. To sum it all up, Jamie Raeburn was easy to be with, he was good looking with big, dark brown eyes and long brown hair, and he was fit. But, and it was a big but, she suspected he didn't take life too seriously and that was why she had the feeling she would be hurt. But…it was another but, she reflected, maybe her own problems and personal baggage would hurt him too.

For the first time since the tingle had passed through her on seeing Jamie Raeburn on his admission into the Intensive Care Unit, Kate thought about her husband and her family back in England. Tom Maxwell, the man she had married four years before, wasn't the man who occasionally came home to her now. He was a stranger. His drinking had been insidious, eating away at their relationship slowly but surely. The few pints he had taken at the weekends became a few pints every day and before Kate really knew what was happening, drink had taken over Tom's life. They stopped sleeping together. He stayed out at night, initially just the odd night, then two or three and eventually he would disappear for days on end. They drifted apart and now he didn't seem to have any interest in her at all.

In the beginning she had wondered if he was seeing another woman, or worse, other women, but rationally she knew that couldn't be the case. He wasn't taking care of himself; he rarely shaved or washed and his personal hygiene had deteriorated badly, not the sort of thing you did or allowed to happen to you if you were chasing other women. Four years and the fairy-tale had all gone horribly wrong. They hadn't slept together for months now and, if she was honest with herself, she didn't want him anywhere near her. What had happened, she asked herself? Had he simply grown bored of her? If so, whose fault was that, she wondered, his or her own? Or was it the arrival of Lauren? Ever since Lauren's birth Tom had seemed unable to cope. It was as if he was jealous of her but that was such an outlandish notion that Kate continually pushed it from her mind. But it refused to go away.

Thinking about it, leaving Lauren behind in Calverton with her mother when she and Tom moved to Glasgow had been Tom's idea. She had baulked against it, argued with him over it, but she had given in…eventually. He said it would a temporary measure; promised her that once they were settled in Glasgow Lauren would join them…and she had believed him. Admittedly, the first few months in Glasgow had been good. They found a nice house, Tom was working hard, he was drinking less and he was attentive to her…loving even. She had been excited at the prospect of Lauren joining them and of their being a family again but when she had raised it with him, Tom had made excuses; the house wasn't ready, he was working long hours and Kate had her job in The Royal, childcare would be a problem. And so on and so on. And as Kate persisted, his drinking started again…with a vengeance. She could see it all clearly now; he wanted her all to himself and couldn't share her, even with his daughter. If that was true, things would never be normal again.

These thoughts brought her back to Jamie Raeburn. Was having an affair with him really a good idea? Yes, she was attracted to him…she had already admitted that to herself. Why else was she popping round to Ward 2 like a love struck schoolgirl? But was a fling worth the risk? What would Tom do if he found out? And, more to the point, how would Jamie react when he learned that she had a two year old daughter?

'You've got that look on your face again, Kate,' Barbara Laing said gently, interrupting her meditation. 'Having second thoughts?'

'Yes…and third, and fourth and fifth,' Kate replied, forcing a smile.

'What's worrying you?'

Kate shook her head slowly. She needed to talk to someone and Barbara was closer to her than anyone else in Glasgow…by a long way. But where could she start? No one here knew about Lauren and Kate wanted to keep it that way if she could. She felt guilty at leaving her behind. Again, nobody other than Barbara knew about Tom's drinking or how she now felt about Jamie Raeburn. That part made her feel foolish, awkward, like a silly schoolgirl.

'It's easier if you talk about it,' Barbara continued, her voice still gentle, persuasive. 'Take it from someone who knows,' she added tellingly.

Kate forced another smile. 'You told me not to get burned but I think that's what's going to happen,' she replied, keeping her voice low to match Barbara's.

'You already have been, Kate,' Barbara said softly. 'How long did you say Tom's been drinking?'

'God,' Kate retorted with a pained sigh. 'It's been a long time…it seems like forever.'

'And you still think he'll come out of it?' Barbara continued with a cynicism that took Kate by surprise. She shook her head sadly as Kate nodded in response. 'I'll let you into a secret,' she said quietly. 'My first husband was…still is, an alcoholic. Like your Tom, he promised he would stop, time and time again, and I believed him every time…because I wanted to believe him. We had a son, Mark, who was growing up seeing his father constantly drunk and both of us arguing and fighting. My husband was always feeling sorry for himself; always looking for money for "just one more beer", always saying he was sorry and that he loved me and Mark…and I think that, actually, he did love us. A deep sadness seemed to descend on Barbara then and she paused, biting a finger nail for a moment before carrying on, her head down and her voice softer, more reflective. 'Truth is, he didn't love us enough to stop drinking and eventually, I just couldn't take it anymore. We were in serious debt and he was missing days at work…then he lost his job. He found somebody else to blame for that too, the man who reported him. Drunk in charge of a welding torch,' she laughed bitterly. 'It's a dangerous enough job when you're sober, I imagine.' She paused, her eyes filling up, but Kate remained silent, struck by the parallels in both their lives. 'It was always "poor me" with never a thought for me or his kid,' Barbara continued, anger creeping in. 'The sad thing is he couldn't admit he was an alcoholic, so I left him.' Barbara paused again and a tear rolled down her cheek. 'It's not easy Kate,' she continued, her voice stronger again. 'I know that…but you have a life too. I was lucky, I met a lovely man who loves me and looks after my son, Mark, as if he is his own…and you can do the same.'

Kate's tears took Barbara by surprise and she pulled her to her to comfort her. 'We're alike in so many ways, you and I,' Kate said enigmatically. Barbara smiled and knitted her brows, thinking about that. 'Do you think I'm being foolish…this fixation with Jamie Raeburn?' Kate continued quickly, preventing Barbara's question.

'No, you're not,' Barbara replied with a soft chuckle. 'He makes you laugh, I've seen that…and he fancies you, even I can see that. No, you're not being foolish, Kate, believe me. Just enjoy him for as long as you can…and if you fall in love with each other, all the better.'

Kate pushed herself up from her seat. 'Thanks Babs,' she whispered. 'I'm going along to Ward 2 to see him.'

Barbara laughed. 'He'll be asleep, stupid.'

'I know,' Kate replied. 'But I just want to make sure he's alright. I won't be long.'

When she arrived at Ward 2 the nurses there were having a break. Kate gave them a little nod of acknowledgement wave as she passed their Station and they smiled back, clearly intrigued. Their curiosity was piqued when she stopped next to Jamie's bed. Then, realising what was unfolding before them they made eyes at each other and giggled quietly.

'I have to admit, he's not bad looking,' one of them said in a loud stage whisper loud enough for Kate to hear.

'Aye…and his equipment isn't bad either!' the other snorted crudely. 'Come on Katie,' she added with a vulgar laugh. 'You're married, don't be greedy.'

Kate turned to them with a faux pained expression on her face which made them laugh even more. Her visit and the reason for it was relieving their boredom but for Kate it was another step into the unknown. *But, they do have a point, she mused with a smile, his "equipment" isn't bad.* She blushed at the thought.

Barbara had been right, of course, Jamie was asleep. Kate stood silently beside him listening to his breathing, wanting to reach out and touch him, to run her fingers through his hair. He turned suddenly in his sleep and her heart leapt. In the next bed the American was awake but he seemed distracted, his mind somewhere else, and she felt sure that he hadn't recognised her. It was the dead of night, the hardest part of night shift, and the ward was quiet. She realised with sudden certainty that she wanted to be with Jamie Raeburn and her thoughts turned to making love with him. *'One day soon', I'm going to lie with you and feel the heat of you next to me,'* she promised. She hoped he heard her through his dream.

As she passed the Nurses again on her way back to the I.C.U. the girl who had joked about Jamie's "equipment", waved cheekily. 'Don't worry Katie; love, I'll keep an eye on him,' she said bawdily and their laughter followed her down the corridor. Kate didn't care; her mind was made up.

*

The routine of the Ward started early. Having tossed and turned uncomfortably for most of the night, dozing at times and sleeping fitfully at others, Jamie had finally fallen into a deep sleep just before five o' clock in the morning. Now, at seven, he was rudely awakened by the nurses busying themselves around the ward. Conor, watching, laughed softly as one of the nurses prodded Jamie gently and Jamie groaned in response.

'It's well seen you're a civilian, kid,' Conor grinned. 'I've been awake for ages,' he said, sounding proud of his achievement.

'Bully for you,' Jamie replied sourly. 'Remind me never to join up!'

Conor's raucous laughter drew a chastening look from a passing nurse but he ignored her. 'You'd love it, kid,' he retorted. 'And believe me, dames love uniforms.'

'Aye, right,' came back Jamie's sarcastic response which was missed entirely by the American. Jamie smiled to himself; only in Glasgow do two positives produce a negative, he mused.

Kate appeared just after eight o'clock. As she walked down the ward towards him Jamie saw some of the Day Shift Nurses exchanging smiles and there were one or two raised eyebrows. She pulled up a seat beside him and lowered herself wearily onto it.

'You're getting some strange looks,' Jamie said, curious.

Kate smiled and reddened slightly. 'I came in to see you during the night when you were asleep and I was teased a bit,' she explained. 'I suppose word has gone round.' She gave him an awkward little smile and he laughed happily. Her mood brightened instantly.

They talked and laughed for a few minutes but Kate was obviously tired. She was fighting it but fatigue was winning the battle. Eventually, she surrendered. 'I need to get to bed,' she yawned, covering her mouth with her fingers.

'There's room in here,' Jamie whispered, easing back the covers with a smile. He hoped he hadn't gone too far.

Kate looked at him coyly and a smile played at the side of her mouth. So far so good, Jamie judged. She bent forward, close to him, and whispered into his ear. 'You're an outrageous flirt, Jamie Raeburn,' she laughed. 'Anyway, you're not fit enough…and there are too many people around. You'll just have to wait a little while longer.' She straightened up again and sighed. 'It's been a long night,' she continued, her voice louder now. 'I'll come back to see how you are tonight,' she added, and slid her fingers tantalisingly across the back of his hand. She winked, pouted her lips out of sight of the others, and stood up. 'Get well soon,' she said. 'I don't want to wait too long for you.' Her voice had dropped again but Jamie heard her and his heart rate jumped. As she turned to leave Jamie took hold of her hand, pulling her back. She smiled broadly and squeezed his fingers. 'I'll see you later,' she whispered.

As Jamie watched her walk away from him he was mesmerised by the rhythmic sway of her hips and the fullness of her bottom. 'She's incredible,' he whispered to himself and turned to see Conor Whelan grinning from ear to ear.

Later in the morning it was time for Conor to leave and Jamie was sorry to see him go. Two U.S. Navy Nurses, spic-and-span in their white uniforms, arrived mid-morning to accompany him on his journey and as they made their way up the ward they attracted myriad looks from the other patients, young and old, from admiring right through to the openly lecherous. Conor watched Jamie, who was nodding approvingly, and gave him a conspiratorial wink. Jamie broke into a broad smile. 'Now I see the benefits of bein' in your Navy,' he laughed. 'Do you think you could get me in?'

Conor responded with a loud snicker. 'yeah, bed baths don't seem so bad now, do they?'

The two American nurses were, to use the vernacular, real crackers and Jamie was surprised some of the older patients hadn't suffered cardiac arrest. 'If you ever need recruits just put up a poster with them on it and you'll be oversubscribed,' he giggled, turning back to the American.

'And why do you think I signed on?' Conor grinned. He was reading Jamie's thoughts. Both girls were blondes, both quite young and naturally tanned, their golden skin glowing against the white of their uniforms. 'You seem to have a penchant for nurses, kid,' Conor laughed as the girls came closer, their hips swinging provocatively. Jamie grinned. He didn't have a clue what a penchant was; *maybe it's American slang for a hard on*, he thought with a smile. Whatever it was, it sounded good.

The nurses glanced at Jamie as they arrived beside Conor, smiling knowingly in unison at the effect they were having on him, then drew the curtain around Conor's and disappeared from sight. Jamie heard muffled chatter and laughter coming from behind the curtain and then, after a couple of minutes, the curtain opened again and Conor was lying on a trolley, ready for the off. He gave Jamie a wave and the smaller of the two nurses, a buxom beauty with uniform buttons straining to contain her ample breasts, came round to Jamie's bed.

'Mr Raeburn,' she said in what Jamie imagined was a deep, sexy, Southern drawl. 'Lieutenant Whelan asked me to give you this.' She said "Lieutenant" as "Lootenant" and smiled, holding out a piece of paper. Jamie took it with a nervous smile and saw Conor's name on it with a telephone number scrawled below. The nurse's voice was seductive and Jamie's "penchant" was swelling beneath the sheets. Wet dreams for me tonight, Jamie smiled to himself, as the girl bent down over him and his eyes were drawn, inexorably, to the deep V between her breasts. She grinned cheekily at Jamie's obvious discomfiture. 'Lootenant Whelan said you're thinkin' of joinin' us…and you might be coming down to the base to see him soon. Maybe you and me could meet up for a little fun,' she breathed sexily, breaking into a throaty laugh as Jamie's face turned beetroot red. She looked him over appraisingly. 'You're sure a good lookin' boy, honey…do you want my number as well?' Her laugh tinkled and Jamie blushed again. Conor's rumbling laugh and his theatrical wink told Jamie that he'd been set up and his own laughter followed Conor out of the ward.

'Don't forget, kid, call me,' Conor shouted back, putting his hand to his ear to mimic a phone call. Jamie waved him off, genuinely sorry to see him go.

Chapter 6

It was another eight days before Jamie was allowed to return home. Eight days of unmitigated boredom broken only by Kate's daily visits. His mother came every night but conversation was stilted. Jack Connolly had visited at the weekend, Gerry Carroll with him, and the Staff Nurse on duty was almost driven to distraction by their jokes and raucous laughter.

Two detectives from Glasgow Police, a Detective Superintendent and a Detective Inspector no less, visited him on the following Monday. The significance of their ranks wasn't lost on him. A Detective Superintendent and a Detective Inspector wouldn't normally be assigned to a case like this even though it had now been classed as a double attempted murder. Conor Whelan, he realised quickly, was undoubtedly their main interest.

They were pleasant enough. He was the victim, or one of them, after all, but the questions soon turned to Conor's reasons for being in that neck of the woods in the first place that night.

'So he didn't mention anything about why he was there?' the Superintendent asked after going over the events of the night.

Jamie shrugged. 'We didn't exactly have time to exchange pleasantries,' he replied, trying desperately to keep the sarcasm out of his voice. 'He was getting the shit kicked out of him when I got there and my time was pretty well taken up then too.'

'Did you hear anything? The men attacking the American, did they say anything you picked up on?'

Jamie shrugged and shook his head.

'And what about afterwards?'

'Afterwards?' Jamie laughed. 'Afterwards, I was unconscious and was being brought in here,' he continued shortly.

The Detective Inspector looked like he could be antagonistic but for now he was simply noting everything down. The Superintendent smiled sourly. 'We appreciate that Mr Raeburn,' he said, and Jamie could see that the effort in being polite was taking its toll on him. 'When I said "afterwards" I was meaning the time you were together in here,' he continued. 'I understand Lieutenant Whelan was in the next bed to you.'

Jamie ignored the question.

'So what *did* you talk about?' the Inspector asked.

Jamie put on his thoughtful face. 'We talked about what happened…he thanked me for coming to help him…we talked about women…and he told me all about Boston,' he said slowly, as though trying to recall.

'But not why he was in Cowcaddens?' the Superintendent interrupted.

'No,' Jamie replied, looking the man directly in the eye.

The detective let out an exasperated sigh. 'Alright,' he said, covering his frustration well. 'Thanks for your time Mr Raeburn. If you remember anything else…'

'I'll let you know,' Jamie broke in, bringing the interview to an end.

The two men rose as one and headed for the exit. They both smiled politely but Jamie could see that they were seething inside. *And if I do find out what he was doing there, you'll be the last to know.* He smiled back in return.

As the detectives disappeared down the corridor Jamie resolved to phone Conor Whelan as soon as he got home. He'd already asked him the same question and Conor had evaded the issue. He obviously had his reasons and Jamie wouldn't pursue the issue if Conor baulked at it again, but he had to let Conor know that he wasn't the only one asking questions.

By the ninth day in the ward Jamie had had enough. He began pestering the nurses about getting home and when the doctor came on his ward round he started on him too. He said he felt stronger, the pain was gone and he felt that lack of exercise was getting him down...so please, could he go home. Dr McLean smiled knowingly and finally relented and at one thirty that afternoon, Wednesday 7th December, Jamie's mother appeared with clean clothes. Jamie dressed quickly before Dr McLean could change his mind and less than an hour later he was home in Knightswood.

He was relieved to be home but as every pessimist knows, every silver lining has a cloud and Jamie's cloud was the fact that Kate was working Day Shift all week and he wouldn't see her again until the following Monday when her shift rota changed. But he did have her telephone number and she had made him promise to call her later when she finished work.

His mother left him at home and went back to her office with a warning that he should remain in bed until she returned home later. Jamie waited until she had been gone for about ten minutes and then hauled himself out of bed and dressed. He had spent almost two weeks lying in a hospital bed and he had no intention of spending any more time in bed...alone at least, he thought with a smile. His mother had known that he would be up out of bed as soon as she left him but she had tried.

He checked his watch. It was just after three o'clock...another six hours before he could call Kate. He thought about how their relationship had developed and the speed of it astounded him. He had asked her about her husband and had discovered the guy was a drunk so he didn't feel guilty any more. He knew that Kate wanted to be with him...they both wanted it, but there was a fly in the ointment. Two flies actually, he reminded himself. First, Kate was on Day Shift until the weekend and didn't start back on nights until Sunday. Second, she was going home to Calverton to be with her family for Christmas. When she had broken that news to him he had been philosophical about it. He had waited almost two weeks already so he could wait another four days and as for Christmas...well, the break would let them know if what they were feeling was the real thing.

Having put his mother's advice on the back burner Jamie pulled on extra layers of clothing to combat the cold. He needed fresh air more than bed and decided to tinker with his motor bike. He hadn't used the bike much over the last few months. The cold and the wet that was winter in the West of Scotland was the main reason for that and he knew that the bike could do with a service. He looked outside. It was bright but still cold and the snow that had fallen the night he had been attacked still lay on the ground, rutted and hard. Jamie pulled on his leather jacket and wound a scarf around his neck before letting himself out of the house, crunching his way over the packed snow and rutted ice to the little hut at the rear of the garden. With tools in hand, he returned to his bike and removed the protective tarpaulin from it, undid the chain that secured the bike to a bolt on the house wall and set to work.

He felt invigorated. He enjoyed the cold, fresh air and fiddling with the machine was therapeutic. He loved this bike, and when he rode it he felt completely free. It was almost as good as sex…almost, but not quite! The day he had brought it home his father had shaken his head with disbelief and had told him it was too big and too powerful for an inexperienced rider like Jamie. Jamie simply smiled and said he would be careful. He knew his old man was secretly jealous but he was probably right; it *was* big and it *was* powerful and there weren't many other bikes on the road that could live with it when it came to sheer speed. It was a gleaming red and chrome 1962 Triumph Bonneville T120 that he had picked up when he finished his apprenticeship at John Brown's, having saved money from his wages religiously, week after week, until he had enough. It had cost him Ninety-five Pounds, twelve shillings and sixpence…a lot of money but worth every penny so far as Jamie was concerned. With its 650cc parallel twin engine and its twin one and three sixteenths inch Amal monobloc carburettors it really was a performance machine. Jamie hadn't pushed it to its limit…yet, but he was fairly confident he could push it past the magical 100mph if he tried.

Working on the machine, wrapped up in the intricacy of adjusting the carburettors, Jamie lost all track of time and before he realised it was after four o'clock and darkness was beginning to fall. His father had arrived home earlier and had joined him for a while. They said little but they were comfortable together now and his father had helped, giving advice which Jamie found, to his surprise, improved the machine's performance. With his father back inside now, Jamie finished up and tidied away his tools. That done, he swung his leg up and over the tank and settled onto the seat then kicked the machine into life, listening to the throaty roar of the big, powerful engine. It would do, he decided. By four thirty he was back inside the house with a fire lit in the grate. He washed and changed so that his mother wouldn't know what he had been up to and hoped his father would keep quiet.

Dinner came and went. His mother tried to keep him interested in what had been happening while he was in hospital but she could see he was preoccupied. Jamie took himself off to his room around seven and listened, somewhat dreamily, to Radio Luxembourg. Time dragged. He looked at his watch repeatedly and each time it was only a minute or so since his previous look. Finally, the time arrived. At eight thirty he picked up the handset of the phone in his bedroom, illicitly installed by Gerry Boyle, a pal who was a telephone engineer with the Post Office, and thrust his index finger into the dial. He was suddenly aware of how much he was already missing Kate even though it had only been hours since he had last seen her.

The ringing tone came back down the line, brrrr-brrrr…brrrr-brrrr…brrrr-brrrr before it was answered and Kate's voice echoed back down the line.

'Hi, it's me,' Jamie said, feeling a little foolish.

'Hello you,' she replied, her voice husky. 'I was thinking about you just then.'

'That's funny,' Jamie replied contentedly. 'I've been thinking about you too. What were you thinking?' he asked. 'Anything exciting?'

'Mmm,' Kate replied with a throaty, seductive laugh. 'I hope you're as good in reality as you are in my fantasies,' she said with a sigh designed to excite him. It worked!

As Jamie thought about being with her an unwanted feeling of doubt crept into his mind. 'Are you sure about all this?' he asked hesitantly. Kate had more guilt to shoulder than he had about the final outcome, after all.

'Oh yes, I'm sure,' she replied immediately, sensing his unease. 'You're not taking cold feet, are you?' She whispered. 'You're surely not scared of being with an older woman?'

She was teasing him now and Jamie laughed with enjoyment, the tension vaporising. 'No, I'm not scared...I can't wait to be with you,' he told her. 'The only question is when?'

'You know I'm on day shift until Friday, off on Saturday and Sunday, and then I start back on night shift on Sunday night. Can you wait until Monday?' she asked wistfully. 'Then we have four full days before I go back to day shift...and home after that for Christmas.' She threw in the last bit reluctantly.

'Another four days?' he said with feigned anguish. 'You're torturing me. What am I going to do for four days?'

Kate laughed, imagining the expression on his face. 'You'll just need to pretend,' she giggled. 'Close your eyes and imagine I'm there with you...and pretend.'

'Pretend, as in give myself a hand job?' he laughed incredulously. 'Isn't that a mortal sin? Won't I go blind?'

Kate choked with laughter. 'I think what we're going to do is a bigger sin,' she said. 'Just don't do it too often, I want you at your best!'

'Oh, don't worry, I'll be at my best,' Jamie murmured quietly. 'And I'll make love to you as often as you want me to.'

'I'll hold you to that,' Kate whispered. 'Now, tell me what you're going to do with me,' she urged. They whispered to each other, describing their dreams and their fantasies. By the end of the call they both knew what Monday would bring. 'That's the first time I've made love over the phone,' Kate laughed, still trying to catch her breath. 'Can we do it again sometime?'

'I'll give you my number,' Jamie laughed. 'Phone me when it's safe rather than risk me phoning you when it isn't.'

That might have been a sobering thought for Jamie but it wasn't for Kate. She knew there was little risk for her and now she had reached a final decision about Jamie there was no going back on it. 'Alright,' she agreed. 'But what about your father and mother, won't they hear us?'

Jamie laughed mirthfully. 'I hope not, I don't want them getting randy and presenting me with a wee brother or sister,' he chuckled. 'Don't worry, I've got an extension phone in my bedroom...we can talk in private.' Jamie finished by reciting his number.

'I'll call you tomorrow...at lunchtime. Okay?' Kate said. 'I'd better go now.'

'Okay, sweet dreams,' Jamie replied. 'Call me tomorrow.'

Jamie heard her say she would and then the line was dead. He closed his eyes and tried to picture her in his mind. He imagined her naked, lying beside him and dreamed of her hands on him. What, he wondered, would her skin feel like against his? He could picture himself daydreaming like this for the next four days. *It won't be too hard to pretend*, he laughed to himself.

Chapter 7

Being at home was, for Jamie, as bad as being in hospital…worse even. The only difference between the two was that in hospital he could ignore the nurses. He couldn't ignore his mother! She worried about him incessantly, as mothers do, and laid down the law, insisting that he stay in bed.

Kate phoned him at lunchtime from a coin box and their conversation was even more intimate, and erotic, than the one they had enjoyed the night before. Afterwards, Jamie wondered how Kate could go back into the I.C.U. and carry on with her work. He doubted if he could. She promised to phone him again in the evening and he was already counting the hours and the minutes.

He spent some time thinking about himself and, in particular, his recovery. He still had some issues but they were psychological more than physical. His body was healing quicker than his mind. Sleep was difficult and he was plagued by a recurring nightmare which was vivid in the extreme. Conor Whelan is surrounded by a screaming, whirling, faceless mob that swirls around him like dervishes in a fog while he, Jamie, looks down from above onto the unfolding scene. He tries to intervene; screaming, shouting and lashing out at the mob but each time he knocks one of the mob down another takes his place…like spring loaded ninepins. Everything appears to him in black and red, no other colour, and the red is in myriad shades and hues…crimson, ruby, burgundy, maroon, dark red, cherry red, pink. And then, with almost preordained inevitability, the mob turns from Conor to him and a thousand knives come lunging towards him. He sees himself bathed in blood…and then he wakes, screaming.

The dream had come to him for the first time the night before. Waking from it, he had sat upright in his bed, his body rigid with fear and bathed in sweat. He had run his hands over his chest before examining them to discover if they were, indeed, covered in blood. His mother and father had rushed to him, concerned. It was just a nightmare, he had assured them, nothing to worry about. But it had come again and now it was, he knew, something to worry about.

During the morning, alone in the house, he struggled with his emotions. Inactivity bred despair so he tried to keep himself busy and his mind occupied. By doing this he could function reasonably well but now he was tormented by flashbacks that came on without warning and presented him with graphic recollections of the incident. He watched it unfold again…and he felt it. He broke out in a cold sweat and his body shook violently.

*

Jack Connolly appeared out of the blue that afternoon with a fistful of comics and the obligatory bunch of grapes. His task, he informed Jamie, was to bring him up to date with what had been happening to the others. They all hoped he would be back to normal soon.

Jack's first impression of Jamie, now that he was home, was a good one. Most of the physical evidence of the attack had faded, he had colour back in his cheeks and his eyes, dark and sunken when Jack had last seen him in the hospital, were now almost back to their sparkling best. Jack could see what girls saw in Jamie Raeburn...lucky bastard, he thought without envy. But he could see something else in Jamie's eyes now, something new, a dark presence, and that worried him.

'You're lookin' good, big man,' Jack started encouragingly.

'Yeah, I'm feeling good,' Jamie replied, a smile lighting up his face. 'It's really great to see you! I didn't expect it.'

'Ach, ah wis at the quack this mornin' so ah decided tae take the rest o' the day aff. Ah thought ah'd come an' cheer ye up.'

'I'm glad you did,' Jamie replied cheerily. 'The company's appreciated; I'm climbin' the walls here.'

Jack looked at him admiringly, astounded by the improvement in him and in his mood. 'Let me intae the secret,' he said. 'Some guys tried tae murder ye a couple o' weeks ago and now ye're sitting here looking like the cat that's got the cream.'

'I've got a new girlfriend,' Jamie laughed. 'That's the secret. I'm in love,' he continued, a wide grin lighting his face again.

'Aw fur fuck sake, no' again,' Jack retorted sarcastically before realising that Jamie was serious. 'Really? No kiddin'? Ye've actually met someone?' he asked incredulously. 'But you've been in hospital...so it's a nurse,' he said finally, with a laugh, as the penny dropped.

'Spot on,' Jamie grinned and filled him in about Kate, watching with delight as Jack's eyes opened wide in surprise. 'I'm pickin' her up at the Royal on Monday morning when she finishes night shift and we're goin' back to her place.'

'Fur fuck sake, Jamie, is that no' a wee bit dangerous? Whit about her man?' Jack cautioned.

'Ach, maybe it could be a wee bit tricky,' Jamie laughed. 'But she's worth it, she's a stunner,' he said. He decided not to get involved in any further discussion about Kate's husband and closed the subject.

Jack got up and wandered over to the front window. He pulled back the curtain and looked out enviously. A girl, not bad looking, short skirt and high boots, long coat flapping open as she walked, strode past the house and into another further down the road. Traffic ran along Great Western Road up to the left and everything seemed green even though the trees lining the road outside had lost their leaves. Trees, for fuck sake! He felt an unexpected twinge of bitterness. It was so different here to what he was used to; grey tenements, busy streets, noise and litter.

'It's nice here,' he said, turning back towards Jamie. 'First time ah've visited the posh side o' the city,' he laughed sarcastically. 'You toffs dae alright, eh? Big hooses, two flairs, a bedroom tae yersel an' gardens at the front *and* the back,' he continued, his bitterness showing. 'An' ah swear tae God, ah passed a park an' a golf course jist doon the road, there. A fuckin' golf course! Christ, ah'm surprised ye even talk tae me.'

'Who's rattled your can?' Jamie replied angrily, stung by the bitterness in Jack's voice. 'You think because I live here I'm any different from you?' he continued. 'Well, fuck you, Jack!'

Jack retreated immediately, regretting his bitter outburst. This was a different Jamie, one he hadn't met before. 'Ah'm sorry Jamie; ah didn't mean anythin' by it,' he apologised. 'Ye know that.'

Jamie ignored him and started to rant. 'We moved here from Townhead,' he continued, his anger unabated. 'From a single-end that makes the flat you live in look like a palace,' he went on. 'You'll remember the type...shit house on the half-landing, bed recess off the livin' room an' my mother had to go to the steamie two or three times a week to wash our clothes. It was so bad at the end even the fuckin' rats were movin' out. Aye, it's nice here…but it hasn't changed me. I'm no' a fuckin' toff,' he finished angrily, realising he was shaking.

Jack held up his hands, shamefaced. 'Keys, big man,' he said, contritely, holding up both thumbs. 'Ah wis oot o' order. Ah'm sorry, honest.'

Jamie closed his eyes and breathed deeply, trying to calm himself. This wasn't like him. *What the fuck is happening to me,* he wondered? His anger was irrational; he knew what Jack was like, his sarcastic, sometimes acerbic, wit was well known and no one took him too seriously. So why was he taking it like this now? *Shit, I'm losing it,* he thought. Opening his eyes he looked at his friend and smiled apologetically. 'Nah, it's me who should be sayin' sorry, Jack. I don't know what's wrong with me. Forget it, eh?'

'Ye were nearly killed, that's whit's wrang wi' ye. Ah thought ah'd lost ye that night; it frightened the shit oot o' me, so whit it did tae you, God only knows. Let's jist get ye back tae normal.' Jack said emotionally, clasping Jamie close in a man hug.

'What's normal?' Jamie asked, hollow voiced. 'I had a nightmare last night…twice in fact. Is that normal? And today I've been getting flashbacks… I see it all happening again and I hear you screaming, again and again. Is that fuckin' normal?'

'Shit Jamie, ah don't know,' Jack replied, troubled. 'Whit about goin' tae the quack?'

'Yeah, but apart from givin' me some pills and tellin' me to rest he's not likely to be much help, is he?'

'Maybe gettin' back tae work will sort ye out,' Jack suggested. 'Or maybe this wee nurse…whit's her name again?'

'Kate.'

'Aye, well maybe this Kate lassie will bring ye oot o' it,' he said, though he suspected that Kate might be the start of bigger problems.

They drifted away from the subject with Jack feeling awkward and Jamie wanting to push it from his mind. The rest of Jack's visit was spent chatting aimlessly. The conversation was banal but at least it took Jamie's mind off his problems.

Jack was worried though he was hiding it well. Jamie had changed. He couldn't say how, exactly, but Jamie wasn't the same. He seemed to have lost interest in everything…other than this nurse Kate, though he was obviously ignoring the fact that she was married. When this fling ended, as it undoubtedly would, what would Jamie do then? He remembered the last episode in Jamie's love life; his break up with Carol Whyte…and that wasn't a happy time. It was depressing…he remembered the old Jamie; cheeky, insubordinate, gallus. *Yes,* that was the word he was looking for, *gallus.* He hoped the old, gallus Jamie would come back soon. After about an hour they ran out of things to talk about and Jamie seemed preoccupied, which only served to prove Jack's earlier thoughts. He left before Jamie's parents arrived home from work, eager to avoid meeting them and having to go over, once again, the events that had led to Jamie being stabbed that fateful night. That he could do without and he left, promising to return soon.

*

On Saturday morning, keeping his promise, Jack returned, only narrowly missing Jamie's mother and father who had gone shopping. He thanked his lucky stars. Following Jamie into the living room he tossed a folded copy of Friday's Evening Times onto the table. 'Ye'll get plenty o' birds noo, Jamie boy,' he grinned. 'Ye're in the papers. "Hero Saves American Sailor" it says, look.'

Jamie picked up the paper and read the article, the headline jumping out at him. 'Christ, Jack, that's all I fuckin' need,' he groaned.

'Whit? Ah thought ye'd be chuffed,' Jack retorted, dismayed by Jamie's reaction.

'Chuffed? Are you kiddin'?' Jamie raved. 'It's a nightmare. Every wee shite from Drumchapel to Easterhouse will be out to show they're harder than me…an' that I can do without.'

'Ah didnae think o' that,' Jack admitted thoughtfully, then tried to steer Jamie towards the positives. 'Look on the bright side,' he pointed out. 'The talent will be aw over ye like a rash…an' let's face it, ye need a new bird.'

'I've got one,' Jamie replied simply.

'Nah, ye don't,' Jack responded cuttingly. 'Whit ye've got is another man's wife. Ye're jist shaggin' her. She's no yer girlfriend.'

'So, what you're sayin' is that sleepin' with her doesn't make her my girlfriend, is that it?'

'Give the boy a coconut!' Jack laughed sarcastically. 'Listen, if shaggin' a bird makes her yer girlfriend, you'd need a fuckin' coach tae take them aw oot. A girlfriend is one ye go oot wi',' he said slowly, as though talking to a slow witted child. 'You know, tae the pictures, oot fur a meal, back tae meet the family,' he continued. 'An' ah don't think this Kate fits that bill.'

Jamie was quiet, reflective, and Jack thought he'd gone too far. Jamie obviously liked the lassie but unless her man worked away from home it wouldn't be much of a relationship. Even then, taking her out would be dicey. It only took one person who knew her and her man to see her with Jamie, and bingo! Rearrange the following words into a well-known phrase or saying…"fan, shit and hitting" he thought caustically. There was another alternative, of course, but Jamie wouldn't be that stupid…would he? Oh shit. 'Ye're no' thinkin' aboot…'

'About what?' Jamie jumped in quickly.

'About getting her tae leave her man?'

'What?' Jamie blurted out, stunned.

Well, if ye like her that much, ah jist thought…' Jack's voice tailed off again.

Jamie drew him a look of utter disbelief. 'I don't believe you!' he laughed. 'Do you think I've lost my marbles?' I like her, she's fun to be with, she's good lookin' and she's got a great body, but we hardly know each other yet…an' we haven't even done the business, so gimme a break.'

'Well, thank fuck fur that,' Jack sighed, relieved. 'So ye're still in the market fur a new girlfriend then?'

'Nah Jack, I've had enough of girlfriends. If I get enough of the other with Kate I won't need one, will I? And if I don't, then I'll just go back to one night stands,' he finished.

'They're no' aw like Carol Whyte,' Jack continued. 'She wis a wee bit o' a slapper; we aw thought that.'

Jamie gave him a pained look. 'Now you tell me!' he retorted. 'Good of you all to let me know.' He felt he should be angered by Jack's revelation but strangely, he felt nothing. Not a thing. Quite simply, Carol wasn't worth bothering about.

'Ye widnae huv believed us, Jamie boy,' Jack fired back at him. 'Ye'd known her fur too long an' the sun rose an' set on her nicely shaped arse as far as you were concerned. Be honest.'

Jamie smiled grimly and thought back to his relationship with Carol Whyte. Maybe he should have seen the signs but Carol was quite a girl and, as Jack said, he had known her for a long time. She had been easy on the eye and nice to be with but, with the benefit of hindsight, she was also a first rate liar. She looked after her body and she knew how to use it so, if he was honest, he probably wouldn't have listened to anyone bad mouthing her. *More fool me*, he thought, but much of the bitterness had left him now and he had learned his lesson. 'Aye, okay, you're right Jack,' he conceded after a pause. 'Don't worry, I've put her and her perfect bum behind me,' he laughed. But the conversation had started him thinking about Kate Maxwell again...and he hadn't been entirely open with Jack. He was seriously thinking about getting involved with her. But could Jack be right? Was there any future in it? That was something he would have to think about but, for the moment, he would happily settle for no strings attached sex.

Jack was talking again and Jamie switched back to listening mode. 'Okay, so ye don't want a girlfriend...yet,' he said. But ye huv tae admit, the birds ye've been pickin' up recently are a bit o' a hotch potch...even fur you,' Jack laughed. Jamie stared at him stonily. 'Whit ah mean is, ye don't need tae go for fat or scrawny birds because ye think they'll be grateful; good lookin' birds like tae get shagged tae...the Carol Whyte's o' this world, fur example. An' that "Hero" bit aboot ye in the paper will help.' An evil smile began to spread over his face. 'And think aboot it...Carol will be fuckin' ragin',' he laughed, taking the newspaper back from Jamie. 'An' another thing, while we're on the subject' he said, continuing with his lecture. 'Ye need tae lighten up a bit, ye're twenty wan, no' sixty wan, so gonnae stop yer fuckin' moanin.'

'Christ Jack, you're worse than my mother,' Jamie laughed. 'An' you're bein' a bit unfair to the girls. Every one I've got off with has been good lookin'. Alright, they might have been a wee bit big, a wee bit skinny, a wee bit small or a wee bit tall...but they were all good lookin', admit it.'

Jack pulled a face and nodded. 'Aye, okay, they were aw pretty, includin' that Loretta that ah slagged off. She wisnae that big...an' ah huv tae admit, she hud tits tae die fur.'

Jamie laughed, vindicated, but he realised now that Jack and the others had been affected by his moods after his break up with Carol. 'Have I been pissin' you all off?' he asked.

Jack gave him a sideways look, a grin on his face. 'Aye, just a tad,' he replied. 'Carol Whyte hus a lot tae answer fur! Anyway, when will ye be up fur a night oot wi' the lads again?'

Jamie hesitated. 'I don't know Jack,' he sighed. 'I don't know if I'll ever feel up to it again, to be honest. It's the flashbacks and the nightmares, seeing Conor, the Yank, on the ground, blood everywhere, and hearin' your voice, all panicky, shoutin' to me.'

'It'll pass, big guy.'

'Oh aye, is that right, Doctor Connolly? You've been readin' up on it, have you?'

'Nah, ah mean, it's bound tae get better...easier, isn't it?'

'Christ, I hope so. I don't want to be walkin' about Glasgow lookin' over my shoulder all the time.'

'It'll be a'right, ye've got me an' the rest o' the boys tae look oot fur ye.'

'I know that, Jack, but you can't be with me all the time,' Jamie replied seriously. They left it at that.

Jamie's mother and father reappeared just before noon and the conversation between Jack and Jamie dried up. The things they wanted to talk about were too risqué to discuss with Jamie's parents present. They invited Jack to stay for lunch but he made his excuses, honestly as it happened, and took his leave. 'Ah'm playin' football this afternoon…an' we're already a centre half doon,' he laughed, punching Jamie playfully on the arm. 'So, ah'll need tae be off.' He heaved himself out of his chair and pulled on his jacket as Jamie escorted him to the front door. 'Next weekend? Are ye up fur it?' he whispered, not wanting Jamie's mother to hear. 'If yer new bird disnae mind, that is,' he added.

'I don't know Jack, phone me, okay?'

Jack nodded and stepped out into the cold, calling cheerio to Jamie's parents. 'It wid dae ye good,' he said in parting. 'When ye fa' aff yer bike the first thing ye dae is climb back on.'

'It's not a bike, ya dummy, it's a horse,' Jamie laughed.

'Aye, ah know that, but you cannae afford a horse,' Jack snickered as he sauntered down the path.

Jamie stood at the front window watching his pal make his way up to Great Western Road and thought about their conversation. Jack Connolly, philosopher, he laughed inwardly. "When you fall off your bike the first thing you do is get back on". But Jack was right, he had to get on with life again but, apart from the prospect of some extra marital shagging with Kate, he had little to look forward to. Even the prospect of getting back to work was unappealing.

He had changed, he knew that, but he also knew that he couldn't hide himself away for ever. He wouldn't anyway, it wasn't in his nature. Having an *affair* with Kate – her words, not his - was a big enough risk, but that element of risk added to the excitement. The same couldn't be said of a night out with the boys. Risk? Aye, plenty. Excitement? Not a lot! He would wait a while before venturing back into the city with the lads, he decided. Keeping clear of Glasgow's gangs was difficult enough these days without the added problem of his new, unwanted, hero status.

Chapter 8

The morning of Monday 12th December was cold but that was the last thing on Jamie's mind. He had risen early and was out of the house before his mother had a chance to ask where he was going. Fair to say she had a shrewd idea given that he had been sprucing himself up the night before and had laid out his clothes…always a sure sign that a girl was involved.

Jamie rode the Triumph into the drop off area in front of the hospital, stopping just beyond the main entrance, and sat astride the bike waiting patiently. He was early, unusually for him, but he couldn't wait to be with Kate again. He was wrapped in his battered leather flying jacket giving him some degree of comfort against the bitter wind and the early frost. He was, uncharacteristically, nervous. Slapping his gloved hands together for warmth he thought about Kate and hoped she was wearing something warm enough to combat the cold otherwise he might have to thaw her out when they arrived at her house. That, on the other hand, could be quite enjoyable. There were quite a number of ways he could think of to warm her up which would bring a smile to his face at least…and hopefully to Kate's.

The time passed quickly and he checked his watch nervously. It was now almost ten past eight and she should have been with him by now. Other night shift staff had filtered past him, coming out the main doors of the big Victorian building to head for the bus stops on Castle Street. He scanned the faces, looking for Kate, and recognised two of the nurses who worked in Ward 2 but still there was no sign of Kate. He began to worry. Had she taken cold feet, he wondered, and changed her mind? But some nurses were still exiting the building so all hope was not lost. The cold was eating into him now, even ensconced as he was in his fur lined leather jacket, and his breath billowed in great white clouds. If their tryst was still on then Kate would have to thaw him out if she took much longer.

Suddenly, there was a flurry of activity and Kate appeared at the main entrance, flanked by two other nurses, one of whom Jamie recognised as the other nurse from the I.C.U, Barbara Laing. All three were wearing long, heavy coats, boots, scarves and woollen hats to ward off the cold and they lingered on the wide stone steps, laughing and joking for a moment. Jamie's heart raced as Kate looked across at him and waved. Barbara Laing smiled at him, knowingly, and he felt himself redden. The three said their goodbyes. Barbara said something to the other girl and all three laughed, Barbara and the new girl looking him up and down, like a specimen in a glass jar, before setting off towards the main road. And then Kate was skipping towards him, her eyes wide with anticipation.

'I thought you didn't want to waste a minute,' Jamie laughed, looking pointedly at his watch. Kate giggled, lifted her face up to his and kissed him, long and hungrily. His pulse raced. It was their first real kiss and it had been worth the wait.

'Sorry, love,' she whispered. 'We had an urgent admission just before finishing time,' she explained.

'I thought you'd stood me up,' he laughed.

'That's never going to happen,' she replied, and Jamie felt good. 'So, are you taking me home now, or what?' Kate continued, smiling happily.

'I hope you can manage onto the back of this?' he said, patting the pillion seat behind him. Kate looked at him with a wide grin, opened the bottom buttons of her coat and swung her leg over, settling behind him and tucking her coat beneath and around her legs.

'I told you before, my brother used to take me out for a spin on his bike,' she giggled happily. 'I even know where to put my hands,' she laughed, wrapping her arms around him.

'I'm not your brother,' Jamie laughed. 'So you can put your hands somewhere else if you like.' Kate giggled and played along, moving her hands down and across his groin, feeling the hardness between his legs.

'I'm flattered,' she murmured coyly. 'Is that all for me?' Her laugh drowned out Jamie's anguished moan. 'Can you control the bike alright if I leave my hands there?' she teased.

'It's not the bike I'm worried about, it's me,' he groaned, turning round to kiss her. 'So, where to then?' he asked.

'Ibrox,' she replied. 'Do you know it?'

Jamie started to laugh. 'You don't really know me yet,' he snorted. 'I'm a Rangers supporter...Ibrox is like a second home to me.'

'Well, take me there,' she instructed. 'It's Number 14, Copland Place, just off Copland Road.' She paused and pulled his face round so that he could see her. 'I know you're nervous, love, but he won't be there, believe me. But if it makes you feel better, drop me at the corner of Copland Road. I'll walk round to the house and you can follow me a few minutes later...alright?'

Jamie laughed awkwardly. 'An' if he is there?' he asked. He was pretty sure he could handle the guy, especially if he was a piss artist like Kate had said, but he was concerned about what might happen to Kate in the aftermath.

Kate laughed and pressed her head against his back. His apprehension wasn't for himself, she realised, but for her and she thought all the more of him for it. 'Tom won't be there,' she assured him. 'But just to stop you worrying, if he is at home I'll close the lounge curtains...that's the left hand bay window on the ground floor, and I'll phone you later.'

'Okay,' Jamie replied, relieved.

'But he won't be there,' she repeated, reassuringly. 'He hasn't been home for days...so I'll expect you at the door no more than one minute after I leave you,' she laughed. 'And no excuses. Come on, Jamie, we've waited long enough,' she whispered in his ear and pressed her hands firmly against him.

Jamie kicked the Triumph into life and pulled away from the hospital, out onto Castle Street and then down High Street towards Saltmarket and the Clyde. Soon, they crossed the Clyde and swung right along Ballater Street towards Kingston and Paisley Road West. The morning traffic was heavy but they were travelling against the rush hour flow and within ten minutes they were in Edmiston Drive and then turning into Copland Road. Jamie pulled the bike to a halt just before the corner with Copland Place and turned round to look at Kate.

Her cheeks glowed in the early morning sun and she gave him a quick kiss. She dismounted from the bike and stood with him for a moment taking both his hands in hers. 'Number 14, one minute...no longer,' she reminded him, laughing. And then she was gone, walking briskly to the corner before turning, briefly, to give him a smile and disappearing from sight.

Jamie counted to thirty and then slipped the bike into gear, riding slowly round the corner behind her. He watched her stride confidently up the garden path to the door then fish around in her bag for her key. Carefully, he took the Triumph past the house and stopped at the end of the cul-de-sac. Two cars sat against the pavement, covered in frost, but otherwise the street was deserted. Dismounting, he secured the bike with the heavy chain and padlock he always carried and set off back down the road in the direction of Kate's house, eying up the adjoining properties. He had walked up Copland Road hundreds of times, he reflected, and couldn't have told you that Copland Place even existed. As he neared the house he saw that the curtains were still open and his heart started to pound in anticipation of what was to come. The waiting was over.

The front door was slightly ajar when he reached it and just as he stretched out his hand it opened fully before him. Kate stood in the hallway, smiling radiantly. Quickly, she took his outstretched hand and pulled him into the hallway, pushing the door shut behind him. It was cold in the house, colder than outside, and as Kate pulled him to her she shivered. Her coat was open and she felt Jamie's arms encircle her. Without warning, he released her and stepped back, shrugging himself out of his heavy jacket, then he pulled her to him again. She pushed her hips against him as her mouth found his, her tongue probing between his lips. His hands cupped her breasts and then her own fingers, as though with a mind of their own, were scrabbling at the buttons of his jeans. There was no turning back now.

Jamie lifted her dress and his fingers brushed the flesh at the top of her stockings. He felt her fingers inside his jeans, manoeuvring beneath his shorts and curling round him. His own fingers teased her lace trimmed briefs loose and he felt the wetness between her legs as the excitement gripped her. Their breathing was harsh with the urgency of the moment. He pushed her back against the wall, kissing her frenziedly, and felt her pull his erect penis from his pants, guiding him towards her. And then they were one, their movements spontaneous, hurried, and frantic. Kate clung to him, her body gyrating against him as he thrust himself into her again and again. He heard her give a little cry and felt her fingers dig into his back beneath his sweater. He came then, exploding inside her, pressing into her until he was spent.

Kate smiled at him demurely, wrapped her arms around his neck and kissed him again, her fingers caressing the back of his neck. 'Where have you been all my life, Jamie Raeburn?' she murmured, and as Jamie withdrew from her she sighed. She watched him tuck his semi-flaccid member back inside his pants then took his hand. 'Come on,' she said simply, leading him to the stairway.

On the landing Kate opened the first door which led to the bedroom situated directly above the living room, with a big bay window looking out onto the street outside. 'Wait here,' she said, leaving him standing in the doorway whilst taking off her coat. She removed the white bib and apron from her uniform and folded them neatly on a chair, the only chair in the room, before lighting a gas fire fixed to the wall. It ignited with a loud whoosh as the air in the room was sucked in by the ribbon of burners along the bottom and blue flames danced up the ceramic elements and glowed on the metal filaments. Kate returned to him then and took his hand, kissing him briefly before passing him and leading him along the landing to the bathroom at the end.

The bathroom was dominated by a big white enamel cast iron bath and a small sink with an old pine unit fitted around it. Kate leaned into the giant tub and fitted the plug then turned on the hot water which spluttered from the tap as air trapped in the pipes forced its way through. Great billows of steam followed as the hot water began to run freely. She turned to him then, twining her arms around his neck and kissing his open mouth. Breaking free from the kiss she nuzzled her head against his neck. Jamie felt the warmth of her breath against his ear. 'Undress me,' she whispered, and stood back from him.

Jamie moved closer, feeling as if he were in a dream. Everything he wanted was here in this room. He fumbled with the top button of her dress and then the second as her eyes bored into him. He leaned into her, his lips caressing the base of her neck as his fingers opened her up, button after button. Kate's fingers stroked the hair at the back of his neck and excitement built in him. His fingers trembled as he fumbled with the elusive fastenings until finally he managed to undo the last button and exposed her fully to his hungry eyes.

They kissed again. Kate closed her eyes and Jamie heard a soft sigh escape from her lips. They said nothing...there was no need, their eyes were saying everything. She came closer, pulling his sweater up over his head and running her fingers across his chest. She undid his belt and the top button of his jeans, pushing them down over his muscular thighs. She felt him harden again and repeated the operation with his pants, freeing him. Quickly now, she slipped out of her dress and stood before him, watching as he kicked off his shoes and stepped out of his denims and pants. They were acting on impulse now, instinctively, each of them knowing exactly what the other wanted and expected.

Jamie stepped away from her and devoured her with his eyes. He was almost convinced he was dreaming. Kate's breath was coming in short, quick pants and as he gazed at her he was rapidly losing control. Everything worn under her dress was in black; a lace trimmed bra with thin straps clung to her shoulders and encased her firm breasts, tiny black lace fringed silk briefs sat atop a black suspender belt with light tan stockings attached, all of these things contrasting vividly with the creamy whiteness of her skin.

Kate smiled happily. She couldn't remember ever feeling as she did now. The bath was almost full and steam filled the room. With her eyes never leaving Jamie, she sat on the edge of the bath and started to remove her stockings. Jamie's eyes were wide and with the steam swirling around them both he felt as though he was in some sort of surrealistic dream. With every piece of lingerie that Kate removed Jamie's desire to have her again increased exponentially.

Suddenly, it seemed, they were both entirely naked, the bathroom floor littered with underwear, and Kate came to him again. Their hands caressed, their mouths teased, their tongues searched. She pulled away and swung to the tap, turning off the water, and then stepped into the deep heat of the bath. She held out her hand and Jamie took it, following her.

They stood still for a moment, their bodies touching, and then sank together into the water. Knees bent, they strained to be close and slowly manoeuvred their bodies intimately together. Jamie stretched out his legs and Kate lifted herself over and on to him, sitting astride his thighs and wrapping her legs around him. His mouth sank to her breasts and his lips teased her nipples. Kate sighed and her hands caressed his neck. She felt the hardness of him again between her thighs. 'Take me,' she whispered. Gently she guided him into her, her hips moving against him, taking him deeper. She was in control now, moving her body intimately in a steady motion. Her breasts heaved against him as his mouth and lips alternated between them, teasing her nipples to hardness. They had no concept of time. Kate came suddenly, another cry slipping from her as Jamie moved faster, bringing himself to climax. Again, she felt him erupt inside her, his spasms continuing on and on until his head sank onto her breasts.

Kate laughed happily as they separated, the warm water washing over them. She leaned forward to kiss him, pushing her tongue out through her opened lips as she met his. They played together now, like children, splashing and creating a covering of bubbles on the surface of the water. They washed each other, touching intimately, caressing, arousing.

As the water cooled they stepped from the bath and dried each other, letting their hands linger intimately to excite and arouse. Their bodies still damp, Kate led Jamie to the bedroom, her lithe body moving ahead of him like a Greek Goddess, and he found himself stimulated again. Every movement of her body, every touch of her fingers, every look she gave him, aroused him and he found himself wondering when his body would give up. Never, he hoped.

As he followed her into the room his eyes quickly took in the surroundings but his attention was focussed almost entirely on Kate. Her movements hypnotised him and his head swam. He gazed at her unashamedly, entranced by her, as she sat down on the bed facing him. He ran his tongue over dry lips and came to her. Kate's eyes bored into him and he sensed she was looking right into his heart and his mind, anticipating his every thought.

He sank to his knees in front of her, his hands resting on her thighs and a tremor of excitement passed through him as Kate's fingers traced their way across the muscles of his chest.

'It's funny,' Kate whispered. 'I've seen you naked before but this is different somehow,' she murmured throatily. 'And I've spent the last two weeks wondering what would happen today.' She paused and leaned forward to kiss him. 'I didn't expect this,' she said.

'What didn't you expect?'

She gazed at him, happy, relaxed. 'I didn't expect you to want me again after we'd made love the first time.'

'Once will never be enough with you,' he whispered, his hands rising to her breasts and cupping them. Gently he pushed her back onto the bed and eased her thighs apart with his hips. Kate lifted her legs, anticipating the thrust of him but instead his head came to her breasts and his chest lay across her belly and groin. His mouth meandered across her breasts, his tongue circling the areola of each, then lower to her ribs and stomach. She felt his tongue probe her navel then drift across her abdomen as his hands slid inside her thighs and eased them further apart. His mouth lingered on the tight flesh covering her hip bones and then, slowly, inexorably, his head moved down across her mound of Venus towards her vulva. She felt his fingers open her and his mouth close on her. She raised her hips towards him and moaned as his tongue traced a path along her labia to settle, finally, on her clitoris.

Kate heard herself moan softly again as his stimulation of her continued and she gripped his hair tightly in her fingers, her hips rising again to press against his mouth and tongue. The exquisite pain of her orgasm started slowly then swept over her in waves. She cried out and suddenly he was above her. The hardness of him was against her and she opened herself to accept it, feeling him penetrate deep inside her. His thrusts were rapid and her orgasm continued, crashing over her like a series of giant waves. She called out his name and her teeth bit into his shoulder as, with a final thrust, he exploded inside her once again. The rhythmic movement of their bodies continued then until both were completely sapped of their remaining energy.

They lay together across the bed, Jamie still inside her, reluctant to withdraw. Their bodies were slick with sweat. They kissed, slowly, their mouths locked together, their tongues dancing a waltz.

'Oh God, Jamie, it's been so long since I felt wanted like that,' Kate murmured softly, her mouth nuzzled against his ear. 'It was like making love for the first time…it was unbelievable.' She lifted her head to look at him and caught his smile.

'I'm still pinching myself to be sure I'm not dreaming,' he whispered. Kate's response was to tighten the muscles of her vulva around him, convincing him. 'It's not a dream,' he sighed aloud.

She began kissing his chest again and her fingers gently traced the curve of his ribcage. They lay together for what seemed an age before Jamie rolled aside and slipped from her. Kate lifted herself up on one elbow and leaned over, kissing him passionately before edging away and tucking herself under the blanket.

Jamie followed suit, pulling her to him again and kissing her sensuously. 'You said it's been so long,' he said casually as they separated. 'How long is so long?' he probed. Truth was, he was curious as to what had driven her into his arms.

He thought he saw a tiny hint of sadness in her eyes before she replied. 'Months,' she said eventually. 'Longer…nearly a year…I don't know…does it matter?' There was irritation in her voice.

Later, Jamie would berate himself for his next question but for the moment he wasn't thinking. 'It matters if you still love him, do you?' he asked.

Kate looked at him steadily and the irritation reverted to sadness. 'Why the questions, Jamie?' she asked, waiting for his response but there was none. She shrugged then, almost imperceptibly, and carried on. 'I married Tom four years ago,' she started slowly, her voice laced with melancholy and Jamie was beginning to regret going down this line. 'When I married him I loved him like mad,' she admitted. 'We met when we were both very young…and he was the only boy I'd ever really known.'

'So what went wrong?' Jamie persisted, unable to leave it. He needed to know if she was still in love with her husband but the why of that escaped him then. It became obvious to him later.

'I don't know,' Kate responded, reflectively. 'He had a good job…he worked for Rolls Royce in Derby, but something happened…I don't know what, but he was unhappy.' There was a faraway look in her eyes. 'He started to drink heavily,' she continued. 'He seemed to be in control of it at first but eventually it took control of him.' She was becoming emotional, paying the price for Jamie's questions and he felt remorseful and selfish.

'One day he came home and told me he'd been offered a better job, here in Glasgow,' she started again. 'He said he was sorry for everything he'd put me through and he wanted to make a fresh start.' Jamie could see she was becoming maudlin. 'I tried, I really tried,' she murmured. 'But it turned out to be just more of the same,' she said sadly.

'What was "more of the same"?' Jamie kept on, ignoring his regret.

Kate hesitated, as though weighing up how far to take him, and then carried on. 'Tom doesn't just drink,' she confided at last. 'He can't help himself, he's an alcoholic.' Jamie waited, sensing that she was about to unburden herself. 'Once, I went along with him to an Alcoholics Anonymous meeting,' she laughed sadly. 'Lots of sad men and women fighting a daily battle to stay sober.' She paused again, the events of that night in her mind. 'Later, at home, here, he said he wasn't like any of these other people…he wasn't an alcoholic. He toasted that piece of news with another beer.' She paused again. 'The difference between Tom and those people was that they were prepared to fight their addiction, he wasn't. 'We haven't been a married couple for a long time. Does that answer your question?' she asked finally, her sadness filling the room.

Jamie's heart told him to stop but his head wanted the answer to the question Kate had avoided. 'Do you still love him?' he asked, perpetuating her torment.

Kate looked into his eyes and saw the uncertainty there. She realised then what was behind his probing and smiled sadly. Jamie deserved to know how she felt...how she *really* felt. *Let's see where this takes us,* she decided. 'Okay, you've asked the question...I still have feelings for him,' she said quietly. 'It's impossible not to when you've been with someone for so long...but do I still love him? I don't know,' she murmured, answering her own question. She drifted away then, putting distance between them, and Jamie thought he had pushed it too far. Suddenly, she was back with him, as though she'd just experienced an epiphany and everything was clear now. 'I'm sorry for him,' she continued, better explaining her feelings. 'I feel affection for him...for what we *used* to have together...but he's not the man he was, he's a stranger, and I won't let him ruin my life too,' she said bluntly.

'But what if he changed?' Jamie continued. *I've started this, so I have to finish,* he told himself.

'He won't change,' Kate replied sadly. 'He promises he will but they are empty promises...he can't change. Until he accepts that he *is* an alcoholic, he'll never get better. I don't think he wants to.

Jamie's regret at starting out on this journey was now full-blown. Nothing was simple anymore and he had no idea what to do or think. His feelings for Kate now were far beyond anything he had anticipated. He felt awkward and realised his questioning like that her had been crass. He hadn't wanted to know how she felt about her husband, he wanted to know how she felt about *him*, so why hadn't he simply asked her that question? The answer was simple...he was scared of what she might say because, contrary to what he had told Jack Connolly, he had fallen in love with her.

'What are you thinking?' Kate asked, registering in his pensiveness.

'Nothing, really,' Jamie lied.

'Come on, Jamie,' she pried gently. 'I've seen that look before,' she laughed quietly. 'What's up?'

What's the point in avoiding it, Jamie asked himself? I need to know where I stand, he decided. 'Where do I fit into your life?' he asked quietly. 'Am I likely to be around for a while...or am I just a temporary distraction?'

Kate regarded him thoughtfully. She knew what was behind the question and could see that it unsettled him. 'That depends on you,' she replied softly. 'What do you want?' She held his eyes and trailed her fingers slowly and deliberately across his stomach.

He gazed back into her eyes, sure that she was reading his mind again, looking into his soul, and she would see the jealousy that was tearing him apart. Why am I jealous of a man she won't let near her, this stranger that comes back to her from time to time? What *do* I want from this; am I in love with her, he asked himself? Yes, he thought, giving himself the answer, I am.

'Alright,' he said at last. 'I'm thinking about us...the future,' he said.

'What future?' she asked, playing him.

'Our future,' Jamie sighed. 'Do we have one?' he asked gently, his fingers trailing absent mindedly along the inside of her thighs.

Kate stared back at him, forcing him to hold her look, and a smile played at the corners of her mouth. 'Seriously, is that what you really want?' She whispered. 'A future…with me?' She lifted her hand and touched his face gently with her fingers.

'Yes, that's what I really want,' he said decisively. 'I want all of you.' He had crossed the Rubicon now and there was no going back. In the physical sense, he wanted her all the time and that would never diminish, he was certain of that…but there was more to it. He needed her emotionally as well as physically. He waited impatiently for her calls every day, desperate to hear her voice. He wanted to be with her all of the time. She was under his skin, in his heart, in his head and in his soul. She was his life now.

'Meaning?' Kate prompted.

Jamie hesitated, apprehensive that his next words might be too much too soon, but he was committed. He drew a deep breath and started. 'You asked me what I want…well, I want you to be mine, I want everyone know that you're mine and I want everything to be out in the open…not hidden away,' he said quietly. 'I don't want a sleazy affair, Kate. I want to be with you…and that's why I need to know if you still love him.'

Jamie held his breath. Kate smiled though there were tears welling up behind her eyes as she took hold of his hands and lifted them to her lips, kissing his fingertips. 'God, Jamie…that was a speech and a half.' She was still smiling and leant forward to kiss him firmly on the mouth. Her fingers stroked the back of his neck. 'I suppose I do,' she said thoughtfully, and Jamie's shoulders sagged. 'But not in the way I used to.' Jamie waited for the next twist or turn, holding her hand to his lips and kissing the tips of her fingers just as she had done to his. 'I still have feelings for him, I told you that' she continued. 'But I'm not in love with him. Do you understand?'

'No, not really,' he bridled, missing the subtlety of her point. 'You either love him or you don't,' he continued bluntly.

'That's unfair, Jamie!' Kate retorted, angrily. 'There's a difference between *loving* someone and *being in love* with them,' she continued. Jamie's obvious scepticism invited more. 'You love your Mother, don't you?' Kate continued, 'And I love my father…but *you're* not *in love* with your Mum and *I'm* not *in love* with my Dad. Don't you see?' There was a brief pause, but not enough for Jamie to get a word in. 'You wouldn't sleep with your mother, would you?' she added with a sardonic laugh. 'There's a big difference between loving someone and being in love with them.' She paused again and took a deep breath to steady herself. Jamie made to speak but Kate stopped him, placing her fingers firmly over his lips. 'I'm sorry for him, Jamie,' she continued. 'I feel guilty about what I've done to him…about what I'm doing now, with you,' she explained, becoming tearful. 'I don't really want to hurt him…and I know that what we're doing will do just that,' she said, resigned to the fact.

'I'm sorry,' Jamie responded gently. 'I didn't mean to spoil things between us…but my feelings for you…I can't explain. I was curious.'

'Curious?' Kate threw back quickly. 'Curious about what, Jamie, my married life…or our future?'

'Curious is the wrong word,' he retorted, trying to dig his way out of the hole he had dug for himself. 'I don't want to know about your married life, though I suppose that's part of it,' he continued. 'I wanted to know why you allowed me to get close to you.'

The question hung in the air for a while. 'Truthfully?' Kate asked eventually and watched him nod in response. She smiled and took a deep breath. 'The first time I saw you something happened to me,' she whispered. 'I couldn't take my eyes off you. I began to fantasise and wondered what it would be like to feel loved again by someone like you. The feelings took me completely by surprise. I knew I was behaving like a silly, love struck schoolgirl, but I couldn't stop myself.' She took both of his hands in hers and gazed intently into his eyes. 'When you said you'd like to see me again my heart raced...and nobody has made me feel like that for a long time,' she murmured. 'That's not true,' she whispered after a heartbeat. 'No one has *ever* made me feel like that...including Tom. You make me feel like a woman again, wanted.'

'You're kidding me. You're beautiful,' Jamie whispered back to her. 'There's probably a queue of guys who want you, believe me.'

Kate laughed at last and the tension that had been building between them was broken. 'You make me feel *so* good, baby,' she said contentedly.

'But you're wondering about me, right? You're not sure about me,' Jamie murmured, sensing what was in her mind.

A mixture of amazement and guilt flitted across her eyes. How did he know that, she wondered, surprised by his insight. 'Maybe,' she admitted. 'You're good looking, after all. You're young, you're charming and you're not vain...'

'Oh yes I am,' Jamie interrupted her with a laugh.

'No, you're not...you're confident, not arrogant, you're not full of yourself...there would always be other women trying to tempt you away from me...and I made a big mistake before.'

Jamie knew she was watching his reactions carefully, waiting for his response. 'Other women don't interest me,' he said, smiling reassuringly. 'You do.'

'After you moved out of the I.C.U. I didn't know whether or not to come to see you...but in the end, I couldn't stop myself,' she admitted. 'Barbara was great...she told me to enjoy you. I came to Ward 2 every night when you were asleep and just stared at you. The other nurses teased me but I didn't care,' she went on. 'I wanted you then...and I want you now. I haven't felt loved for a long time and you make me feel loved...but if we were married I'd be scared of losing you and I'd be jealous all the time,' she finished off, voicing her fear.

Jamie chose his words carefully. 'In the beginning, I thought this would turn out to be just a harmless fling,' he started gently, trying to put his thoughts into words. 'But everything has changed. It's more...I don't know how to explain it,' he murmured, his voice trailing off.

'Are you trying to tell me you're in love with me?' Kate asked, her voice mirroring her surprise.

'Yes, I suppose I am.'

'But you don't really know me,' she threw back. 'What about our ages for a start...I'm older than you are? Doesn't that matter?'

Jamie laughed easily for the first time since the conversation had begun. 'No, it doesn't...not to me anyway,' he confirmed. 'Does it matter to you? Do you think I'm too young?'

'No baby, you're not,' Kate replied sincerely, leaning forward to kiss him. 'I just never imagined you would get serious about me. What changed?'

Jamie gazed at her intensely. She had been reading his thoughts from the beginning and he wanted her to read them now. 'I don't know what changed...I just know that something did. You're under my skin,' he laughed lightly. 'All our chats, the telephone conversations, and your visits to me in hospital over the last few weeks…they made me realise that I want you, need you, more than I ever believed possible.' His talk with Jack flooded back to him; Jack's question about him taking her away from her husband and him pouring scorn on the idea. It wasn't so ridiculous now, he mused. 'What age are you anyway?' he asked. Kate laughed again, filling him with delight.

'A gentleman doesn't ask a lady her age,' she giggled, fluttering her eyelashes.

'Aye, well, we've already established that I'm no gentleman,' he responded, laughing.

'I'll be twenty-five in February…an old woman compared to you.'

Jamie gave her a look feigning shock. 'That just means you can retire nine years before me to look after the grand-kids,' he grinned. 'Seriously, your age doesn't matter.'

Kate yawned and Jamie remembered, guiltily, that she had just finished twelve hours in the I.C.U. That and the frenzy of their love making was taking its toll on her. She yawned again and tried to stifle it.

'I'm sorry sweetheart, I should've realised,' he apologised. 'You must be shattered. I'll head home if you like and let you sleep,' he offered.

'No, please Jamie, stay with me,' she pleaded, wrapping her arms around him. 'I want you here when I waken…beside me.'

Jamie looked at her and raised his eyebrows. 'Are you sure about that?' he asked. 'What about the Lord of the Manor?' he continued, trying to sound nonchalant.

Kate smiled. 'What about him?' she asked, pulling a face. 'The last time I saw him was over a week ago,' she said, the sadness creeping back in again. 'And I can't remember when he last came home before I left for work.'

'Then I'll stay,' he whispered, kissing her again. 'Right here beside you.' He kissed her gently on the top of her head and smelt the freshness of her hair. He wrapped an arm around her shoulders and let her lay her head on his chest. His fingertips traced a path down the skin of her arm and minutes later she was asleep, her breathing low and the steady exhalation of her breath caressing his skin.

*

With Kate now asleep in his arms, Jamie surveyed the room. There was nothing at all in it to suggest that a man lived here. A double wardrobe stood against the far wall, its door slightly ajar, and he could see dresses, skirts and a woman's trousers but nothing resembling male clothing. The dressing table was littered with make-up; perfumes, oils and creams, a brush and curlers but again, nothing remotely masculine. Jamie began to wonder if Tom Maxwell lived here at all. He thought back to the bathroom. Yes, there had been a safety razor, shaving soap and shaving brush, but none of those looked like they'd been used for quite a while.

Long, white, net curtains were drawn across the windows allowing the occupants of the room to see out while preventing anyone on the outside from seeing in. There were heavy, bottle green velour curtains hanging at both sides of the window. A straight backed chair sat next to the wardrobe with an underskirt, two pairs of stockings and a pair of sheer nylon pantyhose draped over the chair back and a few pairs of Kate's knickers were stacked neatly in a bundle on the seat. Jamie smiled at this picture of female domesticity and kissed her hair again. The smell of her excited him; the fresh, citrusy smell of her hair mingled with the floral aromas of her perfume produced a heady mix. He inhaled it deeply, enjoying the scent and feeling completely relaxed. His free hand drifted gently across her body and rested easily on her hip. Soon, his eyes began to droop under the soothing influence of her breathing and he felt himself sink into a sound sleep, all thought of confrontation with Tom Maxwell now expunged from his mind. For the first time in days Jamie slept without the nightmare plaguing him.

When he awoke it was dark outside and he was alone in the big bed. He panicked. Sitting up sharply his eyes roamed around the shadowy room. Outside, he could hear the sounds of children playing and traffic passing on the main road. Straining, he could hear the sound of Kate's voice singing softly somewhere else in the house and he relaxed. He stretched his body out on the bed, easing the stiffness from muscles that had been exercised for the first time in weeks. He heard a scraping noise and turned, catching sight of Kate's silhouette framed in the doorway. She was wearing a short, white cotton robe tied round her waist with a belt of the same material.

'You're awake,' she murmured huskily, walking towards him and undoing the knotted belt as she did so. The robe fell open and Jamie caught his breath. He was ready for her when she slipped into the bed beside him. The heat of her body and the softness of her skin against his worked their magic and he reached for her urgently. Her fingers found him, curling around him.

He closed his eyes and felt Kate's mouth drift across his body, her breath tickling the hair on his chest. He lifted her head to him and they kissed, long and hard. She pulled away from him, breathless, and her lips wandered down the length of his chest again, her tongue flitting lightly across his stomach, his muscles tightening in expectation. She paused, momentarily, and looked up at him, her eyes searching his in the semi-darkness.

'My turn,' she said quietly, her tongue running along her lips. The look in her eyes was implicit and Jamie's head swam. His mouth and throat were dry. He closed his eyes and felt the heat of her mouth around him, the tips of her teeth caressing him, her tongue teasing him, and a wave of uncontrollable rapture swept him away. He lost all track of time, the feelings and sensations pulsating through him were like nothing he had experienced before. He fought to keep control, his fingers twisted in her hair, holding her firmly. Her fingers and her lips moved in perfect synchronicity and he felt the pressure build in him, pushing him to the verge of discharge.

Suddenly, she slid up the bed to him, reaching for his mouth with hers, kissing him urgently. She pulled away and knelt over him and he felt her fingers around him again as she lowered herself onto his swollen member. The heat and wetness of her enveloped him as she started to move, her body rising and falling on him as his hands reached for her breasts. She moaned softly and arched her back, leaning backwards, her hands gripping his legs as her momentum increased. He was deep inside her now and thrusting upwards against her downward motions, deeper and deeper. Kate climaxed with a cry, calling his name again. His control already gone, Jamie felt the surge of his semen pulsating through him, filling her with the force of his ejaculation, as he jerked spasmodically inside her.

Kate slumped forward over him, sated, her breathing still fast and her face wreathed in a rapturous smile. 'I love you,' she sighed, her face against his. He was still inside her. 'I've never felt anything like that before...ever,' she moaned softly. 'I can't believe how I feel right now.'

She felt him kiss the front of her throat and then his mouth was against her ear, his teeth nibbling at her lobe. 'I love you too,' he whispered, pulling her round and kissing her again. They had both taken the irrevocable step.

They lay still for several minutes, both exhausted by the frenzy of their coupling, and it was close to six o'clock before Jamie, reluctantly, started to move. He didn't want to drag his body from hers; they were comfortable together, their bodies knitted perfectly. Kate moved above him and he felt her muscles tighten around him again.

'It's late,' he whispered. 'Stop it.'

Kate's laugh was muffled as she buried her head against his chest. She turned her head to the side then and looked up at him. 'Don't you want me?' she asked, pretending hurt. 'You promised you'd make love to me as often as I wanted,' she laughed, reminding him of their conversation days earlier. She giggled at his expression, tightening and relaxing her muscles and driving him out of his mind.

She laughed and lifted herself up, kneeling again, then slowly raised herself from him. Jamie lay completely still as she rolled from the bed and climbed to her feet in front of him, her stomach level with his head. He reached for her, his arms encircling her bottom, and pulled her towards him, running his tongue horizontally across her belly and pressing the tip into her navel.

Kate laughed again, a soft, tinkling laugh that set his pulse racing. 'Don't start something you can't finish,' she said. 'There's always tomorrow.'

Jamie left Copland Place just after six o' clock. He now knew the meaning of the word euphoria and his earlier worries about Tom Maxwell were gone. Kate loved him, not her husband. Why anyone should want to drown themselves in drink when they could come home and drown themselves in the arms of a beautiful wife escaped him. Tom Maxwell was, in Jamie's opinion, a very stupid man.

Chapter 9

Kate arrived at work later with a bounce in her step and dark circles under her eyes.

Barbara Laing had been waiting patiently for news and laughed as Kate came into the ward. 'I take it you had a good time, then,' she said with a smile. 'Think you'll manage to stay awake tonight?'

Kate sat down beside her at the Nurses' Station and the radiant smile on her face gave Barbara the answer to the first part of her query. 'I had a wonderful time,' she giggled, stifling a yawn. 'I can't believe I actually did it,' she confided.

'No regrets?' Barbara asked.

Kate looked at her, the smile still fixed on her face. 'None at all,' she said.

'Good,' Barbara laughed. 'In that case, I can't wait for the break to hear all the juicy details,' she sniggered.

They were about three and a half hours into their shift before they finally managed to take a break. As Kate sank wearily onto her seat, Barbara laughed and slid a cup of coffee towards her. 'Did you get any sleep at all?' she whispered, lewdly.

Kate giggled. 'Actually, I did,' she said wistfully. 'I slept like a baby...in his arms, but when we weren't asleep it was intense. Honestly, Babs, I've never felt anything like it.'

'Come on then,' Barbara fired back quickly. 'Spill the beans.'

'Use your imagination,' Kate laughed. 'I just love being with him. The sex was incredible...but it's not just that. I feel contented when he's with me and I don't want not to be with him.'

Barbara smiled. 'Sounds like you're falling in love, Katie, watch it.'

'Yes, I know,' Kate replied dreamily. 'It scares me a bit.' Barbara looked at her questioningly and Kate caught her expression. 'He's the first guy I've really looked at...really wanted to be with, in years, and I'm scared I'm getting it all wrong,' she said quietly, unleashing her anxiety. 'My life's so complicated, I wonder if I'm clutching at straws. And there's Tom to think of.'

'No, there isn't Tom to think of,' Barbara retorted firmly. 'Tom's an alcoholic who, from what you've told me, isn't likely to get any better. He's the only complication in your life.' Barbara carried on, spelling out what she saw as the reality of Kate's situation. 'If Tom keeps drinking, and he probably will, then he'll kill himself. You can't stop him, Kate. Only he can do that and, from what you've said, I don't think he can. Get out while you still can...and if that can be with Jamie Raeburn, then take the chance.' Barbara watched Kate closely as she said all of this, unsure of how she would react, but the look of deep sadness that her words seemed to evoke in Kate was unexpected.

Kate's eyes suddenly filled with tears, her earlier happiness and elation of her time spent with Jamie Raeburn seemingly expelled from her mind. 'Tom isn't the only complication, Babs,' she whispered. There was a pause as she considered whether or not to go on and unburden herself of the torment that was rending her. Maybe Barbara was right, she reflected, perhaps talking it out would help. She looked at the other woman and saw only concern in her eyes and instinct told her that if she could trust anyone, she could trust Barbara Laing. 'I've got a baby daughter,' she whispered.

Barbara sat dumbstruck. Kate had never mentioned anything about having a family to her...or to anyone else, come to that. 'God Kate,' she sighed, sympathetically. 'How do you cope? Who looks after your little girl when you're at work?' she asked, more questions forming rapidly in her mind.

'I don't cope,' Kate admitted. 'She's down south with my Mum and Dad...and I miss her so much.'

Barbara put her arm comfortingly around Kate's shoulder, still trying to assimilate all of it and at the same time recover from the shock. 'What's your little girl's name?' She asked, her voice soft and gentle now.

'Lauren,' Kate sobbed. 'She's two...and I've hardly been with her since she was born. It's all getting too much.'

'And have you told Jamie?' Barbara continued, teasing information from her.

Kate shook her head sadly. 'No,' she admitted. 'He knows about Tom but not about Lauren.'

'Has he asked?'

Kate laughed sadly. 'We've only known each other for a couple of weeks. It's hardly the sort of question you'd expect a boy to ask on a first date.'

No, it isn't, Barbara admitted to herself, but what do I tell her now, she wondered? She had helped push Kate into this relationship with Jamie Raeburn, after all. And what about him, she wondered, as a picture of Jamie came into her mind? He was younger than Kate...how would he cope with the introduction of a two year old child into the relationship? Would he still want Kate? God, what a mess, she groaned inwardly, feeling partly to blame. But only Kate could judge how Jamie would react. If he loved her, only she could gauge the strength that love and, if Kate kept Lauren's existence from him, what then? 'What does your instinct tell you about Jamie?' Barbara asked finally.

Kate looked at her with furrowed brows. 'What about?' she asked.

'About everything, Kate,' Barbara continued, hugging her closer. 'About how he feels; does he love you? What sort of man he is...good, kind, that sort of thing, and about how he'll react when you tell him about Lauren?' she explained.

Kate appeared to understand and drifted into a thoughtful trance. 'I think he loves me,' she said quietly. 'We talked about Tom and I think he's jealous of him but I suppose that's natural. He says he loves me and wants to be with me...and I believe him. He's gentle, thoughtful and kind...but he's young, Babs, how can I land him with a two year old child?' she asked, and it was almost as if she was asking herself.

Barbara hugged her. 'If you keep on seeing him you'll have to tell him eventually,' she counselled softly. 'You're going home next week...for Christmas and New Year, aren't you?' she continued. 'Why don't you wait and see how being apart affects you both? You'll be with Lauren and your family and Jamie will be up here in Glasgow, alone. If he's still waiting for you when you get back then you've got a decision to take, my girl,' she said firmly, though her eyes were gentle. 'And go with your instinct. My mother always said that a woman's instinct is far superior to a man's,' she laughed, trying to bring Kate back from her self-imposed despondency. 'And know what? My Mum was right. It's not easy but if you follow your gut instinct, and don't let your head get in the way, things usually work out.'

When Kate left work the following morning Jamie was waiting in the same place, sitting majestically astride the Triumph like a medieval knight on his charger. She hugged Barbara on the steps. 'Remember,' Barbara whispered. 'Follow your instinct.' They kissed, cheek to cheek, and then Kate ran across to Jamie, a smile on her face.

Chapter 10

Jamie spent the next few days in a dream. He picked Kate up every morning at eight, took her back to Copland Place, and they made love as if the world was about to end. He was falling deeper in love with her with every passing day but at the back of his mind was the fact that Kate was heading down south for Christmas to see her family and the old green eyed devil, jealousy, was rearing its ugly head again.

There was something subtly different about Kate's attitude towards him since their first day together…not in a bad way, he reflected, but it was there. Did she still think that he would tire of her, he wondered? He laughed at that but he could understand her doubts. He still harboured doubts of his own, after all. Prime among those were Kate's continued feelings for her husband. She said she loved him once and what was to say that that love was dead? Tom Maxwell would be going down south with Kate for Christmas and no doubt he would play the family guy, the loving husband, stay sober, and get her back. Jamie tried to push these thoughts to the back of his mind but he couldn't quite manage to get them out of it completely. The only certainty, he accepted, was that he would have to deal with all of this at some point. But there was still a week to go before Friday 23 December, the day she was leaving, and he was determined to make the most of those remaining days.

Friday the 16th of December produced a surprise. When he picked Kate up that morning Jamie heard her tell Barbara Laing that she would see her on Monday and he remembered that Kate had two days off now before going back on day shift. But would he see her over those two days, that was the question?

They returned to Copland Place that morning as usual and made love slowly, sensually, savouring the delights of each other. Afterwards, Kate slept soundly, wrapped in Jamie's arms as usual. Jamie dozed, on and off, listening to the sounds from the street and the creaking of the timbers in the old house. Nothing had changed in all the days he had been coming here and, happily from his point of view, there was nothing to suggest that Tom Maxwell had been at home at any point. When Kate woke, late in the afternoon, they made love again.

As they lay together, exhausted after their second coupling, Kate laid her head on Jamie's chest. This was their favoured position, their bodies touching, pressed close to each other, almost morphing into one.

'My night shift finishes tonight,' Kate whispered. 'And I start day shift on Monday.'

Jamie lifted his head from the pillow and looked down at her, her twinkling eyes meeting his. There were two points to that, Jamie thought, one good and one bad. It was a double edged sword. On the plus side, Kate wouldn't be working on Saturday or Sunday and that might give him an opportunity to be with her but, on the down side, what was he going to do when she was on day shift? Especially as she was going home in seven days!

Her next words lifted him. 'You said you wanted to take me out…so how about tomorrow night,' she suggested.

'Seriously?' he asked, the delight in his voice impossible to hide.

'Yes, seriously,' she laughed. 'Out in the open, the way you want it to be.'

'But what about…your husband?'

Kate gave a little laugh. 'If he comes home at all he probably won't even notice I'm gone,' she replied. There was still a tinge of sadness in her voice and Jamie felt that old twinge of jealousy. 'But I don't think he'll come home,' she added.

It was a bitter sweet moment for Jamie; jealousy and ecstasy entwined. But at last he felt that Kate was truly his and that he wasn't just her bit on the side. 'Where would you like to go?' he asked, his accompanying grin lighting up the room.

'I don't care, as long as we're together,' she replied. 'That's what you want, isn't it? To be seen with me?'

Jamie pondered that, a little put out. Did she think he just wanted to show off, he wondered? 'You're not a trophy,' he responded defensively. 'I don't just want to show you off, I just want us to be a couple.'

'Then that's exactly what we'll be,' she whispered, kissing him softly. 'What do you want to do?'

'Well, apart from the obvious,' he laughed. 'Why don't we go for a meal, then a drink…and finish off at the dancing. The Locarno, maybe, or one of the Discos…the Maryland or Joanna's?'

'And afterwards? What about "the obvious"?' Kate asked, smiling coyly. 'Back here?'

Kate laughed. 'Probably best. I don't think your mother and father will be too happy if we spend the night together in your bed,' she continued. 'Will you stay the night with me?'

'Is the Pope a Catholic?' Jamie laughed. 'I can't imagine a day without you…unless it's forced on me,' he sighed.

As he sat on the edge of the bed dressing he saw Kate watching his reflection in the dressing table mirror. He sensed uncertainty in her, some indecision perhaps, or was it guilt? Something was troubling her but she wasn't ready to let him into the secret…not yet, at least. She was doing her best to hide it but Jamie picked up her negative vibes…a legacy of his relationship with Carol Whyte. He finished dressing and rose from the bed, pulling his jeans up over his thighs and buckling his belt. He turned and bent down to kiss her, conscious of the shadow that had passed across her beautiful face. 'Are you going to call me tonight?' he asked quietly.

'You should go out with your friends,' she suggested, 'and you can boast about your conquest of an older woman.' She laughed nervously.

Jamie looked at her again, perplexed. Was she joking or was she serious? Did she really think he would boast about her being a "conquest"? 'I won't boast,' he said firmly. 'I'll tell them I've got a new girlfriend…but that's all I'll tell them.'

Kate pulled him down to her again, her lips parted, her mouth hungry for his. 'I'm joking. I'll call you if you want me to,' she said as she released him. 'But you should go out…it'll do you good.'

'Okay, maybe I will,' he agreed. 'But please, stop going on about this older woman thing. It doesn't matter…I don't care!'

He left her in bed, his eyes lingering on her as she stretched luxuriously, and lifted his jacket from the chair. On his way out he stopped in the doorway, wanting to tell her that he loved her, but what he had sensed earlier stopped him. Instead, he blew her a kiss, turned and made his way down the stairs. As he stepped out into Copland Place he looked back and saw her at the curtains, a sad smile masking her beautiful face.

Jamie rode home with his head in a whirl. The rush hour traffic was streaming through the city and out to the suburbs but he wove the Triumph deftly in and out of the jams, quickly eating up the miles. His mind was filled with thoughts of Kate and what she had brought to him...and had brought him to. He wondered what was worrying her. Guilt was the prime suspect but he couldn't really criticise her for that. She was helping him to live again. The flashbacks were waning, the nightmares with them. When he slept now his dreams were mostly sweet and the bitterness that had engulfed him after his break up with Carol Whyte was gone. He had loved Carol but that love bore no likeness to what he now felt. This was the real thing.

The changes in him had been swift. A week earlier he had doubted whether he would ever be able to meet with the boys again but now, with Kate's encouragement, he was about to do just that. With Kate beside him he could do anything.

Chapter 11

'You're home,' his mother called from the kitchen, surprised, as he pushed open the front door. At least she's happy tonight, he thought. Since his return from hospital she had fussed over him like a mother hen, but her discovery that he was seeing Kate had relaxed her. Her happiness was undoubtedly down to the fact that Kate was a nurse and would be looking out for him but, and Jamie knew it only too well, she would be less happy if she knew all of the circumstances. But that could wait, he decided. For the moment, the fact that he was constantly grinning like a Cheshire cat and managing to sleep at night seemed to be enough for her. She hadn't, as yet, cottoned on to what was causing his early evening fatigue.

Jamie returned her greeting and made his way up to his room. He rummaged in his wardrobe and chose a suit for the evening...an old one, but still perfectly serviceable. The suit he had been wearing the night he ended up in hospital had been consigned to the bin and he hadn't yet had time to go into town for a new one...for obvious reasons! He washed quickly then dressed, ready for his night with the boys.

Dinner was on the table when he came down from his bedroom but his mother was still in the kitchen. His father eyed him up and down, surmising his intension. 'You're going to be popular, son,' he whispered.

His mother appeared, wiping her hands on her apron, her eyes mirroring her concern at finding him dressed like this on a Friday night. The last time she had said goodbye to him when he had been dressed like this, he hadn't come home.

He decided to break his plans to her gently. 'I'm taking Kate out tomorrow night,' he said, filling his mouth with a forkful of minced beef and onions, and watched his mother's face light up just as he knew it would.

'That's nice, son,' his mother chirped. 'She seems to be making you happy. What do you think, Dad?' she continued, bringing Jamie's father into the conversation. His father gave a grunt which his mother took as affirmation. 'And are you going out with her tonight too?' she asked.

'Ah...no,' Jamie replied quietly. 'I'm going into town to meet Jack and the lads tonight.'

He watched the smile crumble from his mother's face as her earlier concern reappeared. His father looked up from his plate, waiting for the inevitable explosion. 'Don't you think it's a bit early for that?' his mother suggested, agitated, her fingers tapping on the table top. 'You're just out of hospital,' she added, as if reminding him of that would change his mind.

'I'm just going for a couple of pints,' he replied. 'I'll be home early...I'm not going to the dancing, honest...and I'll stay out of trouble. I promise.'

His mother wasn't convinced, he could see that. Saying he would stay out of trouble was like telling her it wouldn't rain in the next seven days...it might happen but it was highly unlikely!

'You didn't go to the dancing last time either,' she replied, with more than just a trace of anguish. 'And what does Kate have to say about it?' she continued, using everything in her arsenal in an effort to change his mind.

'It was Kate who suggested it,' he threw back, stopping her in her tracks. His mother looked at him, trying in vain to think up another argument against his going and he could see a huff coming on.

His father decided to throw in his tuppence worth. Jamie heard the little cough as his father cleared his throat, and waited for the pearls of wisdom. 'He has to go back out sometime, Mary,' he said softly. 'He can't sit about the house all the time.'

Am I hearing this correctly, Jamie questioned himself, amazed? Has he just backed me up? The look on his mother's face confirmed that he had.

'Oh, I should have known you'd take his side,' she stormed. 'You men always stick together when drink's involved.'

Now, that's a bit below the belt, Jamie thought. Never once had he sided with his father when he got himself tanked up. The opposite was true. In fact they'd come to blows over it on occasion. He looked at his old man now and raised his eyes to the ceiling.

'I'm not taking his side,' his father protested. 'But you can't expect to wrap him up in cotton wool for the rest of his life…he's twenty one Mary, not ten.'

Jamie's mother was crying now and that made Jamie feel like shit. He could see it from her point of view. He was her only child and he had almost died a few weeks earlier. What it must have been like for her then, the knock on the door and opening it to find two policemen there with the news that he was in the Royal and she should get there as quickly as possible, he couldn't imagine.

'I'm sorry, Mum,' he said. 'You're right, I won't go.'

His mother smiled back at him through her tears. 'No love, your Dad's right…you're and adult and I can't wrap you up in cotton wool. Go out. Just be careful.' She lifted her hand off the table and placed it over his and in the background he heard his father sigh quietly with relief.

*

The familiar sounds and smells of the Waldorf welcomed him as he stepped in from the cold. The bar was full as usual and the familiar, heady reek of beer and tobacco smoke mingled with sweat, men's aftershave and women's perfumes, filled his nostrils. He took in a deep breath and let out a satisfied sigh.

Walking along Cambridge Street his eyes had lingered on the spot where he had been stabbed only four weeks earlier and he was pleasantly surprised to find that the building that had sat beyond the alley was now gone. The demolition work had finished and all that remained was an enormous pile of rubble, twisted cables and wood.

The face of Glasgow was changing quickly these days, he mused, but there were still other alleys, murky lanes and dark closes where danger lurked. It wasn't a change of landscape the city needed, it was a change of psyche. There were people out there who didn't give a shit about life. It was cheap. What had happened to him wasn't unusual, far from it. In reality, it was something that was hard to avoid. What was it his father said…discretion is the better part of valour? Well, from now on that would be his watchword. That, of course, didn't mean he would turn his back on trouble if it came along, only that he would approach it from a different angle.

He paused inside the pub door, a comfortable feeling enveloping him. He let his eyes drift over the crowd, saw familiar faces and listened to the ribald chat of the regulars. Two guys, long haired and bearded, with guitars were setting up in the far corner and a group of girls were ensconced at a table near the door. He looked them over appreciatively; long legs, big boobs and pretty faces, and received a couple of appraising glances in return. If he wasn't with Kate now he could have a good time tonight, he mused.

Manoeuvring past the girls he saw two who had smiled at him eyeing him up. He squeezed along the bar, flattered by their attention. A few of the regulars recognised him and turned to welcome him, pumping his hand and slapping his back. Welcoming words were coming to him from all sides; "Saw the bit about you in the paper, big man" – "Welcome back, Jamie boy" – "Didn't expect to see you back so soon, great to see you". He fielded them all, smiled and shook hands, felt his shoulder pummelled by well-wishers, but all the time, inside, he was grimacing. He didn't like all the attention.

Over in the far corner of the bar his mates were congregated around the usual table and even from where he was standing near the bar he could hear their banter and jokes. They were all there; Jack, Tony Boyle, Gerry Carroll, Jim Campbell and Vinnie Boyd, and it felt good to be here with them again. Eventually, he managed to escape from the well-wishers and made his way over to the lads, approaching Jack from the side and laying his hand on his friend's shoulder. Jack jumped and turned, his face immediately breaking into a wide grin. 'Well fuck me!' he exclaimed, standing up and grabbing Jamie in a bear hug. 'Ah wis jist tellin' this lot we'd probably huv tae come tae yer hoose an' drag ye oot,' he beamed. The rest were all around him now, slapping his back, grinning and laughing, wanting his news.

A barmaid, a nice girl but quite shy, appeared beside them, her tray laden with pint tumblers. 'Welcome back, Jamie,' she said shyly. 'Mrs Gray sent these over…they're on the house.' She flashed him a smile and started placing the glasses on the table, one by one. Finishing, she planted a kiss on Jamie's cheek and headed back to the bar. The lads let out a whoop of delight and Jamie looked across to the said Mrs Gray, standing in her usual place beside the till. He raised his glass in thanks and watched as her face broke into a wide grin.

A chair was quickly found for him and everyone started talking at once, all of them wanting to let him know their news. He sipped his Guinness happily, his first in four weeks, and told the guys that he was on the mend. They were all surprised that he had turned up, none more so than Jack, who kept looking at him and shaking his head in disbelief.

'So, how come the change o' heart?' Jack asked when the hubbub had finally settled down.

'I'm feeling better, that's all,' Jamie replied, but the twinkle in his eyes told Jack there was more.

'The sex cure's workin' then?' Jack threw back with a laugh.

Jamie spluttered and laughed. 'Did you tell this lot?' he asked, almost choking on his Guinness.

'Aye,' Jack confirmed. 'Ah telt them ye'd discovered a new miracle cure.'

'It is, right enough,' Jamie grinned. 'I'm sleepin' better, the nightmares are gone and the flashbacks aren't coming around quite so often,' he told him.

'Well then, that almost fa's intae the miracle category,' Jack responded, laughing heartily. 'We'll be lookin' oot fur three wise men on camels comin' frae the East next,' he joked.

'Impossible,' Jamie laughed. 'Where would you find three wise men from Parkhead?'

'Aye, funny,' Jack retorted sourly. 'An' whit about yer wee nurse?' he asked.

'She's fine,' Jamie replied, smiling happily. 'We've taken things a wee bit further.'

Jack was suddenly interested, wondering what Jamie meant. 'And whit wid that be?' he asked.

'I'm takin' her out tomorrow night,' Jamie replied, watching in amusement as Jack's eyebrows shot up.

'Going oot? Th'gether…as a couple?' Jack probed disbelievingly.

'Nah, separately, she's going to the Locarno and I'm going to the pub,' Jamie replied sarcastically. 'Of course we're going as a couple you daft bastard!' he laughed.

'Is that a good idea? Whit aboot her man?' Jack continued, ignoring the sarcasm.

'It's a long story, Jack.' Jamie replied. 'Let's just say I don't need to worry about him.'

'Fur fuck sake, Jamie,' he shot back. 'Ye never stay at peace. Everythin' changes wi' ye in a week!'

'She's brilliant, Jack,' Jamie enthused. 'I'm in love.'

'Aye, but she's still married,' Jack retorted flatly, putting a dampener on Jamie's enthusiasm.

Jamie nodded slowly, considering his reply and wondering how much to confide in Jack. 'Aye, for the moment,' he said eventually.

'For the moment?' Jack exploded. 'Nah Jamie, please. Tell me ye're no thinkin' whit ah think ye're thinking,' he muttered, pulling a face. Jamie smiled enigmatically but said nothing. Jack tactfully changed the subject. 'Are ye comin' wae us tae the dancin' th'night?' he asked.

'Nah, not tonight Jack. I've had a tiring week,' he smirked. 'And I need all the rest I can get to build up my strength for tomorrow night.'

'Ah'm surprised ye were able tae grace us wae yer presence th'night then,' Jack replied, a little bit of sarcasm edging in again.

'It was Kate's idea… she said I should come out with you lot again.'

Jack's eyes opened wider in surprise. 'Did she? Really?' he asked, amazed. 'Ah'm changin' ma mind aboot this lassie…rapidly.'

The two of them laughed at that. Jamie smiled to himself. Jack would be curious now and he would be desperate to meet her. Jamie would need to break Kate in gently to that. The others learned about Kate, piecemeal, throughout the evening, and Jamie spent a lot of time repeating himself, describing her, telling them how they had met and what he thought of her. And the more he repeated the story, the more he realised he really was falling in love with her. Everyone was pleased for him but he knew they would reserve judgement on Kate till they knew her better; they remembered his tortured breakup with Carol Whyte only too well. It was them who had helped him pick up the pieces and them who had put up with him when he had been a complete pain in the arse.

Vinnie summed up their feelings perfectly. 'Ye seem happy, big man,' he said. 'An' if nothin' else, she'll keep ye out o' trouble.'

They left the pub for the dancing around nine thirty. The last time Jamie had been here with them he had been the one pressing them to leave but tonight he just followed along, staying with them as they made their way along Sauchiehall Street and taking his leave outside the Beresford Hotel at the junction with Elmbank Street.

As Jamie walked away from them Jack detached himself from the others and caught up with him. 'Listen Jamie,' he started earnestly. 'Ah'm takin' Teresa O'Brien oot th'morra night.' He was smiling and it was clear that he had made a breakthrough with Teresa. But there was a little nervousness there too, so what was coming, Jamie wondered? 'Dae you an' Kate fancy a wee foursome?' Jack blurted.

So that was it, Jamie laughed to himself. He still needs me to hold his hand…only this time I get to go with my girl and not one of Teresa's wee pals. 'You'll behave?' Jamie quipped, grinning. 'No sarcastic comments? And no telling stories?' he continued.

'Aye, of course. Whit dae ye take me fur?' Jack replied, pretending to be hurt by Jamie's suggestion that he wouldn't be. 'Ah jist thought it wid be a good time tae get tae know her.'

Jamie laughed. 'You're just bein' nosey,' he teased. 'I know you so well.'

'Aye. That tae,' Jack grinned. 'So, how about it?'

'I'll talk to Kate in the morning when she phones me,' Jamie agreed. 'Call me about ten o'clock,' he continued, breaking free from Jack and heading down Elmbank Street for his bus. 'Enjoy yourself tonight,' he called back over his shoulder.

*

Jamie arrived home just after ten and his mother almost expired with shock. 'You're home early,' she remarked, quickly recovering her composure.

'I said I would be, didn't I?' he admonished her. 'The lads were going to the Locarno,' he smiled. 'Any tea going?'

'And you came home?' his mother queried, her amazement resurrecting itself.

'Yeah, well…Kate's working,' he explained. 'So I didn't think I should be going.'

His mother smiled happily. She was looking forward to meeting this girl. She rose from her chair to make tea whilst Jamie's father snored over a programme that was droning away on the television. 'Are you bringing Kate back here tomorrow night?' his mother threw at him as she disappeared into the kitchen.

Panic filled him. 'Don't know, maybe,' he replied quickly, thinking on his feet. 'We might be going back to Kate's place.' That wouldn't be the end of it, he knew that. He heard his mother fill the kettle and light the gas. Still no further comment…but it would come.

'You could bring Kate back here,' she said eventually, just as Jamie knew she would.

Oh fuck, Jamie thought, almost forgetting himself and saying it aloud. 'We'll see,' he replied, trying to dream up something to knock the idea down.

His mother ignored him and carried on. 'She can have your bed and you can sleep in the spare room,' she persisted. 'And I'm looking forward to meeting her.'

You're looking forward to interrogating her, you mean, was what sprung to Jamie's mind. He was facing a quandary. His feelings for Kate were still like little green shoots and he surmised that Kate probably felt the same. An interrogation by his mother could be a frosty affair and frost kills green shoots. He didn't want that to happen. And if it came out that Kate was married then the shit would really hit the fan.

'She's shy,' he fired back, hoping that would be enough.

But when his mother got something into her mind she was like a dog with a bone. She wouldn't let go. 'She can't be that shy,' she threw at him as she returned to the living room with the tea. 'Why don't you ask her?' she insisted.

Jamie wasn't going to win this particular battle. It was time for full scale retreat masquerading as a strategic withdrawal. 'Okay, I'll ask her,' he capitulated. 'She's phoning me in the morning when she finishes her shift,' he continued. 'I'll ask her then.'

Satisfied with her victory, his mother sat down and sipped her tea, a broad smile on her face. Kate's situation would have to come out sooner or later but later was better…much better! And when it did, he would have to break it gently…very gently. It wouldn't be fun but it would have to be done. He drank his tea and listened to the dulcet tones of his father's snoring. And there's another reason for not bringing her here, he thought.

Chapter 12

"The best laid schemes o' mice an' men gang aft agley" as Robert Burns, Scotland's most famous son, once so aptly put it. Jamie didn't get the chance to ask Kate about his mother's suggestion the next morning…his mother beat him to it. He had set his alarm for just before eight o' clock, knowing that Kate would phone as soon as she finished work. The house was quiet and he assumed that his mother was still in bed asleep. His father was at work delivering the morning post so there shouldn't have been a problem. But there was…his mother was wide awake and waiting for Kate's call because he, foolishly, had told her the night before that Kate would phone when she finished her shift.

The phone rang twice and Jamie reached out for the handset but before he could pick it up the ringing stopped…and so did his heart. 'Shit, shit, shit,' he kept repeating under his breath. From the living room below him he could hear his mother's voice twittering away happily. So the damage was done. All he could do now was try to limit it. He lifted the handset and put it to his ear only to hear the voices of the two women in his life chatting away happily.

The click in his mother's earpiece alerted her to his presence on the line. 'Hello son,' she chirped. 'I've just been saying to Kate that she's welcome to stay here tonight,' she raced on. 'Isn't that right, dear?'

'Hi Jamie,' Kate said, joining the conversation. 'Your Mum says I can stop over tonight,' she continued, clearly amused. 'I've said I'll ask if I can stay out,' she added.

Ask if you can stay out, Jamie thought, going out of his mind. Christ, when she meets you, my mother will wonder why a twenty-five year old siren has to ask if she can stay out.

'That's great, thanks Mum,' Jamie replied, defeated.

'Well, just let me know,' his mother came back, addressing them both before hanging up.

'Your Mum caught me by surprise there,' Kate fired at him, laughing aloud. 'She said she asked you last night…what did you tell her?'

'I said you were shy but I'd ask you,' he replied and heard her choke with laughter. Jamie joined in with her despite himself.

When the laughing finally stopped the flirting began. 'Did you miss me last night?' Kate whispered.

'You know I did,' Jamie confirmed. 'But not as much as I'm missing you this morning,' he added archly. 'I'm having withdrawal symptoms.'

Kate laughed again. 'Then don't withdraw,' she giggled. A yawn followed. 'If we're going out tonight I need to sleep,' she informed him. 'Did you go out last night? she asked.

'Aye, I went for a drink with my mates,' he told her, quickly adding. 'But I was home around ten thirty, honest.'

'So you didn't go dancing?' Kate continued, sounding pleased. Jamie could imagine her smile.

'No, I needed my sleep,' he laughed. 'I've had quite a week.'

Another tinkling laugh tumbled down the line to him. 'So,' Kate continued. 'Where are we going tonight?' she asked.

Jamie crossed his fingers, hoping she wouldn't mind the surprise he was about to spring on her. 'How do you feel about going out in a foursome?'

'Seriously? she queried, unsure.

'Yes, seriously,' he confirmed. 'But if you don't want to, it's okay.'

'Who with?' Kate asked.

Jamie breathed a little sigh of relief. At least it wasn't a straight "no", he noted. 'My pal, Jack, and his new girlfriend,' he told her. 'He collared me last night, just before I headed home...and I said I'd ask you,' he continued apologetically. 'He's just being nosey; he wants to see what you look like.'

There was a short pause before Kate replied and Jamie guessed she was wondering what he had told Jack about her. 'What have you told him?' she asked with ominous quiet. His pause confirmed he had said more than simply that she was his girlfriend.

'He knows you're married,' Jamie admitted eventually.

'And my age?' she demanded. 'Did you tell him that?' The hint of irritation was back in her voice.

'No, I didn't tell him your age,' he replied defensively. 'But he knows you're older than me,' he added, honestly.

When Kate spoke next she sounded hurt. 'You said it didn't matter, Jamie,' she responded. 'But the first thing you do is tell your mate.'

'It wasn't like that,' Jamie retorted, grovelling now. 'He worked it out from the fact that you're married...and when he asked me right out I couldn't lie, could I?' There was silence and he suspected that Kate was simply racking up his guilt. 'It doesn't matter to me, I told you. Please believe me.' He knew he was pleading but he didn't care.

'I don't want to be a freak in a sideshow, Jamie,' she said quietly.

'Jack's not like that. He just wants to meet you.' He hoped he was winning her round but the continued silence wasn't a good sign. He ploughed on regardless, trying to explain. 'He's just started going out with this girl, Teresa, and I think he needs me to hold his hand,' he said and started to laugh almost immediately at the absurdity of that. When Kate laughed with him he knew he was winning.

'Alright,' she said, relenting. 'But you'd better make it up to me afterwards.'

'I'll do whatever you want,' he responded quickly. 'What do you want?'

Kate's laugh continued. 'I'll think of something, don't worry. But what are we going to tell your Mum?'

'Shit...who knows?' Jamie said despondently. 'She'll be annoyed if you don't come back with me because she's dying to meet you,' he explained. 'But she'll interrogate you relentlessly if you do.'

'Tell her I'm coming,' Kate replied immediately, flooring him. 'I'd like to meet the other woman in your life.'

'You're kidding me, aren't you?' Jamie said, incredulous.

'No, I'm serious,' she laughed again. 'You want me, don't you? And I want you, so I have to meet her some time.'

'Christ...'

'Uh,uh,' Kate broke in, stopping him from going on. 'No swearing.' She paused. 'There is one thing though'

'What thing?' Jamie asked, worried. 'Your husband?'

'No, don't be silly, don't worry about him,' she laughed. 'Something much more important,' she said, leading him on. 'You promised you'd make love to me…how are we going to manage that?' she giggled.

Jamie breathed a sigh of relief. Everything had worked out. 'Don't worry,' he said confidently. 'I'll find a way!'

'You'd better,' she chuckled. 'I don't want to miss a day.' She yawned again, louder this time. 'I'm going home now, baby,' she said. 'I need my beauty sleep.'

They arranged to meet later, at four thirty, to give them time alone together before meeting up with Jack and Teresa and Kate left everything else up to Jamie. 'Surprise me,' she replied when he asked where she would like to go.

'Alright,' he agreed cheerily. 'Meet me at Boots Corner at half past four.'

'Okay. I love you,' was all Jamie heard as the line went dead.

Chapter 13

Jamie arrived at "Boots Corner" – the corner of Argyle Street and Union Street, in Glasgow's City Centre – early, having come into the city before his rendezvous with Kate to be measured for a new suit. He felt better than he had for a long time but there was a gamut of feelings pounding in his brain; excitement mixed with nervousness, anticipation melded with bashfulness. Standing here, all spruced up in a grey wool worsted herringbone suit, a light blue Byford shirt, dark brown Clark's brogues and a double breasted woollen overcoat, he wondered what Kate would think of him. She had never seen him suited and booted before and, come to think of it, he had never seen her in anything other than her uniform.

As he waited he cast his eyes around the other hopefuls; four guys dressed up like him and two of them looking apprehensive, a couple of girls, heavily made up and with Buffon hair do's and a handful of lads there just to watch the girls go by. Andy Williams had a lot to answer for. The two worried looking guys appeared to have missed the boat, their glum expressions and the fact that they were constantly checking of watches tended to give the game away. All dressed up and nowhere to go, Jamie thought, feeling a little sorry for them. Boot's Corner, or "Dizzy Corner" as it was sometimes called, got its name from the big Boots Department Store that sits imposingly on the corner. It was probably the most popular meeting place in Glasgow for courting couples but it was also a place where dreams were shattered. Hence its name, Dizzy Corner, the place where disappointed guys and girls waited for dates who didn't turn up, and then slunk off dejectedly.

He spied Kate coming along Argyle Street from the direction of St. Enoch's Square and smiled to himself. Heads turned; guys drooled, and girls turned green with envy…and it was little wonder, she looked stunning. The short black dress she was wearing clung to her body like a second skin and showed off an impressive length of thigh beneath her long black maxi coat which flapped open as she walked briskly towards him. The black, high heeled, knee length boots finished the picture and made her just about the sexiest female in Glasgow today, Jamie thought, *and she was coming to meet him.* Her dark hair hung loosely down to her shoulders, curling just under her chin, and as she came closer Jamie could see that judicious use of eye makeup had made her big, green eyes appear even bigger than usual. She wasn't tall, he reflected, but she would never be overlooked in a crowd.

She stepped up to him and placed her hand on his shoulder, kissing him long and hard, producing a collective sigh of envy rise from the men milling around them.

'Hi sweetheart,' she said, loud enough for the others to hear, her voice sultry. 'You look great…I think I'd rather just take you home than go out with you tonight.' Jamie suspected she knew what her appearance was doing to the men around them and she was winding them up. He grinned. Lust was all around and wet daydreams would be on the menu for a couple of those guys at least. He slipped his arm under her coat and around her waist, kissing her again.

'Where do you want to go?' he whispered, nuzzling his head against her ear.

'I don't care, anywhere, but first I need to go to Lewis's,' she said, still loud enough for general consumption. 'I want to buy a new nightdress for tonight or I'll be sleeping naked,' she giggled. She wasn't playing up the audience any longer, only Jamie, but still her words piled on the agony. Jamie imagined he was now being described as "the lucky bastard". He was tempted to say 'no' to her request and let the poor buggers imagine her with him, naked as God intended, but the poor buggers had suffered enough.

Instead, he nodded and took her by the arm. 'We've got plenty of time,' he said happily. As he steered her away towards Lewis's further along Argyle Street, he leaned close. 'That wasn't fair,' he said, stifling a laugh. 'Some of those poor guys back there wet themselves.'

'What poor guys?' she grinned cheekily. 'I didn't see any other guys…there's only one I'm interested in.' Jamie's response was a happy laugh, his ego suitably inflated.

At Lewis's, that big four storey white walled department store that dominated Argyle Street, Kate lead him straight to the lingerie department and watched him blush awkwardly as she took her time browsing through the range of sexy underwear. For Jamie, it was a first. Never before had he visited the lingerie department of any big store and the range of knickers, camisoles, suspenders and night dresses on show was mind boggling, in addition to which the mannequins looked almost lifelike. He felt his cheeks warm and averted his eyes then blushed even more when he caught Kate watching him. She laughed and teased him viciously.

'And I thought you were a man of the world, Jamie Raeburn' she joked, kissing him on the cheek.

'I thought the models were human,' he spluttered. 'I was waitin' for them to speak! The closest I've ever seen so many scantily dressed women at one time was in my mother's Littlewoods's Catalogue.' The memory of his early brush with women's underwear made him blush even more and started Kate laughing uproariously. Kate suddenly realised they were the centre of attention and rose up on her tip toes to plant a kiss firmly on his lips.

'I'm sorry sweetheart,' she whispered, but she was still laughing.

Jamie joined in, beginning to relax and enjoy himself. 'It's alright,' he grinned. 'But just remember that I'm an only child and I don't have any half-naked sisters running about the house.'

'Don't fret, my sweet, you've got me now,' she purred, teasing him again.

'Oh yes, you'll do nicely,' he laughed and pulled her close, upsetting two elderly spinsters standing nearby who tut-tutted loudly.

After that, Kate quickly chose a pink cotton nightdress, a white silk camisole and a pair of matching white silk French knickers, holding them in front of herself for Jamie's approval. The thought of her in those made his heart race again and he wondered if his rapid nods of admiration made him look like a lecher to the two old dears who were now keeping a close watch on them. But he also figured it was his turn to do some teasing and as Kate waited in the queue to pay for her purchases, with the two old loves queuing up close behind, he leant in close. 'I can't wait to see you in those,' he said in a loud stage whisper and smiled at the stereophonic gasps from the two old spinsters and the quickly camouflaged giggle from the sales girl.

Kate smiled coquettishly and turned round, playing the game with him. 'I thought you preferred me without them,' she said, knowing exactly what would happen. The salesgirl sniggered and turned away and the two old dears almost died of shock, thunderstruck by Kate's brazen effrontery.

They left the store, still laughing, and crossed over to the Argyle Arcade with its array of jeweller's shops. Jamie's destination was Sloan's' pub which nestled off to the side of the Arcade but as they passed the first of the jeweller's shops Kate stopped to admire the window display. She scanned the various items and pointed out a couple of rings that she liked. Jamie looked at her curiously, wondering if there was anything behind this but there was nothing in her expression to suggest it was anything more than simply appreciating the rings. He said nothing but took note of the ring she seemed to like most…someday…maybe, he mused.

They had a coffee in Sloan's and then made their way, hand in hand, up Buchanan Street and into St Vincent Place towards George Square and the city's magnificent Victorian City Chambers, built at a time when Glasgow was the "Second City of the Empire". The Square and the streets around it were all decked out in Christmas lights and there was an air of joy and fun all around them. If Kate was worried about being seen with him it didn't show, Jamie noted happily, and anyone watching could see they were in love.

In George Square, foraging pigeons strutted around the feet of the festive crowds that meandered around taking in the splendour of the lights and the giant Christmas tree which was shipped over year after year from Norway, a "Thank You" from the Norwegian people. The birds, experienced in the ways of the crowds, hopped nimbly from side to side, pecking crumbs of food and avoiding the crushing feet of the horde. Others, pigeons and starlings, sat majestically atop the statues that dotted the square, coating sculpted heads and shoulders with a liberal dose of bird shit.

Jamie pointed out the various took the time to point out the various sculptures, identifying them collectively and deprecatingly as the "so called great and good" of the Victorian era. Great phalanxes of Starlings swooped around the Square and perched from time to time on the window sills of the adjoining buildings to leave their mark in the form of and undulating white stain that seeped down the ancient stonework.

'The birds have got it right,' Jamie laughed, pointing Kate to the top of Gladstone's statue. 'William Ewart Gladstone, Prime Minister of this once great country in the late 1800s' he said knowledgeably, and not a little sarcastically. 'Like all politicians, he made a career out of shitting on the ordinary people. The birds are our way of getting our own back,' he chortled.

For the first time, Kate was seeing Glasgow properly and she was enjoying herself. She found herself laughing at Jamie's jokes and his irreverent commentary on the various buildings and statues, deciding that there was more than a just a little bit of Republican in Jamie Raeburn and a big chunk of Socialist too. Her father would love him.

'I've lived in Glasgow for two years,' she said reflectively as they made their way along West George Street to Buchanan Street again. 'And I've seen practically nothing of it...it's wonderful. Her husband had brought her into the city at the beginning but he quickly lost interest when his drinking started up again, but his knowledge of the place was scant, unlike Jamie's, who seemed to be a mine of information. Jamie was looking at her with a degree of scepticism…"wonderful" wasn't the word he would have chosen to describe the place.

He had decided to introduce Kate to the delights of The Waldorf and had arranged to meet Jack and Teresa there at six o'clock. It was reasonably quiet when he ushered Kate through the door at ten to six, a few regulars dotted around the bar and Mrs Gray, the landlady, in her usual place behind it. Mrs Gray's plump and worldly wise face registered surprise when they appeared but Jamie suspected that it was the sight of Kate on his arm rather than the timing which surprised her.

She greeted them warmly, pouring Jamie his usual tipple without prompting before turning her appraising eyes to Kate. Kate smiled radiantly and asked if she could have a gin and tonic and Jamie could almost read the older woman's thoughts as she smiled back at her. This wasn't some starry eyed teenager, she was thinking.

Jamie carried their drinks to the table normally shared with Jack and the boys and Kate followed, quietly taking everything in. 'So, this is where you spend your weekends,' she smiled as she lowered herself onto a chair. 'It's really nice, I love it,' she added, turning to give the formidable Mrs Gray a winning smile. 'And I think the lady behind the bar likes you too,' she whispered mischievously. 'You really do have a way with older women, don't you darling,' she added, teasing him.

Jamie had no time to respond. The door opened and Jack arrived with his usual flourish, ushering Teresa O'Brien, timid and shy, before him.

'Well, well, ' Mrs Gray chirped. 'Two of you tonight and with two lovely girls, I must be getting old,' she laughed as she poured Jack a pint before he had even opened his mouth. Teresa asked for Vodka and lime and that, to the astute Mrs G, placed her firmly in the "starry eyed teenager" category.

Jack brought an anxiously smiling Teresa to them and pulled out a chair for her next to Kate. Quite the little gentleman, Jamie thought, amused. Kate was assessing him but if Jack kept this up she would almost certainly get it wrong. For once, Jack was behaving impeccably and even Mrs Gray was looking at him with an expression of surprise bordering on shock.

Jamie started the introductions, leaning over to kiss Teresa on the cheek as Jack did with Kate and soon they were chatting easily. Kate brought out the items she had bought in Lewis's and there was a lot of oohing and aahing and not only from Teresa…Jack's eyes too were wide with wonder Jack caught him watching and winked, a broad smile on his face. Kate, it appeared, had passed the Connolly test!

Choosing a restaurant that suited all of them was easier than Jamie had feared. Their tastes were cosmopolitan but they settled for "Traditional British", deciding on The Whitehall at the corner of West Regent Street and Renfield Street, just opposite Burns' Howf, the new "In Spot".

They left the Waldorf at half past six and Mrs Gray asked if they would be returning later. The answer she gleaned from the lads' expressions was a definite maybe, but leaning towards no. She laughed and waved them off and then, on impulse, called Jamie back. He excused himself and sauntered back to where Mrs Gray was leaning on the bar, smiling. 'That lassie's special, Jamie Raeburn,' she whispered. 'If I were you I'd hold on to her.'

Taken aback, Jamie laughed but recovered quickly. He smiled disarmingly. 'I intend to,' he replied. Mrs G. was a shrewd judge of character and Kate passing her scrutiny made Jamie a happy man.

He ran to catch the others and when he did Kate grabbed hold of his arm and tucked herself against him while Jack quizzed him with a look, intrigued.

'What was that all about?' Kate murmured, asking the question that was interesting them all.

Jamie laughed. 'Mrs G. likes you,' he chirped happily. 'She told me to hold on to you,' he added, kissing the top of her head. 'I told her I intend to,' he smiled as Kate cuddled closer.

They sauntered down West Regent Street, four abreast, taking up most of the pavement. The city was filling up and Jamie saw Kate taking in groups of boys and girls with looks that varied between amusement and disbelief. He and Jack were watching the groups too, particularly the boys, but from a different perspective.

There was a nervous edginess in the air, different factions gathering and scanning other groups for evidence of rival "Teams". Glasgow, as Jack and Jamie both knew all too well, was a dangerous place, something that he imagined Kate, as a nurse in The Royal Infirmary, probably knew too.

A skirmish broke out nearby and Jamie felt Kate grip him tightly. He could see the fear filling her eyes and drew her protectively closer, seeing Jack do the same for Teresa. The fight spilled out into the middle of West Regent Street, bringing cars and buses to a halt with squealing brakes and blaring horns. There was a lot of noise but not much in the way of violence.

Kate looked up at him, expecting to see her fear reflected in his eyes but he appeared relaxed. Was he really that hard, she wondered? Jamie eyed her quizzically. 'You amaze me,' she responded. 'Aren't you afraid? You seem almost…' she paused, searching for a word. 'I don't know…blasé almost.' Jamie simply shrugged. 'My husband would have dragged me away from here by now,' she continued. 'But the two of you,' she said, nodding towards Jack. 'You seem to take it in your stride.'

'It's just Glasgow…a wee contretemps. It was nothing serious, sweetheart,' Jamie replied quietly, kissing her tenderly on the brow. 'My mother throws bigger tantrums than that.'

Kate laughed, forgetting her fear, and hugged him tightly. 'Inexplicably, she felt both safe and frightened at the same time and a truth revealed itself then. She felt completely safe with Jamie beside her and her fear had been for him, not for herself. It was then she realised she really was in love with him.

They reached The Whitehall and made their way down the wide stone steps, savoury aromas of grilling meats, roasting vegetables, garlic and herbs wafting out to meet them. A small, rotund man in a tuxedo and scuffed black shoes met them led them to a table, strutting imperiously around and between tables and chairs with their menus held out in front of him. As they took their seats he preened himself, sweeping back his thinning Brylcreemed hair with one hand while admiring his reflection in the mirrored wall behind them. He was full of himself and seemed to imagine he was God's gift to womankind. Jamie shook his head sadly and gave a wry smile and Kate wrinkled her nose and smiled at him knowingly.

The man handed each of them a Menu, paying more attention to the girls and hovering for a moment with the Wine List before passing it to Jamie. Jamie took it awkwardly, flicking it open as the man sashayed, self-importantly, away.

Jamie looked at the Wine List knowing he was about to make a fool of himself. *Here I am, trying to make an impression, and I don't have a fucking clue*, he thought nervously. Wine wasn't his thing. Kate recognised his predicament and laughed privately as he scanned the List, his face a picture of bewilderment. Red, white, rosé; French, Italian and Portuguese. *What's the fucking difference*, he wondered, beginning to panic? Kate finally leaned across and looked down the Wine List with him before pointing to an Italian Chianti, not too expensive.

I think Teresa and I would like that one,' she said quietly and smiled appreciatively as Jamie mouthed a silent, relieved "Thank you". When the waiter reappeared, he ordered the bottle of Chianti for the girls and beers for Jack and himself. The meal itself was wonderful! They laughed and chatted happily through it and Jamie couldn't remember feeling better. His earlier worries about Kate fitting in evaporated quickly. She was relaxed and at ease with Teresa, despite the difference in their ages, and Jack was still on his best behaviour.

It was still reasonably early when they left the restaurant and made their way back up through the town to the bustle of Sauchiehall Street. It was much too early for the dancing so they headed for the Royal Hotel in Sauchiehall Street to take in the Cabaret. The town was busier now, the Christmas lights bringing families into the city in hordes to enjoy the colour and the festive spirit…fathers, mothers, grannies, grandpas and screaming kids, all enjoying Christmas.

But some people get their fun in different ways. As they neared the Royal Hotel another fight broke out ahead of them. This one was different from the first and Kate felt Jamie tense this time. These weren't boys this time and weapons glinted in the light of the Christmas decorations that hung above them. Mayhem broke out all around them and Jamie quickly moved Kate protectively behind him. Women screamed and pulled crying, frightened children away while fathers herded their families to safety. The fighting spilled closer and a young man fell heavily on the ground in front of them, a muffled groan escaping his lips and blood seeping onto the road from beneath his now inert body. The youth who had inflicted the telling blow was only a few feet away and his cold, unsmiling eyes locked on to Jamie's for an instant before he turned and lost himself in the swirling melee.

Kate was frozen with fear and Jamie pulled her close, shielding her from sight of the dying man. Abruptly, she snapped out of the terror and struggled with Jamie, instinctively wanting to reach the bleeding youth but Jamie guided her forcibly away towards the hotel entrance. Gradually, her struggling eased and Jamie moved her gently up the stairs to the hotel's reception area with Jack and Teresa close behind.

Teresa appeared on the verge of hysteria but Kate had calmed, though tears were running down her cheeks. She had dealt with the outcome of gang fights more often than most but this was the first time she had seen someone knifed in front of her…it seemed personal this time even though she didn't know the victim. Jamie pulled her to him again and cradled her in his arms, whispering soothingly, while outside in the street the carnage was over and the blue lights of police cars flashed intermittently across the walls of the hotel's ground floor foyer.

When Jamie finally brought Kate into the Cabaret Lounge Jack had already found a table. He rose from his seat as they arrived and made for the bar, leaving Jamie and Kate to calm a still weeping Teresa. Jack returned quickly with drinks and sat down beside her, moving closer and taking both of her hands in his. Jamie watched him, amazed at his gentle manner, and as he leaned his head forward to touch hers, Jamie heard him whispering calmly and reassuringly.

Kate pulled away from Jamie then and was staring at him with a look of puzzlement in her eyes, as if trying to work something out. Jamie knew what was coming.

'You knew that boy, didn't you?' she asserted finally, keeping her voice to a whisper. 'The one who looked at you.' Her eyes were boring into him, searching into his soul, and he realised that she was waiting to see if he would lie to her or not.

'I know both of them,' he admitted. 'And a few of the others involved in as well.' His blunt honesty made Kate gasp.

'But…' She was starting into another question when Jamie stopped her with his fingers across her lips and a plea in his eyes.

'I know them, know *of* them…they're not friends, but they're not enemies either. They're just guys that Jack and I both know…and we steer clear of them,' he whispered.

'But that boy out there might be dead,' Kate whimpered, growing distressed again.

Jamie looked across the table and saw Jack staring anxiously back at him. 'Aye,' he agreed. 'But he had a knife in his hand too…he wasn't just an innocent victim out for a night with his girl or boozing with his mates. He was there looking for trouble…and he found it.'

Kate was wringing her hands nervously. 'I should have helped him,' she whispered. 'I'm a nurse…I should have helped him. And shouldn't we have waited for the police? We were witnesses, for God's sake!' Her voice was growing louder now and a couple at the next table looked over towards them.

'Kate,' Jamie responded softly, stroking her cheek. 'Listen to me. This place is like the Wild West, and sometimes it's better not to see anything. It's dog eat dog in this city and the big dogs eat the wee dogs. Those guys out there, both teams, are the big dogs and Jack and me, we're the wee dogs,' he continued, explaining the reality of life in Glasgow. 'What you saw were two gangs fighting for supremacy…it happens all the time. You know that…you see the results in the hospital every day.'

'But how can you just accept that?' Kate demanded, bewildered and becoming angry. 'You, of all people, Jamie? You were almost killed four weeks ago!'

'That was different,' Jamie retorted lamely.

Teresa, calmer now, was taking an interest and listening intently to the developing argument. Then, suddenly, Kate's shoulders slumped and she began to cry, sobbing quietly. 'I'm sorry…I was so scared,' she sniffed. 'I thought for a horrible minute you were going to get embroiled in it…the look that boy gave you terrified me.'

Jamie hugged her, letting her cry against him, and stroked her hair. A piano burst into life, announcing the start of the Cabaret. He bent closer. 'We'll talk about it later… don't be scared, please love.'

Kate smiled bleakly and wiped her eyes. 'That's easy for you to say Jamie, but I love you,' she sobbed quietly. 'I can't stop being scared…I don't want to lose you.'

As good as the early part of the Cabaret was it couldn't quite lift the mood back to what it had been earlier. The incident was no longer a topic of conversation but it had cast a shadow over the evening and each of them was wrapped up in private thoughts about it. *Sometimes I hate this fuckin' place*, Jamie thought angrily.

The singer, a thirty something buxom blonde going by the name of Trishia Keyes and with what the more discerning gentlemen in the audience would describe as a "fuller figure" sang some old standards and some new songs, accompanied by a piano player and a three piece band. And she was good! The mood gradually lightened and just before the interval Kate slid her chair closer to Jamie's and took hold of his hand. She smiled and mouthed a silent "sorry", squeezing his fingers gently.

When the singer left the stage Jamie headed for the bar while Kate and Teresa made for the "Ladies" leaving Jack to guard the seats. Returning, Jamie placed the glasses with the drinks carefully on the table and caught Jack's worried look. It was obvious he wanted to talk and with the girls having disappeared to powder their noses, he took advantage of their absence. 'Did ye see who that wis oot there?' he whispered gravely. Jamie nodded and sipped his beer. 'Huv we got a problem?' he continued. 'Dae ye think they'll want tae make sure we don't say anythin' tae the polis?'

Jamie shook my head and smiled grimly. 'Nah,' he replied, keeping his voice low. 'Relax, they know us an' they know we'll keep quiet…an' we didn't hang around. It's cool.'

'Christ, ah hope ye're right, these guys ur evil bastards,' Jack murmured, clamming up quickly as Kate and Teresa returned to their seats. *So do I*, Jamie reflected anxiously.

As they waited for Alicia Keyes to return they discussed the venue for the remainder of the evening. Inevitably, the Locarno came up in the discussion and Kate, in particular, wanted to go there. She had heard a lot about it but had never been there before. Jamie didn't give it much thought and nodded his agreement but Jack's expression spelled a warning. All became clear when Jack leaned close to him and whispered furtively. 'Is the Locarno a good idea, big man?' he muttered quietly. 'There might be some birds there keen tae huv a chat wi' ye,' he added cryptically.

Jamie considered it. It was five weeks since he had last been there, the night he'd picked up Loretta, and the dust should have settled by now, he imagined. He laughed softly. 'It'll be fine,' he replied quietly, aware of Kate watching him curiously. 'When they see me with Kate they'll all steer clear,' he added. Jack's left eyebrow rose a fraction. Clearly, he didn't believe that.

The second part of the Cabaret was even better than the first. They were all totally relaxed again, happy in one another's company, and the fight earlier was now just a fading memory. The girls got on well, an added bonus for Jack and Jamie as there were no pregnant silences fill.

When Trishia left the stage for the final time the audience began to drift away and Jack and Jamie waited patiently in the foyer for the girls who had disappeared into the "Ladies" once again. 'Yer Kate's a cracker, Jamie,' Jack whispered when the girls were out of earshot. 'But whit's the story wae her man? If she wis ma wife I widnae let her oot of ma sight,' he continued. Jamie turned slowly to face him, grimaced and shook his head. This wasn't a subject he wanted to get into, not now anyway.

They arrived at the Locarno just after ten o' clock when the queue had shortened. Kate had her coat fastened tightly around her to ward off the cold but even dressed like that she was attracting admiring looks from other guys in the queue and Jamie was still finding it hard to believe she wanted to be with him.

Once inside, standing on the edge of the dance floor, Kate held onto Jamie's arm and took in the scene. They had spoken about the place and she knew it held a few secrets for him but she didn't care about his past, only his future…with her, and a warm glow filled her.

The dance floor was an enormous rectangle with a stage at one end where the big dance band was set up. The air was heavy with smoke and a blend of scents and the floor was awash with young men and women, bodies moving rhythmically to the sound of the music. Hanging above the dance floor, in the centre of the high ceiling, a giant spinning, mirror facetted orb revolved slowly throwing little squares of light in cascades across the dance floor. Kate smiled happily. She loved the place. It had been so long since she had last been dancing and being with Jamie now enhanced the experience.

Jamie looked at her and smiled contentedly, basking in the glow of her beauty. They walked around the edge of the dance floor and as she moved lithely through the crowds ahead of him he couldn't take his eyes from her. Her black dress clung to her, emphasising every delicious contour of her body. She was naturally beautiful, he realised, and the way she dressed simply added to her glamour. As for sex appeal, on a scale of 1 to 10 Kate came in at 11!

The band swung into a Glen Miller number, Pennsylvania 6-5000, and a host of Yank sailors flooded onto the floor near the stage accompanied by the usual collection of tarts and good time girls who hung around them. It was busy tonight…but it was just before Christmas so it was only to be expected. Small groups of girls, two, three or four in number, danced around their handbags which lay on the floor at their feet. The unattached guys, usually hanging around in similar groups of two or three, prowled the edge of the floor like predators waiting to pounce as soon as a girl gave them the eye.

Two girls with skirts barely covering the essentials passed them, giggling, and Jamie watched their progress through the crowd. Kate laughed and tugged at his arm. 'Hey! You're with me,' she teased, but she wasn't jealous. She knew now that he was hers.

Jamie lit his first cigarette of the evening with a sideways look at Kate. From the moment she discovered that smoking was one of his vices she had been trying to persuade him to stop…and she was winning. Normally, he would have smoked five or six ciggies by now, especially when he had been drinking. He smiled guiltily as she drew him a look and shook her head slowly, but it didn't deter him. He drew heavily on his Players Navy Cut and pulled the unfiltered nicotine and tar laden smoke into his lungs then exhaled theatrically through his nostrils. With his second drag he blew a big white ring above him, like a halo, and grinned at Kate like a kid.

She laughed in spite of herself. 'A saint you're not!' she giggled. 'You're incorrigible, but I love you.' That was the third time she had said she loved him in the space of a few hours and he was beginning to believe she actually meant it.

They found seats and settled at a table but Kate wanted to dance and so too did Jamie, just to hold her. Jack and Teresa, on the other hand, were happy to sit and cuddle. Kate left her bag on the table next to Teresa's and stood up, holding out her hand. They drifted out onto the dance floor and folded themselves into each other's arms, Kate entwining her arms around Jamie's neck as he pulled her close. The scent of her perfume filled him and he felt himself harden. Kate felt it too and responded, pressing her hips gently but firmly against him. Her head rested on his chest and her fingers teased the long brown hair at the nape of his neck. It was like making love with clothes on, he reflected happily. He smiled and kissed her and the look in her eyes told him she was thinking along the same lines.

The music changed tempo and the singers with the band broke into a Beatles number, a slow rendition of "That Boy". The floor was instantly filled with couples, all clinging close and drifting slowly around the hall doing the ubiquitous "Moonie". Where the name for that dance came from Jamie had no idea but it was his favourite, and he wasn't alone in that. When the sequence of slow dances started the wolves usually pounced on their prey and if the girl stayed with the guy when the slow dances finished then he knew he had clicked.

When "That Boy" ended they remained on the floor, their bodies still locked together. He nibbled the lobe of her ear and she turned to him, kissing him urgently, as the band broke into "Moon River". She pressed her body into him again, arousing him even more, and his head swam. She turned her face up to him and Jamie saw her lips move but her words were lost in the sound of the band. He gazed down into her eyes and knitted his brow questioningly.

'I said "thank you for making me feel good about myself again and for bringing me here",' she repeated, and kissed him hungrily. Jamie responded instantly, losing himself in her as he had before and, as they separated breathlessly, Kate said it again. 'I love you,' she murmured and pulled him to her, thrusting the tip of her tongue between his lips.

There were those words again. They were words that he normally took with a pinch of salt. To some people they were just a tool, a means to an end, and he had used them himself before to get what he wanted from a girl. But when Kate said them he knew that she meant them...it was in the intensity of her look and the fierceness of her kisses but, frighteningly, he didn't know how to react. Wasn't this what he had really wanted from the moment he had first set eyes on her, he asked himself? Wasn't it what he had been hoping for over the last week? The answer to both questions was a resounding "yes" but, strangely, he was apprehensive.

Maybe it was because he had been down this road before and the memory of that disaster was still fresh in his mind. The possibility that this relationship with Kate could end the same way didn't bear thinking about. He had told her he was in love with her but those were just words. Now he needed her to believe it but something was making him hold back. But the more he thought about it the more he knew that this love was real; it wasn't just a fling, he wanted her. It was more than that...he *needed* her. He was overwhelmed by her...but still he couldn't express to her how he really felt. So he said nothing, simply held her close, caressed her gently, returned her kisses and hoped that she knew how he felt.

It's one of those certainties in life, Jamie reflected later. Think about something and it invariably comes to pass...and it's not always something you want! As the final chords of "Moon River" faded away Jamie allowed his eyes to drift aimlessly around the dance floor. He wasn't looking for anything or anyone in particular, he was simply gazing around dreamily until, that is, his eyes flitted past her, registered her stare in his sub-conscious, and then snapped back. It *was* her, he realised, emerging from his dream like state. *Carol fuckin' Whyte*! What the hell was she doing here, he wondered? She hated this place...at least she had always hated it when she was with him; always refused to come to the Loc' when he suggested it. Physically, she hadn't changed much. She was still beautiful but her beauty, as Jamie knew only too well, was flawed. The blonde hair...a bit longer now, the long shapely legs, the soft white skin and the ruby lips couldn't hide what was beneath...Kate without the charm, he thought grimly. Whyte might be her name but black was her nature...and her fucking heart.

Kate sensed the sudden tension in him and noticed he was distracted. She was suddenly afraid and turned to look back over her shoulder in the direction of Jamie's troubled gaze. Seeing Carol Whyte staring back at her with sad, expressionless eyes, she relaxed. 'She's lovely,' Kate murmured. 'Who is she?' she asked as she turned back to him.

'She's not lovely,' Jamie retorted bitterly. 'An' she's a nobody.' He knew that response wouldn't be enough and Kate would expect an explanation...but that could wait. One thing was sure, from his expression and the harshness of his words Kate couldn't doubt that he meant it.

She looked at him for a moment then stretched up on her toes and placed a peck him on his cheek. Jamie glanced back across the floor. Carol Whyte was still there, her vexed face cold as marble. As he stared emptily back at her she was joined by two other girls, both known to him, and by three young guys, all about his own age. He smiled coldly and thanked his lucky stars. Thank fuck, he thought, they should keep her occupied.

Kate kept Jamie on the dance floor for the next dance, another slow one...Nat King Cole's "When I Fall In Love", and as they enjoyed the intimacy of the dance Jamie put Carol Whyte out of his mind. He blamed himself for tempting fate in any event...simply thinking about her earlier, even in passing, had brought her out from under her stone. She's a fucking witch, he thought bitterly, surprised by how he still felt when he thought he had got over it.

A few dances later Kate saw Teresa waving to attract her attention and she pulled Jamie off the floor. Another trip to the "Ladies" to powder noses again seemed to be on the cards and Jamie wondered, absently, why girls always had to go in two's. As the girls left them Jamie turned to Jack. 'Carol Whyte's here,' he hissed. 'She was givin' me the evil eye.'

'Yeah, ah know,' Jack nodded, directing his eyes over Jamie's shoulder. 'An' she's comin' over.'

'Aw fuck!' Jamie swore viciously. 'I can do without this.'

'Hello Jamie,' he heard Carol say behind him and turned to face her, trying desperately to control the emotion raging inside him. As usual, her makeup had been applied with almost clinical precision. Her lipstick, a deep crimson, stood out vividly against the soft, cream coloured skin of her face and her eyes, sparkling blue beneath her finely plucked eyebrows and her liberally applied mascara, bored into him. She certainly has the looks, he had to admit. Her blonde hair tumbled down over her shoulders in waves and the dress she was wearing was giving every guy in the Locarno who wanted to look...and that was most of them, a glimpse of what was on offer.

'What do you want?' he demanded bluntly, trying to fight the bitterness that was forcing its way back to the surface. Why was he allowing her to affect him like this, he chided himself? She means nothing to me now yet she still manages to bring out the worst in me. Why was that? The answer, when it came, unsettled him. It was pride...she had hurt him badly and it was his pride that had been hurt most of all.

'I just wanted to say I'm sorry,' she said softly. It was put on, he thought; the sad, diffident voice, the contrite look. 'I know I hurt you,' she continued, and if he hadn't known her for what she was, he might have believed her. 'I'm sorry, Jamie...I never meant it to happen. I miss you,' she said and put her hand tantalisingly on his arm.

Jamie ignored the last bit and shrugged off her hand. 'Right,' he replied, trying to keep his voice even. 'You've said it. Apology accepted, now why don't you fuck off and leave me alone.'

That should have been the end of it...and probably would have been but for the appearance of Carol's new boyfriend and her little group of sycophants. The boyfriend hadn't heard the whole exchange between them, didn't know the history, and maybe if he had things might have turned out differently...but he hadn't. All he had seen was Jamie's angry expression as he had shrugged Carol off and all he heard were the words "fuck off and leave me alone". When you only know half the story chances are you get things wrong, Jamie reflected later. Add to the mix the fact that you want to show your new girlfriend how much of a man you are and the potential for making an arse of yourself is multiplied exponentially. The guy came rushing towards them, foaming at the mouth, and Jamie's worst fears were realised. Where the fuck did she find this one, he wondered?

'Leave her alone,' the guy shouted and reached out to grab Jamie but Jamie, anticipating the aggro, swerved aside and the lad missed him completely, lost his balance and only managed to stay on his feet by catching onto Carol. This had a domino effect with Carol tottering away on her high heels and the guy trying desperately to prevent her from ending up on her backside. Carol's face said it all and Jamie could imagine the conversation that was going to take place later. Jack was grinning openly and, in normal circumstances Jamie too might have laughed as the farce unfolded, but the circumstances weren't normal and the girls would be returning shortly so he suppressed the urge.

The bouncers were hovering now, watching events unfold, and Jamie caught sight of them in his peripheral vision. It was time to take evasive action, he told himself. 'Leave her alone?' he repeated. 'Listen, I'm not interested so do us all a favour and take her away…and tell her to leave me alone,' he added icily.

The guy's face reddened. Jamie could see him weighing up his options, thinking about it. He didn't like this situation any more than Jamie but for entirely different reasons. He'd been made to look like a prick and his pride was hurt…and Jamie knew how that felt. Given a little more time she'll make a proper job of hurting you, he was tempted to say, but kept his mouth shut. They stood there, eyes locked together, like two gunfighters at the O.K. Corral waiting for the other man to blink. It was all about intimidation…the famous Glasgow look, and that was something Jamie was good at. It was all in the eyes.

'Come on Bobby, leave it,' one of the others said and one of the girls looked at Jamie and raised her eyes to the ceiling. She wasn't impressed either, it appeared. Carol then tried to defuse the situation; she took hold of the boy's arm and started to pull him away but he wasn't quite ready to cave in, not yet.

'Take your pal's advice, Bobby,' Jamie said disrespectfully, upping the ante. 'She's not worth it, believe me.'

Bobby seemed ready to lunge but his two mates caught hold of him and hustled him away. Jamie smiled grimly. Bobby had been ready to have a go and that would have ruined the whole evening. And he was still raging, turning back to glare malevolently at Jamie and shrugging off his friends' restraining hands. Carol turned too but her eyes were filled with regret and there was a forlorn little smile playing at her lips.

Jamie turned back to Jack. 'Evil bitch!' he spat angrily, then caught sight of Kate and Teresa watching the events from the edge of the dance floor, their faces inscrutable. 'Shit,' he murmured, wondering how much of the spat they had witnessed.

Kate and Teresa walked towards them and Jamie caught a nervous glance from Jack out of the side of his eye. The expression on Kate's face now told him that his "she's a nobody" response to her earlier question now needed much more explanation. Before that though, he needed time to think. and Kate was looking at him searchingly.

'I'm goin' to the Gents,' he said quickly and pushed through the crowd to avoid the immediate confrontation but as started away he heard Kate posing her question to Jack.

'Who is she, Jack?' she murmured and Jamie picked up the anxiety in her voice. Jamie turned back quickly and took in Jack's "what the fuck do I tell her?" look.

'Just tell her the truth, Jack,' Jamie said with a note of resignation and pushed on through the crowd. As he turned towards the foyer he looked back again and saw Jack talking as Kate and Teresa listened intently.

When he returned calm had been restored and all three were sitting down at the table waiting for him. He pulled out his seat and joined them, reaching out for Kate's hand. 'I'm sorry,' he whispered. 'Honestly, I am. What did Jack tell you?' He searched her eyes for a clue to where he stood.

Kate smiled and squeezed his hand. 'Ex-girlfriend, bad news sums it up, I think,' she replied with a sardonic laugh. 'Silly girl.'

'Silly girl?' Jamie repeated, surprised. 'Why silly?'

Kate laughed and a perceptive look appeared on her pretty face. 'You must be blind, Jamie Raeburn,' she said with a chuckle. 'That girl is still in love with you.'

Jamie shook his head in disbelief. How much Jack had told her about his sorry relationship with Carol, he wondered? 'I doubt it,' he said quietly. 'If she had loved me she wouldn't have slept around, would she?' he murmured, trying to keep the bitterness out of his voice, and turned away, scared that Kate would see the hurt in his eyes.

Kate put her hand to his cheek and turned him back to her, forcing him to look into her eyes. 'Do you love me?' she asked.

With the question framed like that there could be no "maybe" answer. It was yes or no and there was no avoiding it any longer. 'Yes,' he said quietly, gazing into her big, green, expectant eyes. 'I love you.'

'Then that's all that matters,' she said softly and kissed him before dragging him back on to the dance floor. 'Come on, dance with me.

Chapter 14

It was almost midnight when they left The Locarno. The sky was clear, the stars were out and the temperature had dropped but they barely noticed it. They tried to get into Joanna's Disco, at the foot of Bath Street, but it was full so they gave up and made their way towards the City Centre and the late night buses. Staying out of the shadows, they hugged closely, girls and boys together. It was surprisingly quiet so maybe the Spirit of Christmas was catching on, Jamie thought.

Reaching George Square at around quarter to one they huddled together in a doorway out of the cold wind, and waited. The late buses started at half past midnight and ran every hour so they had about 45 minutes to wait. There were the usual weekend late night sights and sounds around the Square; interludes of relative calm interspersed with shouting and swearing and, occasionally, the screams of girls, drunks holding on to lamp posts, people throwing up, and couples necking. All in all, a fairly normal Saturday night.

About twenty past one the crowds began to disperse towards the various bus stops sited around the big Square and Jack and Teresa headed for the Lambhill bus stop while Jamie, with some trepidation, led Kate to the stop for the Drumchapel bus on the opposite side.

Trouble comes in three's it is said and that was about to be proved true for Jamie. As he and Kate crossed the Square to the bus stop Jamie spied Carol Whyte and her little group of acolytes congregating. There. With hindsight, he should have expected it. Not wanting another confrontation with the short tempered Bobby he slowed his and Kate's pace and hung back a little.

Kate sensed his unease and began to search for the reason, her eyes finally settling on Carol's little group. She gave Jamie a gentle squeeze around the waist. 'Are they waiting for the same bus as us?' She asked, a little anxiously.

'Yes,' Jamie replied with a grim smile. 'Unfortunately.'

'Wow!' Kate laughed. 'Is this a new Jamie Raeburn I'm with? Where's the brash, bring it on guy I used to know?' she teased, trying to make light of it but all the while concerned herself. Suddenly, it dawned on her that he was worried and her anxiety increased. 'What are we going to do? You're not worried, are you?' she asked, conscious that her voice was shaking a little.

Jamie laughed, trying to release the tension. Trouble comes in all shapes and sizes, he knew that from experience, and this was one of the bigger kind, but uppermost in his thoughts was the fact that he didn't want Kate to be scared again…there had been enough of that already tonight. 'Nah,' he laughed. 'I'm not worried…I just don't want *you* worried…and I don't fancy another slangin' match with that dick, that's all.'

'Then we'll just ignore them,' Kate replied, as if it was as simple as that.

Ignore them, Jamie smiled. Yeah, it's as easy as that, my love, he thought. Just then the buses started to arrive…a convoy of green, white and gold vehicles percolated around George Square and the crowds surged towards them. Carol Whyte and her friends were amongst the first to board the Number 2 for Drumchapel and

Jamie held Kate back until the six had taken their places before helping her on, hoping to get seats as far away from them as possible. *Just stay clear and avoid the problem*, he told himself. Easy! He hoped that he and Kate could board the bus unseen but it wasn't to be. Carol, his female nemesis, and her new boyfriend, if that's what he was, had seats right at the front of the bus with the other two couples sitting in the two rows behind them and as Jamie helped Kate up onto the platform he glanced along the lower deck just as Carol and her new man turned to talk to the couples behind them. *Perfect fuckin' timin'*, he thought angrily. Two pairs of eyes met his and he knew in that instant that the earlier trouble hadn't been forgotten. If Bobby's looks could kill then Jamie would be stone dead. All conversation at the front of the bus stopped and another four pairs of eyes swivelled towards him. Kate looked up at Jamie, worried now, and he smiled grimly.

They climbed to the upper deck and Jamie indulged in another cigarette. This time Kate didn't complain; she knew he could probably do with it. They snuggled close together, Jamie's arm around her, and said nothing. Kate seemed content and Jamie's thoughts were concentrated on the coming morning when she would be subjected to some gentle and some not so gentle probing by his mother.

The lynch mob on the lower deck were firmly in the back of his mind until the bus reached Anniesland Cross and he saw Carol step down off the bus onto the pavement with her two girlfriends. Unfortunately, there was no sign of the three boys which meant they were still on board. Jamie watched edgily as the three girls waved goodbye to the lads and, as the bus started to pull away, he saw Carol toss her mane of blonde hair and look up at the upper deck, searching for him, a sad smile on her face. Was it a warning, he wondered? If Kate's assessment of Carol was accurate then maybe it was and it was a sobering thought.

Half a dozen stops and a few minutes later Jamie and Kate got off. He had tried to time it in the hope that he and Kate could alight unnoticed but the three guys on the lower deck were waiting and there could only be one reason for that. It certainly wasn't because they fancied a long walk home. On seeing them, Kate gave Jamie an anxious look but said nothing.

Jamie and Kate set off, arm in arm, towards Lincoln Avenue, about thirty to forty yards away, making a conscious effort to ignore the three. Some other passengers had alighted from the bus with them but they quickly dispersed and Jamie sensed they were now alone with the three boys following them. He looked back casually over his shoulder and spied Carol's new man swaggering ahead of the others who were flanking him, one on either side.

Jamie leaned in closer to Kate and whispered an instruction. 'If anything kicks off, you keep walking to the corner, turn left and cross the road. It's number 401, the last house,' he smiled encouragingly

'I'm not leaving you,' Kate retorted adamantly.

'Please Kate, let me handle this,' he pleaded. 'I can't do it if I'm worrying about you.' His heart sank as she shook her head defiantly.

'No, I'm staying with you,' she said, and Jamie knew there was no point in arguing with her. He'd seen that look in his mother's eyes before…and it conveyed unbridled stubbornness.

'Hey, smart arse,' Carol's boyfriend call out dragging Jamie's mind back to the problem in hand.

Jamie stopped dead in his tracks and Kate felt him tense. 'Go,' he whispered urgently. 'I'll be alright,' he promised, but Kate was staring defiantly back at him and refusing to budge.

'You insulted my bird,' the boy continued, coming closer.

'Leave him alone,' Kate shouted before Jamie could respond. She tugged at Jamie's arm, pulling him away and Jamie started to follow her without thinking until Carol's new man stuck his oar in again.

'That's right, ya shitebag...listen to yer Mammy,' he laughed derisively. 'Where did ye find her anyway, grab a granny night at the Plaza?' Jamie's blood began to boil.

Kate sensed the change in him and pulled at his arm again. 'Ignore him,' she pleaded, but she knew she was losing the battle.

'Listen you...Bobby, isn't it?' Jamie started, and then carried on before the lad could respond. 'You've just accused me of insulting your bird and now you've insulted mine...so we're even. Now, I suggest you just fuck off before I really lose my temper!' The words came out quietly but the menace in them was obvious.

Bobby started to redden. 'We're no' even,' he spat. 'Not by a long shot. You called my bird a tart, ya bastard,' he continued, working himself into a fury.

Jamie laughed and Bobby reddened some more. 'I was just tellin' the truth, dickhead...so, as I said, why don't you just fuck off,' Jamie continued. He felt Kate tug at his elbow, willing him to come away with her. Jamie knew she was worried and knew too that for her sake, if for nothing else, he should walk away from this. He doubted that Bobby would let him do that, but it was worth a try. 'Right then, if you've said your piece, I'm goin' home,' he said, turning his back on Bobby and taking Kate's arm again. He felt Kate relax almost immediately and hoped she wasn't going to be disappointed. Turning his back on a nutter like Bobby wasn't the wisest option, he knew that from experience too, but with any luck he would get away with it.

He didn't have any luck. He had taken no more than two steps when he felt Bobby's hand on his shoulder. 'Don't you walk away from me, ya cunt,' the boy shouted angrily, pulling Jamie back viciously. Jamie turned to face him and locked eyes with him, staring implacably. Who would break first was the question and only Jamie knew it wouldn't be him.

Intervention came unexpectedly. One of the two guys with Bobby, the one who had tried to pour oil on the troubled waters back in the Locarno, tried to calm things down again. 'Leave it, Bobby,' he pleaded. 'You hardly know that Carol lassie and this guy's out for a quiet night with his girlfriend...he's no lookin' for trouble, so let it go.'

Divine intervention...blessed are the peacemakers for they shall be called the children of God, Jamie smiled coldly, but he had the feeling that this was more Sydney Devine than heavenly Divine and the poor lad was likely to end up "Nobody's Child". It wasn't long before that proved correct and Bobby shrugged him off and rejected his advice. It was all quite simple as far as Bobby was concerned; Jamie had insulted his bird and his pride wouldn't allow him to let Jamie away with it. Ah well, Jamie sighed and prepared himself for the coming battle, such is life.

For Kate's sake Jamie tried once again to walk away, giving Bobby one last chance to back off, but, just as he expected, Bobby wasn't in a walking away mood. Bobby's hand settled on Jamie's shoulder again but this time Jamie was ready. He spun round quickly, took a step closer to Bobby and head butted him sickeningly on the bridge of the nose. There was a muffled squeal and Bobby staggered backwards, his hands covering his now bleeding nose, and Jamie followed up.

Everyone was caught out by the speed of Jamie's retaliation. Kate stood frozen to the spot as though mesmerised and struck dumb. She had suspected beforehand that Jamie could handle himself but, like the others, she was caught off guard and shocked by the speed and the violence of his attack. The quieter one of Bobby's friends reacted first and stepped forward menacingly but the other, the unsuccessful peace keeper, put a hand on the boy's arm and stopped him. Jamie smiled, relieved. He had suspected all along they were reluctant allies of Bobby but he hadn't been sure. Now, he was and it was time to finish it. Grabbing hold of Bobby's lapels, Jamie pulled him forward and sank his knee hard into the Bobby's groin. His legs buckled under him and he sank to the ground like a rag doll.

Jamie stood threateningly over him and kept a wary eye on the other two. He didn't expect them to intervene now but he was ready, just in case. Neither of the others moved and Bobby tried to struggle to his feet. Jamie shook his head in disgust and turned away, quickly taking Kate's hand and pulling her along with him. He looked down at her and saw the fear in her eyes. She was petrified. He put his arm protectively around her and felt her lean against him, sobbing quietly. The tension in her was palpable.

He whispered to her soothingly, trying to bring her out of it but the nightmare resumed. They had covered only about 10 yards when a pounding of feet could be heard coming towards them. There was a shouted warning from the peacemaker and Jamie reacted intuitively. Gently but forcefully he pushed Kate out of harm's way and turned to face the threat. Bobby was now only a few feet away, a crazed look in his eyes and a thin metallic blade clutched in his right hand and thrust straight out, pointing right at Jamie's chest.

Jamie swerved aside and grabbed Bobby's wrist, his right fist then thrown with force into the boy's already damaged nose. Bobby let out a scream and pulled away but the blade was still firmly in his hand and, from Jamie's point of view, he was still dangerous and Jamie was right. Bobby came at him again, shouting and swearing loudly and slashing wildly with the blade.

Jamie moved back out of range. He heard Kate screaming and found himself with his back against a lamp post with Bobby circling, the blade, like a stiletto, being thrust at him repeatedly. Jamie watched him carefully, waiting for the tell-tale signs that he was about to attack and looking for an opening. When the attack finally came, Jamie was ready. He caught Bobby's knife wrist with both hands in an iron grip and twisted it violently but still Bobby stubbornly held onto the weapon. Jamie changed tack. Pulling Bobby towards him again he smashed the boy's hand and knuckles against the lamp post, repeating the operation again and again until Bobby's broken and bleeding fingers could no longer hold the blade and it dropped, tinkling metallically, onto the pavement. Jamie kicked the blade away and Bobby lashed out with his good fist in one last desperate effort to inflict damage, but his strength and his will to carry on the fight were both ebbing fast. Jamie grabbed him by the lapels of his coat again and pushed him violently backwards to crash through a beautifully trimmed privet hedge and onto a snow covered lawn.

Suddenly, he was aware that Kate was still screaming and lights were coming on in the windows of nearby houses. Jamie picked up Bobby's discarded weapon; a steel comb, the type with a long handle used by girls to tease out their French combed hair and the handle of this one had been honed to a fine point. Bobby was on his feet again and was lurking behind the safety of the hedge. He looked cowed. Jamie walked slowly towards him, the steel comb still in his hand, and watched with satisfaction as Bobby backed off fearfully. 'You try anythin' like that again,' he whispered malevolently so that only Bobby could hear. 'An' I'll stick this right up your fuckin' arse so ye'll be shittin' in slices.'

He turned away from him then and faced the other two. There was no fight in either of them but had there been, Jamie knew he would have been in trouble. 'You better get him away,' he suggested quietly, nodding in the direction of Bobby. 'The cops will be here in jig time...and I've got no argument with you two.'

Both lads nodded and made to help Bobby from the garden but their friendship had fallen on hard times. He shrugged off their efforts sullenly and started to dust himself down. Jamie stared at him, holding his look until Bobby looked away, before re-joining Kate. Her screaming had stopped but she was crying now, sobbing quietly. He took her by the arm and kissed her softly on the cheek, then guided her away to safety.

A gamut of emotions filled Kate's mind; bewilderment, shock, fear, sadness, awe, and finally, relief. As the drama unfolded before her she had been frozen with fear, her heart racing, but, as before, the fear had been for Jamie and not for her. She was finding it hard to accept what she had just seen...and the way Jamie had dealt with it. What was it about him, she wondered? Trouble followed him closer than his shadow...it was as if trouble actively sought him out. And why can't he just walk away; why does he always have to face it, her mind screamed at her?

Her feelings were running wild. She loved him, God how she loved him, but could she live with the fear his temperament brought with it? She held on to him, tightly, and felt the rapid beat of her heart against him. He stroked her hair, teasing his fingers gently through it, as though he knew her thoughts and understood her fear. His smile revived her...relieved her too; it wasn't the smile of a man smug with his victory but rather it was forlorn, filled with sadness and stoical resignation. The sound of raised voices made her jump and her heart raced again. She turned nervously to find the three boys arguing loudly amongst themselves and relief flooded through her again.

'It's alright, sweetheart, it's all over' Jamie whispered, his arm tightening around her. The tension in him was gone, like an unwound spring, but she knew that the adrenalin was still pumping through his system. She lifted his hand, horrified to find Bobby's steel comb still clutched there; she had seen the damage these combs could do to people and a flashback to the stabbing earlier that night caused a shudder to run through her.

'Spoils of war,' Jamie said quietly, seeing her look at it. 'The weapon of choice for lots of would be hard men like Bobby back there,' he continued. 'Looks innocent and it's easily hidden, but it's lethal.' As Kate watched, he gripped the comb in both hands and bent it back and forth again and again until the metal sheared in two. Kate sighed with relief as he walked to a nearby bin and deposited the pieces there. She was smiling again when he returned to her and she lifted herself up on her toes and kissed him. 'I love you,' she whispered. 'I really, really love you.'

*

The house was warm when they stepped out of the cold night into the hall. Jamie closed the door quickly, and quietly, to retain the heat inside and ushered Kate into the living room. This room was bathed in a warm, red glow from the coal fire which had been banked up earlier by his Jamie's father and Kate immediately felt the strain of the earlier part of the night leave her. As Jamie moved to switch on the ceiling light she stopped him, taking hold of his outstretched hand. 'Leave the light off, Jamie, please. It's lovely as it is...it reminds me of home,' she said wistfully. 'My mother's house is just like this.'

Jamie took her coat and carried it back out to the hall to hang it up and when he returned Kate had settled on the rug in front of the fire. The red glow of the fire shone on her skin and she looked like an angel, Jamie thought. He didn't recognise the feeling that swelled in him but he had no doubt it was all to do with love…and there was no going back now. She turned to him with a smile that made his heart melt and patted the rug, inviting him to sit beside her. He sank happily to the floor and gazed into her eyes, watching the dancing flames of the fire reflected there. Looking at her was like looking at a work of art by Rembrandt or one of the French Impressionists…and he would never tire of looking…ever.

Kate leaned towards him and kissed him again, her fingers loosening his tie and starting on the buttons of his shirt. 'Can we?' she asked nervously, keeping her voice low.

'It's safe…as long as we're quiet,' he whispered, smiling as his hands caressed her.

'I wish you were sleeping with me tonight,' she continued, nuzzling her mouth against his neck and pressing her hand down between his thighs, arousing him. Jamie let out a soft moan and Kate pressed her lips to his, stifling it. 'Ssssh,' she giggled softly as she broke away from him.

They made love there on the rug. There was something especially erotic about it, their bodies partly dressed and their clothes in disarray. Kate felt the weight of him and eased herself into position, ready to accept him. Their breathing grew faster as their fingers explored and excited and then he was inside her, their bodies moving rhythmically as they had when dancing earlier though this time it wasn't make believe. Kate matched his thrusts, lifting her hips to him, taking him deep inside her as though wanting to morph into him as one being. The scent of her filled Jamie with an uncontrollable craving, an overwhelming lust for her. They moaned softly, smothering the sound with kisses, and Kate gripped his head firmly, her fingers locking in his long brown hair. She held her breath as her passion mounted until suddenly, as Jamie brought her to climax, it was expelled from her in a rush. She twisted her fingers in his hair and pulled his head backwards as the orgasm crashed over her, leaving her gasping and fighting the urge to call out.

Jamie smothered her with kisses as she held onto him with an intensity he had never experienced, her finger nails digging hard into his back. She was still moving in time with him, the peak of her orgasm past, and how he felt himself on the verge. He gripped her hips firmly and felt her hands pull him into her as the tempo of his thrusts increased and then he felt the surge of heat through him, the release as he came. He heard Kate moan softly as a second orgasm or a continuation of her first took her and they were oblivious to everything then except each other. They climaxed as one, stifling their cries.

Spent, Jamie sagged on top of her and gazed down into Kate's eyes. Her arms encircled his neck and her lips and tongue brushed along his collar bone beneath his opened shirt. Her breathing was still fast, the passion still alive in her.

'I wish you could sleep beside me tonight,' she repeated. 'I want to wake up with you there, close and warm.' She was looking at him longingly, thinking about how far they had come in the few weeks since they had met, wondering if he did really love her as he said he did. Was she fooling herself, wanting to believe him? She felt him move inside her again and she tightened the muscles of her vulva around him, urging him on. Oh God, please, please, I want him love me, she prayed silently.

They coupled again, Jamie deep inside her. He heard her gasp as she reached the pinnacle of her ecstasy again. His hands gripped her and his lips and tongue traced crazy patterns across her neck. The exquisite pain of another orgasm filled her and her nails tore at Jamie's back until he came again, the spasms of his ejaculation filling gradually dying inside her. Jamie cried out her name carelessly, but he was beyond caring now.

Both of them were drained this time and Jamie sank down onto her. Kate twined her arms around him and held him close, feeling the soft, damp sheen of his sweat on her hands. Absorbing the animal musk of their love making she realised she had never felt like this before.

They moved apart at last, Jamie smiling sheepishly. 'Sorry,' he said softly. 'I came too quickly, didn't I?'

She laughed softly. 'No, you didn't,' she replied, kissing him again. 'I've never ever felt like this.' She moved up onto the settee and smoothed out her dress before Jamie joined her there, Kate resting her head on his shoulder. 'I'll never get enough of you,' she laughed, her voice low. 'And to think I wasn't sure at first.'

'I know,' Jamie replied. 'You really made me work to get you,' he laughed, leaning over her to kiss the top of her head.

The heat of the fire and the tiny blue and green flames dancing in the red glow of the banked coal were having a hypnotic effect on both of them. Is this what love is, Jamie wondered? He was content and indescribably happy and he hoped Kate felt the same. She said she was in love with him...but was she? There was still the unresolved problem of her husband and, try as he might, Jamie couldn't shake that. Yes, he loved her, but could he trust her? Come to that, could he trust himself?

'Why are you like you are?' she asked suddenly, taking him by surprise.

'How do you mean?'

'Why do you take on everyone else's fights? You never walk away...why are you like that?'

'Why does that matter?' he retorted, on the defensive now.

Kate smiled, trying to put him at ease. 'It matters because I love you, Jamie. If you really want us to have a future I need to know what that future will be like...I don't want to lie awake at night worrying about you.'

There was a moment's silence as Jamie laid his head against her. His head was spinning as he sought an answer. 'It's hard to explain,' he stated, his voice a whisper. 'I'm not a mindless thug,' he said. 'I don't go out looking for trouble.'

Kate lifted his head to look at him. 'I know that, Jamie,' she said gently. I wouldn't be in love with you if you were.'

Relieved, he smiled and Kate's resolve melted. 'It's late sweetheart,' he murmured. 'Can we talk about this tomorrow? I'll tell you why, warts and all...I promise.' He hesitated, waiting for her reaction. 'I really do want to be with you,' he added. She smiled and nodded and Jamie kissed her again, tracing his fingers lightly down her neck. 'Come on, you're tired, I'll show you to your room,' he said gently. 'You're to have the pleasure of sleeping in my bed,' he added with a sardonic smile.

'Where's the pleasure if I'm all alone?' Kate mouthed silently.

Jamie gave her an apologetic smile and she giggled. 'It's alright baby,' she whispered. 'You've already made me very happy tonight.'

He took hold of her hand and led her upstairs to his bedroom. 'My mother decided you'd be better in here,' he grinned, waving his arm expansively around the room. 'I'm relegated to the spare room downstairs...or, rather, the ice box,' he said, pretending to shiver. 'I'll freeze while you roast in my nice warm bed,' he added, making an unhappy face.

'I could keep you warm if you'd let me,' Kate laughed softly.

'Not a good idea,' he retorted, laughing with her.

'Well, don't say I didn't offer,' she said and kissed him quickly, teasing him with her tongue. 'I'll see you in the morning.'

'Yeah, the morning,' Jamie said, lowering his voice still further. 'Prepare yourself for interrogation...the Spanish Inquisition has nothing on my mother,' he laughed. 'Sweet dreams.' He was moving away when he remembered one very important matter. Turning round, he took hold of her left hand and pointed to the wedding band on her third finger.

Horrified, Kate let out a small gasp and quickly tugged the ring from her finger. 'Keep it for me,' she whispered, pressing it into his hand. Jamie looked at it nestling in his palm and felt uneasy. Kate read his mind again. 'Please, Jamie, I don't want your Mum to know...not yet, and if it's in my bag I might forget and let it fall out if I'm rummaging about for anything,' she added. Jamie thought that unlikely but there was no point in arguing. He shrugged and slipped it into his pocket, kissed her again, then made his way back down the stair, taking care to avoid the treads that creaked.

Kate listened to his footsteps fading on the stairs and looked around the room...his room, she reminded herself. It was very masculine but surprisingly tidy; probably his mother's handiwork, she surmised with a smile. Football posters adorned the walls and photographs in frames stood on the chest of drawers...pictures of Jamie as a toddler with his mother, Jamie dressed in a football strip with his father, a couple of photographs of football teams with Jamie involved, one of them recent, she thought, with Jamie one of the bigger players in the team and Jack Connolly there too. She picked this photograph up to study it and another picture, obscured from her view behind it, caught her eye. Replacing the original, she picked up this one and gave a little gasp of surprise. This photograph was of a young man in Army uniform...a Scottish soldier, wearing a kilt and a dress uniform tunic with three stripes on the arm, white spats around his ankles and a glengarry bonnet with a red hackle sitting proudly on his head. His expression was serious, more serious than she had come to expect of him, because the soldier in the picture was Jamie. She studied the photograph in growing amazement. He looked so handsome and his confidence came across clearly, almost jumping out of the photograph...even with that serious look on his face, she smiled. Why had he not mentioned this, she wondered? And then his promise to tell all came back to her.

She replaced the photograph in the place where it had been and examined the room again, taking in more of it now. A small display cabinet stood near the window, filled with trophies and rosettes. She was tempted to open it for a better look at the contents but resisted. She could ask him about all of this in the morning, she decided.

Undressing, she pulled on the new nightdress she had bought in Lewis' and wished that Jamie was here with her. As she turned to switch off the bedroom light her eyes came to rest on an old, worn and thread bare teddy bear which sat proudly on the high backed chair placed next to the bed. She smiled to herself. Jamie Raeburn really was enigmatic. On the one hand he was fearless, prepared to take on the world at the drop of a hat, and on the other he was kind and gentle, a proper gentleman her mother would say, but finding this old teddy in pride of place next to his bed was a paradox. She laughed to herself in disbelief but she wasn't laughing at him, she was laughing with delight. Any man of Jamie Raeburn's age who had the nerve to keep his old teddy in full view was worth holding on to, she told herself. She knew for sure now that in choosing to get to know him she had made the right decision. Picking up the bear she clutched it close to her face and cuddled it, sure she could smell Jamie's scent from the fur. Keeping it tightly in her hands she slipped beneath the bedcovers and drifted off to sleep, conscious of Jamie's deposit still warm inside her.

*

Alone in the spare room Jamie shivered and kicked off his shoes. Sitting on the edge of the bed he started to undress then remembered Kate's wedding ring. He removed it from his pocket and examined it, holding it between his thumb and forefinger. It was a simple gold band but it must have meant something to her once, he mused, allowing doubt to fill his head yet again. She was still wearing it so it must still mean something to her. He suddenly felt cold but not from lack of heat. If the guy was such a wanker…and if she *wasn't* still in love with him…why was she still wearing the ring?

He tormented himself then, oblivious to the cold which wrapped itself around him, as he tried to rationalise his thoughts. He contemplated the events of the past and considered the future and everything became clear to him…all the things he and Kate had spoken of and everything they had done together led him to one conclusion; Kate did love him. But this ring, he thought angrily, rolling it in his palm, would always be a source of doubt. There was a simple solution…if Kate would agree; get her another one to replace it.

Unable to sleep, He wrestled with the problem. Should he confront her or surprise her with a new one. Whilst, normally, confrontation with most people didn't bother him, confronting Kate on this issue wasn't too appealing. But how could he surprise her without knowing the size? He tried slipping it onto his pinkey but it was too narrow. He puzzled over how he could size for an age before an idea finally presented itself. He was in the spare room, the "glory hole", and all the junk collected over the years was kept in here. He remembered an old jewellery box his mother kept filled with old rings, gold chains, hat pins and both his grandfather's medals. It had to be around here somewhere. His search didn't take long, quickly finding the box secreted away on top of the wardrobe. He lifted it down from its hiding place and tipped the contents out onto the bed; gold and silver chains, brooches and rings as well as the medals with their brightly coloured ribbons still attached, littered the blanket. Excited now, he separated the rings from the other items first of all and then he sorted out the rings by size. The larger rings, those clearly his father's or grandfathers', he pushed to the side and concentrated on those he knew to belong to the women of the family. To his amazement, all of these rings were a perfect match with Kate's. It was an omen, he decided. Quietly, he replaced all of the jewellery and other items back in the box, retaining only one of his mother's old rings which he slipped, together with Kate's, into his trouser pocket. Content at last, he finished undressing and slid beneath the bedcovers, drifting quickly into a dream laden sleep.

Chapter 15

Jamie's exertions of the early hours following the fight kept him in bed longer than he had intended and it was the noise of dishes clattering in the kitchen sink through the wall that finally wakened him. Groggily, he rubbed his eyes and stretched, yawning. He could hear his mother's voice, muffled by the wall, and Kate's too though what they were saying was unclear. Suddenly, he was wide awake, panicking; he needed to be there. As he threw himself out of bed the sound of laughter filtered through to him and he relaxed again. If they were laughing, then things couldn't be going too badly, he thought.

He pulled on his underpants and trousers then made his way upstairs to the bathroom. A quick wash before sneaking into his own room for a change of underwear and a clean shirt, and he was ready. His room, he noticed, had been tidied, the bed made up, and there was still a hint of Kate's perfume lingering in the air. Everything was where it had been the day before with the exception of his old, battered teddy which now lay on the bed, tucked under the top blanket. He laughed softly and picked up the soft toy, detecting the residue of Kate's perfume clinging to it. He smiled to himself, tucked "Ted" back under the cover, and made his way downstairs.

Kate and his mother were sitting together in the living room, talking, when he walked in and they were smiling and relaxed...a big plus from Jamie's point of view. If his mother had started her interrogation then Kate seemed to have weathered it well. It was a good start.

Jamie's father joined them later in the morning, Jamie smiling to himself as the old charmer started on Kate. At one point his father gave him a long, pointed look that said he was impressed with Jamie's choice...not only was Kate good looking but she could hold a conversation in words of more than one syllable. Neither his father nor his mother had been overly impressed by Carol Whyte but Kate was clearly giving a better account of herself. Carol's first visit to the Raeburn home had been a bit of a disaster, he remembered, and subsequent visits had failed to improve her image. His father had been impressed by her looks but nothing else, apparently, and his mother hadn't been impressed at all. Maybe I should have taken the hint, he mused ruefully.

It was around mid-morning when his mother produced a bag full of old photographs and Jamie let out a little moan. This could be the start of a period of torture, he thought. He knew what was coming...the usual embarrassing photographs of him taken when he was too young to know better and protest...pictures of him wearing a little knitted swim suit, bucket and spade in hand, him sitting in a tin bath on the kitchen table, him on holiday at Rothesay with his tiny head stuck through a hole in a board which was painted to make him look like a cartoon Mexican, complete with sombrero, astride a grinning donkey. They had all been brought out before and shown to various family friends and relatives so the embarrassment factor wasn't really an issue now...though it was Kate who was being introduced to them now, he reminded himself.

But there was a surprise in store. Kate was examining an old photograph and out of the blue she mentioned the Army. Jamie looked up with a start to find her holding up an old photograph of him with the other platoon N.C.O's when he had been in the Cadets. He had forgotten all about that one. He heard his father laughing but his amusement was cut short by a warning look from Jamie's mother and he started coughing to cover it.

'It was the Army Cadet Force,' Jamie explained, hoping the subject would be dropped. 'I wasn't in the Army.'

'But this photograph…and the one up in your room,' Kate stuttered, picking up on his reluctance to talk about it and wishing she hadn't brought the subject up. 'What age were you?' she asked.

'Eighteen,' he came back quickly. 'It was my last year. I joined when I was twelve, when all my pals were joining the Boy's Brigade and the Scouts, and I left when I was eighteen,' he said, hoping that would be enough…but it wasn't.

'Why didn't you join the Army,' Kate persisted, intrigued. He had obviously been well thought of…you didn't get stripes on your arm otherwise, she imagined.

It was his father who provided the answer to that. 'Our Jamie has an aversion to authority,' he broke in, defying his wife's warning glare. 'He was great at giving orders…a brilliant N.C.O, they said, he just wasn't too good at following them.'

Jamie bit his tongue. It had all been said before but he was sorry Kate was now getting it. Silence is golden, he reminded himself…if I say nothing, it'll just dry up.

Kate felt his awkwardness and decided it was time to change the subject…or at least she tried to change the subject. 'The cabinet in your room, it's full of trophies, what did you win these for?' she asked, waiting for Jamie to tell her, but again it was his father who responded.

'Marksmanship,' his father said, and Kate could detect pride in his voice now. 'Our Jamie can hit a pea on a man's head at 400yards,' he joked. 'He would have been quid's in in the Army,' he reflected dreamily before his disappointment returned.

Jamie was stifling his anger for Kate's sake but he couldn't resist one barbed dig. 'I won them for rifle and pistol shooting…I'm a "natural", apparently. Some people like to live their lives through their kids and find it difficult when their kids don't go along with the plan,' he continued, his sarcasm clearly aimed at his father. He turned back to Kate then. 'The Army just wasn't for me, that's all,' he said quietly. 'And I'm glad…if I'd joined I'd never have met you, would I?' Kate smiled at him and the subject was closed but the air remained a little frosty between his father and mother for a while.

It was a tradition in the Raeburn house that they did without breakfast on Sunday and had an early lunch, brunch, instead and today was to be no exception. To Kate's surprise, Jamie turned out to be the cook and she watched in disbelief as he brought the fare through from the kitchen on numerous dishes which he placed carefully on the table. There were fried eggs, rashers of bacon, slices of black pudding, square sausages and egg coated cod roe, like French toast, and all of that accompanied by baked beans and fried tomatoes. The disbelief factor was racked up again when she saw Jamie heap four fried eggs and two pieces of everything else onto his plate together with liberal helpings of beans and tomatoes, not to mention two slices of buttered toast. How he managed to keep his shape and wasn't hitting 16 stones in weight she couldn't imagine. His mother came up with the explanation but it sounded more like an excuse. 'He plays football,' she said, seeing Kate's amazement and jumping to his defence. 'He hasn't played for a few weeks,' she continued and Kate remembered the photographs in the bedroom, giving a little smile in response. 'He hasn't been getting enough exercise,' his mother continued and Kate heard Jamie splutter. She caught his smirk in her direction and coughed to cover her urge to giggle. *Oh yes he has*, she smiled to herself.

'He's not all that good at the football,' his father laughed, getting a little of his own back Kate imagined. 'But as a centre half, not many get past him.' The pride was back again.

Talk around the table was friendly and easy and Jamie was relieved that his parents were getting on so well with Kate. If there had been a question and answer session between Kate and his mother earlier it seemed that Kate had weathered it. Breaking the news that she was married was going to be difficult, especially when it came to his mother, but the runes were good. He would cross that particular bridge when the time was right, he decided.

Kate and Jamie cleared everything away when the meal was over and washed and dried the dishes together, laughing and joking. When Jamie broached the subject of how she was getting on with his mother and father he was met with a happy smile and a simple "great". So far, so good, he thought happily.

Outside, the sun was shining but the grass was covered in a thick white layer of frost. Jamie wanted Kate alone for a while, remembering his promise given to her in the early hours. There were things he had to explain linked to places he wanted to show her and he hoped that the two would help her understand. His suggestion that they go for a walk was accepted by Kate enthusiastically and, well wrapped up against the cold, they set off.

Once outside the house, Kate linked her arm through Jamie's and cuddled against him. 'Have I told you how much I love you today?' she murmured, smiling contentedly.

'You have now,' he laughed. 'And I love you too.'

'Where are we going?' she asked, conscious that he was following some plan.

'It's going to be a voyage of enlightenment, sweetheart,' he grinned. 'I said I'd tell you everything and that's what I'm going to do.'

Kate took in her surroundings as they walked. She hadn't realised the night before how neat and tidy it was here, so different from Ibrox where she lived now. Even the village of Calverton where she had been born and brought up, though rural, wasn't like this. It was so green here, she marvelled, with grass verges and trees lining the main roads and houses with neat gardens. As Barbara had said, it had a sort of middle class feel to it, yet Jamie didn't seem to fit into that pigeon hole...not your average semi-detached suburban Mr Jones, she thought, the words of the Manfred Man song repeating over and over in her head. Having said that, she mused, Jamie Raeburn could fit in anywhere...drop him into any situation and he would blend in, like a chameleon. He could even change his voice, she had noticed.

They passed Knightswood Cross and walked on towards Anniesland for about a quarter of a mile before Jamie steered Kate left off the main road and into a side street. There was a car showroom on the other side of the road right on the corner and ahead of them was a big, old wood built building that fronted onto the road. Jamie stopped and pointed to the wooden building. 'That's my old Primary School,' he said. 'And that's where my mother works,' he continued, nodding over in the direction of the showroom. Kate waited, knowing instinctively that there was something more to come.

'There used to be a cinema where the showroom is now,' he continued. 'The Vogue, it was called, and there were old garages next to it, between it and the school. One day, on my way home from school, I saw three boys throwing stones at something over there,' he mumbled, pausing as the memory of that day flooded back. 'They were laughing and shouting...and there was a little girl standing near them, crying. I went over to investigate and discovered the boys were throwing stones at a little kitten. I shouted at them to stop but they just laughed and kept on throwing the stones. They were bigger than me...I was nine years old and they were in the year above me at school, probably ten or eleven. When they finished the little cat was dead and I found myself crying beside the little girl. The three boys called me a cissy...a softie, but I didn't care...not then, anyway. I helped the girl, picked up the little kitten...it was her cat, and I carried it back to her house for her. Her mother took us both into the back garden and we buried the little thing there.'

He was quiet now but still Kate knew the story wasn't finished. She had her arm around his waist and squeezed him gently, encouraging him to go on.

'Next day, at school, the three boys told everyone that I was a cry baby. They teased me and bullied me all day, and other boys, boys I thought were my friends, began to join in. Everyone thought it was funny and they expected me to cry again, but I didn't. I just bit my lip and took it. When school was finished the three of them followed me and kept on bullying me until I couldn't take it anymore.'

Kate was listening intently now, engrossed in the story, and tears were building up behind her eyes. She pictured him as the little boy facing up to the bullies and suspected he was going to tell her he had broken down and that the bullying had become worse but when he spoke again, the timbre of his voice had changed.. 'I went into an alley over there - between the cinema and the garages - and I waited for them to come...and, when they did, I picked the biggest of the three and I hit him...and kept hitting him, again, and again and again, until I got all of my frustration out.' He laughed wryly then before going on. 'In ended up with a black eye, a split lip and a few bruises...but I didn't cry. The boy I hit, he cried, but he came out of it worse off than me...and the other two had a few bruises between them,' he added, as though he'd forgotten that. The start of a smile appeared on his face. 'After that, nobody at school called me a cissy or a cry baby ever again.'

He paused, a frown edging in. 'It's a sad thought, though,' he continued eventually. 'If I'd faced up to those boys the day before maybe the kitten would have lived and the little girl would have been saved the heartache,' he said quietly.

Kate looked at him, spellbound. This was a different Jamie she was seeing now. 'And what about the little girl?' she asked, innocently. 'Did you stay friends with her?'

Jamie laughed and Kate puckered her brow in surprise. 'You could say that, I suppose,' he said. 'She was my first real girlfriend...the little girl was Carol Whyte.'

Kate gave a little gasp of astonishment. Everything was falling into place now. She had puzzled over why Jamie had been so wound up the night before when Carol Whyte had appeared and now the answer was there in front of her. When he and Carol had broken up it had been more than just a simple falling out; Jamie had expected more of her and she had let him down, badly it seemed. It wasn't just hurt pride on Jamie's part; she imagined he had felt betrayed.

'So that's what last night was all about,' Kate said quietly, pulling him close to her again. 'She still means something to you, doesn't she,' she suggested gently.

'No, not really,' he replied, leaning down to kiss her. 'I don't still love her, if that's what you think...it's just that she let me down, hurt me. I just...' He was struggling for words.

'I know,' Kate broke in, helping him. 'And I understand.' She paused for a heartbeat, debating whether or not to continue, but the words slipped out. 'I think *she* still loves you...and she knows she hurt you. When she came to say sorry last night, I think she meant it.'

Jamie smiled. 'You're amazing, you know that?' he said quietly. 'Don't you feel jealous or threatened by her?'

'No, I don't,' Kate smiled. 'You've said you love me and you mean it, don't you, so why should I be jealous of her? Carol is the jealous one, I think,' she whispered.

He pulled her into him and they kissed. Yes, I mean it, he told himself, and held onto the thought. 'Come on,' he said at last. 'There's somewhere else I want to take you...another part of the jigsaw.'

They set off again, arms around each other, back the way they had come until they reached Knightswood Park. Kate's eyes opened wide as she took in the wide open space with its big boating pond, now frozen over, with a big flock of swans sitting majestically on the grass beside it. Small children skated on the ice under the anxious, watchful eyes of their parents. The sight of the children tugged at Kate's heart strings as she thought of home and her daughter. Jamie mistook her look for one of concern for the children on the ice and laughed. 'The water's only a foot deep beneath the ice,' he grinned. 'They won't drown.' Kate responded with a smile but her heart was torn. She knew she should tell him the truth but she didn't have the courage...not yet anyway.

Her time to worry was short lived as Jamie wrapped his arms around her and lifted her off the ground, spinning around with her. She laughed and looked at him quizzically, wondering what had brought on his show of affection. He grinned happily as he put her down again. 'I've never felt so happy,' he told her. 'Going to help Conor that Friday and ending up in the Royal was meant to happen,' he laughed. 'It was fate...and I really love you,' he finished, his voice soft again.

'I'm sorry I'm going home for Christmas now,' Kate murmured. 'But I really do *have* to go.'

Jamie looked down on her and smiled, wondering if there was some hidden message in her words. He felt he was missing something but her words sounded sincere. 'Don't worry,' he retorted lightly. 'I'll wait for you.'

'You'd better,' Kate laughed, punching him playfully on the arm. 'But won't you be lonely all on your own?'

Jamie looked at her sideways, smiling archly. 'Who says I'll be on my own?'

Kate pretended to be hurt but there was a real hurt there too, Jamie sensed. She appeared to be wrestling with something, something that affected him. 'I'll worry about you,' she said eventually but it was more than that, it showed on her pretty face.

Jamie laughed it off. 'Don't worry about me,' he said. 'I'll be good...and I'll stay out of trouble. There's nothing for you to worry about.'

'But there is, Jamie,' Kate threw back quickly. 'You just don't realise it,' she continued, leaving him confused.

Jamie didn't like what was developing and moved the conversation on. 'We're almost there,' he said sombrely, 'the final part of the mystery of Jamie Raeburn.'

They walked for another two hundred yards before Jamie stopped next to a small copse of trees. 'See that tree there,' he said, pointing to a gnarled ancient hawthorn. 'When I was a fourteen I was playing football here on the grass with some pals when a gang of boys appeared...they were a bit older, and they were looking for someone. They surrounded us...and unfortunately the "someone" they were looking for happened to be one of my older cousins, Andrew Raeburn. Andy is, always has been, a bit of a tearaway, not like me,' he added with a mischievous laugh. 'Anyway, it all got a bit heavy. I kept quiet but one of my pals kept looking at me nervously and the gang sussed out they were on to something. They started to give me a really hard time and my mate, the one who had been looking at me, blurted out that I was Andy's cousin, hoping they'd leave me alone. What is it they say…the road to hell is paved with good intentions?' he laughed bitterly. 'It was open season on Raeburns after that. They tied me to that old tree with my own belt…my arms behind my back and round the trunk, and then they proceeded to beat the living daylights out of me. They punched me on the stomach and face, laughing, having a contest to see which of them could hurt me the most. I was screaming and trying to kick out with my feet but I was wasting my time. And then they just left me…still tied to the tree. My face was a mess. They all had a good laugh and one of them, a really sadistic wee shite, said that if he saw me again I had better cross the road away from him or he would give me more of the same. I didn't tell my Mum or Dad about it…I told them I'd got into a fight with one of my pals arguing about football.'

A couple of weeks later I bumped into that wee psycho again. He was out with a girl and wanted to show her he was a real hard man. I was on the other side of the street and he was grinning at me and telling the girl what he had said to me. They both thought it was funny but he stopped laughing when I came across the road towards him. There was no walkin' away…the lassie was expecting him to show her what he was made of and he wanted to impress her.' Jamie paused again, remembering the incident clearly. 'The bugger fixed on his grin again and walked right up to me…gave me the old Glasgow stare and told me, loud enough for his girl to hear, that he was going to "sort me out". What should I have done, Kate?' he asked.

Kate looked into his eyes. She knew what was coming.

'I couldn't run away…could I?' he demanded. If I had then I would probably still be running now.' He was facing her now, their eyes locked, and Kate saw the fire there. She wrapped her arms around him, just to hold him. 'It's this bloody city,' he said sadly. 'All the violence…we're brought up with it, fed a diet of viciousness and aggression…and we're proud of it. It's a part of us…and we either embrace it or we're dead.' Kate hugged him tighter, beginning to understand what it must be like. 'Even the good guys who live here need a wee streak of badness in them,' he murmured.

'And last night…with that boy, Bobby, was that your "wee streak of badness" coming out or was it a wee streak of jealousy?' she asked gently.

'Jealousy? Christ no, it wasn't that. Besides, he made all the running, remember? Was it just badness on my part? I don't know…probably,' he said, laughing cynically, and then he was the quiet Jamie again. 'I'm not a thug, Kate. I don't go out at night wandering the streets looking for trouble…like some I know.'

'I know that, I told you that already,' she interrupted quickly, cutting him off. 'But you don't walk away from it when it finds you, do you?'

'No, you're right, I don't,' he conceded, giving a nervous laugh. 'But if you walk away you end up looking over your shoulder for the rest of your life.'

There was a lengthy silence before Kate spoke again and when she did her eyes searched his face, making him feel uncomfortable. She had a knack of reaching right inside him, he thought, to all his private little spaces and dark corners. 'That's what scares me, Jamie,' she said softly. 'I keep seeing you lying there in the I.C.U that first night…and I don't want to see that again.'

Jamie pulled her closer to him, his arm tight around her shoulders. 'You won't.'

'You don't know that,' she retorted quickly. 'You take risks, stupid, thoughtless risks...and one day...'

'One day I'll die,' he said, finishing it for her. 'But that's going to happen someday anyway...crossing the road, lying in my bed asleep. When your time's up your time's up...it's all preordained...it's all on Saint Peter's time sheet,' he laughed.

Kate looked at him lovingly. She didn't quite understand where he was coming from with that remark but it didn't matter; all that mattered was that they loved each other. 'You know I mean it, don't you?' she whispered, pulling his head closer.

'What, that you're scared I'll be killed?' he teased, pretending he didn't understand.

Kate laughed sadly and her fingers traced a path down his cheek. 'No, sweetheart, not that you'll be killed,' she whispered. 'That I love you.' But as she said those words she realised that there were still so many things she didn't know about him, amongst these being just what he was capable of.

The rest of the day was spent contentedly in each other's company and, at Jamie's mother's insistence, Kate stayed with them for dinner. As a result, it was late when Jamie dropped her outside the house in Copland Place, reluctant to leave her. He wondered if her husband was at home but the windows were all shrouded in darkness.

Kate had clung close to him, pressing herself into his back, as they sped along the quiet night roads and now that they were here in Copland Place she didn't want to leave him. She dismounted from the bike and stood beside him, their breath mingling and drifting upwards in huge white clouds in the cold night air. Jamie placed his hands on her hips as she wrapped her arms around his neck and nuzzled into him. He smiled contentedly...Kate had committed herself to him and even seemed prepared to risk being seen with him and he wondered if Tom Maxwell knew about their affair. In a way, Jamie hoped he did but he was still concerned for Kate's safety.

'I don't want to leave you because I don't know when I'm going to see you again,' Kate whispered, her lips caressing his ear. 'I'm back on day shift tomorrow...and I'm going home on Friday,' she added plaintively.

That thought had been in Jamie's mind for most of the evening. When she headed south on the 23rd he wouldn't see her again until the beginning of January. He hadn't expected to be feeling the way he was now but as the date of Kate's departure came closer he found himself sinking into a state of depression.

'Can I stay with you tomorrow night?' he blurted in response, more in hope than expectation. The spectre of her husband was still drifting around in the back of his mind.

'All night?' she asked, a soft smile appearing on her face as her eyes watched for his reaction.

'Yes, all night.'

She leaned into him and kissed him hard. 'Alright,' she agreed, and blew him away.

*

The next week passed quickly for both of them, too quickly in fact. Jamie picked Kate up from the hospital when her shift finished on Monday and whisked her home to Copland Place and they spent the evening the way Jamie imagined a couple should, relaxed and content in each other's company. He was surprised by how comfortable he felt.

Kate prepared dinner for them and Jamie hovered around her as she moved confidently around her kitchen. Over the last year she had all but stopped cooking…what was the point in preparing lavish meals for herself, she decided one day. Now she was revelling in the opportunity to show Jamie how good her culinary skills were. She seemed completely happy, he noted.

They ate at the small table in Kate's living room, a candle glowing in the centre and a large dish full of piping hot macaroni cheese between them, the crust golden and crunchy. Kate watched him devour a large plateful of the creamy pasta and smiled contentedly. Her mother had told her that the way to a man's heart was through his stomach and the proof might be in front of her now…but she was pretty sure she had found her way into his heart via another route…and it wasn't his stomach! She giggled at the thought.

The meal over, Jamie helped clear up and, as on the day before, they washed and dried the dishes together. Ordinary little things like that were drawing them closer. They listened to music later, wrapping themselves together on the settee and allowing the music to wash over them…The Drifters, Beach Boys, Dusty Springfield and The Beatles filling the room and they began to explore each other's past with searching questions.

The prospect of Tom Maxwell appearing had gone from Jamie's mind and Kate was now considering the prospect of spending the rest of her life with him as more than just a possibility. She was intrigued by him. Yes, he was younger than she was but she rarely thought about that now…and when they made love he seemed so much older. He took her to places she had never been and did things she had never done. And it wasn't just sex, he made love to her. She had only been with one other man in her life and she knew that Jamie had been with more than one girl…but that didn't matter. He was *her's* now.

When the last disc on the record stack clicked off at the end of the final track Kate rose from the settee and reached down to take his hand. Until now they had spent the time petting gently, arousing each other, their clothes in disarray and their eyes filled with anticipation. She led him upstairs to the bedroom where they had made love during their first days together but tonight, for Kate, was another first. She knew there was no going back…the wreckage of her marriage was behind her now and no matter what the future brought she wanted it to be shared with Jamie.

They made love as sensuously as ever, their hands, mouths, tongues teasing and arousing, continuing late into the night with neither of them wanting it to finish. With each climax, lying sated beside each other, it took only a touch to arouse them again and lead them, inevitably, to fervent coupling. The night was silent when they finally drifted into sleep, wrapped securely in each other's arms.

Kate was preparing breakfast when Jamie appeared next morning. She looked fresh and happy, smiling constantly…ravishing, he thought. She kissed him softly as he came to her, pushing the tip of her tongue tantalisingly between his lips and feeling him react, just as she knew he would.

'Don't tease,' he laughed. 'You're dressed and ready for work and five minutes is never enough for us, you know that.'

Kate laughed and ran her hand down across his groin, feeling the hardness of him. 'Mmmh,' she sighed. 'And I thought I'd tired you out completely last night.'

'Yeah, you did,' he grinned. 'But that was last night, today is today,' he continued, slapping her playfully on the bottom.

They drank coffee and chatted, both of them avoiding the subject that was causing them the most torment. It was Jamie who broached it, eventually, after skirting around it for a while. 'What about tonight and the rest of this week, especially Thursday night…before you leave me?' he asked quietly. His mind had started to contemplate Tom Maxwell coming back to the house, particularly as he feared that her husband would be there on Thursday night intending to leave with Kate for England the next day. The thought tortured him and as he waited for Kate's reply he searched her expression for a hint of what she was thinking. He couldn't resist the question that bothered him most…he had to know. 'Will he be going with you?' he queried, apprehensively.

Kate slid her hand across the table and placed it on top of his, her eyes on his and she knew he would see the sadness in her. And from his look she could tell he was sorry he had raised this particular ghost. She smiled. What else should I have expected, she asked herself? She knew what Jamie was thinking; she understood his uncertainty and his jealousy, but Tom was still a part of her life, like it or not, and would be for a while yet. Jamie had to accept that and maybe what she was going to say now would help. 'Tom isn't coming with me,' she said softly and watched relief spread across Jamie's face. 'And yes, I want you to be with you all this week, especially Thursday night.' She leaned across the table and kissed him.

Chapter 16

Kate left for Calverton on the afternoon of 23 December. Jamie picked her up at The Royal at lunchtime and had taken her home to Ibrox for her bag and they made love, quickly and urgently, the thought of being apart driving them into each other's arms again.

At the Central Station he walked with her to the ticket barrier and there was a tear in Kate's eye as she made her way along the platform to the waiting train. She turned as she climbed up into the carriage, smiling wanly to Jamie who had remained, forlornly, at the barrier. Neither of them enjoyed the parting.

The night before, they had made love again until the early hours, but even at the height of their passion Jamie had sensed sadness in Kate, something she was still reluctant to share. Whatever it was, it wasn't in their love making, she gave herself completely to that, and it wasn't the thought of their being parted, they had both accepted that…but something *was* troubling her. He could work out what it *wasn't*, but what it *was* eluded him.

He wrestled with it as he made his way home from the station through the late afternoon traffic and it continued to bother him well into the evening, dispelled only when the telephone rang just before ten o'clock and Kate's voice echoed down the line.

'Hello sweetheart,' she said, sounding exhausted. 'I just wanted to let you know I arrived safely…and I wanted to hear your voice.' She was talking quietly and Jamie could hear noise in the background, voices, music, and laughter. 'I'm missing you already,' she whispered sadly. The background noise grew louder, a door opening somewhere, and a man's voice called out her name, instantly filling Jamie with jealousy. 'My brother,' Kate said immediately, anticipating Jamie's reaction and taking the sting out of it. 'Everyone has come to see me,' she continued and he could hear happiness in her voice…but there was loneliness in it too.

The torment was real for both of them. Jamie seemed so far away now and, even with her family and her daughter beside her, Kate felt alone and lonely. She was constantly worried now about Jamie's reaction to news of Lauren and how it might affect their relationship? In the space of only a few weeks she had fallen so deeply in love with him that the thought of being without him now was worse him painful. Could she tell him about Lauren and still manage to keep him? That was the question dominating her thoughts.

'They'll be happy to see you,' Jamie said, wishing he was with her. 'But not as much as me when you come back,' he added quietly.

'Are you missing me?'

'What do you think? Of course I'm missing you,' he replied dejectedly. He heard her brother shout out her name again and listened as Kate responded, saying she wouldn't be long.

'I'll be back with you soon, I promise,' she said gently, trying to cheer both of them up. 'I've only been away from you for a few hours and already it feels like forever…it hurts.'

'Do they know who you're calling?'

'My Mum suspects I've met someone…she's very perceptive,' she laughed. 'But the others think I'm phoning Tom…they don't know about his problem yet and I don't know how to tell them. They all think so much of him.'

Jamie could hear the despondency in her voice as she said these words and he felt sorry for her. 'I'm sorry, love,' he said softly. 'I know it can't be easy.' There was a moment's silence before he continued. 'Will you be able to phone me again?'

Kate dragged herself out of her melancholy. 'Wild horses won't stop me,' she laughed quietly. 'I don't know what I'd do without you.'

'Nor me, sweetheart,' he replied sincerely. 'You'd better get back to them before your brother has a fit.' He paused, wanting to let her know how he felt. 'I love you, Kate,' he said softly.

'I love you too, baby,' she replied quickly. 'More than I thought I'd ever love anybody again.'

As he replaced the handset Jamie closed his eyes and pictured her in his mind. He *was* missing her more than he had expected and that begged the question; how would he survive if he lost her now? He no longer cared what anyone thought, Jack especially, he was in love with her.

Jamie now had another minor problem to deal with, however. His mother would have heard the incoming call and she would have assumed, quite rightly, that it was Kate. She had asked him earlier about Kate's plans for Christmas and he had told her, without thinking, that she was going south to visit her family. He should have thought it out, he realised. Everything his mother knew about Kate implied that her family was with her in Glasgow and he had seen the question in his mother's eyes when he had said it. He would have to think of something…for her family read the rest of the family, maybe? That might do. But his mother had been quiet all week, due no doubt to his nights with Kate. He smiled…he was still his mother's little boy and probably the thought of him spending nights alone with Kate upset her. What did she and his father do when they were young, he wondered? Were they just like him and Kate? It didn't bear thinking about.

Jamie passed the following days in a state of limbo. Events seemed to take place around him but he was oblivious to them, his mind almost constantly on Kate. He went to a party in Jack Connolly's house on Christmas Eve and although surrounded by friends and not a few good looking girls, he felt out of place and lonely. He had joked with Kate that he wouldn't be lonely but that was exactly how he felt.

Kate called him on Christmas Day and his spirit was lifted but the days seemed to be getting longer now. He was counting the minutes until she was back in Glasgow and the thought of another eight days without her tormented him constantly. Only her daily calls were keeping him sane but each time she hung up, his spirits sank again.

Kate called on 29th of December and her news took him completely by surprise. He had been expecting her back with him on 2nd January and had been preparing himself for a miserable New Year. He had phoned Conor Whelan on Boxing Day in an effort to cheer himself up and Conor had appeared genuinely pleased when Jamie told him of his romance with Kate. But Conor too had things to tell. "Why don't you come down for New Year's kid?" Conor suggested amiably before springing his surprise. "I'd like to introduce you to my wife to be."

Jamie had been flabbergasted and pleased in equal measure but he declined the offer gracefully, suggesting that he probably wouldn't be good company without Kate there. Conor had teased him then. "I could fix you up, Buddy" he laughed. 'Those two little nurses are still available.'

Jamie had laughed with him and conceded that if he hadn't fallen for his own "little nurse" he might have taken Conor up on that. The call ended with Conor insisting that Jamie bring Kate to Dunoon soon to meet "my Mary" and Jamie agreeing that he would.

So, it was Mary, Jamie had noted after the call and wondered what she was like. Conor Whelan was a man of secrets so the lady would have to be pretty special, he surmised.

And now here he was, Thursday 29th December, and Kate just off the phone with the news that she was coming home early. "I'm missing you," she had said. "So I'm coming back early." Just like that, and the sun came out in Jamie's world again. And by "early" she meant the next day, 30th December. Jamie had flipped with joy; his New Year was going to be memorable after all. It was a good omen, but before then he had a call to make.

*

Jamie waited by the barrier at Platform 1 and watched the big locomotive come to a halt in clouds of steam. Kate would be with him in minutes and he was on cloud nine. He saw her as soon as she stepped down onto the platform. If he could have run to her he would but the barrier was closed and manned by two burly ticket inspectors. Kate was scanning the crowds on the concourse, searching for him, and he watched her face light up as she found him. She tried to walk faster but the weight of her case was slowing her. Jamie smiled to himself. It had been bloody heavy when he brought her here the day she left for England and it didn't appear to be any lighter now.

She reached the barrier, struggling through the crowd, and rummaged in her handbag for her ticket, smiling as she retrieved it and held it out for inspection…and then she was through the barrier and throwing herself into Jamie's arms. They smothered each other in kisses and he swung her around with delight, the crowd parting to avoid her whirling legs. As he lowered her back down onto terra firma Kate noticed the small holdall sitting on the ground between his feet and her eyes posed the question.

'I hope you can face another train journey?' Jamie said anxiously.

'Where are we going?' she asked, surprised. When they had spoken on the phone Jamie hadn't mentioned anything about this and she had been anticipating a few days with his parents.

'It's not far,' he said. 'We're going to Dunoon. Conor Whelan, the American sailor, remember him? He's invited us down there for New Year.'

'But I thought we were spending New Year with your Mum and Dad,' she came back quickly, and Jamie thought there was a note of disappointment in her voice. 'What does your Mum have to say?'

'She isn't best pleased,' Jamie admitted sheepishly. 'But I didn't fancy spending four nights wanting you and not being able to get to you,' he added persuasively. 'I told her we would come back on New Year's Day and that mollified her. Are you alright with this?' he continued, conscious of Kate's uncertainty.

'But I won't know anyone,' she said plaintively.

'You know me, am I not enough?'

Kate laughed at last. 'I can't say no to that, can I?' She shook her head, still amused. Jamie could manoeuvre her into accepting just about anything…in fact, he could probably charm the birds out of the trees if he wanted to, she mused wryly.

'So it's okay' he asked and saw her nod. 'Great, let's go! The train leaves Platform 15 in ten minutes,' he said, checking his watch. Quickly, he slung his bag over his shoulder and picked up Kate's case before wrapping his free arm around her and guiding her across the station to the Gourock train.

Settled on the train Kate started to tell him about her holiday. The carriage was empty and she curled up on the seat against him, overjoyed to be with him again, but still consumed with guilt at what she was keeping from him. But now wasn't the time to tell him…that would come soon enough. Why is life so complicated, she asked herself?

Jamie couldn't believe she had come back for him and the fact that she had dispelled any doubts he had about her love. He stroked her hair and caressed her, whispered endearments and told her how much he had missed her. It was already dark when they stepped down off the train at Gourock to find the ferry waiting at the pier, thick white smoke rising from its funnel into the black void above. The sail to Dunoon took only twenty minutes during which they huddled together at the deck rail, braving the cold and looking out over the dark waters of the Clyde, glass like beneath the silvery moon, to the lights of Dunoon in the distance.

With the ferry finally tied up they walked hand in hand down the gangplank and onto the wooden pier. Beyond the white pier buildings they could see the car park and the hill with the statue of Robert Burns' "Heilan' Mary" sitting proudly on its crest. A few cars waited in the car park but Jamie had no difficulty in finding Conor. An enormous blue Oldsmobile sat imposingly between a MacBrayne's bus and an old Ford Anglia and that, Jamie surmised, had to be Conor's. As he and Kate plodded towards it, the driver's door opened and Conor Whelan's voice boomed out over the noise of the car's purring engine.

'Hello ma'am,' he said with a grin, taking Kate's hand and kissing it. Kate blushed. 'I'm glad you could both make it,' he continued. 'Mary's really looking forward to meeting you both…especially you kid,' he enthused, grabbing Jamie in a bear hug and forcing the breath out of him. 'Jeeze, it's great to see you,' he went on and his pleasure was painted all over his face. 'Mary has got something special for us tonight,' he said as he let Jamie go. 'And your room's ready and waiting.' He opened the back door of the car and ushered Kate in, giving her the full treatment. Jamie made to join her but Kate nodded to the front seat, indicating that he should sit with Conor and as the American deposited the bags in the boot (which he insisted in calling the trunk) Jamie settled into the deep plush seat. It was hard to believe they were in a car, the seat he was on was as big as his father's favourite chair back home, he thought. Conor quickly joined him, grinning at Jamie's expression, and drove out of the car park, turning right towards the Argyll Hotel then out along the Esplanade towards Toward Point and the Holy Loch.

Kate sat quietly in the back of the car looking dreamily out over the dark water and the whitecaps of the waves and listening absently to the conversation between Jamie and Conor. They laughed and joked and Kate realised they were like brothers now, closer than she had imagined they could be given their differing backgrounds. She closed her eyes and thought of her family back in Calverton and her mother's tears when she had broken the news that she was returning early. It had been a spur of the moment decision but being separated from Jamie had been torture. It was hard to believe that in the space of only a few weeks she had fallen so completely in love with him. If she could resolve the one problem that remained her life would be perfect.

There had been lots of questions about Tom. Her mother knew he was a heavy drinker but no one, including her mother, had any inkling of how bad his problem had become. Her mother had also guessed she had met someone else though she said nothing. Her daily phone calls had probably given her away, she deduced...this based on the looks her mother gave her each time. But the anguish at being separated from Jamie was as nothing compared to the torment of leaving Lauren again; that filled her with an almost indescribable pain. Lauren wasn't a baby any longer and Kate realised that her daughter was growing up so quickly. Her mother hadn't said anything but Kate knew what she was thinking and soon she would be pressing Kate to return to be Lauren's mother again. And where would that leave her with Jamie, she agonised?

Conor's voice announcing their arrival at the house brought her out of her reverie. She saw Jamie looking at her, a worried expression on his face, and she smiled to reassure him. The front door of the house was open and a woman in her late twenties stood on the doorstep, her face wreathed in smiles. She was fashionably dressed and her blonde hair was combed high on her head. As they emerged from the car she strolled down the garden path to greet them and Kate had time to take a closer look at her. She really was quite beautiful, Kate noticed, her skin fair and smooth and her eyes a piercing pale blue.

'So, this is Jamie Raeburn at last,' she sang out happily with a soft Scottish lilt. 'I thought I'd never get the chance to thank you.' She placed her hands on Jamie's shoulders and kissed him on the cheek before turning to Kate. 'And you must be Kate,' she continued. 'I'm so happy you could both make it.' A hug followed and Kate was immediately taken by the gentleness of the woman's manner and the softness of her voice.

'Thanks for inviting us,' Kate replied. 'I hope we haven't put you to too much trouble.'

'Oh, it's no trouble at all,' Mary gushed. 'But you must be exhausted...when did you set out this morning?'

'The train from Nottingham was at five past eight,' Kate told her. 'I left the house about seven fifteen and my father drove me to the station. I am a little tired,' she agreed.

'Come on, I'll show you to your room and you can rest for a while before we eat,' Mary suggested and her eyes were on Jamie as she said it, an impish smile dancing in the irises. 'You two will have a lot of catching up to do too,' she laughed merrily and Jamie, uncharacteristically for him, blushed.

The bedroom they were shown to was big; the walls were decorated in a soft pastel green and there was a dark green tartan carpet on the floor. A big double bed dominated the floor space and the window looked out over the front garden down to the shoreline beyond.

'The bathroom is at the end of the hall there,' Mary informed them, pointing to a white door set into the wall. 'If you want a bath or a shower, help yourself, and there are towels for you in the wardrobe.' Kate's eyes were wide with pleasure. 'We can get to know one another at dinner. Okay?'

'Thank you,' Kate responded, speaking for Jamie as well. 'I'm looking forward to that.'

As the sound of the Conor's and Mary's footsteps faded down the carpeted stairway Kate threw herself into Jamie's arms. 'Hold me,' she urged. Their hands roamed quickly over each other and they kissed hungrily. 'I've missed you so much,' Kate moaned as Jamie's hands started to undress her feverishly, eagerly seeking the touch of her skin against his own.

Urgently, Kate's fingers went to his shirt buttons and she pulled the garment from him, kissing his exposed shoulders and chest. She felt his hand unclip her brassiere and slip it from her and then his fingers caressed her breasts. She struggled with his belt and zip as Jamie undid the button at the waist of her skirt and with the noise of her zip she felt the material of her skirt slip down her thighs. She caught Jamie looking at their reflections in the mirrored wardrobe door and felt him harden against her. His breathing was fast and loud in her ear as his hands slipped between her thighs onto the flesh above her stocking tops. She stepped out of her skirt which was now around her ankles and fell back onto the bed, pulling Jamie with her.

Jamie rolled away from her and slipped out of his remaining clothes. He was devouring her with his eyes. Naked, except for her suspender belt, knickers and stockings and still wearing her thigh length boots, she raised her hips towards him. Lust for her filled him and he tore at her underwear, his need to have her now uncontrollable. They made love frantically, both climaxing quickly, then lay passively, entwined in each other's arms, and with Kate's still boot clad legs curved around Jamie's back. He slipped from her and gently pulled the boots from her shapely legs then settled back onto the bed beside her and kissed her shoulders, neck and breasts. They lay under the covers and caressed, petting heavily until they were ready to mate again, and this time they made love more slowly, moving together sensuously until all control was lost.

Lying together afterwards they listened to the sounds of domesticity from below as Mary and Conor talked and laughed happily, and Kate placed her head on Jamie's chest. Her lips played across his pectoral muscles and she nibbled gently on his nipples as his hands stroked her bottom. She felt herself drift off to sleep and tried to fight it but the soothing rise and fall of Jamie's chest was tranquilising. 'I love you,' she murmured softly before giving up the fight and letting her eyes close.

*

Dinner that night was, as Conor had said, special. Mary had prepared Cullen Skink to start and there was roast chicken with roasted and boiled potatoes and a selection of vegetables to follow. Dessert was apple pie and cream and Conor had produced a couple of bottles of wine for the girls and American beers for himself and Jamie. The evening was relaxing, each of them enjoying the company of the others and chatting away like old friends. Late in the evening Conor and Jamie slipped out to the garden to enjoy a smoke and drew looks from both girls who, they knew, would have preferred that they didn't.

'I'm really glad you're here, Jamie,' Conor started when they were alone. 'Mary has been dying to meet you...and me,' he paused, looking at Jamie affectionately. 'Well, you know how I feel, kid,' he finished.

'You're embarrassing me again, big guy,' Jamie laughed. 'But you still haven't told me why you were there that night.'

Conor laughed nervously. 'If I tell you I'll have to kill you,' he joked, taking a long drag on his cigarette. He looked up into the heavens seeking Divine guidance. How much can I trust Jamie Raeburn, he wondered?

'The police asked me all about it,' Jamie continued, jolting him back to reality. 'No, that's not strictly true,' he said then, correcting himself. 'They asked me all about *you*...a Detective Superintendent and a Detective Inspector, no less,' he added, hoping Conor got the picture. 'I'd be lucky to get a Constable asking about me.'

Conor looked at him again and Jamie detected indecision. 'What did you tell them?' Conor asked quietly.

'Nothing,' Jamie laughed. 'I told them I couldn't remember a thing.'

'And can you...remember anything, that is?'

'Enough. Bits have been coming back to me...little things,' Jamie replied, watching Conor's reaction. 'Don't worry, your secret's safe with me,' he added lightly, still watching. There was that nervous look on Conor's face again, he observed.

The American shook his head slowly, pulled hard on his cigarette once again then flicked the stub out across the garden, its tip glowing like a miniature comet as it spiralled through the darkness to hit the ground in a little shower of sparks. He sighed heavily. 'Like I said, I *was* meeting someone that night, but it wasn't a woman.'

Jamie's eyebrows lifted in amusement and that broke the tension. Conor grinned awkwardly. 'No, not like that!' he laughed.

'Thank Christ for that, you had me worried for a minute there,' Jamie retorted and then they both started to laugh hysterically.

'Can I trust you, Jamie?' Conor asked, becoming serious again.

Jamie knitted his brow. 'You have to be the judge of that, Conor,' he replied, matching Conor for seriousness now. 'But unless you're a serial killer or a Russian spy, you're safe.'

The big American nodded and laughed softly. 'Okay, later then, when the girls go to bed you and I will have a drink...and a talk. Alright?'

Jamie regarded the big American shrewdly. 'Aye, alright,' he agreed, finishing his cigarette and dropping the butt-end to the ground where it sizzled on the frosty grass.

*

'So, there you have it,' Conor said, finishing his tale with a sigh and a large gulp of Whyte and Mackay whisky, heavily laced with Coca Cola. 'I'm not cut out for field work...I'm a desk jockey, an analyst, for Christ's sake.'

Jamie was shaking his head in disbelief. 'So, let me get this straight,' he said slowly. 'You're in Naval Intelligence...but someone in the C.I.A. got you involved in some deal with the I.R.A?' Jamie was struggling to come to terms with it all. Conor's revelations had taken him completely by surprise and now he felt he was involved, by default. Conor *was* a spy...just not a Russian spy. 'And what about Mary, does she know all this?' he demanded, keeping his voice low.

'Christ, no!' Conor retorted. 'I'm a sailor. She knows I work in Naval Intelligence but she thinks I sit behind a desk...Christ, what am I saying; I do sit behind a fucking desk all day.' He was growing edgy. 'Mary doesn't know about this...and I want to keep it that way. This whole thing is a one off...I just happened to be here and fit the bill for the guys at Langley; Irish American, you know, easy to play the sympathiser role. The whole deal has been set up to lead us to Irish sympathisers in the States so that we can control the flow of money and guns if anything blows up in the North. We don't want trouble with our English Allies, do we?'

Jamie ignored the "English" bit. It was a fact of life that nobody out with Britain called it British; it was always English or England. 'Why the fuck tell me all this now, Conor?' he asked, his voice climbing an octave before he managed to control it again.

Conor regarded Jamie cautiously, hoping he had judged him correctly. 'You asked kid,' he sighed. 'Listen, you're no fool. I knew that as soon as we started talking in the hospital. You knew something was out of kilter that night and if I hadn't told you, you would have kept on wondering till it festered. Like I said, I'm not a field man; I'm an analyst. I take Intel and I work out what the enemy is going to do. That's what I do…I'm not a spook and lying doesn't come naturally. When you said the police had asked questions I knew you already suspected something,' he continued, his eyes never leaving Jamie's face. 'You saved my life that night…and I guess I'm entrusting you with it again, kid.' He paused, anxiously hoping he hadn't destroyed their friendship.

'Do you expect me to believe this shit, Conor? How do I know you're *not* an Irish sympathiser?' Jamie asked, his voice hard.

'Jesus Jamie, I'm not, you have to believe that…if I was, would I tell you all this, for Chrissake?' he urged, scared now. 'I'm marrying Mary, would I do that if I was?'

'For fuck sake, Conor, what do you expect me to do now?' Jamie asked plaintively.

'Just stay my friend.'

'Shit, shit, shit, shit!' Jamie mumbled quietly. He looked Conor over, taking in the American's expression and examining his body language. Conor Whelan was telling the truth; it was as clear as day, but this was still a shitty mess. 'And if it all comes out?' he asked.

'Then you tell them you know nothing about it…and you walk away. You were just being a Good Samaritan, that night. You're not involved kid, and I won't involve you.'

'What is it you Yanks say?' Jamie murmured rhetorically. 'You're a son of a bitch, Conor Whelan…but I believe you…just don't get caught,' he said, holding out his hand. Conor pushed it aside and grabbed him in another of his signature bear hugs.

'Thanks buddy. I know that you saved my hide that night and for that, I owe you…I won't let you down, I promise.' He picked up the bottle of Whyte and Mackay and poured another two large measures into their tumblers, and clinked his glass against Jamie's. The matter was closed but Jamie was conscious of carrying a weight that hadn't been there before their conversation.

Kate was asleep when he finally reached their room, the top bed cover having slipped down over her shoulders and across her breasts exposing one of them to his adoring eyes. She took his breath away. Every time he looked at her he knew he would never take her for granted. He undressed quietly and crawled into bed beside her, turning to his side to be able to look at her in the moonlight filtering through the curtains. He followed every contour of her face and watched her breasts rise and fall gently in time with the rhythm of her breathing. He was, he realised, a very lucky man.

It was still dark when he awoke. The house was silent, everyone still asleep. Kate moaned softly and turned to him, twisting her arm around his neck and pulling him close to her. He buried his head in her breasts, absorbing the residual scent of her perfume. Kate's fingers played with his hair as he pressed himself against her, wanting to bury himself deep inside her again.

'Make love to me,' she whispered, sliding her body beneath him and feeling the hardness of him as he entered her. They moved slowly, the bed creaking quietly beneath them, coming almost as one. In the aftermath of their passion they lay quietly, caressing and kissing. Kate's next words came from the blue, bringing confusion. Please, never leave me, Jamie,' she whispered, and it was the anxiety in her voice that threw him. Why, he wondered? What made her think he would?

*

New Year 1967 came in with a bang! A mixed crowd of local people and American sailors descended on Mary Campbell's home on New Year's Eve and Kate and Jamie danced, sang and drank with everyone. Kate had settled and was mixing well but her eyes rarely left Jamie. At one point in the evening, when Jamie was with the men and Kate part of a group of women, their eyes met across the crowded room through a haze of cigarette smoke and marijuana joints and they both knew they had found the person they wanted to be with for the rest of their lives.

As midnight chimed they clung to each other before going around wishing the others a happy new year. They danced on into the early hours until the party ended and people drifted off to their own homes or to other parties while some, stoned or simply drunk, crashed on Mary's floor and the available chairs. As Kate and Jamie climbed the stairs to their room, exhausted, Mary called out. 'We'll see you when we see you in the morning...not too early,' she laughed, blowing them a kiss which Kate returned with a tired smile.

In the room they undressed each other, their exhaustion forgotten. Kate's lips meandered down his chest as Jamie's fingers teased her nipples. They made love again, being separated the week before the incentive, until finally they slept, their bodies still locked together. Jamie's last thought before drifting off was no matter what it took to keep her with him he would do it.

They returned to Glasgow in the early afternoon, Conor and Mary insisting on driving them. Jamie invited them to join his family for a while but they passed on it, opting to return home for some badly needed sleep.

Jamie's father and mother were waiting patiently for them, the dinner cooking and drink waiting. Mary Raeburn beamed happily when they arrived and her mood remained high for the rest of Kate's visit.

It was later that evening after Jamie's parents had retired to bed, slightly the worse for drink, that Kate produced a little package from her bag and passed it to him. His curiosity piqued, he examined the carefully wrapped box curiously. 'What is it?' he asked, guiltily.

'Open it and see,' she smiled.

Gingerly, Jamie tore at the wrapping and prised open the box. Nestling inside on a pad of dark blue satin was a strange looking silver cross. It *was* a cross but it had an unusual, elliptical loop at its, and it was one that Jamie had never seen before. The light caught it and it gleamed brightly. 'It's beautiful,' he whispered, taken aback. 'I've never seen anything like it before.

'It's an Ankh,' Kate replied, smiling happily at his reaction. 'It's an ancient Egyptian charm that signifies life.' She laughed then. 'Some say it is a phallic symbol for man entering woman...the loop represents the woman and the long shaft...' She laughed again, letting Jamie draw his own conclusion. 'I want you to wear it all the time so that each time you see it you'll remember me.' She stared deeply into his eyes. 'I love you,' she whispered.

Chapter 17

March 1967

Kate picked up the telephone with a shaking hand, and then hesitated. The dial tone filled her ear and all she had to do was dial but she couldn't find the courage. She replaced the handset with hot tears stinging her eyes. She struggled to bring her emotions under control, sobbing uncontrollably. That was her problem, she realised, Control or, more accurately, lack of it. Everything had spiralled out of control and she had no way of influencing events. If only she had met Jamie earlier; if only she hadn't married Tom Maxwell; if only, if only...too many "if onlys" she mused dejectedly.

She had to get out. There was no alternative. But it was a painful solution because it meant giving up Jamie and her love for him would tear her apart. Jamie didn't deserve this but neither did he deserve to be landed with another man's child. She had tried to tell him about Lauren so many times but always stopped herself...the fear of losing him was always too great. And now, ironically, she was contemplating leaving him. Nothing was simple. She had tried working round it, searching for a solution, but nothing she thought of seemed to fit. Guilt was consuming her...she hadn't deceived him, she told herself continually, but it didn't help to ease her conscience. At one time the thought of being rejected by him had been her greatest fear and now it was the fear that Jamie would think she was rejecting him. It would break his heart...it would break both their hearts.

She thought about Tom Maxwell. Once, she had worried about him and love had kept her with him for a while, but as his drinking ran out of control so too had she run out of love. She still worried about how Tom would end up but she no longer loved him. Everything that was bad in her life now, other than Lauren, was down to Tom and everything that was good was because of Jamie. Fate had played its hand, Jamie told her; he had been destined to meet her...but if Tom hadn't sunk so low and given up on life with her and Lauren in favour of beer and cheap vodka, would she have taken the chance to be with Jamie? She shrugged the thought away...in a perverse sort of way some good had come out of Tom's addiction.

But now the worst consequences of her husband's drinking were finally hitting home. With no job and no money coming in she was finding it difficult just keeping her head above water but somehow, God knows where, Tom still found money for drink. She hid her purse and all her money from him but still he managed get drunk. She hadn't given it much thought after meeting Jamie but how could she have missed it? The discovery that he had borrowed money from a loan shark had floored her. How could he have done it, she had raged? She was working long hours to pay all the bills; the rent, rates, gas and electricity, the food...which Tom rarely ate, and, most importantly, to send money to her mother in Calverton, for Lauren. The loud banging on the door earlier, waking her from her sleep, had heralded the beginning of this nightmare.

She had jumped from her bed, excited, and had run down the stairs expecting to find Jamie at the door but, instead, she had been confronted by two strangers; two hard faced men wearing cheap, ill-fitting suits and smelling of even cheaper after shave, standing on her doorstep. Their faces lit up leeringly at the sight of her in her short nightdress and the smile of anticipation on Kate's face had quickly disappeared. Something about these men scared her. She had crossed her arms defensively in front of her and stepped back into her hallway as a shiver of fear had run through her.

'Well, well, well, this is nice,' the older of the men had started as the younger man eyed her openly with a rapacious stare. She sensed him mentally stripping her and had looked away from him. 'You'll be *Mrs*. Maxwell, I take it?' the speaker had continued and Kate, numb with fear, had nodded dumbly in response. 'Is yer husband at hame?' he added.

Kate's fear metamorphosed into panic as she thought that she was entirely alone and at the mercy of these two thugs entered her head. If they knew that, what would they do? The thought petrified her. The spokesman had thrust his foot into the doorway preventing her from closing it and she had felt seriously threatened. She head was spinning and she was on the verge of hysteria when the roar of the motor bike had rent the afternoon quiet. Only one bike that made that throaty roar and she had grasped at that hope as a drowning person grasps a rope.

The roar of Jamie's T120 disturbed the men momentarily, the younger of the two turning towards the sound. His older companion, more worldly wise, had kept his eyes riveted on Kate's face and had picked up the sudden glimpse of hope in her eyes. She remembered him smiling coldly and her fear had returned.

'That'll no' be yer man,' he had said with a laugh. 'Frae whit ah remember, he'd huv a problem gettin' oan a bike, never mind ridin' wan.' He held Kate's eyes for a moment longer, watched her fear subside, and then had added. 'If that's yer boyfriend comin' fur a wee bit slap an' tickle then ah take it yer man's no' at hame...so we'll be back. Tell him he's got seven days tae get the money, an' if we don't get the cash... it's Two hundred and sixty five pounds, twelve shillings and sixpence by the way, then we'll take payment in kind...maybe frae you. Ma young friend here wid like that, but you widnae, hen, believe me,' he had said evilly. 'So yer man better find the money.' And with that they had left, the younger man hesitating a moment to grin salaciously at her, displaying decayed front teeth that made him look even more loathsome and wafting his bad breath over her. With this silent threat he had trotted off behind his older partner.

Jamie had seen them emerge from the garden gate and passed them just as they climbed into a gleaming Rover. An expensive car, he had thought, and they didn't look the sort who would own one...their suits screamed that out; but although they appeared hard and suspicious, he hadn't seen any trouble so he had ignored them.

Kate was waiting inside the hall when he arrived. She was trembling and the look of naked fear on her face hit him like a slap. He pulled her to him, feeling her body quiver. He turned angrily as the Rover pulled away and caught sight of the younger man grinning at him contemptuously as the car turned into Copland Road. His was a face Jamie wouldn't forget.

Kate remembered throwing her arms round him and feeling him draw her close and only then had her fear begun to ease. She had cried then, tears coursing down her cheeks as the realization of what had taken place fully hit her. Jamie had held her, soothed her and listened to her as she blurted out the history of what had happened. When she had looked at him his face was white with fury. That was when she should have told him everything...that would have been the sensible thing to do, but she couldn't, in much the same way that she couldn't explain to her mother now.

Steeling herself, she picked up the handset once again. This time, the constant hum of the dial tone was strangely comforting. She inserted her forefinger into the dial and started to make the call. The tiny electrical pulses clicked back to her as the number was fed down the wires to the telephone exchange. A series of echoing clicks filled the earpiece as her call was routed to her mother's phone in Calverton and then the ring tone filled her ear. Brrr brrr…brrr brrr…brrr brrr…on and on it seemed to go without an answer. Her resolve was fading and she was about to hang up when her mother's voice came to her at last. 'Hello Mum,' she said quickly, controlling her nerves and determined now to see it through.

'Kate, what a lovely surprise!' her mother replied, her voice chirpy and reflecting her happiness at hearing from her. 'Little Lauren's missing you,' her mother continued, tearing at Kate's heart strings with those words. 'How are you and Tom?' The silence that followed took her mother momentarily by surprise and then, instinctively, she knew Kate's answer wasn't going to be good. 'What's wrong love?' she pressed, concerned now. She should have expected this, she chided herself. Ever since Christmas, she had worried about the two of them. Kate had spent the days making excuses for Tom not being there and had been quiet and withdrawn much of the time, crying a lot. Her numerous telephone calls to a Glasgow number hadn't been to Tom, of that she had been fairly certain and when Kate had returned to Glasgow early her worry had soared.

'I don't know where to start, Mum" Kate sobbed eventually, her voice breaking.

Her mother waited, fighting her growing anxiety, to give Kate time to control herself before continuing. 'Start at the beginning love…it's usually best,' she said softly.

There was another long pause which told its own story. Things must be really bad, her mother realised, because this wasn't the Kate she knew…not her Kate, her bubbly, happy daughter who had always coped so well with life. She heard Kate take a deep breath, as though steeling herself, and then her words began to flow.

'My whole life is upside down, Mum,' she said, barely able to control her sobbing. 'I can't live with Tom anymore…I can't, it's over.'

Her mother gave a little gasp. 'Why, what's happened…what has he done?' She asked, fearing the worst.

'He's an alcoholic,' Kate replied. 'It has been going on for a long time…even before we moved to Glasgow, and now it's just too much,' she sobbed and was sure she heard an answering cry from her mother. 'He lost his job months ago but he's still drinking all the time.' It was all tumbling out now, the dam breached. 'We haven't been together for ages and when he does come home he avoids me…except to pester me for money for drink. He's on a different planet most of the time.'

'Oh my poor baby, what are you going to do?' her mother asked anxiously. 'Do his father and mother know? What are they saying?'

'I think they know but they haven't been in touch with me…and there's no way they can be in contact with Tom. They're in denial. She paused, the pain of the next part almost too much. 'It's more than his drinking now; Mum…he borrowed money from a loan shark here in Glasgow,' she said quietly, paused, took a deep breath, and raced on. 'And now this man wants his money back.' She heard her mother gasp again then carried on, reluctant to stop now. 'Two men turned up yesterday demanding the money and threatening us…threatening me, because Tom's wasn't here…it was horrible,' she sobbed again. 'We haven't been together as husband and wife for more than a year now.' She was repeating herself, she knew, but that was her nerves causing that. Delivering all of this news had been bad enough but the next bit was going to be even thornier and she was terrified of her mother's reaction.

Emily Edwards listened to her daughter's tale in growing alarm. The news was shocking and the threat to Kate now made things even worse. For that alone she would find it difficult to forgive Tom but she was still unsure of how Kate truly felt. She said her marriage was over but that was hard, if not impossible, to believe…Kate and Tom had been married young, certainly, but they had been so much in love and Lauren's birth soon afterwards seemed to confirm it. She was at a loss as to what to say now. Tom was still Kate's husband and it wasn't normally a good idea to come between a husband and wife, but she knew she had to say something. For Kate to have called like this, things had to be really bad. As things stood there appeared to be only one thing Kate could do but putting this to her wouldn't be easy. She wanted Kate back with her where she would be safe, not hundreds of miles away…and Lauren needed her. 'Why don't you come home love?' she said finally, her voice filled with concern. 'That might bring Tom to his senses,' she added, hoping to reinforce her plea, but Kate's next words added to her distress and consternation.

'I don't care if he comes to his senses or not, Mum,' Kate said plaintively. 'I have to get away from him…but…'

Her flow was cut short by her mother. 'It's an illness Kate,' she interrupted, breaking into Kate's explanation.

'I'm a nurse, Mum, I know it's an illness,' she replied irritably. 'But it's an illness that only the patient can cure and Tom doesn't *want* to get well and…' She paused again, building to the moment. It had to be now, she realised, now or never, before her mother cut her off again. 'There's something else…' Another moment's hesitation and then she plunged in. 'I've met someone else,' she said quietly. She imagined her mother frowning but there was no gasp of surprise and no sharp intake of breath this time, she noted. Her nervousness increased as she awaited her mother's response.

Emily Edwards digested the news easily enough and, if she was honest with herself, she had suspected something like this. She thought again of Christmas and her assumptions about Kate's telephone calls had now been proved correct. For it to have gone this far, the situation with Tom must be irreconcilable. Kate wouldn't have been unfaithful on a whim, she wasn't that kind of girl, and if she had looked elsewhere for love then her marriage was well and truly on the rocks. But the shocks of the day weren't over for Emily and the biggest was still to come.

'That's not all, Mum.' Kate continued, speaking slowly, sounding almost reluctant. 'I think I'm pregnant.'

The import of Kate's words struck home immediately. If, as Kate said, she and Tom hadn't been together for a year then Tom wasn't the father. 'Oh Kate love,' she cried. 'How…I mean why?' She stumbled then, words failing her.

There was a long silence with both of them struggling over what to say next. It was Emily who took the plunge. 'Does he know…the baby's father, does he know?' she asked, breaking the silence.

There was another long pause before Kate responded. 'No, he doesn't…and I don't want to tell him, not yet anyway,' she replied. 'I don't even know for sure yet that I am.'

'How late are you?' Her mother probed, reality kicking in for both of them.

'Twelve days,' Kate replied. 'But I've been late before,' she added. The silences were becoming longer. 'If I am pregnant I'm keeping the baby.' She asserted.

Her mother responded instantly to that. 'Of course you are,' she replied sharply. 'That's not even open for discussion...but what about the father, do you love him?'

Kate laughed softly, amused by the irony contained in the question. 'Yes Mum, I love him, more than I thought I would ever love anyone again. If I leave here without him I don't know what I'll do,' she said unhappily. 'But he doesn't know about Lauren and I'm scared to tell him because I've left it so long.'

Her mother sighed, understanding of Kate's plight now dawning on her and flooding her mind. 'So, you love this boy but you don't know if he loves you? Is that it?' she pressed on, oblivious to the subtle cruelty her suggestion caused.

Kate laughed softly again. Her mother's bluntness wasn't unexpected. 'No, Mum, that's not it,' she replied. 'Jamie loves me, I know he does. I wouldn't be with him now and I wouldn't have slept with him in the first place if I wasn't sure of that.'

'So tell him the truth, love. If he loves you, he'll understand.'

'I can't, Mum. I've tried but I keep losing my nerve at the last minute. We've talked about us having children but he thinks he's too young to be a father...'

'What age is this Jamie, then?' her mother broke in.

'He's twenty one, almost twenty two,' Kate replied, waiting for the anticipated explosion. When the response came it was less of an explosion and more of a whimper.

'That's not so bad,' her mother laughed guiltily. 'I had visions of an eighteen year old when you said he didn't think he was old enough,' she continued. 'But that doesn't get you anywhere, love. You *have* to tell him.'

'If I am pregnant and I tell him he'll want to do right by me and the baby...I know he will, he's a good man, but how long would it be before he thinks I trapped him into it? And there's Lauren...why should he be landed with another man's child?' She was racking up the negatives, convincing herself that telling Jamie about Lauren and the fact that she might be pregnant with his child wouldn't be fair on him. 'It's too much, Mum, and I don't want him getting involved with the loan shark either. He's not like Tom in that respect, he would confront them and probably get hurt; and that wouldn't be fair...all because of Tom's stupidity.'

'And what about Tom?' Her mother asked, changing tack, 'does he know all of this...about this Jamie and the moneylender looking for his money?'

'No, I don't think so,' Kate admitted. 'To be honest, I don't think he knows what day it is.'

'If you leave him up there what will happen to him? Is he in danger?'

'I don't know...I don't like to think,' Kate replied, sobbing again. 'Is he in danger?' she repeated. 'Yes, probably,' she confirmed.

'Come home, Kate,' her mother said softly. 'And get Tom to come with you...you can't leave him there.' Her mother had taken over. This suggestion provided a solution that satisfied her but it wasn't one that Kate could easily accept.

'And what about Jamie, what if I *am* pregnant?' She heard her mother sigh again.

'I haven't forgotten about him, love, but I'm thinking about you...and Lauren. Lauren needs her mother with her, not her Nan. If this Jamie really loves you he'll understand and you can sort everything out from here...where you're safe. I'll get your Dad...and Harry, to come for you. Maybe they can persuade Tom to come...I don't like the idea of him and this money lender. It's Easter this weekend...and Lauren would love to see you for that.'

So there it was, Kate reflected, problem solved, and she wasn't to have a choice in the matter. She thought about it. She had two problems now. Her mother was right in one respect; if she left Tom here to the mercy of the loan shark she wouldn't be able to handle the guilt if anything happened to him…and what would she tell Lauren when she was older and asked about her father? She had to try to get him to leave, even if it meant taking him with her, but that didn't mean she had to stay with him. The second problem, the one surrounding Jamie, was much more complex. She was in love with him and she might be carrying his child. Her mother's assertion that if he loved her he would understand was too trite. Why should he understand? Wouldn't he simply think she had been deceiving him all along? In any event, she couldn't just disappear; she had to tell him, she owed him that, even if she couldn't tell him about Lauren and about the possibility that she was pregnant. If her father and her brother, Harry, came to get her without Jamie knowing there could be problems, confrontation, and she didn't want any conflict between him and her family. She had to tell him.

Kate finally surrendered to her mother's suggestion. 'Alright, Mum; ask Dad to come for me this weekend…Friday would be best.' An all-consuming sadness engulfing her as she said it…but what was the alternative. 'If Dad comes early in the morning we can be back by Friday evening,' she carried on miserably.

'Will you be safe until then?' her mother asked, still concerned.

'I'll be alright…they gave Tom seven days from yesterday to find the money,' Kate replied, trying her best to reassure her. 'And Jamie will look after me,' she added, hoping that would still be the case.

'Alright love,' her mother agreed, still uneasy. 'Your Dad will be there on Friday…and Kate, don't worry darling, everything will be alright.'

It was done, the decision taken, but Kate still had one more request. She had always been close to her father and now filial guilt filled her; a feeling that she had let him down. 'And Mum,' she re-joined quietly. 'Don't tell Dad about the baby, please.'

At the other end of the line her mother smiled sadly. 'I won't love, I'll leave that to you when the time comes, if it comes…and you're ready to tell him yourself.'

'Thanks Mum. I'll see you soon then,' she finished gratefully, relief sweeping over her. That part of her ordeal was over at least.

Now she was filled with a fusion of emotions…relief, sadness, exhilaration, despondency; good followed by bad followed by good. She had dreaded making that call but her mother's reaction had been unexpected. If anything it was the opposite of what she had expected but the relief at that was counter balanced by the thought of what this was going to do to Jamie. And how could she explain it? Self-reproach and guilt ate at her again. How could she expect him to understand? She was leaving him, the man she loved and the man she knew in her heart loved her more than anyone else ever would. But she couldn't stay in Glasgow. She was alone here, though Jamie would dispute that, and she was afraid now…really afraid, both for herself and for the baby she was now convinced was growing inside her.

Jamie had said he would always take care of her and she knew that he would. He had already asked her to leave Tom, had all but asked her to marry him. But all of these things were said without knowing about the existence of Lauren. If she stayed, and deep down she wanted to stay, she would have to tell him the truth and he would have to accept Lauren as part of their family. There was also the problem of Tom's angry loan shark and problems like that didn't just go away. Those men who had come looking for Tom were vicious individuals who made a living out of violence and if she stayed then Jamie would become embroiled in the brutality protecting her. She couldn't bear the thought of him being hurt by them but the irony of *that* wasn't lost on her either; the hurt her leaving would inflict would be much worse.

She no longer loved. She had given up on him simply because she believed he had given up on her but when she had started her relationship with Jamie there had been guilt. That was an understatement...the guilt she felt had been almost unbearable, but she had seen a future with Jamie that she would never have with Tom. As Tom's drinking got worse love for Jamie had grown and the guilt had faded. She didn't wish Tom any harm and his drinking was a disease, she knew that, but taking money from that money lender to satisfy his addiction had exposed her and, by extension, the baby she was sure she was carrying, to danger. She could never forgive him for that.

There it was again, she mused; this belief that she was pregnant and this feeling of fear for her unborn child. But notwithstanding that and Tom's part in it, she couldn't leave him to the tender mercies of those men. Violence was second nature to them and if Tom didn't pay up...and there was no way he could, then they would kill him. She believed that beyond any shadow of doubt and if it happened she wouldn't be able to live with it afterwards. He had been a good, kind and caring man once so she had to talk to him if she could and persuade him to come back to Calverton, even though their marriage was over and she couldn't stay with him when they arrived there. Her mind made up she knew then what she had to do.

Now her thoughts reverted to Jamie. He was coming to her tonight straight from his work and the joy of being with him again was now overshadowed by the thought that it could be their last night together. She wanted him to stay, to lie beside her, and to waken next to him in the morning...but would he stay? The few months they had been together had been filled with nights like that, nights full of passion and happiness, but tonight had to be more. Tonight was about showing him how much she loved him before she set him free to love someone else or, please God, follow her. The tears came again. Later in Jamie's life, when he looked back on tonight, she hoped he might realise how much he had meant to her and that in leaving she was losing as much, if not more, than him.

She spent the rest of the day preparing for their "special" night. At one point she felt like Mary Magdalene preparing for The Last Supper and, like the original Last Supper, this one had to be unforgettable. There was one big difference however; tonight she was playing two parts in the drama...Mary Magdalene and Judas. An involuntary shiver ran through her at the thought.

She went shopping to buy some things for the evening but was plagued by a fear that she was being watched and cut her outing short, returning home just before three o' clock in the afternoon. She felt anxious...even here in the house with all the doors and windows firmly shut, she couldn't shake her trepidation.

Occupying her mind was the answer, she decided, and busied herself by choosing her dress for the evening, picking out the one she knew Jamie liked best; the scarlet halter neck dress he had bought for her on St. Valentine's Day. Another tear trickled slowly down her cheek at the memory of that. Tonight wasn't going to be easy but then she had never tried to fool herself that it would be. The feeling of melancholy that was burgeoning inside her mind was weighing her down and she knew she had to snap herself out of it before Jamie arrived. *'Please God,'* she prayed aloud, *'help him to understand why I'm doing this...I need him to understand.'*

The steady knock on the front door brought her back from the edge of despair. She checked the time; it was just after four thirty and it had to be Jamie, but living in fear was part of her life now. She eased back the bedroom curtain furtively and peeked out of the bay window, relief flooding her as she saw Jamie's muscular frame on the doorstep and his face smiling up at her. She descended the stair at a run.

As she opened the door she wanted to throw herself into his arms but he fended her off, leaning forward instead to kiss her and producing a bunch of flowers from behind his back with a flourish. 'I'm not nice to be near, sweetheart...it has been hot and hard all day,' he said apologetically then choked with laughter his unintentional double entendre.

Kate laughed, forgetting her anxiety for the moment. 'I'd keep that quiet if I were you,' she giggled in a loud stage whisper, 'or there will probably be a queue of sex starved women at the door and I wouldn't like that.'

'I doubt it,' he grinned. 'I smell like a Turkish wrestler's jock strap. I need a shower, urgently,' he continued, kissing her again. 'I'll be quick, I promise.' He squeezed past her and made his way up the stairs, his overnight bag swinging in his hand, and Kate went to find a vase for the flowers.

The flowers smelled beautiful and she inhaled their perfume as she placed them in the white porcelain vase she had found in the kitchen and arranged them on the small table which sat, ostentatiously, beneath the wall mirror in the hall. Taking a last look at them she smiled and then climbed the stairs to her bedroom. She could hear Jamie singing as he showered and the sound evoked a bitter sweet feeling. This should have been another blissful day but the shadow of what she had to do crept back into her mind and smothered her euphoria. Happiness and sadness were irretrievably mingled, one with the other, and she sensed her life would always be like that now. She was going to miss him but she had no other choice but to leave.

She shunted these thoughts from her mind and changed quickly, slipping out of her top and jeans and pulling on the red dress. The noise of the rushing water of the shower stopped abruptly heralding Jamie's imminent arrival and warning her she didn't have long to finish her preparations. Quickly, she removed her bra, deciding to go "au natural", and then slipped her stockings up over her calves and thighs, fastening them deftly her suspender straps. She smoothed her dress down over her body and examined herself in the wardrobe mirror before reaching behind her to fasten her zip. Her favourite red leather high heel shoes, adding two inches to her height, slipped snugly onto her feet just as she heard the bathroom door open and Jamie's bare feet padding, almost silently, down the hall. The bedroom door opened and he was there, pausing in the doorway as he took in the sight before him. He let out a low whistle and Kate smiled, flattered.

He made a handsome picture himself, she thought appreciatively, standing there framed in the doorway with his chest bare and his hair tousled and damp, a towel tied loosely around his waist. She saw the tiny red, raw, burn marks on his wrists and forearms where sparks from his welding torch had seared his skin and she remembered Barbara Laing explaining these to her all those months before...a lifetime ago, she thought. The skin of his naked torso was pale compared with the weather beaten tan on his lower arms and face and the muscles of his chest were firm and taught beneath the light coating of dark hair. As he walked towards her now the muscles of his abdomen rippled and she wanted him, as always. Leaving him here was going to be the most painful thing she had done...she loved everything about him.

'You look fantastic,' he whispered admiringly. 'Red suits you. What's the occasion?'

Kate fought back her feeling of wretchedness and forced a smile. 'You look great too, baby,' she murmured. 'Naked suits you,' she whispered with a little laugh, her eyes now caressing his body. She felt him pull her to him and kiss her deeply, lingeringly and some of her misery slipped away. She gripped him tightly then, needing the feel of his skin and the warmth of his body against her.

'You're going to stay tonight, aren't you?' she asked hopefully.

'I'm staying,' he replied, kissing her again.

She sat on the edge of the bed watching him dress and anticipating the pleasure of making love with him but, at the same time, she was dreading the revelation she had to make. They made their way downstairs and Kate busied herself in the kitchen while Jamie selected music for the evening. He knew exactly what she liked now loaded L.Ps onto the record player stacker; Dusty Springfield and Gene Pitney for Kate, The Beatles and The Four Tops for him. He hit the play button, saw the first disc drop and watched the stylus swing over and settle on the record. There was a hiss as the needle picked up the initial groove on the record, quickly replaced by the mellow voice of Dusty Springfield singing one of her signature sad love songs. Jamie walked into the kitchen and came up close behind her, wrapping his arms around her waist and burying his face in her hair, savouring the scent of her.

He kissed her neck then stood back and looked at her. She was truly beautiful, he thought, even with the gaudy striped apron covering her dress. He smiled, staggered by how their love had grown and life couldn't get much better…except; he felt the little box nestling in his pocket and wondered when to ask her. Tonight, he decided; he didn't want to wait any longer. Breaking the news to his mother was going to be difficult but she would accept it, he knew that, she loved her too. Kate was constantly a topic of conversation in the Raeburn house with his mother telling him how much she thought of her and his father agreeing wholeheartedly. The fact that Kate was older than Jamie didn't bother them in the least…her marriage might, but somehow he doubted it.

They chatted and flirted over the meal but although Kate appeared outwardly happy and content, Jamie detected the sadness in her. He had picked it up before, particularly over the last few weeks, but it seemed more pronounced tonight. It could be the shock of the debt collectors turning up at her door a few days earlier, he mused, but the aura of wretchedness that surrounded her from time to time had been there even before their appearance.

After dinner they settled on the settee, Kate's head resting on Jamie's chest as they listened to the music. Please God, let it be like this forever, he prayed; I don't need anyone else, just let me be with her. They kissed and caressed, totally engrossed in each other, their bodies pressed close and they danced to the music, floating around the tiny space where the chairs and settee had been, but throughout it all Jamie could sense dark shadows descending.

As the last song on the final L.P. on the stack faded away and the needle of the record player returned to its rest, Kate took him by the hand and led him upstairs to the bedroom. They made love with an intensity Jamie would never forget, Kate giving herself like never before and murmuring, over and over, how much she loved him. He was swept away by the passion of it and wanted her to experience each and every sensation, every nuance of their love that he himself was feeling.

When Kate climaxed she called out his name and gripped his shoulders with her nails, clinging to him fiercely, wanting the orgasm to last forever. She cried as he withdrew from her, unable to control her emotions any longer and she saw the questions in Jamie's expression through her tear filled eyes. Any doubts that she had harboured about his love for her were dispelled in that moment…but she had made her decision and the die was cast.

They lay quietly, Kate's head resting on his chest and her tears wetting his skin. Jamie was perplexed. He couldn't understand the reason why she cried or comprehend the sense of despair that seemed to be radiating from her. He stroked her shoulder and kissed her sweat dampened hair but her tears continued, unabated.

'Tell me what's wrong, Kate?' he whispered gently at last. 'You're scaring me.'

Her sobbing intensified. 'I…love…you,' she murmured, the words enunciated separately between sobs.

'I know,' he said soothingly, smiling. 'But that's not a reason for crying…so why the tears?'

Kate raised her head up from his chest slowly and Jamie could see from the tortured look in her eyes that something was seriously wrong and, as he waited for her explanation, he was filled with a growing sense of helplessness. She look was haunted and she was averting her eyes from him.

'It is a reason to cry,' she sobbed almost incoherently. 'I'm leaving…I'm going home to Calverton. I can't stay here any longer.'

Jamie felt as though his breath had been squeezed from his body and he struggled to take it all in, half expecting to wake from a nightmare.

'I *have* to go, Jamie…my life is a mess,' Kate continued, her fingers tracing their way gently along his lips. There was a moment of silence, broken only by the mournful sound of the wind as it whistled through the partly opened window.

Jamie knew then that what happened in the next few moments was going to change his life. 'You're not making sense Kate,' he started, his voice shaking. 'You've said you love me…and you know I love you; I'd die for you.' His voice sounded strange to him, like someone else, a stranger, speaking. 'Leave him, Kate. Come away with me…marry me.'

Kate's tears continued to stream from her eyes as she leaned over and kissed him tenderly. 'It isn't Tom,' she replied sadly, wiping the tears from her eyes with the back of her hand. 'There's another reasons…one I haven't been able to talk to you about…something I've been scared to talk about.'

Jamie found himself growing angry. He loved her; she loved him, what else mattered. He fought the urge to shout to get it out of his system. 'I scare you? Christ Kate, I love you….when have I ever done anything to scare you? Give me the reason…you can't just leave it like this. Tell me why.'

'I love you,' she sobbed, 'you know I do. I'm not scared of you…it's nothing like that. I couldn't talk to you because I was scared I'd lose you.' She was distraught now.

'How? How would you lose me?'

Her sobbing intensified, her body shaking with emotion. 'Because I'm scared you'll end up hating me.'

Jamie lay back and stared at the ceiling. His world was collapsing around him…again, he thought, and he had no control over it. Resentment was growing inside him, threatening to boil over, but he managed to restrain it. 'None of this is making sense, Kate. What has brought it on…I thought you were happy with me…is it the money lender?' he asked.

'I am happy with you…those men coming here are only part of the reason.'

'This is bullshit, Kate. You say you love me but that's not how it looks from here,' he said angrily, his voice rising. 'If you don't love me and you want to stay with him, just fucking say it!' he shouted, shaking now, and Kate pulled back from him, shocked that he could think that.

He started to rise from the bed but she caught his arm, holding him back. 'It's not that!' she cried. 'You *know* it's not that...you *know* I love you,' she whimpered, feeling that everything was going wrong.

Jamie sat on the edge of the bed, his head in his hands and she tried to put her arm around him. He shrugged her off but his anger was spent. His shoulders shook and Kate realised he was crying. Kate sighed, hurting. 'I'm doing this because I love you,' she whimpered. 'And it's breaking my heart as much as it is yours.'

'Aye, right! You're dumping me because you love me...that's a new one,' he threw back at her sarcastically, shaking his head in disbelief. 'So when is this all happening?'

'My father is coming to take me home this weekend.'

'This weekend...Easter Weekend?' Jamie repeated incredulously. It was all beginning to look clear to him now. 'And Tom?' he continued. 'Where does he fit in?'

Kate looked away from him, unable to look him in the eye, confirming the suspicion that had already taken seed inside him. 'I can't leave him here,' she mumbled, knowing the effect her words would have. 'Those men will kill him,' she whispered, trying desperately to mitigate it.'

'Aye, and the bastard will swear that he'll give up the booze and be a good guy again and you can live happily ever after,' Jamie retorted sarcastically. 'Does he know about us? Did you use me just to get to him, is that it?' His angry words were tumbling out of now, his bitterness and resentment making him say things he would regret later but his control had gone.

Kate looked at him sadly, her face drawn and pale. She felt terrible. The guilt she had felt in the beginning when she had been unfaithful to Tom was as nothing to the guilt and the pain she was feeling now. Her resolve began to waver...but there was Lauren and Lauren needed her more. Tell him, at least let him know the truth, her heart screamed out at her. 'You know I don't love him, Jamie,' she said, her voice so low Jamie struggled to hear. 'But there is someone else...' That was as far as she got before Jamie interrupted her, his face filled with rage.

'For fuck sake, you've had three of us on the go!' he spat out furiously.

'Listen to me,' she screamed back at him, beating him with her clenched hands. 'Don't assume anything...I'm not a whore.'

Jamie shrank back, unable to look at her, ashamed, her reaction telling him he'd got it all wrong. He hadn't meant that and he didn't believe it either, he had just struck out blindly. 'I'm sorry, Kate, honestly...I'm sorry,' he mumbled. 'You know I don't believe that.' He reached out for her and she took his hand, clinging to it desperately as her tears came again.

'The "someone else" is my daughter, Lauren,' she whispered, the fear of telling him now gone. Things couldn't get any worse now, she realised. 'My mother has been looking after her since Tom and I moved up here.'

Jamie stared at her dumbly. Tonight was a night for shocks and surprises, and they weren't pleasant ones. 'How old is she?' he asked softly, still holding onto her hand. She was shaking, the pain of the confrontation raw in her.

'She's almost two...I know I should have told you, but I didn't know how you'd react and I didn't want to lose you.'

Jamie laughed at the irony. 'So instead of losing me you decide to leave me...don't I get a say in this Kate?'

'I love you Jamie, you know I do,' she reiterated, 'and I don't know if I can live without you.' She stopped, holding his stare now. 'I have to go back to Lauren and I can't expect you to be a father to her,' she said slowly, stating her position for the first time. 'I'm scared that every time you looked at her you would see Tom...and that's why I think you'd end up resenting Lauren and hating me.'

Jamie smiled sadly and his resolve crumbled. Kate clearly believed she was doing the right thing but she was wrong; all she was doing was tearing them both apart and he had to convince her. 'You could have asked me, Kate,' he started, still keeping his voice soft and low. Maybe you don't know me as well as you think...your daughter is part of you and you know I love every bit of you, so doesn't it follow that I can love her. Maybe I'd make a good father...you don't know. Give me a chance, please...at least think about it...I don't want to lose you.'

Kate leaned over him, kissing him again, her fingers stroking his temples. 'It's so unfair, Jamie. I love Lauren and I love you...I don't know what to do. I'm scared...and my Mum is insisting I go back.'

He took her hand and raised it to his lips, kissing her fingers. He always did that to show he loved her, she realised. 'Just tell me you'll think about it...that's all I ask.'

She nodded slowly, her eyes still wet with her tears. 'Alright, I will, I promise,' she murmured and pulled him to her.

They made love again, mindful now that it might be their last night together. Their passion knew no bounds as they coupled again and again until they were finally sated and spent. Jamie lay still, his weight spread across her, wishing he could lie like that forever and so prevent her leaving. They lay in silence, only the sound of their breathing disturbing the peace. And as they lay there he wanted her again. He tensed his muscles to send that message to her and felt the muscles of her vagina tighten around him in response, like fingers gripping him. They repeated the action again and again, arousing each other. Slowly, Jamie began to move inside her, deep inside her, wanting to be absorbed into her body so that they would never be apart. His mouth found her breasts, his tongue traced circles around the aureoles of her nipples and he felt them swell between his lips. Their rhythm increased, their bodies coming together in a crescendo until, with a final explosion of rapture, they climaxed together as one.

As the crashed back to earth Kate pressed her mouth close to his ear. 'I love you,' she whispered. 'You have to believe that, Jamie...I'll always love you.'

They slept fitfully then, their bodies warm and glistening with the soft sweat of their love making. Jamie awoke around three o'clock, his mind still in turmoil. It was dark outside and the wind was blowing gently at the curtains, causing them to sway gently in the draught. He lay quietly, listening to Kate's breathing, thinking about the dark days ahead because he had accepted she would go...as much as he accepted that she loved him. And when she did go, what then? Follow her? What was left for him here without her?

His thoughts back over the weeks since they had met; the things they had done together, the fun they had shared. Looking at her now evoked a memory of the first night he had taken her back to his parents' home, hiding her wedding ring, making love to her clandestinely before taking her to his room and leaving her there alone. He smiled as he recalled looking in on her later and seeing her curled up in his bed, her hair spilled across the pillow and his old teddy bear clutched close to her breast.

The idea came to him suddenly. Rising from the bed carefully so as not to disturb her, he dressed and slipped from the room, silently making his way downstairs, avoiding the treads he knew would creak. Once outside, he locked the door and walked quietly down the short garden path and out into the street to the waiting Triumph. He lifted the bike off its stand and manoeuvred it quietly around the corner and into Copland Road before bringing it to life.

Asleep in the bed, Kate moaned softly and turned, the faint roar of the Triumph's 650cc engine momentarily disturbing her dreams. She turned, called out Jamie's name softly, and fell silent again.

As Kate sank back into her dream filled slumber Jamie was racing through the Clyde Tunnel heading north. The dark streets were deserted as he sped, unhindered, to Anniesland Cross and then onto the main artery running west, Great Western Road. Less than 15 minutes after leaving her he pulled up outside the house in Knightswood. It was shrouded in darkness but that would not be the case for long. His father, he knew, would be rising for work in less than half an hour and Jamie wanted to avoid him if he could. Time, therefore, was of the essence.

Switching off the engine he dismounted and made his way silently into the house, creeping carefully up the stairs to his room to retrieve the bear from its habitual spot next to his bed. He tucked it inside his heavy jacket and left the house again, his short visit passing completely unnoticed.

The sun was tinting the eastern sky with pink as he let himself back into the house in Copland Place and climbed back upstairs to the bedroom. Kate still lay prone on the bed, her body stretched to its full length. Her head lay in the centre of her pillow and her hair was still spilled all around. She had thrown back the bedcovers in her sleep to reveal the pink firmness of her naked breasts, rising and falling gently with the slow inhalation and exhalation of her breath.

As quietly as when he had left her, Jamie undressed and crawled back into the bed beside her, placing the furry bear on the pillow next to her before pressing himself close and curling his right hand over her to cup her breast. She moaned softly in her sleep and turned towards him, her left arm settling on his hip. How can you let her go, a little voice in his head screamed out at him, fight for her, keep her.

They awoke around six, a gut wrenching sense of dread already growing in Jamie's stomach. Was this to be his last morning with her, he wondered? He started work at eight and the journey to the Yard would take him around twenty minutes, maybe twenty five. He would have to leave her at around 07.30…and leave her was the last thing he wanted to do.

As Jamie stirred, Kate stretched and opened her eyes, a smile spreading over her lovely face before disappearing beneath a mask of sadness. She twisted her head towards him, her eyes coming to rest on the bear, and gave a little gasp of surprise. 'Where did you come from?' Lovingly, she picked up the soft toy and held it close.

'If you are going away then Ted here is going with you…that way you'll never forget me.' He was smiling but his despair was palpable. There was a moment of quiet before he spoke again. 'And when you're ready, I'll come for you…all three of you.' Kate knew when he said the words he had included the little bear in the three but she shivered none the less.

Jamie started to rise but she reached for him. He felt the gentle but firm pressure of her fingers gripping his arm and turned back to her, forcing back his tears.eaning over to kiss her hair. Kate's arms curled around his neck and he felt himself pulled down to her.

'Make love to me,' she pleaded. 'Don't leave me like this, Jamie…I love you; I'll always love you,' she whispered, as if sharing a secret, her eyes watery and heavy with tears.

'I know,' he mumbled incoherently through his own anguish before their lips met. 'I'll always love you too, baby,' he said more clearly then as he raised himself over her and his mouth drifted to her waiting breasts. Gently, he cupped her bottom with his hands and eased her up towards him and entered her.

Chapter 18

As he rode to work, weaving in and out of the morning traffic, Jamie's thoughts never left Kate. He was on autopilot, aware of other vehicles and dangers around him but oblivious to everything else. The little box with the ring pressed against his chest; the ring he had hoped would change his life...and Kate's. Yet he hadn't shown it, even as he had asked her to marry him...why? Would it have made a difference? Probably not. Kate's priority wasn't him, it was her daughter and that made acceptance of the situation easier...not bearable, just easier. 'There's still hope,' he said aloud but deep down he knew he was deluding himself and his thoughts tortured him.

He should have seen the signs earlier, he rebuked himself, they had been there...he had sensed something was wrong but he'd been afraid to confront it. He should have asked her, made her tell him, rather than let her be dragged down by it. The last week, in particular, she had been withdrawn, clearly worried, but refusing to be drawn on what it was. He should have forced it from her then...but maybe by then it was already too late. When they made love there had been an intensity to it that was new...as if Kate was making love each time as though it may be their last.

And now he was on the verge of losing her. Realistically, he thought he already had. The day passed slowly, frustratingly so. Being unable to contact her he felt lost. He needed to convince her to stay but how could he do that if they didn't talk? When the horn sounded bringing the shift to an end he was first out of the yard and was racing home before most of the workers had left the yard. He had toyed with the idea of going to The Royal and waiting for her there but decided against it. It wasn't a good plan, he had concluded eventually but that encapsulated his problem...he didn't have a plan!

It was rare for him to be home after work before his mother and the sight of him sitting alone in the living room as she breezed in, his face shrouded in anxiety, troubled her. She tried to talk to him but he refused to be drawn. His father had joined them and caught her eye, shaking his head warningly. With a mother's instinct, she knew immediately that whatever was wrong involved Kate. The girl had almost become part of the family and her son had been changed by her and in a good way. The boy who had found trouble everywhere had become a man who shied clear of it. But she too had sensed a change in Kate in recent weeks and she had been uneasy. Whatever! It would all come out in the wash, she told herself, and set about preparing dinner but she was unable to push her feeling of disquiet from her mind.

Jamie remained quiet over dinner, morose almost, and his mother suspected the worst. His father too noticed his mood and, never one to avoid posing the direct question, asked if everything was alright between him and Kate. Jamie's grunted response convinced them that all was not well.

There was a sense of relief later when they heard the tell-tale tinkle of the phone in the lounge as Jamie picked up the extension in his room. Normally, it annoyed them but on this occasion it brought relief...if they were still talking then all was not lost.

Alone in his room, Jamie went over what he wanted to say, repeating it like a mantra, and then, his plea ready, he dialled Kate's number. She answered almost at once, sounding breathless; and was there was relief in her voice, he wondered...or was he kidding himself?

She was sobbing quietly. 'I'm sorry Jamie,' she sniffed. 'I was so afraid you wouldn't call.'

'Listen Kate,' he started urgently, 'I've been thinking about you all day, planning what to say to you to you now so please, baby, don't stop me...let me get it all out.'

'You sound serious, Jamie,' she sniffed again.

'You leaving me is serious,' he replied quickly. 'And I need to convince you that you can't...we love each other.'

'It's not just about you and me, Jamie,' she interrupted and heard his deep sigh.

'I know that, sweetheart...I know that. Lauren is your first priority, and I accept that,' he continued, trying to follow the argument he had formulated earlier. 'But I can love her too...you have to believe that.'

Kate was torn. Lauren *was* her priority but her love for this man had reached a height she had never believed possible. Lauren had suffered too because of Tom's drinking, deprived of both her father and her mother and Kate knew she had to be her mother again. But could she do that and still have Jamie? She believed him when he said he could love Lauren too, but it wasn't as simple as that...she wished it were. Tom was still Lauren's father and, if he stopped drinking, wouldn't he want to see his child again? Part of her hoped that he would...not because she still loved him, but for Lauren's sake. And the consequences would be unbearable; for all of them. She knew how Jamie felt about Tom and she knew too how Tom would react to another man taking his place...both as her husband and as Lauren's father. There would be endless arguments, fights, quarrels and rows, all of which would put her relationship with Jamie under intolerable strain...leading, inevitably, to a bitter finale. And yet, she wanted Jamie so much. 'I do believe you, Jamie, and I know you'd make a good father...but can't you see the pressure we would be under? I don't think we could survive it...and I'm scared we'll end up hating each other. That would kill me.'

'Oh Kate, Kate,' Jamie responded forlornly. 'No matter what, I'll never hate you. You're my life, don't you realise that. I'm not giving up on us.'

'I'll never give up on us either, baby...I don't want anyone else.'

'Then give me a chance. You said you'd think about it but don't just do it for me, do it for us. Please sweetheart, *really* think about it.'

'I'm doing nothing else, Jamie. I am thinking about us...and I'm thinking about you; I want what's best for Lauren and what's best for you...because I love you both.' Her sobbing started again as she wrestled with the burden of it all and Jamie's heart broke.

Chapter 19

Friday, March 24ᵗʰ 1967 (Good Friday)

Kate left Glasgow in the rain, her father's little red Austin 1300 loaded with all her worldly goods in two suitcases and a selection of cardboard cartons. Her brother Harry sat in the front beside their father and Kate cocooned herself in the back, wrapped in a coat of melancholy, feeling that part of her had died. Her father and brother attempted to cheer her up, tried to involve her in conversation, told her about Lauren, but she sat in silence watching the grey east end buildings of Glasgow pass by outside but seeing nothing. Her mind was with Jamie. She had given him her decision the night before and she could still feel the pain that had radiated down the phone line to her. He had pleaded, begged even, and had then fallen into silence. She prayed that he would be alright, that she could live with the consequences of what she had done and that it didn't turn out to be the biggest mistake of her life.

It was almost an hour before she started to come out of her shell and then the tears came in a gush. She had been fighting against them from the moment she pulled the door closed at Copland Place but now the dam burst. Neither her father nor her brother knew the cause of her grief but assumed it was the breakup of her marriage. Tom Maxwell hadn't been at home when they had arrived but Kate's father, a shrewd judge of character, had discovered a hoard of empty bottles and had taken a quick peek into the room Kate said Tom used. That had confirmed his worst fears but he said nothing, simply pulled the door firmly closed and returned to comfort his daughter. Inside, he felt a strange mix of emotions; rage, anger, sympathy and despair…and a feeling of having let Kate down.

The story started to trickle out from Kate as they passed the border and drove south through Cumbria and by the time the Austin turned onto the A1 at Scotch Corner, Stan and Harry Edwards knew almost all there was to know about the breakup of her marriage…but they still didn't know that her tears weren't about that. They knew nothing of her love for Jamie Raeburn.

*

Good Friday was anything but good for Jamie. He had been tempted to miss work that morning but it was better to be active than to sit around and mope, he decided. Work had been tortuous; his mind had been far from focused and he had burned himself a couple of times, though not seriously. He cried briefly behind his mask, grateful for the privacy the steel helmet and visor gave him, as his angst engulfed him. Why, he kept asking? She loved him; he knew she did, so why? Where had he gone wrong? He wondered where she was, what she was thinking and if she regretted her decision. At the end he had accepted her decision stoically, realizing he couldn't change it. Lauren was the deciding factor and it was better that his, and he hoped her, heart was broken than that she feel she had failed Lauren.

Kate called him that evening. It hadn't been her intention to call him so soon, better, she thought, to give him time, but her loneliness and despair were almost unbearable. The call had been awkward; what else should she have expected, she reflected? And she could still hear the hurt in his voice. But he still loved her…it was in everything he said, every nuance of every phrase. But she learned something else too...she had to let him go, set him free. His parting words, "I love you", tore her apart and she cried herself to sleep with Lauren snuggled tightly in her arms.

Jamie had been unprepared for the call and it had exacerbated his unhappiness. It also convinced him that Kate regretted it but she still saw it as the "right" thing to do. That didn't help and he couldn't accept the idea of "being free" as Kate had put it. He didn't want to be free. He'd been there, during the hiatus in his life between his split from Carol and meeting with Kate...and it wasn't all it was cracked up to be. He didn't want to go back to being the Jamie that had existed then; too much booze, too many one night stands and too many confrontations. Kate had changed him...and he wanted her back.

Saturday morning dawned brightly and Jamie awoke early after a difficult night. After Kate's call he had joined his parents and told them all that had transpired. Much of it had come as a shock to them but, strangely, his father seemed to have suspected something and sat up late with him, talking. During the tale his mother had remained quiet, hurt mainly by his feeling unable to tell her about Kate's situation earlier, and as he spoke he realised he was making excuses for her, defending her against any criticism his mother might decide to levy. When he thought about that later he realised the sole reason for doing so was the hope that one day they would be together again. When his mother had eventually spoken Jamie had been consumed with guilt for not being honest with her before. Her words were not what he had expected and it was clear that Kate still held a cherished spot in his mother's affections. To Jamie, it appeared almost as if she admired Kate for what she had done. The sting in the tail for Jamie, however, was the fact that if he had been honest earlier his mother would have supported his efforts to keep Kate with him and that thought tortured him for the rest of the night.

Saturday was no less painful than Friday had been. He remembered early on that he didn't have Kate's telephone number in Calverton – she had always phoned him at Christmas time - nor did he have an address for her. He cursed himself for his stupidity. That afternoon, wanting to be alone, he took the Triumph for a run, racing down the A82 past Duntocher, Dumbarton, Renton and Alexandria and along the western shore of Loch Lomond, to Luss, attempting to clear his head. The roads were busier than usual with Easter holiday traffic and he wove dangerously in and out of the convoys of slow cars, easing back on his speed only when forced to do so, in an effort to vent his frustration. As a remedy it didn't work. If anything, he became more and more confused and his mind returned, again and again, to the hope that Kate would return to him.

Sitting alone on the loch shore at Luss, oblivious to the crowds of visitors milling around him, and gazing across the flat calm and glassy waters of the loch to the mountains beyond, he reached a decision. Quickly returning to the bike he fired it into life and set off on the return journey to Glasgow, following the low road this time, the A814, which would take him through Clydebank and on to the Clyde Tunnel, his destination fixed in his mind. As he sped past John Brown's yard the giant bulk of the Q.E.II towered above the high walls casting deep, cold shadows over Glasgow Road. A shiver ran down Jamie's spine and he wondered, fleetingly, if it was the cold of the shadow or the coldness of loneliness which caused it.

Less than fifteen minutes later he emerged from the Clyde Tunnel at Linthouse and turned the big bike towards the Fairfield Shipyard, Govan and Ibrox and ultimately to Kate's home in Copland Place. It was approaching four o'clock, with only a couple more hours of sunlight remaining, when he pulled to a halt outside number 14. Everything appeared normal; the lounge curtains pulled back allowing him to see into the room itself. It appeared to be deserted but his sixth sense told him someone was inside. He looked to the floor above, the bedroom, and the curtains were similarly wide open but again there was no sign of life.

He sat for a while, listening to the ticking sound of the bike's hot engine as it cooled and contemplating his next move, then heaved the machine onto its stand and dismounted. At the Copland Road end of the cul–de–sac a group of small boys were playing football in the street, passing the ball around skillfully and using the dwarf walls fronting the gardens to beat opponents, smacking the ball off of it and controlling the rebound as they skipped past. Two piles of jackets and sweaters sat in the middle of the road as the goal which was being guarded, fairly well, by a portly boy of about nine. The boys noticed him watching and stopped playing, returning his look suspiciously. He grinned, took a cigarette from his pocket and lit it with his Zippo lighter, then dismounted from the bike and walked purposefully up the garden path as the boys resumed their game. One thing was certain, they would remember him, he thought.

Standing on the doorstep he hammered the door with his fist...three loud, distinct knocks. There was no sign of life and he tried again, battering his hand against the wooden panel again and again but still there was no response. 'Why should I expect anyone to be here?' he mumbled to himself? Kate was now in Calverton and Tom Maxwell, for all he knew, had gone with her. That had been her intention after all, he remembered, but again his sixth sense told him it hadn't worked out that way. He stepped off the path and walked through the weeds to the bay window, peering into the sitting room and straining to see through to the dining area beyond. Suddenly, he heard the sound of the lock being turned and stepped back onto the doorstep just as the door swung open.

A man, or what Jamie imagined had once passed for a man, with a gaunt, jaundiced face and eyes screwed tightly shut against the glare of the sinking sun, stood framed in the doorway. Jamie looked at him coldly, trying to hide his shock. This creature had to be Tom Maxwell, Kate's husband, and Jamie couldn't rationalise this fact in his mind. His hair was greasy, matted and tangled and he had many days growth of beard on his face. His clothes were wrinkled and stained, as though he had been sleeping in them, and his shirt, once white Jamie imagined, was now grey and covered in food and drink stains. The smell of stale alcohol on the man's breath and the distinct, tart smells of urine, faeces and body odour were almost overpowering. A brown tinted stain covered both legs of his creased and wrinkled fawn trousers, from crotch to knee, indicating the source of the obnoxious smell. Jamie wrinkled his nose in disgust.

'Wha' you want?' the man slurred incoherently, swaying precariously and holding onto the doorframe for support while trying to focus his eyes on Jamie. How could Kate have loved this wanker, Jamie pondered angrily?

'I'm looking for a Mrs. Maxwell, Mrs. Kate Maxwell,' Jamie replied and watched the man's expression change with the mention of his wife's name. His eyes narrowed warily, suspiciously, as Jamie's words registered in his drink sodden brain.

'Who are you?' Maxwell demanded, his speech still slurred but his brain beginning to function, albeit slowly. And then, in a heartbeat, his expression changed again, anger replacing his bewilderment. 'It's you!' he cried, as though suddenly enlightened. 'You're the guy who's been fucking my wife.' His voice grew louder, angrier, but there was despair in it as well as anger.

The footballers, hearing the commotion, had stopped playing and were watching the drama unfold. Jamie looked down the street towards them and decided to steer clear of confrontation. He wanted a telephone number or Kate's address and he wouldn't get either if Maxwell hung onto the belief that he was Kate's lover. 'What the fuck are you on pal?' he fired back at him. 'I'm only here because my sister asked me to come to see if I could get an address or a number for her,' Jamie lied easily. 'Your wife borrowed money from her...and my sister wants it back, so get a fuckin' grip.'

Tom Maxwell stared blankly back at him, his eyes glazing over again and his vacuous expression returning. The lie appeared to have worked but it produced another problem. Believing now that Jamie wasn't the one fooling around with his wife, his mind had slipped back into neutral and Jamie's words were no longer penetrating his drink saturated brain.

'So, is she here?' Jamie persisted, 'and if not, where can I find her?'

'Who are...what do you want?' Maxwell repeated, seemingly confused again and looking at Jamie as if seeing him for the first time.

'Kate...Maxwell...money...for...my...sister,' Jamie said, enunciating each word singly as if speaking to a retarded child. 'I want an address.'

'She's not here, she's gone,' Maxwell mumbled miserably and began to eye Jamie suspiciously once more. 'And you can fuck off too,' he muttered.

Jamie stared at him malevolently until Maxwell averted his eyes. He needed to get inside the house, try to find something that would let him get to her. He looked out to the roadway. The small boys had resumed their game and had lost interest in the disturbance and there was no one else about. Maxwell tried to close the door, swaying precariously as he did so, but Jamie jammed his booted foot inside the doorframe and forced it back. Throwing Maxwell off balance, he forced his way into the hallway, pushing Maxwell ahead of him. They entered the living room, Jamie still pushing and Maxwell glaring at him, his eyes wild.

'So where is she?' Jamie demanded again. '*Where* has she gone?'

'She's not here; I told you...she's left me.' Maxwell started to weep before breaking down completely and staggering backwards to fall on the couch. Jamie looked at the pathetic creature lying scrunched up in a ball in front of him, arms wrapped around his head, but he felt no pity for the man. He left Maxwell lying where he had fallen and made his way through into the kitchen, searching for anything that would point him to Kate. There was nothing. The bedrooms were next. He made his way upstairs to Kate's room, the room he had almost begun to regard as "their" bedroom, strangely afraid of what he might find there, but it was empty and the bed made up. Nothing had been disturbed. He searched the wardrobe. All of Kate's clothing was gone and as his eyes swept over to the dressing table he saw that her makeup, lipsticks and perfumes had been cleared as well. The chest of drawers was likewise empty. Next, he moved to the second bedroom but the smell that met him when he opened the door repulsed him, making him gag, and he shut it quickly. The thought of searching in there was too much and he wondered how anyone could live in a state such as that. Finally, having already given up hope, he checked the bathroom before returning downstairs to the lounge.

Maxwell was where he had left him, sitting now, shoulders slumped and his eyes red rimmed by crying. Jamie felt anger well up in him again and he wanted to hurt Maxwell now, to punish him...but what good would that do, he asked himself? He gripped him by his shirt front and hauled him up to glare into the man's face. Maxwell averted his eyes. 'Where can I find Kate?' Jamie demanded again, shaking him roughly. He had given up all presence now and it slowly began to dawn on Maxwell, even in his advanced state of drunkenness, that his first thought on seeing Jamie had been correct. This was his wife's lover.

'I knew there was someone else,' he slurred, all fight gone out of him. 'Why, Kate...why?' he muttered incoherently, his voice trailing off.

Jamie shook his head in disgust. 'You honestly expected her to stay with you?' he retorted scathingly. 'Have you had a good look at yourself recently? You're a dribbling wreck...and don't kid yourself, I didn't take her from you, you gave her away...*and* your daughter.' he spat viciously, watching the reality of his words sink in. 'So I'll ask you again; where is she?'

Maxwell started crying again, his shoulders shuddering and the tears coursing down his grime stained cheeks. There was still a lot of self-pity in him but not, so far as Jamie could see, any self-loathing and without that the guy was going nowhere. 'You can't...you can't find her,' he muttered and Jamie detected defiance. 'She's gone back to her mother...asked me to go with her,' he added, now wanting to hurt this man who had caused him so much grief. 'But I didn't go...I knew she was playing around.'

'Did you hurt her?' Jamie asked menacingly and watched Maxwell shrink back from him. There was terror in his eyes and for the first time Jamie could smell the fear in him.

'No, no,' he spluttered, we argued...she pushed me, slapped me...and I lashed out. I pushed her away from me and she fell...but that's all. She was alright, I swear.'

Jamie drew Maxwell's face to within inches of his own, the man's foul breath wafting into his face. 'If I find out you're lying and you've hurt her, I'll come back and I'll kill you, you useless piece of shit,' he hissed viciously. 'And that's not a threat...it's a fuckin' promise.'

He pushed Maxwell away then and watched, callously, as he crumpled back onto the settee in a broken heap. Standing in the lounge doorway and looking down on the wreck that was Tom Maxwell, Jamie realised they were both losers. Kate had gone and for that he was as much to blame as Maxwell. Why hadn't he taken her from this hell hole earlier? Why couldn't she believe that he loved her and would look after her and her child? But he thought he was beginning to understand why; all Kate had seen, all she had learned of him, showed Jamie Raeburn the hard man...the guy who took nothing in life too seriously and who treated it all like a bad joke. He cursed himself softly.

Darkness was falling as he left the house, leaving the front door open to the elements. The small boys were gone and lights were coming on in windows up and down the street, but the light was going out of Jamie's life.

Chapter 20

One Week Later.

Jamie parked the Bonneville and looked around. Everything seemed just as it had been the Saturday before; the same small boys played football in the street though this time the goalposts were designated by chalk marks on the road. There was an argument going on about a shot that appeared to Jamie to have been just inside the chalk marks but the goalkeeper, the same little fat lad, was arguing vociferously that it had missed. There was heaviness in the air, malevolence even. A roar went up from Ibrox Park which sat just behind the houses where Rangers were playing Dundee and judging by the wall of noise that engulfed him, Rangers had just scored.

He sighed and looked at his watch; 3.17pm on 1st April, April Fool's Day, he smiled grimly...but who was the fool? Another roar went up from the stadium, not so loud this time so either Rangers had just missed or Dundee had scored but he realised that he really didn't care. Since meeting Kate he had lost interest in football...and if he was honest, he had lost interest in most things. His life had simply revolved around her. He sighed again and realised that sighing was becoming a habit. Further along the street, three little girls were playing with prams and dolls...pretending to be little mothers. Little boys with footballs and little girls with dolls...stereotypes, he thought, but who would have it any other way.

He fished out a Lucky Strike and flicked his lighter, continuing to survey the street as he guided the flame to the tip of the cigarette. He was smoking heavily again...too heavily, Kate would have said. He shook his head sadly and then, finally satisfied that nothing was out of place, he dismounted from the Triumph and walked casually towards the house. The rusty hinges of the garden gate creaked in protest as he pushed it open then made his way over the broken paving stones to the door. As he reached out to knock he noticed it was slightly ajar; not open as such...more like it hadn't been closed properly. He stopped, listening intently, but there was nothing to indicate anything out of place and only the background noise of several thousand football supporters, the boisterous shouting of the small boys and the joyous laughter of the girls disturbing the calm.

Tentatively, he placed his hand on the door and pushed it open. There was a loud creak as the heavy wooden door, like the gate outside, swung inwards on its worn hinges, making him cringe. He waited, listening for movement and sounds of life, but there were none. He scanned the dim hallway...and again there were no signs of trouble. Taking a final look around outside, he stepped into the hall, picking out the small table against the wall on his left and the mirror above it. That was where Kate had placed the flowers he had brought on their last night together...in the little white vase, he remembered, then stopped. On his last visit, the week before, the vase had still been there with the flowers dry and wilting. Maxwell didn't strike him as house-proud so where were they now?

He edged forward a couple of paces and found what was left of the vase scattered across the floor; tiny shards of white porcelain on the threadbare carpet, glittering in the light from the open door, small, sharp slivers of pottery left behind when larger pieces had been hastily removed. The first sign of trouble since his last visit or simply evidence of Maxwell's drunken carelessness? Or had Kate returned and they had argued? Hope was suddenly revived...maybe Maxwell had confronted her after his visit the week before. But still the house was silent with only the sound of the Venetian blinds in the kitchen rattling in the draft.

He waited again, breathing deeply, trying to control the tension building in him. A faint scent of Kate's perfume lingered in the air, reminding him of her and why he had come back. He shook his head slowly to clear it. All that mattered to him now was that Kate was alright. He walked slowly up the hall, his boots crunching on the small pieces of broken porcelain. The living room door was closed and the relative silence which surrounded him only served to heighten his unease. Finally, he pushed the door gently and as it swung inwards he was able to look towards the front of the house and the bay window.

He gasped sharply, the scene before him like something from a horror movie. The living room had been trashed; the standard lamp lay smashed on the floor, the light fitting dangled precariously from the ceiling rose, its shade broken and its bulb smashed. Ornaments were scattered across the floor and the back of the easy chair nearest to him was torn, a jagged rent in the fabric ran from top to bottom, and it was bloodstained. But the silence continued, un-nerving him further. Pushing the door further, as far as it would go on its hinges, he stepped slowly into the room and turned right, towards the arch separating the living room from the dining area and the kitchen beyond, before releasing the handle.

One more step and his view extended through the arch and the sight which greeted him now made his stomach churn. Maxwell, for it could only be Maxwell, was sitting at the far end of the dining table with his torso slumped across the table top and his face down on the veneered surface, but it was his hands that caught Jamie's attention. They were stretched out on the table, palms down, with blood seeping from beneath each and, looking closer, Jamie could see the heads of two large nails protruding from the flesh on the back of each. The job had been carried out none too carefully, by the look of it, and Maxwell's hands were swollen and bruised where the hammer had struck him rather than the nails. Jamie fought back the urge to retch.

Suddenly, he heard movement behind him and as it registered in his mind a figure, a man, emerged from the kitchen, an evil grin spread across his pudgy, pock marked face.

'Well, well, well,' the man said icily. 'If it isn't lover boy...come to join the party?' he laughed caustically.

Jamie recognised him instantly as one of the men at Kate's door a couple of weeks earlier...the loan-shark's heavy brigade. He had been leaving that day just as Jamie arrived and he had eyed Jamie with open contempt as they passed at the gate. His cheap, flash suit and his callous expression gave away the nature of his "profession"...a hard man, confident in his ability to handle people and happy to meet out violence when needed...and even when it wasn't. There had been two of them, he remembered, and Kate had been freaked out as she sobbed her way through the story. Loan sharks were relentless in pursuit of debt and Jamie prayed now that Kate *hadn't* come back.

Jamie made to move but immediately he was pinioned from behind, both arms held in a steely grip. The second man, the young one, he realised immediately, cursing his stupidity. 'Let go,' he growled angrily but the response was a cruel laugh and a tightening of the grip on Jamie's arms, the man's fingers digging painfully into his taught muscles.

'You're no' in a position tae gie orders,' the thug behind hissed into his ear and gripped him even more tightly. Jamie grimaced and allowed his shoulders to sag, trying to give the impression of being cowed. The man laughed and Jamie could smell tobacco from his breath. 'Told ye,' he chuckled to his partner. 'He's jist a fuckin' pussy.' Both men started to laugh.

It had to be then, or never. Slowly, so as not to draw attention to what was coming next, Jamie lifted his right foot six inches off the ground then brought it crashing down heavily, the steel heel of his boot crushing the metatarsal bones of the thug's right foot. There was a loud scream, cut short when Jamie's head, thrown viciously backwards, connected with the cartilage of the thug's nose. A gurgling sound came from the man's lips and the grip on Jamie's arms loosened. That was his cue. Spinning quickly, before either man could react, he took hold of the injured man's arm and propelled him, head first, against the edge of the door. He held onto the thug for an instant, supporting him, and then let him drop to the floor in a crumpled heap.

The older man was moving, picking up the hammer from the table and advancing on him menacingly. Jamie stared at him, a cold smile on his face, and moved his boot over the fallen man's throat. 'You take another step,' he hissed, 'an' I'll break his fuckin' neck.' The man stopped dead and held up his hands in a gesture of surrender but his angry, vicious eyes were sending out a different message.

'That wisnae too bright son,' he said. 'Ye've nae idea whit ye're getting yersel intae.'

'Oh, I've got a pretty shrewd idea,' Jamie laughed coldly.

The man shook his head with a hard smile. Clearly, he disagreed, but he decided to settle for the placatory approach. 'Listen son,' he started. 'We're jist doin' a job...this fucker here,' he continued, grabbing Tom Maxwell by the hair and yanking his head up off the table. 'He owes oor boss money...big money. We've no' got any argument wi' you.'

Jamie looked over at Maxwell's limp head. The man's eyes were screwed tightly shut and his face was contorted with pain even though he was, mercifully, anaesthetised to some degree by alcohol. For the second time in a week Jamie found it hard to believe that Kate had married this scarecrow.

'And where's his wife?' Jamie demanded, praying that Kate hadn't returned and that these men hadn't already harmed her. The man beneath his foot groaned, coming round. 'Quickly,' Jamie continued, lifting his foot again, the threat obvious. 'Or your pal here loses all his teeth.'

The older man looked at his pal nervously. He wasn't used to this, people didn't fight back. And worse, he was just the "negotiator"; the blunt instrument was on the floor beneath Jamie's boot. If the boss found out about this shambles there would be hell to pay. He jumped as his mate on the floor moaned once more.

'Time's running out,' Jamie hurried him.

'Ah don't *fuckin'* know...that's why we're still here,' the gangster shouted. 'We were jist huvin' a word wi' her man when you turned up. Listen pal, a' we want is the money.'

Jamie laughed frostily. Bending down, he gripped the collar of the recovering thug's jacket and used it to propel the man's head against the door a second time then dropped him back onto the floor. 'Your pal's gonnae have a sore head...but at least he's still got his teeth,' he said with a malicious grin.

'You're a *dead* man son,' the older guy said with outward calm but his expression showed fear bubbling away close to the surface.

'Listen auld yin,' Jamie said in a voice laced with menace. 'I don't give a shit about that prick,' he continued, nodding towards Maxwell, 'but as you've already guessed, his wife means a lot to me…so just convince me that she's not here, or so help me, I'll kick the livin' shit out of both of you.'

'Ah *fuckin'* told ye…she's no' here,' the man whined. There was a cold sweat on his body now and he imagined this must be how his victims usually felt. This fucker was something else, he realised, and he seemed to have no fear whatsoever. Worse, he looked more than capable of handling both of them, he thought nervously.

Jamie knelt down and fished around in the unconscious man's jacket, removing the hoodlum's wallet. Opening it ostentatiously for the other man's benefit, he pulled out the man's driving license. 'Robert Hood,' he read aloud, waving the tiny red folder in the air. 'Great name for a guy in your line of work,' he laughed coldly. 'And it's got just what I'm looking for…his address,' he said, smiling. 'Now, give me yours.' He held out his hand.

The thug hesitated for a moment. 'Fuck off,' he mumbled, defiantly.

Jamie laughed, sending a shiver down the man's spine. 'You don't really want me to come over and take it from you, do you?' he suggested, grinning. The implied threat was enough and the man quickly brought out his wallet and threw it over, watching belligerently as Jamie caught it one handed and then leafed through it, finally extracting the man's National Insurance Card. He smiled frostily and tossed the wallet back.

'Christ, it gets better,' he laughed, spluttering as he read the details. 'William Hardman! Robert Hood and William Hardman…are you guys for real? he continued, laughing aloud. It was a struggle to regain his composure now. 'Christ, you two are made for this game…or did you pick these names specially; like stage names?' he snickered. Hardman looked back anxiously. He wasn't finding any of this funny. 'Okay,' Jamie continued, finally controlling his mirth. 'That's phase one out of the road…now I know where you and this dick live,' he said, prodding Hood with his toe. 'So now we can move to stage two.'

Jamie backed away carefully towards the telephone which sat, apparently undamaged, on the coffee table in front of the fireplace, his eyes fixed unwaveringly on Hardman. He picked up the handset and almost sighed with relief when the welcoming purr of dial tone filled his ear. His eyes flitting between the dial and Hardman across the room, he dialled Conor Whelan's number from memory and prayed that the American was at home. The ring tone came back down the line, just loud enough for the hardman to hear, before the call was answered by Mary Campbell.

'Mary,' he said quickly. 'Is James there?' The tone of his voice and the use of Conor's middle name told her that Jamie was in some sort of trouble.

'Yes, he is,' she replied instantly. 'I'll get him.'

There was silence for a moment and Jamie filled it by gazing stonily at the unhappy enforcer. Hardman returned his look warily, unused to being in this position, and found himself intimidated. It wasn't the first time…the boss had that effect on him sometimes, but this guy was different.

Conor came on the line a few seconds later. 'Jamie, what's up kid?' His voice came down the line loud enough for Hardman to hear and his accent was clearly American.

'I've got a wee situation here, James,' Jamie replied, sticking to Conor's middle name to signal the gravity of the situation. 'It involves that little nurse I met a few months ago. Her husband has been stupid enough to borrow money from a loan shark,' he went on, 'and I've got myself involved. I want to take out a wee bit of life assurance,' he added, looking directly at Hardman who was staring back at him, puzzled as to where this was going. 'I'm going to give you two names and addresses,' Jamie continued. 'And if anything happens to me, anything at all, or to the girl, then I want these two guys sorted…permanently. Can you fix that?'

Hardman studied him, bemused. Jamie's voice had changed completely. The working class Glaswegian he had been dealing with at the beginning had disappeared and now he was listening to a posh, middle class bastard from the West End. How can he do that, he wondered? Up until now he had thought they were dealing with just another wee Glasgow ned but he had got it wrong. *There's more to this guy*, he warned himself, *be careful*.

That thought coincided with Conor's evil laugh as he picked up on Jamie's lead. 'I can fix it right now if you want kid…I'll send over a couple of my boys,' he said. 'Where you at?' His voice was casual, matter of fact, which had the effect of worrying the hapless William Hardman even more. Sending a couple of his boys sounded like something he did every day and a shudder ran down his spine. His fear was showing openly now.

Jamie saw it and smiled coldly, his eyes never leaving Hardman's face. 'No James, I think they've got the message,' he said quietly, grinning contemptuously at Hardman as relief, of a sort, flooded the man's face.

'Okay kid. Keep in touch. Call soon,' Conor laughed and hung up.

Jamie replaced the handset and gazed over at the now clearly frightened Hardman, pleased that the man couldn't hold his look. He imagined Hardman was seething on the inside but fear was keeping him in line.

'Right Willie…or is it Bill or Billy?' Jamie started, but Hardman just stared back at him sullenly. 'Whatever,' Jamie shrugged. 'Anyway, I think this is what's called a Mexican standoff,' he laughed.

'So whit dae ye want?' Hardman asked bitterly, breaking his silence.

'I want all of this to go away,' Jamie replied simply. 'You go back to your boss and you tell him that this wanker,' he paused, indicating Maxwell again, 'and his wife, have disappeared…because as far as you're concerned, she already has and he's about to.' He paused again to allow Hardman to come to terms with that part before carrying on. 'You just tell your boss you can't find them and he'll need to write it off. Simple. How you explain this clown's wee accident is up to you,' he finished, prodding Bobby Hood again with his boot.

'Simple? Ur you aff yer fuckin' heid? Ah cannae dae that,' Hardman whined.

'Of course you can,' Jamie laughed softly. 'Or would you prefer my American friends to pay you and Bobby a wee visit?'

Hardman swallowed hard and tried to face Jamie down but the menace in Jamie was unmistakable…and he remembered clearly what the Yank had said and how he had said it. He could imagine what would happen if he and Bobby Hood didn't go along with this. From Jamie's point of view, that was the key. Fear is usually born out of imagination and what you *think* will happen, and Hardman thought that Conor, or James as he knew him, would snuff him and Bobby Hood out without compunction…like crushing beetles under his foot. He looked away, defeated.

'Good,' Jamie said, taking his silence as acquiescence. 'Now, before you go, take the nails out of that poor bastard's hands. He'll be leavin' with me an' he won't be comin' back, so there's nothing left for your boss, here…got it?'

Hardman nodded sullenly and moved forward to the table, picking up the hammer again and slipping its claws round the first nail. Tom Maxwell moaned loudly as Hardman levered the hammer against his damaged hand, sending a pain searing through him. Hardman forced the nail out, moving it viciously from side to side with the hammer until it worked free of the table, taking some pleasure out of inflicting more pain on Maxwell. He would rather be inflicting it on the young fucker facing him, he mused, but that wasn't going to happen, so he would settle for venting his spleen on Maxwell instead. Jamie read the look in the man's eyes and smiled icily, doing nothing as Hardman repeated the process on Maxwell's other hand. When this nail too was free of the table and had been pulled roughly through the wound in Maxwell's hand, he tossed the hammer and blood stained nail back onto the table, smiling surreptitiously as the vibration made Maxwell moan. He looked at Jamie then. 'You'd better leave Glasgow as well,' he said, endeavouring to reassert some authority but he knew as he said it that it was futile.

Jamie laughed at it. 'Don't make empty threats, Willie,' he retorted. 'You know what'll happen to you if anything happens to me…and some of these American boys are just back from Vietnam so they can probably teach you an' Bobby here a thing or two about killin' an' hurtin' people.' He waited a moment to allow that to sink in. 'Now, pick up this piece of shit and fuck off,' he finished, prodding the unconscious Hood again.

Hardman looked down at his hapless colleague. 'Gie us a brek,' he whined. 'How the fuck dae ye expect me tae lift him?'

Jamie laughed. 'I'll give you a hand if you like.' Hardman looked at him in disbelief and Jamie knew he had misunderstood. 'I don't mean literally,' he continued, laughing still. Leaving Hardman with Maxwell and the unconscious Hood, Jamie disappeared into the kitchen. The sound of running water came through to Hardman and then Jamie reappeared, carrying a basin of water firmly in both hands. Without saying a word he walked to the prone body of Bobby Hood and tipped the contents over him in one quick movement. Hood began to choke and splutter and spat water out of his mouth, cursing. He sat up unsteadily, the water trickling down across his face. His jacket and his trousers around his groin were soaked and he was sitting now in the middle of a puddle. Rubbing his eyes, he looked up at Jamie menacingly. 'I think you'll need to explain the finer points of your predicament to yer pal,' Jamie said casually to Hardman. 'Otherwise he might end up gettin' you both into trouble.' His accompanying smile said it all. 'Right,' he continued, 'you're finished here, so get to fuck.'

Chapter 21

Jamie watched from the window as the two men stumbled down the path, Hardman supporting the heavier man with an arm around his waist and the other's arm draped around his shoulder was struggling and was directing a tirade of abuse at Hood. It was all Hood's fault as far as Hardman was concerned...if he hadn't been so fuckin' complacent allowing Jamie to catch them on the hop they could have sorted him before he'd had a chance to phone that Yank for help. But now the shit really had hit the fan...and he was left to explain the whole fuckin' fiasco to the boss!

Hood, clearly the brawn rather than the brains of the two, was beginning to collect his wits again and his face was infused with anger. His clothes, particularly his shirt and jacket, were soaked through and blood streaming from his nose and a gash above his left eye was dripping onto his white shirt and forming a pretty, pink stain. His right foot, the one Jamie had stamped upon, was throbbing with pain and he couldn't put his weight on it. He wasn't having a good day and scowled sullenly at Hardman as the older man continued to berate him.

Their car, a black Humber Hawk, was parked at the corner with Copland Road about forty yards away and Jamie was surprised he hadn't spotted earlier, when he had arrived but his mind had been on other things at the time. Hardman propped the unsteady Hood against the car while he opened the driver's door and then leaned in to open the rear door from inside. Jamie watched as the two men continued to argue, Hardman doing most of the talking, and he imagined Hood was being enlightened as to the painful reality of the events in number 14.

Hardman tried to get the younger man into the back of the car but Hood shrugged him off angrily and limped heavily around the car to the front passenger seat. Before getting into the vehicle he turned back to look at the house, sensing that Jamie was watching, and his eyes burned with naked hate. Jamie pulled back the net curtains so that the man could see him clearly and stared back at him, his expression stonily cold. Hood didn't have a monopoly on hatred. When he finally did sink into the car he paused, raised his hand thrust his first and second fingers in the air in a classic V sign. "Up yours" the message said but Jamie simply smiled. Robert Hood, he decided, was one guy he didn't particularly want to meet again.

Jamie's thoughts now returned to his remaining problem. Tom Maxwell was unconscious again, slumped in an untidy heap across the table. His face was badly bruised and there was swelling around both eyes. Hardman and Hood obviously enjoyed their work. Jamie surveyed the room, fully taking in the carnage for the first time. As well as the damage to the easy chair and the broken light fittings, the record player wouldn't be playing records again. Add to that the blood stains on the settee and the broken ornaments littering the floor and you got the impression a bomb had hit the place. Jamie shook his head in despair. He was still worried about Kate but at least he knew she had avoided this. What he still didn't know was whether or not Maxwell had hurt her before she left and that was something he intended to find out.

There was a plan forming in his head but to put it into effect he would need Maxwell to be semi-conscious and looking half-human, at least. First, however, he had to speak to Conor who, he knew, would be waiting for a call. Leaving Maxwell where he was Jamie sank into the battered easy chair and picked up the phone. Surprisingly, the easy chair, like the phone, seemed to have survived the worst of Hardman and Hood's visit. Settling back, he dialled the Dunoon number again and Conor answered immediately, his anxiety showing.

'Jamie,' he said immediately, sounding relieved. 'What the hell's goin' on, kid?'

'It's a long story Conor...short version is I need to get a guy out of town and he's in pretty bad shape just now.' It sounded melodramatic, like a scene from an old Western movie.

'Where are you?' the American demanded.

'Ibrox...I'm at Kate's place.'

'Shit Jamie, is she with you?' Conor responded quickly, worried again.

'No, that's all part of the long story. She's gone back home to England...I think,' he replied, the sadness in his voice giving Conor all the clues he needed. 'She's safe there,' he added.

'You think she's gone home?'

'Yeah, well I'm pretty sure,' Jamie said reassuringly. 'She wasn't here when those goons arrived and all her clothes and things are gone.'

'What happened, kid?' Conor probed gently.

'Her maternal instincts kicked in,' Jamie replied.

'Maternal instincts?' Conor paused, confused. 'What? She wants kids and you don't...or am I missing something?'

'You're missing something,' Jamie laughed bitterly. 'She's already got a two year old daughter...and the baby needs her.'

'Shit Jamie, I'm sorry kid,' Conor replied sounding shocked. 'I thought you two were solid.'

'We were Conor, that's the sad part. We still are.'

Silence swallowed them up for a moment before Conor came back, all business. 'So who's the guy you need to get out of town?'

Jamie laughed, unable to keep the bitterness out of his voice when he replied. 'Her husband.'

'Give me the address,' Conor instructed, deciding not to comment on that revelation. 'Stay put and keep the door locked till I get there,' he continued quickly, taking command of the situation. 'I'm leaving now.'

'Bring bandages,' Jamie added before giving him the address.

Replacing the phone handset on its cradle Jamie turned his attention to Maxwell. The man was a mess and looking as he did there was no way Jamie's plan would work. Wearily, he hauled himself to his feet and went through to the kitchen, filled a kettle with water and lit a ring on the gas cooker. He rummaged through the cupboards, finding the usual things; salt, pepper, sugar and some jars of marmalade and jam and, tucked out of sight at the back, a jar of Maxwell House coffee. It might have his name on it, Jamie thought, but he doubted if Maxwell had ever tasted it. One thing was sure in Jamie's mind though; he would have to acquire a taste for it now.

Leaving the kitchen he carried out a quick search of the rest of the house, beginning with Kate's bedroom as before. Nothing had changed, confirming his belief that Kate hadn't returned. Next, he visited the second bedroom, better prepared this time. The stench from the room hadn't abated any in the course of the week...if anything, it was worse. The tightly shut windows made the air fetid and heavy with an obnoxious combination of sweat, stale beer, urine and crap. Jamie gagged, wondering how Kate could have lived next to this but, on reflection, he hadn't noticed the smell when he had spent the nights with her. There had been no outward signs of the state of this room until he had opened the door. Breathing through his mouth rather than his nostrils to lessen the effects of the malodorous stench, he ventured in and searched through the wardrobe and drawers.

From below he heard sound of the kettle coming to the boil, its shrill whistle piercing the quiet of the house. He ignored it and continued to rummage until he found what he was looking for; a reasonably clean shirt, clean underwear and a suit. They had all seen better days and all looked a bit on the big side for Maxwell but they were clean and serviceable...and had all probably fitted Maxwell before the drink took him, he surmised. He grabbed the items in his arms and left the room, shutting the door firmly behind him. '*I should have shut Hardman and Hood in there for a while,*' he murmured to himself, '*that would have sorted them out.*'

Downstairs, he laid out the change of clothes in the living room to air and then went into the kitchen to silence the angry, whistling kettle. He made a large pot of coffee, thick and black, and added several spoonful's of sugar to sweeten it, then took it through to the dining table along with a mug. He placed the pot in front of Maxwell and shook the man roughly but with little effect. Losing patience, he lifted Maxwell's head up off the table, gripping him by his hair, and hit him, open handed, across the cheek. That, at least, brought an instant reaction. Maxwell whimpered and tried to pull away but Jamie held tightly to his hair and shook him roughly until his eyes opened and he began to focus.

The pain returned then. It surged through every nerve ending of his damaged hands and he started to scream, hysterically. It was unrelenting and Jamie knew that if he kept it the police wouldn't be long in arriving. That left him only one option. Hauling Maxwell's head up again he slapped him hard, once on each cheek, and silenced him. The red marks left by his slaps blended in with the bruising already there but the imprint of Jamie fingers on his flesh was clearly visible. If the police arrived now Jamie would have some explaining to do.

Maxwell was looking at him uncomprehendingly, trying to identify him. He looked down at his hands, his expression vacant, and saw the raw, ugly red holes where the nails had pierced them. He was clearly unable to remember or understand what had happened. Finally, he managed to focus on Jamie and saw before him a man a few years younger than himself, with dark, piercing, contempt filled eyes and a sense of familiarity came to him. Where had he seen this man before, he wondered?

'Wha' ha..ppen..ed to me?' he mumbled incoherently, his speech slow, deliberate, disjointed and slurred. 'Who...are...you? I know you, don't I?"

Jamie ignored his questions and poured coffee into the mug, lifting it to Maxwell's mouth. The man turned away, retching, the smell of the thick, treacle like liquid attacking his olfactory senses. 'Drink it,' Jamie insisted, and something in his voice made Maxwell start. He opened his mouth and Jamie poured a large quantity of the hot, sweet coffee down his throat, making him gag. He spluttered and spat some of the black liquid out onto the table, splashing Jamie's jacket.

Jamie eyed him with utter contempt. 'Drink the fuckin' coffee,' he shouted at Maxwell. 'An' do that again and I'll drown you in the fuckin' stuff.'

Maxwell glowered up at him...but he drank the remainder of the coffee in the mug. When he replaced the empty mug on the table, Jamie refilled it. Jamie didn't need to say anything this time, his look was enough. Maxwell lifted the mug in his shaking hands and drank down the contents.

'Keep drinking it,' Jamie ordered. 'As if your life depends on it…and it probably does,' he added ominously. Leaving Maxwell he climbed back upstairs to the bathroom and filled the bath with lukewarm water. When he returned he was pleasantly surprised to find that Maxwell had finished most of the coffee and his eyes were beginning to show signs of life after death.

'Right,' Jamie started on at him again. 'Now get yourself upstairs and reintroduce your body to soap and water…you fuckin' stink!' he continued brutally. 'And I'm not puttin' up with the stench of you any longer.'

'But my hands…' Maxwell whined, lifting them up for Jamie's inspection.

'Cleaning them will probably help…so just get on with it,' he said coldly.

Maxwell was leaving when Jamie passed him the clothes from the bedroom. 'An' when you're finished washing, put these on,' he instructed. The beard would have to go, he thought. 'Do yourself a favour,' he added, 'if you can keep your hands from shakin' for long enough, have a shave; you might just pass for human after that.'

Maxwell took the clothes. If he felt any resentment at the way Jamie was treating him he hid it well. The time passed slowly as Maxwell bathed and Jamie's anxiety grew with each passing minute. If Tweedledum and Tweedledee returned, mob handed, he would be in big trouble…and he knew it. It was now half past four and the football fans would soon stream out of the stadium, their noise covering the sound of anything happening here in the house. He looked anxiously out of the window, repeating this every few minutes, remaining behind the net curtains to avoid being seen. Everything remained quiet, for now at least.

Maxwell hobbled back into the living room, his long hair damp and lank. Every piece of clothing, as Jamie had suspected, hung loosely on his emaciated frame and he looked more like a scarecrow now than before. His shirt hung open, the buttons too intricate to fasten with his injured and shaking hands. Jamie regarded him with an unexpected feeling of pity but it was short lived…all of this was of Maxwell's own making, he reminded himself.

The sound of a big car pulling into the street made Jamie jump and he leapt quickly to the window, his heart beating faster, afraid that the Hardman and Hood were back, but coming to a halt right outside the house was a big black and blue Oldsmobile and lounging in the front was the tall frame of Conor Whelan. Jamie let out a sigh of relief and ran to the front door, throwing it open. The engine was turned off and a degree of peace settled on Copland Place again just as 60,000 plus football supporters greeted the final whistle in Ibrox Stadium with a roar that filled the heavens. Conor hauled himself from the car and turned towards the sound.

Jamie grinned then turned his attention then to the man accompanying his friend, watching in awe as the man pulled himself from the car and stretched. The man was a giant; a big, black giant with a gleaming bald head and a wide grin. 'Fe, fi, fo, fum, I smell the blood of an English man' Jamie laughed, remembering the old fairy tale, and this guy probably could grind bones to make his bread, he thought.

They came into the house, Conor grabbing Jamie in his usual bear hug before introducing his enormous companion.

'This here is Leroy,' he announced. 'I thought it might be a good idea to have him along…he tends to scare trouble away,' he continued with a laugh. The giant stepped forward and offered his hand which Jamie took gladly, grateful that Leroy was on his side.

In the living room, Maxwell sat silently, his face betraying the fear in him. Both Americans looked at him, taking in the bruises and the sunken eyes in his thin, wasted face. Maxwell gazed back at all three, afraid to speak.

'He's been in the wars,' Conor acknowledged grimly. 'They're obviously not nice people.'

'Scum,' Jamie agreed. 'But this clown brought it all down on himself…and Kate, unfortunately.'

'So, what's the plan?' Conor continued, turning away from Maxwell as Leroy began to check out the man's injuries.

'There's an overnight train to London leaves Central Station at 11.00pm tonight. I'm going to get him on it…get him home,' Jamie replied.

Conor look was a study in astonishment. Jamie Raeburn never ceased to amaze him…he was the last of the Knights of the Round Table. 'Why are you doing this, Jamie?' he asked quietly.

Jamie laughed. 'You know something, Conor? I haven't got a fuckin' clue. All I know is that Kate would be distraught if this clown gets killed…and if he stays here, that's exactly what's going to happen,' he said sadly, pausing. 'And there's the kid to think of…she needs a father, even a bad one, as well as her mother. Who knows, he might even stop drinking.'

Conor Whelan looked down at the man. He had met a few alcoholics in his day. Some he even counted as friends…but these men had reached the bottom of the pit and knew it, and they had the strength of character to drag themselves back up. Looking at Maxwell, he didn't think he had it in him.

*

Jamie sat quietly in the tearoom beside the morose frame of Tom Maxwell and looked anxiously around the station concourse. They had left the house at Copland Place just after eight, Conor and Leroy escorting Maxwell in the car while Jamie followed them on the Triumph. They left the vehicles in Gordon Street and Conor had brought Jamie and the hapless Maxwell here to the tearoom while Leroy stood guard at the station entrance. It had all been worked out with military precision. Once inside, Conor left them while he moved the car, fearful that it might draw the bad guys to the station and, without Conor around, Jamie felt exposed. The sight of Leroy lingering near the ticket booths at the main entrance eased his anxiety but there was still a sliver of fear gnawing at his insides. He smiled as the giant glanced over in his direction and caught his eye, winking. Leroy was on the game.

It was reasonably quiet; a few boisterous American sailors wandered past heading for the nightlife but other than that, no one. Jamie looked at the large four faced clock suspended above the concourse. It read 8.45pm and the London sleeper didn't depart until 11.00, though they could board at 10.30, but that still left an hour and forty-five minutes to kill. He laughed grimly...not the best expression given his present situation. He asked himself for the umpteenth time why he was doing this but the answer was always the same...he loved Kate; and if that meant saving the life of the snivelling, dribbling wreck beside him, then so be it.

Conor appeared from the Union Street entrance and sauntered casually to the ticket office. Jamie watched nervously as he approached an empty counter and began talking with the clerk. The transaction was completed quickly and Conor joined Leroy by the Gordon Street entrance. They carefully avoided contact with Jamie and Maxwell and settled to watch. Conor was pretty sure they hadn't been followed but, just in case, they waited, keeping an eye on the ticket clerk. A discrete pound note slipped to the man would buy the destination for the tickets that Conor had purchased, but no one came.

The next hour and a quarter was nerve wracking for Jamie and Tom Maxwell added to his anxiety and frustration by whining about the pain in his heavily bandaged hands. Jamie listened patiently at first but his nerves frayed eventually and he finally gripped Maxwell by his shirt collar and pulled the man's face close to his own. 'Listen arsehole,' he hissed threateningly, 'you're lucky to be alive, so shut the fuck up.'

Maxwell looked at him sullenly and lapsed into silence. An elderly couple, sitting nearby and surrounded by luggage, watched them with a mixture of shock, curiosity and distaste. Jamie returned their look, smiling apologetically but in truth, he couldn't care less what they thought. He pushed himself up from the table and made his way to the counter, returning with two more coffees, black and sweet for Maxwell and white for himself.

'Drink this,' he ordered, placing the cup in front of Maxwell who looked at it with distaste and began to retch. Jamie watched him impassively, feeling no sympathy for him and knowing that things would get worse for him before they even started to get better. The alcohol was working its way slowly out of his system and, from what Kate had told him, Maxwell hadn't been dry for weeks, if not months. The delirium tremors, the dreaded D.T's would start soon, the hangover of all hangovers. Serves the bastard right, Jamie thought, but he knew that his own already stretched patience would wear thin when the effects of all that kicked in.

At ten twenty Conor parted from Leroy and joined them. He pulled out a seat and sat down beside Jamie. The cafeteria was deserted now, the old couple having departed ten minutes earlier, and the staff was making noises about clearing up for the night.

Conor laid the tickets on the table in front of Jamie. 'One return, one single,' he said. 'The station is clean Jamie, no one followed...do you really want to do this?'

Jamie smiled his stony smile. '"Want" isn't the word I'd use Conor, but I *have* to do it...for Kate.'

The American shook his head slowly. 'What does she see in this?' he asked, looking across at Tom Maxwell with undisguised disgust.

Jamie looked down at the now stirring Maxwell. 'Love is strange Conor...love is strange.'

They rose slowly and Jamie leaned over to shake Maxwell's shoulder roughly. 'Come on, time to go,' he said harshly, pushing the untouched, and now cold, cup of black coffee in front of the man. 'And drink this first,' he commanded. Maxwell wrinkled his nose. 'Drink it or I'll pour it down your fuckin' throat,' Jamie threatened again. Maxwell was growing used to his threats, none of which he had carried out, but Jamie's tone advised him that compliance was best. He picked up the cup and swallowed the cold, black liquid, gagging as before.

Conor laughed coldly. 'Not as palatable as beer or a big glass of Jack Daniels, but better for you in your state,' he opined.

Between them, Jamie and Conor dragged Maxwell to his feet and, as Conor held the man steady, Jamie lifted the small bag containing Maxwell's clothes and swung it over his shoulder then together, they escorted Maxwell across the concourse and onto the platform.

'I'll help you get this guy on board and then I'll wait on the platform till you're on your way...if anyone follows, I'll climb back on board,' Conor said reassuringly.

'Thanks Conor, I appreciate all this.'

The big American smiled broadly and gave Jamie his usual bear hug. 'Nada,' Conor smiled. 'There's no need kid; I'm still on this planet thanks to you. Now, let's get this guy onto the train and into a bunk.'

Working together they manhandled Maxwell up onto the train and found the compartment, lowering his thin and fragile body onto the lower bunk. Jamie had suggested putting him on top but Conor, more worldly wise, pointed out the dangers of gravity. 'If this guy has an accident, kid...you don't want to be beneath him,' he advised, and Jamie grinned gratefully.

With Maxwell settled Conor took Jamie back out into the corridor. He hugged him again, Jamie more and more like a younger brother to him now. 'You're a big guy, Jamie Raeburn,' he said sincerely. 'I hope the little lady appreciates what you're doing.'

Jamie smiled wryly and shrugged. Conor held out his hand. 'Almost forgot,' he chirped. 'I'll need the keys for the bike. Leroy's going to follow me to your place and I'll put the keys through the door...your Mom knows, doesn't she?'

Jamie dug out the keys and handed them over. 'Yes, she knows you're dropping off the keys...but not what I'm doing, so if they're still awake when you get there, you don't know anything, okay?'

'Don't know anything about what?' the big American joked. 'Listen kid, phone me when you get there and let me know when your train gets back here...I'll come pick you up.'

'There's no need, you and Leroy have done enough already,' Jamie protested. 'Thank the big guy for me.'

But Conor was having none of it. 'No argument kid,' he declared. 'Phone me.' Jamie nodded in acquiescence. 'Good. Okay kid; look after yourself...and good luck.'

Conor turned away and opened the carriage door, stepping down onto the deserted platform. He looked up and down the length of it and then, satisfied, gave Jamie a thumb up sign and strolled off towards the main concourse. Jamie leaned out of the window, watching him go. Conor stopped at the ticket barrier, still alert, but nothing untoward took place and, as the train pulled away from the platform, he waved. Jamie smiled and returned the gesture.

Suddenly, Jamie felt exhausted. The adrenalin that had been pumping through his system for most of the day was gone and he was overcome by fatigue. He pulled up the window and returned to the compartment, surprised to find Tom Maxwell awake and looking almost human. Or maybe it was just the dim ceiling light that made him look like that, Jamie reasoned. Looking closer, it was the light, or lack of it, that made him look human. His eyes were rimmed by dark circles and the whites replaced by a patchwork quilt of red blood vessels. He was trembling, but at least he seemed to be aware of what was going on around him. He lifted his bandaged hands. 'Thanks,' he mumbled, almost incoherently.

Jamie regarded him coldly, trying to keep his emotions and his distaste for the man under control. He despised Maxwell but he tried to keep that out of his eyes. 'Don't thank me,' he replied. 'I'm not doing this for you.' His voice was low but Maxwell caught it.

'I know,' he murmured quietly, taking Jamie by surprise. 'It *is* you, isn't it?' he continued.

'What's me?' Jamie demanded shortly, irritated.

'It's you that Kate's been seeing over the last few months,' he continued, voice breaking.

Jamie back stared at him, his gaze piercing into the man. *What is the point in lying,* he wondered? Maxwell knew Kate was seeing someone, why shouldn't she, given his behaviour? The only thing Maxwell didn't know was the identity of his wife's lover so why keep him in the dark?

'Aye, okay, it's me,' Jamie responded. 'But you've only got yourself to blame,' he added, keeping his voice low and steady. He expected a reaction...anger, hatred maybe, but instead there was only resigned acceptance in the man's eyes. Strangely, it was Jamie who was angry. *Doesn't this clown realise he has won,* he thought bitterly? *Kate has chosen him...after all he has done, all he has put her through, she decided to take him home with her and he threw it back in her face.* Jamie clenched and unclenched his fists, forcing the anger away. Maxwell began to weep and suddenly Jamie suddenly felt inexplicably sorry for him. Unable to watch, he turned to the compartment door and left.

He made his way along the corridor to the carriage door and slipped the window down on its leather strap. The slipstream of the speeding train sucked air from the corridor and took his breath away before the pressure equalised. Outside, the lights of Glasgow were receding behind them and soon they would be in Motherwell. He found his Lucky Strikes and lit one, savouring the flavour of the toasted tobacco and the hit of nicotine. Conor had given him two extra packs...and he'd need them tonight, he thought. He probably wouldn't sleep so he'd smoke plenty. That meant he'd spend a lot of time in the corridor, which was just as well; he wouldn't be able to put up with the wreck in the lower bunk feeling sorry for himself.

The train began to slow and the engineering works on the approach to Motherwell flashed past. Jamie took a final drag on the cigarette and flicked the remains of it out of the window, watching the tip glow a bright red in the slipstream and then disappear in a flurry of tiny sparks.

When he returned to the compartment Maxwell was asleep. Relieved, Jamie climbed up into the top bunk and stretched out. The clickety-click of the wheels on the rails slowed in tempo, there was a hiss of air and a squeal of brakes and the big locomotive came to a halt. Doors banged, voices called out and feet padded down the corridor. He pulled back the curtain and surveyed the platform. A porter pushed a luggage trolley past the carriage, its rusty axles squeaking in protest, but otherwise the platform was deserted. A whistle blew, more doors banged and then there was a jolt and the loud puffing of the heavy locomotive as it hauled the carriages away from the station into the Lanarkshire countryside.

Jamie settled back onto his bunk and stared at the ceiling above him. Beneath him, Maxwell breathed heavily, his breath rasping irritatingly in his throat with every exhalation. Even if sleep were possible for him he doubted he could manage it with that racket going on. His thought back over the past few days. *Life, he decided, had a nasty habit of kicking him in the balls...just when he least expected it.*

He thought about Kate. He knew she had gone home, but where, exactly, was home? Was she thinking about him...or was he already a fading memory? His pride wouldn't let him accept that; when she had told him she loved him and had cried in his arms, she had meant it, of that he was sure. He felt he was missing something. What it was he couldn't say what...but there was something more to all of this.

Astonishingly, he drifted off to sleep lying fully clothed on top of the bunk. He woke an hour later, disorientated and sweating in the stifling, fetid heat of the compartment. The atmosphere stank of the alcohol seeping from Maxwell's pores and Jamie decided a cigarette was needed to clear his head. Maxwell was still asleep, snoring loudly. Jamie took up his smoking position at the carriage door and lowered the window, inches this time; just enough to take away his exhaled smoke. The train raced south, swaying gently from side to side on the rails and its wheels tapping steadily over the joints like a metronome. The moon was out in an almost clear sky and fields, hedgerows and stone dykes flashed past. Darkened farmhouses stood like sentinels guarding the silent countryside while herds of cows and flocks of sheep patrolled the fields.

A station flew past, the noise changing as the carriages hurtled through the enclosed space at around 80mph. Jamie strained to see the signage giving its name but the speed of the train defeated him. He looked at his watch. It was after midnight now so they had to be somewhere in England, he reasoned, but had forgotten to consider stops en route when he had been asleep. They were now approaching Carlisle but it was of no consequence. They had to get off at Crew and change to another train which would then take them on to Nottingham, but that was not until after six o' clock in the morning, still a good five hours ahead. He finished his cigarette and returned to the compartment where Maxwell continued to snore. It was going to be a long night!

*

A series of shuddering jolts woke Jamie just after five thirty. Maxwell was still snoring soundly below him and he shook his head in disgust. His eyes were nipping and he rubbed them with the heels of his hands. He felt like shit. Pulling back the curtain he looked for a sign and found one about 50 yards away with "CREWE" in bold black lettering against a white background. Where had the night gone, he mused? He felt dirty and he needed a wash to freshen up but the facilities on the train were restricted to one small wash basin in each sleeper compartment. In any event, there probably wasn't enough time as they had to change trains here.

He shook Maxwell roughly and was surprised when the man woke immediately. 'Time to get off,' he said, lighting up another cigarette. His mother's idea of breakfast was a fag and a cup of coffee and that would have to do him today...he hoped the station cafeteria was open. Maxwell coughed and made a face as the acrid smell of the tobacco caught his throat. Smoking, apparently, wasn't one of his vices. Jamie eyed him dispassionately and ignored him.

The station was virtually deserted when they climbed down from the sleeper. A few other passengers joined them on the platform and Jamie spied the elderly couple who had given him grief earlier at Glasgow Central. 'Fuck!' he muttered under his breath. 'That's all I need.'

Maxwell looked terrible but at least he could walk in a straight line now...without support. Jamie guided him off the platform into the main hall of the station and searched for the tearoom. He found it near the main entrance and it was open...at least something was going right. They took a table near the window and Jamie bought tea for Maxwell and a coffee for himself.

'Why are you doing this?' Maxwell asked when Jamie returned from the counter with the cups.

'Doing what?' he replied, being intentionally obtuse.

'Bringing me here...home, to Kate.'

Jamie regarded him sourly. *Good question, he thought to himself, why am I doing this?* But he knew the answer. 'Kate didn't want to leave you to the loan shark,' he said, holding up Maxwell's bandaged hands. 'She thought he would kill you...and she was probably right,' he said, nodding at Maxwell's wounds. 'She didn't want that on her conscience.'

Maxwell looked at him blankly; it was his turn to be obtuse. 'Those would be Kate's reasons,' he replied. 'Why are *you* doing it?'

Jamie smiled grimly. 'Because I love her,' he stated bluntly. Maxwell lifted his cup and drank his tea. His questions had dried up.

They arrived in Nottingham at five past seven. Being Sunday morning, the station was almost deserted, just as Crewe had been, but the cafeteria was open. *I'm beginning to live in fuckin' cafes*, Jamie reflected grimly as he bought another tea for Maxwell and another coffee for himself. He didn't feel like eating so if Maxwell was hungry that was his bad luck. As they sat drinking the hot beverages Jamie fished loose change from his pocket and slapped it onto the table; a half-crown, a florin, two one shilling pieces, three sixpenny pieces, a threepenny bit and a few pennies.

'Are you phoning or am I?' he asked, as Maxwell examined the money.

'I'll do it,' Maxwell replied, but made no attempt to pick up the coins or to rise from his chair.

'Well, any time this week will be fine,' Jamie said sarcastically. 'I don't want to spend any more time with you than necessary…there's a coin box over there,' he continued, pointing to a row of red Post Office telephone kiosks. 'And tell them to come right away,' he added as Maxwell rose to his feet. 'There's a train back to Glasgow at nine fifteen and I want to be on it.'

Jamie watched as Maxwell made his way to the telephone kiosks, lifted the hand set and dialled. Who is he phoning, Jamie wondered, Kate or his father and mother? It nagged at him as Maxwell spoke into the phone, his head turning towards Jamie from time to time, and then he replaced the phone and trudged slowly back to the café and slumped into his chair.

'Well?' Jamie demanded.

'They'll be about forty minutes.'

'Who will?'

'My father…he's coming. My family knows…about my drinking,' he stammered, as if Jamie would be interested. 'Kate must have told them.'

'Good,' Jamie replied, attempting unsuccessfully to kill the conversation.

'Why did she leave you?'

Jamie sipped his coffee and looked at Maxwell over the top of the cup. Fuck you, he thought bitterly, breaking into an embittered laugh. It was another good question though and one he still hadn't been able to find an answer to.

'Moral responsibility,' he tendered eventually. 'You've got a daughter…and for Kate she comes first. Maybe you should take a leaf out of Kate's book and start thinking about both of them rather than about yourself.' Maxwell returned his look and Jamie, surprised, imagined he saw shame in the man's eyes.

They sat in silence then and Jamie smoked another cigarette. Time dragged. The station entrance was about 100 yards away from the café and it was Jamie who saw them first. Kate came into the concourse, an older man with her. It could be her father, Jamie thought, but then again, it could be Maxwell's. 'Kate's here,' he said quietly, trying to control his anger. 'You lied to me.'

'What? No, I didn't,' Maxwell stammered, panicking. 'I spoke to my mother; I swear…she said my father would come for me…she must have phoned Kate.'

Jamie looked at him sourly. He had wanted to avoid this, knowing that meeting would be painful for both of them, especially with Maxwell present. He watched unhappily as Kate and the man stopped and scanned the concourse, looking for Maxwell, he presumed. Just looking at her now was sending arrows straight to his heart. She looked pale and drawn but she was still beautiful. A few minutes passed and Maxwell remained beside him. It was as though he was afraid to go to her with Jamie there. Then, another man appeared and this one *was* Maxwell's father, the family resemblance unmistakeable. The two men shook hands and Maxwell's father hugged Kate. The little cameo was too excruciatingly painful for Jamie to watch and he turned away. Just looking at her now filled him with angst. He had lost her.

'They're waiting for you,' he said softly. 'Go on.' Maxwell stared at him for a moment then rose slowly, holding out his hand. Jamie looked at it and then at him, his expression saying it all. 'Just fuck off,' he said, and, as Maxwell hesitated, pushed his hand away. 'Get out of my sight,' he continued coldly and turned his attention back to his coffee.

Maxwell stood there, unsure of himself, not knowing what to do. He suspected he had lost Kate and the man sitting opposite him was the man she loved, but here he was being told by that man to go to her. He didn't even his name, other than what the American had called him…Jamie. He wanted to say something, thank him, but he knew that wasn't a good idea. He hovered there, waiting, watching Kate and her father and his own father walking towards the cafeteria. Jamie was looking at him, he sensed it, and he turned back to face him.

'Go to them,' Jamie shouted angrily. 'Don't let them come in here…I don't want Kate to see me.'

Maxwell nodded slowly and made for door, knowing Jamie's eyes were following him, waiting to see what transpired. As he stepped out of the door Kate's father spotted him and pointed him out and both men then strode purposefully forward to meet him. From the dim interior of the cafeteria, Jamie watched Kate hold back. She stood still, her eyes pointing directly at him but he knew she couldn't see him. She knew he was there, he felt it. Why could she not just leave it?

But Kate couldn't just leave it. Her father had taken the message…Tom was at the train station in Nottingham with a man from Glasgow who had brought him home; he was injured and needed help. She had tried to hide her elation but it was impossible. Her father misinterpreted but her mother knew exactly what she was thinking. Instinctively, she knew the "man from Glasgow" was Jamie and her heart beat faster and faster. She could feel his presence there in the darkness. She already regretted leaving him but still clung to the belief that she had had no other choice. But none of that mattered because she still loved him…and she always would. When Tom emerged from the café alone her intuition told her that Jamie was avoiding her and her heart broke. She waited, tears welling up in her eyes as the three men came to her. Tom was almost unrecognisable; he was nothing like the man she had married and he really was a stranger to her now and she knew in her heart she couldn't spend the rest of her life with him. The man she wanted to be with was in the café but she knew she had burned her bridges with him. That left her feeling desolate and empty.

Her father looked at her and saw the pain in her eyes. The sadness emanating from her was like a force field, letting nothing else through to her. He knew about Tom's drink problem, that had come out on the car journey south with Kate but he was still in the dark about her relationship with Jamie. As they made their way to the exit he watched his daughter look over her shoulder, again and again, as though willing something to happen and there were tears on her cheeks.

Suddenly, Kate stopped. She hesitated for an instant, looking at the faces of the three men around her, and then she started to run back towards the café. The older men looked at each other awkwardly, both tempted to follow, but Tom Maxwell held them back. 'Leave her,' he said. 'She needs to be with him…alone.' He said nothing more…there was no need; they knew and all they could do now was wait.

Jamie saw her running to him and rose from the table. The young waitress who had served him watched the little cameo develop in front of her. It was a true love story, a love triangle, she realised, being played out before her very eyes and she wasn't going to miss the finale. It would be something to tell her friends about later.

Kate pushed through the door and spotted Jamie immediately. She stopped then, let out a little cry, and then ran to him, thrusting chairs aside and throwing herself into his arms. 'Why Jamie, why, why, why?' she sobbed, burying her head in his chest.

He held her, the watchful eyes of the waitress wide with anticipation. 'You couldn't leave him,' he said gently, stroking her hair. 'And I didn't want his death on my conscience any more than you,' he continued. 'Lauren needs her father…you were right on that too. I love you Kate, but I know I can't have you…not now anyway.' He placed his fingers gently on her chin and tilted her face up to his, looking into her green eyes, awash with her tears. 'I love you…now go,' he said. She pulled him to her and kissed him, refusing to release him. 'Go!' he repeated, pushing her away.

She walked dejectedly away, her shoulders slumped and tears coursing down her cheeks. Her father put his arm protectively around her and looked towards the cafeteria but he could see nothing of the man she had gone to. Tom's father studied her with sad eyes and then looked at his son. Their marriage was over, of that he had no doubt. He took hold of Tom's arm and led him away, Kate and her father following slowly, but separately, behind. Kate turned back again as they reached the exit, hoping for a final glimpse of Jamie…but he was gone.

Chapter 22

Kate's letter arrived on Wednesday after Jamie left for work and it was sitting, accusingly, on the mantelpiece when he returned home that night. His mother was waiting eagerly to tell him about it the minute he walked in the door. She was perplexed. She had believed that Kate and Jamie would get back together but for some reason, which Jamie refused to divulge, it now looked unlikely. Jamie appeared to be taking it calmly but she knew it was a façade. He was hurting badly. He refused to speak about it, even though she probed relentlessly, simply sticking to his pretence of acceptance.

She watched him wander into the living room and pick up the envelope. He turned it over and examined the postmark…just as she had done when she found it behind the door earlier. Nottingham, on Monday…so it *had* come from Kate. When she and Kate had talked she had learned that Kate's family came from a little mining village, Calverton, somewhere near Nottingham, so the letter had to be from her.

Disappointed, she watched Jamie slip the envelope, unopened, into his pocket. He seemed reluctant to open it, she noted, and she was concerned for him. When he had returned home on Sunday his face had been like granite. She had asked what was wrong and he had replied simply that he and Kate had split up. That was all; no explanation, nothing. She had tried to wheedle information from him but he refused to say anything. He took after her in that respect and would say nothing unless, and until, he was ready…and at this moment, he wasn't ready.

Jamie pulled out a chair and sat down wearily at the kitchen table. If his mother wanted to know what was in the letter she would have to wait. Dinner passed normally with the usual small talk, his father and mother doing most of the talking; complaining about the weather, complaining about prices, Jamie and his father discussing football…discussion about everything under the sun except the one subject his mother wanted to broach.

When the meal was over, he excused himself and made his way up to his room, taking his father and mother by surprise. Normally, he would sit with them and watch the news on the television but tonight he had other things on his mind.

Alone in his room Jamie lay back on his bed, examining the envelope, turning it over in his hands again and again, reluctant to open it to read it. He thought he knew what the letter would say, would learn Kate's feelings for him at the end, but he was afraid to read it. He still saw it all as his fault. Why hadn't he made her stay? Why couldn't he convince her she was better with him? Was it his propensity for getting involved in trouble that had chased her away? He had calmed down a lot since he met her but there had still been occasions when trouble sought him out. The heavies at her door looking for money were part of it but not all of it. He should have taken her away from Tom Maxwell when he had the chance, should have married her…but he hadn't, and now all he had to show for the relationship was an engagement ring that she would never wear, a silver ankh around his neck…and his memories.

Mustering up the courage he ran a finger nail along the flap of the envelope, tore it open, and pulled out the folded sheet of paper inside. It smelled faintly perfumed, the same as the scent Kate habitually wore, and he wondered absently if she had sprayed some of it onto the paper before sealing it in the envelope. With trembling fingers he opened the folded sheet and began to read.

My Darling Jamie,

My heart broke again yesterday when I saw the hurt in your eyes. I pray that one day you'll be able to forgive me, even though I can't forgive myself.

As much as I love you, and I do love you Jamie, I felt that I was trapping you into something you weren't ready for. You told me you loved me and I know it now, I saw it in your eyes yesterday, but my life is a mess. Maybe I just lack the confidence to believe we could make it together. I've already made one enormous mistake in my life and I didn't want to make another - but I think that maybe I have.

I've cried myself to sleep every night since I left you and last night was even worse. Do you really want me? I keep thinking that if you did you would have made me stay – or at least tried to get me to come back to Glasgow with you on Sunday.

You said you'd look after me through everything and that you'd care for Lauren but I didn't know if you were saying that because you felt you had to – because it was the right thing to do – or because you really love me.

If I'm wrong I'm sorry but there are other things I just couldn't deal with if I was alone in Glasgow. I love you Jamie, I always will. I haven't come home because I don't love you. I just didn't know if our love could survive the problems.

Maybe it just wasn't to be. I'll never stop thinking about you and I'll never stop loving you. Take care of yourself my baby.

Kate.xxx

He read the letter again and a tear rolled down his cheek. Later, he took the small box containing the engagement ring he had bought from the drawer where he had hidden it and removed the ring. The diamonds sparkled brightly. He found a little piece of cotton wool and wrapped the ring carefully in it then folded Kate's letter in two, then four, and slipped the ring between the folds. Meticulously then, he folded the letter again and again into ever smaller parts before placing it finally inside his wallet. What he would do with it now he had no idea. His fingers went to his neck, searching for the ankh and then toying with it. The ring, the letter and the ankh were the only tangible remains of a love that now survived only in his head and his heart.

Chapter 23

Friday 21 April 1967

Another Friday night. They all blended into a oneness now, none any different from any other. And the same could be said of every other day in the week since Kate had left, Jamie mused miserably. He had lost interest in everything and even a night out with the boys had lost its appeal.

A week earlier at this time he had been sitting on a coach with Jack, Jim Campbell and fifty other Jocks heading south for the England v Scotland football match at Wembley, and even a quickie with a nice blonde girl he'd met in a Soho Club after the game hadn't done much to lift his spirits. If anything, the trip left him even more restless.

George Square was relatively quiet tonight but it was still early, he reminded himself, and the dance halls didn't close until after midnight. He shifted his bottom uncomfortably on the cold stone dwarf wall that surrounded the Square's floral arrangements and munched a lukewarm chip from the bag in his hand. His watch read 10.52pm and he shook his head gloomily. The rest of his mates would be enjoying the Locarno but he just couldn't hack it tonight. When was the last Friday night he had gone home this early? Things had to change, he told himself…and he had to stop feeling sorry for himself.

'Hello Jamie.' He knew the voice instantly and recognised the legs, sheathed in nylon and fitted snugly into black high heeled shoes. 'Can I sit with you?'

He looked up into Carol Whyte's tentative eyes and shuffled his bum along the stone. His anger at what she had done to him, to their relationship, had burned out long ago and the fight in him was gone. 'Be my guest,' he said, patting the stone and offering her his bag of chips.

Carol sat down and stretched out her long shapely legs. She picked a chip from the bag and slid it into her mouth. 'I didn't expect to see you here,' she said, as she chewed on the deep fried potato chunk.

'Likewise,' Jamie replied, turning to look at her. She gazed back defiantly, expecting an outburst, then softened when she realised he had mellowed.

'Where's your girlfriend tonight?' she asked, and Jamie knew from her tone that it wasn't a barbed question…just an innocent, though hurtful, one. She looked at him quizzically, suddenly conscious that she had struck a nerve.

'Nottingham…she left at Easter,' he replied quietly.

'God, I'm sorry Jamie, I didn't know, honestly.'

'It's alright, I know you didn't,' he said gently.

'She was really lovely,' Carol said absently and furrowed her brow when Jamie started to laugh.

'Funnily enough, she said the same about you,' he snickered. 'Seems I manage to find beautiful women but I can't manage to keep them.' There was sadness in his voice Carol didn't recognise and she was shocked when she realised he was referring to her as well as his girlfriend.

'What happened?' she continued, curious now. Everything she knew about Jamie and the English girl, and she had kept up to date through mutual friends, had led her to believe their relationship was solid.

'She's married...her husband won,' Jamie replied glumly. 'Her family...or his, who knows, put the pressure on...but hey ho, life goes on. What about you? Whenever I see you I expect to see a guy trailing along. Where is he tonight?' he asked, laughing softly.

It was Carol's turn to offer a sad smile and there was silence between them for a moment. Jamie scrunched up the now empty chip bag and tossed it, skilfully, into a litter bin nearby. He dug out his cigarettes and offered one to Carol. She took it gratefully and inserted it between her full, crimson lips, and waited for him to raise the flame of his lighter to it. Jamie spoke then, breaking the silence. 'Had a fall out?' he asked. 'Is it still that Bobby character you were with before Christmas?' he pressed on, saying nothing about his altercation with the said Bobby or the fact that he thought Bobby was a bit of a tosser. There had been enough bad feeling between himself and Carol without adding to it.

'Sort of,' she said. 'But I only kept seeing him because Jennifer...you remember Jennifer?' she laughed, waiting for his response before carrying on. Jamie nodded. 'Well, Jennifer is going out with one of his pals and she asked me to go out with him.' Jamie smiled knowingly in response to that. Jack had done the same to him, numerous times. 'We were out tonight,' she continued, 'the four of us...at that new pub near the Locarno, and we were going to the dancing later, but Bobby sort of laid it on the line...too much beer gave him false courage, I think. He wanted me to sleep with him tonight, miffed that I haven't let him already,' she laughed nervously.

Jamie returned her look, dead pan. He found that hard to believe but then again maybe it was just his natural suspicion after what she had done to him.

Carol sensed his disbelief even though he thought he had concealed it well. 'I told him I wasn't ready,' she continued, 'but then he got abusive...told me I'm "just a cock teaser" and I'm "always giving other boys the eye"...and he brought you up too.'

'Me?' Jamie retorted, amused. 'What did he have to say about me?'

'Well, it was more about me, I suppose. He said that from what he'd heard I had been only too ready to "drop my knickers" for you...and if he wasn't getting the same then it was all off.' She was angry now.

'And you said?' Jamie asked, trying to keep his amusement in check.

'I told him you were worth dropping my knickers for and he wasn't,' she laughed nervously.

Silence fell between them again. Jamie felt her eyes boring into him but resisted the temptation to look at her. He finished his cigarette and flicked the butt out into the street, managing to curb the urge to laugh at the scenario she had just painted and Kate's words, from that night in the Locarno when she had first seen Carol, came back to him..."silly girl, she still fancies you".

'Will you take me home?' The words startled him. Six months earlier he could have strangled her and now she was asking him to take her home.

'Maybe not a good idea,' he suggested. 'After what happened between us...and Bobby might get the wrong idea.'

'I don't care about Bobby,' she retorted quickly. 'But you're right, I know, and I'm sorry Jamie, really. I never meant to hurt you. I never wanted to lose you.'

'And if I hadn't caught you at it that night what would you have done? Kept on seeing me and have him on the side?'

A tear trickled down Carol's cheek. He hadn't raised his voice, hadn't seemed angry, and yet his words had the effect of a slap. 'For what it's worth, no...I wouldn't have seen him again,' she replied quietly, and strangely, Jamie believed her.

'Then why did you do it, Carol? Why?'

'I don't know...I was stupid. I took something at the party and my head was all over the place and I wondered what it would be like being with someone else. Despite what everyone thinks about me, you were the only boy I'd ever been with...and again, for what it's worth, apart from that night, you still are.'

Jamie shook his head slowly. This was all too much to take in. 'What was it you took?' he asked, curious.

'I don't know. Pills...a boy at the party had them. Speed, I think,' she replied guiltily. 'Didn't you know?'

Jamie shook his head. Pills being available at the party was news to him. 'So, you took these pills and then decided to hold a wee competition,' he suggested cruelly. 'If he was a better fuck than me then you would dump me...I suppose I should be flattered, if what you've just said is true.'

Carol's tears were in full flow now and Jamie was suddenly full of remorse. 'I'm sorry,' he said softly, reaching out to comfort her though expecting her to pull away. 'I was out of order,' he added as Carol leaned against him, sobbing and saying "I'm sorry" again and again.

Jamie took her home. They left the bus at Anniesland Cross and walked the rest of the way to her parents' flat in Great Western Road. The matter of her unfaithfulness that night wasn't raised again and, even though they didn't walk arm in arm, there was a certain closeness between them again.

When they reached the entrance to the flats Jamie looked up at the windows. There were no lights on in Carol's flat and the living room curtains were still open. It appeared that no one was at home.

'Do you want to come up?' Carol asked softly, putting her hand on his arm. Jamie wrestled with his thoughts. There was no future in starting this all over again but he still found her desirable. She *was* beautiful but she didn't have the natural beauty that Kate had, he thought, comparing them; Carol's beauty was more clinical, more artificial, but she was beautiful none the less. And the hardness between his legs gave him its own opinion. But if he went with her now he'd simply be using her; he wouldn't be making love to her, just fucking her.

Carol seemed to read his thoughts. 'No commitment, Jamie. Just see how it goes,' she said. 'And I won't eat you...unless you want me to,' she laughed coyly.

Jamie smiled and looked up at the darkened windows. 'When will your father and mother be home?'

Carol smiled temptingly when she replied. 'They've gone up to Perth for a Silver Wedding Anniversary. They won't be home until tomorrow afternoon.' And with those words the die was cast. Maybe he could make love to her, he thought, he had loved her once before after all.

When he left her just after dawn she watched him from her bedroom window. She had thrown a dressing gown over her shoulders but it hung open showing her firm breasts, highlighted in the early morning sun. She was smiling sadly. Their love making had been frantic. For Jamie, it was an attempt to eradicate Kate from his mind and for Carol it was an attempt to make amends to the man she loved. Neither of them succeeded. In the final minutes before he left her, Carol asked if she would see him again. His silence gave her his answer.

Jamie walked the mile and a half home engrossed in his thoughts. He despised himself for what he had done. No matter how he tried, he couldn't justify it. If he hadn't actually cheated on Kate he had, at the very least, cheated on her memory. He hadn't felt like this the weekend before in London but that girl had been a stranger and it had simply been sex, a casual shag with a stranger and neither he nor the girl expected anything more from it. But tonight with Carol, it had been different. Carol was no stranger; they had been close once and she had hoped they could be close again. Despite how he still felt about Kate, he had made love to Carol. And he *had* made love to her. It hadn't been the "no strings attached" fuck he had meant it to be and he knew that if he kept seeing her she would pull at his heart strings until she enticed him back to her. But it could never be, *would* never be, what it had once been. 'An exquisite blow job and a night of rampant sex doth not love make,' he said aloud, parodying Shakespeare. The realisation that he couldn't stay around here any longer came to him in a flash, like Saint Paul's conversion on the road to Damascus. He slept fitfully that night, his mind filled with images of Kate, her eyes rebuking him.

Chapter 24

I've had it with this place,' Jamie spat vehemently. 'You can't even have a quiet night out without some wee shite wantin' to show you how tough he is!' Jack Connolly nodded, rubbing his left cheek gingerly and examining his bleeding knuckles. Jamie looked at him, concerned. 'You alright?' he asked, noticing the graze and the dark bruise around Jack's left eye for the first time.

'Aye, I'm okay,' Jack returned, annoyed. 'That wee ginger heided bastard caught me wi' wan before ah downed him. Whit aboot you?'

Jamie looked himself over, checked his hands ran his eyes over his suit. There was a dark stain on the front of his jacket and a similar mark on his trousers, just above his right knee. 'I'm fine,' he replied, but his voice betrayed how he really felt. Another good suit ruined!

The detritus of their skirmish with the four lads lay scattered about the roadway; two short wooden staves, an empty Lanliq bottle and a steel comb. Jamie picked up the comb, turning it over in his hand as he looked up the now deserted and dark street. They were near the bottom of Abercrombie Street, about 150 yards from London Road, a sort of "no man's land" between the territories of the Calton Tongs and the Baltic Fleet. It was half past one in the morning and they still had a dangerous journey ahead of them. He slipped the steel comb into his inside jacket pocket and sighed.

'Where did they wee arseholes come fae, that's whit ah want tae know?' Jack whispered, as if normal conversation might attract other "wee arseholes" to them.

'Probably saw us with the girls and decided to wait till we left them. Might have thought we're Tongs or that lot from Dennistoun…the Monks, and didn't like the idea of us ridin' the local talent,' Jamie laughed coldly.

'Speakin' of which,' Jack followed up quickly. 'Did ye?'

'Did I what?' Jamie laughed.

'Shag the lassie?'

'Don't be daft…is the Pope a Catholic?' he laughed again. 'An' I heard you at it, ya dirty bugger.' He started to giggle. 'It was probably the noise you were makin' that attracted those wee shitebags, aw yer puffin an' pantin' an' shoutin' out "yes, yes, yes," like you'd just scored a goal. Right enough, I suppose you had,' he grinned then became serious again. 'Come on, better get away from here; I'm gettin' nervous.'

That was enough for Jack. If Jamie was getting nervous then he should probably be shittin' himself, he thought. They made their way up Abercrombie Street, keeping to the shadows, their eyes and ears wide open as they checked the road ahead and turned round anxiously to watch their backs. Jack began talking, regaling Jamie with the details of his conquest to cover his nerves.

'An' does Lillian know you're a Tim?' Jamie asked when he could get a word in edge ways.

'Whit?' Jack asked, surprised. 'Nah, why should she? She wisnae bothered…why ye askin'?' His response was drowned out by Jamie's laughter. 'Whit's so funny?' he demanded, exasperated.

'Her old man's a...,' Jamie started then broke down again, spluttering with laughter.

'Whit? Her old man's a whit?' Jack was becoming annoyed.

'He's the Master of the local Lodge,' Jamie chortled.

'Ya bastard!' Jack retorted loudly. 'And you knew?' He started to laugh then too. 'Christ, that's a first,' he chortled. 'How did ye find oot?'

'Val told me when we were dancin'...but I thought we were on to a good thing so I didn't let on...didn't want you pullin' out.'

'Nae worries there, pal,' Jack grinned. 'The only pullin' oot ah wis doin' came after ah poked her,' he laughed.

'Better not tell your Ma though, eh? She'd have a fit,' Jamie giggled. 'It's bad enough her findin' out you're a wee whore maister but if she finds out ye've shagged a Proddy she'll get ye ex-communicated.'

They laughed, nervousness evaporating, and continued on their way up towards the Gallowgate. It was still quiet, too quiet maybe, but as they reached the Gallowgate junction a police car, blue lights flashing, raced towards them from Parkhead. It slowed as it reached them, the two cops on board checking them out, and then sped off up Abercrombie Street towards Dennistoun. Jamie and Jack looked at each another, each reading the other's thoughts; just another normal Saturday night in the great metropolis.

The tenements of Calton sat to their left, Dennistoun lay ahead and Parkhead was off to their right. The big question now was whether to head down through Calton or to carry on up towards Dennistoun 'Whit way?' Jack asked, deferring to Jamie on this one.

Jamie scanned the roads to left and right, checking potential trouble spots along the Gallowgate. There were lights still on in some of the tenement flats and music and laughter drifted on the night air. Everything seemed peaceful enough but that, as Jamie well knew, could be deceptive. Peace was a rare commodity in this city.

'If we go down Gallowgate we pass The Barras...right through the heart of Calton; if we head up to Dennistoun we need to take Duke Street and George Street to get to George Square...that could be dicey with guys comin' out from the centre...could be trouble either way,' Jamie murmured, thinking aloud.

The sound of raised voices from the Gallowgate made their decision for them. Six or seven young guys with a like number of hard faced, loud mouthed girls, spilled out of a tenement close about into the middle of the road about 200 yards away. They were all the worse for drink and an argument was brewing. Their blood was up and battle was imminent. As Jamie had thought earlier...just another Saturday night.

'Abercrombie Street, ah think,' Jack said quietly.

'Aye, let them fight one another rather than us...c'mon.'

They walked across the junction, trying not to draw attention to themselves until they reached the high walls of the City Abattoir and Meat Market, and then broke into a jog.

Jack spotted them first. Three lads about their own age emerged from a close about fifty yards ahead and were eyeing them belligerently. 'Shite!' Jack muttered under his breath and caught hold of Jamie's arm. 'Bandits, two o'clock,' he warned; he had always wanted to be a fighter pilot.

You've been watchin' too many war movies, wee man, Jamie mused as he slowed to a walk, assessing the threat. But turning back wasn't an option. He made up his mind. 'If they decide to take us on just run right through them...hit the fuckers hard an' keep goin', don't stop, right? He instructed. 'An' stay close to me.'

Jack nodded. Here we go again, he thought. They walked on steadily with practised nonchalance as the gap between them closed. Suddenly, one of the three let out a blood curdling cry and all of them ran towards the two friends, the streetlights glinting on the weapons in their hands.

'Here we go,' Jamie shouted. 'And the fuckers have got chibs...so remember, don't stop.' They started to run, Jamie slightly ahead and Jack, cursing quietly under his breath, following. Their bravado threw the others into confusion and, for a fleeting moment, doubt set in and that fleeting moment was all that Jamie and Jack needed. Remembering Jamie's mantra; hit first and hit hard, Jack followed his instructions to the letter.

Running fast, Jamie body checked the leader off and knocked him to the ground, his long bladed knife skittering away across the roadway. Another of the trio was coming at him but his pal's quick demise had un-nerved him and he swung out wildly at Jamie with his weapon. Jamie, now in warrior made, caught his wrist and spun him, propelling him face first into the abattoir wall. But the boy held onto the knife and, despite his now bleeding face, came at Jamie again. His knife arm flicked out and Jamie gripped it tightly, stepped close and slammed his forehead into the lad's face, smashing his nose...a perfect Glasgow kiss, and the boy's scream echoed off the tenement walls. Out of the corner of his eye he saw Jack drop the third lad with a vicious kick to his left knee. There was a sickening crack, like a twig snapping, and the young man fell to the ground with a sob.

Jack slowed momentarily then, caught out by the speed of what had just taken place, and was grabbed immediately by Jamie. 'I told you, don't stop...fuckin' keep runnin',' he shouted, pulling Jack with him. The value of Jamie's words was proved seconds later as another team of boys charged out of the tenement close and gave chase.

They raced up Abercrombie Street, breath rasping. Duke Street was tantalisingly close but the gang was closing on them. Jamie hadn't stopped to count them but he reckoned there were five or six in the group and if they were caught a severe kicking was on the cards. The blood stains on his suit would be as nothing then, he thought morosely. Suddenly, car headlights swept round from Duke Street and a white Ford Anglia, with blue lights flashing, sped towards them. A tidal wave of relief flowed over them as the car skidded to a halt only in front of them, its front doors flying open as it disgorged two burly cops. Jamie sighed with relief and turned smugly to face the gang only to discover that they were alone, their pursuers and their three injured mates having melted away.

The two policemen approached and stood in front of them as they bent over, their hands on their knees, and caught their breath.

'Thanks,' said Jamie, still out of breath. 'That was close.' The two cops smiled mirthlessly, the younger of them swinging his baton casually.

'What was close?' the bigger man asked in a soft Highland accent that was at odds with his size.

Jamie pulled himself up straight, telling Jack with his eyes to keep quiet. He had been in this sort of situation before...and in Glasgow it didn't always matter who actually started a fight. Often, the victims ended up in the local nick if they opened their mouths out of turn charged with breach of the peace with the only witnesses being the cops who arrested them...the infamous two cop breach! They were waiting, notebooks and pencils poised, and the young cop was clearly growing impatient. A good cop, bad cop scenario was developing and Jamie hoped the big Teuchter, the good cop, was in charge.

He started to explain. 'We took two lassies home to Brig'ton and were headin' back to George Square when that lot started chasin' us,' he said, still panting from the exertion of the chase and confident the cops must have seen the gang behind them. 'That was the second lot to attack us tonight,' he added. 'Lucky for us you showed up when you did.' It didn't do any harm to fawn a little.

'Names and addresses,' the young cop demanded, Jamie's explanation having fallen on stony ground. The way he said it made it clear it wasn't a request, it was an order, and they had no alternative but to comply. They gave him their details, trying desperately to keep insolence out of their voices. Sometimes in Glasgow, even the innocent are guilty, a fact they accepted with that brand of stoicism peculiar to Glasgow and the West of Scotland...not so much change what you can change and accept what you can't, more change what you can change and if you can't change it just kick the shit out of it…that always makes you feel better.

'Alright, on your way then,' the big Teuchter said, surprising them.'

They turned towards him, mouths open, and Jamie spotted the look of anger and resentment that appeared on the young cop's face. His baton was swinging furiously now.

Jamie didn't need a second invitation. Grabbing Jack by the arm he pulled him away, mumbling his thanks, towards Duke Street without looking back. The two cops returned to their car and the big Teuchter leaned against his door as Jamie and Jack disappeared into Duke Street.

'What the fuck was that all about?' the younger man challenged indignantly. 'We could have had them.'

The big Highlander smiled back at him. 'You didn't want to do that,' he said cheerfully. 'Chief Constable wouldn't have been pleased.'

The young cop looked at him as if he'd lost his marbles. 'What are you going on about?' he asked.

'James Raeburn…does that name not ring a bell with you?'

'No, why the fuck should it?'

'The Chief Constable praised a James Raeburn to the hilt in the Press last November. Spoke of the Good Samaritans of this fine city…don't you remember? An American sailor it was…attacked in Cowcaddens and one James Raeburn came to his rescue. There was a big piece in the Evening Times…and The Record too, I think.'

The young cop's face paled a little. 'Shit! James Raeburn, do you think it's the same one?'

'Aye, well, that James Raeburn came from Knightswood too…bit of a coincidence if it's not the same one, eh? Why take the chance? Bit of a hero, he was…might be embarrassing if we had arrested him, eh?

'Aye, right Donald…thanks.'

The big Teuchter grinned and heaved himself into the car. 'Turn round and follow them,' he instructed. 'We'll just make sure they're okay.' The young cop settled behind the wheel and started the engine. 'And after that,' the big Highlander laughed. 'You can buy me a cup of tea.'

Jamie and Jack were about 200 yards along Duke Street with Tennent's Brewery at Wellpark on their right when the police car turned out of Abercrombie Street and stopped. Jamie looked back over his shoulder and smiled without breaking his step. 'It's like the fuckin' Dodge City, this place,' he laughed grimly. 'Wyatt Earp an' Doc Holliday are making sure we're safely out of town.'

'Aye, you're right,' Jack replied. 'But thank fuck they were on our side,' he quipped. . Were they, Jamie wondered? Well, maybe one of them, he conceded

At George Square they waited for their busses and watched, disinterestedly, as another fight broke out. 'I've really had enough of this shit, Jack,' he said quietly. 'It's gettin' me down...I need to get away,' he continued, waiting for Jack's reaction. 'I met Carol last night,' he said, before Jack could come in. Jack stared at him. If Jamie expected surprise he was disappointed. 'I took her home,' he added lamely.

'Whit? Doin' yer knight in shinin' armour bit again?'

'No, it wasn't like that. We just met here, waiting for the bus, and we got talking. She'd walked out on her boyfriend, that prick I had the run in with that night we met them in the Locarno, mind?'

Jack nodded. 'And?' he asked bluntly.

'And...I ended up spending the night with her.'

Jack shook his head slowly. 'An' ah take it ye shagged her?' he said. 'Ye're aff yer heid, ye know that?' Jamie said nothing. 'Remember whit she did tae ye last time?' Jack added.

'Aye, we spoke about that to, Jack, an' that's another reasons I have to get away. If I stay, I'll end up back with Carol or I'll spend more nights like tonight bein' chased through Springburn or Easterhouse or God knows where else, running away from God knows who...it's shite here, Jack, be honest.'

Jack turned towards him and looked him over, weighing his response. A young girl, probably 17 or 18 was throwing up nearby, momentarily distracting him and he wrinkled his nose in disgust. He had to agree, getting back together with Carol Whyte or fighting your way through bandit country for the rest of your days weren't particularly appealing. Tonight had been scary and the prospect of Jamie getting back with Carol again, whilst it might be fun for a while, would end in tears. *Personally, ah'd rather fight ma way through bandit country, he thought ruefully.* Okay, apart from them shaggin' Lillian and Valerie, tonight hadn't been much fun but it was nothing unusual so, other than escaping the clutches of Carol, there had to be another reason for the big man's sudden decision. 'It's Kate, isn't it? he said suddenly. 'Ye're goin' tae England tae find her, aren't ye?' he continued, voicing his suspicion. He had been here before with the big man. 'She's gone Jamie,' he continued wearily. 'Ye cannae start searchin' all over fuckin' England lookin' fur her. Let her go mate.'

Jamie smiled wryly. Jack was astute. Kate *was* part of it. Since she had left him he had been trying to come to terms with it but he simply couldn't get her out of his mind. He heard her voice and imagined her speaking to him; he dreamed about her – longed for her to be beside him when he woke....and he saw her in crowds - only for her to fade away before his eyes as he went towards her. And, if all that wasn't bad enough, now he was burdened with the guilt of sleeping with Carol. If he couldn't get her back then he had to exorcise her from his soul. He knew Jack's thoughts on the matter; they had discussed it often enough...Jack was a pragmatist and he was a dreamer. 'I'm not going to be searchin' the whole of England, wee man,' he replied, eventually in a tired voice. 'Okay, she might be part of the reason I'm going but she's not all of it.' He paused for a long moment, looking reflectively around him. 'I started thinking about it last week after Wembley...out on the town with no fightin' and a couple of birds that knew what they wanted...and told you,' he said, laughing at the memory. 'Then, last night I meet Carol and I can see my past becoming my future, if

I'm not careful. And tonight…Christ, I'm getting' too old for this shit, Jack, really…it's time for a change.'

They sat quietly for a while, watching the sights around the Square. Some guys were running amok at Queen Street; girls were screaming and police cars were coming from all sides. Nearby, a drunk was throwing up and two girls were arguing loudly, shouting abuse at each other as friends tried to pull them apart. The girl who had been sick earlier was still swaying precariously and holding onto the lamp post…looking like death heated up.

'Look at all this, Jack,' Jamie said, breaking the silence and sweeping his arm around to take it all in. 'Last weekend we were in London; we had a great night out in Soho, wandered the streets with some lassies, and we weren't bothered by anybody. The only fight I saw that whole weekend was between two drunks from up here.'

'And yer point is?'

'I'm moving South, Jackie mate.'

Jack shook his in disbelief. 'Jist like that…whit aboot a job? Ye'll need money. Where ur ye gonnae stay?' he fired at Jamie.

Jamie was ready. He removed his wallet from his pocket and pulled out a piece of folded newspaper, passing it over.

'Whit's this?'

'It's an advert from the Nottingham Post.'

'Regular reader, ur ye?' Jack laughed.

'Just read it, smart arse,' he retorted, laughing with him.

As Jack read the advert Jamie fished out two Lucky Strikes from an almost empty packet and offered one across. Jack took it. His eyes were glued to the advert and he turned it over, reading the words on the back. 'Where'd ye get this?' he asked.

'Last Sunday, on the way home…that wee roadside cafe outside Nottingham, remember? There was a newspaper lyin' on the table we sat at…it was in that.'

Jack nodded, remembering the cafe and the two young girls serving in it. They were memorable, if nothing else. 'So whit ur ye gonnae dae?'

'I'm handing in my notice at the Yard on Monday,' Jamie replied. 'I phoned the number in the advert this morning, they interviewed me over the phone, an' I start work at Ratcliffe on Soar Power Station on 16th May. I'm goin' down to Nottingham on the 15th.'

'Fur fuck sake, Jamie…yer in a bit o' a rush, ur ye no?' Jack spluttered. 'Whit aboot transport…digs an' that?'

'All sorted. The Company arranges it all.'

They were quiet for a while then Jack let out a sigh this time. 'Ye're right, big man, this place is gettin' worse. Ah nearly shit masel th'night. An' since ah broke up wae Teresa ah've been at a loose end…an' ah'm no gettin' much…ye know.'

'Aye, I know,' Jamie laughed, apart from last weekend and tonight. I bet lots of guys wish they were "no gettin' much" like you.'

'They twins last weekend, Phyllis an' Janey…ah'm still no' sure which wan ah shagged,' Jack said with a giggle.

'Probably both,' Jamie chortled. 'I couldn't tell the difference…an' we did it twice, mind?'

'They wir somethin' else,' Jack laughed, brightening. 'Ah kinda fancy comin' wae ye…if that's a'right wae you?'

Jamie smiled. He knew all along that Jack would come with him. He had lost Kate, Jack had dumped Teresa. They were both in purgatory; they had just taken different routes to get there.

'Keep the advert an' phone them first thing Monday mornin',' Jamie said. 'Tell them you spoke to me. The money's great...much better than here, an' if you don't like it you can always come home.' He grinned and put his arm around Jack's shoulder. 'I'm glad you're coming. I need my wingman to watch my back.'

Part II

The Journeymen

"If you don't know where you are going, any road will get you there." <u>Lewis Carroll</u>

Chapter 25

Nottingham/Derby May 1967

The club was hot and sweaty. Cigarette smoke drifted lazily up through the subdued lighting and The Temptations blasted out over the giant speakers on both sides of the little stage which sat at the far end of the dance floor. The atmosphere was heavy with an amalgam of smells, scents and odours; cigarette smoke, perfumes, the musk of male sweat and the sweetish, distinctive smell of cannabis.

The clientele tonight was predominantly male and a queue had formed early. The billboard outside the club and flyers posted all over Derby and distributed in pubs in the town gave the reason. "The Enchantresses", a female dance troupe known for their raunchy, erotic and evocative dance routines, were performing tonight and they sold out wherever they appeared. They had been appearing all over the Midlands over the past nine months and tonight they were back in their home town.

As the strains of The Four Tops' "Shake Me, Wake Me" faded away an expectant hush fell in the hall and there was a surge towards the stage. The music started again, the tempo faster, and the stage curtains opened slowly to reveal the girls, one by one. Men pushed and shoved, trying to get closer to the stage, and the air was filled with testosterone now. Each of the girls was blonde with short, cropped hair and their bodies were slim and athletic, sheathed in flesh coloured body stockings which, beneath the fluorescent lighting, left nothing to the imagination. They gyrated mystically, casting a spell over their audience, and swayed erotically with the music, their bodies shimmering with sweat and liberally applied glitter in the heat of the stage lights. As the tempo of the music increased to a frenzy so too did their routine. They had sexual magnetism in abundance and mesmerised their audience. Every man there believed that they were performing only for him and for no-one else and when the curtain closed at the end a collective sigh of unfulfilled lust filled the room.

Lucie Kent skipped from the stage and rushed to the dressing room. It was the end of their second, and final, routine of the night. The other girls were going on to another club to enjoy themselves, *incognito*, but Lucie had an early start the following morning at the hospital where she worked and had to get back the Nurses' Home. She stripped off her stage outfit and pulled on her normal clothes, a tight fitting top and jeans, then threw the body stocking and other bits and bobs into her duffle bag. She would shower back at her room as she usually did. Brushing back her short blonde hair she caught it in a clasp at the back of her head, pulled on a white crocheted tammy, applied a skim of dark red lipstick to her lips and pulled on her jacket, her appearance now completely changed. Quickly hugging and kissing the others, she left the club by a side door and made her way down the lane to the main road.

Outside, the cool evening air stroked her skin, refreshing her. It was just after ten o'clock and twilight was settling on the city and the roadway outside the club and the surrounding area were quiet. She felt safe. The doormen were still in view and one of them, an older man with cropped grey hair and a lived in face, gave her a wave. Lucie smiled back and waved in return before disappearing into the anonymity of the bus shelter. She estimated she had around five or six minutes to wait before the bus arrived but she didn't mind. She was happy tonight. Earlier that evening her best friend, another nurse, Julie Bradley, told her they had been invited to a party in her mother's house at the weekend. Julie's mother, known affectionately by Lucie as Auntie Jo, and her father Brian, ran a large lodging house in Beeston, near Nottingham, and threw regular weekend parties for their lodgers and family friends. An invite for the girls usually meant that there were some new boarders that Jo thought they might find "interesting". Hopefully, this time the guys would be more her own age and not older and married! Jo Bradley was an incorrigible match maker who never stopped trying to find a "nice boy" for each of them. Unfortunately, Jo's idea of a "nice boy" didn't always match the two girls' aspirations.

She was happily contemplating what the new lodgers might be like when the sound of a car pulling up alongside her brought her back to reality. The car was instantly recognisable; a 1966 black Rover 2000TC. A shiver of apprehension run through her. Three men lounged in the vehicle with Max Kelman sitting arrogantly in the driver's seat with another man beside him and the third sprawled in the back. As she looked into the car, all three men leered at her. She pulled her coat tightly around her and stared back defiantly. The driver's window wound down and the faux angelic features of Max Kelman smiled up at her, like a crocodile that has just spotted lunch.

'Hello Lucie,' he started smoothly in a voice that brought back nightmare memories for her. 'Long time no see.'

Not long enough, she thought privately, and smiled back frostily. He made her skin crawl and, like most people who knew him or knew of him, she was afraid. Being antagonistic towards him wasn't a good idea so she remained polite, cool and distant. Once upon a time she had thought him handsome and sophisticated but, she remembered bitterly, she had been so wrong. And that mistake had led to disaster. 'Hello Max,' she replied quietly, her eyes watching the road for her bus which she prayed would arrive soon.

'Get in,' Kelman continued pleasantly. 'I'll run you home…there's a little matter I want to discuss with you.'

Lucie's heart began to race as she looked around despairingly for a way out of this. Max Kelman was never pleasant just for the sake of it, there was always an ulterior motive behind it, and she began to panic. The man in the back of the car was smirking at her and she feared the worst now. Unsurprisingly, the doormen at the club had disappeared from sight. The arrival of Max Kelman's black Rover usually had that effect on people. Max had the knack of making people disappear.

Her bus arrived, pulling to a halt behind the Rover and disgorging a group of young men who were heading for the club. Lucie didn't wait or look round and ran for the bus immediately, the laughter of Max Kelman's two thugs ringing in her ears. Significantly, however, Max remained silent and as Lucie swung up onto the platform the Rover roared away with a squeal of tyres and the smell of burning rubber.

She found a seat on the lower deck and watched anxiously for any sign of the black car following. She was trembling, her heart was beating fast in her chest and her skin felt clammy. She thought she had erased the nightmare from her mind but even a glimpse of him brought it all back. And it had been more than a glimpse tonight. She felt sick. What could he want? she asked herself, but she suspected she already knew the answer. As her journey ended so her anxiety increased and before the bus had even come to a halt, she jumped from it and ran for the safety of the Nurses' Home about 50 yards distant.

The elderly night concierge lifted his head from his newspaper as she raced past and shook his head at the antics of the young, and then resumed his reading. She climbed the stairs to her room on the second floor two at a time and once there, locked and bolted the door. Only then did she break down and cry, the dark memories flooding her mind and forcing everything else aside. She looked in the mirror and saw a frightened child with a tear stained face staring back at her. She didn't recognise herself in the image but she knew that was how she had looked that fateful night two years earlier and she knew too that Max Kelman would always have this effect on her. Despair was in her again, drowning her in its dark and malevolent tide, but something inside her refused to die and she managed to pull herself back. She stripped and showered then, scrubbing her skin roughly as though by doing so she would wipe all thought of Max Kelman from her mind.

As she dried herself in front of the full length mirror in the bathroom she looked at her reflection in the glass. She saw nothing special in herself when compared with the other girls in the troupe. *They're special, but I'm not, so why me, she wondered?* Her modesty was another of her graces. She didn't consider herself as special in any way and she had no idea of the effect she had on men. She wished her mother was still alive which brought more tears from her eyes. Sadly, she pulled on her nightdress, returned to her bedroom and slipped beneath the sheets, pulling them over her head. She tried to blank all thought of Max Kelman from her mind but his words and the look of evil on his face haunted her. She cried herself to sleep.

Chapter 26

15 May 1967, Beeston, Nottinghamshire.
The train clanked to a halt in a hiss of steam and a cloud of white smoke. Jamie threw his bag down onto the platform and climbed wearily from the carriage, stretching his aching muscles. An early afternoon sun beat down from the cloudless sky and he was sweating heavily, his shirt clinging to him like a second skin. His bleary eyes half closed against the sun's glare, he scanned his surroundings and spotted others not unlike himself and Jack Connolly, all lost and trying to get their bearings.

It was warm here, much warmer than home, and the humidity was oppressive. His hangover didn't help. Jack hovered beside him and he wasn't faring any better, his face contorted and his eyes closed to narrow slits. He too stretched his stiff and weary muscles and shaded his eyes against the brightness with his hand over them like a permanent salute. They were both in bad shape, their drinking session of the night before still taking its toll. It had been an impromptu booze up, organised at the last minute by some of their mates who insisted they join them in the Beresford Hotel Bar in Sauchiehall Street, to say goodbye. On the positive side, their earlier nausea, dry boak, throbbing headache and raging thirst had abated a little leaving them with mild headache, aversion to the bright sunlight and overwhelming exhaustion.

'Ah'm knackered,' Jack complained as the heat hit him. 'Why the fuck did we drink sae much last night?'

Jamie tried, painfully, to force a grin. 'Why do we ever?' He was suffering badly but he suspected that Jack was in an even worse state. Pints of Guinness and double whiskies in equal measure were a potent combination and Jamie had lost count at six of each.

'Fur fuck sake!' Jack muttered. 'Can somebody no pull the curtains or turn aff the light? That thing's burning right intae ma brain…like a fuckin' weldin' torch,' he moaned. The "thing" he was referring to was the sun which sat like a smouldering orange in the sky above them.

Jamie laughed and instantly regretted it. His head started to pound again and a new wave of nausea swept over him. He fought it back, swallowing hard. 'That "thing", as you put it, is the sun. You must remember it…it comes out a couple of times a year back home,' he said sarcastically.

'Aye, but it disnae shine like that,' Jack retorted. 'Or if it does, it's usually hidin' behind a cloud or some other shit risin' frae the chimneys.'

A whistle blew, the guard waved his flag, and the train pulled away. There was still a crowd of guys milling about and looking as lost as before but other than them there was no-one. Jamie picked up his bag and sauntered over to the nearest group which consisted of three lads. 'Are you guys startin' work at Ratcliffe Power Station, by any chance?' he asked as he joined them, Jack in tow.

'Yeah,' one of them, a big, dark skinned older lad, replied, sounding relieved. 'Do you know wha' we're supposed t' do now?' he asked, in a thick, nasal Scouse accent.

'Wait here, I suppose,' Jamie replied, waving his envelope. 'The letter says someone will meet us.'

They set about introducing themselves. Jamie dug out his Lucky Strikes and offered them around. The big Scouser was Terry Hughes and he, like Jamie, had been working in a shipyard, his being on the Mersey, till he found this job at Ratcliffe. He was a big, jovial Liverpudlian and Jamie sensed immediately that they would get on well. If the rest of the crew working at Ratcliffe were like him then things would be alright.

Next to introduce himself was a small Glaswegian who Jamie and Jack had spoken to briefly on the train out of Glasgow earlier in the day. He was about 5'2" in height with a narrow waist and broad, powerful shoulders and a warrior's face set atop a thick, bull like neck. His eyes sparkled, a feature which drew attention to the fading black, brown and blue remains of a large bruise around the right one.

'Ah'm Andy Lynch,' he said, thrusting out his right paw. 'But ma pals call me Benny.' He was grinning broadly.

Jamie took the proffered hand and shook it. 'I'm Jamie, Jamie Raeburn, and this recovering alcoholic here is my pal, Jack Connolly,' he said, putting his arm round Jack's shoulder. 'Why do your pals call you "Benny"?' he asked innocently. 'Is it your middle name?'

'Naw,' the little guy laughed. 'It's after the boxer...Benny Lynch,' he replied proudly. 'Ye *must've* heard o' him... undisputit world flyweight boxing champion, an' he came fae the Gorbals, like me.'

'Oh that "Benny Lynch"!' Jamie smiled, covering his embarrassment. 'Aye, I've heard of *him*. So you're a boxer then?'

Benny laughed easily. 'Well, ah didnae get this keeker walkin' intae a door,' he snickered, pointing to his black eye.

'Wae that accent ye could've got it walkin intae anythin',' Jack interjected with a grin of his own and shook the little guy's hand.

The third member of this disparate group was a Geordie. Michael Brown (who insisted they call him Mick but persisted in introducing himself as Michael). He was an unlikely looking welder. His dress sense was, to say the least, bizarre and he was overweight by at least two stones. His stomach hung over his belt and Jamie suspected the last time he had seen his feet was a couple of years earlier, at least. His face was puffy with pasty white skin and heavy jowls that made him look much older than the twenty three years he claimed to be. He did, however, have one saving grace; he had a happy go lucky attitude and an easy going style which was easy to be around.

They were onto their second cigarettes before an overweight gent in a dark suit trotted along the platform, waving furiously to attract their attention and the attention of the other small groups of men gathered on the platform. The other groups migrated towards them and the suited man, sweating heavily from what appeared to be uncustomary exertion, was quickly surrounded. There were twelve now waiting expectantly for instructions.

The man looked them all up and down and turned his attention to his clipboard. 'Right, you're all here,' he started. 'All starting at Ratcliffe on Soar?' he asked. But as there was no one else on the platform and he had been expecting twelve men, it was a pretty safe bet. Running down the list of names on his clipboard alphabetically he had them identify themselves, one by one, and gave them the names and addresses of their lodgings. Jamie discovered that he was sharing digs with Benny, Michael (just call me Mick) and Terry Hughes but was disappointed to find that Jack was billeted elsewhere. Still, Beeston didn't seem to be a big place so that wouldn't be a problem. And then, having given out his information, the man quickly disappeared, leaving them still bemused and without directions.

Without thinking, Jamie took charge and made his way to the ticket office where he found the Station Master, a neatly uniformed little man with a close cropped hair and a military style moustache, reading a paper behind the ticket counter. Jamie quickly explained their predicament and the man laughed. 'Same thing happens most Mondays,' he chortled. 'Where are you staying?'

'Bradley, Devonshire Place,' Jamie replied quickly.

'Jo Bradley,' the little man laughed. You'll be alright there, lad,' he said reassuringly and gave him directions to find the place. 'Send in the others, and I'll sort them out too,' he continued merrily as Jamie departed.

Leaving Jack with his own group and promising to meet later, Jamie and the others made their way to the house in Devonshire Place. It took about ten minute to walk there and the fresh air and the sunshine started to have a recuperative effect on Jamie. By the time they arrived at the boarding house, he felt almost human again. At the door, the others unconsciously deferred to him and left him to do the introductions. When Mrs Bradley opened the door they found themselves face to face with an attractive woman in her mid to late forties. She nodded as Jamie went through their names and then looked them up and down like an army sergeant major before leading them upstairs to their rooms.

'The three of you will be sharing this room,' she started immediately, pointing to Jamie, Benny and Mick. 'And you will be in the room next door,' she told Terry. The other two lads in your room are at work just now and the freshly made bed is yours.' She then rhymed off a list of "do's and don'ts" – mostly don'ts as far as the lads could tell. 'There's no smoking allowed in the bedrooms; no drinking in the rooms; no loud music after nine o'clock at night; the room is to be kept clean and tidy at all times…and no women are allowed in the rooms.' She paused, just long enough to let that lot sink in and to catch her breath, and then she was off again. 'Breakfast is between six thirty and seven, dinner at six thirty at night, and if you're late, you won't be fed. The bathroom is at the end of the hall on this landing, just there, next to the stair leading up to the attic bedroom,' she said, pointing along the landing. 'Alright? Any questions?' she asked, but they all got the impression that questions weren't welcomed. The four of them stood there, like dummies, looking at one another and lost for words. 'Right then,' the formidable Mrs Bradley continued. 'In that case, I'll let you all settle in and I'll see you at dinner.' She left them and headed back down the stairs to her kitchen, her face wreathed in a mirthful grin.

'Fuck sake!' Benny mumbled despondently, breaking the stunned silence. 'Ah left hame tae get away fae the likes o' that.' Jamie and Mick were still shell shocked.

Terry smiled grimly. 'Reminds me of my wife,' he said wryly. 'Ah'll feel right at 'ome.' He plodded off to his room and disappeared inside.

There was no argument over the beds. Jamie picked the bed nearest the door, Benny the bed facing the door and Mick ended up sleeping underneath the window. There was a high backed chair next to each bed, one large antique wooden wardrobe – big enough for all their jackets and trousers – and a three drawer chest against the far wall, one drawer for each of them. Jamie lay down on his bed and wondered how Jack was getting on. They suspected before leaving Glasgow that they would be allocated to different digs but at least they were in the same town and, as it happened, Jack was in a house only about ten minutes' walk away.

'Anybody fancy goin' fur a walk?' Benny asked after a bit. 'Maybes we can find a pub that's open. Ah need a drink efter aw that,' he added morosely.

Jamie hauled himself off his bed. A hair of the dog might be a good idea, he thought. They tried to rouse Terry but the big Liverpudlian was already sound asleep on top of his bed. Leaving him snoring like a wart hog, they set off, tip-toeing quietly down the stairs to avoid being spotted by the intimidating Mrs Bradley. They failed miserably though they were unaware of the fact. Jo Bradley was still in her kitchen as they passed down the hall on their tip toes, and she took immense delight in their apparent anxiety. She liked to put the fear of death into her new lodgers before they discovered that her bark was infinitely much worse than her bite.

'We're no' likely tae find a pub open at this time in the efternoon. Whit about yon factory doon near the station, it hud a big Social Club, mind? Mibees it'll be open,' Benny remarked and a look of utter confusion appeared on Mick's pudgy face. 'Whit's wrang wi' you?' Benny demanded.

'I couldna understand a word you said, bonny lad.' Mick replied with a shrug and Jamie creased up with laughter. Benny drew him a dirty look and shook his head.

'Jist…follow…the…two…o'…us. Right?' he said, spelling the words out slowly and deliberately as if speaking to a slow witted child. Mick nodded in time with each word, a cheeky grin on his plump face.

They meandered into the town, enjoying the early summer weather. It was quiet. An urban oasis, away from noise and grime and the people they saw, mostly women, seemed happily content with life. 'No' like Glasgow, eh big man?' Benny observed, directing his comment at Jamie.

He nodded. It did all seem so different…and he was one of the lucky ones, he reflected; Guys like Benny and Jack lived in dark, grey tenements, cheek by jowl with their neighbours…to them it must seem like the promised land. And the sun was shining. 'Take a deep breath Benny…enjoy it, you won't choke, unlike home' he replied, a sense of contentment reviving in him.

'An' where ur aw the men? Huv ye seen any…apart frae that wee fat guy at the station?' 'It's like we're the only men here,' Benny grinned. It wasn't difficult to see where he was going with it.

'Now *that* could be fun, bonny lad,' Mick chipped in, the underlying suggestion astounding Jamie and Benny, both. Benny looked at him, open mouthed, and Jamie raised a dubious eyebrow.

'So you're a ladies' man then?' Jamie asked, scepticism dripping from every word. He hadn't thought of Mick as the Don Juan type but first impressions can be misleading, he reminded himself…but taking another look at the rotund Geordie he thought he'd probably got it right. Mick was short, about five foot four inches tall - or short - depending on how you looked at it, and his girth was about the same. He looked like an oversized Munchkin, Jamie reflected. His trousers were supported by a leather belt which could just be seen beneath the sagging overhang of his ample belly. And his jacket, fastened by one remaining button, had definitely seen better days. But that wasn't all; his fondness for psychedelic colours was…well, *unusual* was probably the least offensive way of putting it. His trousers, flared hipsters, were a fawn and brown check and his jacket dark blue, sort of mid-way between royal blue and navy. The *piece de resistance* however was his mustard yellow button down shirt with a wide Paisley Pattern tie in shades of green. The whole outfit could do with a volume control. But Mick had one saving grace…his face which could almost be described as cherubic and he had, beneath his heavy black glasses, two clear, almost translucent, green eyes.

Overall, Jamie couldn't imagine him attracting many women...unless they were colour blind and had a predilection for men with tits. Takes all types, he thought with a laugh. 'Stick with me, then, Micky boy an' we'll see if we can find you one,' he grinned. Benny's astonishment rose to a different plane.

Benny was a horse of a different colour, to quote The Wizard of Oz. He was even shorter than Mick, coming in at five feet two (wearing Cuban heels!) and weighing around nine stones. He was like a coiled spring and, despite his size, his latent strength was obvious. His face looked as if it had been sculpted from granite with prominent cheek bones and sparkling blue eyes which never seemed to be at peace. In his three piece herring-bone patterned grey suit and immaculate white shirt and plain blue tie he was quite the little dandy. And Jack had said the same at the station earlier. Benny, though, just might be a ladies' man – for little ladies, or big ladies - if they liked small guys!

They were three very different guys; Jamie, tall and well-built with long, brown hair and dark brown, almost ebony coloured eyes like bottomless pits. Benny, smaller than the other two but dressed like a tailor's dummy and looking every bit the athlete he undoubtedly was, and Mick, the colour bandit who clearly liked his beer...and probably his grub, the man for the myopic "bigger" girl. Something for everyone!

They didn't make it to the factory Social Club. The sun was out and there were women to look at so they wandered aimlessly around, exploring, until at five o'clock they discovered The Spinner's Rest, a big pub on Woolaton Road. The Spinner's Rest had one major point in its favour; it was only minutes from Devonshire Place if they skipped through the church grounds opposite. The landlord looked surprised when he opened the doors to find them waiting patiently and then, with three pints of warm bitter before them, they sat contentedly looking out at the evening traffic.

'Whit brought ye doon here?' Benny quizzed, sensing a story behind Jamie's mask of conviviality. Jamie sipped at his beer and looked at him blankly. Undeterred, Benny ploughed on. 'Ur ye runnin' away fae somethin', or somebody?' he pressed. 'If ye ur, ye'd be better aff joinin' the Foreign Legion.' He swallowed some beer, watching Jamie's reaction.

The laugh didn't surprise him. 'I'm not runnin' away from anyone, wee man,' he replied, 'I just fancied a change.'

'So, if ye're no runnin' away, ur ye tryin' tae find yersel?'

'For fuck sake, Benny, give it a rest,' Jamie exploded with amusement. 'I thought you were a welder and an amateur boxer, no a fuckin' part time psychiatrist.'

Mick broke in. 'He's got a point, bonny lad, you've got the air of a man of mystery,' he said, laughing through a mouthful of bitter.

'Don't you start,' Jamie fired back. 'I'm here for the money and the women...end of story. If you two keep bangin' on, the fuckin' Foreign Legion might be my next stop.' Benny and Mick shared a look and burst out laughing. 'What I do have is the air of a thirsty man.' He finished his beer and nodded at Mick. 'An' it's your round,' he said. As Mick waddled over to the bar, Jamie reflected on that little discussion. *Is that why I'm here, he wondered, to find myself?*

They returned to Devonshire Place just before the time set for dinner, washed quickly and joined the other boarders in the dining room. Introductions followed, Jamie struggling to remember names as the others introduced themselves one by one. With the newly arrived quartet there was now a total of twelve; an eclectic mix of Londoners, Liverpudlians, Geordies, Mancunians and Irishmen...and, of course, Glaswegians. A sort of United Nation of journeymen, welders, sparks, plumbers and joiners all working at the newest and most advanced Power Station in the country. Maybe he had found himself right enough, Jamie thought.

*

The first weekend came quickly. Work finished early and Mick announced on the journey back to Beeston that he was going home and when the works bus deposited them in the town centre he was off like a greyhound out a trap. The others sauntered along slowly in the warm afternoon sunshine. Before they reached the digs Mick was already on his way, racing past them back towards the town to catch a bus into Nottingham and the connecting train for Newcastle. 'See you all on Sunday night,' he shouted back as he disappeared down the road.

Jamie watched him go, bemused. 'I can't see the point,' he said, shaking his head. 'We've just got here an' he's off home.'

'Maybe he's got a bird there,' Benny opined.

Jamie looked at him theatrically, his face a picture of disbelief, and the others howled with laughter. 'Are you for real? You probably think the moon's made of cheese too, eh?' he replied caustically. 'But hey, you never know,' he added, apparently mellowing and becoming serious. 'My mother says there's somebody out there for everybody…but, then again, she's never met our Mick.' His words were swallowed up in a roar of laughter.

'Aw, come on, he's no' that bad,' Benny admonished, jumping to Mick's defence.

Jamie was still laughing. 'I'm jokin' Benny, honest. Mick's alright, strange taste in clothes, but he's alright.'

'Okay, point taken,' Benny agreed, joining the communal hilarity. 'He's like a clown oot o' yon Chipperfield Circus…a big rid nose an' he'll huv a new career.'

'If he keeps shiftin' bitter the way he is he'll have one of those soon enough,' Jamie chortled as they all filed into the house. 'Right, enough about Coco,' Jamie said when he and Benny were alone. 'Are you comin' out to play tonight? Jack and I are headin' into Nottingham to see what it's got.'

'Nah, ah don't think so. Ah'm no' too good wi' burds. Ah leave that sort o' thing tae shaggers like you.'

Jamie grinned. 'Well, if you change your mind, I'm getting' the half seven bus.'

'Nah, ah'll leave it, big man; ah'm aw fingers an' thumbs when it comes tae burds.'

Jamie bent double with laughter again. 'Listen Benny, some birds I've met love a guy that's "all fingers and thumbs"…I'm quite good wi' them myself,' he chuckled. 'Stick with Jack and me an' we'll find you a nice wee lassie you can practise your talents on.'

Benny blushed and shook his head slowly. 'Nah, thanks aw the same, ah'll jist stay here.'

As he was leaving later, Jamie tried again to cajole Benny into coming with him and Jack but the wee man steadfastly refused. Jo Bradley, hearing the exchange from the kitchen, joined them and she too added her encouragement but Benny was having none of it. She gave up and then looked Jamie up and down, giving a low whistle. 'Some girl is going get lucky tonight, she teased. 'If I was twenty years younger I'd fancy a bit of you myself.'

'If you were twenty years younger folk would think I was a baby snatcher,' he threw back flirtatiously. 'I've always liked older, more experienced women,' he laughed, flickering his eyelids and watching her blush. 'If I don't get lucky in Nottingham I'll be back for you,' he grinned.

'You cheeky monkey,' she snickered. 'But with six women for every man around here you're bound to attract at least one, so I won't stay up,' she laughed.

'How many? Six did you say? Really?' he spluttered.

'Yes, really,' Jo .chuckled.

Jamie turned again to Benny. 'Six to one, Benny; come on, you have to be up for it now, surely'

Benny blushed and lowered his head. 'Nah, ah'll jist stay here, go fur a pint.'

'Ah well,' Jamie sighed. 'Don't say I didn't ask.' And with that, he stepped out into the warm evening air.

'Enjoy yourself,' Jo called as he disappeared down the road. *Oh I will, he thought happily, I certainly will.*

Chapter 27

Jack waited impatiently at the bus stop, pointedly looking at his watch in frustration as Jamie arrived. 'Dae ye ever turn up on time fur anything, you?' he moaned. 'We're wastin' good drinkin' time.'

Changed days, Jamie thought, and ignored him, turning instead to the lad who was with Jack. 'How you doin'? I'm Jamie,' he said, smiling and thrusting out his right hand.

'Davie Miller,' the lad replied. 'Jack's been tellin' me all about ye, eh?' His accent said he came from Edinburgh.

'Well, don't believe everythin' *he* tells you,' Jamie grinned. 'So, you up for it tonight? It's Friday.'

Friday night habits die hard. First, a drink…or four. Next, move on to a club or the dancing and last, but not least, try to pull and, if you're lucky, get your leg over. They decided to stick with the formula. As they sat on the upper deck of the bus, smoking Jamie's Lucky Strikes, Davie gave Jamie his story. He wasn't working at Ratcliffe, like them, and was, instead, a telephone engineer doing a course three month course at the big Erikson Telecoms factory near the station.

'That's good,' Jamie said, picking up on this. 'You'll be able to get us in to the Social Club then?'

'Oh aye, no problem, eh,' Davie replied enthusiastically. 'It's good; they've got pool an' billiards tables, cards and bingo…an' the beer's cheap, eh,' he confirmed.

Why do Edinburgh folk always finish a sentence with "eh" even when they're it's a statement they're making and they're not asking a question, Jamie wondered? Probably for the same reason we say "aye right" when we mean "no", he concluded. 'Did you two know that the lassies outnumber the men down here by six to one?' he said, imparting Jo Bradley's news.

Both turned to him instantly. 'Aye, right!' Jack laughed dubiously.

'Seriously…Jo told me,' Jamie confirmed.

'Who's Joe?' Davie asked, bemused.

'Naw, not Joe, Jo…it's short for Josephine. She's my landlady.'

'She's a bit of alright, your landlady,' Jack chipped in grinning.

'Aye, she is,' Jamie agreed. 'I told her that myself tonight before I came out. Made her blush.'

'Ooooh, now that could be dangerous, big man. Her man's a bit o' a bear an' apart fae that, she'd probably suck ye in an' blaw ye oot in bubbles,' Jack guffawed, attracting attention from the other, seemingly staid, passengers. 'Mind you, it wid be worth it cos ye'd always be well fed!'

At the stop for Nottingham University a crowd of students, mostly guys, clambered noisily onto the bus. From their conversation, they were heading for a pub and then, later, going to a club. The three Scots boys shared a look. Just the business, they all agreed, and when the students rose to get off they followed. It turned out to be a wise move. A few minutes' walk took them to Nottingham Castle and a pub, "Ye Olde Trip to Jerusalem", which claimed to be the oldest pub in

England, dating back to the time of the Crusades. 'If that's right they should know how tae pour a good pint, then,' Jack declared. 'A few o' those doon oor throats an' then we can look fur six lassies…though two wid be enough fur me.'

'Is that right?' Jamie laughed. 'If you can handle two how come you always needed me to take Teresa's wee pal, Bernadette, off your hands? You could have shagged the two of them.'

'No, no, no,' Jack responded, putting it on. 'Ye *were* essential. Ye huv tae remember,' he continued furtively, as though divulging a secret, 'is that Teresa and Bernadette are two good Catholic lassies. Bad enough traipsing along tae Confession tae admit ye've hud a shag but confessin' tae a threesome, nae chance! They'd be sayin' Hail Mary's an' lightin' candles furever.'

'You two are mad,' Davie chortled loudly. 'Ye're both Catholics, then?'

Jamie and Jack looked at each other and then turned in unison to look at Davie. 'I take fae yer question ye're no?' Jack said gravely and getting a look of awkward embarrassment from Davie in return.

Jamie saved his blushes. 'Ignore him Davie, lad…he's a Tim,' he laughed, flicking his thumb in Jamie's direction. 'Me, I'm a Hun, like you…we're on the side of the angels.' His laugh grew louder and he grabbed Jack round the shoulder as his friend pretended hurt. 'There's only one condition of membership to our wee club…Religion is taboo. We don't talk about it – not in a serious way anyway – and we don't let it stop us havin' a good time. Jack here even uses condoms an' he shags Protestants.' His laughing was out of control as he gripped Jack's shoulder tightly. 'Would you like to join?'

Davie beamed and thrust out his hand. 'Oh aye, I'm in!'

'No' like that big man,' Jack laughed, showing a clenched fist. 'Like this!' Jamie put his fist on top of Jack's and Davie, catching on, placed his on Jamie's. 'Jist like the Three Musketeers,' Jack laughed, forcing his arm upwards to throw all three still clenched fists into the air. 'One fur all and all fur one,' they shouted together to the bewilderment of passers-by, some smiling and others shaking their heads incredulously. To them, it appeared, the lunatic had been allowed out of the asylum.

A pleasant surprise awaited them at the pub. Six to one Jo had said but in here that ratio was well surpassed. There were girls everywhere; tall girls, small girls, fat girls, thin girls, blonde girls, brunettes and redheads, girls in miniskirts and girls wearing practically nothing at all. The three lads stood there, open mouthed, blocking the doorway.

'Fur fuck sake! Jack exclaimed with delight. 'Ah think ah've jist died and gone tae heaven.'

More girls jostled past them as they fought their way into the already heaving pub. Davie spotted a small space near the bar and they squeezed through the crowd towards it while their eyes moved appreciatively from one group of scantily clad girls to another and it wasn't long before they themselves were attracting attention. Men were certainly in the minority and the ones who were here looked mostly like students. Jamie bought a round of drinks and they then pushed their way, as gently as possible, through the crush of female bodies to a relatively quiet spot near the rear which happened, fortuitously, to be right next to the Ladies' Toilets. As Jack remarked, succinctly, this was the best spot in the house as at one time or another just about every girl there would have to pass them. It promised to be a good night.

Chapter 28

Soon, they noticed they were drawing looks from all directions. Some were admiring…from girls, and some were hostile…from the few guys which was a bit unfair as there were more than enough girls to satisfy demand. But male pride and jealousy has no rational basis and they were different; they stood out. Their clothes were stylish and looked expensive, indicating that they had money, and, to add insult to injury, all three were what the girls would describe as "fit". Animosity was only to be expected.

'Well, it's aw here an' it's aw up fur it,' Jack announced with a grin. 'It's Showtime!'

A group of six girls took up a spot nearby and began to show interest, casting admiring glances in their direction. Jamie smiled. Now he understood how girls at the Locarno felt when the wolves were on the prowl. The six girls were eyeing them up openly now and Jamie caught one of them brazenly looking him up and down. He smiled at her and she blushed but kept on looking. 'I think I've found mine,' he announced, elbowing Jack in the ribs. 'The tall one with the long dark hair and the low cut black dress…just look at those tits!' he said salaciously

Jack and Davie looked at her, ogling her appreciatively, and she blushed more then, her cheeks turning a deeper red.

'She's alright, eh,' Davie agreed.

Jack nodded absently…he had spotted another that took his fancy. 'That wee blonde in the light blue crochet dress is a bit of alright,' he murmured. 'Ye can see everythin' that's on offer beneath that frock she's wearin'?'

Jamie followed the direction of his friend's gaze and saw immediately what Jack was referring to. 'Fuck me!' he exclaimed quietly. 'Is she wearin' anythin' at all under that dress?'

'Ah hope no!' Jack replied with a laugh.

Jamie turned back to the tall girl in black. She was staring at him again. The blushing was over and she was waiting for him to make a play, flirting with him openly. She was tall, about 5' 8" or 5' 9", Jamie guessed; tall and slim. Her black dress she was barely covering the essentials, exposing long, shapely legs which appeared to be naturally tanned and unspoiled by nylon so far as he could see. He was aroused already and he suspected she knew it. He looked at her face again. Her jet black hair, cut with a straight fringe above her eyes, fell down below her shoulders, feathered at the front to frame her face perfectly and curving in wisps under her chin. It highlighted her long, slender neck and settled just above her breasts. Wow, he thought, the stirring of desire building between his legs. He thought of The Hollies' song, "Long Tall Woman in a Black Dress" and the guy who wrote it must have been looking at a girl like this at the time. He was beginning to fantasise, always a good sign when it came to women. Pulling his eyes, reluctantly, back up to her face he saw her smile, sure her expression was saying "come on then, what are you waiting for?"

'Come on Davie,' he muttered impatiently. 'Jack and me are sorted…there must be at least one of that lot you fancy,' he pressed. Davie looked at him awkwardly, and then turned back to the girls.

'Ah didnae realise you guys fae Edinburgh were sae slow. Dae ye need a haun?' Jack asked cheekily.

'No, it's alright,' Davie replied quickly, his mind made up. 'I fancy that wee lassie in the red mini skirt and the white top, eh?' he announced finally. 'What do you two think?'

Jamie and Jack turned their attention towards the chosen one, their eyes appraising her expertly from top to bottom and bottom to top. Being a big lad himself, Davie had chosen wisely. A "wee lassie" she wasn't, but she was definitely well proportioned and good looking…not as overtly sexy as the girl in black or Jack's blonde but there was something erotic in the way she sipped her drink.

'Aye, very nice,' Jack replied, tempted to tease Davie. 'Ah think ye might jist huv the best chance o' the three of us o' gettin' yer leg ower.'

Jamie laughed, perpetuating the joke. 'To be fair Jack,' he chirped. 'I would.'

'Aye, but you wid wi' anythin' wearin' knickers,' he laughed, and then, seeing the hurt on Davie's face, relented. 'Ah'm kiddin' Davie, honest, she's nice. Go for it, big man,' he said encouragingly and Davie's expression brightened immediately. 'Right, that's us sorted,' Jack declared. 'Let's go. Let the dug see the rabbit.'

They moved in like well-trained Collie dogs separating individual sheep from a flock. The six girls watched and waited, all of them wondering what was about to unfold. Only the girl in the black dress had any inkling of that, her eyes on Jamie as he came towards her. He approached her directly; his eyes on hers, and saw the smile of anticipation appear on her face. She, for her part, had decided she was having him and cut the rest of the girls out by stepping forward to meet him, her message abundantly clear. They faced each other and Jamie placed his hand possessively on her hip.

'What kept you?' she asked huskily.

'They did,' he laughed, jerking a thumb at Jack and Davie who had now closed in on their chosen targets. 'I'm Jamie,' he said, leaning forward to kiss her on the cheek. 'What do I call you?'

'My name's Charlotte but you can call me Charley,' she replied with a warm smile.'

'I like that,' he said smoothly, both hands on her hips now.

'Where are you from? I haven't seen you in here before,' she asked, resting a hand on his shoulder. Her voice was soft and sexy, increasing Jamie's craving. Everything was all going to plan…for both of them.

'Glasgow,' he replied, wondering if the city's reputation might frighten her off, but she didn't seem fazed.

The small talk and flirting continued as they sussed each other out. 'What are you doing down here?' she asked, sounding genuinely interested. He considered spinning her a porky…he could be anything, after all; professional footballer, singer in a rock band, a junior doctor, maybe…with a good bedside manner, or even a pilot. But Charley didn't look the type who would be impressed by any of those, so he plumped for the truth.

'I'm a welder,' he said, trying to make it sound exciting. 'I'm working at the new power station over at Ratcliffe on Soar.' She looked like she was impressed but she could have been kidding. In any event she probably didn't have a clue what a welder did so he explained, trying to make it sound more exotic than it really is.

She seemed to be hanging on his every word and the vibes were good. She was making all the right noises…his clothes were "really stylish" and the local boys "don't really care" because they thought they "didn't really have to" which Jamie took as a reference to the number of girls for each guy in the area. 'We don't have many Mods like you around here,' she continued, casting a disdainful eye around the pub.

'I'm not exactly a Mod,' Jamie replied, gently disabusing her of the notion…Mods, after all, wore Parkas and drove around on scooters, like sewing machines with wheels, whereas he rode a Triumph T120 and wore leather.

'Oh, I think you are,' Charley replied, preventing him from saying more on the subject. If she wants me to be a Mod, I'm a Mod, he decided. 'You look really good,' she added, massaging his ego.

Time for a compliment of his own, he decided. 'You look better than good,' he whispered. 'I love your dress…what you got on under it?' he posed cheekily, anticipating a slap.

Charley smiled coyly and leaned towards him. 'Take me home later and you might find out,' she laughed sexily and gave him his first kiss of the night. As they came up for air Jamie looked around the pub, checking out the local lads. Charley was right, he noted; he, Jack and Davie made the locals look scruffy, which probably accounted for the hostility he was beginning to pick up.

With Jack and Davie having made their choices the other girls drifted away. Jamie swung Charley around to join the others in a little group and introductions followed. The "wee lassie" Davie was fawning over was Donna and the blonde bombshell with the see through crochet dress was Angela.

Time to impress, Jamie decided, and pulled a thick wad of Pound notes from his jacket pocket. 'What would you girls like to drink, girls?' he asked, smiling impishly as the others, with the exception of Jack, looked at the money with open astonishment. Jack suppressed a grin. He out of all of them knew the trick that Jamie had pulled. Surprised, because they usually had to buy their own drinks, the girls chattered away excitedly and all for dark rum and black which, Jamie discovered, was dark rum topped up with blackcurrant cordial. It was a new one on him but, if that's what rocked their boat, so be it.

Jack followed him to the bar with an offer to help with the drinks and, when out of hearing range, doubled up with laughter. 'Did ye see the look on Davie's face?' he chortled. 'He'll think ye're a fuckin' gangster wi' all that cash.

Jamie grinned as they waited for the barman to pour the drinks. 'Aye, it works every time…as long as I don't spend more than six quid.' It was a trick he and Jack pulled occasionally to impress girls, usually the ones they decided were "gold diggers" but that wasn't the case tonight. Twenty or so bits of newspaper cut to exactly the same size as Pound notes with a few real one pound notes on top and the bottom looked, when folded over, remarkably like a wad of at least twenty pounds. 'Should we tell Davie?' he asked.

'Aye, ah think that's a good idea,' Jack spluttered. 'If ye don't he'll expect ye tae buy the drinks aw night.'

When they returned and Jamie passed round the drinks, Jack eased Davie aside and whispered in his ear. Jamie laughed to himself as the big Edinburgh lad's face was wreathed in a wide grin and he looked over, giving Jamie a conspiratorial wink. Jamie grinned, raised his pint, and winked back.

Davie and Donna really seemed to be hitting it off and Jamie watched, a little enviously, as they chatted away secretively. With a flourish, Davie finally let them into the secret that he and his new love had been discussing though Jamie had the impression the other two girls already knew it. 'Donna was sayin' that her house is empty,' Davie said, trying to sound nonchalant and keep the excitement out of his voice while wrapping his arm, meaningfully, around Donna's waist. 'If you guys are up for it, we can go back for a wee party, eh?'

It was obvious then that Angela and Charley did already know the score and they seemed to be "up for it" as Davie had put it. Result! Jamie thought with a broad smile and saw that Jack had reached the same conclusion. When he turned back to Charley there was a tell-tale twinkle in her eyes. She leaned forward to kiss him and his eyes were drawn, as she knew they would be, to the deep cleft between her breasts. He moaned, almost silently, and then looked up quickly, guiltily. Charley laughed at his embarrassment and continued with the kiss as she had intended, then whispered huskily in his ear. 'Donna's Mum and Dad are on holiday and her brother is away at some camp or other,' she murmured. 'We can spend the night together...and you can see what else I've got beneath my dress...if you want?'

Jamie grinned. 'Yes, I want,' he said. 'But what about this?' he asked, lifting her left hand and holding it in front of her eyes, the diamond ring on the third finger sparkling in the light.

'I'm engaged,' Charley replied quietly, 'but he's away just now. Is it a problem?'

Jamie was taken aback by her directness and was, unusual for him, almost lost for words...almost but not quite. As Charley made to pull away he caught her and pulled her to him, kissing her firmly on the mouth and tasting the flavour of the rum and blackcurrant on her tongue as she responded. No, it's not a problem, and yes, I still want to.' Charley's face lit up and for a heartbeat, Jamie thought of Kate. Engaged? Married? Same difference, he told himself, but this time it definitely was just for fun.

Chapter 29

It was still early when they left the pub, all of them keen to get to Donna's house; but as they were leaving a nasty confrontation threatened to spoil the party. Some local lads decided to take the piss, jealousy and resentment at the back of it. It was nothing too serious but Jamie, being Jamie, couldn't ignore it. The ringleader was mimicking a Scottish accent, badly, with lots of "hooch aye the noo" being thrown in. It was something and nothing but Jamie could sense the girls were worried. He stopped in front of the instigator and turned to face him, Charley tugging forcefully at his arm to keep going and leave. He ignored her and stared coldly at the guy, said nothing, just looked contemptuously at him and disregarded the others who all appeared to be waiting in anticipation. Davie was edgy, ready to say something, but Jack held up his hand and silenced him. Nerves began to fray as Jamie kept staring at the guy with a look of complete disdain. Who would blink first, was the question?

Jack smiled perceptively as the scenario unfolded; he had been in this situation with Jamie before. Gently, he took hold of Charley's arm and eased her away.

Jamie moved closer to his protagonist and whispered softly, so low that only the lad himself could hear. 'Try it, an' I'll break yer fuckin' arm...in fact, I'll break both yer fuckin' arms,' he said amiably, but there was no mistaking he meant every word. From the side, Jack smiled as the smug grin on the arrogant shit's face started to fade and seeds of doubt took root. Watching closely, knew what was going through the guy's head...this wasn't in the script, and his smile widened.

The retreat came abruptly. The lad's eyes started to blink nervously and his eyes flicked round his mates looking for support...but they too were sensing the menace emanating from Jamie, and none came. His arrogance had evaporated and he wanted to get away from Jamie's cold, threatening eyes but loss of face still held him there. Suddenly, his nerve cracked, and in the blink of an eye he was gone, pushing his friends aside as he made for the perceived safety of the toilets. Jamie's eyes followed, and then swept back to the others, still hard, cold and threatening. The sense of menace was now the reality of menace and they started to back away, none of them was prepared to take Jamie on. He shook his head scornfully and turned to go, Charley once again clinging to his arm.

Outside, they all started talking at once. 'How the fuck did you do that?' Davie asked, still trying to come to terms with what he'd just witnessed. Jamie just smiled. 'That guy was shittin' himself,' Davie persisted.

Jamie shrugged. 'Sometimes a look an' a few kind words is all it takes,' he smiled. 'As long as the other guy knows you mean it.'

Charley gazed into his smiling, ebony eyes, still overawed. 'He believed you...and I still can't believe it,' she said. 'That crowd are bullies,' she continued. 'We've seen them do that to other boys before...and all *you* did was look at him. I still can't believe it.' Donna and Angela were nodding in unison. Charley dropped her voice and whispered. 'Then again, you've been looking at me all night, and I think I got your message too,' she continued, hoping she was right.

Jamie laughed quietly, riveting her with a look. 'So what's the message now?' he asked and watched her blush. 'Exactly,' he whispered and leaned forward to kiss her.

She rose on her toes and pulled his head down, her lips next to his ear. 'All night?' she whispered.

Jamie grinned and pulled her close. 'Yes, all night,' he murmured as she rose onto her toes again and kissed him lingeringly.

Donna, it transpired, lived in Arnold, a suburb to the north of Nottingham and taxis were the fastest option. They had to split up but that too was a bonus as far as Jamie was concerned. He offered to take Charley while the others shared a second cab and Jack grinned. Jamie wasn't missing a trick...as usual. On the way to the taxi rank Charley leaned close against him, her arm possessively around his waist. 'I still can't believe what you did back there,' she said admiringly. 'There were six or seven of those lads...weren't you afraid?'

'Not really,' he replied. 'The lad who was instigating it didn't expect us to face up and when we did, he got cold feet...I just had to convince him that no matter what went down, he was gettin' it. When it comes to convincing guys like that a good, hard, Glasgow stare usually works,' he laughed. 'We've got a reputation folk think we live up to.'

'But it wasn't "we", it was you,' she replied. 'You're amazing.' She hugged him closer, already thinking ahead to the rest of the night. She had never met anyone like him and what she had witnessed clearly hadn't just been bravado. All joking aside, she knew she was going to sleep with him and wondered what he would be like. If his confidence and control of the last half hour were anything to go by, it would be a wonderful night.

So early in the evening there wasn't much demand for taxis and there were a few waiting at the rank. Jamie and Charley took the second, allowing the others to go on ahead. They sat close together in the back of the car, kissing and petting to the disconcertion of the middle aged driver whose eyes spent more time in the rear view mirror than on the road. Fortunately, they made it to Arnold in one piece, pulling up at Donna's home just as the first was leaving, and joined the others on the pavement. It was impressive; a nice semi-detached villa with a garage and a big garden surrounded by shrubs and trees. Daddy must do alright to afford a pile like this, Jamie mused. Night was falling and some of the houses already had lights on but Donna's home, and the adjoining semi, were in darkness.

'The neighbours are on holiday too,' Donna chirped happily, satisfied that her decision to bring them all to the house wouldn't get back to her parents. None the less, she asked them to keep quiet and they all crept up the garden path, the girls giggling and the boys muffling their laughter

Once inside, they congregated in the lounge and waited while Donna pulled closed the heavy curtains in the bay window and shut them off from the expanse of front garden and the street beyond. That done, she switched on the lights and pointed to a large drinks cabinet set against the wall. 'That's where my Dad keeps his booze...help yourself, but just remember I'll have to put it all back,' she said, 'and there's beer in the fridge in the kitchen, if you want.'

Davie and Jack looked at each other wondering if things could get any better. Jamie, on the other hand, knew they would.

And Davie didn't have long to wait to discover it either. Donna wrapped her arms around his neck and put her lips close to his ear. 'My bedroom's upstairs,' she whispered, 'come on.' She took him by the hand and pulled him towards the door as his eyes filled with expectation.

Jack was already opening the drinks cabinet and finding an Aladdin's Cave of booze. Angela settled on the settee, letting her little crochet dress ride high up her thighs, and Jamie took the opportunity to have a good look at her. She was quite small, about 5' 2" or 5' 3" with shoulder length blonde hair, startling blue eyes, nice full lips and a perfect body. The only thing that nagged him was her similarity in look and appearance to Teresa, Jack's ex back in Glasgow. *She's a clone*, he mused, *and Jack just can't get her out of his mind*. But who was he to judge.

While Jack rummaged through the bottles in the cabinet, checking labels and letting out little whistles of appreciation, Charley pulled Jamie close. He felt the contours of her body press against him through the thin fabric of her dress and he began to harden, just as he had in the taxi. The gurgling of liquid distracted him momentarily and he turned to see Jack pour a glass of white wine for Angela. 'Whit aboot you two?' Jack called over, grinning.

'I'll have a glass of wine too, please,' Charley chirped.

'An' I'll have a whisky, malt if there's any,' Jamie added.

As Jack poured, Charley rose up on tip toe to whisper conspiratorially into Jamie's ear. 'There are another two bedrooms upstairs,' she said huskily. 'Donna's Mum and Dad's and her brother's…her Mum and Dad have an enormous double bed but her brother has a pokey little single…and he's untidy, so guess where we're going?'

Jack brought their drinks and returned to the cabinet to pour one for himself. En route, he spied an expensive stereo system set on a long wooden cabinet, with a collection of LP's stacked beneath. 'What music do you fancy? he called out and turned, just in time to see Charley pull Jamie into the hall.

'Sorry Jack, somethin's come up,' Jamie laughed, pulling the door closed behind him.

'Ah well,' Jack retorted. 'Ah suppose we'll jist huv tae make dae wi' the sheepskin rug an' the settee.' Angela's giggled response was the last thing Jamie heard before Charley whisked him upstairs.

*

Charley pulled him into the bedroom and turned on the light. The décor took his breath away and he let out a low whistle of admiration. As he suspected, Donna's parents weren't short of a bob or two. The carpet was a thick luxurious Axminster pile and his feet sank deep into it. The curtains were heavy, satin velour by the look of them, and they were held back against the wall on each side of the window by heavy brass rings. And the bed – it was bigger than any bed he had ever seen - was covered in a thin top-sheet with a lace throw over it. Solid wood bedroom furniture, modern stuff, and expensive by the look of it, completed the image. It could have come straight out of a magazine, he thought.

He suddenly felt uncertain; not about what they were about to do but where they were about to do it. 'Are you sure it's alright to use this room?' he asked, certain they were taking a liberty.

Charley smiled and pulled back the throw, looking at him coyly. 'Don't worry, I told Donna I would clean up after us…and her mum and dad aren't back for two weeks.' She stood at the edge of the bed and slipped off her shoes. 'Well?' she murmured huskily, crooking a finger and summoning him. 'You said you'd make love to me all night.'

Jamie didn't need a second invitation. Sometimes dreams *do* come true, he thought happily. With her shoes off Charley was only a couple of inches shorter than him. She had lightly tanned skin that seemed to glow in the light; her arms were slender and her fingers were long and graceful, her nails sculpted and painted a deep scarlet. Her legs were long and shapely; her hips just wide enough to leave a tantalising gap at the top of her thighs, and her stomach was flat and firm. And her breasts, as he already knew, were superb. When he finally managed to take his eyes off those two magnificent orbs he looked at her pretty face; oval shaped with high cheekbones and dark brown, almond shaped eyes encompassed by long, black eyelashes which were accentuated by expertly applied mascara. Her mouth was full and inviting, her sensuous lips made fuller by her dark red lipstick, and the image was completed by her raven black hair that framed her face and spilled down over her shoulders to end half way down her back. Throw in the scent of her perfume and she was simply sex on legs!

He pulled her to him and she slipped her arms around his neck, kissing him hungrily and pushing her tongue between his lips while her fingers stroked the back of his neck. Jamie responded immediately, his hands moving to her breasts, cupping them, caressing them and teasing her nipples to hardness between his thumbs and forefingers. Clothes were removed in a rush, with frenzied urgency, and then they were on the bed, their hands exploring. Charley twisted over onto her back, pulling him with her, her back arching up towards him as he rose above her. 'You promised and I've been waiting all night,' she whispered breathlessly. 'Don't make me wait any longer, please.' Her mouth was on his again, her tongue probing.

He entered her, his hands pulling her to him as he moved inside her, her hips gyrating against him, taking him deeper and deeper. Time stood still…and then he felt her fingers on his back, gripping him, and her nails raking his skin as she climaxed, her body pressing hard against him. She was whispering again, whimpering, pleading. 'Come baby…come now, pleeease.'

He couldn't stop himself even if he had tried. He erupted inside her, his body convulsing spasmodically as he ejaculated and the strength of his orgasm dissipated. Exhausted, he slumped on top of her.

They lay wrapped in each other's arms then, bodies glistening with sweat, breathing rapid and hearts racing. It had been so spontaneous and so natural, Jamie marvelled, with no awkwardness, no misunderstandings and no embarrassment. They had only just met and yet they made love as if they had been together for a lifetime. He ran his fingers down Charley's spine, stepping them one by one over the discs, and felt her arch her back to push herself against him. He lifted his head and smiled into her sultry eyes. 'All night…remember?' Charley laughed softly and stretched up to him, kissing him long and sensually, with her fingers entwined in his hair locking him to her.

Jamie's mind spun in a whirlwind of sensations; the smell of her, the touch of her fingers, and the softness of her skin against him…all of them pulling at him and he knew he could fall her if he wasn't careful.

In time, Jamie slipped from her and rolled onto his back beside her, reaching for her hand and kissing her fingers. They said nothing and the silence was comfortable. Everything had been as perfect as it had been spontaneous.

She pulled away and slipped from the bed, floating rather than walking across the room. Jamie was dazzled by her physical attractiveness; she moved like a cat, her limbs moving sensuously with feline grace and her bottom swayed before his eyes, tantalising. He felt himself harden again.

Charley was aware of his eyes following her progress and it excited her. Before turning off the light to plunge the room into darkness, she turned and posed provocatively, hands on hips and legs tantalisingly apart. Her laugh came to him as she threw the switch and moonlight flooded in through the window. Her body seemed to glow then, a silvery sheen radiating from her body as she made her way back. She crawled into the bed and slid close to him, her fingers reaching for him again and her breath warm on his face as she snuggled close. 'Make love to me, she murmured. 'Let me feel it all over again.'

'It takes two,' he replied, pushing a lock of black hair away from her eyes.

They made love again, time standing still as before, and then they slept, locked together in a tight embrace. About four o'clock in the morning Jamie awoke to the sound of a cock crowing in the distance and early sunlight flooding into the room. Charley lay across him, her legs entwined in his, both of them lying naked on the big bed. He devoured her with his eyes, wanting her again…and he hadn't felt like *that* for a long time. Her breathing was slow and regular and her eyelids flickered as she passed through some part of a dream. He didn't want to disturb her but he had to go. 'Too much beer,' he muttered softly as he slid his arm gently from beneath her and disentangled his legs. He slipped as quietly as possible from the bed and tip toed across to the door, leaving her to her dream.

Charley awoke as Jamie turned the door handle and ghosted out of the room. She looked around groggily, willing herself awake. Their clothes were scattered across the floor where they had been dropped in their haste that first time and she smiled as the memory of it returned. The sound of water running and the toilet door opening and closing came to her and then Jamie was back, framed in the doorway. She propped herself up on an elbow and watched him wistfully as he came across the room, in the same way as he had watched her earlier…and with the same thoughts. She took in the powerful muscles of his legs, the tightness of his stomach, his broad shoulders and his handsome, angular face framed by his long brown hair. He was smiling, just as she had done, and his eyes locked onto hers. *Oh those eyes*, she sighed, darker brown than her own – almost black - like two deep, black, mysterious pools. There was something about them, something special. All of his emotions seemed to be reflected there and it was that, she realised, that had drawn her to him. It had been his look, his eyes making love to her, and she had known in that instant that she would be with him tonight. As he eased himself back into the bed there was another message in his eyes, a longing that matched hers.

They locked together at once, fingers and mouths caressing, teasing and arousing. They coupled slowly, relishing the moment, taking each other to the point of climax then pulling back only to attain higher levels of arousal, again and again, until they could no longer contain themselves and climaxed together in an explosion of ecstasy.

It was after six o' clock when Jamie woke again. The voices of Davie and Donna in the next door room pulled him from his slumber. Charley was sprawled across him and the bed, her head on the pillow close to his and her long black hair spread over his chest in giddy profusion. He looked reluctantly at watch and saw the hands read five minutes to six; it was time to leave. If they stayed much longer the neighbours would be awake and tales of their debauchery would abound, returning eventually to Donna's parents. There was no point in killing the goose that laid the golden egg.

He pulled away from what he thought was her sleeping form but immediately felt her hand on his arm pulling him back. He turned around to kiss her, his hand cupping her breast and she responded, covering his hand with her own and pressed his fingers against her, prolonging the kiss. 'We should go,' he whispered. 'We don't want to cause Donna any problems.'

'I know,' Charley replied, stretching her body and arching her back. Jamie could feel the sap rise again but fought the urge knowing that a quickie was impossible with her. 'I just want a kiss before you leave me,' she continued, locking her lips onto his. As their mouths parted, she stared into his eyes. 'Will I see you again?'

'Yes, if you want to,' he murmured. 'But do you *really* want to? What about your fiancé?'

She smiled sadly as though seeing his question as an excuse. '*He's* not here…and *you* shouldn't have to ask if I want to,' she whispered huskily, pointing out the obvious.

Jamie felt a twinge of guilt. Somebody was going to be hurt and it wasn't him; but Charley had wanted him as much as he'd wanted her, hadn't she, he thought? Why was he torturing himself about a guy he didn't know and would probably never meet? They had been good together and he wanted more of her. So *what* if she was engaged? All would be fine so long as her fiancé didn't find out and he, himself, didn't get too involved. *You've been here before*, he reminded himself, *but this time, there would be no commitment.* 'Yes, I want to see you again…I want you again,' he said, kissing her. Charley's eyes scrutinised his face when they separated, searching for the truth and what she saw there made her heart beat a little faster. *He meant it*, she thought, *it's there in his eyes.* She heard him speak and her soul sang out in delight. 'How about tonight, then?' he suggested, his voice soft. 'Same place?'

She grabbed him tightly around the neck, kissing his face all over. 'Oh yes, babe, yes,' she purred.

'Half past seven then,' he said as he rose from the bed and began picking up his discarded clothes.

Charley nodded happily and, as she watched him dress, she began, ashamedly, to think about her fiancé. She had pushed him from her mind since meeting Jamie Raeburn in the "Trip" and had amazed herself. She had expected to be riven by guilt at this stage but she felt none of that, so what did that tell her, she wondered? What was she going to do? If she really loved Derek why had she thrown herself at Jamie last night? She smiled again as her thoughts returned to Jamie's advances; he hadn't seduced her…she had wanted it to happen. So instead of worrying about what she was going to do with Derek, maybe she should be thinking about what she wanted with Jamie Raeburn…that was a much more pleasant dilemma. She got out of bed and pulled her dress over her head then sat down beside him on the edge of the bed as he pulled on his shoes.

'I'm missing you already,' she said softly. 'Do we have to wait until tonight?' She wrapped her arms around him and pulled him to her again, enticing him. He sighed but managed to resist the temptation of her charms…but only just.

They headed downstairs, Jamie knocking hard on Donna's bedroom door as they passed.

'We're just comin',' Davie shouted in response and Jamie laughed.

'Too much information, Davie,' he retorted, grinning. 'Just go for the one, multiple orgasms take too long and we need to get out of here…so get your arse downstairs as quick as possible.'

'Very funny,' Davie's laughed and Donna giggled.

Jack was stretched out on the settee, semi naked, when they entered the lounge, his legs draped over Angela's thighs as she leaned back on the sofa wearing only her panties and a broad smile. Her hair was recklessly dishevelled and her breasts were pert and firm. Charley grinned and put a hand across Jamie's eyes as Angela looked at her, eyebrows arched with an unspoken question. Charley's smile pointed to only one thing; she had enjoyed herself too.

Donna and Davie arrived minutes later, stopping in the doorway to kiss. Donna was glowing and Davie was tucking his shirt into his trousers. Everyone, it seemed, had had a great night. But Donna and Davie couldn't stop and were at it again within seconds. 'Right, big man,' Jack laughed. 'Leave some for later.' They stopped and grinned then kissed again for good measure.

After the last goodbyes the three lads stepped out into the early morning sunshine, stealing away from the house as quietly as possible. Jamie turned and looked back, hoping to catch sight of Charley and found her peeking from behind the curtains in the lounge. He waved and she blew him a kiss.

Chapter 30

'So, a good night wiz it?' Jack asked, stifling a yawn. They had caught a bus soon after leaving the house and were now in Nottingham, transferring to another bus to take them out to Beeston.

Jamie smiled. 'You could say that; and you?' Jack's smile matched Jamie's and Davie was grinning like a Cheshire cat. They didn't bother asking him.

'So, same again tonight?' Jamie asked, fairly sure of the answer.

'Aye, but I'll need to sleep all day. That Donna was quite demandin', eh' Davie replied. It sounded like a complaint and Jack and Jamie creased themselves with laughter.

'Ah'll tell ye wan thing,' Jack laughed. 'If we keep shaggin' at this rate, shares in Durex will go through the roof.' The others joined his laughter but Jamie's laugh was suddenly a little hollow.

Shit, shit, shit, shit he repeated over and over in his mind. Please God,' he prayed, 'let her be on the pill or usin' that Dutch Cap thing. If she isn't, why didn't she ask me to use a Johnny? He asked, torturing himself for a while before convincing himself that everything would be alright.

As they separated in Beeston they arranged to meet again later to return to Ye Olde Trip to Jerusalem. Jamie had gotten all about Charley's engagement and the potential problem of having made love to her without using a condom and he was whistling happily as he entered the yard outside the house. He caught a glimpse of Jo at the kitchen window and grinned at her, knowing she would come to meet him at the door.

'Been out for a morning stroll?' she teased.

'Nah, I'm just gettin' back from a night on the tiles…enjoyin' myself', just as you said I would.' he grinned. 'Hope you didn't wait up for me? He joked and checked his watch. 'Good God, is that the time? Have I missed breakfast?'

Jo burst out laughing. You are one cheeky lad, Jamie Raeburn,' she grinned like him. 'No, you haven't missed it which is just as well judging by those dark rings under your eyes. You're going to need it…and a sleep. 'Away and get changed…nice perfume by the way,' she threw in as he made for the stair.

Jamie sniffed theatrically. 'Aye, it is right enough.'

*

At breakfast, Jo announced that there would be a party in the house that night and the old hands roared with delight. 'For you new boys,' she started to explain, 'we often have parties on a Saturday night… and *everyone* is invited. So if you're not doing anything special tonight we'll expect to see you,' she concluded, looking pointedly at Jamie. 'What about you, Casanova, will you be there?' she asked, and the other hooted with laughter…his reputation was spreading.

'Ah…no, sorry Jo, I've got a date again tonight,' he replied sheepishly.

'Ah well, that's a pity, I had a nice surprise lined up for you,' she said tantalisingly. 'Never mind, maybe next time.' She carried on serving the meal. Jamie thought she looked disappointed, though she was trying to hide it, and he wondered why. Truth was, she had been hoping that Jamie would be there but playing matchmaker didn't always go smoothly.

Jamie slept for most of the day, rising at four o'clock, and at dinner rushed his meal and headed for the bathroom before the hordes descended on it. He showered quickly, shaved and was back in the bedroom pulling on his Wranglers when Benny pushed through the door. 'Ah, the very man,' he said smoothly, laughing at Benny's suspicious look.

'The very man fur whit?' the wee man demanded slowly.

'It's my back,' Jamie explained. 'I've got a wee problem with it. Do you have any of that iodine stuff left…the stuff you use for cuts?'

'Aye, but whit dae ye need it fur?'

'It's my back, like I told you, look!' Jamie said, turning round.

Benny looked him over, his eyes widened in horror and he let out a low whistle. 'Jeeze-oh, Jamie, whit the fuck happened tae ye?'

'I was shaggin' last night…it's called collateral damage. Birds wi' long nails can do a lot of damage to male flesh,' he warned.

'Wiz it worth it?'

'Are you kiddin'? Of course it was worth it,' Jamie replied, grinning broadly. 'An' it'll be worth it again th'night.'

Shaking his head despairingly, Benny found his training bag and searched for his little bottle of iodine. Giving a little whoop of joy, he held up the little blue bottle of iodine for Jamie's inspection and found some cotton wool. 'This is gonnae sting, big man,' he said with a malicious grin. 'Grit yer teeth!' Jamie did as instructed and felt the initial cold of the liquid iodine against his skin and then, quickly thereafter, then the nipping started. Benny was right, the stuff did bloody sting.

'Let it dry in afore ye put yer shirt on or ye'll stain it,' Benny advised. 'An' ye don't want that on yer good shirt, dae ye?'

Jamie took the advice and sorted out the rest of his clothes for the night ahead. He placed his suit jacket, the light grey worsted herringbone, on the bed beside his pale blue Ben Sherman shirt with the button down collar. Light tan moccasins and light grey socks finished his outfit.

Benny watched admiringly as Jamie pulled on his shirt and slipped on his socks and shoes. He particularly liked the jacket. It was longer than standard, three buttons with five on each cuff, hand stitched lapels, slanted pockets with a small ticket pocket on the right and a 15" centre vent at the back. 'Ah like yer style, big man,' he said appreciatively. 'Ah wish ah could dress like that.'

'Give over,' Jamie laughed. You're a wee dandy, Benny. Tell you what though, I'll take you to a tailor next weekend if you want an' we'll get you sorted with some nice threads,' he promised. 'But for now, duty calls.'

Jo was in her usual place in the kitchen when Jamie vaulted down the stairs with Benny trailing behind. He stuck his head in through the door to say goodbye, still intrigued by her comments at breakfast.

'What was that nice surprise you were talking about this mornin'?' he asked inquisitively.

She laughed, knowing she had hooked him. 'Oh, I can't tell you,' she teased. 'But I can guarantee you would have liked it. Same girl tonight, is it? Can we expect you back before tomorrow?'

'Possibly, in answer to your first question and unlikely to the second,' he replied, laughing cheerily, and skipped out the door.

*

Nottingham was busy again. The good weather of the last few weeks was bringing people out in droves and men and women, singly and in couples, wandered around the city, filling the restaurants and bars. Jamie looked Davie and Jack over approvingly. Charley had been spot on with her assessment of them the night before…when it came to style, they were streets ahead of the locals and were already attracting admiring glances from the single women.

'So, what's the plan for tonight?' he asked as they made their way to the pub.

'Don't know,' Jack replied. 'Ah huvnae thought aboot it, but as long as ah end up doin' what ah wiz doin' last night, ah'll be a happy bunny.'

'I think ye'll be a happy bunny then,' Davie laughed. 'Seein' as how Donna's expectin' us back at her place again eh.'

Jamie smiled happily, contemplating another night of full on, erotic sex with Charley. How she could contemplate gettin' married when she was carrying on behind her fiancé's back bemused him, but he wasn't going to analyse it. She seemed to be enjoying him and he was enjoying her and that was enough. He didn't give his double standards a moment's thought as he patted the two packets of condoms he had purchased earlier.

They early and found stools near the bar to wait. Jack ordered three pints of warm bitter, paying the required six shillings and ninepence, and they settled down. Just before the appointed time of seven thirty Angela and Donna pushed their way through the door but there was no sign of Charley. Jack and Davie exchanged worried looks and arched their eyebrows.

The two girls smiled apologetically as they came over and Jamie swung round to face them. Donna placed a hand gently on his leg. 'Charley can't make it Jamie, I'm sorry,' Donna said apologetically. Jamie smiled ruefully and shrugged, resigned to a night on his own. 'Derek came home on a surprise 24 hour leave,' Donna raced on, trying to explain.

'Derek?' Jack enquired. 'Who the fuck's, Derek?' he continued, lifting his pint to his mouth.

'Charley's fiancé,' Jamie replied before either of the girls and Jack almost choked.

'Fiancé? She's engaged? An' ye knew?' he asked, incredulous.

'Aye, I knew,' Jamie conceded. 'He's in the RAF an' he's away doin' his initial training. I was just keeping the home fire burning,' he said, a little cruelly.

'Fur fuck sake, Jamie!' Jack mumbled under his breath. 'Dae you never learn? Remember Kate?'

'Drop it Jack,' Jamie said coldly and Jack dropped it.

'So what do we do now?' Davie queried. 'We can't leave you on your own, eh?'

Jamie lifted his eyes to the ceiling in exasperation. 'I'm no' a fuckin' kid, Davie,' he said vehemently. 'I can look after myself…so I'll just sit here an' have another pint or two an' eye up all the girls; an' the four of you can do whatever it is you were goin' to do. No arguments,' he said, closing the subject. But they were still hesitant about leaving him so he accepted another pint from Davie, conscious that his presence was holding them back. He downed his beer quickly and stepped down off his stool.

'Right, I'm off,' he said.

'Where to?' Jack demanded.

'Back to Beeston…there's a party on tonight so I'll just head back there an' get pissed, enjoy yourselves,' he said with a smile and set off, waving casually as he disappeared through the door.

'Well girls,' Jack said, turning to Donna and Angela. 'Whit dae you two fancy doin' now?' The girls laughed and headed for the door. As they stepped out into the evening light Jamie was nowhere in sight.

Chapter 31

Jamie arrived in Beeston just after half past eight. He felt awkward, embarrassed even, at returning to the house early after saying he was meeting someone. Getting a "dizzy" wasn't something he was used to and, accordingly, another pint was called for. He stopped off in The Spinner's Rest and realised that it was quickly becoming his local. He ordered a pint of Guinness and stood alone at the bar, drinking slowly. He began to feel morose and his heart wasn't in it. Had Charley really got so close to him? Her failure to turn up had upset him, yes, and he realised, with some surprise, that he had actually been looking forward to being with her again. And to cap it all, she was with her fiancé. *Fuck it*, he mumbled into his pint, *I'll just head back and sneak up to the room and get a good night's sleep.* That way he could avoid the awkward questions and the jokes. Finishing his pint, he nodded to the barman and left the pub, taking the short cut via Foster Avenue and through the grounds of the Church of Our Lady of the Assumption which brought him out next to the house.

There was no one around but loud music was pumping out from the lounge at the rear of the house, filling his head Roy Orbison's "Pretty Woman". He'd almost had one of them tonight, he smiled wryly. Maybe he should join the party, he thought, but anticipating incessant leg pulling from the rest of the guys and Jo he decided against it. So it was back to plan one; sneak up to his room, sharpish. The outside door opened quietly and he slipped into the empty hall, the music louder now and there was loud laughing and singing. Everyone was getting well-oiled and having a great time by the sounds of it. Silently, he closed the door and made for the stairs, fingers crossed that he wouldn't bump into anyone.

He made it to the stair undetected and was about to begin the climb when movement on the landing above caught his eye. He stopped and looked up, gradually taking in the vision in front of him and realised with a start that he was staring rudely. Standing on the landing looking down at him with an amused smile on her face was a girl. Her form was framed by the light from the window behind her, the dying sun placing her in shadow, so that he couldn't make out her features. He thought she was smiling at him but couldn't be sure because of the blinding effect of the sun. Who was she...and where had she appeared from, he wondered?

He beckoned to her to come down. 'It's bad luck to pass on stairs,' he called, trying to break the ice, but she stood still, hovering there and waiting for him to ascend.

He started to climb and as he came closer everything about her became more defined. Her hair was golden, the colour of set honey, and with the sun behind her she appeared to be bathed in a deep amber glow. Her smile widened as he approached and his heart began to race. *Who is she, he asked himself again?* He couldn't find a word to describe her...even "magnificent" seemed to fall short. He knew he was still staring but, what the hell, she was worth it. She was tall, almost as tall as him, and slim, her body perfectly toned and with legs that seemed to go on forever from perfect ankles, the left one adorned by a thin gold chain, to magnificent thighs. And she was *almost* wearing a dress; a short, dark crimson little number that stopped about half way down her thighs and gave him a tantalising glimpse of a tiny white triangle at the top of her legs. The rest of it was every bit as alluring, the front plunging in a deep V shape that showed off breasts which, though not big, were perfectly formed. He tried to focus on her face then. Her eyes, a dark blue, indigo might be closer, had a depth to them the like of which he had never seen before and they seemed alive, fluttering constantly, never at rest. Her eyes were beautiful...*she* was beautiful and stunning was the word he had been looking for earlier, he realised right away.

Only one girl had made him feel like this; Kate, and a momentary sadness swept over him. Sub-consciously, he found himself comparing them. Physically, they were complete opposites but beauty comes in all shapes and sizes, he told himself. Very profound, he thought with a laugh.

The girl moved aside as he reached her, allowing him to squeeze past. Her eyes twinkled and she was smiling at what she perceived to be his shyness. Jamie held her eyes for a moment then his gaze drifted downwards, taking in the fullness of her breasts cupped in a white frilly bra which emphasised the depth of her cleavage. His mouth was dry and his tongue felt thick, making it difficult to speak.

He had never been completely speechless before, even with Kate. And Charley, she too was quite something but she hadn't left him speechless either. He didn't normally go for blondes but for this girl he would make an exception.

'Hi,' she chirped happily as he passed her. 'You must be Jamie,' she continued, and threw him completely. 'Are you coming to the party?'

Completely flummoxed, he began to stammer. 'Aye...yes, I'll, eh, I'll be down... in a minute,' he managed. 'I came back especially.' The lie came out automatically in his effort to cover up the fact that he'd been stood up.

'Great,' she replied, giggling happily as she descended the stair. When she reached the bottom she threw him a backwards look. 'We were hoping you'd show up,' she said throatily.

"We?" Jamie thought immediately. Was that a Royal "we" or could there be more than one like her at the party? He gazed at her admiringly as she walked away, holding her body like a model on the catwalk and swaying her hips seductively from side to side. Her perfume lingered around him, excited him, and he stood there watching her lasciviously and feeling like a pervert. Even at this distance she was beautiful. At the lounge door she stopped, turned again and gave him a wave and a shy smile, then went in to the lounge to join the party.

Jamie stood stock still, stunned by the thoughts that were emerging in his head and realised, a little self-consciously, that she had aroused him more than just a little. 'Down boy,' he muttered quietly, conscious of the result of that arousal. Suddenly, his face lit up with a smile. Tonight might just turn out to be a good night after all, he thought. 'Sorry Charley,' he murmured.

A quick wash, teeth brushed and Old Spice liberally applied, he raced back down stairs, taking them two at a time. The lounge door opened just as he reached it and Frank and Henry, two of the other lodgers, swayed past him, grinning inanely en route to the kitchen. He grinned back, happy they hadn't asked the question why he was here, and Frank pressed a glass into his hand while Henry patted him boisterously on the back. Pissed as newts, he thought with a laugh.

The lounge was crammed full of bodies, all drinking and some dancing – or doing what they thought passed for dancing - to the crackling music being belted out by an ancient record player. The French Windows were open to let in fresh air and even more people were on the patio and the grass. Now this is what I call a party, Jamie grinned.

He searched the room for the girl in the red dress but there was no sign of her. Benny was there, away on the far side of the room, talking animatedly with a man and a woman, both in their early thirties and trendy by the look of them. He didn't recognise many of the others but that wasn't a worry. What was a worry was the fact that he couldn't find "the girl" and his heart sank. His run of bad luck was going on, it seemed. He started to cross the room to Benny when Jo Bradley's velvety and ever so slightly slurred voice stopped him in his tracks. He turned, awaiting the inevitable sarcasm, but Jo had more important things on her mind.

'Jamie Raeburn, come here immediately,' she slurred out, like an angry schoolmistress about to chastise an errant child, but she was grinning broadly. 'We didn't expect you,' she said, an oblique reference to the fact he was supposed to be somewhere else, 'but I'm glad you are because these two lovely girls have been dying to meet you…though God knows why after what I've been telling them,' she laughed raucously.

Jamie's eyes turned in the direction of the "two lovely girls", a diffident smile on his face, and saw the brunette first. Jo hadn't been kidding! This one, at least, was lovely; tall, pretty face, blue eyes, big breasts, short dress…and then, stepping out from behind her was a short haired honey blonde in a red dress, smiling shyly…the girl from the stair! *'Thank you God,' he murmured.*

'You decided to come then?' Jo smiled, avoiding any reference as to why.

'I couldn't face the night not knowing what your "nice surprise" was,' he chirped back, smiling charmingly. The blonde girl was still smiling shyly but the dark haired beauty was looking him over, brazenly, appraising him like a prize bull at a stud auction. He laughed; can't complain about that, he thought. He had to admit, the dark haired girl was good looking but the blonde had the edge. Ever the gentleman, he tried to focus equally on both as Jo started the introductions.

'This is my daughter, Julie,' she said, placing an affectionate hand on the dark girl's shoulder, 'and this is Lucienne…but we call her Lucie.' Jo, even though a little tipsy, was watching Jamie's reaction closely and she spotted quite easily that even though he was trying to keep his attention on both girls his eyes were glued to Lucie. She looked at Lucie then and smiled; the girl was looking at him as if he were the reincarnation of Adonis. It wasn't to be Julie's night, she sighed, but Julie could look after herself, she was her mother's daughter. Lucie, on the other hand, tended to be withdrawn and shy around men most of the time, something of a paradox given that she was a professional dancer who spent time titillating male audiences all over The Midlands. She stopped herself then. It wasn't shyness, she reflected, it was something more…a reluctance to get caught out again, fear even, and it was only to be expected. She had built a wall around her, keeping boys at bay. Others had tried to storm it in the past but eventually gave up. Jamie Raeburn, however, seemed to be making progress where the others had failed and there might even be cracks appearing in Lucie's wall. Jamie was a rogue, definitely, but he could be a very loveable one, and what Jo saw in Lucie's eyes augured well.

Jamie was into his patter, flattering. 'If Jo had said you two would be here I would have been first through the door,' he laughed. 'I don't think your Mum has a very high opinion of me,' he said, addressing Julie, 'so maybe she was trying to keep us apart.' He said it as a joke but quite clearly he was addressing Lucie now.

'I doubt it,' Julie replied, giggling. She could see which way this was heading. 'My Mum is an incorrigible matchmaker,' she laughed, 'and I suspect that's what she's up to now.'

'Is that right?' Jamie came back, giving Jo a sideways look. 'I hope she hasn't filled your heads with malicious rumours about me,' he laughed, cheekily sticking his tongue out at Jo.

Julie was into it now but she knew who Jamie fancied. 'No,' she giggled, 'apart from telling us she thinks you're a bit of a Casanova,' she added quickly, grinning now. She looked at Lucie as she said this and saw a little flicker of annoyance flit across her friend's face. *She fancies him*, she though instantly, *she actually fancies him. Wow!* It was time to change tack. 'Actually, she said a lot of nice things about you…didn't she Luce?' she said, trying to bring Lucie into the conversation but the poor girl was love struck, her eyes locked intently onto this dark haired, brown eyed, handsome boy.

Jo Bradley watched everything unfold with a warm glow of contentment. She thought Jamie Raeburn would be good for Lucie. Actually, it was more than that; she knew he would be good for Lucie. She smiled inwardly and settled back to let things take their course.

Julie, on the other hand, wasn't for waiting. Lucie's reaction was so out of character she, Julie, couldn't let the opportunity pass. It was time to give her friend a helping hand. Taking Lucie by the arm she eased her around till she was facing Jamie directly. 'I think you two should get to know each other better,' she said. 'You haven't stopped looking at each other since *you* came into the room,' she laughed, directing the latter part at Jamie and poking him playfully on the chest. 'Go on, dance!' she instructed, pushing them together then taking hold of her mother and pulling her away. 'Come on Mum,' she said, 'I think we should leave these two lovebirds in peace.'

Jamie held out his hand and saw Lucie hesitate. 'I don't bite…not on a first date at least,' he joked, and saw the smile come back. He was confused. On the stairs, when he had met her earlier, she had seemed bubbly and confident, if a little shy, but now her confidence seemed to have evaporated completely.

The music changed then, the fast tempo, to which a number of drunken guests were attempting to do the Twist, dropped and the voice of John Lennon singing "Yes It Is" calmed everything down. Jamie glanced across to where he knew the record player to be and saw Julie return his look with a giant grin. He couldn't resist smiling back even though the words of the song were painful; Lucie was in red tonight just as Kate had been the night she broke the news of her leaving, wearing the red dress he had given her on St. Valentine's Day. He closed his eyes and a picture of her appeared; and his heart lurched. When he opened his eyes again Lucie had moved closer and she was smiling shyly at him again. Could he forget Kate and all the plans they had made, he wondered? Could he find happiness again with the girl in front of him now? He placed his hands on Lucie's hips and she moved closer still, wrapping her arms around his neck. '*Forgive me Kate, please forgive me,*' he muttered silently.

*

Lucie and Jamie danced the rest of the night away. Talking became easier and Lucie's bubbly character came to the fore. They talked about themselves, learning a lot about each other, but some secrets remained hidden. At one point, when the heat in the house became oppressive, they strolled out into the garden and lay on their backs on the grass, gazing up at the diamond encrusted heavens.

Jamie couldn't believe what was happening to him. He usually chatted up girls with one thing on his mind but for some strange reason that wasn't what he was doing now. And, strangely, he felt awkward and shy. Getting Lucie Kent to sleep with him wasn't the most important thing on his mind just now…that would happen;

he knew it would. Right now, he just wanted to get to know her and not frighten her off. For the first time since losing Kate he was thinking about a new relationship…a long term relationship, and it was frightening him.

When the time came to say good-night he escorted Lucie to her room, the room she was sharing with Julie, and stood there awkwardly. They hadn't even kissed yet and he wondered whether to try for one or not. That decision was resolved hen Lucie wrapped her arms round his neck and pulled him towards her. Their lips met and a tingle of excitement coursed through him. Tentatively, he pushed his tongue between her lips and a wave of exhilaration swept over him as she responded.

The kiss might have led to more but for the appearance of Jo, squeezing past them on her way to her own room. She said nothing but her smile told its own story. They smiled shyly at each other before Lucie finally said "goodnight" and slipped through the bedroom door. As he made his way to his own room he heard Lucie's voice, breathless and excited, behind the bedroom door and Julie Bradley's tinkling laughter.

Chapter 32

With the morning, Jamie was awake early. In truth, he hadn't slept much. He rose from bed, listening to Benny snoring, and washed, shaved and dressed before any of the other lodgers were even awake. His mind had been filled by Lucie for most of the night but there had been interludes involving erotic thoughts of Charley and fleeting, aching memories of Kate, but neither had displaced Lucie for any length of time.

The dining room was empty but the mess from the party had been cleared and the big table set. He was hoping Lucie Kent would be there and his disappointment at finding he was alone was almost palpable. Pulling out a chair near the window he sat down, his back to the door, and toyed with the cutlery. The door opened and he turned, hoping his prayer had been answered, but it was only Jo checking to see who had arrived. She popped her head into the room and smiled broadly. If she was hung over, it wasn't showing. 'Well, well, well, you're up early,' she said cheerily and he smiled back, hoping his disappointment wasn't showing. 'Couldn't sleep?' she asked, cheekily.

'How did you guess?' he laughed, blushing a little. 'Why am I acting like this,' he asked himself, 'she's just another girl.' but even as the words registered, he knew he was kidding himself…Lucie Kent wasn't just another girl.

Jo returned with his breakfast minutes later; a full English with all the trimmings, and he sat alone munching his way through it. His appetite, at least, hadn't been affected. She escaped the kitchen for a later and joined him, ready to chat. He suspected she wanted to know how he and Lucie had got on but he didn't mind. Without Jo he would never have met her.

'Did you have a good night?' Jo asked with a smile.

'I think you know I did,' he replied, laughing at her approach. 'It was a nice surprise, by the way."

Her laughter bubbled up and enveloped him. 'I knew you'd like it…you did, didn't you?'

Jamie laughed. 'No, I *loved* it,' he replied and Jo beamed with delight.

Their conversation was interrupted by the arrival of one of the other lodgers, his face grey and drawn and his eyes dark and rheumy. Now there was a face that would make a great poster for Alcoholics Anonymous, Jamie smiled wryly as the newcomer slumped into the chair across from him. Jo looked him, pulled a face, winked at Jamie and scurried back to her kitchen; here was a man who needed food…urgently.

Jamie liked Jo Bradley. After their first meeting, when she had read out the house rules leaving Benny, Mick, Terry and Jamie shell-shocked, he had quickly realised that she had been winding them up. Since then, he had got the feeling that she actually liked him. Even describing him as a rogue…correction, a likeable rogue, was part of that. He hoped that she was happy he and Lucie had hit it off.

He sipped his coffee and indulged himself with a Lucky Strike, the face of his companion on the other side of the table changing colour from pasty grey to sickly yellow. The dining room door opened again and he swung round, his face transforming this time as he saw Lucie. She was no less stunning now than she had been the night before. Today she was wearing a pale blue "A" line dress which was even shorter than the red one of the night before and the only other accessory was a broad smile. For a second time, Jamie found himself speechless and all the more so when she came to him, leaned down and kissed him softly on the cheek. She settled herself on the chair next to him then and looked at him longingly, a smile playing at the corners of her eyes and the edges of her lips. Her eyes were talking to him again. Without speaking, she picked up Jamie's coffee, sniffed it and downed what was left of it, smiling impudently. 'Let's go for a walk,' she whispered, holding out her hand. Jo smiled in surprise as they passed her, hand in hand, at the kitchen window. Her match making efforts had worked, it seemed.

The sun was already above the rooftops and they could feel its heat on their faces and bodies. They walked together, closer now, their arms around each other, and Jamie was already contemplating the future. They lay on the sun scorched grass in the local park and embarked on another voyage of discovery, carrying on from where they had left off the night before.

Lucie spoke of her family again, adding detail to the basic picture painted by her the night before. Her mood sank when she told him of the loss of her mother in France when she was very young and how she still missed her, but it rose again when she recounted life with her aunt and uncle, her father's sister and her husband, in Derby after moving from France to England. She told him too of her affection for her younger cousins and her lifelong ambition to be a nurse, something she put down to her mother's early death. When she spoke of her mother's side of the family in France she enthused about life there and told him how much she loved the country. She said little about her father other than that she loved him and wished that she saw more of him. She finally talked herself out and turned expectantly to Jamie, wanting to know everything about him. She had never met anyone like him and had known right from the beginning that he was different; special was a more appropriate word, she reflected. The other Glasgow boy, the little one, Benny, had been almost impossible to understand most of the time but Jamie was entirely different. It was as though he and Benny came from different planets rather than the same city…and yet, she recalled with a smile, there had been times, listening to them conversing, when she hadn't been able to understand either of them. Jamie intrigued her. He had told her what he did for a living but why he did it was another matter. She could see he was bright and intelligent. He could probably be anything he wanted to be, she mused, so why had he chosen to be a welder? It fascinated her.

'Why did you become a welder?' she asked, unable to contain her curiosity. They were lying side by side, holding hands, and looking up into the clear blue sky.

Jamie eased himself up onto his elbow, looking down on her, and laid his other arm over her stomach and around her waist. 'Economic necessity,' he replied with a smile. 'It was going to take too long to qualify as brain surgeon.'

She laughed. Did he ever take anything seriously, she wondered? 'Be serious…I really want to know,' she insisted, laughing.

'I *am* being serious,' he grinned, 'well, maybe not about the brain surgeon bit,' he admitted, pretending contrition. 'When I was younger I really wanted to be a pilot.' He laughed again but she could see he was being serious. 'Truth is,' he added then, 'my folks couldn't afford to let me stay on at school so I had to leave and find a job…simple.'

'But why a welder?' Lucie persisted.

'Now that's a good question,' he replied, laughing again. 'To be honest, I didn't choose the job, it chose me,' he said after a moment's pause. 'In Glasgow, the shipyards and the heavy engineering works are where most young guys like me end up working. John Brown's was taking on apprentices, my father knew one of the foremen, and that was it.'

'What did you enjoy doing at school?'

School, he thought. That was a lifetime ago though the memories were mostly good. What did I enjoy, he ruminated? 'Languages,' he replied eventually. 'I took French and Russian…can you believe that? And I was quite good at them too. If I'd been able to stay on at school I suppose I would have gone to University to study those.'

'That's a shame,' Lucie replied quietly. 'You can do anything you want to do, you know,' she smiled genuinely. 'Maybe one day you will.'

'Aye, maybe…si je gagnerais les pools,' he laughed, breaking into a little Franglais.

'You can practise your French with me, si tu veut…if you want,' Lucie responded as she pushed him back onto the grass and laid her head on his chest. For the first time in years she felt safe with a man. Not just safe…completely safe! She felt Jamie's arms around her, sensed the strength in him and hoped that something would come of this. The realisation that she was attracted to him didn't come as a surprise. The attraction had been instantaneous when she had passed him on the stairs and she was sure that he had felt the same. Their first kiss, as he had left her at the bedroom door, had left her breathless and tingling with excitement, and she wanted to feel like that again. She lifted her head up from his chest and saw him looking down at her, a smile teasing the corners of his mouth.

'What?' he asked softly.

'Nothing,' she whispered and stretched up to kiss him. From that moment on they were inseparable. When they returned to the house just Jo fussed around them and Julie laughed in amusement at her mother's antics. But her mother, she realised, was genuinely happy for Lucie…they both were, come to that. It had been so long since either of them had seen her so happy and if Jamie Raeburn needed any encouragement to keep her looking that way then she, and her mother, would make sure he got it. Somehow though, she didn't think he was going to need too much of that.

For Jamie…for both of them in fact, Sunday evening came too soon. Jack came to visit during the afternoon to check on Jamie after the disappointment of the night before and had been introduced to Lucie and Julie. One look at Lucie holding on to Jamie like a leech told him that his friend's night had turned out much better than anyone had expected. Jamie avoided the subject of Charley and Jack played along…the reason for Jamie's reluctance was standing beside him and Lucie Kent was a stunner. Jack's discretion was assured but he had a problem and he needed to speak to Jamie alone…and soon, because Charley was hoping that Jamie would be able to meet her later.

The opportunity presented itself when Jack was leaving later in the afternoon, a brief interlude when Jamie saw him off. All three had escorted him to the door but Jamie alone walked with him to the yard gate. Jack snatched his chance. 'Charley phoned Angie this mornin',' he whispered, casting a furtive look over Jamie's shoulder to make sure the girls were out of earshot. 'She wants tae see ye th'night…ur ye comin'?'

Jamie pulled a face. Were his sins coming back to haunt him, he wondered glumly? He wrapped his arm nervously around Jack's shoulder, wondering what to do next. 'The girls are going back to Derby at seven,' he breathed almost silently. 'I'll meet you at half past at the Cross…but I don't know if I'll be coming into Nottingham with you.'

Jack looked at him incredulously. This wasn't the Jamie Raeburn he knew but he wasn't going to argue the point with him here. He shook his head slowly, looking directly into Jamie's eyes. 'Right,' he said quietly.

Jamie spent the rest of the afternoon in a quandary. He liked Lucie…a lot, it had to be said. There was something about her that kept pulling him to her. He hesitated to admit that he was falling in love with her but he suspected that he was. But Charley had been good with him too…better than good. Keeping the two of them going wasn't a good idea but…he pushed the dilemma to the back of his mind and concentrated on Lucie, for the moment at least.

*

Jamie escorted the girls to Beeston railway station that evening and waved them off on their return journey to Derby. Lucie had clung to him on the platform, telling him she couldn't wait until the next weekend to see him again, and they had kissed passionately. He felt strangely desolate as the train disappeared down the track and even the prospect of seeing Charley later did little to cheer him up.

Jack was waiting patiently with Davie by his side when Jamie arrived. 'So, are ye comin' or no?' he asked brusquely. He knew he was being selfish but all three girls would be at Donna's house and Jack didn't fancy having to console a sobbing Charley when he could be wrestling with the athletic Angela.

Jamie looked at him askance. 'Aye, I'm comin,' he replied, and Jack brightened up immediately. Atta boy, Jack smiled gratefully. 'It wouldn't be fair not to, would it?' Jamie added, grudgingly it seemed. 'I should give her a chance to apologise for standing me up last night.'

Jack looked at him sardonically. 'She didnae really huv much choice, did she?' he retorted caustically. 'Her fiancé turned up, remember?'

'Easy Jack, easy…I'm windin' you up,' Jamie laughed. 'I do want to see her.'

'Oh aye? An' whit aboot Lucie?'

'I want to see her too…but she's not back till next Friday.'

'Ye're gonnae to keep seein' both of them?' Jack queried, stupefied, and Davie, who hadn't a clue as to what had happened, looked on in amazement. 'Ah don't believe ye,' Jack said dubiously

Jamie laughed. 'What would you do then? They're both crackin' birds an' I don't know which one I want to be with most…it's only been 24 hours. I'm no gonnae keep them both goin'…no for long anyway, just till I make up my mind. But Charley's engaged remember…she's got a decision to make too. I think she's got a mountain to climb, right enough, but while she's climbin' it I'll just give her a wee hand up.'

Jack shook his head. He didn't know what to make of it all. Jamie was going to be a right bastard, he thought, but it was only a few weeks since Kate had left him and maybe that was influencing him. He decided to give him the benefit of the doubt, for now anyway.

An hour later, Jamie was in the parental bedroom of Donna's house with an apologetic Charley. He had seen her at the window as he walked up the path behind Davie and Jack and she had run to the door, waiting for him, her eyes wet. Her apology had been accompanied by a hungry kiss and she hadn't waited for anything else before leading him upstairs.

'I'm really sorry, baby' she started again. 'He said he wanted to surprise me…and he did, but it wasn't a pleasant surprise. I was frantic. I didn't want to let you down…I really wanted to be with you, honestly.' She was looking at him pleadingly, on the verge of tears, and he felt awful.'

He stroked her hair gently and edged her towards the bed. 'It's alright,' he whispered. 'I understand, honestly. Forget it.'

'What did you do? Did you miss me?' she continued.

'I went back to my digs and there was a party on. I had a few drinks and went to bed. A quiet night…I needed a good sleep anyway after Friday night,' he lied, covering it with a laugh.

Charley pulled him to her and began to kiss him urgently; and running her hand down between his legs she felt him harden. 'You'll need a good sleep tomorrow night too, then,' she laughed, happy again.

They made love, Jamie trying to put Lucie out of his mind and Charley wondering what she should do about her engagement to the hapless Derek.

Chapter 33

'So, what do you think?' Jamie asked. Lucie and Julie had just left him with Jack in Yates' Wine Lodge to enjoy some "boy talk" as Julie put it. Two weeks had gone by since Jamie and Lucie's first meeting and in the intervening time Jack had latched onto Julie. Today they had come into Nottingham on a foursome, with the girls intending to do some serious shopping.

Jack toyed with his glass, swirling the beer around thoughtfully. 'Ye want the truth?' he asked, raising a quizzical eyebrow.'

'What else?'

'Okay, ah'll start wi' the bit ye want tae hear,' Jack said, then paused, waiting for a reaction but got none. 'Lucie's a cracker...if ye played poker ye'd always win cos ye've got three Queens, ya jammy bastard. Christ, ah wish ah could pull like you,' he murmured enviously. 'It must be yer little boy lost look, they aw seem tae want tae mother ye.'

'Get on with it,' Jamie laughed, but his ego had been well massaged even though that hadn't been Jack's intention.

'Ah'm getting the feelin' that Lucie's gettin' tae ye,' Jack continued, raising a questioning eyebrow, but Jamie remained quiet. 'A'right; ah think she's oot o' yer league, Jamie boy,' he pressed on, getting a reaction this time. 'Hear me oot,' he added quickly, stopping Jamie's angry retort. 'Dae ye really think ye can make it work wi' her, big man? She lives on a different planet fae the likes o' you an' me. She comes fae money...an' the class difference between the two o' ye is massive. She's upper middle class...and that perfume she wears prob'ly costs mair than ye earn in a week. And you, Jamie boy? Ye're jist a fuckin' workin' class welder, like me. Ask yersel...where can the relationship go? Charley's mair yer type.'

Jamie stared at him stonily for a while before replying. 'You're wrong Jack,' he said eventually. 'You know your problem? You're just a fuckin' cynic...and in case you'd forgotten, Charley's engaged.'

Jack's immediate response was a chortling laugh. 'That didnae stop ye afore...but ah'll give ye the bit aboot me bein' a cynic,' he continued with a grin. 'But that's jist because all us Catholics huv a head start on you Proddies when it comes tae cynicism. It's aw tae dae wi' us havin' accepted the fact that we're part o' the downtrodden masses, the great unwashed, unlike you Proddies who huvnae cottoned ontae the fact yit,' he countered philosophically. There was a pause and Jamie waited expectantly, suspecting Jack had another gem to add. He did and it came as a bombshell. 'Rumour has it that Charley's thinkin' aboot dumpin' the Air Marshall,' he said quietly. Jamie looked at him, shock etched across his face. 'Whit fit does the beautiful Lucie kick wi', by the way?'

'What the fuck does that have to do with it?' Jamie demanded angrily, completely off balance now.

'Jist askin', jist askin', Jack retorted quickly.

'She went to a girls' school run by nuns, a convent school, so I presume she kicks with the left foot, just like you,' Jamie replied. 'Satisfied?'

'Ah,' Jack smiled in response to that titbit.

'Ah? Is that it? What the fuck does "ah" mean?' Jamie insisted, getting another cheeky grin from Jack in response. 'Ach, forget it…I've been out with good Catholic girls before, remember? Helpin' you out? Anyway, what the fuck's this about Charley breakin' off her engagement…where did you hear that?'

'Where dae ye think? It wiz pillow talk wi' Angela the other night.'

Jamie moaned and sunk his head in his hands. 'Shit Jack, what am I going to do?'

'Have ye shagged her yet?' Jamie drew him a puzzled look. 'Lucie,' Jack continued. 'Have ye shagged her?' The puzzlement was replaced by anger and Jamie's eyes blazed but Jack wasn't in the mood for backing down. 'Well?' he persisted, and watched Jamie deflate.

'No, not yet,' Jamie admitted, picking up his beer and taking a long pull on it, watching Jack all the while over the rim of the glass.

Jack followed suit, wiping his lips with the back of his hand. 'That's no' like ye, big man,' he laughed. 'Ye normally get their knickers aff in jig time. Ah'd think ye were losin' yer touch if ah didnae know whit ye've been up to wi' Charley.'

'Aye, you're right,' Jamie conceded reluctantly. 'It isn't like me…but Lucie's not like other girls. I feel differently about her but there's something not quite right. I think she wants to…you know, wants me to, but she's scared. It's as if she thinks I'll hurt her and drop her as soon as we've done it.'

'An' will ye?'

'No, that's the thing. When you said earlier that it couldn't work for us it made me angry because I think it can.'

'An' whit about Charley? Are ye gonnae keep seein' her?'

'She's engaged Jack, you know that,' Jamie replied. 'Dumpin' her fiancé is just a rumour, you said that yourself, an' you know what happened the last time I got involved with a girl in a relationship.'

'Aye, but Kate wiz married tae a piss head…there's a difference.'

'Look, I like Charley but I don't love her…and she doesn't love me, *or* the guy she's engaged to. It's a relationship that won't last.'

'Whit relationship won't last, the one wi' you or the one wi' him? We already know whit's on the cards fur him.'

'Both, probably,' Jamie acknowledged grimly.

'But ye're still seeing her?'

'Aye, I'm still seein' her, but I want Lucie, Jack, seriously. An' I'll wait till she thinks the time is right.'

'An' meantime ye're still getting nookie with Charley. That could be interestin' if ye manage tae crack it wi' Lucie. It's tirin', take it from one that knows.' He paused there, just to let the message sink in. 'Ah hope Lucie disnae keep ye waitin' too long or ye'll end up a right grumpy bastard,' Jack said, bringing a semblance of a grin to Jamie's face again. 'Let's huv another drink…same again?' he asked. 'Ye might as well, brewers' droop willnae matter tae you th'night, will it?' he laughed, and ducked to avoid the playful slap that he knew Jamie would direct at him.

Chapter 34

Two cars pulled up outside Clouds Dance Club in London Road, Derby, and eight young men piled out onto the pavement. Of the eight, Jamie Raeburn was the youngest at 22 and Terry Hughes, the big Scouse welder, the eldest at 33, and all of them, to a man, were looking forward to the night. Jamie had started out a reluctant participant now he was enjoying himself, particularly the company and the humour of the other seven. His leg was pulled about his relationship with Lucie and there were numerous leading questions, but he just grinned back enigmatically. Let them think what they want to think.

The club was busy but they had expected that; the Enchantresses had a big reputation and guys, like them, would be coming from far and wide to gawp and fantasise. It promised to be a hot, sweaty and erotic night!

Jack and Jamie found a space by the bar and settled down for their first pint of the evening. 'These lassies th'night, ur they no' the wans your Lucie wiz wae?' Jack mulled as he surveyed the heaving crowd.

Jamie smiled and nodded. He'd never seen Lucie dance and felt he had missed out on something. Maybe he should ask her for a private performance; that could be fun, he mused. 'Aye, they're the ones,' he replied, 'wish I'd seen her perform.'

Jack choked and started to laugh. 'Speakin' o' which,' he came back cheekily, 'huv ye managed tae get her tae perform fur you yit…or is yer right haun still gettin' its exercise? he laughed irreverently and carried on. 'If these lassies th'night ur as sexy as they're supposed tae be ye'll prob'ly end up wankin' yersel tae death later. Right enough, ye've still got Charley on the go; ye could always gie her a wee call.'

Aye, but not for long, Jamie reflected, giving Jack an acidic glare. Breaking it off was going to be hard but it would be almost impossible if he kept seeing her for much longer…though he wasn't seeing much of her now anyway.

'So, whit hus Lucie telt ye aboot this lot?' Jack continued. 'Ur any o' them go'ers?'

'Oh aye,' Jamie responded in a conspiratorial whisper. 'They're all stunners apparently; they're all about 5'7" an' blonde wi' big tits…an' they're all up for it,' he said with a wink. 'There's only one problem…' he paused, luring Jack into his trap.

'Aye? Whit's that?' Jack asked, walking right in.

'They don't like wee red headed Scotsmen, so you're fucked!'

Jack burst out laughing, totally unabashed. 'That disnae matter tae me, Jamie boy, ah'm already gettin' plenty…you're the wan that's oan a diet.'

'Aye, right,' Jamie responded sourly. 'But maybe I'll get one of these th'night,' he joked, producing a loud guffaw from Jack.

The club was full now and it *was* hot and it *was* sweaty – and that was without the appearance of The Enchantresses. There were some girls in the clientele and some were gyrating wildly to the music. The Beeston guys had congregated around the small bar but a couple of them had their eye on local girls. They'd be gettin' taxis back. Everything in life has a price. There was a feeling of excitement pulsating through the club as the appointed time approached and as the band finished its last number there was a surge of bodies towards the stage. The two friends remained at the bar, Jack observing Jamie carefully. He wanted to see his reaction to the girls…maybe it would give him a pointer to how Jamie really felt about this new love of his life. Apart from anything else, he still found it hard to believe Jamie had managed to put Kate behind him and he still wasn't sure about Lucie.

The music started up again and the sound of Motown blasted from the giant speakers around the stage. The curtains began to open, revealing the girls one by one, and a collective sigh of lust from the males in the audience almost lifted the roof. The outfits the dancers wore; the skin coloured body stockings, made them appear naked and as they swayed wildly and gyrated provocatively Jack's eyes widened. But it wasn't the eroticism of their routine or the shimmering body stockings that caused his surprise; it was the girl gyrating wildly on the left side of the troupe. 'Is that no' your Lucie?' he said, disbelievingly, turning to Jamie.

Jamie was transfixed, his eyes following every movement of her body and his expression was a mixture of shock and awe. All of the girls were stunning but he couldn't take his eyes off Lucie, the girl hoped would be his. Terry Hughes looked back at him, alarmed, and there were some awkward looks from the others but Jamie was oblivious to all of it. His earlier remark to Jack that he might try for one of them tonight had been prophetic and he began to laugh at the irony of it.

The routine continued for fifteen minutes and the music ran, nonstop, through numbers by Smokey Robinson, Diana Ross and the Supremes, The Temptations and The Four Tops. The girls glistened with sweat and seemed to glow on the stage, smiles fixed on their beautiful faces and their eyes seeming to pick out individual men in the audience. Wet dreams were on the cards for many later and, as the curtain began to close, an all-encompassing moan of male misery filled the tiny club.

Jamie remained at the bar throughout. He saw the surreptitious looks and guessed what the others were thinking but he knew he had nothing to worry about. Before they had set off from Beeston earlier Lucie had called him and he clearly remembered her parting words so, no, he didn't have to worry. He painted a smug grin on his face and prepared to deal with the inevitable comments.

Those, it happened, didn't transpire. Either his mates believed his smug look or they were too embarrassed to raise the matter and when the band returned to the stage a few minutes later he slipped outside for a smoke. He chatted jokingly with one of the bouncers, an older guy with short cropped hair, and explained he was only going out for a smoke and would be returning. The door man smiled, nodded and grunted his agreement.

He strolled down the stairs to the pavement and lit a Lucky Strike, filling his lungs with the smoke and thinking about what he had just seen. Suddenly, from an alley at the side of the club, Lucie appeared and made her way towards the bus stop about thirty yards away. She was wearing tight blue jeans and a black polo neck sweater, which emphasized her figure, and she had a duffle bag slung over her shoulder. This wasn't the girl he had just seen bring hordes of lusty men to the verge of orgasm. She looked at her watch and hurried along, turning to look up the road beyond Jamie but failing to see him there. He watched her, filled with indecision. Should he try to catch her, talk to her, or keep his visit to the club a secret for the moment? He took another drag on his cigarette and had decided to let sleeping dogs lie when a sleek black car passed him and pulled to a halt beside the bus stop. He saw Lucie take a step backwards, seeming to distance herself from the car and its occupants, and a sense of her fear radiated out towards him.

He was moving before the black car had fully stopped, covering the ground between them quickly. He saw the front window of the car wind down and caught a glimpse of the driver, a suave, smug looking guy. He was saying something to Lucie but Jamie couldn't hear but he was close enough to see the look on her face and was closer still when she replied, hearing most of her response.

Lucie was still unaware of his presence, her attention taken up by the sudden reappearance of Max Kelman. Her heart was racing and she could feel her whole body trembling with revulsion. Just when everything seemed to be going right for her this animal had to appear and spoil it. 'Leave me alone,' she said, her voice shaking.

Jamie heard the callous laugh of the man and his blood boiled. He was only a few feet away now. The car driver was talking again and Lucie's face was a deathly white. 'The lady told you to leave her alone,' Jamie said loudly, walking up close to her. Lucie turned to his voice and her eyes opened wide in surprise. The driver laughed again, a thin, evil laugh, and spoke to someone in the car. The far passenger door opened and a large man hauled himself out, smiling like a hyena.

Jamie looked at Lucie and saw the mix of fear and hope in her eyes but the hope part seemed to be fading with the appearance of this big man. Jamie gave her a smile, hoping she would take heart from it, but panic appeared to be setting in. She hadn't said a word since his intervention and her fear was clearly burgeoning.

The big man came round the back of the car and positioned himself in the opening, blocking Jamie's way out. Jamie regarded him dispassionately. He was big, right enough, with the look of a man used to handing out beatings but he was running to fat and complacency had set in. That comes when people don't resist and he didn't expect resistance now. Jamie slipped his hand into his pocket and felt for the ever present folded paper and his three pennies. Seconds later and his makeshift knuckle duster was ready. As the big man closed in on him Jamie raised his hands in what appeared to be a gesture of surrender but the bruiser ignored him and lumbered closer. What happened next shocked everyone. The man swung a punch but Jamie simply stepped inside the arc and drove his fist straight up and into the guy's throat below the chin. There was a moment's silence and then a gagging sound came from the man's mouth; he clutched at his throat and a look of pained surprise flooded his face. Jamie didn't wait to let him recover. He stepped in closer and hit the big man again, driving his fist hard into the man's unprotected solar plexus. There was a coughing noise as air was expelled from the man's diaphragm and his eyes opened wide just as Jamie's third punch landed and finished him. A straight right, delivered to his chin, sent him staggering backwards and he crashed to the ground, his head cracking against the unforgiving concrete.

Jamie knew he was down and turned back to Lucie and the driver. Lucie was dumbstruck, her eyes wide with shock. The driver looked at his fallen champion and then into Jamie's eyes and decided it wouldn't be prudent to hand around. The car engine screamed and there was the squeal and acrid smell of burning rubber as the car pulled away in a cloud of smoke. The timing was perfect, or so Jamie thought, when a bus pulled in at the stop where the car had been. He turned to Lucie, smiling, but her eyes were full of fear and darted frantically between him and the fallen giant lying on the pavement.

'Oh no, Jamie...what have you done?' she cried, sobbing uncontrollably, and then she swung onto the bus and away from him. He saw the fear still etched on her face but there was something else there too and as the bus pulled away, he stood there wondering what the hell had just happened.

The big man was still out cold but it wouldn't be long before he started to come round, Jamie realised. He still wouldn't be much of a threat but Jamie anticipated the return of the car and he doubted if the driver would be alone when it did. He took another look at the man. His breathing was regular and apart from a sore head and a sore throat he would survive. Jamie lit another cigarette and returned, pensively, to the club, pondering the strange turn of events. Whatever had happened it wasn't just a casual attempt by a guy to proposition Lucie, he was sure of that. He rejoined the others at the bar but said nothing. Better they didn't know unless they had to and he would take it up with Lucie on Friday…if she turned up.

Chapter 35

That night brought another change to Jamie's life. It had been in flux already, it has to be said, but he had reached a hiatus. The question was how to move forward. He was with Lucie only at the weekends and was rarely with Charley now...they were together on Sunday nights, no there, and he guessed she suspected that there was someone else. It didn't curb their passion when they were together but Jamie was feeling more and more guilty felt guilty now and the time was coming to end it. The "Wing Commander", as Jack called Charley's fiancé, was almost finished his basic training so things would have to change in any event. The result of all that was that mid-week evenings were quieter for Jamie now, though that couldn't be said of the night before and the events of it troubled him. He sat alone in the garden turning everything over in his head yet again.

Lucie being on the stage had been a surprise but that was all; it was the incident with the guy in the car that really bothered him. He kept thinking about Lucie's reaction when she found him beside her. He was missing something, but what? She had been distressed, that part he could understand, but why rush off and leave him...and her words, "Oh no, Jamie... what have you done"; what was that all about? He had said nothing to anyone, but tomorrow night, Friday, he would get to the bottom of it...it could wait until then.

He heard the French Doors open behind him and feet padding out onto the patio. 'Hey, sleepy head! Benny and Mick are waiting for you,' Jo Bradley informed him as she sat down beside him at the table. Jamie sighed and lit another cigarette, offering the pack to Jo who took one and waited for him to light it. 'Moping about on your own isn't good,' Jo continued, drawing thoughtfully on her cigarette. She could see that something was troubling him...it had been there on his face all day. 'Go out, have a drink, play some pool...and Lucie will be with you tomorrow,' she counselled, hoping she could bring him out of it.

Jamie sensed rather than saw her inquisitive looks; she had covered them well. He knew that if he stayed her natural curiosity would lead to questions and he wasn't ready for that. Jo was doing everything she could to cement his relationship with Lucie and he thought he was missing something there too, but she cared, about both of them it seemed, and because of that he could forgive her anxious curiosity...though he wasn't up for a question and answer session tonight. 'Okay, okay...I'm going,' he smiled, resigned, 'but if Lucie throws a tantrum, it's your fault,' he said, forcing a smile.

Jo laughed. 'Lucie won't...she knows you're not the hermit type; go out, enjoy yourself.'

So he had done just that and being with Benny and Mick took his mind off things. He had started to unwind and a couple of pints and a game of pool with some of the usual crowd in the Social Club helped. It was the Thursday night bingo session and the club was reasonably busy, mostly middle aged men and women, but there was a younger crowd in tonight too. He had been to the club on a few occasions now after Davie Miller introduced him. Davie was spending most of his time with Donna now and was hardly ever there but the committee members manning the door knew Jamie and the others well now and welcomed them with open arms...they spent money and caused no trouble.

The bingo was about to start and some of the younger crowd drifted into the bar. Three girls were casting glances and he smiled back but romance was certainly not on his mind but Mick seemed up for it. Mick had toned down his "adventurous" dress style over the last few weeks, courtesy of some gentle pushing by Jamie, and he'd lost a bit of weight...so he might be on a promise tonight, Jamie laughed, and that wouldn't have happened before. One of the girls was becoming a problem however and it looked like it was going to be Jamie's problem. She had started to flirt openly with him: brazen looks, fluttering eyelashes and pouted lips which had started to annoy her boyfriend and that could prove troublesome. Jamie ignored her hoping she would get the message but her antics continued and her boyfriend was doing his best to divert her attention. It suddenly struck Jamie that she was winding the boy up. Some girls would go to any lengths, he mused. She would be about 17 or 18 he reckoned, no older, with long, jet black hair and her eyes heavily made up with a dark blue eye shadow and mascara. Her lips were a dark red and her fingernails were painted black, matching the top and trousers she was wearing. Obviously a girl from the dark side, he smiled to himself, but underneath the sombre makeup and the black clothes he could see that she was quite pretty. Her boyfriend, also about 18, maybe a little older, was beginning to lose the plot and kept drawing Jamie warning looks but Jamie kept his head down. He'd been trouble free almost since leaving Glasgow, apart from a couple of minor disagreements and that carry on in Derby, and he wanted to keep it that way. He liked coming to the club from time to time and upsetting the members of the committee wasn't on the agenda.

The younger crowd, which included Jamie's young admirer and her boyfriend, left the club at quarter to ten and Jamie and the two others followed shortly after them. Jamie had relaxed again, sighing with relief when the crowd had departed, conscious that the girl in black had almost pushed her poor boyfriend to the limit and Jamie had sensed trouble brewing.

Benny, as usual, was complaining of hunger. For such a small guy he could certainly eat and tonight was no exception. 'Anybody fancy a fish supper?' he suggested. There was a Chippie near the Social Club, close to the railway station, and it did a good bag of chips but Jamie wasn't interested. Benny and Mick, however, went into the shop and joined the queue while Jamie waited outside, lighting up a smoke.

A young mixed group of four lads and three girls came from the direction of the Social Club and entered the Chippie behind Benny and Mick. Jamie didn't recognise any of them from earlier but his antennae picked up bad vibes as they passed him. He gazed through the shop window, picking out Benny and Mick easily. The group had closed in on them and the proprietor was watching developments, uncomfortably, from behind the counter. Benny's face was set hard and an argument was clearly underway. Jamie's hand went to his inside jacket pocket and he felt the comforting, cold shape of the steel comb nestling there. *What the fuck am I doing*, he reproached himself angrily? *This isn't Glasgow, it's Nottingham. Get a grip!*

One of the girls looked out of the window at him and the boy with her drew him a look. The girl looked familiar, he thought, and then he realised why...she was almost identical to the girl in black earlier, so much so they could be twins, he realised, but this one dressed in lighter hues.

The argument inside the shop was heating up and Jamie swithered about joining in but that, he reckoned, would simply make matters worse. So he waited, growing impatient and angry. Benny stormed out a few minutes later, chips in hand and his face red with anger, and Mick followed in his wake, clearly disturbed.

'Fuckin' arseholes,' Benny muttered as he joined Jamie.

'What happened?' Jamie asked, looking back into the shop and seeing the group engaged in a discussion.

'They wir jist tryin' tae wind me up,' Benny fumed.

'Looks like it worked,' Jamie laughed, patting him on the shoulder. 'C'mon, let's get home.' Benny grinned sheepishly and offered Jamie his bag of chips and Jamie picked out a couple of steaming chunks of potato and slipped them into his mouth, enjoying the tart flavours of the salt and vinegar which coated them.

They had managed to cover fifty yards before Jamie realised they were being followed by the group from the chippie. It could simply be that they were making their way home in the same direction but Jamie suspected not. The group stayed well behind but as they neared the town centre they were joined by more, another three boys and three girls...including the lady in black. Jamie knew, instinctively, that things were going to kick off as the gang, because by now it was a gang, started to close in on them. Mick was showing signs of panic and Jamie put his arm around the big Geordie's shoulder in an attempt to calm him. 'Relax Mick,' he said easily, 'there's no' enough of them yet.'

Mick looked at him wide eyed then back to the group, counting them mentally. 'There are seven of them, bonny lad,' he spluttered, 'how many does it take?'

Benny smiled coldly. 'Dae ye think they'll come, big man?' he directed at Jamie who kept on walking, not looking back.

'Aye, probably,' he replied. 'When you're finished your chips give me the wrapping,' he continued, pointing to the wrapping of the carry out.

Benny raised one eye quizzically then peeled away the newspaper, the outer wrapping, and handed it over. 'Ah'm finished wae it noo,' he said, interested to see what Jamie intended doing with it and watched, intrigued, as Jamie tore the paper in two and began to fold it in strips, doubling it over and over until he was happy with it, then tucked it into the palm of his right hand. Benny and Mick exchanged curious looks as he clenched the strip tightly in his hand and then, with his left hand, he fished some coins from his trouser pocket. He selected three pennies and replaced the rest, then carefully inserted the pennies between the clenched fingers of his right hand.

Benny grinned and Mick turned pale. 'Nice one, big man,' the small Glaswegian commented with a low whistle.

'Aye, it's effective,' Jamie smiled icily, 'but I'll only use it if I have to.' He thought back...the last time he used this he had ended up in The Royal and met Kate. What would tonight bring?

'Gie us the other piece o' paper,' Benny came back, holding out his hand.

'I didn't think you'd need it,' Jamie laughed. 'You keep tellin' me your hands are lethal weapons.'

'Aye, they ur, but a wee bit o' help disnae go amiss,' Benny retorted, and Jamie passed the paper over, watching with a hint of amusement as Benny folded the paper just as he had done and gripped it tightly in his hand. Jamie had already dug out another three pennies from his pocket and handed them over.

'What about me?' Mick asked nervously. 'What can I do?'

'I don't know; what can you do?' Jamie retorted.

'I've never been in a fight before,' the Geordie admitted nervously.

'If it moves, hit it,' Benny laughed. 'But ye'd better take yer specs aff first.'

They kept walking, serious now, but not hurrying. Jamie knew that the gang was coming closer but he continued to ignore them. More people joined them and Jamie turned at last to count them. There were eight boys and five girls now closing in on them. Thirteen, he smiled grimly, unlucky for some.

'We need to keep them talkin' till we get close to home, right?' Jamie instructed, automatically taking command. 'If we start battlin' with them here it'll be a long slog home.'

They were about a quarter of a mile from the house…in Chilwell Road now and then into Devonshire Avenue…say three hundred yards down Devonshire Avenue to Devonshire Place, he calculated, then another hundred and they would be home. He nodded his head sagely. 'If we can make it to the corner of Devonshire Place before it all kicks off, we'll skoosh it,' he said confidently. 'It's tight in there and they won't have room to get round about us. He turned to Mick. Are you alright?' he asked, concerned.

'Aye, fine bonny lad,' Mick responded, his Geordie accent even thicker than normal now, but he didn't sound fine…and he didn't look it either.

The gang came for them as soon as they turned off Chilwell Road into Devonshire Avenue. 'Here we go,' Jamie smiled grimly, clenching his right fist around the pennies. 'Remember, keep talking and keep walking till we get to the corner,' he instructed. Benny nodded but Mick seemed to be in a state of panic.

Devonshire Avenue being a wide thoroughfare, they were quickly surrounded. A quick look told Jamie they were mainly youngsters, between 16 and 18, and he settled for the biggest lad in the group who just happened to be the boyfriend of the black widow as Jamie now thought of her. The lad who had been winding Benny up in the chippie stood belligerently in in front of the wee man now, walking backwards and threatening with gestures as Benny followed Jamie's advice and kept moving towards Devonshire Place.

'Took yer time,' Jamie laughed, goading his chosen opponent, his accent reverting to strong Glaswegian. It didn't hurt to let them know what they were dealing with. 'Enough o' ye now, ye think?' he continued, staring intimidatingly at the guy.

'You Jocks think you're big men, don't you?' the lad fired back, his confidence swollen by his supporting act.

'Big men?' Jamie laughed and pointed at Benny. 'He's aboot 5 foot nothin',' he chortled and then his face became serious again. 'Huvin' said that, he's still big enough tae take that prick,' he said caustically, looking dismissively over at the lad backtracking in front of Benny. 'Whit we ur is hard men…an' if ye think we're no' then come ahead.' To some it might have sounded like bravado but it produced a flicker of doubt in the boy's eyes none the less. They kept walking, edging ever closer to Devonshire Place, with Jamie keeping up the verbal pressure.

'You Scotch bastards think you can come down here and take our birds,' the big lad blustered, causing Jamie to give the girls a disdainful look.

'Frankly pal, ah don't fancy any o' that lot,' he replied dismissively. 'In fact, ah widne even shag them wi' your dick.' The boy's face reddened with rage but still he didn't make a move.

Jamie glanced over at Benny once again. The wee guy was needling away at his tormentor, keeping with the tactics. Jamie paid no attention to what was being said;

Benny, he knew, could take care of himself. Mick, on the other hand, was more of a problem and he was already drifting away from the centre of the confrontation towards the garden hedges and walls facing onto the road. He was feeling his way along and Jamie suddenly realised that without his glasses, the big Geordie was as blind as a bat. For fuck sake, Jamie thought anxiously, I'll need to look out for him too. But for the moment, everyone seemed to be ignoring him.

At last they reached the corner of Devonshire Place. Jamie gave Benny a quick look and saw him nod. The time had come. Coincidentally, it coincided with Jamie's rival deciding he was ready to take Jamie on having been goaded into it by the others, in particular his girlfriend, who were screaming at him to do something. He made his fatal move and reached out, grabbing Jamie's lapels and pulling him round.

Jamie looked down at the boy's hands and smiled coldly. 'Big mistake, pal,' he hissed. 'Let go.' The boy stared at him uncertainly. He wanted to do something but quite what, he didn't know but he didn't let go as Jamie had instructed. 'Ah've hud enough o' this shite, Benny,' he said loudly. 'Just hit that fucker and let's get this ower wi'.' He took hold of the boy's lapels and pulled him in, his head jerking forward and connecting viciously with the bridge of the boy's nose. There was a moment of stunned silence. The boy staggered backwards, blood streaming from his damaged nose and Jamie followed up, landing a punch on the boy's stomach with his right fist. The pennies sank deep into the lad's abdomen and he sank to his knees. Benny, watching in admiration, said something to his antagonist and the boy exploded, swinging a wild punch which Benny sidestepped easily, laughing. The guy swung another and Benny swayed to the other side, making the guy miss again. He was making the boy look stupid which made the lad angrier and more impulsive. The boy, screaming now, threw another haymaker and again Benny sidestepped but on this occasion, instead of moving out of range, he stepped in close and head butted the lad solidly on the bridge of his nose, an exact replica of Jamie's assault on the other. There was a sickening thud and a scream as the boy's nose broke and blood and gore splattered everywhere.

The shocked silence descended on the scene again but not for long. 'Now they know what Glasgow Kisses are, wee man,' Jamie laughed, his blood up. His own opponent was rising to his feet when Jamie hit him again. The pennies drove upwards and impacted on the boy's ribs, cracking two of them, and a second punch, thrown with his left hand this time, landed on the guy's right cheek and sent him spinning back to the ground. 'Time tae go,' he screamed at Benny, at the same time searching for Mick. Mick, he discovered with some relief, had already begun making his way down Devonshire Place but he was still vulnerable. 'Mick,' he bellowed at him. 'Run, for fuck sake, run.'

They took off, running for the house at the end of the cul de sac before the gang recovered and came to grips with the situation. They gate to the yard was closed and the mob was now closing, forcing them to search out defensive positions. Benny stopped with his back against the high fence and Jamie stood under the big elm tree which stood at the edge of the pavement. What happened now was in the lap of the Gods and they awaited the onslaught. Benny, like Jamie, was street wise and knew to protect his back but Jamie couldn't see Mick anywhere. He began to panic, fearful that the Geordie had been caught and left further down the street. He spotted him then and breathed a sigh of relief. Mick stood calmly at the door, ringing the bell, and Jamie surmised that the gang had decided he wasn't worth the effort and concentrated their attack on Jamie and Benny. That, as far as Jamie was concerned, was the only explanation but he had an immediate problem to deal with. Six of the boys were still fighting fit and they split into two threes, coming for Jamie and Benny now in a concentrated attack. He lashed out with fists and feet, feeling his blows land and taking a few in return.

The air was blue with cursing and swearing and the pressure was beginning to tell. One of his attackers broke off a wooden fence post and came at him, swinging it viciously above his head. Everything moved in slow motion then; he saw the stave ready to descend on him, watched as Benny went down under a kick and then the door opened and a swarm of hairy welders, plumbers and electricians dressed in vests and pants, some barefooted and some in socks, piled out of the house to their rescue. The noise itself was enough to scare Jamie let alone the local boys and soon the street had reverted to its normal calm as the pack made off, haring down Devonshire Place as fast as their shaking legs would carry them.

Jamie sagged back against the tree and looked over at Benny. The sight which met him would have scared a lesser man. Benny, his face and shirt covered with blood and snot, was grinning like a demon, his white teeth and eyes blazing out of a crimson background. One by one, the men who had chased off the mob returned and gathered round the two combatants, vexed by their appearance. Jo and Brian Bradley emerged and surveyed the battleground, Jo's eyes finally settling on Benny; she broke down immediately, tears bursting forth while Benny looked at her in total bemusement.

'Whit's up Jo?' he asked, puzzled.

She returned his look, still in shock., and she too was puzzled Why, she wondered, was he asking *her* what was wrong when he looked as if he'd been through a mincer? 'You're covered in blood, Benny love,' she sobbed. 'Where are you hurt?'

'Hurt? Me? Ah'm no hurt, Jo,' he laughed. 'Aw this blood isnae mine,' he assured her, looking over at Jamie. 'Ur you a'right, big man?' he asked solicitously.

Jamie laughed coldly. 'Never better, wee man,' he replied bitterly, 'but I thought I'd got away from all that crap.'

Jo, still distraught, quickly ushered them into the house and insisted, immediately, that Benny take off his shirt to satisfy her that he really wasn't injured. The blood had seeped through the cotton of his shirt onto his torso covering his chest in swathes of red, like some futuristic form of art. Beneath the slick coating of blood there wasn't a mark on him and he grinned broadly. 'Telt ye,' he said triumphantly.

They all turned to Jamie then and he became aware of them looking at him with the same concern shown for the wee man. His jacket and shirt too were spotted with blood and he, unlike Benny, was showing some signs of battle. His cheek was grazed, his left thigh throbbed and his ribs ached but he had escaped major injury. He looked down at his right hand and realised, with alarm, that the pennies were still there and his knuckles were covered with blood. Surreptitiously, he slipped the coins into his trousers pocket and casually placed the folded paper into the waste bin.

'Take off your jacket and shirt and I'll soak them,' Jo instructed, holding Benny's shirt between thumb and forefinger for the same purpose. Without argument, Jamie slipped off his jacket, pulled the expensive Byford top over his head, and handed them over. Benny came to him, grinning inanely, and hugged him, like two victorious gladiators, while the others looked on in amazement. Beer was produced and, to the sound of cans opening, Benny toasted him and started to cavort about the floor. Jamie laughed at the expressions on the faces of the watchers. They already thought Glasgow was full of nutters and it looked like two of those had ended up with them, here in Nottingham.

Jo shepherded them all out of her kitchen and into the lounge, promising to bring more beer. Brian, her husband, looked at her anxious face and smiled reassuringly. 'They're fine,' he said. 'Don't worry.'

Jo watched as her brood filed out towards the lounge, the two Scots boys bringing up the rear. They were so young, she thought, and yet they seemed so hard. As if to reinforce that thought her eyes picked out the two ugly scars on his naked back, just above the waist band of his trousers, and a small shudder ran through her. Jamie, it appeared, was no stranger to violence and it didn't take much imagination to guess what had caused those scars...a knife. Stab wounds, fairly recent by the look of them, and here he was in another fight which could have had serious consequences.

Looking at Jamie and Benny now, Jo was staggered by what appeared to be their calm acceptance of something she and, she suspected, the others would consider alarming. Were they so used to that sort of thing they simply didn't think about it? And was Glasgow really as bad as everyone said it was, she wondered? She had lived through the war and had been in Coventry at the time of the blitz and she had seen a lot...but she would be the first to admit that she was shocked by tonight's events. It wasn't so much the blood that shocked her.; like Julie and Lucie now, she had been a nurse and had seen plenty of that. It was the boys' acceptance of it as normal that scared her. Things like that rarely happened here in Beeston and it was hard to accept that they did even in bigger cities like London, Birmingham and Glasgow. She had been shocked tonight and now that shock had been worsened by the scars on Jamie's back. She gasped, drawing in a sharp breath which Jamie heard and he turned to her, seeing instantly the concern on her face.

'What happened to you?' she asked softly.

'Long story,' Jamie replied, his voice steady and his expression serious. 'Maybe I'll tell you all about it one day,' he said over his shoulder as he left the room. Jo gave an involuntary shudder and her husband hugged her. The thought came to her that Jamie Raeburn might be more of a handful than she had first imagined...and she feared the impact of that on Lucie. Jamie Raeburn was no stranger to trouble.

Jo loaded beer, whisky and glasses onto a tray and headed for the lounge. The lodgers were spread around the room listening to Benny's version of the fracas and she had come in just at the tail end of the story. She looked for Jamie and found him, still stripped to the waist, sitting in one of the easy chairs with his eyes closed. He looked calm, as though nothing had happened.

'Jamie hud it aw sussed out,' Benny said, looking at Jamie admiringly. 'He telt us that if we made it tae the corner at the end o' the road we'd be a'right,' he continued, 'an' he wiz spot on. Ah wiz brickin' it but the big man wiz cool...an' it wisnae till we were closer tae hame afore the shit hit the fan.' He spied Jo in the doorway then and blushed. 'Sorry Jo, ah didnae see ye there,' he spluttered. Jo smiled, but her eyes were still on Jamie.

Benny was about to launch into the story again when Jamie silenced him. 'Enough Benny, everybody's bored...can it,' he said quietly but Benny got the message. He might be a good boxer but he didn't fancy an argument with the big man. He turned sheepishly to the crowd. 'Sorry everyone,' he said. 'Ah'm jist a wee bit hyper, know? It's the adrenalin.'

Jamie smiled behind his closed eyes. Does Benny even know what adrenalin is, he wondered? But he knew what it was and he knew what happened when it wore off. He opened his eyes and rose to his feet then grabbed Benny in a hug. 'Stay cool, wee man,' he said with a tired smile. 'I'm going to bed and I'll see you all in the morning,' he finished, saluting them.

A chorus of grunts acknowledged him and he headed for the door, glancing over at Jo. The worry and the questions were still there in her expression and guessed the sight of the stab wounds hadn't helped. He sighed, gave her one of his disarming smiles, and padded off to the stairs and up to his room. She smiled wanly at his disappearing back. He was like two different people and she preferred the one she thought she knew...the likeable rogue.

She joined the others and poured herself a whisky. With Jamie gone she could quiz Benny about him. 'Do you know what happened to his back?' she asked casually.

Benny knitted his brow. 'Naw Jo, sorry, ah don't,' he replied. 'Ah've only known him since we arrived here. Ah asked him once but he disnae talk aboot it,' he continued. 'The best wan tae ask wid be his pal, Jack. They've been mates fur years,' he added helpfully.

'Thanks Benny,' she returned softly. Yes, Jack would probably know the truth and Julie has been seeing him, she remembered. She would ask Julie.

Lying on his bed, Jamie listened to the muffled conversation from below. He was in a contemplative mood now, thinking about life and wondering why he always ended up battling. A quiet night out for him more often than not ended up in a Donnybrook...or a "Jamiebrook", as Jack would say! Kate came to him. She had been right to worry about the future with a guy like him, a guy who had trouble for a friend. But he could stay out of it...when he had been with Kate he had stayed out of it. Was that the answer? Maybe, now that he had Lucie things would get better. Then the look of horror on Jo's face came back to him. His scars had really scared her and putting those alongside tonight's little fiasco she probably thought he was a total wanker. He needed her on his side if he wanted to keep Lucie and if he didn't? Well, maybe she would encourage Lucie to end things...and he didn't want that.

Sleep was difficult but when it finally came he fell into a deep slumber and when Benny and Mick tip-toed into the room an hour later, he was dead to the world.

Chapter 36

The knock on the door just before 4.30pm took Jo Bradley by surprise. Friday afternoons were usually quite relaxing. Some of the boarders went home at weekends and, as a result, she had less people to cater for and more time to herself. The door was always on the latch; family and boarders knew that and didn't stand on ceremony, just pushed it open and came in. So who was there bothering her at this time in the day?

Mildly annoyed, she rose from her chair with a deep sigh and made her way down the hall. Opening the door with the look of annoyance still imprinted on her face, she caught her first glimpse of the uniforms and her look changed from annoyance to shock in an instant. Two policemen stood patiently on the doorstep, sweating profusely in their heavy uniforms under the warm afternoon sun.

'Mrs Bradley?' the older officer, a sergeant, enquired. The other didn't even look old enough to shave let alone be a policeman, she thought, her mood changing again. I must be getting old, she laughed to in response to that thought.

'Yes, that's me sergeant,' she acknowledged, knitting her brow questioningly. 'How can I help you?'

'I'm Sergeant Blackman and this is Constable Thomas,' he replied, getting the formalities out of the way. 'It's about a disturbance last night,' he continued. 'There was a report from one of your neighbours. Do you happen to know anything about it?' he asked in a low monotone, sounding bored.

'Well, actually, I do,' Jo replied immediately, astonishing him. 'Would you like to come in?'

'Thanks,' Sergeant Blackman replied quickly, his face breaking into a smile for the first time. He was grateful to get out of the sun and into the cool of the big house for a while. Both men removed their helmets and mopped their brows as they stepped into the hall and followed Jo through to the cool of the lounge.

'Some local boys set about three of my lodgers,' she explained as they sat down. The sergeant looked at his young colleague who immediately took the hint and pulled out his notebook. He licked the tip of his pencil and held it poised, ready.

*

Lucie Kent and Julie Bradley caught the four twenty Derby to Nottingham commuter train, both buoyed by thoughts of what lay ahead that night. It had been a bad week for Lucie, disastrous even, but the thought of being with Jamie again later brought a smile to her face. Her only worry was in the memory of Wednesday night and the questions that Jamie would pose. What should have been a pleasant surprise for her, Jamie's sudden appearance, had, in actual fact, been a nightmare. Max Kelman wouldn't forget Jamie's intervention and consequences were inevitable. She still couldn't come to terms with what had actually happened...one minute Max Kelman was accosting her and in the next instant Jamie was there beside her, protecting her. The shock of his appearance had been indescribable but even that was eclipsed by what happened next. Tony Abrahams, Max's muscle, had been despatched from the car to take care of Jamie but it hadn't worked out that way. And it had all been so quick. She could remember Jamie raising his hands as though signalling defeat; could remember too a fleeting sense of disappointment…and then Tony Abrahams was on the ground and Max was away. Panic had engulfed her and she had run, jumping onto the bus that had just arrived. She had shouted something to Jamie but couldn't remember what now…but the look on his face would stay with her for the rest of her life. Everything was there; tension, confusion, anger, dismay, questions…even exhilaration. So why had she run? Fear, of course; but for herself? Yes, she was afraid for herself but there had been more to it…there had been fear for Jamie. He'd come to her, like some knight in shining armour but he had no idea what he was getting into. If Max Kelman linked her in any way to Jamie then he would be in danger, terrible danger…and that was why she had run. Never in her wildest dreams had she imagined meeting anyone like Jamie Raeburn; someone fearless who would jump to her aid the way he had done. And when she thought of that a thrill electrified her…but it was tempered by the knowledge of what Max Kelman would visit on him now. Max knew only one way to respond to a challenge and Jamie had set that challenge.

She had been anticipating another visit from Max. His authority had been challenged and his ego dented and he would want to know who the stranger was and if she knew him. She kept going over it in her mind; had she, in the heat of the moment, called out Jamie's name? It tortured her. But try as she might, she could not remember. She prayed not and the more time went by the more she clung to the hope that Max didn't suspect anything.

This weekend in Beeston served two purposes. Apart from being with Jamie again it was an opportunity to be out of Max Kelman's reach. She would, she knew, have to deal with the problem Max Kelman presented sooner or later. Whether she could deal with it with Jamie by her side or not was another question. She baulked at the thought of involving…and not simply because of the danger to him but because she would have to tell him everything…and she didn't know if she could.

She smiled across the compartment at Julie who was studying her intently. Since meeting Jack Connelly, Julie had an added incentive to visit her family every weekend, but even before that she had been happy to accompany Lucie on her weekly trysts. But now there was a quizzical look in her eye.

'What are you going to tell Jamie?' Julie posed eventually. A very frightened Lucie had come to her on Wednesday night and had sobbed her way through the details of what had taken place. Even now, almost 48 hours later, Lucie was still uptight about it, her nerves taught. It wasn't surprising, Julie reflected. It had taken Lucie a long time to find someone she thought she could trust, someone she had true feelings for at last, and now all of that was in jeopardy. The next few of hours would be interesting. How would Lucie handle it, she wondered? 'What are you going to tell him?' Julie repeated, forcing Lucie to deal with it.

Lucie gave her an anxious look. 'I don't know Jules,' she replied hesitantly, using Julie's pet name. 'What *can* I tell him?'

'The truth might be a good idea,' Julie fired back. She had expected Lucie's reluctance. Over the last three weeks she had regaled Julie with all her hopes and dreams about Jamie and now she feared she might lose him. Julie had formed a different view. Apart from anything else, he was in love with Lucie. Unfortunately, the only person who couldn't see it was Lucie herself. But she was walking a fine line; if she kept the truth from Jamie now it would make everything so much worse when it did come out…and it would, eventually. That, in Julie's view, was a recipe for disaster. 'Like I said, I think you should tell him the truth,' she said finally.

'I don't think I can,' Lucie replied forlornly. 'It's too painful…and I'm scared of what he'll think.'

'I know it is, honey,' Julie continued, putting an arm caringly around Lucie's shoulder. 'But he has to know about it sometime if you keep seeing him…and that *is* what you want, isn't it?'

'Yes, that's what I want.'

Julie smiled, she had won her point, but she could still see reluctance in Lucie's eyes. 'What do you see in him?' she asked.

Lucie looked at her quickly, stung by her words, then realised that Julie wasn't speaking of Jamie in a derogatory way. She smiled awkwardly at her mistake. 'He's not what I expected,' she laughed, 'especially after the way your Mum described him. I expected some sort of Don Juan, with arms like an octopus, that I would have to fight off…but he's not like that. Not at all,' she said dreamily. Julie looked at her sceptically and Lucie picked up on it. 'He's not,' she repeated, laughing. 'That's not to say he isn't romantic…he is; and he's kind, he's considerate and he's gentle…and he's shy.'

'Shy?' Julie laughed incredulously. 'Jamie Raeburn is never shy!'

Lucie blushed a little. 'He is…at least, he's shy with me.'

'Are you telling me you've never…you know?' Julie continued, unsure how to phrase the question and feeling a little naughty at prying. Lucie blushed even more. 'My God, you haven't!' Julie exclaimed with a shriek. 'I don't believe it…especially after what Jack has told me.'

Lucie looked at her angrily. 'Have you been talking about us with Jack?' she asked indignantly.

Julie retreated. 'No, nothing like that,' she replied defensively. 'It's just that Jack has told me things about what the two of them and their friends get up to in Glasgow, that's all.'

Appeased somewhat, Lucie softened. 'No we haven't, not yet,' she said, overcoming her reluctance to discuss it. 'He tried at the beginning but I just couldn't…and he didn't push. That's what I meant when I said he's kind and gentle.' The dreamy look was back in her eyes.

'Do you want to?' Julie asked quietly.

Lucie smiled sadly at that. 'Yes, of course I want to…but I'm scared too.'

Julie pulled her closer. Considering what Lucie had been through it was only to be expected that she would be scared, but Jamie wasn't Max Kelman and, in Lucie's own words, he was considerate and gentle. 'I don't think you need to be scared, Luce…Jamie won't hurt you, you must know that.'

Lucie's smile was sad still. 'It's not Jamie I'm scared of, it's me. What if I freeze up and he thinks I'm frigid.'

Julie could see where Lucie was coming from with that but putting off the day wouldn't help. And if Jamie was as hot blooded as Jack said, how long would he be prepared to wait? She spoke out, almost thinking aloud. 'Waiting isn't going to help either, Luce. If you don't…you know…maybe he'll look elsewhere.' As the words came out she hoped she hadn't gone too far.

But a look of panic rather than anger at the suggestion appeared on Lucie's face. 'Do you think he will?' she asked fearfully.

Damage repair time, Julie recognised instantly. 'No, I don't think he will…he's in love with you, you silly cow,' she laughed lightly. 'You're the only one who doesn't see that. He'll wait till you're ready, I'm sure he will…but I don't think you should keep him waiting too long.' She left it there and Lucie slipped into a thoughtful silence. 'Let her think about it,' Julie told herself.

Lucie was doing just that. She wanted him, more than anything, and he wanted her...she had seen the evidence of that with her own eyes and had been secretly pleased. When she had stopped him that first time...when their petting was getting too heavy, he had backed off immediately. He seemed to sense her insecurity...and perhaps even her fear. But there was something else too, something about him; what was it, a fear of rejection or of commitment, perhaps? She wondered what Jack had told Julie about him. Was he a Casanova? She looked over at Julie who was gazing disinterestedly out of the carriage window. Julie had been great. The moment Jamie had walked into the room that first night they had both fancied him but as soon as Julie had spotted the way he was looking at *her*, she had bowed out gracefully. Since then she had done everything she could to bring them closer together. If only she had Julie's confidence she and Jamie would be lovers by now...but she didn't.

Julie looked back from the window as if sensing Lucie's thoughts and feelings. 'If you want to use the room tonight, just say,' she said quietly. 'I'll get Jack to take me out for a while.'

Lucie smiled at the thought. 'Maybe,' she said.

It was Julie's turn to ruminate. Jamie Raeburn wasn't your average boy and she sensed that Lucie had grasped that too. There was something very different about him and the more she thought about it the more he became an enigma. The Jamie that had taken Max Kelman's man apart on Wednesday night wasn't the considerate and gentle boy Lucie described, nor was he the soft talking, suave boy they had met that first night. The Jamie of Wednesday night was a different breed entirely...hard and violent...brutal almost. Reading between the lines of what Jack had told her, neither he nor Jamie were strangers to that dark world. And yet, the Jamie who laughed, joked and chatted with them was none of these things.

Lucie's problems would never leave her until max Kelman was completely out of her life...it always came back to him. If only Jamie could whisk Lucie away, far away out of Kelman's reach, then maybe they could have a future together. Please God, she prayed, let that happen.

'I should have told him I was still dancing with the group, shouldn't I?' Lucie sighed, interrupting Julie's thoughts and bringing her back into conversation. 'Do you think he'll be mad?'

Julie laughed in disbelief. Here *she* was thinking about the consequences of Jamie's fight with Kelman's thug and all Lucie seemed to be worried about was the fact that Jamie had seen her flaunting her body erotically in front of a crowd of panting men. *That isn't the problem*, she thought to herself but she realised it was camouflage...Lucie just didn't want to think about Max Kelman.

'I told you already, he's in love with you,' Julie sighed. 'I don't think seeing you flaunting your body in front of a bunch of randy guys is going to change that,' she continued, pointing out what she thought should have been obvious. 'Your real problem, and Jamie's, is Max Kelman,' she went on, trying to make Lucie face reality. 'You have to tell him the truth.' She knew she was pressing hard and knew too the pain Lucie felt. She had lived it with her. And as she watched, Lucie's happiness evaporated to be replaced by the shadow of all her fears.

'I know,' Lucie replied, her voice shaking. 'But I'm scared, Jules, so scared. 'I don't know *what*, or *how*, to tell him...I don't know what he'll think of me or how he'll react...it's not something that's easy to talk about,' she sighed, her voice dropping to a whisper.

So she does understand, Julie thought and slipped back across to hug her again as Lucie began to sob. 'I know, honey, I know,' she whispered soothingly. 'But if you love him…and if you want to keep him, then you *have* to tell him…and it will be alright.'

Lucie nodded slowly, her head bobbing up and down against Julie's shoulder. Her mind was in turmoil. Julie didn't know the half of it; she knew nothing of Max's call after she had run from him four weeks earlier. She had laughed at him, safe at the other end of the telephone line, but his veiled threats had been playing on her mind ever since. She wanted to ignore the menace in his words or at least be able to live with it, and then she had met Jamie and everything had changed. Max's threats had involved only her and her family and if she did what he wanted everyone would be safe, but now? How could she go through with it when she was in love with Jamie? And what would Max do when he found out?

Julie's voice broke into her thoughts again. 'You're in love with him, aren't you?' she said with a soft laugh. It was framed like a question but it didn't need an answer. There was no need to say who "him" meant; there was only one man that could refer to and Julie already knew the answer.

Lucie pulled away from her, her face flushed, and a smiled edged tentatively back onto her face. 'Yes, I think I am,' she acknowledged with a sigh. 'I didn't think I'd ever find someone I could trust again…and he makes me feel safe,' she continued pensively. 'I want to be with him all the time and when I'm not, I get scared…so scared.' The tears were forming again.

Julie pulled her back and hugged her tightly again. 'Listen to me,' she said firmly. 'Jamie's not an animal like Max Kelman.' Her voice was fierce and angry. 'Jamie's a really nice guy…and we both know he's in love with you,' she continued. 'He'll never hurt you…but you *must* tell him the truth,' she repeated, again, emphasising the point. 'He'll understand.'

Lucie wiped the tears from her eyes with the back of her hand. 'I can't tell him *everything*, Jules,' she sobbed. 'If I do, I'll lose him…I know I will.'

'I think you're wrong,' Julie responded quickly. 'Jamie doesn't cares what other people think or what they say, but he cares about you,' she continued relentlessly. 'You *have* to tell him. If he finds out from anyone else he'll be hurt because you haven't told him…it's about trust, Lucie, and he'll begin to doubt you. Tell him. He'll believe *you*,' she finished persuasively.

Lucie looked back through red rimmed eyes and shook her head. 'I can't Julie,' she whispered, her spirit sagging.

The rest of the journey was passed in silence, both deep in thought about Lucie's quandary and both with diametrically opposed ideas on how to deal with it. Julie worried about Lucie as she would worry for a sister and she wanted what was best for her, but she wasn't getting through to her. She began to sink into despair like Lucie until the train approached Beeston Station when Lucie began to smile. The closer she came to Jamie the better Lucie felt, Julie smiled and breathed a silent sigh of relief. By the time they arrived at Devonshire Place both of them were happy and smiling, but another shock was in store.

Chapter 37

As they entered the hall voices filtered to them from the lounge. The conversation was muffled but they recognised Jo's voice and that of a man...or perhaps two men. Although the words were indistinct, the tone seemed serious. They looked at each other, intrigued, and pushed open the door, Julie sticking her head into the room. Her mother was standing near the French Windows and two men in police uniforms were sitting in chairs facing her with their backs to the door. Jo saw Julie's head appear and smiled, beckoning for her to come in. The policemen turned, unsmiling, and waited as Julie and Lucie filed into the room.

'What's wrong?' Julie asked, her eyes darting between her mother and the policemen. Lucie had a sinking feeling in her stomach, a sixth sense telling her that whatever had brought the policemen here, it involved Jamie.

'It's alright, girls,' Jo started to explain. 'Three of the lads were set upon outside the house last night, that's all.'

'Jamie?' Lucie interrupted quickly, already anticipating the answer.

'Yes love,' Jo confirmed, 'and Mick and Benny too. Some local boys apparently took a dislike to them.'

Lucie's head began to spin. If the police were here it had to be serious and she clung onto Julie's arm for support, her emotions on a rollercoaster and her heart pounding.

'Is he alright?' she asked, her voice shaking.

'Yes, he's fine,' Jo smiled reassuringly. 'There's nothing wrong with him, Lucie.'

The older policeman, a middle aged sergeant, smiled benignly. 'It's alright Miss,' he added calmingly. 'We're following up on a call from a neighbour last night, is all.' He sounded bored. It was hardly the sharp end of investigative policing. 'No one appears to have been badly hurt...at least none of the three lads living here.'

'The same can't be said for the other lot, apparently,' the younger cop, probably in his early twenties, interjected, only to receive a reprimanding glare from the sergeant. He clammed up and resumed his appraisal of the two girls.

'We're just trying to find out what happened last night, Miss,' the Sergeant continued. 'There really is nothing to be worried about.'

But to Lucie it couldn't be as simple as that and his assurances fell on deaf ears. She was worried, no matter what the policeman said. Even if Jamie wasn't hurt she had seen what he was capable of. If any of the other boys had been injured, as the young policeman seemed to suggest, Jamie could be in trouble. Why else would the police be here, she argued? She slumped into the nearest chair and began to sob quietly, throwing the police officers off balance. A look passed between them and the younger policeman raised his eyes to the ceiling.

The sergeant coughed, a small embarrassed cough, and tried to take control again. 'Thanks for your help, Mrs Bradley,' he said, turning to Jo. 'I think you've cleared everything up...we shouldn't need to come back.' He turned to the younger man then. 'Come on Sid, we've got enough.'

Jo escorted the two police officers from the room and the girls could hear muted conversation in the hall before the outside door banged shut and Jo returned. Lucie was still sobbing and even Julie was concerned now.

'They were only here because one of the neighbours reported the fight,' Jo reiterated as she came back into the room. 'It's nothing to worry about, honestly.' She crossed to Lucie and bent down to her, lifting her head up to look her in the eye. 'Jamie's not hurt, other than a black eye, I swear...and he's not in any bother either,' she said with a smile. Lucie tried to return it but her emotions were all over the place. Jamie was the most important person in her life now. She couldn't express or explain her feelings to them but there was something special about him and she had fallen in love with him the moment she saw him. The last four weeks had been spent on an emotional rollercoaster between heaven and hell and now she felt as if her world was falling apart...again.

Jo was perplexed. She couldn't understand Lucie's reaction to what had really been a minor skirmish the night before but a whispered explanation from Julie about Jamie's involvement in Lucie's confrontation with Max Kelman on Wednesday made things fall into place. If it involved Max Kelman it was bad. This might be a good time to find out what Julie knew about the scars on Jamie's back, she decided. 'I don't think Jamie's a stranger to trouble,' she breathed quietly. 'Has Lucie said anything to you about his back?'

'His back?' Julie replied vacantly. 'No, she hasn't. What's wrong with his back?'

'He's got two nasty scars...low down. They look like stab wounds...and they're fairly recent by the look of them,' she whispered softly, not wanting Lucie to overhear.

Julie looked at her mother in shock, her brow furrowed in disbelief. 'No, she hasn't said anything.'

'And his pal Jack; he hasn't mentioned anything to you?' Jo continued. Julie simply shook her head.

Jo's concern for Lucie was growing and she bent down in front of her again to console her. As she hugged her and soothed her, the boisterous noise of the returning lodgers filled the room. They filed into the hallway and some of them wandered through to the lounge to relax, retreating quickly when they saw Lucie's distress. Last to arrive, as usual it seemed, were Benny and Jamie, with Mick trailing behind. The Three Amigos the others called them, the title bestowed on them after the shenanigans of the night before.

Jamie spotted her the instant he stepped into the lounge. Her head was down in her hands and her body was shaking with silent sobs, with Jo beside her, comforting her. What had happened? He wanted to rush to her, to hold her and make things better but he guessed that he was in some way the reason for her distress. He caught Julie's eye and his assumption was confirmed, but there was something else in Julie's eyes beyond the perplexed and confused, something deeper, and it was something he couldn't work out.

Lucie sensed him there and looked up. Without a word, she pushed herself up from her chair and away from Jo's encircling arms, and rushed to him. She was crying; her make-up smudged and her eye shadow smeared across her temples. The mascara that normally accentuated the length of her eye lashes was now running in tiny rivulets down her cheeks...but she was still beautiful. He opened his arms and she threw herself into them, sobbing uncontrollably, then pulled him down and kissed him fiercely, taking him completely by surprise. As she pulled away, she beat her tightly clenched fists against his chest, tears still streaming down her cheeks.

'Why didn't you call me?' she sobbed. 'You should have called me, why didn't you?' she demanded angrily, continuing to beat her fists against him until her anger was spent.

Jamie cast his eyes around the room. Everyone looked embarrassed but waited, none the less, for his response. 'There was nothing to tell you,' he reasoned, stroking back her hair and running his fingertips lightly across her cheek. Her head was buried in his chest and he lifted it up, looking deeply into her eyes. They were like a deep, dark blue sea...*I could drown in there*, he thought. She returned his gaze with an intensity that shook him, searching for the truth. 'I'm alright, honestly,' he told her gently and pulled her into his arms again, holding her tight against him. 'Why are you so upset?' he asked.

'The police were here,' Julie said, overhearing the question.

'Ah,' Jamie replied, understanding now. 'And you thought I was in trouble,' he whispered for no one but Lucie.

She nodded. 'And I was worried about Wednesday.'

'Don't worry about Wednesday,' he murmured, kissing her softly. She tried to speak again but he stopped her, placing his fingers lightly across her lips. 'What did the police say?' he asked, kissing the lobe of her ear. He had forgotten about everyone else in the room now.

'They said you were alright and that you weren't in trouble,' she replied.

'And what did Jo say?'

'The same really,' she admitted, drawing a quiet laugh from him.

'There you go then...I'm alright, and I'm not in any trouble,' he said gently.

She averted her eyes. 'I'm sorry,' she whispered, 'I was just so scared...Jo said you had a black eye, but that was all.'

Jamie laughed again. 'Aye, that was all.'

She studied his face, noticing the dark blue and brown smudge around his left eye that she had missed earlier, and lifted her fingers to brush them over the bruise. 'Does it hurt?' she asked.

'Don't change the subject,' Jamie continued, laughing again and teasing his fingers along the back of her neck. 'If I *had* telephoned, you would just have worried all night and all today until you got here...so there was no point,' he argued, 'and no, it doesn't hurt.'

'Okay, maybe I would have worried,' she admitted, 'but I would probably have come to make sure you were alright...and I still need to explain Wednesday night.' She had forgotten about everyone else now and Jo's eyes arched suspiciously.

'If I'd thought you'd come to nurse me I would have phoned,' he joked and stroked her cheek again. She responded instantly, stretching up to kiss him. 'I'm alright; everything is in perfect working order, honestly,' he said, oblivious to the others, and she smiled for the first time. Jamie caught her quick glance towards Julie and Julie's imperceptible little nod in response and wondered what she had planned. He was about to find out. Abruptly, she pulled away and took his hand, glancing nervously at Jo who returned her look with a smile, unperturbed.

Jo had guessed what was about to happen, she had been young herself once. Her only concern was what would happen if Jamie wasn't Prince Charming...but they were both old enough and they would be lovers soon anyway...if they weren't already. She smiled demurely and gave them her silent blessing.

Lucie pulled him from the room, his look of surprise and uncertainty amusing her, and guided him towards the stairs. Her heart was racing but Jo's smile and Julie's little nod encouraged her. She was ready but as they climbed to the top of the stairs and emerged onto the landing, Jamie pulled her back. 'Are you sure about this?' he asked, sensing what was in her mind.

She smiled, remembering the moment she had first set eyes on him at this very spot and the look that had passed between them then. She recalled the instant attraction and the fluttering of her heart…and all of those things were in her again now. She pressed her body against him and felt the hardness of him. He wanted her, she knew it. She gripped his hair in her fingers and pressed her mouth to his, the kiss seeming to go on forever. When they eased apart at last, both breathless, she gazed at him. 'Yes, I'm sure,' she replied, kissing him again. 'I don't want to wait any longer…I love you.'

He followed her meekly now, anticipation filling him, as she took him to her bedroom. They kissed again in the doorway and then she pulled him inside, pushing the door closed with her foot. Her mouth was locked onto his, her tongue pushing between his lips and finding his. Her fingers caressed his neck then, quickly, she pulled away from him reached down for the hem of her dress. Jamie watched, transfixed, his heart racing, as she eased the dress up over her body and head and dropped it casually on the floor. She gazed at him, willing him to touch her, as she pulled his T shirt from his jeans and stripped it from him.

They had touched before, petted heavily, but Lucie was ready to go further and she hoped Jamie believed that. When they had done this before he had known when to stop…would he stop now or would he know that she wanted him, all of him? He pulled her to him and she felt the warmth of his skin against her. Her doubts evaporated as his fingers nimbly undid the fastening of her bra and his hands moved to her breasts, firm beneath the flimsy cotton of her bra, and she felt her nipples swell with his touch. Their mouths met again, their tongues like rapiers, and his hand slid down across the flat of her stomach then paused. Lucie pulled away from the kiss, her lips now pressed against his ear. 'Go on,' she urged, 'don't stop now.'

Jamie moved his fingers under the top band of her panties and found the tiny, tight blonde curls beneath. Slowly, he pressed his fingers between her thighs and heard the soft sigh of her response. They had come this far before and he had wanted this moment but now, bizarrely, he was suddenly afraid.

Lucie sensed the change in him and encouraged him on with her hands, arousing him and listening to the gasps of his breath as he hovered on the edge of control. 'I want you to,' she urged, her own breath warm in his ear.

'I *want* to make love to you,' he moaned softly, kissing her neck. 'I'm just scared it doesn't work and I let you down.'

Lucie smiled incredulously. He was scared too and she had been thinking it was only her fear that had been stopping them. She knew in that moment that it would be perfect. 'It will work for us, baby, it will,' she murmured. 'Go on, pleeease.' She started to undo his belt, wanting to reach for him.

Jamie felt her fingers take him and move slowly then, filling him with pain and pleasure in equal measure. He groaned softly, all his fears dissipating with the touch of her fingers. Soon they were beyond the point of no return, tearing at each other's clothes now, their breathing fast and urgent.

Lucie pulled him onto the bed, her arms entwined around his back and her legs wrapped around him. She was thinking about nothing now other than having him make love to her. The fear had gone. He was over her, looking down into her eyes, and moving gradually downwards as she arched her back towards him.

For Jamie the moment had been the same. He wanted her now more than he had imagined possible and tonight, perhaps, the ghost of Kate would be laid to rest. When he and Lucie had been together in the past he had caressed and explored her, bringing her to orgasm, but he had always stopped short of intercourse. That, he knew, would come and now the moment had arrived he prayed that he would be able to maintain it without the curse of premature ejaculation spoiling it for both of them and leave Lucie disappointed.

He raised himself, his hands sliding beneath her and gripping her tightly. His mouth sank to her breasts, alternating between her nipples, sucking and nibbling. He felt her spread her thighs beneath him, experienced the sensation of her legs encompassing him and her ankles locking behind him and the touch of her fingers guiding him into her. They moved together, slowly at first, their bodies in harmony, thrusting against each other and then they were morphing into one. Jamie couldn't believe that they were making love at last but the sensation of Lucie's fingers gripping him, her long, sculpted, red varnished nails digging into his back and the exquisite pain they produced told him it was real. Subtle changes in their breathing, in the tempo of their coupling and in their body positions brought them to climax almost simultaneously and he heard Lucie give a small cry, a millisecond before he came inside her.

Spent, they lay there, perfectly still, the only sign of life emanating from their bodies coming from their breathing, the filling and emptying of their lungs, as they descended from the height of their passion.

It had been perfect. Lucie's fear of what might have been had evaporated the instant Jamie's fingers had touched her. She hadn't known what to expect. Yes, he had brought her to orgasm before but that had been through the touch of his fingers and her imagination anticipating the real thing, but "the real thing" had surpassed even her wildest expectations and she prayed that Jamie felt the same.

Jamie moved gently on top of her, turning to look into her eyes. He hadn't failed, hadn't left her wanting, and his unspoken fear hadn't materialised. He kissed her and felt her respond, her fingers twisting in the hair at the back of his neck once more. Their tongues danced a slow waltz in each other's mouths with mutual arousal following naturally. Fingers, lips and tongues, caressing and licking, all played a part until they were ready and made love again, slower this time, more sensually, their bodies moving rhythmically against each other.

Later, as they lay side by side, their bodies slick with their sweat and their hands still stroking softly, Jamie broke the comfortable silence. 'When we spoke on the phone on Wednesday, before…you know, you said…'

'Yes, I remember and I meant it,' Lucie answered quickly, anticipating his question.

'Do you *really* mean it?' he persisted, the incident on Wednesday night still casting a cloud over him.

'Yes, I really mean it,' she whispered quietly. 'I'm in love with you. When I went back to Derby last weekend, I cried. I didn't want to leave you and I've never felt like that before. Julie must think I'm going crazy. When I called you on Monday night it was just to hear your voice.' She paused then, turning towards him before continuing. 'I wanted to know if I'd have the same feelings just by talking to you.' She stopped, gazing tellingly into his eyes.

'And did you?'

'Oh yes,' she laughed softly. 'Love at first sight maybe isn't such a crazy notion after all. I know it has only been three weeks…but I can't imagine my life without you now,' she said quietly. 'Do *you* love *me*?' she asked, hoping she had judged him correctly.

Was he hearing this correctly, Jamie wondered? Had she just said that she was in love with him and asked him if he loved her? Christ, he thought...yes, I love you, but I've been here before. He had been in love with Kate...he still was, he imagined, and look what happened there. "I love you"...three little words that he had used from time, usually with an ulterior motive, but if he said those words to Lucie now it would have to be the real deal...as it had been with Kate and, to a lesser degree, with Carol. But there was no point in debating it with himself; he had already fallen for her...hook, line and sinker. 'I love you,' he said quietly.

But deep inside him the presence of Kate was still alive and she was re-emerging from the dark shadows of his mind. He had thought her memory would be laid to rest tonight but she was still there, hiding deep in his head and in his heart. Lucie was the girl with him now...and he wanted to be with her, he did love her, but Kate was still there in his soul, haunting him. How long would it be, he wondered, before he could finally exorcise her? He'd come down here with the intention of seeking her out and winning her back but he hadn't tried very hard, had he, he reasoned? So what the hell was he doing?

When Kate left he had resolved to return to his old ways; drinking with the boys, one night stands and no commitment...definitely no commitment. And then up pops Lucie Kent...and no more one night stands. Well, that wasn't strictly true, he reflected, there had been and still was Charley...not exactly a one night stand but a relationship that wasn't going anywhere. If he and Lucie were going to make it, then he had to expunge Kate from his mind and break up with Charley. Breaking with Charley should be simple enough, if a little painful, but erasing Kate from his memory was a much bigger challenge. He remembered Jack's opinion on that; getting over Kate would take a while, he said, and going with other girls was simply papering over the cracks...covering his grief. Jack was wrong though...in part at least...Charley might be an exercise in "covering up" but Lucie was different...so very different, even though Jack thought they had no chance of making it last.

Kate had breached the defences he had built up around himself after Carol, getting under his skin, piercing his heart and lodging herself in his head. If he had a soul, which he seriously doubted, she had taken up residence in it. Could his life ever be the same again? When Kate left him he had vowed never to get into a situation where he could be hurt again...but with Lucie he had to take the chance.

Downstairs, someone was playing an LP on the record player and a track drifted up to him; Yes I Will, The Hollies, he thought absently. The other sounds of the house were muted; faint voices, the movement of furniture, feet padding around on the carpeted floors. Only the words of the song were relatively distinct. He turned towards her, took her hands in his and pulled her to him, kissing her and then letting his lips drift to the lobe of her ear. He whispered the words of the song to her then and as the final words of the chorus faded away he turned to face her again, hoping she could read his eyes. 'Yes, I love you,' he repeated.

She contemplated his look and smiled contentedly. She knew then that he was hers. Jamie would be her salvation, her deliverance from evil. She felt herself lose control, the physical need to feel him inside her again intensifying with every passing second.

'I love the feel of your skin,' Jamie mumbled hoarsely.

'I love the feel of all of you,' she whispered intensely in response. 'Make love to me again,' she said without thought, without fear...the past meant nothing now.

She moaned again, softly, breathlessly, growing wetter as he caressed her, explored her and aroused her. Her control was lost as his touch teased her, bringing her rapidly to climax again, her body shuddering convulsively. She closed her eyes as he took her left breast in his mouth, feeling her nipple swell once more under his kiss and savouring the sensations created by his lips as they wandered down across her stomach and onto her hips. Her head swam. She arched her back, enticing him to take her again, wanting him inside her. Suddenly, she felt him retreat from her and her heart almost stopped before a tidal wave of ecstasy crashed over her as his mouth descended on her again, his tongue flitting over her and into her. She was electrified, minute tremors cascading through her, wave after wave of desire washing over her skin and as the initial shock of what he was doing faded it was replaced by a craving for the feeling to continue. The tingling excitement created by his mouth and tongue seared through her, taking her beyond anything she had ever imagined. And it felt so natural for him to be doing this and for her to want him to do it. There was no sense of guilt or shame, just an overwhelming desire to have him...to have all of him. The thundering waves of ecstasy continued to sweep over her and an almost primeval moan fill the room which, she realised with surprise, had escaped from her own mouth. She felt him tease her with his lips, arousing her more and more and she locked her fingers into the tangled locks of his hair as she arched herself towards him.

'Please,' she murmured. 'I want you inside me.' Her voice was shaking with the overwhelming force of her longing. She felt him move and suddenly he was above her, the fire in his eyes again. She reached for him and guided him into her again, feeling the thrust of him and then the withdrawal, again and again, faster and faster, penetrating deeper into her with every forward motion. She gasped with each thrust, feeling him fill her, and clung to him fiercely, her fingers gouging into the tightened muscles of his back. They were moving together now, losing themselves in each other and in the ecstasy of the moment. She heard Jamie's rapid breathing in her ears and felt the frantic beating of his heart against her...or was it her own heart she felt, they were so close, their bodies melding together as one.

'Now, Jamie! 'Please, now.' Jamie wondered if he had heard the words or imagined them but the answer with Lucie's next breath. 'Please Jamie...pleeease!' she repeated, moaning softly as her nails raked down across his back. He lost control, his body tensing as he erupted inside here again, jerking spasmodically and pulling her tightly to him.

Lucie gripped his shoulders and felt the fluttering sensation inside her as Jamie came, her own climax sending her spirit soaring. She heard him call her name and it seemed to hang in the air for an age, reverberating around her, echoing in the corners of her mind as love and lust intermingled there until, with a final sigh, Jamie sank gently down on her, completely spent.

They lay still, so close they were almost indistinguishable one from the other, their breathing rapid and their hearts racing. Their bodies glistened with the sweat of that last frantic union. Oh that this feeling could last forever, Lucie dreamed.

Jamie nuzzled his head in her hair, inhaling the scent of flowers there. He felt her move beneath him, her legs around him, and her ankles locked behind his thighs as she tried to keep him inside her forever. Finally he slipped from her, rolling onto his side and gazing down into her eyes. He saw her smile up at him contentedly, her lips slightly apart. He leaned forward and kissed her, feeling her push the tip of her tongue into his mouth again.

All her fears and her earlier despair, the result of the nightmare she had faced at the hands of Max Kelman, had gone, fading to nothing with Jamie's first touch, the softness of his hands on her body and the feel of his skin against her. She kissed him again. 'On the way here tonight I decided I really wanted you,' she confided, pausing. 'I wanted you to make love to me…but I never expected it to be like this,' she whispered. 'I love you so much. You made me do things I never thought possible.'

'I *made* you do things?' Jamie repeated, perturbed. 'I'll *never* make you do anything, Lucie.'

'No, I don't mean you forced me,' she stammered, realising how her words had sounded. 'I wanted to do everything,' she said. 'What I meant was, I only want to do them with you. Tell me you understand.'

'Yes, I understand,' he replied quietly, mollified.

Lucie looked at him coyly. 'Are you happy now?' she asked shyly.

'Yes, very happy…but I was worried I wouldn't be able to control myself because I wanted you so much. I do love you, Lucie.'

She looked searchingly into his eyes. He had already told her that he loved her but she still harboured a tiny element of doubt, probably because she knew he had been with other girls before her. 'Do you really mean it?' she asked. 'You really love me?' His eyes answered for him and she relaxed.

'So what do we do now?' Jamie asked, 'go back downstairs and face the music?'

Lucie regarded him flirtatiously. 'Well, we could make love again…if you want to, but I think four times might be pushing my luck,' she said with a grin. 'Or we can just lie here and talk and later we'll go back down and pretend we've been a good boy and girl,' she giggled.

'I know what I *want* to do but I probably wouldn't be able to walk afterwards…let's talk.'

Lucie giggled happily, snuggled close to him and felt better than she had ever felt before. 'Will you still love me when I'm old and grey?' she teased.

'As long as we can keep doing it like that, yes!' he promised.

They lay side by side, their bodies touching, holding hands. Lucie watched him, his eyes closed and a smile on his handsome face and it was then, for the first time, she wondered about the thin silver chain with the Ankh around his neck. She had seen it before but had thought little of it so why was it an issue now? Irrational jealousy, she wondered? 'Have you been with lots of girls?' she asked quietly, wondering immediately why she had started down this road.

'Are you serious?' Jamie laughed, turning to look at her. 'Does it matter? I don't know how many guys you've been with and I don't care…they're the past, I'm the present…and the future, I hope.'

'I'm sorry, I didn't mean…' she whispered, clearly embarrassed. 'Where did you get this?' she continued softly, picking up the Ankh from its resting place. Something told her it was important to him and the dark shadow that passed across his eyes confirmed it.

'Someone gave me it,' he said quietly, watching her reaction.

'A girl?'

He nodded. He had wanted to exorcise Kate tonight, he remembered; maybe this was the way to do it…bring her out into the open. 'Yes, a girl,' he said and saw her face crumble. That wasn't what he wanted…he wanted Lucie to trust him and love him, not be jealous of his past. Confession is good for the soul, he told himself, and carried on. 'Before I came down here I was close to a girl but things didn't work out. She was married,' he added as if that explained things which, in a way, it did.

'Did you love her?' Lucie continued, following her masochistic course. She almost added "Do you still love her" but resisted the temptation.

'Yes, I loved her...but it's over. I told you, that's all in the past, she's my past...and you're my present. I love you.'

Lucie dipped her head, unable to look him in the eye, angry with herself. 'I'm sorry,' she whispered. She wanted to say more, to let him know it didn't matter but she couldn't because his mouth was on hers again, kissing her passionately.

After a moment, he broke away from the embrace and leaned out of the bed, searching for his jeans, looking for his cigarettes. As he stretched away from her Lucie ran her fingers across his back, her eyes taking in the scratches left by her nails as they had raked his skin and finally coming to rest on the two ugly scars defacing his lower back. She traced her fingers softly along them.

'What caused those?' she asked, though she already knew part of the answer. What sort of nurse would she be if she didn't, she mused.

'Your nails,' Jamie laughed, rolling back onto the bed.

'You're avoiding the question,' she continued.

He looked at her for a moment then rolled onto his back and stared at the ceiling for what seemed an age. He opened the cigarette packet and, without thinking, offered one to Lucie, forgetting that she didn't smoke. She shook her head, waiting patiently as he lit his cigarette and lay back again, inhaling deeply. A plume of smoke came from his mouth, forming a ring above him, but he continued to look at the ceiling and another dark shadow settled on his face, like some slow moving cloud blocking out the sun that had been there minutes earlier.

'I think you know,' he started, 'you're a nurse, after all.' He was gazing intently at her now and he could see the worry and concern in her eyes. 'I was stabbed last December; it was nothin',' he went on, trying to belittle the seriousness of what had taken place. 'In Glasgow,' he added, as though that fact explained everything.

'It wasn't "nothing", Jamie. Please, tell me what happened?' she probed, and he detected her anxiety.

He sighed and filled his lungs with another drag on his cigarette, blowing out the smoke again as he started to explain. 'I was out for a night with Jack and some pals and I went out of the pub for some fresh air and a smoke...it was snowin' and the whole place was covered with it.' Lucie could almost see his mind creating pictures of the night, his eyes fixed on the ceiling again as though it were a giant screen. 'I heard a noise and someone calling for help so I went to find out what was causin' the ruckus...and found a guy bein' beaten up. There were four of them...kickin' the poor sod...I didn't think about it, just ran in to help him...'

'Were you on your own?' Lucie interrupted, horrified.

'Aye...bit stupid that; but you don't think, do you? Lucie just shook her head slowly, trying to imagine that.

'Anyway, I managed to help the guy a bit, he was an American sailor, and we almost got away...but there were more of the bastards and they came after us.' Lucie could hear the bitterness now and sensed the rawness of the memory for him. She regretted asking the question now as Jamie returned to the story. 'We almost made it...ran out into the street...I remember a burnin' sensation, and then...the last thing I remember was the 7th Cavalry arriving – Jack and my other mates – before I woke up in hospital in Intensive Care...end of story,' he said, carefully omitting all reference to Kate.

'God, that's terrible...you were lucky,' Lucie remarked softly, her fingers and eyes taking in the position and the nature of the scars.

'Aye,' Jamie laughed, trying to break the tension, 'that's exactly what the doctor said. I was just a ba' hair from death, he said.' Seeing Lucie's puzzled look, he burst out laughing. 'A ba' hair…it's how we measure tiny things…there's the ba' hair, the pico ba' hair an' the micro ba' hair an' they're all tiny, tiny fractions of an English inch,' he said, teasing her and trying to keep a straight face but almost choking with the effort.

'Is it really that bad…Glasgow, I mean?' she replied, ignoring his mirth.

Jamie looked into her eyes again and once more she saw myriad dark memories swamp him. She waited, watching him intently. She was scared by what she was seeing and wondered how she could bring him back.

'Yeah, it's a pretty bad,' he conceded at last. 'What happened to me isn't rare.' He was drifting away again; she could see it in his eyes. They seemed distant, as though focussed on things she could never see. It changed me,' he went on, thoughtfully. 'I decided never to let anyone do that to me again…but I still can't run away. An old guy I worked with in the shipyard – he was a Commando during the war – gave me some advice.' He stopped, deciding it would be better not to let Lucie know what that advice was; the penny trick, and others, would remain his secret. He laughed. 'Now I get my retaliation in first.'

They were quiet for a moment and Lucie detected a change of direction coming from him and something told her she wasn't going to like it. Jamie was looking at her strangely, as if weighing up what to say next, and when he did speak, she didn't like it.

That guy on Wednesday night, Quasimodo, he's a good example,' he said, watching her reaction. 'What was that all about anyway, by the way?' he asked, instantly regretting it. He'd already said it didn't matter yet here he was, interrogating her. She would tell him when she was ready; he didn't need to force the issue. 'I'm sorry, ignore that,' he apologised softly. 'You don't have need to explain…I've got baggage too.'

Lucie looked at him for a long moment then kissed him gently. 'No, I can't ignore it. I should have told you I was still dancing with the girls…but that was my last night, I promise.'

She saw him shake his head slowly. 'It's not the dancin' I'm talkin' about and you know it…but while we're on the subject, you were fabulous and I wasn't jealous…so you can relax.'

'I was thinking about you all through the routine,' she smiled, refusing to let go.

Jamie raised an eyebrow and smiled. 'So, tell me about the guy in the car,' he said, returning to that thorny topic and bringing Lucie down to earth with a thud.

She paused, unable to look him in the eye, scared that lies and omissions would be seen by him. She wrestled with it, thinking about Julie's earlier advice, and then sighed. 'His name is Max Kelman,' she started. 'He's an ex-boyfriend.'

'Did you love him?' he asked, interrupting and throwing back the question she had posed to him earlier about Kate. It was a cheap shot and he regretted it immediately.

Her eyes were hurt by it and he sensed there was more to this than just some teenage romance. It was deeper than that. 'I split up with him more than two years ago,' she said eventually, her voice almost a whisper, 'and no, I didn't love him. His father is a local "businessman" in Derby.' There was a sneer in her voice when she said "businessman" that hinted at something else. She was still holding something back as though reluctant to invite him into some private place.

'And?' he persisted, and her forced smile faded from her face.

'And I haven't seen him since we broke up and then he just turned, up out of the blue, on Wednesday.'

There's somethin' not quite right about all of this, Jamie thought. I'm missin' somethin'…but is this Kelman guy anything to worry about? The last hour…no, forget the last hour, every second we've been together, says he's not. But I'm still missin' somethin'.

He knew he should let it go but something impelled him on. 'So, what did he want when he turned up out of the blue?'

'Can't we just drop this, Jamie?' she asked quietly, pleading almost, but there was uncertainty in her voice too. He said nothing but she could see he wasn't going to agree. Her mind raced. He wasn't going to let this go but she couldn't tell him the truth; not yet at least. 'He asked me to go out with him,' she lied, still avoiding Jamie's eyes. 'He said he'd been thinking about me and that he was sorry for the way he had treated me.' The lies were spilling out now but, unfortunately for Lucie, Jamie didn't need to see her eyes; from bitter experience, he knew a lie when he heard one.

Why is she lying to me, he wondered? She was trying to play down what had happened but he could still see the fear that had been on her face before he had turned up. And that wasn't just because an ex-boyfriend asked her out.

'And?' Jamie used the single word prompt again, his voice colder now, insistent.

'And nothing!' Lucie replied angrily, looking at him but still avoiding his eyes, then forced another little smile. 'I told him I wasn't interested, honestly….and I told him to leave me alone, and that's when you turned up! My knight in shining armour,' she laughed, but that too was forced.

'And the big guy with him?'

The laugh came again, genuine this time. 'His name is Tony Abrahams, he's one of Max's heavies,' she said. 'Max Kelman never goes anywhere without someone like Tony at his side…Max isn't the most popular of men so he likes to have guys like Tony around for protection.' She shuddered a little, and then tried to laugh it off, recalling the incident. 'That didn't work with you though, did it?' she said thoughtfully. 'You really hurt him…and I don't think anyone has done that before.' There was a hint of admiration in her voice but it still couldn't mask the fear he knew was there.

He looked at her, softening. He had pursued this far enough - for now anyway. But a seed of doubt had been sown deep inside him now. Lucie had lied to him but the truth would surface eventually…it always did. Until then, there was no point in spoiling the rest of the weekend. He smiled warmly again and pulled her to him, kissing the top of her honey blonde head. 'Let's go down and face the music,' he said, climbing out of the bed and pulling her up onto her feet.

'This hasn't changed anything between us, has it?' she asked anxiously. She pulled him close, pressing herself against him. 'You do still love me, don't you?' she whispered.

'Yes, I still love you.

Chapter 38

Jack appeared shortly after dinner and joined Julie, Lucie and Jamie in the garden where Jamie was enjoying an after dinner cigarette. The girls were scheming and Jamie was sitting at the patio table with his eyes closed and a contented smile on his face. Lucie had recovered her composure after his question and answer session and she too was smiling radiantly. At dinner, everyone around the table seemed happy for them judging by the smiles and looks that did the rounds.

Inside the house bedlam had reigned as all of the remaining lodgers vied for the use of the bathroom at the same time to prepare for a night on the town. Jamie left them to it. There was no rush as far as he was concerned. He had sauntered out into the garden with Lucie at his side and they sat together at the table, hand in hand. Julie joined them there after helping Jo with the clearing up and sank gratefully into a chair beside them. 'You both look happy,' she laughed mischievously. 'Anything you want to tell me?' Her giggle was infectious and they both laughed with her. 'Is Jack coming tonight?' she asked, looking at Jamie.

'You should know…it's you he's coming to see, not me,' he replied with a grin. 'What is it they say…one man's loss is another woman's gain?'

'Cheeky!' Julie retorted, punching him playfully on the arm. 'If you're not careful I'll withdraw my offer,' she whispered archly.'

Jamie raised an eyebrow and Lucie laughed with glee. 'What offer…what have you two been plotting?' he asked with a grin.

'Well, I was going to let you have my bedroom all to yourselves,' she whispered, looking over her shoulder to make sure no one was listening. 'If I can stay with Jack…what do you think?'

Jamie's eyes twinkled. 'It's a great idea but there's only one drawback; Jack's landlady's a Rottweiler and she's as thick as thieves with your mother,' he replied.

'Actually, I was thinking we could use your room,' she came back coyly.

Jamie laughed at the thought of that. 'If you like an audience, be my guest,' he spluttered. 'Benny and Mick are sure to enjoy a spot of voyeurism.'

'No, I haven't forgotten them…but I've got a plan,' she confided enigmatically.

'Then we accept,' Jamie agreed with a laugh. 'But there are two beds in your room so we can double up if your plan falls through…though we might keep you awake all night,' he grinned happily.

'That's plan B,' Julie giggled. 'But if that's the way it has to be then at least I'll get to see this amazing body that Lucie and my mother have been raving about,' she quipped.

'Flatterer,' he laughed. 'And do I get to see yours?' he added, to a duet of protest. 'Nah, I didn't think so.'

*

When Jack arrived the four of them remained in the garden for a while until the house quietened down. They decided to stay local rather than go into Nottingham centre and The Spinner's Rest won the popular vote. Julie had a quiet word with jack then sloped off to corner Benny and Mick before they left the house, following up on her "plan". Jo joined the three of them and enjoyed one of Jamie's cigarettes. She was uncharacteristically quiet, he noticed, and wondered, belatedly, if she was upset about what had obviously taken place under her roof. Jamie decided to excuse himself to freshen up now that now that the rush for the bathroom was over and left Jack alone with Lucie and Jo, feeling a little guilty that he was leaving Lucie to face the prospect of Jo's wrath on her own. He soon forgot about that when Julie passed him and gave him a beaming smile and a surreptitious thumb up sign. His day was improving with each passing minute.

Jo watched him go and wondered how to tackle her problem and it was made all the more difficult because of what had happened that afternoon. Lucie was clearly in love with him but Jo was still concerned that Jamie might not be all he seemed. She was posing a question to Jack just as Julie returned. 'Did Jamie tell you all about the fight outside last night?' she asked. Jack nodded but made no comment. 'Benny's been raving about him,' she continued, 'seems he's quite a lad.'

'Aye, he is,' Jack replied this time, intuiting more behind the question. 'If ye ever get intae trouble, Jamie's the guy ye want standin' beside ye.'

'What happened to his back...those scars?' she went on. 'They look serious.'

Lucie's intervention took Jo by surprise. 'He was helping someone,' she said, and saw Jo's eyes widen.

'That's right,' Jack agreed, amazed that Lucie knew this. 'It wis an American sailor...the guy wis bein' attacked by some thugs an' Jamie went tae help him. Jamie ended up bein' stabbed...an' he nearly died...the newspapers were full o' it. They made him oot a hero but he disnae like that...he disnae talk aboot it.'

Jo looked round the faces, all of them staring at her now. 'Does he make a habit of that?' she asked, knowing she was overstepping the mark but feeling justified because of her concern for Lucie.

Jack returned her look with a sardonic smile. 'If ye're askin' if he's a ned, the answer's naw,' he said quietly. 'Jamie's no' a thug...he disnae make a habit o' getting' intae fights.'

'Two in two nights, is that not a habit?' Jo threw back at him.

'Two in two nights?' Jack repeated, confused. 'Whit ur ye talkin' aboot?'

'You didn't know about Wednesday night, then?' Jo continued.

Lucie drew Julie an angry look and Julie jumped down her mother's throat. 'That's unfair Mum,' she interrupted angrily. 'Jamie was only looking out for Lucie...you're making him sound like a gangster.'

Jo began to retreat. 'I'm only thinking of Lucie,' she said defensively. 'I don't want her to be hurt.'

'I can look after myself,' Lucie interjected angrily, her annoyance breaking through.

It was left to Jack to pour oil on the troubled waters. 'Listen Jo, believe me,' he said softly. 'Jamie isnae a thug, he disnae go around lookin' fur trouble and he'd rather avoid it if he can...but he willnae walk away fae it...an' if ye're in trouble, Jamie will be there fur ye,' he said, finishing off.

Jo gave them an embarrassed look. She had her answer. 'Forgive me?' she pleaded, looking directly at Lucie. 'I just worry about you...you're like a daughter to me.'

Lucie smiled and hugged her. 'I know you do Auntie Jo, but you don't need to worry about me where Jamie's concerned.'

Jo smiled gratefully and rose from her chair, passing Jamie in the doorway as she made her way into the house. 'Look after her,' she said, hugging him. 'She needs you.'

Jamie saw the disquiet in Jo's eyes and wondered what it stemmed from. He was to learn about it later but at that moment he passed it off. Instead, he held on to her a moment, smiling. 'I will,' he said quietly.

Chapter 39

Three months' later. Friday, 1ˢᵗ September 1967.

Jamie stretched and yawned, turning as he always did to look at Lucie curled up on the bed beside him. Each morning he woke at the same time and each morning he was still tempted to pinch himself, sure that he was dreaming. Six months earlier his life had been a mess, turned upside down by Kate's departure, but then this beautiful girl lying next to him arrived. She was the dream at the end of the nightmare…the pot of gold at the end of the rainbow.

The alarm clock on the bedside table read 06.15 and he silenced it before its jangling racket could disturb her. The morning sun was shining through a gap in the window blind above, sending a shaft of light across the room like a laser beam. It was going to be another warm weekend, perfect for their trip to London, but before that he had to put in another day's work at Ratcliffe Power Station and Lucie would be busy in Derby Royal. They had moved in together to the small self-contained attic flat at the top of the Bradley house in Beeston at the beginning of August and the novelty still hadn't worn off.

After the contretemps with Max Kelman in early June, Lucie had refused to let him come into Derby to meet her, saying she was afraid for his safety. Jamie had laughed it off but over time he realised she was seriously scared and there was something darker, and deeper, disturbing her. When he thought back, he hadn't considered Max Kelman to be much of a threat but his henchmen were a different kettle of fish. The guy he had floored that night had been caught out by complacency and over-confidence and that wouldn't happen twice. If there were others like him in Kelman's stable then he had to concede that Lucie might have a point. He didn't particularly like the idea of avoiding Kelman, but if it kept Lucie happy, so be it.

But in forcing Jamie to avoid Derby, Lucie had created other problems and frustrations for them. They wanted to be together, never apart, but they were restricted to weekends or fleeting mid-week trysts in Nottingham or little villages and towns served by the train line between the two cities. And time was always the enemy.

It didn't take long for the subject of them moving in together to be raised. Jamie had been amazed by the dramatic change in her over the weeks since they had met. Her shyness and reticence, always competing with her natural confidence at the beginning of their relationship, had all but gone and now she was confident enough to take the lead in things that concerned them both rather than wait for Jamie to raise it. Agreeing with her proposal that they live together had been easy for Jamie but breaking the news to "Auntie" Jo had filled them both with trepidation.

As it turned out, they needn't have worried. They broke it one Sunday afternoon when the house was quiet and Lucie, speaking for both of them, let Jo into their plan. She had listened, stony faced, as Lucie told her that they were in love and being together was part of that. 'We want to live together,' she had said, waiting for the explosion but Jo simply maintained her serious expression throughout, her eyes flitting between the two of them, and Lucie suspected that Jo's problems, if any, would concern Jamie rather than the plan itself. She suspected, too, that Jo still wasn't sure of him and she was still being protective. There was a lengthy silence when Lucie finished and Jo had nodded her head thoughtfully. Lucie and Jamie prepared themselves for the coming argument. *This is our decision, not yours,* Lucie was ready to say when Jo's face suddenly split into a wide grin. They had been standing in the kitchen at the time and Jo had turned on her heel and beckoned them to follow. They had looked at each other in confusion then followed her quietly, hand in hand. She lead them along the hall and then up the stairs with their curiosity mounting.

When Jo stopped outside the door opposite the bathroom, the door that was never open, their interest piqued. This was the door to nowhere, Jamie thought. In all the time he had lived in the house, seven weeks at that point, he had never seen behind that door. It was always locked and he knew that for a fact because he had tried it more than once. Jo had produced a key ring and chose a key from the big bunch attached to it. With an air of theatrical mystery, she slipped the key into the lock and turned it, then slowly pulled the door ajar. Lucie and Jamie gazed through the opening and saw a steep flight of stairs leading up into the roof space.

'On you go then,' Jo had said, ushering them ahead of her. At the top there was another door, the twin of the one below. Jamie was in the lead now and reached out for the handle, more and more curious. Turning it, he pushed the door inwards to reveal an enormous room with natural light streaming in through two big Velux windows, one set in each side of the sloping roof. He heard Lucie's sharp intake of breath and he, himself, was speechless. There was a heavy carpet on the floor and some old, but solid, bedroom furniture. A big, double bed with a metal frame and headboard sat to one side, directly beneath one window. Jo pushed them into the room ahead of her and Lucie gasped while Jamie stood transfixed.

Jo waited patiently until they had recovered. 'This was the room Brian and I used when we took on the house and started doing it up. It hasn't been used for years but I come up every week and clean it...not that it needs much,' she had said. Lucie and Jamie were dumbstruck, neither of them able to comprehend why Jo had brought them here. 'You're going to be together no matter what I say or do.' she had continued, 'so you might as well stay here...it's yours if you want it.' And that was it! Lucie had hugged her, both women beginning to cry and Jamie stood there dumbstruck.

That had been six weeks ago and they had moved into the room the following weekend. Idyllic was the word Jamie used to describe his life now. He leaned over and ran his hand down the length of Lucie's arm, waking her gently.

Her eyes fluttered and she smiled sleepily, reaching up for him and snaking her arm around his neck to pull him to her. 'What time is it,' she asked, still drowsy.

'Quarter past six,' he murmured, kissing her neck.

Lucie eyed him brazenly. 'Well, we don't have much time, do we? So what are you waiting for?'

Jamie laughed and pulled her closer still, her naked body warm against his. They slept naked most nights, drifting off to sleep in each other's arms after making love. The thrill of it hadn't lessened for either of them and making love in the mornings especially was still a novelty, though it tended to be fast and furious. And today was no exception, reducing Jamie to a frenzied dash as he prepared to leave for work, rushing out the door after the other lodgers as they left for the seven thirty bus to Ratcliffe.

Lucie pulled him back. 'Remember, I'm going straight to Nottingham with Julie tonight and the train to London is at six, so don't be late…and don't forget anything,' she called to him as her raced away. He waved without turning and ran on.

Lucie returned to their room and prepared her bag for the weekend. She wouldn't have time to return here after finishing work and was taking her bag with her, not trusting Jamie to remember. She packed quickly, neatly folding underwear and nightwear and laying it flat in the bag then laying dresses and a pair of pink trousers on top. She thought about what she was going to do and, though she didn't relish it, she knew she had no option. Julie had warned her that it would be difficult to tell Jamie the truth about Max Kelman if she left it too long and she realised now how right Julie had been. She had pushed it from her mind over the last few weeks and with Jamie close to her all the time that had been easy. She was happier than she had ever been, but storm clouds were never far away.

Max Kelman had intercepted her more than once when she was leaving work, insisting that they talk. His anger when she refused to entertain him was obvious and she knew that she was walking a fine line. She knew what he wanted, although he hadn't spelled it out, and she knew the lengths he would go to, to get it. She was worried for herself, naturally, but that worry was eclipsed by the fear of Max Kelman's reaction when he finally learned of her relationship with Jamie. She had managed to keep it a secret at work…even though she tended to have a permanent smile on her face each morning and again each night as she left for home. Even Julie knew to keep the secret.

But Jamie had to know the truth. She had arranged the trip to London as a way of getting Jamie away from everything familiar so that she could break her news to him without distraction, but Julie had overheard her discussing it with Jamie and now the four of them were going. It made no difference; Jamie had to know and when the weekend was over would either still be with her or he would be gone.

*

Soho, London, same day.
The restaurant was fairly busy when they arrived from their hotel around 8.30pm but they managed to get a table without too much difficulty. It helped that Lucie knew the owner; a friend of a friend of her father. It was small eatery, with only thirty covers, but it was clearly popular and Jamie liked it immediately. The ambience was serene and the decoration was relaxing; soft pastel shades covered the walls and ceiling and hidden lighting gave the place a discrete warm glow. Animal carvings adorned the walls a large carved, hardwood elephant's head, guarded the entrance to the kitchen. The name – Blue Chilli – conjured up a melange of hot and cold foods in Jamie's mind and he was looking forward to the meal. Jack and Julie were making the most of their last weekend together following Jack's decision to return home to Glasgow. The reason Jack had given her for his sudden decision was a lie and Jamie, who knew the truth, felt awkward. He liked Julie but decided to keep Jack's secret, even though he felt Jack was being unfair.

Jamie had worries of his own. Something was brewing; he could feel it in his water. For the last week or more Lucie had been edgy, worrying about something but trying to hide it. She wouldn't discuss it with him when he probed and, outwardly at least, she seemed happy. Her stock reply when he tried to raise it was "don't be silly" and she would move swiftly on to something else. It wasn't anything he had done, he was sure of that, but in some way it affected him, he was sure of that too. He could read between the lines and Lucie's suggestion that they come to London to "get away from it all" was, he suspected, simply to give her an opportunity to open up with him. When Julie had asked if she and Jack could join them Lucie had tried to remain nonchalant but Jamie detected the disappointment in her. But Julie and Jack were here with them so Lucie was going to have to make the best of it.

As they were shown to their table by a petite waitress wearing a dark red, sarong like dress, Jamie cast his eye over the other diners. There was a couple of suited businessmen sitting at a table facing out onto the street outside, downing bottled beers and helping themselves to food stacked high on two platters set in the middle of the table. They were talking animatedly, probably discussing some deal or other, he surmised. The other diners were all mixed couples and Jamie subconsciously divided them into two groups; courting couples and newly-weds in one and those married for at least two years in the other. Identifying which group a couple fell into was easy. The courting couples and newly-weds were overtly tactile, laughing and joking, their conversations bubbly, and their hands constantly touching. The longer married couples sat quietly, hardly speaking at all, preferring their own company to that of their spouses and probably thinking about their lovers, Jamie imagined. *Christ, I hope Lucie and I don't end up like that*, he prayed silently.

Lucie was gazing at him, a smile playing on her lips, reading his mind. 'I hope so too,' she said with a soft laugh. Reading his mind was becoming all too easy for her, he reflected.

Their table was at the back of the restaurant near the kitchen and right beneath the carved elephant's head. Jamie and Jack looked worryingly at the carving as they sat down. 'If that thing fa's on us we're deed,' Jack joked, casting a wary eye at it again.

Lucie and Julie laughed, but Lucie seemed distracted and Jamie slid his hand across the table, letting his fingers rest on hers, stroking them. The restaurant was cosy and if the food was as good as it promised to be then the evening would go well. The tables, bamboo frames with glass tops, were positioned close together and a small glass, filled with blooms of fresh flowers, stood at a corner of each. In the centre there was another small glass, this one containing a candle which the waitress lit for them before departing. As the waiting staff hurried past, in and out of the kitchen, the flame of the candle danced in the disturbed air. From the kitchen came the sound of pots and pans rattling and the aromas of spices and freshly cooking meats and fish made them salivate.

'I like it,' Jamie enthused.

'You'll like it even more when you've tried the food,' Lucie assured him. 'My father says it's the best Thai food he's tasted outside Thailand itself,' she continued, very matter of fact. As if everyone spent time in Thailand, Jamie thought with a grin.

When the little waitress returned with the menus she hovered, waiting for a drinks order. Again, Lucie took over and again the others let her. Jamie heard her ask for a bottle of something with a name he instantly forgot while he and Jack asked for beers. When the waitress returned with a bottle of champagne and four glasses as well as two bottles of beer, Jamie turned to Lucie in amazement. 'What's this, no rum and black?' he teased.

'I thought I'd educate you about champagne,' Lucie shot back. 'And you'd better enjoy it.'

'I'm more of a beer man,' Jack interjected.

'Not tonight you're not,' Lucie retorted and Jamie grinned. 'Tonight you're going to learn how to appreciate the better things in life,' she laughed.

'I already do,' Jack responded, eyeing up Julie lasciviously and Jamie cringed.

As the waitress poured the champagne Jamie looked across at Lucie. The soft lighting in the restaurant and the flickering light from the candle cast varying shadows across her face and added to her allure. She really is beautiful, he thought, and counted himself lucky. If he lost her now his life would be empty…again. Lucie caught his look, read his mind again, and smiled, her even white teeth glinting in the candlelight. God, how he loved her, he mused.

When Lucie had suggested the trip Jamie had baulked at the idea and had thrown back a number of arguments against it; they couldn't afford it; they were saving up for a place of their own; they were saving for the future; London was big and smelly…he had tried them all but nothing would sway her. She had worked on him, as only she could, and finally he had given in. She told him she wanted time with him alone; just the two of them, no Julie, no Jo, and no Jack. No anyone. All of them, she said, took up too much of their precious time together. She knew this little hotel that she and her father had stayed in when he was on leave, not too expensive, and right on the edge of Soho near all the nightlife. She also hinted that there were things they had to discuss privately and she didn't want any of the others around. Unfortunately, her plans had been scuppered as Julie and Jack were here, but Jamie knew that whatever was bothering her would soon be out in the open.

They toasted one another with the champagne and wished Jack a safe trip home. Julie told Jack to come back soon and Jamie winced. Lucie caught his reaction and looked at him questioningly but he simply shook his head. She would work on him later, he knew. As Lucie extolled the virtues of champagne Jamie struggled with the menu. She watched him surreptitiously and smiled to herself. Mr Independent, she thought, typical man…too proud to ask for help. 'You'll like just about everything that's on there,' she suggested helpfully, including the others in the comment. 'You like spicy food, don't you?'

'Aye, but there's spicy food and there's *spicy* food,' Jamie retorted. 'And I'd like my taste buds to be alive for later,' he laughed.

'Why? What's happening later?' she fired back, teasing him.

He leaned across and whispered in her ear. 'Later, I'm going to eat you.'

'Ssssh,' she laughed, looking at the others with a happy smile spread across her face. She was excited by the prospect but there was still the other hurdle to cross first. *Why can't it always be like this, she wondered? When I'm with him I can almost forget. Don't do this; remember why you're here but don't spoil this moment she told herself.* She snapped her mind back to the here and now. 'Tell you what,' she proposed. 'Why don't we all have the mixed starter and then I'll order for all of us? And that is what they did.

The food was superb, just as Lucie had promised, and Jamie discovered flavours and aromas he had never experienced before. Lucie had been conservative in her choices and the three novices to Thai dining were impressed. Jamie and Jack had steak and the girls both had fish. The selection of starters was wonderful, the sirloin amazing and, encouraged by Lucie to try some of her dish, Crispy Sea Bass in a spicy sauce with jasmine rice, Jamie had to admit that it too was sensational.

'So you're all happy I brought you here?' Lucie asked as they finished, getting smiles and a nods of approval all round as they munched happily on the last of their meals.

They spent the rest of the evening in the restaurant, downing another bottle of champagne and they were amongst the last to leave. The little waitress, delighted with the tip that Jamie and Jack had left her, smiled and bowed to them as they passed her at the door. It was still warm outside even though it was now late and they strolled happily amongst the late night clubbers and revellers as they made their way back to the hotel. Jamie was amazed at the mix of nationalities thronging the streets, all of them apparently enjoying themselves. On a couple of occasions they heard raised voices and arguing, sounds Jamie and Jack knew all too well, and Lucie quickly steered Jamie away. He had an unhealthy habit of getting involved in things like that, she remembered.

Without knowing it, Jack helped Lucie to achieve the aim of her plan for the night. As they neared the hotel he suggested going on to a club and Julie jumped at the idea, leaving Jamie and Julie alone at last. Jack and Julie's look said it all; it went something along the lines of *you'd think they would be tired of doing it by now; they've been living together for three months.*

Back at the hotel Lucie picked up the room key from reception while Jamie flicked through some leaflets on a display stand near the door. He heard Lucie laugh and smiled over, seeing her blush in response. He started over and noticed the receptionist's looking at him a little too closely and it wasn't missed by Lucie. A flash of annoyance and jealousy flitted across her eyes as she wrapped her arm around him and pulled him away towards the lift door, sending out a clear "hands off, he's mine" message but when Jamie looked at her the jealousy and annoyance were gone and all that was left was uncertainty, as though she was agonising over something. He pulled her close.

As the lift door closed, shutting them from the amused look of the receptionist, Lucie kissed him fiercely, almost as though the world was about to end and he was still locked in her embrace when the lift shuddered to a halt and the doors opened on the second floor. There was no one there but it wouldn't have mattered to Lucie if there had been, her mind too involved with what she was about to do. She lead him to their room and passed him the key and again the look in her eyes was disturbing…it wasn't anticipation of forthcoming passion Jamie saw but something else entirely. He unlocked the door and pushed it open to let Lucie pass but she paused, removed the "Do Not Disturb" sign from behind the door and placed it over the door handle.

'I don't want us to be disturbed…I need your full attention,' she whispered, but again, the look Jamie expected to accompany those words was hidden behind a mask of uncertainty. She seemed to read his mind and forced a laugh. 'We don't want them coming into clean the room in the morning and disturbing us…I don't enjoy "coitus interruptus", she giggled but it did nothing to assuage his mounting fear.

She pulled him into the room and pushed the door shut behind them. Lucie was taking the lead in everything now. She needed him physically before she made her disclosure…it wasn't part of a plan, just an overwhelming, gnawing need. She kissed him hungrily, pulling at his clothes exciting him as she led him slowly but steadily towards the big bed. Jamie was engulfed by her, his mind discarding all thoughts of worry as he responded to her and a trail of clothing littered their route. Finally, they stood by the edge of the bed, both fully naked, and clung to one another, kissing and caressing ravenously. Lucie felt the strength of his arms around her and the heat of his skin against her. She wanted him and every nerve end of her body tingled.

'I love you,' she whispered, kissing him fiercely again. The message she conveyed said more than that but, swallowed up by lust as well as his own love for her, Jamie missed it.

His eyes were on fire as he eased her onto the bed, sitting her on the edge and kneeling in front of her. 'I want you,' he whispered, his voice thick, as his fingers tripped lightly up her legs and prised them gently apart. Lucie gasped softly and lay back on the bed as his hands moved to her breasts and his lips made little butterfly kisses up the insides of her legs before he went down on her.

'I love you,' she sighed and this time there was no accompanying meaning.

They made love slowly, their passion reaching new heights, as they strove to fulfil each other's dreams and fantasies. Lucie controlled him, gripping his manhood tightly when she sensed he was on the verge of exploding inside her, lying still with him and then encouraging him to take her again, slowly and deeply. When she was ready she brought them both to the edge and then let out a quiet moan, the orgasm engulfing her as Jamie lost the last vestige of control, his body rigid against her as he deposited his seed.

'I love you so much,' Lucie murmured as he lay, unmoving, on top of her, her legs still entwined around him. 'Tell me you love me...really love me,' she continued. It was almost a plea, Jamie thought instantly, and the anxiety was there in her voice again. '*What is going on,*' *he asked himself?* '*How can she possibly doubt it?*'

'You know I do,' he replied, kissing her open mouth. 'And I always will.' He was trying to sound reassuring even as his own anxiety grew. He couldn't avoid it now; couldn't ignore the nagging doubts gnawing at him any longer. 'Tell me what's wrong, love,' he insisted, his voice low and soothing.

'There's nothing wrong,' she responded quickly...too quickly, she realised immediately and then she started to crumble. 'I'm scared I'm going to lose you,' she said softly.

Jamie laughed gently and squeezed her tightly. 'Hell will freeze over first,' he said, smiling, but the smile did little to ease her anxiety, he could see that. It was all getting out of hand. What had he done to make her feel so insecure...and then another, darker thought crept into his mind; was it her, something she had done?

She nuzzled her head against his chest as he ran his fingers down the curve of her spine. She kissed his nipples, nibbling him gently and let her hand wander across the taut muscles of his stomach. 'I don't want to lose you,' she murmured, gazing up at him.

Jamie kissed her waiting lips. 'You'll never, ever lose me sweetheart,' he said lovingly. 'Why should you?' She was silent and as she rested her head on his chest again he could feel the wetness of her tears. He eased her face round, making her look at him and the tracks of her tears were etched into her makeup, coursing down her cheeks and gathering below her chin like dark rainbows gathering on leaves. Her lips trembled and she sobbed silently as he wiped away the tears with his fingertips. 'Tell me what's wrong, Lucie,' he urged, his voice gentle but firm. 'It's why you brought me here...so tell me; it's tearing me apart. 'I love you; whatever it is it doesn't matter as long as we love each other.' He kissed her gently on her eyes and a sudden thought flashed into his mind. 'You're not pregnant, are you?' he asked softly.

'No, I'm not pregnant,' she smiled sadly. 'Would it be a problem if I were?' she sniffed.

To her surprise, he was smiling. 'No, that wouldn't be a problem...not at all,' he told her honestly. She lapsed into silence again and this time he waited. Whatever it was, he would know in the next few minutes; there was no need to push her. Outside in the corridor the peace was broken by a sudden noise; someone trying a door nearby, a man's voice, cursing loudly then silenced by a woman's laugh. Jamie had felt her tense with the drunken cursing and relax just as quickly with the sound of the woman's laugh. Why, he wondered, perturbed?

*

The room was dark, only the meagre light from the streetlamps outside giving form to the furniture and furnishings. Every few seconds a flashing neon sign, fixed to the wall on the building opposite, bathed the room in a deep multi-coloured glow, which seemed to last for a heartbeat, then faded into the gloom once more. Lucie moved to close the curtains but he stopped her, mesmerised by the kaleidoscope of tints and shades that filled the room and washed over their naked bodies like an incoming tide. Lucie's voice broke into his thoughts then, drifting disembodied out of the darkness, startling him.

'Long before I met you I went out with Max Kelman – the guy in the car,' she began hesitantly, waiting for a reaction, but Jamie simply continued stroking her hair. She kissed his shoulder and continued. 'It was more than two years ago…I had only turned sixteen.'

Wherever this was leading, whatever was coming, it was going to be bad, Jamie surmised, and sensed it was something they would have to resolve it and put it behind them or it would fester and poison everything they had. Meantime, the story was coming out haltingly in short, painful bursts.

'I suppose I was flattered…an older boy fancying me,' she continued slowly, her voice low and sad with the opening of old, painful wounds. 'People warned me but I didn't listen…I didn't believe the stories…just thought they were jealous. He took me out…and he was nice to me at the beginning…didn't try to make me have sex or anything like that…and I thought he really liked me. But after a while, when we were out together, I started noticing that people were afraid of him and I saw them looking at me as if I was some sort of tart; it was as if they despised me and it upset me.' The story was starting to flow now and Jamie knew this was what she had kept from him when they had spoken after making love that first time.

'It was Julie who finally made me see him for what he is. I told her I was seeing him and she looked at me as if I'd lost my mind…didn't I know who he was, she asked me? And when it was obvious I didn't, she told me…she said I must have been living on a different planet for a while because *everyone* knew who he was. The tears were filling her eyes again, ready to flow. Jamie stroked her face gently. 'He's a gangster,' she said at last…and that's why people were afraid of him and why they hated me,' she sobbed.

'And that's why you're scared now? Jamie whispered.

She smiled sadly but didn't respond to that. Instead, she continued with the story. 'His father is the real gangster; Max is just his little boy, his little helper,' she said bitterly. 'He runs the protection and money lending side of the business…and the prostitution, I think. There are lots of guys like Tony Abrahams working for him and they're all vicious thugs who enjoy hurting people.'

'Abrahams, the big guy at the club?' Jamie interrupted.

'Yes, he's one of the gang's chief enforcers. They're loan sharks and they run a protection racket, extorting money from businesses,' she repeated. 'When Julie told me all these things I felt sick. I knew what people were thinking about me then and I was scared about how I would end up…so the next time we met I told him I didn't want to see him again. He stopped being nice then…though he tried not to let it show…but he was furious; he could hide it in his eyes. He said he'd booked a table at a restaurant and it would be a shame to miss it. I was naïve and scared, scared to say no, so I agreed…I should have walked away.' She broke down then and the floodgates opened. Jamie held her and let her cry it all out but he was getting a bad feeling about all this.

When she regained her composure she started again, hesitantly now. He started driving but when we arrived at the restaurant he had spoken of he didn't stop…just kept driving…taking me out into the countryside. I asked him where he was taking me and he laughed; said he knew another little place where we could talk it through. I was really scared then and told him I wanted him to take me home but he started to laugh again and it wasn't a nice laugh…and he said we were finished when *he* decided, and not before. We were out in the countryside, on narrow country roads…deserted. I was crying then but he didn't care. Suddenly, he turned off the road onto a track into some woods.' She stopped again then and Jamie could see the pain behind her eyes.

She had a strange faraway look in her eyes as if she was facing a final hurdle. The tension in her was palpable now and Jamie had already guessed what was coming. He didn't want to hear it; he wanted her to stop but it was too late…it had always been too late…it all had to come out for them to deal with it and bury it forever. But inside he was like a ticking bomb; rage, fury and resentment all ready to explode.

Lucie started to sob uncontrollably and he could see her wrestling with the magnitude of it all, the painful memories crowding in on her. It was then he realised how much it was taking out of her and he knew in that instant how brave she was.

'He stopped the car amongst the trees,' she mumbled, sniffing back tears. I started scrabbling at the door handle…I was hysterical…desperate to get away from him. He leaned across me, grinning, and locked the door…and then he slapped me hard across the cheek. I thought he was going to kill me…sometimes I wish he had. I started to scream and he hit me again, harder this time, and told me to shut up.'

Jamie tried to pull her closer but she resisted, pushing him away from her, detaching herself from his love almost as though she felt she didn't deserve it. The tears flowed from her in a deluge but he could see that she had passed the point of no return. She was going to open her soul to him; no matter what…that was why she had brought him here, after all.

She fought back the tears and started once more. 'He got out of the car and came round for me…he was grinning like a hyena   and then he unlocked the door and dragged me out. It was dark and we were in the middle of nowhere…I screamed and screamed, but he just laughed. He told me I could scream my head off but no one would hear me…and then he picked me up and carried me into the trees.' There was a long period of silence now as she searched for the courage to complete the final part of the story. 'And then he raped me.' Her voice was faint, distant almost, but Jamie sensed that a great weight had been lifted from her…she had managed to tell him and whatever happened now was in his hands, not hers. But then the tears came again, with a vengeance now, her body racked with her sobs and her shoulders heaving. 'I'm sorry Jamie, I'm sorry,' she mumbled through it.

Jamie wrapped her in his arms and pulled her tightly against him. This time she didn't resist. 'I'll kill him,' he whispered, his voice barely audible and his eyes mirroring the cold fury raging inside him. He pulled her closer, crushing her to his chest. 'Never, ever say you're sorry for that again,' he whispered. 'You did nothing wrong.'

'Do you still love me?' she asked and he knew it was a plea.

He lifted her face to him again, gazing directly into her eyes. 'You always say my eyes tell you the truth,' he said gently. 'Yes, I still love you,' he whispered. 'Do you see the truth?'

She lifted her fingers and touched his face, tracing the lines of his eyebrows, running her fingertips along his lips. 'You still love me,' she said with a melancholy smile. 'But I could still lose you.'

Jamie looked at her, perplexed. 'You won't lose me...I know it all now...and it makes no difference; I love you.'

'But you don't know it all,' she whispered. 'There's more...and that's why he was talking to me that night at the club.'

Jamie sat transfixed. How could there be more, he gasped? He felt cold, detached. He looked at her, nodding his head slowly. 'Tell me it all, Lucie. If I'm going to deal with it I need to know what I'm up against.' The anger in him had plateaued earlier but now it was threatening to erupt again, like a volcano. The way he felt now, if Kelman appeared in this room nothing would stop him from ripping the man's heart out. He began to breathe deeply, trying to control the anger. 'I didn't come here to leave you...or to lose you,' he told her. 'I'm not givin' up on us...so tell me the rest.' The sadness was still in Lucie's eyes when she looked at him but he could see strength returning too.

She wiped the tears away. What was it about him, she wondered, that made her feel almost invincible with him there by her side? Her head was telling her she would still lose him but her heart was telling her something else entirely.

'It's a long story and it's complicated,' she started.

'We've got all night, haven't we...so tell me everything.'

She smiled nervously. 'You already know a bit about me but there are some things you don't know.'

'What things? Don't talk in riddles Lucie.'

She looked away, nodding slowly. 'My mother died when I was seven, just over ten years ago, she said, profoundly sad. 'She was French, you know that, and my father met her just after the end of the War. It was love at first sight,' she said with a wan smile. 'Just like us, I suppose.'

'Well, if she looked anything like you it's understandable,' he interrupted and watched her smile, warmer now.

'My mother was an only child...like us,' she continued. When my mother was born there were complications...and my gran couldn't have any more children afterwards. I don't think my grandparents were best pleased when my Mum fell in love with my Dad because they wanted her to carry on the family business.' Jamie's quizzical look stopped her and she digressed to explain. 'My mother's family owns land in France...near Epernay; they grow grapes and make champagne...blanc de blancs, Grand Cru,' she smiled, allowing a little pride to show. Jamie smiled in response but it meant nothing to him being strictly a Guinness and Newcastle Brown man. It did, however, explain Lucie's attempt earlier in the evening to educate them all about champagne. 'My grandmother died when I was ten years of age and my grandfather died when I was fourteen, leaving everything to me.'

'What exactly is everything?' Jamie asked, intrigued now.

'Everything,' she repeated, 'the whole estate.' 'Whole estate?' Jamie repeated, struggling with the concept. 'What exactly does that mean?'

'I don't know,' Lucie replied truthfully, 'but the vines seem to cover the whole place.'

'And who looks after them?'

'My mother's family,' she replied and saw Jamie's confusion resurface. 'A second cousin runs everything...his family have their own vines.' She paused...this was where the complications started. 'When I say everything is mine, it isn't really…not yet, at least; it all comes to me when I reach my 25th birthday…if I marry before that time it comes to me then…as long as I'm 21.' Jamie was beginning to get the picture. 'When I was 18 the family started paying money to me…an allowance; it gets paid to a lawyer here and he pays it into my account.'

'Christ, Jack was right,' Jamie mumbled. 'You *are* an heiress.' Lucie's eyebrows arched questioningly. 'I spoke to Jack about you and me,' he admitted, 'not long after you met him…the Saturday we all went to Yates…remember? Lucie nodded and he carried on. 'He said we wouldn't make it together…because we come from different worlds…he actually said you were probably an heiress,' he finished with a wry smile.

'Well he got one bit wrong…we have made it, haven't we?' She didn't allow him to reply before carrying on. 'I suppose I am an heiress,' she said reflectively. 'I hadn't thought of it like that…but it doesn't change how I feel about you,' she continued, suddenly anxious again as a new thought emerged. 'It doesn't change how you feel, does it?' she asked, voicing her fear.

He laughed softly. 'I told you; nothing will change how I feel about you,' he said reassuringly as she looked into his eyes, analysing his response. Satisfied, she smiled.

But she was still wrestling with her next revelation…all she had said up until now was background.

They lay quietly for a long moment, Lucie tracing her fingers across his chest and then circling the nipple of his left breast with her forefinger. Jamie was still full of rage against Max Kelman but he was managing to control it. His biggest weakness had always been impetuosity but there was no room for that. If he was going to take revenge on the man, *and he was going to take revenge*, then he would have to plan it carefully. It was then he realised that Lucie hadn't yet said anything remotely disturbing and she had said Kelman was still involved. 'So, where does Kelman fit into this?' he asked quietly.

She smiled sourly. 'He wants my land and the vines…he thinks they'll make him rich,' she said simply.

'What, he wants you to sell them to him?' Jamie asked, incredulous.

Lucie laughed coldly then. 'No baby, that would be too easy,' she replied sadly. 'If he can get me to marry him he gets it all for nothing.'

'You're joking!' Jamie laughed mirthlessly, but the look in Lucie's eyes told him it was no joke. He was speechless. In any other circumstances he would admire Kelman's audacity but this was Lucie he was talking about. 'That's not going to happen,' he said forcefully. 'You told him to get lost, didn't you?'

'Yes, of course I did…but it's not that easy Jamie,' she replied dolefully and the tone of her voice told him worse was yet to come. 'When he raped me he told me not to bother going to the police, I'd be wasting my time…he said they wouldn't believe me and I got the impression that he is paying some of them off.'

'Go on,' Jamie prompted.

'He said he'd make my family pay if I was stupid and *did* go to the police.'

'What? Your father?' Jamie said quietly, finding that hard to believe.

'No,' Lucie murmured, 'he's not that stupid…my aunt and uncle, and my little cousins. And he took great delight in telling me what he would do to them.' Her tears welled up again.

Jamie was shaking with anger now, his face white. 'He's dead,' he said quietly, 'I'll kill the bastard!' Lucie looked at him and saw the other Jamie Raeburn then. Some people made empty threats and promises…he wasn't one of them.

Somehow, his cold fury gave her the strength to go on. 'Two weeks before we met, about four months ago, he met me outside the hospital.' She paused, and Jamie watched her steel herself. 'He was his usual obnoxious self I wanted to get away from him…as I tried to leave he caught hold of my arm and said he'd heard a rumour…a "little bird" had told him that I had come into money and would soon be a "very rich" little girl. I tried to laugh it off…said I didn't know what he was talking about, but he must have seen it in my eyes. He laughed at me…said he "had his sources" and there was no point denying it.' She was wrapped up in it now, her voice cold and rapid. 'When I calmed down later and thought about it, no one knew about it other than my father, my aunt Emily, my uncle…and the lawyer. My family wouldn't say a word to anyone, let alone Max Kelman, so who does that leave?' she said bitterly. 'You can't trust anyone,' she murmured.

'You can trust me,' Jamie said softly, taking her hand gently in his.

Lucie smiled wanly and her eyes brightened behind the screen of tears. 'Yes, I know,' she whispered as the tears began to fall and her body shook with her sobbing. Jamie thought she would shatter and break into smithereens. He pulled her close, letting her take her time.

After a while she had regained her composure and started again. 'When you saw him at the club he was trying again…he tries to get me alone…no witnesses. He managed it two weeks ago and that's when he told me what he was going to do…I told him he makes my skin crawl and I'd rather be dead…' She shuddered visibly and Jamie thought it was all getting too much for her again but she seemed to shake herself and carried on. 'He laughed at that…said that could be arranged, but it would spoil his plan…he had a better idea.' The look on her face was bleak and the strain was showing but she forced herself to carry on. 'He said he would kill my uncle first…followed by my aunt Emily…and then my cousins, all one at a time "to give me a chance to come to my senses". He said they would all have "nasty accidents" but I didn't need to worry…he only wants the land in France and the money…he doesn't want me…he can get all the sex he needs without forcing me to do it,' she laughed hollowly. 'Thank God for small mercies.'

She was at breaking point and Jamie pulled her to him again, kissing the top of her head. He wondered how she had managed to keep all of this bottled up but it explained everything; the quiet moods, the distraction, not hearing him when he spoke…and the subtle sense of dread that seemed to fill her sometimes. Her strength astounded him but she couldn't face it alone. 'It's not goin' to happen, sweetheart, I won't let it,' he said defiantly.

Lucie looked at him fondly but her mind was already considering the consequences of Max Kelman discovering they were lovers. 'If he discovers we're together he'll have you killed, Jamie,' she said desolately. 'That's why I never, ever, let you come to meet me at work, you know that, don't you?' she continued. Jamie nodded…yes, he knew, but he didn't like it. 'He's had men looking for you since that night outside Clouds.'

'He won't get me,' Jamie replied, his voice hard as steel, 'but I'll get him…I just have to find a way.'

Lucie shook her head hopelessly. 'He's never alone…it's too dangerous, sweetheart,' she warned, 'and if I lose you I might as well be dead.'

Jamie pulled her to him again and kissed her gently and they lay wrapped in each other's arms, letting the silence and the darkness envelope them, as if those two elements could heal them and take away the scars.

'When is all this supposed to happen?' Jamie asked eventually.

'I don't know,' Lucie replied quietly. 'He knows I don't inherit the estate before I'm 21 so I don't think he'll be in a rush...he just likes to remind me of it to frighten me. He's a sadist,' she sobbed angrily.

'I won't let it happen,' Jamie repeated. 'You're my life now...an' that bastard isn't takin' you away from me.' Lucie lifted her head up off his chest and gazed into his eyes again. 'Do you trust me?' he asked.

She smiled sadly. 'Yes, Jamie...with my life,' she answered calmly.

'Then let me deal with the problem...and I will.'

A smile blossomed in Lucie's cheeks. It was irrational and she couldn't explain it but she felt safe again. She had dreaded telling him all of this, frightened by what his reaction might be...partly because she feared he might abandon her to her fate but her greater fear had been the thought of him rushing, unprepared into the lion's den seeking vengeance and ending up dead himself. Neither of those fears had materialised...he was still hers; and a cold, calculating Jamie Raeburn would be a dangerous opponent for anyone as Max Kelman might soon discover.

By now, the traffic noise outside had died down and the clubbers had departed. Jack and Julie had returned an hour earlier, their laughter disturbing the other guests, but peace had descended now and the city was asleep. Lucie lay snuggled against Jamie, her breathing settled and regular, the tension gone from her. The neon light on the building opposite was no more and the room was in shadow, what scant light there was settled on Lucie's face and hair, giving her an ethereal, almost angelic appearance. Jamie kissed her softly and smiled, content that she had finally given in to sleep.

His own brain continued to churn, searching for solutions, and sleep refused to come. He closed his eyes and listened to the sound of her breathing, hypnotic in its regularity, and inhaled the spicy floral fragrances of her perfume and the musk of their entangled bodies. Sleep came to him just as the early sunlight filled the room.

*

It was late and daylight was fading when they stepped down from the train in Beeston. Grey clouds filled the sky and rain threatened. It was Sunday evening, barely 48 hours since Lucie's traumatic disclosures which had caused her so much pain and misery but already her love for Jamie and his for her had grown more solid. There had been an almost immediate change in her and she felt that an enormous weight had been lifted from her shoulders...and the fear that had filled her and built a barrier around her, disappeared. The change in her was dramatic.

Other passengers descended from the train with them and had immediately run for the cover of the Waiting Room to avoid the rain but the four of them laughed and played in it like children, enjoying the cooling sensation of it after the sultry, oppressive heat of London. They skipped, arm in arm along the road, jumped in puddles, screamed and laughed and made their way to Devonshire Place.

At the house, Lucie pulled Jamie under the big Oak tree at the road's edge, his protection when he and the others had been attacked weeks earlier, and let Jack and Julie go in ahead of them. They listened to the rain cascading onto the umbrella of leaves above them and Lucie twined her arms round his neck. The rain had flattened her short blonde hair against her head and dulled its lustre, her T-shirt top clung to her body and her mascara was smudged, but she was still the most beautiful woman Jamie had ever laid eyes on. The thought of Max Kelman taking her from him and forcing her to marry him was all too much but with the thought came the solution to their problem.

He smiled grimly and turned Lucie to face him. 'I'd rather we had time to do this properly,' he said quietly and saw the question in her eyes. 'But I...we haven't got time,' he stopped, and knelt down on the rain soaked pavement. Holding on to her hands he looked lovingly at her. 'Will you marry me?'

Lucie's bewilderment flitted to uncertainty and then delight and she pulled him to his feet, kissing him hungrily. 'You mean it?' she asked huskily. 'You want to marry me?'

Jamie laughed. 'Yes, I want to marry you...we're already livin' together so it's the next logical step, isn't it? And if we're married, then Kelman can't have you.'

Lucie suddenly saw his plan and doubt flooded in. 'Is that the only reason?' she asked him unhappily.

'No, that's not the only reason,' he laughed awkwardly. 'The only reason is that I love you...Christ Lucie, you can't doubt that...marry me.' He watched her and saw fear raise its unwelcome head again. 'What's wrong? Tell me,' he said gently. 'I don't want your money, I just want you...and then we can both tell Kelman to sling his hook.' The rain was falling heavier now and he felt it trickle down his back as he waited for her response. What is the problem, his mind screamed? 'If you love me as you say you do, why do you even have to think about it?' he asked, the words sounding harsher than he intended.

She smiled and touched his cheek. 'I'm thinking about it *because* I love you and *because* I don't think you've worked this out properly,' she said softly, kissing him gently on his open mouth. 'I want to marry you, more than anything in the world, but what about the consequences? You haven't thought this out, Jamie.'

'What consequences? If we're married he can't make you marry him, it's as simple as that.'

'No, my love, it's not. We're not dealing with a normal person here; we're talking about an animal with an animal's cunning and an animal's morals. If we marry and he finds out, he'll kill you. There's nothing to stop him marrying a widow, is there?'

'Shit! He wouldn't,' Jamie spat out angrily.

'Yes, he would,' she said sadly. 'You don't know him, baby...he wouldn't think twice.' Jamie's shoulders sagged and Lucie could feel the frustration exuding from him. She hugged him tightly.

'So, you won't marry me?' he said sadly, his head dropping.

She lifted his face and made him look at her, smiling and kissing him again. Julie shouted from the house, telling them to come in out of the rain, but they ignored her plea. The rain was nothing, this moment was everything. Lucie gazed into his eyes and reached her decision. 'I'll marry you, because I love you and I want to be your wife, but no one can know. If you promise me that then I'll marry you as soon as we can get a licence.'

Jamie brightened instantly and swung her up off her feet, spinning her around in his arms. 'Someone will have to know,' he said. 'We can't do it without witnesses.'

Lucie nodded. She had thought of that too. 'We can tell Julie, she can keep a secret...and Jack can be your best man,' she said.

Jamie shook his head. 'No, not Jack, sweetheart...he's going home to Glasgow, remember?' In the end they settled on Terry Hughes. The big Scouser knew about Jamie's trouble at Clouds and he was more perceptive about things than the others. More importantly, Jamie knew he could trust him to keep his mouth shut.

And so, Lucie Kent married Jamie ten days later, 13th September 1967, in Nottingham Registry Office with only Julie Bradley, Terry Hughes and the Registrar there to celebrate it and that night they spent their honeymoon in their little flat at the top of the house in Devonshire Place. Nothing could spoil their happiness now.

Chapter 40

Jamie was still working on his problem of how to deal with Max Kelman four weeks later when matters came to a head, and it was pretty much his own fault. Ignoring Lucie's warnings, he ventured into Derby one Monday night to meet her when she finished work. It was partly bravado, he knew that, but more so it was his refusal to be cowed by Kelman that drove him to it, he would admit later. His intention was to surprise Lucie and he did…but for all the wrong reasons.

He had cadged a lift from a workmate who lived in Derby and arrived at the hospital about ten minutes before Lucie finished her shift. He bought a bunch of red roses from the florist's shop across from the hospital and waited, enjoying a cigarette and imagining the look of surprise on Lucie's face when she spotted him. He had wanted to do this for a long time to show her that he wasn't afraid of Kelman and his thugs but, with hindsight, he would realise it was reckless and rash.

And fate and bad luck follow those who are reckless and rash. This time it was bad luck. Another five minutes and he and Lucie would have been gone but as he lounged outside the hospital, waiting, a car pulled up on the other side of the road and stopped outside the florist. That was the first piece of bad luck; the second was that Tony Abrahams was in that car and he had every reason to remember Jamie…his face was etched into the man's memory and he was still smarting from the humiliation inflicted on him all those weeks earlier. Here was a golden opportunity to even the score. The fact that Jamie was waiting outside the hospital where Lucie Kent worked with a bunch of red roses in his hands didn't register with him at the time. He didn't care who Jamie was waiting for, that was the last thing on his mind; the first thing…the *only* thing on his mind, was how to inflict the maximum amount of pain on the Jock bastard standing across the road.

Abrahams turned to his three companions, a look of undisguised glee on his pudgy face. 'See that cunt across there,' he started, pointing Jamie out. 'That's the Jock bastard that sneaked up on me at Clouds weeks back.' All three had heard about the incident though Abrahams had carefully sanitised it. In his version of events, Jamie had attacked him without warning and had caught him unawares. The true version had, however, filtered out courtesy of Kelman himself, but no one, least of all the three in the car now, had the bottle to put him straight about it. Even now the truth was best left dormant. They simply took in what Abrahams said and nodded sagely. 'I want that bastard sorted, right?' Again all three nodded. 'Right, Ted, you stay with the car…and you two will come with me.' There was a moment's hesitation then both men, thinking Abrahams was ready to go, started to exit the vehicle before he called them back. 'Wait a minute, for fuck sake,' he hissed. 'I don't want this cocked up. The two of you head off down the road a bit then work your way back behind him. I'll get out when you get close to him and I'll make sure he sees me…that'll distract him enough for the two of you to grab him and then I'll sort the little shit out,' he grinned, wolf like. 'I've got a fucking score to settle. Right, on you go.'

The men stepped out and strode off down the street, chatting casually and avoiding looking at Jamie. About twenty yards beyond him they crossed over the road and began their walk back towards him, cautious now. Tony Abrahams hauled his muscular body from the car and stood on the pavement but Jamie was still relaxed, smoking his cigarette, and hadn't noticed him. He would, however, soon be aware of the other two men closing in on him so he had to act fast. Quickly, he walked round behind the car and stepped into the street before calling back over his shoulder to Ted, the driver. As anticipated, Jamie spotted him immediately and his ruse had worked; Jamie's attention was on him and not on the others. He kept walking towards Jamie, surprised that he didn't react, then grinned triumphantly as his two henchmen closed on him, gripping his arms and locking them behind his back.

Abrahams let out a roar of delight and ran the last few yards, lashing out and catching Jamie with a solid punch to the right temple. Another haymaker landed on Jamie's solar plexus knocking the wind from him just as Abrahams' knee landed solidly in his groin. The two men behind Jamie were laughing harshly as he struggled to free himself, kicking out blindly at them to no effect. As blow after blow rained in on him the lights started to go out and he remembered the phenomenon from the last occasion in Glasgow...but at least this time he hadn't been stabbed, he thought absently.

Suddenly, there was a flurry of activity at the hospital entrance. Women were screaming and the security men on duty at the gate were running towards the fracas. Abrahams landed another crushing punch on Jamie's face and looked over his shoulder at the advancing crowd. Amongst the nurses and others coming towards them was Lucie Kent and the look on the little tart's face told its own story. She screamed out Jamie's name but the look on her face made the shout superfluous. Tony Abrahams' face lit up. *She didn't need to shout out this bastard's name, he thought, she knows him...and they're not just friends.*

Even someone as intellectually challenged as Tony Abrahams could add one and one and come up with two...she didn't just know him, they were an item. A frisson of excitement ran through him. He turned back to his henchmen. 'Right, show's over...let's get out of here before somebody decides they should identify us.' He let out a shrill whistle, beckoning wildly for the car, and with a roar of exhaust and a squeal of tyres Ted swung across the road towards them. The men holding Jamie dropped him and ran for the car, followed by Abrahams who waited just long enough to take a last kick at him as he tumbled to the ground.

With another squeal of tyres and smoke from burning rubber the car raced away. Tony Abrahams looked back at the scene just in time to see a tearful Lucie cradle Jamie in her arms. Her eyes looked down the road after the speeding car and Tony Abrahams was sure that they met his. He smiled happily; the boss was not going to be pleased.

*

Lucie saw the assault as she emerged from the main door of the hospital with colleagues. It was obvious that someone was being attacked and the girls with her screamed. Lucie stood transfixed, her heart in her mouth, as she recognised Jamie and then she started to run with the others, calling his name. Two of the security guards on duty at the hospital, both ex-soldiers, started to run with her. She saw Tony Abrahams look at the people running towards him and saw the flicker of recognition in his eyes, and in that moment she knew that her relationship with Jamie was no longer a secret. Max Kelman would know of it within the next few minutes and he would do what he always did when things didn't go the way he wanted. Jamie's life was in danger. She suspected that Tony Abrahams wouldn't finish Jamie now because Max himself would want that pleasure, but still Jamie was getting a severe beating. Lucie almost cried with relief when she saw the men release him but Tony Abrahams' final kick horrified her and she screamed out in anguish.

She kept running, oblivious to the danger now. She saw Abrahams smile sneeringly at her and then he was gone, the car making off in a spin of tyres and burning rubber. Jamie was prone on the pavement, his face covered in blood, but he was still conscious. She sank to her knees beside him and slid her hands beneath his shoulders to raise him up onto her lap as her tears fell onto his face and mingled with his blood. Her eyes followed the speeding car and she caught Abrahams' knowing look, her fears confirmed. 'Oh Jamie, Jamie, why did you come?' she sobbed as she wiped blood from his face. Friends and colleagues crowded around her, all eager to help and all realising immediately that the young man lying bloodied on the ground was close to her.

Supported by Lucie and one of the security guards, Jamie was helped to his feet and taken into A&E where, forty minutes later and with bruises now showing vividly on his face, he re-emerged to a waiting Lucie and a concerned Brian Bradley. Lucie ran to him and threw her arms around his neck, failing to see his grimace of pain. 'What have they said?' she demanded, 'is anything broken?'

Jamie smiled through the pain burning in his chest and his head. 'No, nothing broken...only my pride,' he mumbled awkwardly, casting his eyes at Brian who gave him an encouraging smile.

'I'm your taxi,' Brian laughed. 'Lucie phoned and told us what happened and I was dispatched immediately. Come on, let's get you home...you look like you've been through a mincer.'

Jamie winced. He was sore all over but he hadn't yet seen himself in a mirror and Brian's words gave him an insight into what to expect. 'That bad?' he asked.

Brian pulled a face but it was Lucie who replied. 'Yes sweetheart, that bad.'

Jamie looked at her apologetically, ready to take the flak for ignoring her warnings and coming to Derby to surprise her, but he could tell that there was something else on Lucie's mind. He arched his eyes questioningly but she glanced at Brian and shook her head imperceptibly. Whatever it was on her mind, she obviously didn't want Brian to be party to it and the drive back to Beeston was completed in silence.

Chapter 41

Tony Abrahams had an undisguised look of delight on his face as he stepped from the car outside a phone box in Derby City Centre. In his eyes, Max Kelman was a bit of a dick but his old man paid Tony's wages and if that meant cow towing to the arrogant little turd that was Cyril Kelman's son, then so be it. But tonight he had information that would upset Max no end and he intended to enjoy the moment. It was going to be worth every penny of the sixpence to make the call and enlighten Max to the fact that his little bird was nesting with the Scots lad.

Telling the others to wait in the car he stepped into the phone box and dug out some change from his trouser pocket. The call was answered immediately, the supercilious voice of Max Kelman echoing down the line. 'Hello boss,' Abrahams started, faking obsequiousness. 'It's Tony…'

'I know it's you, what the fuck do you want?' Max interrupted brusquely. 'I'm busy and I haven't got all fucking night.'

Tony Abrahams smiled at the other end of the line. He was just about to spoil the little shit's evening and he was determined to savour the moment. 'We spotted that Scotch git in Derby about ten minutes ago.'

Kelman was instantly interested. He'd had men looking for "that Scotch git" for months and the bastard needed to be taught a lesson. If Tony Abrahams had missed the chance to give the fucker a good hiding then he'd have his balls. 'So, you spotted him, but did you get the fucker?'

'Yeah, I got him,' Tony laughed. Worked him over real good, I did,' he confirmed. 'He was standing outside the hospital and we had to leg it when some nurses came out…but I hurt him.'

'Fucking excellent, Tony, there's a bonus for you in this,' Kelman enthused. His night was getting better. *Maybe I'll treat myself to one of the girls locked up in the house, he thought…have a little celebration.* He'd begun to think the Scots git had buggered off because he hadn't been seen in Derby since that night outside Clouds. He was ecstatic…no one messed with Max Kelman and got away with it. But Tony Abrahams was still on the line and a tiny alarm bell started to ring in Kelman's head. 'So, what else have you got to tell me?' he demanded.

Tony Abrahams pictured Kelman sitting in his office, full of his own self-importance and conceit, and grinned. *Fuck you Max, he thought silently, it's time to have some fun.* 'That little nurse you've been keeping an eye on,' he said quietly and knew that Kelman's ears would have pricked up with that intro. 'She came out of the hospital with a bunch of other nurses just as we were disposing of the Jock and she clocked me,' he continued, spinning it out.

'Relax Tony,' Kelman fired back. 'She won't say a word, she knows better,' he laughed.

'No, it's not that boss…I know she won't talk, but I think you'll want to have a chat with her about the company she's keeping,' he said seriously whilst inside he was enjoying the moment.

'What the fuck are you on about Tony? Stop talking in fucking riddles…what company?'

'She's seeing that Scotch bastard,' Tony Abrahams said, delivering his coup de grace. 'Real cosy, it appears.' The silence at the other end of the line filled him with glee. He'd waited quite a while to give little Max a virtual kick in the balls and now that he had done it he was filled with an exquisite sense of delight.

The silence dragged on and Tony revelled in it but it was only a matter of time before the explosion, he realised. But, to his surprise, when Max did eventually speak his voice was controlled, level and without any hint of the rage or fury that Tony had expected.

'Thanks for that Tony,' Kelman said. 'I *will* have a word with her. As a matter of interest, how do you know they're cosy?'

'She was screaming his name as she ran towards us and as we were driving away she had him in her arms, crying all over him. Looked cosy to me, boss,' he replied, twisting the screw just a little bit further. But it was a dangerous game he was playing, and he knew it. If Max Kelman suspected for even a second that he was enjoying delivering this little tit bit of information then he would get his own balls to play with.

'Right Tony, thanks. I think we'll need to sort this guy out again…permanently this time. See if you can find out where he lives. Okay?'

'Yes boss, okay,' Tony Abrahams replied and the line went dead.

Everything moved quickly after that. Three days later Lucie was intercepted as she left the hospital and was bundled into the back of Max Kelman's car by two of his goons, and then driven to Cranston Hall, Cyril Kelman's pile on the outskirts of Derby. Fear numbed her as she sat in the rear of the car between the two rough looking men who had grabbed her. Max Kelman, sitting in the front, said nothing throughout the journey and his silence only heightened her anxiety. She had been half expecting something to happen now that Max knew about her and Jamie but she hadn't expected it quite so quickly and she hadn't expected this. She knew Max would assume she was living with Jamie, that was the way his mind worked, and she had assumed that he would have her followed. In Max's warped mind Jamie was a threat…Jamie was *the* threat, and when Max found out where Jamie was he would come for him. Tony Abrahams knew about her and Jamie so Max must know…and he would be furious. He wasn't a man to allow his plans to be scuppered like this and he would already be planning his way to recoup the situation. Lucie was worried but she knew it wasn't her life that was in danger…Max needed her alive, but that didn't apply to Jamie and she shuddered at the thought, steeling herself for what was to come.

Max stopped the car at the big wrought iron gates outside Cranston Hall and one of the men sitting beside her out and punched a code into a little keypad set into one of the stone pillars supporting the gates. The gates began to swing inward and seconds later they were sweeping up the long tree lined drive to the imposing Georgian house. *Who said crime doesn't pay, Lucie thought bitterly.*

Max pulled up outside the main door and got out. The men sitting either side of Lucie followed suit and one of them then hauled her roughly from the car.

'Take the car round to the garage,' Max ordered one of the men. 'And bring her into the house,' he told the other as he made his way up the wide steps to the door. The man gripped Lucie tightly by the arm, making her gasp, and manhandled her up and through the door behind Max. Inside, Lucie was stunned by the opulence of her surroundings. A wide marble stairway led up to an upper floor and everything was painted in gleaming white and pale grey. The whole place oozed wealth and luxury and in any other circumstances she would have been impressed. Someone had taste but her limited knowledge of Max suggested it wasn't him.

Max turned to her with a conceited smile on his face and Lucie stared back at him defiantly. 'If you play your cards right all this could be yours,' Max laughed. 'We could marry our fortunes together,' he smiled coldly. Lucie glared back at him with an expression of pure loathing and a flash of irritation passed across his face. 'Take her upstairs to the room that's been prepared for her...and lock her in,' he ordered.

'What are you going to do to me?' Lucie shouted as she was led away, struggling.

'To you...nothing,' Max responded with an evil laugh. 'To your boyfriend...well, that's another matter,' he said quietly and walked away, leaving her there alone with her fear.

Chapter 42

That night Jamie waited for Lucie at Beeston station. The bruising around his eyes was still bad but the aches and pains of his beating at the hands of Tony Abrahams had lessened and he was moving freely again. He was still smarting from the humiliation inflicted on him and realised, with a degree of shock, that he wasn't unlike Max Kelman in that regard. Neither of them could accept humiliation.

Lucie had ripped into him when they were finally alone in their room that Monday night until finally she had relented and began to cry. Jamie accepted that the thought of Max Kelman taking revenge on him was uppermost in her mind and it made his efforts to neutralise Kelman all the more important. Only then would Lucie be able to relax.

They had made love later that night with Lucie doing most of the work, Jamie had hardly been able to move but the closeness of Lucie's body had been therapeutic. Sexual healing wasn't just a concept, it actually worked, and for a moment he remembered the effect Kate had had on him all those months earlier. He wondered how she was and if she thought of him, the way he was thinking of her just now.

The Derby train appeared further down the line and he pushed Kate from his mind. Lucie would be with him in minutes and she was his life now. His whole world revolved around her. The diesel locomotive squealed to a halt and the passengers began to disembark, rushing along the platform towards the gate and out to the main road beyond. But there was no sign of Lucie. Normally, she was amongst the first off the train, eager to be with him, and because of her height he could usually see her blonde head bobbing above the others…but not tonight, and he experienced a sudden feeling of disquiet.

She had been late home before this, but not often. It could have been an emergency in the ward which had kept her late, he told himself, trying to shrug off his unease. That had happened once before, he recalled…but on that occasion she had telephoned.

He pulled a cigarette from his packet and lit it, drawing in the smoke to calm his now fragmented nerves. No matter how hard he tried to rationalise the situation, deep down he knew that something had happened to her. Sixth sense, premonition, some psychic link between them, call it what you like, but Jamie knew.

The next train from Derby was due at seventeen minutes past six so it made sense to wait rather than return to the house. He passed the time in the empty waiting room, trying to keep up his spirits by making plans for their future together.

The time passed slowly. About ten minutes before the train was due, and bored with staring at the four whitewashed walls of the waiting room, Jamie rose and wandered outside onto the platform. There were only so many times he could look at posters extolling the virtues of Filey and Skegness as holiday destinations without going crazy!

It was a damp evening with a mist was beginning to settle after the heat of the afternoon, and a haze softened the glare of the sun. He stood at the edge of the platform looking down the tracks which were now burnished a deep antique gold by the dying sun and allowed his eyes to follow their lines until they joined in the distance. He was almost in a trance like state now, his whole existence concentrated on Lucie's failure to appear. Footsteps on the platform jogged him back and he turned his head to see the portly station master, still resplendent in his dark blue uniform, checking the floral displays along the boundary fence separating the station from the road beyond. The man nodded to him genially and Jamie returned the greeting, but his mood was far from genial.

He lit another Lucky Strike and filled his lungs again. Normally he would have appreciated the hit of the nicotine but tonight his mind was distracted and the feeling of unease which had started earlier was growing stronger with each passing minute. He knew what his mother would say. A native of the West Highlands of Scotland, she swore by the power of Second Sight which, to the rest of the world, is Sixth Sense. She would say that if his Second Sight was telling him something was wrong, then something *was* wrong and he would ignore it at his peril.

He glanced nervously at his watch and looked again down the line. The incoming train started as a speck in the distance, just where he had seen the lines converge earlier, growing in size with each passing second. It was on time but its arrival did nothing to shake the anxiety that was building inside him and refusing to budge.

With a hiss of steam and a squeal of metal on metal, the train glided to a halt. Doors were flung open and weary commuters, fewer of them this time, stepped down onto the platform and hurried towards the exits, back to their homes, their wives, husbands and children. He searched the faces frantically, his nerves frayed. Still no Lucie and his spirit sagged. There was only one rational explanation but it was one he didn't want to accept…Kelman had her. He cursed himself for ignoring her warnings and going to Derby to surprise her earlier that week. That had been the trigger. It was his fault; now he was on the back foot and Kelman had the upper hand.

With the bitter taste of his stupidity in his mouth he made his way home; his only hope now, and a frail one, was that Lucie had managed to get a lift from a colleague and was waiting for him back at the house. But that frail hope disappeared with Jo's puzzled look as he stepped over the threshold. Lucie wasn't there and the anguish on his face prompted Jo to drop what she was doing and come to him immediately. 'What's wrong?' she asked, apprehensively. 'Where's Lucie?'

'I don't know,' he whispered, sounding lost. I take it she hasn't phoned?'

'No, she hasn't.' Jo was looking at him intently now and the worry etched on his face was mirrored in hers. Something was seriously wrong, she sensed intuitively. She started for her private room at the rear of the house, dragging him with her. 'I'll phone Julie and get her to check…maybe she's been held up, maybe there's been an emergency,' she continued, her words tumbling out.

Jamie smiled bleakly. 'She won't be there Jo…she left at her usual time.'

You don't know that, Jo thought, finding herself strangely angered by his certainty. It was only then that the truth began to dawn on her. 'You don't think that Max Kelman…' She started to voice the fear that was creeping into her mind but couldn't finish it, unable to utter the words. But there was no need…what she saw in Jamie's eyes confirmed it and the cold, calculating intensity she saw there frightened her. She began to cry and a scream left her lips.

Jamie held her, trying to ease her pain, but he had to *do* something. 'Can I borrow your car?' he asked quietly, bringing her back to reality. 'I have to find her.'

Saying "no" wouldn't stop him, she realised. She had guessed what was on his mind and was fairly sure where he would go. Something had been brewing for weeks; she had seen it, sensed it, but then everything had changed four weeks earlier after the trip to London. Lucie had changed…changed back might be truer…she had been happy and bubbly again, until…her memory flashed back to Monday night…Lucie's frantic telephone call and the look on her face when she returned to the house later with a badly battered Jamie. Everything changed again in that moment, Jo realised. The withdrawn and worried Lucie had come home instead of the vibrant, happy girl who had skipped off to work that morning. She smiled sadly. If Max Kelman had Lucie and Jamie went to Derby looking for her, he would be walking right into the lion's den. 'Why don't you let Brian take you, he can drive while you look,' she suggested, but she knew it was futile.

Jamie shook his head slowly. 'This is my fight,' he said quietly. 'I don't want Brian, or you, or anyone else for that matter, involved. It's personal…an' I'll fix it my way.'

'You don't know what you're taking on,' she came back quickly, her voice mirroring her anxiety and her fear.

He smiled grimly, his mouth lop sided. 'Yes, Jo, I do…I know exactly what I'm takin' on…an' it's somethin' I should have done long before now.'

Jo shook her head in despair. Max Kelman was not just another thug. He was evil personified, a pitiless, inhuman gangster. Jamie Raeburn was a fighter…and he was brave, but he wasn't in Max Kelman's league when it came to mindless violence. The man had no conscience and he would use anyone. Jamie's insistence on doing this himself set him apart from Max Kelman…a classic case of good versus evil, but it also meant that her Brian wouldn't be involved and that, she realised guiltily, was a blessing.

Jamie set off for Derby in the Bradley's little Austin 1100 ten minutes later. His only concession to Jo was that he would keep in touch, promising to telephone every hour to let her know he was alright and he would call the instant he found Lucie. Jo had insisted on telephoning Julie at the Nurses' Home, asking her to check with Julie's ward but by this time she knew it was a forlorn hope. Jamie's final concession was his agreeing to meet Julie at the hospital before he did anything else.

Twenty five minutes later he was with Julie. She was a bundle of nerves and was verging on hysteria. She had gone to Lucie's ward immediately after her mother's call but, as Jamie had known, Lucie had left at her usual time and hadn't appeared concerned about anything. In fact, the nurses who had come on duty told Julie that she had been anxious to get home to her boyfriend. Julie's next port of call had been at the security desk at the main door and that was where she learned the bad news. One of the security guards, the same man who had helped Lucie take Jamie into A&E a few nights earlier, said he had seen Lucie getting into a black car. He couldn't say what make of car it was but it was, in his words, "a big black car". That sealed it for her. Max Kelman drove a big, black car.

Jamie took the news stoically. In truth, it was no more than he had expected. His problem now was no different from what it had been since Lucie had told him everything in London. How could he get to Kelman without being killed in the process?

But right now, Julie was losing it and he had to calm her down. She was the first to have discovered what Kelman had done to Lucie two years ago so her anguish and concern were only to be expected but she wasn't privy to the man's current scheme. Julie would keep quiet. He trusted her, and so did Lucie. She was one of only three people who knew about their secret marriage and she could keep this new secret too.

'Shouldn't we call the police?' Her voice, heavy with emotion, cut into his thoughts.

Jamie wrapped his arms around her and pulled her close, feeling the heaving of her chest against him as she fought back the tears. 'I don't think that would do any good,' he said with a sigh. 'Lucie suspects that some of them are in his pocket and even if they're not and she is with him, he will have threatened her family and she'll simply say that she's there of her own free will. He's not going to hurt her,' Jamie added and the certainty of his words hit her immediately. She looked at him, her eyebrows knitting together in a question.

'There's an element to this you don't know,' he explained, and saw light appear in her eyes as she backed away from the verge of breakdown. 'It concerns Lucie's inheritance which Max Kelman knows about…and he wants to get his hands on it. He's been trying to coerce her for months and has threatened to kill her family if she doesn't agree to marry him.'

'Marry him?' Julie hissed, her eyes blazing.

Jamie smiled bitterly. 'Yes, marry him…and that's one of the reasons I asked her to marry me. Foolishly, I thought that if he discovered we were married he would back off but Lucie agreed only if we kept it a secret. She knows that bastard better than I do and she reckoned that instead of backing off he would simply eliminate the problem…me. So at the moment, Lucie is safe. He can't afford to harm her.' Jamie watched hope reignite in Julie's eyes and smiled grimly. She hadn't picked up on his "at the moment" statement and it was better that she didn't think too far into the future.

'So what *are* you going to do?' she asked eventually.

'I'm going to find her, make sure she's alright and do everything I have to do to get her back with us.' The words came out as a statement of intent which Julie thought misplaced.

She looked at him askance and started to sob again. Even if Jamie was able to find Lucie, getting her out of the clutches of Max Kelman would be something else entirely. He wouldn't stand a chance against the sheer number of Kelman's thugs. She felt him wrap his arms around her again and she buried her head in his chest. There was no fear in him that she could detect. Lucie, and Jack, had both told her, on separate occasions, that Jamie Raeburn feared no one and that he had an almost fatalistic attitude to death…worrying about it served no purpose, he had told them both, when it comes, it comes. She prayed that his time wasn't coming now.

Julie was calmer now and he felt he could leave her. 'Don't stay here tonight,' he said quietly. 'Go home and stay with your mother in Beeston. I'll keep phoning in.' Julie nodded and Jamie walked away.

She stood in the doorway watching him as he set off into the night. She doubted that there was anyone else like him in the entire world. But what could one man, even Jamie Raeburn, do against the army of thugs that Max Kelman had at his disposal? That thought filled her with dread. The last she saw of him was as opened the door of her father's car. He turned and waved to her and she returned it, hiding her face lest he should see the tears that were now coursing down her cheeks. This might, she reflected, be the last time she saw him alive.

*

Finding Lucie was going to be simpler than Julie, or Jo, thought, he was sure of that. Kelman's men would be out looking for him so he would simply let them find him. What he did then, of course, would depend on Kelman but he was sure that he would see Lucie soon.

As he stepped out of the hospital car park three pairs of eyes followed his progress. The three men who had been with Abrahams the night Jamie was assaulted watched him from a car parked opposite the hospital gates. They had been told to wait there and report in if they saw "the Scotch bastard". Without a word the man seated in the back seat of the car opened his door and climbed out, heading for the hospital where he knew there was a bank of public phone boxes. The others stayed with the car, kept on watching Jamie, and were ready to follow if he moved off.

Passing close to the Austin the thug averted his face, afraid that Jamie might recognise him, and in doing so he didn't see the grim smile that appeared on Jamie's face. When he returned to the car minutes later after making his call, Jamie was still sitting in the car smoking a cigarette, but now the watchers were the watched.

The thug settled back into the car and the others turned to him expectantly. He smiled. 'We've to pick him up without fuss and take him out to Cyril's place. Max wants a word with him,' he grinned.

The others looked at him in amazement. Picking the Scotch git up hadn't been on the menu when they had set out earlier and the order to take him out to Cranston Hall was an even bigger surprise. But they knew better than to question an order from Max.

'The car park is quiet,' the driver of the car said quietly. 'We could do it now.'

'No fuss, the boss said,' the man in the back retorted.

'There won't be any. You're tooled up, aren't you?' It *wasn't* a question. They were all "tooled up". 'Do you think he'll create a fuss if he's looking down the barrel of a Beretta?' That *was* a question and both the other men in the car shook their heads in response. No one in their right mind would create a fuss in those circumstances.

Leaving Ted, the driver, the other two left the car and made their way across the road. Jamie watched them come. There was a certain swagger to them and it was clear that they didn't expect any trouble from him. So why give them any…just yet at least. *Welcome to my world, said the spider to the fly,* he thought, and smiled icily.

Jamie opened the car door as they approached and saw them hesitate, one of them sub-consciously reaching inside his jacket. He climbed out and flicked his cigarette stub away then waited for them, leaning casually against the Austin. 'What kept you?' he said with just a hint of insolence. The men looked at each other, uncertainty creeping in and their swagger slipping away. They hadn't expected trouble but Jamie's relaxed pose unsettled them. 'As we're in a public place, I'm presuming you're not intending wasting me,' he said easily. 'So what do you want?'

'The boss wants a word,' one of them said quickly. 'We're to take you to him.'

'Great,' Jamie smiled coldly. 'That saves me the trouble of looking for him.' He slammed the car door shut and locked it then started to walk past them towards their car, momentarily wrong footing them. 'What are you waiting for?' he called back over his shoulder and laughed as they hurried to catch up with him.

He walked quickly to the car, a Ford Cortina, and pulled open the back door, slipping into the back seat before either man had a chance to think. His calm demeanour settled them and they began to relax. They thought he was crazy. No one usually came to see Max Kelman without kicking and screaming but this guy actually seemed to be looking forward to it. As the car pulled away from the kerb Jamie dug out his cigarettes, flicked one from the packet and lit it then lowered the window and blew the smoke out into the slipstream.

The man sitting alongside him now in the back seat, the one who had done the talking, shook his head and laughed. 'You won't be so fucking relaxed when Max starts on you,' he grinned. Jamie smiled and the man started to laugh. 'Enjoy your fag, Jock, it might be your last,' he said finally and sank back into the seat.

Jamie drew in a lungful of smoke and let his eyes wander. The driver and the man in the front were talking easily and his companion in the back was resting his eyes. It was as if they had forgotten all about him already…he was just a package to be delivered and he hadn't caused any trouble. They were letting their guard down. Jamie continued smoking…and waited.

The car drove out of the city and into the countryside. They had been driving for about fifteen minutes, in a westerly direction Jamie reckoned, when the car finally began to slow. They were on a narrow country road now with no houses in sight. A high stone wall ran parallel with the road and about five yards back from the road edge. Up ahead, Jamie saw an access road off to the left and the wall was further back there. The driver swung left onto the access road and drove on about fifteen yards, stopping in front of double iron gates. There were trees and overgrown bushes on both sides of the roadway, a thick screen of vegetation which stretched all the way back to the perimeter wall.

The front passenger opened his door and levered himself out of the car and sauntered towards the gates. There was no urgency in his stride and Jamie watched and waited. All three men appeared to be totally relaxed, just the way he wanted them. The man now at the gates had his back to them when Jamie pulled his cigarette packet from his pocket once again, this time offering one to the man beside him. The man smiled and reached across and then his face contorted. Jamie had turned quickly, his right hand gripping the man's throat in a vice like grip while his left snaked inside the man's jacket and withdrew the gun from its shoulder holster. The man was gagging as Jamie crashed the butt of the gun into his temple and his resistance ceased immediately. Ted, the driver, caught unawares, started to turn and his hand moved automatically to his left armpit but the cold barrel of the Beretta, now in Jamie's hand, and pressed against the nape of his neck stopped him. 'Shhh-h,' Jamie whispered. 'Just keep both hands on the wheel and shut up and you'll be alright.'

The third man was walking back to the car in the failing light, completely unaware of what had taken place. Jamie tapped the barrel of the automatic against the driver's head. 'Don't try anything,' he warned, 'it isn't worth it.'

Ted swallowed hard and kept his hands on the steering wheel and his eyes focussed on the gates which were now swinging inwards. The third man pulled at the door and swung himself in. 'Right, let's go,' he said, turning to the driver and seeing Jamie, in his peripheral vision, grinning and laughing at him. He turned angrily, ready to shut Jamie up, then caught sight of his unconscious pal and the ugly nose of the automatic pointing directly between his eyes. Even in the half-light Jamie saw the colour drain from his face.

'Take out your weapon and pass it over…carefully. I don't want to shoot you but I will if I have to,' Jamie warned, waving the nose of the Beretta just enough to emphasise his threat.

'Shit!' The man cursed angrily and withdrew the weapon, passing it back over his shoulder without turning round. Jamie was silent as he pocketed the gun beside that of the driver. The men stared straight ahead, reluctant to look at him in case they provoked a reaction, and waited for the next step. They were already in deep shit no matter what happened now. Max Kelman would have their guts for garters for allowing this to happen…if they managed to stay alive long enough.

'Your boss wants to see me, you said,' Jamie said eventually. 'So why are we still sitting here at the gates. Drive.' The last word came out viciously and Ted jumped. Quickly, he slipped the Cortina into 1st gear and drove forward through the gates and as they passed through, the gates began to close automatically. Some sort of beam, infra-red, Jamie guessed. Ahead of him he could see lights on in the rooms of a large house and the façade was bathed by floodlights. The driveway was about 400 yards long, tree lined, with stob and wire fencing behind the trees and fields stretching beyond on both sides. The trees ended about thirty to forty yards short of the house and a manicured lawn filled the remaining space. Jamie let out a low whistle.

The car drew to a halt on a gravel forecourt in front of a wide stone stairway leading up to the front door. There was no one about but two other cars were parked haphazardly on the gravel. The gangsters were reluctant to move, fear of the man behind them with the gun and fear of Max Kelman's reaction to their bungling fighting a well-balanced battle in their heads.

'Time to go, boys,' Jamie laughed, opening his door. 'Out!' The two men climbed out sullenly, leaving the unconscious third man still sprawled on the back seat, and started to climb the stairs. 'Just remember that I've got all the guns,' Jamie reminded them. He followed them up the steps and waited behind them at the door. Ted, the driver, pulled brass handle and chimes could be heard tinkling in the interior. After a moment he pulled it again and the door was eventually opened by a disinterested middle aged woman sporting peroxide blonde hair and showing a cleavage that a Panzer Division could have hidden in. She might have been attractive once but she was now well past her "sell by date". She looked at them, saw Jamie behind the two men, and turned away into the house. 'He's waiting for you,' she called back over her shoulder and pointed to a door set into the left hand wall of the enormous hallway.

The house was enormous, Jamie noted, with a broad central stairway leading up to a landing above and two further flights of stairs, one at each end of the landing, rising to the second floor. It was expensively furnished and decorated even if the modern style didn't compliment the building itself. The woman disappeared up the stairway and Jamie followed the two men towards the door that she had indicated. The leading thug knocked and a voice, slightly higher pitched than Jamie expected, told them to enter. This should be fun, Jamie thought grimly, suddenly coming to terms with the fact that he had no escape route worked out.

Chapter 43

'Your boyfriend won't be much good to you now,' Kelman sneered, and grabbed Lucie by the neck. 'So you'd better get used to the idea.'

Lucie eyed him with contempt, her insides churning with abhorrence. She made no attempt to hide her feelings, saying nothing but letting her eyes tell him what she thought of him.

'You used to like me,' Kelman continued with a grin. 'So you can grow to like me again.' The way he said it, it wasn't a suggestion or a hopeful plea, it was an instruction.

'I used to like you when I thought you were a man...but you're not a man, you're an animal.' Lucie fired back defiantly.

Kelman kept the smile fixed on his face but he was seething. Didn't this silly bitch realise that he now controlled her destiny. She was his, whenever and wherever he wanted her. 'You're mine,' he said, trying to keep the anger from his voice. 'And I can have you whenever I want you, remember that,' he threatened.

Lucie returned his look coldly. 'Yes, you can take me, force me, whenever you want,' she said quietly, pausing to watch the look of triumph appear on his face. 'But you'll never *have* me, because I'll never give myself to you,' she declared, pleased with her small victory as Kelman's expression turned black again. 'Only one man has ever really *had* me...and he'll come for me, believe me.'

Kelman looked at her with fury filled eyes, tightening his grip on her neck. His fingers dug painfully into her skin and then threw her away from him, down onto the bed. 'I'll be back...I'll leave you to think about that,' he said menacingly; an evil smile playing across his features, and then he turned quickly and left the room.

Lucie heard the key turn in the lock and then the faint padding of Kelman's footsteps as he paced down the hall. He was whistling one of her favourite tunes, a song Jamie had sung to her sometimes when they danced to its music, but now it turned her blood to ice.

She looked around the room, seeing it properly for the first time. It was comfortably furnished. The bed she was on was a double, the sheets clean with an expensive quilt on top. There was a big wardrobe, solid wood, against the far wall. It looked new and expensive and there was a matching drawer unit, four high. She smiled grimly. There was no need for the wardrobe or the drawers as the only clothes she had were those she was wearing. The final items of furniture consisted of a dressing table with a mirror and a low oblong, velour covered stool.

There were two doors, one leading to the hallway and another set into the adjacent wall. She rose from the bed and tried the handle of this door. She expected to find it locked but the handle turned freely and the door opened inwards to reveal a bathroom. She found the light switch and turned on the light. There was a bath with an overhead shower, toilet and wash basin with towels and a selection of expensive toiletries laid out on a small vanity unit.

She turned off the light and returned to the bedroom, walking over to the window then. There was an expensive organza curtain covering the entire window and heavy satin drapes hung at each side. She looked down into the grounds which stretched into the distance towards the high stone boundary wall which surrounded the property. She had only been in the house once before, a fleeting visit, not long after going out with Max Kelman for the first time. It seemed like a lifetime ago. She tried the window and was surprised to find it opened easily but the room she was imprisoned in was on the second floor so escape via the window was out of the question.

She returned to the bed and lay down, staring up at the ceiling and thinking about Jamie. She wondered what he would do, never doubting for a minute that he would be trying to find her even now. But what could he do? Her spirits sank then. Max Kelman was surrounded by hard faced men who wouldn't think twice about killing Jamie. All it would take was a nod from Kelman. They had already beaten him badly, Tony Abrahams and another two, kicking and punching him until the crowd had descended on them.

Despair engulfed her. Being in Kelman's clutches filled her with dread and the horror of what he had done to her was still fresh in her mind even after two years. When she had met Jamie Raeburn she had pushed all of that from her mind and his love had healed her, but Kelman's return and his recent threats had brought it all back. What could she do, she wondered wretchedly?

Tears welled up in her eyes but she fought them back. Her fingers found the small gold cross on its chain around her neck, given to her by Jamie as a Wedding present. She had to be careful not to let Max know that she and Jamie were married…if he found that out she knew what would happen. She gripped the tiny cross tightly and prayed that somehow this nightmare would end.

*

Lucie didn't know how long she had been in the room. Sounds from outside filtered through to her; voices, laughter, and the sound of a car driving over the gravel driveway. Car doors banged, voices were shouting. Doors opened and doors closed below her, deep in the bowels of the house and the faint murmur of muted conversation filtered up to her. The room was darkening as the sun sank towards the horizon in the west. She lay still, unable to summon up the will to move. The house was silent again and then there were footsteps on the stairway and padding heavily along the landing before coming to a halt outside. A key turned in the lock and the door swung open to reveal the substantial frame of Tony Abrahams, his face wreathed in a cold smile.

'Come on, you're wanted,' Abrahams said with a smile which, to her surprise, she found was surprisingly gentle. 'The boss has a little surprise for you.'

Lucie looked at him with contempt. The expression on his face told her it wasn't a pleasant surprise. She wished Jamie was with her. 'You can tell him to keep his surprise,' she said defiantly.

His smile grew colder then. 'Don't be an ungrateful little tart. You'll like this surprise,' he lied easily. 'Come on, get a move on!' he instructed and stepped threateningly into the room.

Lucie rose to her feet wearily and started to move, wanting now to get whatever it was that Max Kelman had waiting for her over and done with. Abrahams moved aside to let her pass and she could smell his body cologne but behind it there was a faint manly musk. Some women might actually find him attractive, she thought abstractedly, but to her he was simply a thug and no amount of cologne could cover the obnoxious smell of his chosen "profession". It hung around him, clung to him, like a shroud.

Once out into the long hallway, Lucie could hear faint traces of conversations once more, muffled voices, faint sounds of apparent normality, a woman's shrill laugh, but nothing in this house could be normal, she thought. Abrahams followed her along the hall and down the thick carpeted stairway, like a sheepdog herding an errant ewe, and she could feel his presence. Lucie refused to look at him. She stared ahead and made her way down the stairway to the floor below and then, on a gentle prod from Abrahams' hand, down to the ground floor. The voices were louder now and there was cold laughter. She suddenly felt it; the certainty, because that's what it was, came to her gently at first, stirring her senses, then grew steadily until it crashed over her. Jamie was here! Her heart pounded in her chest as Abrahams smiled and leaned past her to open a door. With a gentle push, he guided her into the room.

She saw Max Kelman first. There was a cold, strained smile on his face and Lucie felt a surge of hope. He was sitting in his leather chair behind his desk and he didn't appear to be enjoying the moment. Lucie's eyes quickly scanned the rest of the room. There were two other men in the room that she could see, both of them standing with their backs to the wall to the right of Max Kelman's desk and both looking distinctly uncomfortable.

She sensed rather than saw Jamie. Abrahams was behind her and she turned, confused, Jamie stepped out from behind the bigger man and took her gently by the arm. Her head swam and she felt as if she was about to pass out, her body swayed and then Jamie's arm was around her, supporting her.

She was disorientated, confused and bewildered. What was happening? How had Jamie managed to get here and, more puzzling still, why did she sense that he was controlling the situation? She felt him guide her to a chair and lower her onto it and then he was kneeling beside her. He was smiling but it wasn't the smile she knew and his eyes remained fixed on Tony Abrahams who was waiting just inside the door.

'Are you alright?' Jamie asked softly and she could hear his concern. 'Has he hurt you?'

Lucie's eyes welled up with tears but she shook her head. 'No, he hasn't hurt me,' she whispered. Everything was so surreal, and then Max's voice broke into the dream.

'This is very touching...the star struck lovers...Romeo and Juliet,' he said, heavy with sarcasm. 'But it isn't going to get you anywhere, Jock. You might have three aces in your hand but I've got a full house, and that beats you every time...and you know what happened to Romeo.'

Lucie looked at Kelman; the cold smile was still there and the confidence that had been missing when she entered the room was re-establishing itself. She felt Jamie straighten beside her and her eyes moved to him. She still didn't understand...until she saw the gun clasped loosely in his right hand.

'We're leaving,' he said quietly and Lucie felt his hand under her arm, gently lifting her from the chair.

Kelman laughed but his eyes were colder, calculating. 'And where are you going to go, eh?' he grinned. The confidence and the old Max Kelman were back and Lucie shuddered. 'Sure, you can leave, but you can't hide. I'll find you and...'

'Not if you're dead you won't,' Jamie interrupted, raising the pistol.

Max Kelman smiled again. It was bizarre, Lucie thought, it was almost as if he was enjoying this. 'You've never met my father,' he came back. 'Lucie here doesn't think much of me...I'm evil, she thinks. She's never had the pleasure of meeting him either, come to think of it, but if you kill me you'll meet him alright. You're a dead man walking Jock,' he laughed viciously. Lucie sank back into the chair, her shoulders heaving as she began to sob. 'Now look what you've done,' Kelman laughed. 'You've upset her.'

The mood in the room was changing. Jamie's control of the situation was slipping and Lucie could sense it. He was tense but, strangely, he still didn't seem to be afraid and that was something that Max Kelman and Tony Abrahams had spotted also.

'So, what are we going to do to get out of this impasse?' Max said and stood up from his desk, wandering round to the front and settling his buttocks on the edge. 'I suppose we could stay like this all night…starve you into submission,' he laughed. 'But Cyril will be home soon and he doesn't like his evenings disrupted.'

He *was* enjoying this, Lucie realised, but then he knows he has won. There was no way out for either of them. She and Jamie had lost.

Max looked over at the two men standing against the wall and their eyes swerved away from him. You could almost feel the fear radiating out from them and Max Kelman's cold eyes gave them an insight into their immediate future. 'Tony, you stay…and you two useless arseholes get out of my sight,' he ordered. The two men avoided his eyes and scurried for the door, almost tripping over each other in their haste. 'Where the fuck did you find them, Tony?' he said with exasperation, shaking his head from side to side.

He waited until the door closed and shuffled his bottom on the edge of the desk, making himself comfortable. Tony Abrahams hovered by the door. He was armed but the Scotch kid had a Beretta already in his hand and Tony didn't fancy his chances. In any event, he realised, Max had something in mind. Whatever it was though it would need to be good because this boy was something else. Even in his present predicament he was showing no signs of fear. Tony Abrahams had seen men here before, shaking in their shoes, willing to agree to anything just to stay alive. This one though, was dangerous. Tony Abrahams could tell, just like any predator can spot another.

Max Kelman started to speak again. 'The way I see it Jock, you're a problem I can well do without. Normally, I'd just have Tony and the boys take you outside and put you to sleep…give you a nice little bed in the woods over there,' he laughed harshly. He was waiting for a reaction but Jamie simply raised the Beretta tellingly and let his eyes rest on it. Lucie shuddered and began to sob but Jamie simply stared back at him disdainfully and a shadow of annoyance passed over Max's face.

Tony Abrahams smiled to himself and tried to hide his admiration for the Scots lad. His earlier thoughts had been confirmed. If Max lets this boy live it will be at his peril, he mused, secretly hoping that might come to pass.

'But if I do that, I'll upset my bride to be,' Max continued, attempting to needle Jamie again. 'And we don't want that, do we?' Again, the jibe was intended to elicit a reaction but still Jamie took no notice. It was as if he knew how all of this was going to play out. 'So, I've decided to be generous…and I'm going to let Lucie here decide what happens.' As he said it, he held out his hand towards Tony Abrahams and gave his fingers a flick. Abrahams, without any need for further elucidation, walked towards him and withdrew his automatic pistol from its holster beneath his left armpit, handing it over. The boy didn't shoot and Abrahams realised that it was simply fear for Lucie's safety that had stopped him. Max had guessed correctly.

Kelman smiled sadistically. 'See, that's the difference between us Jock. I would have fired but you were scared the little lady here would get hurt. And now we're even,' he grinned, hefting the automatic in his hand. He settled back on the edge of the desk as Abrahams sidled back to block the doorway. 'So here's the deal. Lucie here stays with me and you live…simple really.'

'No deal,' Jamie said steadily, his eyes still on Kelman.

'Ah, but it's not your decision, Jock. I told you…it's up to Lucie. She has the power to keep you alive, not you.'

'No,' Jamie repeated, but he sensed the tide turning. He was scared to look at her.

Kelman ignored him, turning his attention to Lucie. 'What's it to be, love?'

Jamie turned towards her, his eyes imploring her to throw Kelman's suggestion back in his face, but he knew the way her mind would be working. Max still didn't know they were married so she still had a way out of this and by agreeing she could buy time. But he knew it was more than that…her biggest fear was that Kelman would kill him and she would agree to anything to prevent that.

She smiled up at Jamie sadly. 'I love you,' she mouthed silently. 'Forgive me.' Turning to face Max Kelman she gave him a look of utter contempt but it washed over him, like water off a duck's back. But still she didn't answer Kelman's prompt.

Max was growing impatient, and it showed. The veneer of reasonableness was wearing thin and he couldn't resist a final dig. 'Lucie, as you've probably guessed, is reluctant to go through with my little plan. Obviously she needs an incentive. I've been reasonable up till now but I'm running out of patience,' he said sneeringly. It was a case of heads I win, tails you lose as far as he was concerned but he still needed to exert his authority. Slowly, he raised his arm and pointed the muzzle of the pistol at Jamie's head.

Jamie stared at him, implacably, and Max grew angry. *You'd better kill me now, Jamie thought, because if you don't, there will be a reckoning…and I'll kill you.* The thought surprised him because it was more than a thought, it was a commitment. He *would* do it. What was happening to him? He let his eyes drift to Tony Abrahams and caught his expression, a faint smile in his eyes hidden from Max Kelman. He knows what I'm thinking, Jamie smiled inwardly.

There was a click and the automatic in Kelman's hand was ready to fire. He turned to face Lucie, a maniacal grin on his now flushed face. 'So here it is, the best incentive ever…either you agree to marry me or I blow this Scotch cunt's brains out right now. Make your mind up, girl.'

'Don't do it Lucie,' Jamie said quietly and the force of his words struck her like a sledgehammer. She was torn…but it wasn't as simple as just saying "no". She saw Max's finger tighten on the trigger. 'Stop!' she cried out, springing from her chair and throwing herself between them, in Max's line of fire. 'I'll do it…I'll marry you; I'll do anything you want, but don't kill him, please don't kill him.' She screamed the words out, sobbing now, almost on the verge of hysteria.

'There you go, Jock,' Kelman grinned triumphantly. 'The little lady's just saved your fucking life. You should be grateful. Say thank you.'

'Fuck off!' Jamie retorted angrily and Kelman gloated sneeringly while Lucie just looked at him imploringly. He smiled and leaned forward, kissing her gently.

'Atta boy,' Max sneered. 'Give the bride to be a kiss.'

Lucie saw Jamie smile bleakly at her and her sobbing intensified. 'I'm sorry, baby, I'm sorry,' she sobbed. 'I can't let him kill you. If he did, I'd have nothing to live for.' She pressed her head close to his and felt the heat of his breath in her ear.

'I'll be back for you, I promise,' he whispered.

Kelman took hold of her arm and pulled her away. 'Very touching,' he sneered. 'But a bargain is a bargain. It's time for you to go,' he continued, giving Jamie a long hard stare.

'If you hurt her...' Jamie said in a cold, steady voice.

'Yeah, yeah, yeah,' Kelman smirked, cutting him off. 'You'll come back and sort me out. Oooh, I'm frightened,' he carried on scornfully. 'Tell you what, she can write to you every day and let you know what a great time we're having...even tell you *everything* we're up to on our honeymoon. Will that make you happy? No? Ah well, you can't please all of the people all of the time.' He was mocking Jamie, baiting him, hoping he would rise to it but Jamie maintained a contemptuous silence. Seeing his efforts fall on stony ground he soon tired of the game. He returned to his desk and dropped the pistol. 'Ted, Terry,' he shouted, 'get your sorry arses back in here.' He was impatient now and wanted Jamie out of his sight. The door opened and the two men he had dismissed earlier slunk back in, their eyes darting nervously from Kelman to Abrahams then back to Kelman. Kelman didn't notice it but Jamie caught the look both men gave Abrahams. Kelman might be the boss's son but Abrahams was the man who had their loyalty. 'Take the lady back up to her room,' Kelman instructed, dismissing them again.

Jamie saw Abrahams nod imperceptibly and smiled inwardly. *There's no love lost between these guys*, he thought. But at that moment it made no difference to him. Lucie was alive, that was all that mattered, and he would get her back, no matter how long it took. As Ted and Terry escorted Lucie from the room she turned back and Jamie smiled, letting her know that nothing had changed. He still loved her.

Kelman turned to Abrahams. 'Take this bastard back into Derby and drop him where he was picked up,' he instructed. He swung round then, addressing Jamie. 'You've got 24 hours to get out of Derby. If you're still here this time tomorrow then it's open season on Jocks.'

Jamie laughed quietly, refusing to be intimidated. 'You've been watching too many Cowboy films,' he grinned coldly. Kelman's face flushed angrily. He was unsettled and it was showing. He had tried everything to rile this Scotch fucker and still the git looked back at him as if he didn't give a shit. He smiled grimly. He had made his promise to let the bastard live so he'd stick with it...for the moment. But what he hadn't said to Lucie was that it was a limited time offer, and accidents happen.

Tony Abrahams waited by the door as Jamie turned towards it and then, abruptly, stopped. He pulled the first of the two Berettas from his pocket with his left hand and both Kelman and Abrahams panicked. Jamie's icy laugh followed. He tossed the pistol onto Kelman's desk, scratching the veneer, and then withdrew the second, repeating the process. 'I'll keep this one until I'm back in Derby and then I'll give it to your boy here,' he said, raising the third pistol in his hand, grinning as drops of cold sweat gathered on Kelman's brow.

Abrahams was a different animal altogether. Kelman was brash, Abrahams was shrewd. When Jamie had told Max he would come back if he hurt the girl, Max had laughed it off, but Tony Abrahams had noted the look in Jamie's eyes. When the Jock said he'd be back, he meant it...every single word.

Jamie walked with Abrahams to the car that had brought him here, taking in the house and the gardens, the long tree lined driveway, the security lights. He looked up at the windows, hoping for a sight of Lucie, but all of the upper floor windows were in now in darkness. Abrahams opened the back door and ushered Jamie inside, following him and settling into the leather seat beside him.

'Can I smoke?' Jamie asked, startling the big man with his apparent lack of concern and the simplicity of the request.

'Yeah, why not,' Abrahams grinned coldly. 'You're quite a piece,' he continued, and for the first time Jamie detected admiration in the big man's voice.

Jamie pulled the battered pack of Lucky Strikes from his trouser pocket and flicked one out then offered the pack to the Abrahams, throwing him off balance yet again. Abrahams took one and dug out his lighter, offering the flame to Jamie first. They inhaled the toasted tobacco while they waited for their driver and Abrahams broke the silence. 'Don't come back, Jock,' he offered. 'If you do, I'll probably have to kill you…and I don't really want to do that.'

'I can't do that,' Jamie replied, closing his eyes and blowing a plume of smoke from his mouth.

'No, I didn't think so,' the big man laughed. 'But if I were you I'd take myself back to Scotland…and I'd watch my back…every day from now on.'

Jamie opened his eyes and looked at him. Abrahams was looking straight ahead. He drew casually on his cigarette and gave nothing more away. The arrival of Ted heralded their departure. The man looked at Jamie warily as he slid into his seat, still smarting from the embarrassment of having been disarmed by Jamie earlier, and then looked at Abrahams, waiting for instructions.

'We're dropping him back at the hospital where you picked him up,' Abrahams told him. 'Then you can leave me the car and you're finished for the night.' Ted looked fleetingly at Jamie and Abrahams caught it. He laughed coldly. 'Don't worry…you'll get your piece back tomorrow.'

Ted nodded and turned the key in the ignition. The engine sprang to life and the car began to glide forward, crunching over the gravel. Jamie opened his eyes, casually scanning the surroundings, trying to memorise everything that might be important later. The car pulled up about ten feet in front of the big iron gates and Sid slid out, making his way to the switch on the left hand stone column. His hand drifted swiftly over the keys and the gate began to swing towards them. By the time he had resumed his place behind the steering wheel the gates were fully open. He slipped the car into gear and drove through the gates down towards the main road and turned right towards Derby.

*

Lucie had been taken back to the room on the second floor and left there, sobbing in the darkness; the only vestige of comfort left to her then was the certain knowledge she had saved Jamie's life. That was all that mattered to her. And he would come back for her; he had said it…he wouldn't leave her…but that was cold comfort. She heard the car leave and ran to the window but the tail lights were already disappearing in the distance, far down the long drive. She suddenly felt very alone.

Footsteps approached along the hall, voices, two men talking, and then the key was turned in the lock and the door swung open. Her heart stopped. Light from the hallway spilled into the room and she screwed her eyes tightly shut against the sudden glare. When she opened her eyes again two of the gang, men she hadn't seen before, were in the room. One of them was holding a tray laden with food which he placed on top of the chest of drawers. They said nothing but grinned salaciously at her, revelling in her discomfort. They stood for a minute watching her, their presence intentionally intimidating, and then they turned and left.

With the closing of the door the room was once again in semi-darkness with only the meagre light from the late evening sky giving any illumination. Lucie looked at the food but she had no appetite despite having last eaten at lunch time, almost eight hours earlier. Appetite or not, she knew she should keep up her strength and made her way over to the chest of drawers to survey what was on offer. There was bread, three different cheeses, a green salad with some form of dressing, and a selection of cold meats and chicken. An apple, a bottle of still water, a flask of coffee and a cup finished the offering. She smiled bitterly when she picked up the plastic knife and fork...obviously not trusted with anything that could be used as a weapon or to escape. She lifted the tray and carried it over to the dressing table and sat down on the stool, starting to pick at the food in the semi-darkness, absorbed by her misery and her anxiety. Finally drained, the tears came and her body was racked by endless sobs. Leaving the food she returned to the bed and removed her uniform before slipping beneath the sheets in her bra, pants and underskirt. Her sobbing continued until finally, exhausted by the events of the day she fell into a troubled sleep.

Kelman came for her in the early hours. She struggled awake at the sound of him entering the room and the distinctive smell of his aftershave told her it was him. She pulled the quilt around her and began to scream but a blow across her cheek with the back of his hand silenced her. She felt his weight on her and smelled the alcohol and tobacco on his breath as he tried to kiss her. He pulled at the quilt and her clothes, ripping away her underskirt and tearing her pants from her in his frenzy. Her hands flew to his face and she raked her nails down his cheek, hearing him grunt, and then his fist hit her on the side of the face and blackness enveloped her. Dazed, she slumped back onto the bed and felt his hands on her and his knee pressed between her thighs. She closed her eyes and prayed that it would soon be over. The rape was violent but mercifully quick and she thanked God that Kelman had neither the stamina nor the control that Jamie had. He rose from her, grinning maniacally, and pulled up his trousers then hovered over her as if expecting some form of retort but she lay still, staring blankly at the ceiling. Eventually, he left her, his elation and domination of her dulled by her lack of reaction, and padded off down the hallway leaving her alone in the darkness.

Lucie listened to his footsteps receding down the hall and then on the stairs, she heard a door open and faint music drift up from the floor below then faint conversation and laughter. Confident that he would not return she rose painfully from the bed and made her way into the en suite bathroom. She turned on the light and climbed into the bath and turning up the heat control to as hot as her body could bear she switched on the shower and stood beneath its spray for twenty minutes washing and scrubbing herself vigorously to remove every vestige of Kelman from her. Finally satisfied that she was clean she turned off the water and stepped out, looking at herself in the mirror fixed above the wash hand basin. Her left eye was bloodshot and there were bruises on her cheeks and at the tops of her thighs where Kelman had forced his knees against her to open her to him. Her vulva too was painful but worse than everything else was the shame. The tears came again then and she cried, not for herself now, but for failing the man she loved.

Returning to the bed she pulled off the blood flecked and semen stained sheet which covered the mattress and threw it into the corner of the room next to the wardrobe. She stripped back the top sheet to replace it and finally lay down, pulling the heavy quilt tightly around her once again. She doubted if Max would come back that night but lying there, alone and ashamed, she vowed that she would never let him do that to her again. She would rather die...and if she were dead then his plan to get his hands on her inheritance would die with her. That, and her belief that Jamie would return for her, were the only sources of solace she had left and she clung to both as she fell into an exhausted and fitful sleep.

Chapter 44

The car ride back into Derby was concluded in silence. Abrahams sat with his eyes closed but Jamie knew that the man was fully alert. The driver manoeuvred the car into the hospital car park and came to a halt next to Brian Bradley's little Austin. Jamie flicked open the door and made to exit only to be stopped by Tony Abrahams' big hand on his arm. He turned towards the man, a questioning look in his eyes.

'Just remember what I said Jock, don't come back...and watch your back,' Abrahams said softly.

Jamie smiled grimly and released his arm from the man's grip. 'Like I said, I can't do that,' he replied. 'An' my name's not Jock, its Jamie Raeburn...remember it.' He stepped out of the car and turned to watch as the two men drove off. The last thing he saw of Tony Abrahams was his grin.

When the Ford had finally disappeared from sight he made his way into the hospital and found a free telephone kiosk in the main hall. It had been more than two hours since he had been picked up by Kelman's men and almost three since he had last spoken to Jo Bradley so he knew she would be frantic by now. His call was answered immediately.

'Jamie?' Jo's anxious voice roared down the line. 'Thank God! Where have you been? You promised to phone every hour...we've been frantic here,' she continued, her voice exhibiting her frayed nerves.

'Sorry Jo, but I didn't think Kelman would appreciate me askin' to use his phone,' Jamie answered her wryly.

'Kelman?' Jo almost screamed. 'God Jamie, how on earth...'

'Another long story Jo...short version is that he does have Lucie. She's alright...and I'm alright. I'll tell you everything when I get back...about twenty minutes,' he said and hung up before she could respond.

*

'So that's it,' Jamie said, finishing his account of what had taken place at Cranston Hall. 'He's given me 24 hours to get out of town or he'll set the dogs on me.'

Brian, Jo and Julie Bradley looked at him with open concern. From what they now knew of him, acceding to Kelman's threat wouldn't be something he would easily accept.

'What are you going to do?' Brian asked. 'You're not thinking of staying and taking him on, are you? That would be madness!'

Jamie laughed caustically. 'I've thought about it...but even I'm not *that* crazy. No, I'll go back to Glasgow,' he said quietly, watching some form of relief spread over Jo's and Brian's faces, but Julie sat quietly, her tear stained face white with worry. 'But I'll be back,' he added after a heartbeat, 'when the bastard least expects it.'

Brian Bradley shook his head slowly and Jo looked at him despairingly. 'What can you do on your own, Jamie?' Jo whispered realistically, she thought. 'The last thing Lucie needs is for you to be killed.'

'Jo's right,' Brian chipped in, 'think about Lucie.'

'I *am* thinking about Lucie,' he threw back at them. 'I told her I would come back for her...and I will.' He paused, holding them all with his gaze. 'She trusts me, she'll be waiting for me...and I'm not going to let her down.'

'He's right Mum,' Julie interjected quietly. 'Lucie will expect him to come for her....and that thought alone will keep her going.' Everyone turned towards her and Jamie reached out. She took his hand and smiled bleakly, nodding her understanding of his thoughts.

Jo rose from her chair then and came to him, wrapping her arms in an almost motherly fashion around his shoulders. She felt him shudder and was stunned to find he was crying softly against her. In her eyes he was still little more than a boy but, strangely, his tears made him seem even more of a man. Only a man can weep without shame, she thought, and hugged him tighter.

Brian too was overcome by the emotion flooding out of Jamie. 'Whatever help you need we'll give it,' he said softly. 'Lucie means a lot to all of us too.'

Jamie wiped his eyes with his hand and smiled. 'Thanks, Brian...Jo,' he replied quietly and moved across to enfold Julie in a hug. She sank against him, weeping inconsolably. 'Just get me to the station tomorrow morning for the Glasgow train...then leave it to me. I don't want Kelman to involve you in this...any of you. Let me handle it...if I need help I know where I can get it, don't worry.' He released Julie then returned to Jo, kissing her softly on the cheek. 'Don't worry,' he repeated.

*

Just before nine o'clock the following morning Jo Bradley dropped Jamie outside Nottingham Railway Station. Before getting out of the car he leant across and kissed her on the cheek. 'If you get any chance at all to talk to Lucie tell her that we've spoken and that I'll be back as soon as I can,' he pleaded.

Jo smiled sadly. 'You know I will,' she replied. 'But I doubt if we'll get anywhere near her. Let us know when you're coming. We'll be waiting.'

Jamie shook his head determinedly. 'No, Jo, it can't work like that. I don't want you involved. When I come back I don't want anyone to know...it's best that way.' Jo smiled forlornly and nodded her head. 'Go home now,' Jamie continued, 'and the next time you see me I'll have Lucie with me. He kissed her again and stepped from the car. As he lifted his bag from the back seat he gave her a brave smile then walked into the station without looking back.

As he walked down the platform to the waiting Glasgow train, a small weasel faced man in a black leather jacket and blue jeans watched his progress. Jamie had spotted him as he walked into the station. He had been at Kelman's place the night before but hadn't been directly involved with Jamie but that didn't matter. What did matter was that Kelman, true to his word, was making sure that Jamie didn't stay around. He smiled dourly. He would get even with Kelman. He didn't know yet how he would manage that but he promised himself that he would...sooner rather than later.

When the outgoing train pulled away from the platform the weasel faced man sauntered to a phone booth on the concourse and fed a sixpence into the slot. He dialled the number that was imprinted on his mind and when Max Kelman answered he pressed Button A. The little silver coin dropped into the coin box and the call was connected. 'He's gone boss,' weasel face reported. 'The ten past nine train for Glasgow.' All the sharp featured little man heard from the other end of the line was a cruel laugh and then it was dead.

Part III

End Game

"Being deeply loved by someone gives you strength, while loving someone deeply gives you courage."
Lao Tzu (The Father of Taoism)

Chapter 45

The train journey was slow and tedious despite the fact that it was a limited stop express train and not the "Pennine Crawler" that zigzagged across the country, stopping at just about every town and village that boasted a station. Jamie was despondent, filled with a mixture of anger and misery, thoughts of revenge and plans on how to fulfil them. His night had been turbulent and sleep had evaded him but even now, exhausted as he was, he failed to find it. He chain smoked. The carriage was virtually empty, the only other passenger being an elderly man making the journey north to visit relatives in Aberdeen. He had tried to engage Jamie in conversation, joking that this might be his last opportunity to travel as age was catching up with him, but he quickly caught Jamie's mood and lapsed into silence, settling instead for the comfort of his pipe. The combination of the old man's pipe and Jamie's Lucky Strikes filled the carriage with a pall of smoke that deterred anyone else from entering and they passed the journey in relative peace.

The countryside seemed to drift past; green fields delineated by fences or stone dykes, herds of cows and the little white dots of sheep on the gently sloping hills. Stone farm houses, remote from civilisation, stood out on the landscape as stark reminders of man's constant battle to tame nature, and thin columns of white smoke rose into the still air above them. To Jamie, it was like studying a painting by John Constable, though his tended to be less austere. Apart from the smoke rising from remote chimneys into the leaden grey sky, there was no sign of human activity and he felt his isolation grow.

Towns and villages flashed past and the train screamed through the small stations with a noise like wind in a tunnel, shaking signs and making the buildings close by tremble as though shaken by the hand of God. Soon, they had passed out of The Midlands and were racing through the Red Rose County of Lancashire, stopping to disgorge some passengers and uplift others in Lancaster, and then on towards Cumbria and Carlisle.

The scenery changed subtly. The soft, rolling hills of middle-England became the steeper and higher crags of the Lake District and then they were slowing as the locomotive approached Carlisle. Another stop, more banging of carriage doors, shouting and laughter as people came and went. Faces appeared at the compartment door but the clouds of smoke enveloping the two wraiths inside frightened off even the stoutest of hearts.

The remainder of the journey, for Jamie at least, passed in a flash. In around two hours he would be sitting in front of the fire in his parents' house in Glasgow being subjected to a barrage of questions by his mother. *What the hell do I tell her*, he asked himself? The truth would scare her to death and, in any event, it sounded so far-fetched it would be unbelievable. There would be the inevitable questions about Lucie; what was she like, what did she do, why wasn't she with him, what was her family like? And then there would be the comparisons with Kate. His mother still thought fondly of Kate and comparison with Lucie was inevitable. He prayed that when she eventually did meet Lucie she would accept her in the same way as she had

Kate. She would have to, he told himself, Lucie was his wife after all...but he'd keep that to himself meantime.

The train pulled into Glasgow Central at a quarter to two in the afternoon, five minutes early. It had started to rain as they passed Carstairs Junction and the sky was a dark foreboding grey as they trundled over the Clyde and came to a halt in billowing clouds of steam, the locomotive resting like an exhausted dragon.

Jamie helped the old man transfer his luggage onto the platform and walked with him down to the ticket gate and the main hall as rain battered onto the glass roof high above. Home, the dear grey place, Jamie smiled grimly. The old man was heading off for Queen Street Station and his connecting train to Aberdeen. Jamie had decided on a fortifying pint in the Horseshoe Bar in Drury Lane just round from the station before heading for home. A pint of Guinness would help him finalise his story for his inquisitive mother. He shook hands with the old gentleman outside the pub and his travelling companion, with incredible insight, wished him luck with whatever it was that was troubling him. Jamie smiled and thanked him, but it was more than luck he needed...and he knew it.

Settled by the pint of Guinness, Jamie made his way up to St Vincent Street and waited for a Number 9 bus to carry him home. But where was home now, he ruminated? Probably not here, he decided. He loved the place, was proud to say he was a Glaswegian, but he didn't feel at home here now...there was nothing for him here. Maybe all that would change again when he was settled back in his mother's house, but he doubted it. So much had changed. He had changed. He was still changing...and new gates were opening before him all the time.

His arrival at the house in Lincoln Avenue was less stressful than he had anticipated. He put it down to the fact that he had turned up unannounced and his mother hadn't had an opportunity to prepare a list of questions for the interrogation process. That would come later. It was inescapable...as night follows day, so his mother's questions would follow his arrival home.

His bedroom was just as he had left it. It was as if his mother kept it as a shrine to his memory when he wasn't there. He could imagine her coming here every day and tidying things that didn't need tidying, just to have the sense of being close to him and to convince herself that she hadn't lost him. What she didn't realise was that she would always be close to him and she would never lose him. But perhaps that was the disadvantage of having only one child, he thought, all your eggs were in one basket.

Immediately after dinner that night Jamie pleaded exhaustion, and the drawn lines on his face and the heavy dark circles around his eyes reinforced his plea. Questions could wait. Tomorrow was another day, his mother decided...and it was Saturday tomorrow, she would have all weekend to find out what he had been up to. Jamie climbed wearily up the stairs to his room and kicked off his boots. He lay down on top of the bed, fully clothed, and pulled the heavy quilt around him. Within minutes he was asleep.

Chapter 46

Jamie weathered the weekend. The questions had come, as expected, but he had stuck to his game plan and fielded them with relative ease. The photograph he carried of Lucie looking happily at him had silenced the questions about what she was like and the news that she, like Kate, was a nurse and had to work, was the perfect excuse for her not being with him. But yes, she was dying to meet them and he would bring her with him the next time he came home…God willing, he thought wryly.

He had telephone Jack on Saturday morning and had discovered that he was going out with Teresa that evening and again the following night so the romance was obviously blossoming once again. They made arrangements to meet on the Monday evening at The Byre Pub at the corner of Byres Road and Highburgh Road and now, here he was, strolling down Byres road to the rendezvous, wondering how he would break his news to Jack.

Preoccupied as he was, he failed to notice the short, skinny lad in a Parka and tight blue jeans following him. Nor had he spotted the same lad lurking near the house in Lincoln Avenue for most of Monday and getting on the 20 bus behind him on his journey into town.

When Jamie entered the pub the youth hung back then crossed the road to a bank of red public telephone boxes where he could phone *and* keep an eye on the pub door. Keeping one eye on the pub he slotted coins into the box and dialled a number on the South side of the city. The call was answered almost immediately, the faint sound of a radio programme echoing in the background. 'He's gone intae the Byre Bar in Byres Road,' he reported, without preamble. 'Been in there aboot five minutes. He's wearin' a light tan leather jacket an' a per o' Levi jeans, looks the business.'

'Keep watchin' him,' the voice at the other end of the line ordered. 'We'll be there in aboot twenty minutes. If he comes oot again, phone here an' follae him. Goat it?'

'Aye, right Bobby, nae problem.'

The phone was cut off and in a flat in Kinning Park, Robert Hood, loan shark enforcer and journeyman hard case, beckoned to his two companions and headed for the door. This could prove to be the easiest four hundred and fifty quid he had every made in his life. Even after paying off his henchmen and the wee gnaff who was following the target, and the boss who had got him the job, he'd still have around £300 to himself. With that he could get any bird he wanted…maybe even two. He grinned in anticipation and led the charge down the stairs to the car waiting below.

*

'So, that's all my news,' Jack finished happily. 'Bit o' a shock wiz it?' he chirped.

Jamie smiled despite his melancholy, genuinely pleased for his friend. 'No, it wasn't a shock pal…I expected it sooner or later,' he replied. 'Every bird you picked up down south…with the notable exception of Julie, was a wee clone of Teresa,' Jamie continued with a laugh, but he couldn't disguise the pain behind it.

'Ah didnae expect tae see ye up here fur a while yet, Jamie boy,' Jack continued. 'Whit's the occasion?' he said, looking carefully at Jamie over the rim of his glass, 'an' why is Lucie no wi' ye?' he continued, taking another gulp of Guinness.

Jamie had arrived first, ordered two pints of Guinness in anticipation of Jack's imminent arrival and had then settled into a seat away from the door and waited. He knew Jack surprised to hear he was in Glasgow and his request to meet as soon as possible had piqued Jack's curiosity.

In fact, Jack had been thinking about the call ever since. There had been something in Jamie's voice that suggested his return to Glasgow wasn't entirely for social reasons or for old time's sake. There was an edge to his voice that spoke of bad news but perhaps his own news, and the request he was going to make, would cheer Jamie up.

They had chosen this pub because it was relatively easy for both of them to get to without travelling into the centre of the city and they had drunk together in The Byre before. It was a man's pub, all heavy wood and brass fittings and a solid wooden floor, but it was a bit more upmarket than the pubs in Partick and down along Dumbarton Road.

Jack arrived just as Jamie was taking his first sip of the heavy, black liquid. Almost like drinking liquid tar, he always thought. They spied each other immediately and Jack hurried over, Jamie rising from his seat to greet him. They clasped each other, like long lost brothers, patting each other on the back, neither of them aware of the drama that was going to unfold and engulf them.

Jamie laughed quietly as they separated and sat down. 'I'm sure you were watchin' from across the road an' waitin' till I got the bevvies in ya wee bugger,' he teased, trying to keep it light.

'Don't ah always,' Jack replied. 'Christ, it's good tae see ye again big man…and huv ah got news fur you!' He watched Jamie's reaction, seeing a smile but seeing also the pain behind it. Whatever was bothering Jamie it didn't look good. 'Ah need ye tae dae somethin' fur me,' he said quickly, eager to let Jamie into his secret. 'It's really important…an' ah hope ye can help me out.' He was playing it out, trying to draw Jamie from his shell, conscious of the weight he seemed to be carrying.

Jamie eyed him affectionately. Jack was the best pal he had ever had and he'd do anything for him, just in the same way he hoped Jack would for him when he learned of the nightmare that enveloped him. Meantime, he played the game. 'Well, if it's money ye're after, I've got none and if you're wantin' me out on a foursome with one of Teresa's wee mates, you can forget it,' he laughed.

'Nah, it's no money…an' ah don't need tae go oot in a foursome noo,' Jack replied. 'Though ye will need plenty o' cash tae get me legless on ma stag night,' he laughed and waited to see how quickly Jamie would pick up on it. The reaction was slow, Jack noted, another indication that Jamie had something serious on his mind. But at least he appeared to be genuinely happy, a warm smile changing his features.

Jack proceeded to tell him everything that had happened since he had returned home; meeting with Teresa again, making up with her, telling her he had missed her and that he loved her and finally asking her to marry him. Teresa, as Jamie had always known, was the only girl for Jack Connelly.

And now it was Jamie's turn and something told Jack that he wasn't going to like what he was about to hear. But they had been inseparable for years, as close as two friends could be, and if the big man needed help then he would stand by him. 'So, come on,' he started, 'spill the beans, whit's up?'

Jamie sank about half his glass of Guinness and Jack watched as a myriad of emotions spread across his friends face. 'It's Lucie,' Jamie responded quietly, his face finally collapsing in despair.

'Whit the fuck's happened?' Jack demanded urgently. Instinctively, he knew they hadn't broken up; the despair on Jamie's face was rooted in something else entirely...and apart from that, he had experienced Jamie being "dumped" before...twice. No, that wasn't fair, he chided himself, Kate hadn't "dumped" him. They had been victims of circumstance. 'Is Lucie ill?' he asked, his concern growing. 'She's no' pregnant, is she?' Jamie shook his head sadly. *So she's not ill and she's not pregnant,* Jack ruminated, wondering what else could make Jamie so low. He was about to find out.

Jamie looked at him searchingly. 'Do you remember that night I got involved with that guy down in Derby...outside the club where Lucie was dancin'?' he asked.

'The night Lucie appeared on stage unexpectedly? The barney ye didnae tell us aboot?' Jack replied, the memory returning.

'Aye, that's the one,' Jamie nodded, gathering his thoughts. He'd been wrestling with this since leaving Cranston Hall and he felt guilty landing Jack with it but he needed someone to talk to...no, not just someone; he needed *Jack* to talk to. 'I told you the guy was a gangster, didn't I?'

Jack nodded reflectively. 'Yeah, ye told me that...but ah cannae remember when.'

'He's taken her.'

It sounded too trite, too simple, and Jack stared at him open mouthed. Eventually, he gathered his senses and spoke. 'Whit dae ye mean, "taken her"? Like, as in kidnapped her?' he continued, disbelievingly.

Jamie's explanation came out faster now; the weekend they had shared in London, Lucie's tear-filled story of the rape, her inheritance and Kelman's plan to get his hands on her fortune. Jack listened patiently, growing angrier by the second, feeling Jamie's pain almost as much as Jamie himself. When Jamie finished they sat quietly for a long time, both lost in thought.

It was Jack who broke the silence. 'Whit ur ye plannin' tae dae?' he asked, though he suspected he knew the answer to that.

'I thought if I married her, the guy would give up,' Jamie started, surprising his friend.

'Marry her? Why no'? That might work,' he interrupted thoughtfully, but the look on Jamie's face indicated otherwise.

'I already have Jack; we were married four weeks ago. I'm sorry pal, I should have told you...but the rest of my plan was shelved. Lucie thought that if this bastard discovered we were married he'd have me topped.' He smiled grimly and gave a resigned shrug.

'Fuck!' Jack spat out angrily. 'So whit dae ye want to dae? Take a team doon?' Put the frighteners on the guy?'

Jamie smiled coldly. 'That wouldn't work, Jack. This guy doesn't frighten...he's a fuckin' psycho.'

Jack shook his head in frustration. 'So, whit ur ye gonnae dae?

Jamie finished his Guinness, picked up Jack's empty glass, and started for the bar. 'I'm going to kill the fucker,' he said quietly as he passed.

Jack sat staring at the table. He had thought he knew what Jamie would do; taking some of the guys down, mob handed was his first thought, but killing him. Shit, that was heavy. He looked over to the bar and watched the barmaid pour the second pint as the creamy white head settled on the first. *Fur fuck sake, kill him*, he thought again, but then, going over everything Jamie had said, he reached the same conclusion. If the guy couldn't be talked to, "persuaded", then what was the alternative? Jamie couldn't grab her and run. There was money involved…and a lot by the sound of it, so the guy would come after them. They couldn't spend their lives hiding…so there really only was one answer; get rid of Max…or whatever his name was, Kelman, and you got rid of the problem. But how, that was the question?

Jamie returned with the fresh pints of Guinness and placed a glass carefully before his friend. 'Well?' he asked, noting Jack's thoughtful expression.

'Ye're right. It *is* the only way,' he conceded. 'But how the fuck ur we gonnae dae it?'

Jamie smiled. He could always rely on Jack, but this was his fight, and his alone. 'Not "we" Jack, me,' he replied, noting the disappointment on Jack's face. 'Think about it…one person might get close enough, two probably wouldn't,' he continued, letting Jack down gently. 'I need a gun,' he said without any further hesitation. 'A knife's no good…even if I got close enough his minders would be onto me like a shot and, from what I saw of them, they're mostly tooled up.' He laughed coldly at his unintentional pun.

'Jesus Jamie,' Jack muttered, stunned. He realised instantly that Jamie had worked all of this out in advance, but getting a gun was easier said than done…and it was risky. 'Ye cannae jist walk intae the local gun shop and ask fur wan, can ye?' he said with a worried grin. 'Can ah huv a pistol please, ah'm gonnae kill a guy,' he muttered in a squeaky voice.

Jamie smiled grimly. 'Nah, you're right, an' that's why I need to find someone who can get me one. Any ideas?'

Jack drank his Guinness and looked at the ceiling thoughtfully. A couple of old guys were having an argument over at the bar and he let his eyes wander to them. Football, as per the norm in Glasgow, was the subject of their dispute and the discussion was getting heated. How anyone could get upset about Partick Thistle he couldn't fathom and he smiled in spite of everything. He turned back to Jamie, the smile gone. 'Ah don't know anybody that can get ye a gun, Jamie,' he said under his breath. 'If ah did, ah'd tell ye. Can ye no think of another way? Are ye sure that goin' doon wi a team widnae work?'

'There is no other way. He's surrounded by serious hard men. Aye, we could probably give a few of them a kickin', but it would be like kickin' a wasp's nest…and we'd never get near the bastard himself,' Jamie re-joined. 'No, this is somethin' I have to do myself…up close and personal…but I need a gun…otherwise I'm fucked.'

Jack was distraught. He wanted to help but how could he. Finding someone in Glasgow who would be willing to sell them a gun would be almost impossible. Sure, there were people out there who sold guns but it was a tight market. They only sold to guys they knew or to friends of friends. There was no way they would consider selling a gun to an amateur like Jamie…and even if they did, the cost would be prohibitive.

'I didn't expect you to know anyone,' Jamie said quietly, taking the pressure off. 'But I'm getting' desperate an' I wanted to bounce it off you. I have to get Lucie away from that bastard,' he finished morosely.

They sat in silence for the next few minutes. Jamie realised he had lumbered Jack with a problem and he regretted it, but he had no one else to confide in…and he needed help. There was someone else he could confide in but he had scored him off the list early on. Involving Conor might be a step too far.

And then Jack turned to him with a look that suggested a light had switched on in his brain. 'Whit about yer big pal, the Yank?' he said earnestly. 'The Yanks huv got guns comin' oot their ears. Surely he could fix ye up…an' he owes ye.'

Jamie regarded him thoughtfully. It was true, Conor could probably fix him up but he was reluctant to involve him…the consequences were imponderable. But, on the other hand, he was getting more and more desperate and in the absence of any other solution he might have to reconsider. He nodded silently in response and left it at that.

They left the pub at half past nine and started to make their way up Byres Road towards Great Western Road. Before leaving, Jack had badgered Jamie to allow him to wear his light tan leather jacket; it was the one that Jack particularly liked, and he had given in. It was a mild night for October and a few people were out and about, sauntering along on both sides of the road. They crossed over the street near Hillhead Underground Station and continued north towards Great Western Road.

The three men came for them as they passed the entrance to Ashton Lane and Jack took the brunt of it. It was the jacket…they thought they were attacking Jamie. It took the pals completely by surprise and, as a result, they were slow to react. Jamie saw the glint of light on a blade and a groan came from Jack's mouth and then Jamie watched in horror as his friend slumped forward. The knife flashed again, a stabbing movement, but Jamie reacted quickly this time, catching hold of the wrist holding the knife and twisting violently. The knife missed Jack by inches but the damage had already been done and Jack collapsed to the ground, a pool of blood spreading out from beneath his now still body.

The owner of the knife cursed violently and turned to face Jamie. Their eyes met and a vengeful grin spread over Robert Hood's face when he recognised the face of the man now in front of him. *Two birds with one stone*, he thought gleefully, but he would have to be quick. A crowd was gathering, women were screaming and the two useless pricks he had brought along as backup had legged it.

He pulled his arm free from Jamie's grip and lashed out at him in a wild slashing motion. Jamie stepped back quickly but the sharp tip of the blade sliced across his stomach. Hood moved closer, ready to stab again but Jamie managed to get a hold on the wrist once more and held it firm. Hood's earlier glee at finding the opportunity to get Jamie was quickly turning to panic as he realised that even if he escaped the scene now, his description would be circulated to every cop in Glasgow in no time. There were too many witnesses and this guy, who had humiliated him once before, was still holding on to him. *Ye've already killed once so ye've got nothin' tae lose, his brain screamed, kill the cunt, kill him, and get tae fuck away fae here.*

He swung to the side, throwing Jamie violently against the wall of Ashton Lane, and tried to wrest his knife hand free but Jamie's grip was vicelike now. Their faces came close and then he felt Jamie's forehead crash violently into his nose, breaking bone and cartilage. Tears of anger and frustration welled up in his eyes and when he turned to face Jamie again he saw his own death staring back at him. He began to struggle desperately, kicking out and trying to throw Jamie off balance to give him a chance to bring the knife into play again but time was running out. Summoning up all his remaining strength, he forced his arm downwards towards Jamie's chest and the knife hovered between them, its point angled down towards Jamie's abdomen. Hope returned fleetingly. He stared into Jamie's eyes and expected to see fear but all he saw was the cold, dark abyss into which he was falling. The Police sirens were growing louder and more people had surrounded them; for Robert Hood, all hope of escape had gone.

They had strayed away from Jack's body and some brave souls had gathered round him and were attempting to stem the flow of blood from the wound below his rib cage. Another sound joined the police sirens as an ambulance raced to the scene from the nearby Western Infirmary. Hood was frantic now. Baring his teeth and roaring, he used all his strength to force the blade downwards and into Jamie's chest but his eyes opened wide with shock as Jamie diverted the thrust using Hood's own momentum. He felt the tip of the blade cut through his clothing and slice into his skin. This couldn't be happening. He struggled and twisted furiously, trying to free himself, but Jamie held his wrist, vice like, with the knife point still piercing his skin. And then it all slipped away from him. With an almost gentle push Jamie forced his hand, still gripping the handle of the knife, slowly downwards and he felt it slide between his ribs and pierce his heart. His struggling ceased and a final breath escaped his lungs like a long sigh.

Jamie felt Hood's body grow limp, a dead weight in his arms, and they toppled backwards, still entangled, onto the blood stained pavement. Hood's head cracked hard against the cold paving stones but it was of no consequence; he was already dead.

Then rough hands were grabbing at Jamie, pulling him forcefully from the dead man. He was thrust violently against the nearest wall and reacted instinctively, lashing out against these new attackers, adrenalin still pumping through his veins and a red mist before his eyes. He felt one of his fists land on taught muscle and then both his arms were wrenched painfully up his back. He turned, his eyes blazing, and only then recognised the blue uniforms. He stopped resisting immediately and sagged, exhausted, against the stone wall.

'Easy son,' a big policeman shouted in his ear. 'It's over.'

Jamie's thoughts returned immediately to Jack and he tried to break free to get to him but two pairs of strong hands restrained him. 'You just you stay where you are son,' the big cop ordered, pushing him upright.

His struggling died away and he started to break down. He needed to know that Jack was still alive. 'He's my pal,' he pleaded, nodding towards Jack's body. 'Three of them jumped us and that one there stabbed him,' he spat out, his hate filled eyes locking onto the Hood's face. The man's eyes were open, staring blankly skywards while Jamie's face contorted in latent rage and uncertainty.

The big policeman took in the scene and he sensed the truth in Jamie's statement. 'Stay here,' he ordered Jamie. 'Angus, keep an eye on him while I try to find out about the other lad,' he continued, addressing his colleague. He left them and joined the ambulance crew who were working feverishly on Jack. Jamie saw him bend down, nod two or three times, and then he started back towards them. He stopped, staring at Jamie, and then turned again to the ambulance men. 'Better have a look at this one as well,' he said, indicating Jamie. Jamie thought the cop was referring to Hood, who lay sprawled close by on the pavement, but soon realised it was he who was the subject of the remark. Looking down he saw a quickly spreading bloodstain seeping from the wound on his stomach over his shirt and trousers. Strangely, however, there was no pain.

The ambulance crew placed Jack in the back of the ambulance and one of them then came to Jamie. He examined the wound quickly, noting the length of the slash and the depth of the incision. 'He'll live,' he said, addressing the two policemen, 'but he needs to get that seen to as quickly as possible.' With that, the man sprinted away to the ambulance which had been turned in the street and was now awaiting him. Jamie watched the tail lights disappear and reaction began to set in.

More police arrived and witnesses gave their details and their version of the events. Someone covered the body of Robert Hood with a blanket and Jamie, for the first time, realised that the man was dead. Robert Hood's death was of no consequence to him and he had no regrets...he had no feelings for the man at all, but Jack Connelly was his best friend and he still didn't know if Jack would live or die.

The cop who had asked the ambulance crew about Jack's condition seemed to read Jamie's mind and gave him a sympathetic smile. 'He's alive,' he said quietly, 'and with any luck, he'll make it. Now we have to get you seen to.' He turned away and Jamie saw him speak with a Sergeant and a senior officer, judging by the amount of white braid on the skip of his hat, and all three looked in Jamie's direction. 'Right Angus, let's get this lad down to The Western,' he called over and headed for his car.' As Angus and Jamie joined him, he turned to Jamie with a grim smile. 'Try not to bleed all over the upholstery, son,' he said, without malice, as he helped Jamie into the back seat.

Jamie was whisked straight to A&E at The Western, a padded dressing pressed firmly to his wound. When they arrived, the waiting area was busy and people were sitting, in varying states of distress, on the rows of hard seats. The appearance of the two policemen with Jamie supported between them, his body and trousers covered in blood, had a sobering effect on the people waiting and there was no complaint when they were ushered through to a cubicle in the treatment area immediately. A nurse was washing her hands when Jamie was shown in. Close by, he heard voices, urgent conversations, instructions and then the sound of a hospital trolley being could hear the urgent voices of nurses and doctors and then the sound of a hospital trolley being rushed away. Something told him it was Jack on the trolley, but there was nothing he could do. He felt helpless.

Minutes later, a young female doctor entered the cubicle. There was no warm smile and Jamie could see that she was clearly harassed by the sudden emergency that had taken place. The doctor eased up Jamie's shirt and examined the wound. 'Nasty,' she murmured, 'you were lucky.' Jamie knitted his brow...lucky...again? He considered it and shook his head slowly. Lucky? No, I'm definitely not that, he decided.

The doctor turned to the nurse, a middle aged woman with a kindly face and smiling grey eyes, who had been waiting quietly. 'We'll need to get this cleaned up and stitched...and he'll need a tetanus jab too, nurse,' Jamie heard her say and jumped in quickly.

'I had a tetanus jag in Derby Royal about four weeks ago,' he said. 'Will I need another one?'

The doctor smiled and shook her head. 'No, you should be alright with that,' she agreed. 'They're not the most pleasant of jabs, eh?' she laughed, as relief spread across Jamie's face. He nodded; the memory of getting the injection at Derby was still clear in his mind. "This will hurt", the nurse had said just before plunging an enormous needle into his thigh...and she hadn't been kidding, it had hurt like hell.

'Stitch him up nurse,' the doctor said finally, 'and then he can go.'

The nurse looked out into the general area and saw the two policemen waiting patiently by the door. It didn't look like this lad was going anywhere other than Partick Police Station, she thought. One dead, one critical and this one slashed across the abdomen. He was the lucky one, she told herself. But had she known Jamie better, she would have known that, to him, luck played no part in it...it just hadn't been his time. It had, however, been Robert Hood's time...and Jamie was praying that it wasn't Jack Connelly's as well.

286

As the nurse prepared the needle for stitching Jamie turned to her. 'The lad who was brought in by ambulance, do you know how he is?' he asked softly. She looked at him, wondering what his part in the brawl had been, and Jamie could see it in her eyes. 'He's my pal,' he added quietly, his eyes filling up.

The nurse gave him a kindly smile. 'Let me get you stitched up first and then I'll try to find out for you,' she offered. 'I know they took him straight to theatre,' she added, as she started to work on him. 'What happened?' she asked.

'Three guys attacked us,' Jamie replied. 'And I've no idea why.' That fact had started to bother him. Robert Hood was a professional hard man, so why did he want to kill Jack? He played the whole incident back in his mind and it just didn't make sense. And it wasn't a random attack, that guy Hood didn't do random...so it had been planned. But why?

'What happened to the dead lad?' the nurse asked, interrupting his thoughts.

Jamie looked down at her and watched her slide the needle into his flesh. 'He stabbed my pal and he was about to stab him again when I grabbed him,' he murmured. 'We struggled, and he slashed me,' he continued, nodding down at his partly stitched stomach. 'He was trying to stab me but his knife ended up in him and not in me.'

The nurse was silent for a while, concentrating on her work. She considered what Jamie had just said and thought it had the ring of truth to it. He doesn't look like a killer, she thought, but then again, what does a killer look like in this city?

She had seen it all in twenty years as a nurse; boys barely out of their teens, little boys with baby faces, but vicious killers. She shrugged mentally and gave Jamie the benefit of the doubt. Finally finished her stitching she stood back to examine her handiwork and pulled off the latex gloves she had been wearing. 'Your scar won't be too bad,' she said, 'I'm good at this...the stitches are nice and tight together; you'll hardly know it's there,' she smiled. 'Now, lie still and I'll try to get you some news about your pal.'

She left Jamie lying there and he heard her speaking with the policemen as she passed them. He lay for what seemed an age before she returned and Jamie looked at her face for a sign. She was smiling and Jamie suddenly felt better.

'Your friend's out of theatre and he's being moved to the I.C.U.,' she reported. 'The surgeon is hopeful, but that's all I can tell you, sorry,' she said gently. 'And now I'll have to tell the gentlemen outside that you're ready.'

Jamie nodded gratefully. 'Thanks,' he said, 'he's got the constitution of an ox so he'll make it,' he told her.

Shortly afterwards, the two policemen came into the cubicle. 'Come on son,' the cop who had spoken with him earlier said. 'We need to get you down to Partick. C.I. D. will want a word and you'll probably be charged, but I don't think you've got much to worry about,' he added. 'From what we've heard, you and your mate were jumped and you acted in self-defence...and the knife was still in the dead lad's hand. Come on,' he repeated, taking Jamie gently by the arm.

*

The cell was cold but it didn't matter. They had brought him a cup of tea and a sandwich and he had wolfed them down. He lay on the hard, leatherette mattress and stared at the single bulb on the ceiling encased behind its green painted metal frame. They had taken his belt and his shoelaces and had left him alone. Every so often the metal flap on the cell door opened and an anonymous pair of eyes looked in on him but otherwise he was left in peace. The realisation that he had killed Robert Hood dawned on him slowly at first. He felt that he should be experiencing guilt but, strangely, he felt nothing…no remorse, no regret, nothing. *What should I be feeling, he asked himself? I've just killed somebody…but isn't that exactly what I'm thinking of doing to Max Kelman? What am I becoming?*

It was the middle of the night when Jamie was finally taken to C.I.D. The two cops who had brought him in earlier had gone off duty and new faces wandered around the police station. He was shown into what appeared at first glance to be an untidy, disorganised office, with papers and files strewn on desks and ashtrays piled high with cigarette stubs. Two men in shirt sleeves, ties loosened at the neck, and wearing braces were waiting in the room. One of them indicated a chair in front of his desk. 'Sit down, Mr Raeburn,' he said. His voice seemed hollow, lifeless even, and his expression was unreadable. 'First things first; I'm Detective Sergeant Cooper and my colleague here is Detective Constable Baxter,' he said, getting the introductions out of the way. 'You're not being charged with anything…for the moment, anyway, but a report will go to the Procurator Fiscal. 'You're going to be released on bail until the P.F. makes up his mind about what to do with you, but before that we'd like to hear your version of events. Are you up for that?' Jamie hesitated. 'Listen son, from the statements I've read, nothing is going to happen to you.'

Jamie looked at him doubtfully but felt he had nothing to lose if he told the truth. 'Alright,' he said quietly. 'I'm up for it.'

'Good,' Sergeant Cooper continued, a hint of a smile appearing on his rugged face. 'Right then, before we start, do you want anything? Tea, coffee?'

'Can I get my cigarettes from my belongings?' Jamie asked hopefully.

The Sergeant smiled openly ten and looked at the D.C., flicking his eyes towards the door. The other detective gave an exaggerated sigh then rose from his chair and disappeared out of the room. He returned a few minutes later with a bag, containing all of Jamie's possessions, which he dropped onto the desk between Jamie and the Sergeant, and then produced a sheet of paper which he placed next to the bag.

'If you want to check everything's there and sign the receipt, we can get on,' Sergeant Cooper said, becoming officious.

Jamie tipped the contents of the bag onto the desk and sifted through them, picking out his watch and fastening it around his wrist. The time read 04.42. Taking his time, he unlocked the fastening on the silver chain which held the Ankh given to him by Kate months earlier and fastened it around his neck. His wallet and money were there too. He picked up the wallet and examined it without counting the money in it and then replaced it on the desk. His belt and his shoelaces could wait, he decided. He leaned across the table and took the pen proffered by the big Sergeant and signed the form with a flourish. Finally, he picked up his packet of Lucky Strikes. It had been battered about a bit in the course of the fight with Hood and the first cigarette he pulled from the pack was broken in two. Loose tobacco spilled onto the Sergeant's desk. Jamie withdrew another and found this one intact, slipped it into his mouth and picked up his lighter. As he flicked the wheel to obtain a flame the Sergeant bent forward and blew the loose tobacco off his desk and onto Jamie's lap. Jamie smiled at him wryly.

'Right then, how about telling us what happened last night,' Sergeant Cooper started and leaned back in his chair, his eyes never leaving Jamie's face.

Jamie drew heavily on his cigarette and started, taking the men through the events of the evening from the point when he and Jack had left the Pub at around nine thirty. He was on to his third cigarette by the time he finished. Both men had listened carefully, asking questions from time to time, D.C. Baxter keeping a note of Jamie's statement.

'So, have you any idea why this happened?' D.S. Cooper asked as Jamie settled back. 'It doesn't strike me as a motiveless attack,

Jamie shook his head slowly. 'No, I've got no idea,' he said. 'I only got back from down South on Friday afternoon and Jack Connolly's not the sort of guy to be involved with punters like that.'

'But you are?' D.S. Cooper asked quietly.

'I didn't say that,' Jamie responded quickly.

'Did you know any of these guys,' D.S. Cooper re-joined, watching Jamie shrewdly. 'The guy that was killed, for instance?'

Jamie made a face and shook his head slowly, then took another drag at his Lucky. 'No, never seen him…or any of the others for that matter, before last night,' he lied easily.

There was a pause as the D.S. pulled open a drawer and removed a clear polythene evidence bag, then slid it across the table towards Jamie. Inside was a single sheet of paper with some pencilled writing scrawled on it. 'That's strange,' the detective said softly, 'because he knew you.' He nodded at the evidence bag, inviting Jamie to pick it up. Intrigued, Jamie lifted the bag from the desk and examined the sheet of paper inside. "Jamie Raeburn, 495 Lincon Avenue, Nightswood, £450, 01224 456657" jumped out at him, the words and figures written in a semi-literate scrawl. 'That's you, isn't it?' The D.S. continued.

'Aye, that's me,' Jamie agreed.

'So, any idea why a guy like Bobby Hood should have your name and address on a piece of paper in his pocket?'

Jamie simply shook his head. Everything was falling into place now.

'What about the telephone number?' D.C. Baxter threw in. 'Does that ring any bells?' he asked, laughing at the unintentional pun. Again Jamie shook his head and said nothing. 'It's a Derby number,' the detective carried on. 'You said you just came back from down South on Friday…where were you?'

'Nottingham,' Jamie replied quickly.

'Not Derby?'

'No, not Derby,' Jamie retorted, but he suspected that D.S. Cooper and D.C. Baxter would know that Derby and Nottingham weren't exactly poles apart.

D.S. Cooper let out a heavy sigh. 'It's been a long night,' he said. 'You can go, but don't disappear, we might want to ask you some more questions,' he added, 'because something doesn't stack up…particularly why a nutter like Bobby Hood should have your name on a piece of paper and why it was your pal that Hood and his mates went for. But I'll find out, don't worry,' he finished ominously.

*

It was still dark when Jamie walked out of Partick Police Station and the cold night air hit him like a sledgehammer. Everything was quiet. He made his way up to Dumbarton Road and debated his next move. He wanted to know how Jack was, that was uppermost in his mind, but he was worried about his mother and knew he should go home. The police had telephoned his mother and told her that he was helping them with enquiries. She would be demented, but first and foremost he had to find out how Jack was.

A set of headlights was coming towards him from the direction of Thornwood and he was able to identify the box like shape of a black hackney. The "FOR HIRE" light was illuminated and Jamie quickly reached a decision. Flagging it down, he crossed the road quickly and climbed in, oblivious to the driver's startled stare. 'Saracen Street, Possil,' he called through the partition and sank back into the seat. Taking the car to Jack's house was a gamble but he suspected that Jack's mother, at least, would be awake.

The driver raced up Byres Road, past the spot where he and Jack had been attacked, and Jamie was surprised to see policemen still there and the area sealed off. The driver concentrated on driving and didn't engage in conversation, most unusual for the normally gregarious Glasgow taxi drivers. Jamie smiled bitterly and put it down to the reasonable assumption that the man didn't want to get involved with someone who looked like an escapee from a slaughterhouse. The undisguised look of relief on the man's face when Jamie paid the fare and stepped out onto the pavement in Saracen Street confirmed his suspicion. Jamie stood on the edge of the pavement contemplating the light burning in the Connolly's living room window on the second floor and the taxi driver made good his getaway. With a high revving engine, he drove off at full tilt down Saracen Street towards Keppochill Road and the City.

Jamie pulled out his cigarettes and lit one, steadying himself. He felt like shit. What he had gleaned from his chat with the detectives earlier, explained everything. It wasn't Jack that Hood and his mates had been after; it had been him, and the Derby telephone number showed Max Kelman's hand behind it. Tony Abrahams' words as they had parted four days earlier came back to him…"watch your back". He hadn't thought anything of it at the time but Abrahams obviously knew Kelman better than he did. How could he explain to Jack's mother that her son was lying in hospital because of him? He stood there letting a feeling of desolation drag him down and his eyes filled with tears. Steeling himself, he entered the close and began the long climb up to the second floor.

His knock was answered almost immediately, as if they had been waiting for him. Jack's mother stood there, her face drawn and pale but, at the same time, somehow peaceful. She looked at Jamie, took in the blood stains on his trousers, saw the haggard look on his face and the tears welling in his eyes and pulled him to her. 'Oh Jamie, Jamie,' she cried, hugging him tightly as the flood gates burst and his tears flowed like a river in spate.

She brought him into the living room where Jack's father sat near the fire, his face a ghastly grey. Anne-Marie, the youngest of the family, lay curled on the settee, asleep, while another of Jack's sisters, Bernadette, sat at the end of the settee, gently stroking her sister's hair.

'I'm sorry,' Jamie wept, burying his head in his hands. 'It's all my fault.'

Mrs Connolly quietened him. 'You're not to blame Jamie,' she admonished him gently. 'You didn't wield the knife.'

'But you don't understand,' Jamie mumbled. 'It was me they were after, not Jack.'

Jack's father spoke for the first time, his voice steady, belying the look of anguish on his face. 'It doesn't matter who they were after lad. Evil doesn't differentiate…and it looks like they almost got you too.'

'It's nothing,' Jamie replied. 'A few stitches, that's all. What about Jack?'

Mrs Connolly smiled grimly and ushered him to a seat just as Anne-Marie awoke. She looked up with a start, saw the blood on Jamie's clothes and rose quickly, throwing her arms around him. Jamie grimaced but said nothing.

Jack's mother smiled sadly now. She knew her daughter was infatuated with Jamie Raeburn but Jamie looked on her like a sister. He would do nothing to hurt her but one day, unintentionally, he might. 'Anne-Marie, leave Jamie be,' she said to her daughter. 'Can't you see he's been hurt too?'

Anne-Marie backed away, distraught, and Bernadette came to her aid, leading her back to the settee and settling her as Jamie sank back into the chair.

'They operated on him last night,' Mrs Connolly said, confirming what Jamie already knew. 'He's in Intensive Care and the doctors think he's got a good chance of pulling through.'

Jamie audibly sighed with relief. 'Does Teresa know?' he asked.

'Yes, she knows. She's at the hospital just now with Liam,' Jack's mother advised. 'Dad and I will go in the morning and if we get any news we'll let you know right away.' She paused for a moment, regarding Jamie affectionately. She had four sons of her own but she would gladly have accepted Jamie Raeburn as number five. 'What about your mother?' she asked, 'does she know?'

Jamie nodded. 'The police phoned her...told her I was alright and I wasn't being charged but that they wanted to ask me some questions.'

'You should be at home, Jamie,' Mrs Connolly admonished. 'Your poor mother will be at her wit's end.'

She was right, Jamie thought guiltily. He wasn't being fair to his mother. 'I'll go now,' he said. 'I'm sorry for dropping in like this but I just needed to know Jack was alright.' He started to rise from the chair only to be stopped in his tracks by Jack's mother, her hand pressed gently but firmly against his chest.

'You can't go home looking like that, Jamie,' she said quietly. 'If your poor mother sees you like that she'll have a heart attack. Wait here and I'll get you some of Jack's clothes to change into.'

Jamie didn't protest. A tidal wave of exhaustion crashed over him and he closed his eyes. Anne-Marie came to him again, cradling his head against her shoulder, and she was still with him when her mother returned. Her mother's chastising look had little effect; rather it simply stoked Anne-Marie's defiance. Jack's mother shook her head; arguing would be pointless. She placed a pair of jeans and a woollen jumper in Jamie's lap. 'You know where Jack's room is,' she said, 'you can get changed in there...and give me your bloodied ones. I'll soak them for you.'

Jamie rose unsteadily and made for Jack's room, clutching the clothes tightly against his chest. 'What about a jacket?' Jack's mother asked as he passed her. 'Weren't you wearing one last night?' She continued, ready to chastise him for not looking after himself properly when she saw the dark shadow cross his face.

'Jack was wearing it,' he said quietly and pulled the door closed behind him.

*

His mother was up and keeping herself busy when Jamie opened the front door. She emerged from the kitchen, her face white and etched with worry, and ran to him. He winced as she hugged him but he didn't complain. He had put her through enough over the years.

'Are you alright?' she demanded anxiously. 'The police said you were hurt but that you were alright. Are you?'

'Yes Mum, I'm alright,' he said, reassuring her. 'I wouldn't be home if I wasn't, would I?' he added, hoping that was a persuasive argument.

'What about Jack, is he going to be alright?' she probed.

'I think so. He's in Intensive Care at the Western...they think he'll pull through.' He felt his mother tremble against him and realised this was bringing back memories of his own close brush with death only ten months earlier.

'His poor mother,' she sobbed, tears beginning to flow. Jamie held her tightly and let her cry it out.

Later, as she made him breakfast, she asked if he wanted her to stay with him. Jamie loved his mother desperately but she was the last person he wanted with him today. He had already made up his mind on what he was going to do and having his mother hovering around him all day would limit the scope of that. He thanked her but insisted that she go to work, promising to telephone if he needed her and assuring her that he was going to spend the day in bed asleep. Mollified, she agreed and at twenty minutes to nine she left him alone in the silence of the house.

He climbed the stairs to his room and pulled off the woollen jumper that Jack's mother had given him. He unwound the bandages around his torso to look at the wound. It looked red and angry but apart from the pulling of the stitches there was little discomfort. The hospital had provided him with painkillers and he took another two now. Peeling off the remainder of his clothes, including his blood stained underpants, he slipped beneath the covers and was soon asleep.

When he awoke it was early afternoon. A pale, watery sun was trying valiantly to fight its way through the layers of grey cloud beneath it with limited success. He rose stiffly from his bed and dressed in fresh, clean clothes. Pain was kicking in and the wound was beginning to itch. He had bled a little in his sleep and the bandage was stuck to the wound with dried blood, adding to his discomfort.

He thought about what he was about to do, troubled that he was involving someone else in his personal troubles, and that "someone" was as close to him as Jack Connolly. He hoped his action wouldn't produce a similar result.

*

Jamie listened intently as the ringing tone continued uninterrupted, still vexed. But who else could he ask, he rationalised? Conor had offered him help any time he needed it…and boy did he need it now. But he was still reluctant to involve the big American. He would rather not involve anyone; it was personal; he could do it himself, he kept telling himself, but the fact remained, he needed help to get the thing he wanted to get the job done.

He was about to hang up when the ringing stopped and Mary Campbell answered in her soft West Highland accent. 'Hello,' she said, throwing Jamie off his stride. He had prepared his speech for Conor and he spluttered before responding.

'Hello Mary,' he started hesitantly. 'It's Jamie, Jamie Raeburn. I was hoping to speak to Conor…is he around?' he asked apprehensively.

'Jamie!' Mary replied immediately, her voice filled with obvious pleasure at hearing from him. 'Conor's not here just now, he's up in Aberdeen,' she continued apologetically, 'but he'll be back tonight. Where are you?'

'I'm back in Glasgow,' he replied despondently and Mary sensed instantly that he was in trouble. 'I need a wee bit of help,' he continued, confirming her suspicion.

'I'll get in touch with Conor right away and get him to phone you,' Mary replied immediately. 'Stay by the phone.'

'Thanks Mary,' he managed before she was gone.

It seemed an age but it was only minutes before the phone rang, jangling his nerves. 'Jamie, kid…it's Conor, what's the problem little buddy?'

'I need a bit of help again, Conor, sorry.'

'Forget the "sorry" kiddo, what's wrong? Tell me, I can hear it in your voice,' Conor continued, his thick Boston Irish accent filled with concern.

'It's not something I feel comfortable talking about over the phone,' Jamie threw back to him. 'You offered me help once if I needed it…'

'Yeah kid, like I said, any time,' Conor interrupted, his concern growing. 'If you don't want to talk on the phone, where and when do you want to meet?'

'Mary said you'd be home tonight so I'll come down to Holy Loch on the bike tomorrow, if that's alright. It's kind of urgent.'

'I can tell that from your voice, kid. Okay, come down tomorrow, I'll be here,' Conor agreed immediately. He waited, sure Jamie wanted to say more, and his intuition proved to be correct.

'Listen Conor, the problem's personal...and it's serious...if you can't help I won't be offended.'

'Girl problem?' Conor fired back. He was tempted to make light of it but decided against it.

Jamie laughed softly but there was an edge of bitterness to it. 'Aye Conor, it's a girl problem, but it's not what you think. I need your advice as well as your help.'

'You got it kid. Come to the Navy Exchange. You've got me worried,' the American continued. 'What time will you be here?'

'I'll be down by 09.30, is that okay with you?'

'Sure kid, I'll be waiting,' Conor confirmed.

'Okay, see you tomorrow...and Conor, thanks.'

Before the American could reply the line was dead. He stood for a while, staring into space, wondering what sort of trouble Jamie was in. Girl trouble wasn't unexpected; Jamie was a good looking kid but there was more to this problem than simply girl trouble...that was something Jamie could handle himself. Something in his voice hinted at serious and Mary picked up on it as well. The phone in the borrowed office in Aberdeen began to ring again, returning him to real time. He picked up and heard Mary's concerned voice, calling for an update, and that confirmed it...if Mary was calling him so soon then it *was* serious.

Back in Glasgow, Jamie replaced the handset and gazed vacantly out of the window. It was grey outside, a heavy mist had hung in the air since early morning and the street lights had been on all day. It would probably get worse as the temperature dropped later, he thought, and he worried that it might still be bad the next morning for his ride to Dunoon. But that was a hazard he might have to face on the road back down South in a week or two, so the experience might be worthwhile. He sat alone in the quiet of the house, thinking morosely about Lucie and wondering if she knew about what Kelman had planned for him. If she thought he was dead what would she do, he worried? She had said that if he was killed her life wouldn't be worth living. *Christ, please don't let her do anything stupid*, he prayed.

Anger surged through him again. Lucie loved him...she had sacrificed herself for him and here he was, sitting on his fat arse, feeling sorry for himself. What was it Geordie Irvine always said? Don't get mad, get even. Max Kelman was the root of all the evil that he and Lucie were facing...Kill Kelman, and the problem was solved. It was a simple solution but it wouldn't be easy to achieve, of that he was certain.

He closed his eyes and thought about it. Wherever Kelman went, he always had minders...he had first-hand knowledge of that and Lucie had confirmed it. Walking up to him in the street or anywhere else for that matter was a definite nonstarter, unless he himself was prepared to die and that, he smiled grimly, defeated the purpose somewhat. He had to find a weak spot and then devise a plan around that. But finding a weak spot might take time...and he didn't have a lot of that, but none the less, it was the only way. He had to be able to watch Kelman without Kelman knowing it...and he needed a base to work from; somewhere close to Kelman and somewhere he wouldn't stick out like a sore thumb. A plan began to form in his head but once again it meant involving someone he cared for.

Without arguing with himself this time, he picked up the phone and dialled. Jo Bradley answered on the third ring. 'Hello Jo, it's Jamie.'

'Jamie, at last,' Jo replied, sounding relieved. 'We were talking about you last night and Julie asked if you'd been in touch,' she raced on. 'Have you spoken to Jack yet...I assume you'll be asking him for help? The ominous silence from Jamie sent a shiver through her. 'What's happened, Jamie? What's wrong?'

'Jack's in hospital, Jo. He's critical but stable, that's the words they used.'

There was a sharp intake of breath as Jo came to terms with that. 'God, what happened?' she asked, her voice flat and sad.

How much should he tell her, Jamie wondered? It would all come out eventually, sooner rather than later, he suspected, so why postpone the inevitable? 'We were out last night,' he sighed. 'I told him about Kelman and asked for his help...but when we were on our way home...it wasn't late, and we'd only had a couple of pints, three guys attacked us.' He paused, reliving the horror. 'They went for Jack...it was as if they had targeted him. One of them stabbed him...I fought with the guy and then...' He paused again, longer this time, and Jo waited, her heart and her head pounding. 'I killed him,' he said at last, his voice so faint she almost missed it.

Jo's head spun out of control. What was happening in the world? 'And what about you?' she asked, coming to grips with it, 'are you alright?'

'Yeah, I'm alright,' he replied flatly. 'I've got eighteen stitches across my stomach but I'm alive.' His next words, said quietly and firmly, threw Jo into a vortex of despair. 'It wasn't Jack they were after...it was me,' he whispered. 'Kelman was behind it.'

Jo's gasp reverberated down the line to him. How could Kelman's reach stretch so far? It was almost unbelievable and for a moment she doubted him, imagining him seeing the Kelman's spectre in everything that happened now...but that wasn't like the Jamie Raeburn she knew, was it? 'How can you be sure it was Kelman?' she questioned. 'You only returned home days ago...it's too quick?'

'It was him, Jo, there's no doubt about it. I was arrested last night...the police didn't charge me or anything, and I was released early this morning,' he added quickly to allay her fears. 'Before they let me go two detectives interviewed me...asked if I knew the man who had knifed Jack, the one I killed. I told them I didn't,' he continued, omitting the fact that he did know Hood; there was no point in clouding the issue. 'They seemed bemused by that and I suspected they had something up their sleeve...and then the one conducting the interview, a Detective Sergeant, slipped a piece of paper over to me. It had my name scrawled on it as well as my address in Glasgow, the figures £450 and a telephone number...and the number had a Derby dial code.' He waited a moment, listening to Jo's second gasp of horror from the other end of the line, before finishing off. 'They found that scrap of paper in the guy's trouser pocket...now do you believe me?' There was almost complete silence, only by Jo's gentle sobbing from the other end of the line breaking it. 'I've learned a lot over the last few days...mostly about myself,' Jamie came back again. 'People have been hurt because of me, people I love; I have to sort that.'

'You can't say that about Lucie,' Jo whispered. 'What happened to her was going to happen anyway, Jamie, you know that. You can't blame yourself.'

She heard him laugh bitterly. 'Yes I can, Jo, because I *let* it happen. I knew all about the bastard...and I let it happen when I should have prevented it.'

'There's a big difference between what you think you *should* have done and what you *could* have done, Jamie.'

'I know now what I could have done. I did it last night to somebody else…and now I have even more reason to do it again,' he said with a finality that frightened her.

'You're crazy, Jamie. Do you know what you're saying?' Jo said incredulously. She didn't even want to contemplate what his words meant. 'You don't know what you're up against…you won't stand a chance.'

Jamie laughed coldly. 'He won't be expecting me, Jo…I'm dead, or at the very least he'll think I'm lying in a hospital bed somewhere. The guys who got away will say I was stabbed…and that gives me an edge.'

'I hope you know what you're doing Jamie…two lives depend on it,' she threw back despondently and immediately bit her tongue.

'Let's leave it there just now Jo. If there's any chance at all to get word to Lucie, let her know I'm alive…I'm worrying about what she might do if she thinks I'm not,' he said quietly.

Jo was jolted back to reality. Jamie was right; Lucie was vulnerable and if she found out about last night and thought for a moment that he was dead, there was no telling what she might do. 'I hadn't thought about that,' she confessed. 'We'll try,' she continued, implying Julie's help in it. She hesitated, thinking about everything he had just told her and reaching a conclusion she would rather not have reached. 'If you're set on going to go through with this hare brained scheme, Jamie, don't leave it too long.'

'I won't,' he snorted, and then his voice was quiet again. Is Julie around?' he asked casually.

'No, but she'll be here later. Do you want me to get her to call you?' There was no hint of suspicion in Jo's voice and Jamie felt a twinge of guilt. If she suspected for a minute what he was going to ask Julie to do she would stop him dead in his tracks. 'Thanks, Jo. That would be great…I just need someone to talk to, someone close to both Lucie and Jack,' he lied smoothly. He heard a soft sigh before Jo responded.

'I should have realised, I'm sorry. Give me your number and I'll get her to call you as soon as she gets here, alright?'

Jamie recited the number, thanked her again and hung up before she could ask any more questions which would require him to lie to her again.

He walked to the window and looked out, seeking solace in the familiarity of it all. The bare trees stood stark against the grey light, the green of the grass the only hint of colour in an otherwise lifeless landscape. Self-doubt was creeping in on him again. Could he do this? Even if he managed to get close enough to Kelman could he actually kill him? He stared out into the grey murk, barely able to see the houses on the other side of the broad street through the thickening fog. A couple walked past, arm in arm, their heads bowed against the strengthening wind and their coats pulled tightly around them against the cold. As he watched, a crow swept down and settled on a tree by the roadside, just outside the garden. It sat there, malevolent, its eyes swivelling, searching for scraps of food. *There's something about crows, he thought, they're frightening, ugly birds, black from tip to tail, with piercing, black eyes and large, obscene grey beaks but they're also intelligent…the Max Kelman of the bird world.* A second crow glided into view and settled beside the first, both of them turning in unison to stare at him with their black, lifeless eyes, and an involuntary shiver ran up Jamie's spine. The phone rang and he almost jumped out of his skin with fright.

'Hi Jamie,' Julie's voice said quietly down the line. 'Mum's told me what happened, I'm so sorry,' she sobbed quietly. She still had a soft spot for Jack.

'Thanks Julie…listen, can you talk?'

She was immediately alert. Jamie had said he would be back but didn't want anyone else to know…and she had assumed that included her. But now she sensed he wanted help. 'Yes,' she replied quickly, 'Mum's in the kitchen and I'm alone. What do you need me to do?'

Jamie smiled involuntarily. Julie was sharp. 'I need your help but you have to keep it to yourself,' he said, confirming what she had already deduced. 'No one can know…and I mean no one,' he repeated, to emphasise the point. 'If you don't think you can help me or if you don't want to get involved it's alright, honestly, just say now and I'll figure out another way.'

He heard her laugh softly. 'You can't do it all on your own,' she answered. 'Don't worry, I won't let you down…I'm glad you trust me. What are you going to do?'

'I don't know yet, exactly, but I'll need somewhere to stay.'

'Not here, not with Mum and Brian?' she interrupted.

'No, definitely not with them,' he laughed. 'I don't want anyone close to me involved in this.'

'What about me, am I not close to you?'

Jamie sighed. 'Yes, you're close to me, but you'll be well away from the action. I won't do anythin' to get you hurt, I promise,' he appeased.

'I know you won't,' Julie responded. 'I was teasing, sorry, it's not the time. What do you want me to do?'

'Find me somewhere to stay; somewhere not too close to Kelman's pile but close enough to Derby to let me get in and out of the city quickly…somewhere I won't attract attention. Any ideas?'

'Not right off, no, but I'll find somewhere…when will you need it and how long for?'

Jamie had already thought about that. 'I'll probably need it for a couple of weeks but there are a couple of things I have to do here first. If you can find somethin' in the next couple of weeks and rent it for four, that'll do.'

'Okay, I'll do it. Can I phone you on this number?'

'Yeah, if I'm not here just leave a message with my mother or father and I'll get back to you. I'll let you know when I'm comin' down and I'll meet you…are you sure you're alright with this?'

'Yes, I'm sure…stop worrying.'

'Thanks Julie, but remember…'

'Yes, I know,' she replied, exasperated. This is just between us and nobody else is to know about it.'

'Good girl,' Jamie laughed, despite the circumstances. 'What will I say to Jo if she answers when I call?'

'The same as this time…you just need me to talk to about Lucie and Jack. She'll accept that.'

'Right…one last thing, Jules' he said earnestly. 'If you get any chance at all to get word to Lucie let her know I'm alright. It's important. Tell her you've spoken to me…and tell her I love her.'

'Yes, Mum told me you're worried about Luce,' she acknowledged. 'I'll try…but I don't need to tell her you love her, she knows. If I get the chance can I tell her you're coming back?'

'*Christ, no!* You can't...you mustn't. If Lucie knows I'm coming then the chances are that Max will find out. I want my arrival to be a surprise...a particularly unpleasant one.'

'Okay, I understand,' she said, accepting his logic.

'Good girl. I'll call you soon. Take care,' he finished, and replaced the handset. *Things are moving*, he told himself, satisfied.

*

Julie listened to the silence on the line when Jamie terminated the call but she continued to hold the phone to her ear, lost in thought. She didn't know what Jamie had in mind but she had a fair idea. She had come to much the same conclusion as Jamie and Jack...if you removed Max Kelman from the equation the problem was resolved. But removing Max was a challenge. She already knew he had killed someone in Glasgow the night before, her mother had told her, but killing Max Kelman would be a different matter. For a start, Jamie would have his work cut out simply getting close enough and there were his minders to consider. Could he do it, she wondered? Could he really kill Max Kelman and could she be a part of it? She put the horror of that from her mind. Jamie was right in one thing, she reflected, Lucie couldn't be told he was coming. If she knew Jamie was back she would be petrified with fear and a predator like Kelman could smell that...so she couldn't know. Julie closed her eyes then and said a silent prayer

Chapter 47

Early next day, Jamie set off for Dunoon and his meeting with Conor. He told his mother the truth...or at least part of it; he was going to see Conor, and she accepted that without question.

Mary Raeburn knew that Jamie and the American were close so what was there to question. And yet, there was this nagging doubt in her mind that all was not right...and the cause of that lay deeper than what had happened only thirty six hours earlier. Jamie was preoccupied, quiet, his mind always somewhere else. Maybe it was simply a reaction to what had happened to him all those months earlier, she reasoned, but her maternal instincts told her it was something else.

The traffic on the A82 towards Dumbarton and Loch Lomond was reasonably light, the bulk of it travelling towards him in the direction of Glasgow, and he made good time. The fog of the day before had lifted, blown away by a strong overnight wind, and the sky was a clear, unbroken blue. At any other time Jamie would have enjoyed the ride, but even the spectacular scenery, with the early snow tipped mountains of Ben Lomond and The Cobbler rising majestically into the sky, was failing to detract from the problems besetting him. One day he would bring Lucie here, he promised, and they could enjoy it together.

He turned onto the A83 at Tarbet and passed through Arrochar, skirted Loch Long and the Royal Navy Torpedo Testing Range on the lochside, and began the climb up the "Rest and be Thankful". From there he dropped down into Glen Kinglas, a long straight stretch of road running like a slash in the earth between the mountains to left and right. He crouched low in the saddle and opened the throttle, pushing the speedometer needle up to a staggering 90mph. The wind bit into the exposed skin of his face and roared in his ears as it rushed past him and for a moment he felt exhilarated by it. Slowing rapidly as the road ahead curved gently to the right, he took the sharp left onto the A815 which would take him, eventually, to Dunoon. Racing through St. Catherines with the white buildings of Inverary gleaming imposingly on the far side of Loch Fyne, he reached Strachur and turned left again through the dense woodland of Argyll Forest with the long narrow strip of still, dark water of Loch Eck on his right. Nothing seemed to be moving except him; the sensation of peace was surreal, almost unworldly. By 09.20 he on the shore road around the northern tip of Holy Loch with the leviathan hulk of the U.S.S. Simon Lake filling his vision and small lighters making their way back and forth to the shore leaving small wakes of white on the flat, silvery surface of the water.

A few minutes later he pulled into the open area in front of the big building that housed the U.S. Navy Exchange. Conor Whelan was sitting on a low stone wall bordering the roadway, waiting for him, a cigarette hanging loosely from his lips. He rose and sauntered over as Jamie dismounted from the Triumph and Jamie was reminded of a young John Wayne. Conor grinned and gripped him in a suffocating bear hug. 'It's good to see you, kid,' he smiled. 'Mary and I have been thinking about you. She's worried,' he added tellingly.

Jamie pulled off his gauntlets and his helmet and accepted a cigarette, pulling heavily on it. He was about to involve Conor in something highly illegal, something he was still reluctant to do, even though he knew he had little option.

'Coffee?' Conor suggested, taking Jamie by the arm and leading him up the stone steps and into the building. Competing aromas of freshly made roasted coffee and cooking food assailed Jamie's nostrils and he suddenly felt ravenous. He hadn't eaten properly since the night of the attack and the sight of well-fed Americans tucking into bacon, eggs and steak, filled him with envy. Conor saw the look on his face and guided him towards the serving counter. 'You look as if you could do with something,' the American laughed. 'I'll join you, so don't be bashful.'

Jamie loaded a plate and watched as Conor followed suit. They found a vacant table near a window with a view over the loch and the River Clyde beyond, and settled down. 'It's easier to deal with things on a full stomach,' Conor grinned, beginning to demolish a large slice of steak.

They ate in silence. Finally finished and his hunger completely assuaged, Jamie pushed his plate to the side and concentrated on his coffee while Conor finished off his meal. Placing his empty plate on top of Jamie's, the big American leaned back in his chair and offered his cigarettes. Jamie took one gratefully and lit up, savouring the toasted tobacco and the rich coffee. It was Conor who started the ball rolling. 'So what's the problem, Jamie?' he asked. 'It has to be something special to drag you down here this early.' Jamie dragged on his cigarette and looked surreptitiously around the room, a gesture Conor picked up on instantly. 'Come on kid, if you don't tell me I can't help,' he said encouragingly.

Jamie smiled awkwardly, wondering how to tell him that he needed his help to kill someone. He looked around the room again. The nearest occupied table was a good twenty feet away and the sailors around it were more interested in their food than in Jamie and Conor Whelan. 'I have to kill someone,' he said bluntly. 'And I need your help.'

He watched uncomfortably as the American's face transformed. 'Shit Jamie, you don't beat about the bush, do you,' Conor spluttered. He too looked around the room then. Satisfied that no one was interested in their conversation, he continued in a low voice. 'Do you want to tell me why first, kid?'

Jamie started with the attack on the Monday night and worked back from there. Conor sat, unmoving, his cigarette burning unsmoked between his fingers. He was having difficulty assimilating all of the information coming at him…and he was supposed to be an intelligence analyst, he reflected ironically. 'Let me get this straight,' he said as Jamie finished. 'This mother fucker Coleman, or Kelman, or whatever his name is, has kidnapped your girl because *he* wants to marry her?' He was shaking his head in disbelief as he spoke. Jamie nodded. 'And he tried to have you murdered on Monday night but the plan went sour?'

Jamie nodded again. 'That's about it Conor,' he said quietly.

'Shit Jamie, when do we leave?' the American said earnestly.

Jamie shook his head, a grim smile appearing on his face. 'Thanks Conor, but *we* don't. This is personal…I do it alone, or I don't do it at all.'

'So, how do I help?' Conor retorted, deflated.

Jamie set his face hard and stared at his friend. 'Two ways. First, I need a weapon…a pistol, and Second, I need to know how you would do it.'

The American pushed back his chair and stood up. 'Come on, let's get out of here,' he said. 'It's a beautiful morning; take me up to Loch Goil on that bike of yours…a run through Hell's Glen seems appropriate.'

Jamie hauled himself to his feet and followed the American out into the morning sunshine. He clambered onto the Bonneville and handed Conor his helmet, insisting that the American wear it, and then waited as Conor climbed on board behind him to perch securely on the pillion. Jamie kicked the machine into life and rode slowly out onto the main road then accelerated away. He kept his speed to a steady forty and twenty minutes later pulled into the tiny loch side village of Lochgoilhead.

They sat together on the rocky shore of Loch Goil and threw stones into the still, slate grey water, watching the rings radiate out from the stones' points of impact, intersecting and deviating, until they disappeared. 'Can you do this?' Conor asked, looking sideways at Jamie as he tossed a large rock into the loch. 'Kill a man?'

'Yes,' Jamie answered confidently. 'I've asked myself the same question…an' yes, I can do it,' he said emphatically. He saw the look of doubt on the American's face.

'Have you any idea what it's like to kill someone?' the American asked quietly. The shadow that passed across Jamie's face was more of an answer than any words could give. He would learn all about it later, he assumed. 'Have you ever fired a weapon before?' he came back.

Jamie smiled, almost bashfully Conor noticed. 'You could say that. I was in the Army Cadets till I was 18 and I trained as a marksman…won prizes for it,' he added, without any trace of inflated ego.

'Rifle?'

'Yeah, mostly, but I fired handguns as well.'

Conor stared out over the loch, amazed at what he was learning about the young man beside him. Okay, he could handle a weapon but the nagging doubt was still there…could he kill? 'If it were me, I'd use a rifle,' he said at last. 'From what you've told me, this guy is always surrounded by minders. Getting close enough is the problem so you do it without having to get right up next to him,' he advised.

They said nothing for a while. The calm of the loch was disturbed by a fish jumping and wood pigeons cooed in the distance but otherwise silence permeated the air around them. It was Jamie who spoke next. 'I thought you might say that,' he acknowledged. 'It's the sensible way, I suppose, but when am I ever sensible.' The laugh that accompanied his words was bitter. 'I want the bastard to see it coming, Conor. I want him to feel the same fear he meets out.'

'That could get *you* killed too, kid,' Conor came back swiftly. 'But I can see where you're comin' from.' He pulled his Luckies from his pocket and picked one out, then handed the packet to Jamie. They lit up from Conor's Zippo and sat quietly for a moment. 'Okay,' Conor said quietly at length. 'If you're going in close you'll need to choose the right time and the right place. You'll have to watch him, work out his routines, see who's with him and when, and then work out your approach,' he continued. 'You'll only get one chance at this, kid. You fuck it up, you're dead.'

'I won't, there's too much at stake,' Jamie retorted, smiling again.

Conor nodded pensively. He wanted to talk him out of this but he knew there was no chance of that. Jamie had made up his mind and wild horses probably wouldn't get him to change it now. So, if talking him out of it was a non-starter, the only other option was to persuade him to let him tag along. He would need to work on that. 'What pistols have you used?' he asked, starting down another path.

Jamie looked up into the sky, trying to remember. 'A Browning, definitely…a Beretta, a Lugar and a Walther PPK,' he re-joined hesitantly.

'You win prizes shootin' those too?' Conor threw back cheekily and watched Jamie smile.

'No…but even if I had I wouldn't tell you, I don't want you thinkin' I'm a bullshitter.'

Conor laughed genuinely for the first time since meeting Jamie earlier. 'Oh I know you're no bullshitter, kid,' he grinned, then grew serious again. 'Listen, I can't lay my hands on a gun quickly, least ways not one that isn't traceable…but I know a man who can.' Jamie looked at him sideways, waiting for the follow up. 'Only problem is, it'll cost,' Conor added. 'If it's money, that's not a problem, I'll cover it, but the cost might be a favour…and that might prove difficult for you.'

'Who is he?' Jamie asked quietly.

'His name doesn't matter…if he decides to tell you, that'll be his choice, but he's the guy I was meeting the night you saved my bacon,' Conor replied steadily.

'The Irishman?' Jamie murmured softly

Conor nodded slowly. 'The Irishman,' he repeated.

'I don't really have a choice, do I?' Jamie came back, regarding the American stoically.

'There's always a choice, kid, but sometimes the choice is no choice at all. If you want to go for it I'll set up a meeting…if the price is too high, you can always walk away.'

Jamie nodded, running it all through his head. He had to get Lucie back and he wanted Kelman to pay for everything he had done…and he couldn't do either of those without a gun. So, as he'd already said, he didn't have a choice. 'Okay, Conor, do it,' he said.

They spent another half hour at the loch, talking about everything and nothing, and with Conor sowing seeds he hoped would eventually grow to fruition with Jamie agreeing to let him go south with him. Finally, they mounted the Triumph and set off for Dunoon, Conor in control this time and Jamie clinging to the American as he threw the machine into every corner at speeds Jamie would only think about. As they dismounted outside the Navy Exchange the American's face was wreathed in a gigantic grin. 'That machine is a beast,' he yelled happily, the exhilaration of the ride showing all over his face.

'Well, if I don't make it through this, she's yours,' Jamie said quietly, bringing Conor back to earth with a resounding thud.

*

Conor's call came through at dinner time. Jamie was first to the phone under the watchful gaze of his father and mother and the conversation was brief. 'Tomorrow, one o'clock under the clock in Central Station' Conor said. 'I'll call you in the morning'. Jamie hung up, kept the smile on his face and resumed his meal, feeling his mother's eyes boring into him. 'It was Conor,' he said. 'I'm meeting him again tomorrow.'

Mary Raeburn looked at her son with her big, sad, brown eyes. She knew he was lying, a mother always knows, but it wasn't the fact that he had lied that was worrying her, it was why he had felt the need to lie in the first place. Her feeling of disquiet was growing. Something was wrong, seriously wrong.

Jamie left for the Western Infirmary immediately after dinner, avoiding the awkward questions he could see building in his mother's eyes. But they would still be there when he returned home later and there would be more of them by then. His mother was like a dog with a bone, she never gave up, he smiled wryly; determination, stubbornness, obstinacy, perseverance…he could go on forever. These were all traits he had inherited from her but thankfully they were balanced out, to some extent, by the easy going nature he had acquired from his father. All of that simply meant that he was normally slow to anger, but if the blue touch paper was lit, it was better to stand well clear.

His visit to the hospital did little to lighten his mood. Jack was still in Intensive Care and hadn't regained consciousness, but he was stable. Seeing him lying there, with the various drips and electronic devices attached to his body, filled Jamie with a cold, seething anger. Teresa was by the bed, clinging to Jack's hand, her face drained of emotion. She looked up as Jamie entered the room but her expression was vacant. Jamie didn't stay long. He found it difficult knowing that Jack was there because of him. Wrong time, wrong place, he told himself, but it didn't help.

Jack's father and mother arrived after about twenty minutes and that was Jamie's cue to leave. They made conversation for a while before Jamie excused himself. He needed a drink. It was a still, mild night and he wandered up Byres Road, staring unseeing into shop windows, until he reached The Byre Bar. He pushed the door open and went in, ordered a pint of Guinness and sat at the table he and Jack had occupied forty eight hours earlier. The pub was quiet but the fight nearby on Monday night was a topic of conversation amongst the drinkers who were there. Jamie saw the barman nod in his direction a couple of times and suspected that he had been recognised. Fortunately, the clientele tonight was of an age where incidents like that of Monday evening were of little interest. It was a topic of conversation, nothing more. They had seen it all before. This was Glasgow after all.

Jamie nursed his pint for a while, staring vacantly into space. He thought about his meeting with the Irishman next day and wondered if his decision to go ahead with it was just another example of his impetuosity. He debated it with himself. Conor said that there was always a choice but in this case, was there? It all depended on what, if anything, the Irishman wanted of him.

He bought a second pint. It wasn't thirst or the need for alcohol, simply the desire to delay his return home to a time when his mother would have given up and retired to her bed. When he left the pub darkness had fallen and the streetlights twinkled along the length of Byres Road. He followed the same route that he and Jack had taken on Monday night, stopping to gaze down Ashton Lane as he passed. A dark red stain on the pavement, the remnants of someone's blood, his, Jack's or Robert Hood's, caught his eye and he shivered involuntarily, as if someone had walked over his grave. Where was all of this going to end, he pondered?

His timing was perfect. Mary Raeburn had waited up later than usual but had finally given up and gone to bed only minutes before Jamie returned home. He saw her bedroom light from outside and opened the front door silently, creeping upstairs to his room, like a child playing a game. He stripped off and sank into his bed, gazing at the shadows thrown against the wall by the streetlights and passing traffic. It was going to be another long night.

Chapter 48

Conor phoned as promised just after nine thirty next morning. Jamie had risen from bed before his mother left for work and had endured the opening barrage of questions. She rushed out of the door at eight forty, saving the rest of her interrogation for later in the day.

'I assumed your Mom and Dad were around when I called last night kid, that's why I cut the call short,' Conor started. 'Your meeting is on for one thirty. Wait beneath the clock. You'll be approached, just follow the instructions. Carry a copy of the Evening Times, folded, under your left arm and smoke a cigarette.'

'And that's how they'll know me?' Jamie asked incredulously.

Conor laughed edgily. 'Yeah, clandestine isn't it,' he replied sarcastically. Don't worry; they won't pick the wrong man. Security is one thing these guys are good at…amongst others,' he continued. 'Listen, Jamie, you *are* sure about this? It's not too late to back out.'

'I'm sure,' Jamie replied emphatically.

'Okay. Call me later, alright?'

'Yeah, alright. For Christ's sake stop fretting, you're making me nervous,' Jamie laughed. But the truth was that the unmasked fear in Conor's voice had already unsettled him.

Their conversation over, Jamie prepared himself for his rendezvous. "Follow the instructions" Conor had said, so it looked as if the meeting was going to take place somewhere other than Central Station. If they were as good at security as Conor said they were it stood to reason. But he knew he was walking into the unknown and it worried him; that and the fact that after the meeting he would know the identity of the Irishman and be able to identify him later. If he decided not to take up the man's offer, what then? Would he simply be a loose end that needed to be tidied up or would his link to Conor Whelan be enough to let him walk away? There was only one way to find out.

They initial contact took place in the Central Station as arranged, with Jamie loitering beneath the big clock as instructed. A man approached him at exactly one thirty. He was about forty years of age, well built, with short greying hair and a hard face. All in all he was just another man in the crowd apart from his eyes which were memorable in every respect; cold, blue and piercing. They made him, in one word, intimidating. He asked Jamie for a light, holding up a cigarette in front of him, and waited for Jamie to oblige. As he lit his cigarette from the flame he spoke quietly under his breath, so low that Jamie had to strain to make him out. 'Wait here for two minutes and then make your way to the Isis Cafe at the corner of Bath Street and Dundas Street, just behind Queen Street Station. Go in and find a table.'

Before Jamie could respond the man had melted away into the crowd. He looked around him, feeling conspicuous, but no one seemed to be interested in him or the man. Taking his time, he finished his cigarette and then strolled out of the station into Gordon Street, turning right towards the bustle of Buchanan Street. He walked steadily, feeling all of the time that he was being watched, but he kept his eyes focussed straight ahead. He walked across Buchanan Street and through Royal Exchange Square, past the Stirling Library and left into Queen Street with the Ingram Bar off to his right. The sun was out, unusual for early October, and George Square was filled with office workers enjoying a half hour lunch break in the unseasonal warmth. In normal circumstances he might have stopped to admire the office girls in their short skirts and dresses, but today's circumstances weren't normal.

He made his way through Queen Street Station, keeping his pace relaxed, exited into Dundas Street and then turned right up the hill towards Bath Street and the café on the corner. The Isis was busy but most people were buying sandwiches to take away and he had no trouble in finding a free table. He sat down and was approached almost immediately by a middle aged waitress, heavily made up and with a red slash of lipstick highlighting her thin, mean mouth. When she spoke Jamie caught sight of uneven, nicotine stained teeth and when she forced a professional smile her face was criss-crossed by a multitude of wrinkles...all defeating the recuperative effect of her makeup.

Jamie ordered a coffee, white, and said he was waiting for a friend, thereby avoiding the necessity of ordering something to eat. The coffee arrived before the Irishman. To Jamie's surprise the man who pulled out the chair and sat down next to him wasn't the man who had approached him in the Central Station. Jamie hadn't noticed this man enter the café or seen him approach the table, and only the scraping of the chair legs on the tiled floor alerted him to the man's arrival. Jamie was impressed and a little bit intimidated. His first impression of the man was that he was nothing special and as nondescript as the man who had given him the instructions in Central Station. This one would be about the same age as the first, maybe a little older, Jamie guessed. The haircut was the same; short and grey, but when you looked closer, there was something about this man that made him different. It wasn't something Jamie could put his finger on and it wasn't something he liked, but it was there. He was like a coiled spring.

The waitress was there again in an instant and Jamie almost laughed as she ogled the guy and gave him the full works. Jamie noticed her skirt was well above her knees but her legs didn't merit exhibition. Even in the serious situation he knew he was in, Jamie was finding it hard to keep a straight face. The man didn't waste any time in dismissing her, however, and she trudged off disconsolately to fetch his tea.

The man said nothing, simply watched Jamie closely and waited until the waitress had returned with his tea before starting. 'You're clean,' he said in a distinct and almost refined Southern Irish accent and Jamie realised immediately that his sense of being watched on the walk to the café had been well founded. 'Let's keep this brief,' the Irishman continued. 'I know what you want...and I can let you have one.' He paused, looking casually around the café and watching a man and woman who had just entered. Jamie noticed him glance towards the door and followed his look. His original contact, the man from the Central, had taken a seat near the door and an almost imperceptible acknowledgement passed between the two.

'We need a job done,' the Irishman continued, keeping his voice low. 'You know all about Oxy-acetylene cutters?' he said, but it was a rhetorical question and he carried on without waiting for a reply. 'And we need a safe opened.'

'That's a hard way of doin' it,' Jamie interrupted, hiding his surprise. 'There are quicker ways.'

'Aye, there are,' the Irishman acknowledged, 'but they're also noisier and more likely to attract attention...especially in a busy location.'

'Using an oxy-acetylene cutter produces a helluva lot of heat and smoke,' Jamie advised, his voice low to match the other man's. 'And you could damage what's inside.'

'We know that, but that's our problem,' the Irishman retorted impatiently. 'All you need to do is cut it open. Let us worry about everything else.'

'Who's "us"?' Jamie asked and saw the man look up sharply, his eyes piercing into him. Jamie wasn't easily frightened but this man managed to scare him without too much difficulty and a cold shiver run up his spine.

'You don't need to know that…you don't need to know anything, in fact.'

'And if I refuse to do it?' Jamie queried.

The man smiled coldly once again. 'In that case, I walk out of here, we don't meet again, you don't get the gun and the ammunition you need…and, from what I know of your situation boy, the bad guy wins.'

Jamie stared at him. He needed a weapon, sure, but did he really want to get involved in something like this to get one? As the thought spun around his head he almost laughed aloud at the incongruity of that. *Something like this,* he repeated to himself. He was planning to kill a man; all this guy was asking him to do was cut open a safe.

The Irishman waited, confident that Jamie would come to the right decision, but he gave him a final push none the less. 'Come on son, I haven't got all feckin' day.'

Jamie nodded his agreement and watched the Irishman grin slowly. The man slurped back his tea and made a face. 'Jesus!' he cursed. 'That tastes about as bad as that feckin' waitress looks,' he continued, pushing his chair back and leaning close to Jamie with whispered instructions. 'Be at Benny's Bar in the Gorbals at half past four tomorrow afternoon. 'And bring an overnight bag…you'll be going away for a couple of days.'

'Where?' Jamie asked.

'Over the water,' the Irishman smiled. 'Other than that you don't need to know.' His tone of voice warned Jamie that it would be unwise to probe further. The same ice cold voice came again. 'And you say nothing to anyone…you hear?'

Jamie turned and looked him steadily in the eye. 'Aye, I hear.'

And with that the Irishman was gone, waltzing around the tables and disappearing out into Bath Street, the wistful look of the scrawny waitress following his departure. Jamie turned to the second man seated near the door. This one waited a moment then picked up his newspaper, dropped some coins onto the saucer on his table and followed the Irishman out into Bath Street, giving Jamie a long, hard look as he departed.

Jamie finished his coffee and dug out some change to pay for it before realising that the Irishman hadn't paid for his tea. He fished around for some more coins and paid at the counter. The waitress, sullen faced now, counted out the coins precisely as Jamie watched. He considered whether or not to tip her. *What the hell,* he decided; the service was good even if she had a face like Quasimodo's arse. He left sixpence on the counter as he turned to leave but even that failed to raise a smile.

Out in the street again he felt the afternoon sun on his back. A train was leaving Queen Street Station and a plume of white smoke billowed up from the line below as the locomotive passed under the bridge which supports Cathedral Street, another cloud funnelling up into the sky as it re-emerged on the other side. A bus horn sounded as some errant pedestrians hurried across the road. 'Normality,' Jamie muttered aloud.

He made his way back to George Square. It was empty now, the office workers back at their desks. He found a place on a vacant bench and watched the last of the girls depart but his thoughts were on Lucie. Pigeons strutted carefully around his feet, ready to skip out of the way of moving feet, and pecked at crumbs dropped from hastily eaten sandwiches. Some flew off, circling the Square before settling on the granite and bronze heads of the statues sited all around, proceeding to add to the already thick layer of bird shit already adorning them. *Those pigeons are a lot brighter than most folk give them credit for,* he mused with a smile, but it was bitter sweet as a haunting memory of Kate crept into his mind. They had waited here often, usually late at night, heading either to Ibrox or Knightswood. He still missed her.

*

'I'm going away for a few days,' Jamie announced after dinner that night. He explained it by saying that he had managed to find a few days' work but the inevitable questions followed. Expecting these, he had a story all prepared. 'I'm going up to Nigg,' he lied. 'One of the North Sea Oil Companies needs some welding work done on a platform, bit of a rush job,' he continued plausibly and his mother accepted it without question. He was getting good at lying.

As Mary Raeburn left for work next morning she called up to him, wishing him good luck. *I think I might need it,* Jamie reflected as the door banged shut behind her.

He made a telephone call to Beeston, hoping to speak to Julie but she was at work. Jo wanted to know how he was, repeated again how sorry they all were to hear about Jack and asked him to pass on everyone's good wishes when he saw him again. She went on to ask when he thought he would be returning but he kept it vague…it wouldn't be too long but he still had things to arrange. There had been no contact with Lucie and she hadn't turned up for work at the hospital since the evening of her "disappearance" but, so far as Julie knew, she had been in touch saying that she was unwell and would return as soon as she was better. Jamie hadn't expected anything more but having it confirmed dampened his spirits. He asked Jo to let Julie know he had phoned, explaining that he was going to be away for a few days and would call again when he returned.

The call over, he packed a bag for the trip; the usual things, clean underwear and socks, toothbrush and toothpaste, shaving kit, spare pair of jeans and a couple of T-shirts. He took his savings from the drawer in his room where he kept them and counted out the notes. Seventy three Pounds in a mix of pound notes and five pound notes covered his bed quilt. It was still a tidy sum but it was reducing quickly now. That was one good thing about the Irish job though; it meant he wouldn't have to splash out for a gun.

It was just before four o'clock in the afternoon when he sauntered down Stockwell Street from Trongate and walked over the stone built Victoria Bridge spanning the Clyde and into Gorbals. He was early and spent some time looking in the little shops around Gorbals Cross and killed time by wandering up to The Citizen's Theatre, studying the posters announcing coming events. Romeo and Juliet was playing the following month – "Shakespeare's Tragic Love Story", he read, and remembered Kelman's sarcastic comment the week before. Finally, as the clock approached half past four, he made his way back to Benny's Bar. The Bar was closed, as expected, with opening time still half an hour off and the streets were quiet. He stood outside the entrance and lit a cigarette, looking along Ballater Street in the direction of Bridgeton when a girl approached him from the opposite direction.

'Jamie Raeburn?' she asked, her voice soft, clearly Irish.

Jamie turned towards her, catching a hint of her perfume. She was smiling uncertainly and he saw that she was pretty. Long, curly, dark red hair tumbled down over her shoulders and her face was illuminated by two brilliant, emerald green eyes. She was wearing a long black maxi coat over a bottle green dress, black leather boots up to her knees, and she had a small canvas holdall slung over her shoulder.

Jamie smiled in response. 'Aye, that's me,' he said pleasantly. 'I take it you're here to tell me what's happenin'?'

'Not exactly,' she replied with a smile. 'I'm going with you.'

Jamie looked at her with undisguised surprise and she gazed back, confident now. He could see she was a few years older than him, maybe twenty-five or twenty-six, probably about Kate's age, he reflected. She was attractive…but in a harder sort of way than Kate. Definitely not the sort of girl you'd come home to on a Friday night with an opened pay packet, he mused.

'So what's the story?' Jamie demanded, 'and where are we goin'?'

'You know where you're going,' she replied tartly. 'And if anyone asks, we're on a romantic weekend over in Belfast visiting my mother. You can tell them we're engaged, if you like' she laughed, 'but don't get any ideas.'

'Don't worry, you're safe with me,' Jamie replied quickly, his thoughts now centred on Lucie. 'So how are we gettin' there?'

'The boat leaves the Broomielaw at quarter to seven,' she told him, 'there's a cabin booked for us…you're Dermott Lynch, by the way,' she continued, hauling a wallet from her handbag and handing it over. 'And I'm your *fiancée*, Roisin Kelly…that's my real name.' She cocked an eyebrow at him as she emphasised the "fiancée" bit, waiting for a reaction but got none. Pity, she thought, he's quite good looking and a cuddle would help to pass the night. She'd done the trip before, escorting men across and back, but most of them were old farts that couldn't get it up even if she'd wanted them to, which she hadn't. This one was different though and it had been a long time, she reminded herself. Self-imposed chastity had to end sometime. Maybe she'd try him again later, see if he was up for it. Putting that thought to the back of her mind, she slipped an arm through his. 'Come on then,' she piped, 'you can look through the wallet later. We'll walk along to the Suspension Bridge and then along Clyde Street…it shouldn't take us too long to get to the ferry.'

Jamie slipped the wallet into his inside jacket pocket and they set off. They walked arm in arm, saying little, and arrived at the quay at quarter past five. Roisin rummaged in her handbag again and found the tickets, showing them to a heavily built woman with her hair tied back in a severe bun and just the hint of a moustache on her upper lip. There was a wedding ring on her finger and Jamie wondered what her husband was like…probably a skinny wee guy that she had thrown over her shoulder one night at the dancing, he laughed silently. The woman hardly gave them a glance, simply stamped the tickets and handed them back, a bored expression painted across her pudgy face. Roisin slipped the tickets back inside her handbag and minutes later they were on board, following a steward in an almost white uniform down two decks to their cabin. The steward opened the cabin door and ushered them in, lingering brazenly for a tip. Jamie slipped him sixpence and followed Roisin into the cabin.

It was Jamie's first sea voyage and the cabin wasn't what he expected. The ship would be safe enough, of that he was certain, because a plaque fixed onto the bulkhead as they boarded announced the fact that it had been built at John Brown's Yard. But he was disappointed. He was used to building the hulls and decks, welding giant steel panels, but fitting out was done after the ships were launched and he had never taken the time to see what the finished article looked like. The cabin was a lot smaller than he had thought it would be. In fact, it was cramped; two single bunk beds, a tiny toilet and a small round porthole. It was almost claustrophobic. Roisin pressed down on the beds and chose the softer of the two, the lower one, slipping her holdall from her shoulder and dumping it down proprietorially. 'You can get on top,' she said with a smirk, the double entendre clearly intended.

'Nice!' Jamie exclaimed, ignoring her and unable to keep the sarcasm out of his voice.

'I've sailed in worse,' Roisin replied quickly. 'This one's quite cosy really,' she added, fluttering her eyelashes. 'And if the crossing gets rough, we can share my bunk and hold on tight... that way you won't slip out,' she laughed suggestively and stretched out on the mattress showing an impressive expanse of thigh.

'Aye, right,' Jamie retorted, not rising to the bait. 'So what do we do now?'

'Well, we could stay here and get to know each other better,' Roisin replied. 'Or we could go up to the bar and you can buy me a drink...and get to know each other better.'

'A drink sounds good,' Jamie responded, amused by the undisguised look of disappointment that appeared on her face.

'Ah well, it was worth a try,' she sighed and pushed herself up from the bunk. 'In that case I'll just have to get you drunk,' she laughed.

They spent the next hour in the bar chatting aimlessly about anything that came into their minds, but avoiding the important issue. Jamie wondered if Roisin knew why he was going across but even if she did, he knew it was highly unlikely that she would talk about it. She was his cover for the visit, no more than that. He doubted that anyone would be watching them but he played the part he had been given, just in case. Before they left the cabin to come up to the bar he examined the contents of the wallet she had given him earlier. It contained a driving licence in the name of Dermott Lynch with an address in Royston, an old wage slip from the Caledonian Railway Works at Springburn, a photograph of Roisin and an opened packet of three condoms with two missing. Dermott was either a non-practising Tim or he spent a lot of time at confession, Jamie smiled to himself. He looked at Roisin questioningly as he flicked through the contents. 'Dermott's away with his real girlfriend this weekend in case anyone checks up...memorise his address and date of birth' she said, closing the subject.

The ship left the Broomielaw promptly at six forty-five and they stood together on the deck watching the lights slip past on both sides of the river. Welding torches lit the night sky as they passed the Fairfield Yard at Govan and soon they were passing Yoker, the Renfrew Ferry bobbing up and down in the wake of the bigger ship. John Brown's yard crept up on their right and Jamie nostalgically eyed the tall skeletons of the yard's cranes towering over a new ship with its hull just laid. He could still be there, he thought, welding away from morning to night, carefree, instead of heading for Northern Ireland to God knows what. The Q.E II sat further downriver, her giant bulk filling the skyline and lights shining through her portholes, and Jamie reflected that shipbuilding work was beginning to dry up. Leaving the yard when he did had probably been the right thing to do...for all sorts of reasons.

As the ship passed Dumbarton Rock on the starboard side Jamie and Roisin made their way to the Restaurant and settled into seats at a table looking out towards the lights of Dumbarton which twinkled in the darkening sky. The food was good, if a little pricey, and Jamie was relieved when Roisin picked up the bill. They returned to the bar after that and joined some other passengers for a fortifying drink.

A heavy swell built up as the ship left the shelter of the Clyde Estuary and it started to pitch and yaw in the mounting waves. It was obvious to Jamie that some of the passengers were drinking now solely to curb their anxiety and Roisin too was looking a little green around the gills. He escorted her down to the cabin just after eleven o'clock and sat patiently on the lower bunk while she commandeered the little toilet. He smiled to himself at the sound of her violent retching. Shagging wouldn't be on her mind tonight, he laughed, relieved.

Roisin was pale and drawn when she emerged from the tiny cubicle about twenty minutes later, her hair dishevelled and a trace of spittle on her chin. Jamie took pity on her. He smiled encouragingly and wiped her chin with a handkerchief, tucked her long red tresses behind her ears and helped her into her bunk, pulling the covers up over her. She looked up at him despairingly.

'Don't worry,' he said with a grin. 'This one was built at John Brown's…we'll make it.' He climbed up onto the upper bunk and leaned over to be able to see her, aware of his protective instincts kicking in. *Stop it,* he told himself. *That's your biggest problem Jamie Raeburn; you're always looking out for other people when most of them don't give a shit about you…so stop it.*

Roisin finally fell into a fitful sleep and Jamie lay back on his bunk, falling asleep fully clothed, dreams of Lucie and her plight filling his head.

When the ship entered Belfast Lough the following morning the sea was placid though the sky was still a heavy grey and rain was threatening again. Roisin avoided breakfast but Jamie ate for both of them, taking on board as much as he could, uncertain of when he might next eat. Roisin settled for a coffee but Jamie had to admit that she seemed to have recovered reasonably well.

As they stepped onto the quayside the rain began to fall and they ran for the shelter of the sheds lining the docks, passing straight through to the roadway beyond. It wasn't unlike Glasgow's Clydeside, Jamie thought, grey, industrial, and oppressive. There was something else here though. Some undercurrent that he couldn't quite define but his senses picked up on. He looked around. The streets were quiet, the weather being partly to blame for that, but the feeling still nagged at him.

They joined a queue waiting for the taxis and, for some reason unknown to Jamie, Roisin seemed annoyed. Suddenly, an old white van, held together with rust and a coating of grime, pulled to a halt on the other side of the road and the driver hit the horn. Every pair of eyes in the queue turned to the sound but it was Roisin who reacted. Quickly, she grabbed Jamie by the arm and tugged him across the road as the driver emerged from the van, a broad grin plastered across his face. 'There's nothin' like announcing our arrival, Liam,' Roisin laughed and hugged him. She turned to Jamie. 'Dermott,' she said with a smile, sticking to his cover, 'This is my big cousin Liam.'

Liam looked Jamie over and thrust out a large calloused hand. He was about thirty five to forty years old; it was hard to estimate accurately. A few days' growth of stubble adorned his chin and jaw and a greasy flat cap sat precariously on top of his head. His eyes were a startling blue and Jamie was reminded of the man he had met in Glasgow two days earlier. 'Welcome to Free Belfast,' he laughed quietly, and Roisin drew him a sharp look. Jamie took his hand and felt the strength in his grip as they shook hands.

'Brendan would flay you alive if he caught you saying that,' she warned, looking over towards the dwindling queue at the taxi stand.

Liam laughed carelessly. He made his way to the back of the van and opened the doors. 'Put your bags in here,' he said, holding the doors wide to prevent them closing again. Jamie placed his bag on top of what appeared to be Liam's tool box and surveyed the contents of the van. There were pieces of copper and lead piping, a bag of metal joints, a roll of solder, an old radiator and a gas ring and, tucked at the back, against the bulkhead between the cab and the back of the van stood a gas cylinder and some welding equipment. Liam saw his questioning look and grinned. 'I'm a plumber,' he explained, cum blacksmith, cum welder, cum general dogsbody.'

Jamie looked again at the welding gear. If Liam was a welder, why did they need him to cut open a safe? Liam could do it, he thought, knitting his brow together. Liam caught Jamie's perplexed expression but said nothing, simply slammed the doors shut and ordered them into the cab. Roisin went in first and Jamie followed, Liam returning to the driver's side and hauling his bulk into the worn seat. It was cramped in the front with the three of them but Jamie accepted it stoically. The van might have looked like a rust bucket but Jamie, knowledgeable about engines, was surprised at how sweet it sounded.

'She doesn't look much,' Liam acknowledged. 'But she's never let me down.' He paused, concentrated on an Austin Countryman toddling along in front of them and pushed his foot to the floor, swerving wildly to overtake, then straightened the van up, grinning infectiously. 'Old fart shouldn't be out on the road,' he said disparagingly, referring to the elderly driver he had just cut up. 'You're wonderin' why you're here if I can cut open the safe,' he said, throwing Jamie off balance. 'The answer is simple. As soon as the job is discovered the R.U.C is going to be around at my place, crawling all over me, and at the home of every other volunteer they know is capable of doing the job. Add to that the fact that most of us are watched by the bastards in Special Branch almost round the clock and you start to get the picture. When the job goes off, most of us will have a watertight alibi,' he grinned, 'provided by Special Branch itself. They don't know you and you'll be well away before they even know what's happened.'

Jamie considered this. If Special Branch, whoever they were, were watching Liam "almost round the clock" then presumably they were watching Liam now and that meant they had probably seen Jamie and Roisin arrive. He was about to ask the question when Liam started off again, reading his mind. 'Aye, they saw me meeting you and Roisin, but when they check up they'll find that she *is* my little cousin and they'll learn that you're her fiancée, over to visit Roisin's Auntie Molly...that's my mother, and all the mother Roisin here has had since her own Ma died years ago...an' you'll be seen about town together, doin' all the things that young lovers do,' he laughed.

'All the things that young lovers do?' Roisin repeated with a laugh, 'chance would be a fine thing.'

Jamie ignored her but Liam laughed uproariously. 'Where are we going now?' Jamie asked.

'My mother's house,' Liam replied, beating Roisin to the response. 'I'm dropping you off. You'll spend the rest of the day there until it's time for the job. You'll be picked up and taken to it. Just do exactly what your driver tells you. Roisin will leave the house with you but you'll both disappear for a while after that. You'll meet up again afterwards and you'll go somewhere where you'll be seen. If anyone asks about you later the whole place will swear you'd been there all night.'

'Is all this cloak and dagger stuff necessary?' Jamie asked innocently. Liam stared at him with an expression of total disbelief and Roisin's expression hardened. 'Listen,' Roisin spat out. 'There are things about this place you don't understand…and you probably never will. Things are changing here…they have to.' Her voice was intense, filled with conviction. 'You'll find out all about it soon enough, but for now, you're just here to do a job…and when you've done it, you can go home and forget everything.' She smiled coldly, leaned back in her seat and avoided his eyes.

Jamie looked out of the window. His first impression of the city was being reinforced rapidly…grey buildings and grey, decaying houses, grey sky and grey people trudging along with slumped shoulders. As they crossed the river Lagan the rain stopped but the leaden grey, anthracite sky was still preventing the sun from breaking through but even if it did, Jamie doubted if it would brighten the backdrop. This side of the river appeared to be even more deprived, he noted, and they passed little groups of men waiting outside a big, nondescript building.

'What are they doing?' he asked naively.

Roisin turned her head and looked out of the window. 'They're unemployed and that's the labour exchange,' she replied, pointing to a big, pollution stained red sandstone building. 'They'll be hoping to find work but they'll be lucky…there's not much of that around here if you're a Catholic,' she growled, her voice betraying her bitterness.

Christ, and I thought Glasgow was bad, Jamie mused.

They turned off the main road, Short Strand, and into Arran Street…narrow streets of depressing two storey buildings, small terraced houses lining even narrower pavements. Jamie had spent some time in Liverpool a year earlier and the houses here reminded him of some he had seen there. Some attempt had been made to alleviate the overwhelming sense of drab greyness by painting the outsides of the houses and many windows showed posters, all demanding change. Irish tricolour flags were everywhere so there were no prizes for guessing they were entering a Nationalist conclave.

Jamie kept his thoughts to himself but he was beginning to regret his decision to come. He was wondering what he had got himself into but, if he was honest, he didn't really want to know. *Do what they ask, get home, get the pistol from them and sort out your own problems.* Roisin was right, he didn't need to know.

Liam pulled up outside a fairly ordinary house – no garish paintwork, no posters in the windows and no tricolour. Jamie alighted from the van and looked around, waiting patiently for Roisin who was speaking in hushed tones with Liam. Some raggedy arsed children were playing in the street, a few boys kicking a small ball and a handful of girls skipping with an old rope and he had a sudden flashback to Copland Place six months earlier, the day he had gone to check on Kate. Christ, she was still inside him, still part of him, he realised.

Roisin stepped out onto the pavement beside him and took hold of his arm as Liam swung the van round and headed back towards the main road, giving the horn a toot as he did so. The house door opened just as Roisin lifted her hand to the brass knocker, their arrival obviously anticipated. An elderly woman with white hair tied back in a bun and bright, intelligent, grey eyes, greeted them with a smile, kissed Roisin affectionately and ushered them both inside. Jamie looked back as he stepped over the threshold and caught the twitch of curtains on a couple of houses on the other side of the road. Not much would happen in this neck of the woods without people knowing about it, he surmised.

The old woman caught his look and smiled. 'Don't you be worryin' about them, son,' she said reassuringly. 'So far as they're concerned, ye're not here,' she cackled quietly.

The house was small and cluttered. Roisin obviously knew her way around and led Jamie into the kitchen where a square table sat in the middle of the floor with four chairs positioned haphazardly around it. It was still covered with plates and cups from breakfast and a couple of crusts of toast remained uneaten. A black cat lay curled up on a cushion in one corner of the room, watching them lazily from beneath heavy eye lids. A kettle sat on the cooker, bubbling away but not quite boiling.

'There's a room upstairs for you to use,' Roisin advised. 'You'll be picked up later and taken to the job.'

'An' you?'

'I'll be waiting for you,' she replied with an easy smile. 'Just to make sure you get back here in one piece. Do you want anything to eat just now?'

'No,' he laughed. 'I ate your breakfast on the ferry.' Roisin pulled a face.

The old woman came into the room and pulled a chair out from beneath the table, lowering herself onto it. 'What's yer name, son?' she asked, picking up a piece of the discarded toast and nibbling at it.

'Jam...' He was about to give his own name when he caught Roisin's warning look and stopped himself. 'Dermott,' he corrected quickly. 'Dermott Lynch.'

The old woman looked at him with amusement. 'Well Dermott Lynch, I hope ye're going to make an honest woman out of my little Roisin,' she said with a chuckle.

Jamie looked at both women. The family similarity was strong and they could easily be taken for mother and daughter. The older woman, Auntie Molly, looked well into her late sixties and Roisin was around twenty four or twenty five. Quite an age gap but anything was possible in this crazy place.

'This is my Auntie Molly,' Roisin started, introducing the older woman. 'But as Liam pointed out, she's the closest thing to a mother I've ever had since my own Mammy died. Auntie Molly is my father's eldest sister...and I'm the youngest of the family.'

'She'd be daughter number five and the last of nine,' the older woman added proudly. 'It was Roisin's brother Brendan you met back in Glasgow.'

'Christ!' Jamie muttered. 'I thought he was her father.'

The laughter from both women filled the room. 'For your sake, I don't think we'll tell him that,' Auntie Molly spluttered.

When things calmed down the women suggested it would be a good idea for Jamie to go to his room and rest. Wherever he was going and whatever he was going to cut open was to be started that night. Roisin took him upstairs and opened a room immediately off the landing. The curtains were pulled closed and the room was in semi-darkness but, from what Jamie could make out, it looked comfortable enough. A double bed, neatly made up, sat against the wall below the window. Plenty of room to toss and turn in there, he mused. There was also a three tier chest of drawers against the wall behind the door and a small chair next to the bed. A picture of The Madonna and Child was on the wall above the chest of drawers. He'd seen similar in Jack's home back in Glasgow. Someone must have painted a job lot, he smiled to himself.

'Get some sleep if you can,' Roisin advised. 'You'll need it.' She paused in the doorway as Jamie tossed his bag onto the chair and started to unbutton his shirt. 'If you need a cuddle to help you get over I'll be happy to give you one,' she said impishly, remembering her thoughts of the night before.

Aye, and in any other circumstances I'd be happy to give you one, Jamie reflected. Roisin smiled, as if reading his mind, then blew him a kiss and pulled the door closed behind her.

He lay down on the bed and closed his eyes, a vision of Lucie appearing before him immediately. God, how he missed her. The house was quiet but he could hear the faint voices of two women chattering away in the kitchen below, interspersed with louder laughter. He thought again about what he had let himself in for later but kept coming back to Lucie. No matter what he had to do, he would do it, simply because he loved her and he had to get her back. That dilemma resolved, he drifted into a deep sleep.

Chapter 49

It was growing dark outside when Jamie awoke. He could hear voices drifting up from the kitchen and there was a male voice interspersed with those of Roisin and her "Auntie Molly". It was then he realised he had been awakened by the sound of the outside door banging, probably when the man downstairs had come in. He heard footsteps on the stairs and then the bedroom door opened. He looked over through half closed eyes and saw Roisin framed in the doorway, the light from the landing putting her in silhouette, glowing in her dark red hair and filtering through her curls.

'You're awake!' she said softly, as the light from the landing reflected in his eyes.

'Aye, I'm awake. Is it time to go?'

Roisin shook her head. 'Not yet, but Mammy's made dinner. If you want a wash, the bathroom's at the end there,' she said, turning her head and nodding along the landing.

'Thanks. I'll be down in a minute.' He waited a second then asked. 'Who's the man?'

Roisin smiled. 'It's Liam,' she explained. 'He lives here and you're meeting the family, remember?'

'Surely he's not the one taking me, is he?'

'No, he's not,' Roisin cut in quickly. 'He'll be staying here. If he took you Special Branch would be all over you.'

Jamie nodded but he had detected a hint of anxiety in her voice.

'What's wrong?' he asked.

'Nothing's wrong,' Roisin replied awkwardly. 'It's just that…well, if things go wrong tonight and you're caught.' She stopped short, letting her words hang in the air.

'If I'm caught I'm in the shit, but I won't drop anyone else in it,' Jamie assured her quietly. 'I'm here because I need something from your brother back in Glasgow and it's not something I can tell the police about. Don't worry, I won't grass.'

Roisin smiled sadly. 'People say that sort of thing all the time, but when the pressure's on they change their minds to save their own skins,' she said cynically, looking him steadily in the eye. Jamie waited quietly, letting her reach whatever conclusion she chose. Finally she let out a sigh and her face softened. 'But strangely enough, I believe you,' she said. Her eyes lingered on him as he rose from the bed. She knew what the "something" was that he was getting from her brother and she knew why he needed it. *God, why can't I meet a man like this*, she asked? *Someone who would love me the way he loves that girl.* As she made her way back down the stairs she spoke quietly to herself. *'I don't know who you are love,'* she whispered, thinking of Lucie, *'but you are one lucky girl.'*

Jamie followed her five minutes later, his face washed and wearing a clean T-Shirt. As he entered the kitchen all of the occupants turned to face him and Liam rose from his chair, his hand outstretched and a grin all over his face. Jamie looked him over once again. The family resemblance was strong in this one too but his earlier guess at Liam's age was out, he realised. He revised it downwards. Shaved and tidied up Liam was clearly no older than thirty five but his hair was showing signs of grey and without the flat cap perched on top of his head, Jamie could see he was balding prematurely. His features, like those of his cousin Brendan in Glasgow, looked like they had been chiselled out of granite and his eyes, like those of Roisin, were green, alert and intelligent. He was taller than Jamie, probably six feet tall, and he had a physique to match his height. Jamie thought back to Brendan, the older cousin, and remembered the penetrating, ice cold eyes and the feeling of fear that they had generated. Liam had the physique to put the frighteners on most folk, Jamie considered, but his eyes were softer.

As he sat back down Liam lifted a small backpack from the floor and handed it to him. 'Work clothes for tonight,' he explained. 'After ye've eaten, ye can put this lot on over yer own clothes.' Jamie arched his eyebrows as he took hold of the bag, his question unasked.

'With these on ye'll just be a feckin' shadow in the night,' Liam laughed. 'Ye won't be able to identify any of the other boys ye're workin' with and they won't be able to finger you either...fair enough?'

Jamie nodded slowly, grasping the sense of it. 'Yeah, fair enough,' he agreed, 'but what about you?'

'What *about* me? I'm not goin' with ye,' Liam replied with a laugh. 'You just concentrate on you, it's safer,' he added.

"Auntie Molly" rose from the table and ushered Jamie to a seat before turning to her cooker and the meal she had prepared. Jamie sniffed appreciatively as she placed it in front of him. He had to admit it smelled delicious...and it was! A mutton stew with plenty of potatoes and carrots, and all washed down with a glass of cold milk. It was a meal Jamie's own mother would have been proud of. A pint of Guinness would have gone down well with it but that wasn't on offer, for obvious reasons. He would be doing a dangerous job, working in an enclosed space, and tanking up on alcohol beforehand wasn't a good idea.

The meal finished, Jamie pushed his plate away from him and dug out his cigarettes. 'Is it alright if I smoke?' he asked politely.

Molly laughed. 'Your Mammy has obviously brought ye up well, son,' she complimented. 'The men in this house don't usually ask,' she added, drawing Liam a look to which he responded with a sheepish grin.

Jamie offered the packet round and Auntie Molly and Liam both availed themselves of it, lighting up from Jamie's lighter. They smoked quietly, all of them pensive. Jamie looked around the table and wondered what drove ordinary people like them to do what they were doing. Sure, he knew a bit about Irish history, knew that the Nationalist population in the North wanted a unified Ireland, but would they really use violence to get it? They didn't seem the type...Auntie Molly in particular. But then again, what was the type? Roisin's older brother Brendan, now he was the type.

Jamie finished his cigarette and stubbed it out in an ashtray that Auntie Molly had placed in the centre of the table. Hoisting the bag from the ground, he pushed back his chair and stood up. 'I'll go and get ready then,' he murmured, stating the obvious.

Liam nodded and looked at his watch. 'The car will be here for you in fifteen minutes. It's dark outside so ye can leave the mask off and pull yer own jacket over the top.' He started to chuckle. 'It's not a good idea to drive through Belfast at night dressed in black and wearin' a mask...it attracts unwanted attention.'

'If you're bein' watched...?'

'Don't worry, I'm leavin' before ye an' the Special Branch boys will be followin' me,' Liam smiled grimly.

Jamie nodded then left them, climbing the stairs once more and entered the bedroom. His own bag lay on the chair where he had left it earlier and he opened it, ready to put away the clothes he was now taking off and take out something more appropriate for the work he was about to do. He peeled off his T-shirt and folded it carefully, placing it on top of the other items.

The door opened as he was about to unzip his jeans and, to his surprise, Roisin slipped into the room. 'I just came to warn you to be careful,' she said awkwardly. 'The men you're working with don't know your background…and they don't much like Prods. Don't let anything slip.' She studied him carefully, taking in the muscles of his arms and his stomach before looking up into his eyes. She suddenly envied the girl who had his heart. Jamie smiled at her, as though reading her thoughts, and she blushed, averting her eyes from his.

'I'm flattered,' he said. 'It's just…'

'I know,' she whispered wistfully, 'you're spoken for.'

They stood looking at each other, neither able to speak nor wanting to break away. Finally, it was Roisin who broke the silence. 'Be careful,' she repeated, 'and at least I'll get to spend a night with you on the way back to Glasgow.' She smiled sadly and slipped out of the room.

Voices drifted up from below, the outside door banged and the engine of Liam's van roared into life. Jamie watched from a tiny gap in the curtain. Below him in the street he saw Liam wave and then the van pulled away. Seconds later a Post Office van with two men in the front passed the window, following at what Jamie assumed they thought was a discrete distance. He smiled. What a place, he thought. Quickly, he finished changing and then pulled the loose black trousers and black polo neck jumper over his own clothes. The socks and shoes were next, thick black socks and cheap, black trainers. Standing in front of the wardrobe mirror he looked himself over. The man in black, he laughed, like the advert for Black Magic chocolates on the telly. Everything was black, black shoes, black socks, black trousers, a black polo neck sweater and black cotton gloves. When he pulled the ski mask over his head the only bit of white now on view was a small strip around his eyes. He looked like a delegate at an Undertakers Convention, he laughed grimly. Liam was right, he'd be completely anonymous. He removed the ski mask and gloves and made his way downstairs to re-join Roisin and Auntie Molly.

As he entered the kitchen Roisin looked him up and down approvingly and Molly nodded. 'If ye keep yer mouth shut son, nobody will know where ye're from,' Molly said.

'Is that right?' An' if I talk like this?' he grinned, breaking into a perfect imitation of her accent. Both women looked at him in astonishment then started to laugh.

'Ye've got talent, son, I'll give ye that!' Molly grinned.

Chapter 50

The car, a nondescript black taxi, arrived a few minutes later and Roisin took him by the arm. With his tan coloured leather jacket pulled over the black outfit he looked like any other guy going out to enjoy a night on the town and with a good looking girl like Roisin on his arm, the picture was complete. Roisin slipped into the back seat of the taxi and Jamie followed, pulling the door shut. Nothing was said and the driver pulled away, heading back into the centre of Belfast.

They drove in silence for about fifteen minutes before the driver spoke. 'It's not far now,' he started in a thick, almost unintelligible Belfast accent. 'Ye'll see a row of shops and offices, three storey blocks. I'm goin' to drop ye at the end of an alley between the buildins…it runs down from the road to another alley runnin' along the back.' Suddenly they were thrown to the side as the car swerved violently to avoid a stray dog that had run out into the road in front of them. 'Feckin' stupid animal!' The driver swore vehemently before recovering his composure. Nerves were frayed. 'Go down the alley,' he continued eventually. 'When ye get to the bottom turn left. There's a wall on yer left with doors set into it. The doors are kept locked but the third door won't be, open it and go on through. Ye'll find yerself in a yard at the back of the buildin'. Find the door into the buildin'…it'll be unlocked too and the rest of the Unit will be waitin' for ye inside. Clear?'

Jamie nodded in acknowledgement. 'Names?' he asked.

The driver looked at him as if he was crazy. 'Are ye fer feckin' real?' he asked incredulously, and then laughed nervously. 'Think of them like those Irish jokes youse tell over the water…Pat, Mick and The Irishman jokes, eh? Well, that's who they'll be, Pat, Mick and The feckin' Irishman, but I wouldn't call them that to their faces if I were ye, not if ye want to get out of there in one piece.' He looked anxious. 'Before ye go intae the yard just make sure there's no one's around and then pull on yer mask and gloves,' he instructed. 'Remember, it's the third door…don't hang about if ye miss it. The lane runs on quite a bit and goes intae that park we passed back down the road a'ways.' Even his laugh was nervous now. 'Don't go intae the park…there's a fair bit of shaggin' goes on in there at night, especially at the weekends, an' we don't want ye getting' side-tracked.'

'There's no chance of that,' Jamie responded, laughing grimly. Roisin sat quietly beside him and he realised for the first time that her face was deathly white and she was trembling. He squeezed her arm gently and she turned to him. 'It'll be alright,' he whispered.

The driver turned the car into a busy street lined with bars and restaurants but these soon fell behind them and offices and shops became more prevalent. Suddenly, the car pulled to a halt and the driver gestured in the direction of the alley which appeared as a dark slash against the grey stone walls. 'On ye go! Straight down, don't hang about,' he hissed.

Jamie had already taken off his own jacket and handed it to Roisin. 'See you later…I hope,' he smiled grimly, and then he was out of the car and running down the alley. He met no one and saw nobody. The alley was deserted but the noise from the bars further down the street could be heard filling the cold night air. He was fairly relaxed, sure he wouldn't meet anyone; the only people likely to use the alley would be guys needing to relieve themselves or couples sneaking out of the pubs down the road for a quick shag, but it was still a bit early in the evening for that. The cold would dampen their ardour just now but it might be a different story later, no matter how cold it was.

Reaching the intersecting lane, he turned left as instructed and checked his surroundings. He was still alone. Time for the mask, he told himself. He slipped the tight fitting ski mask over his head and pulled on the black gloves just as he reached the third gate. He skipped over a puddle outside the gate and gripped the handle, twisting and pushing at the same time. It opened easily. Edging cautiously through, he entered the yard and pulled the gate closed behind him. The yard itself was in total darkness, pitch black, and he bumped into a strategically placed rubbish bin and set the lid rattling. In the silence the noise was deafening and he uttered a silent curse as he steadied it with his hand. Feeling his way carefully along the wall and checking ahead of him with his hand for further obstacles, he found the door and opened it gingerly. As it swung inwards a dark shadow appeared in front of him and what little light there was glinted on the barrel of an Armalite rifle.

'Get in here, quick, fer fuck sake!' a voice from the shadows whispered urgently and a hand grabbed him. The door banged shut and a torch was flicked on, its beam shining full in his face temporarily blinding him. When his vision returned he found that he was in a narrow corridor. He could make out nothing of the man holding the torch but, ominously, the Armalite was still in full view.

The man guided him along the corridor and down a narrow flight of stairs into what Jamie took to be the basement. The rest of the group was there, two men dressed in the same clothes as Jamie, waited at the foot of the stairs. The pale, meagre light coming from a naked bulb fixed to the centre of the ceiling by a frayed cable did its best to illuminate the room and cast eerie shadows against the ancient whitewashed walls. In one corner Jamie picked out the cutting equipment which had obviously been brought in earlier.

The leader of the group looked Jamie up and down, trying to intimidate him, but Jamie simply returned his look. The ski masks covered their features but the eyes spoke volumes. Jamie decided this one was "Pat", the leader. 'I hope ye know what yer doin'?' Pat said quietly. 'We want to be in an' out of here quickly.'

'How old is the safe?' Jamie asked, running his eyes over the equipment.

The three men looked at one another. None of them appeared to know the answer.

'Why do ye need to know?' Pat queried. 'It's just a feckin' safe.'

'Aye, I know it's just a feckin' safe,' Jamie replied, mimicking him cheekily and Pat's eyes flared angrily. 'But if it's a new feckin' safe then it's probably been made with copper alloy sandwiched between layers of steel,' Jamie explained.

'And that means?' Pat interrupted.

Jamie looked at him steadily. 'The oxy-acetylene cutter operates at about 6000 degrees Fahrenheit…which cuts through steel fairly easily, but if there's copper in between layers of steel then we've got a problem. Copper has got high thermal conductivity so when it's heated the heat dissipates and this prevents it melting or burning,' he said, remembering the words of an instructor from his college days. He looked at the eyes behind the masks but they all appeared to have glazed over.

'So why has no one mentioned this before?' Pat demanded forcefully, voicing his obvious suspicion.

'Maybe you didn't fuckin' ask,' Jamie retorted, beginning to lose patience.

'Why am I gettin' the feelin' yer tryin' to back out?' Pat hissed back at him.

Jamie laughed harshly. 'Listen pal, I've got my own reasons for bein' here. If I'd wanted to back out I'd have done it back in Glasgow, not here. So get a fuckin' grip.'

Pat thought about that. He didn't like this Glaswegian bastard one little bit but if they used one of the local boys he'd be picked up within five minutes of the job being discovered...and that could be fatal for all of them. The deciding factor for Pat, however, was that Brendan Kelly had sent this guy over and Pat knew better than to question Brendan's judgment. 'So when did they start puttin' copper in the feckin' things?' he asked, backing down.

'Late 1920's or early 1930's,' Jamie told him. 'They realised the old steel safes were too easy to open. I take it none of you has actually seen the safe?' He watched as all of three men shook their heads, confirming his assumption. 'Right, I'll ask you somethin' you *should* know the answer to. How long do we have to do the job?'

It was Pat who answered. 'The office is closed all weekend,' he said confidently. 'Security checks are carried out on the outside but no one comes into the building.'

'You're sure?'

'The place has been watched,' one of the others, who Jamie took to be Pat's second in command, reported. 'So aye, we're sure.'

Jamie nodded thoughtfully. This guy would be "Mick" which left the lad with the rifle as "The Irishman". 'Well that's somethin' at least,' he answered, trying to sound positive. 'If it's relatively new an' there's copper in it, I can still cut it, but it'll take longer.'

'Well, ye've got till early Monday mornin', will that do ye?' Pat asked irritably.

Jamie laughed. 'Aye, that'll do me. I expected to be in an' out in less than two hours. If it's a new safe it'll take longer but I'll still be finished tonight.'

'Thank fuck fer that,' Pat exclaimed. 'Are there any other feckin' problems ye'd like to share with us?'

Jamie smiled beneath his mask. 'Nah, everythin' else is cool,' he replied, keeping his tone light. 'Just remember though that there's goin' to be a lot of heat an' smoke.'

'We know about that,' Pat confirmed. 'Right, let's get movin' then.'

As Jamie watched, bemused, the three men started shifting the cutting gear across the basement and into an adjoining room. Jamie followed carrying the helmet, protective vest and gauntlets. As he entered the second room he was confronted by a scene of work in progress. Tiles had been stripped from the wall and there was a large hole cut into the brickwork behind.

'Where's the safe?' Jamie asked, intrigued.

'Five buildings down from here; we'll be through this lot in a minute,' Pat told him nonchalantly, 'an' then we'll be in the basement next door. There's a manhole in there; we drop down through it into a tunnel an' make our way along to the buildin' with the safe. There's another manhole in the basement floor there and the safe's on the first floor.'

'A tunnel?' Jamie repeated, incredulous.

'It's a sewer,' Mick explained with a smirk.

'Shit!' Jamie said disgustedly.

'Very appropriate,' Mick laughed. 'Breath through yer mouth, it lessens the smell.'

'So, what is this place we're turning over?' Jamie continued his questioning, clearly to Pat's annoyance.

It was The Irishman who came back with the answer on this occasion. 'It's supposed to be an Import/Export Company,' he laughed.

'It's a front business for British Intelligence,' Pat followed up quickly, watching Jamie for his reaction.

Had they not been wearing the ski masks Pat would have seen the shock register on Jamie's face but he managed to keep his voice steady when he spoke again. 'M.I.5?' he asked, hiding his anxiety well.

'Aye,' Pat confirmed with a cold laugh. 'An' they're goin' to get a feckin shock on Monday mornin.' His laugh grew louder as he picked up a sledgehammer. 'Come on, let's get a move on.' He swaggered towards the wall, ushering the others out of the way, and swung the hammer. Two steel rods jutted out from the hole, their heads wrapped in sacking, and the sledgehammer impacted hard against the top one of these. A dull thud filled the basement as metal hit sackcloth. Swinging again he hit the rod once more, watching with satisfaction as it penetrated deeper into the brickwork. Alternating now between the two rods, Pat continued working them through the separating wall. Jamie lost track of time but it wasn't long before there was a crumbling noise as the uppermost steel rod took away a chunk of the brickwork on the other side. Concentrating now on the lower rod, Pat swung the sledgehammer again and again, finally breaking through with it too.

Mick and The Irishman took over, working the brickwork through into the adjacent basement to create an opening big enough for them to move through with the equipment. Mick went through the gap first and Jamie saw a dull glow filter back from the other side. Forming a chain, they passed the equipment through the gap. Jamie left them to it, following through as last man.

Once through, Pat took command again, issuing orders which the other two jumped to fulfill. They knew exactly where the manhole was located and Mick lifted it quickly and easily. Jamie braced himself, but the nauseating smell he anticipated didn't materialise.

'I was kiddin' ye,' Mick laughed. 'It's a storm drain. The only turds floating in it will be dog turds...ye can relax...but watch out for the rats,' he added viciously.

Working quickly, the three Irishmen moved the equipment down into the tunnel and along to the basement of the target building. When they arrived there, Mick climbed up through the manhole and began taking the gear from The Irishman below. When everything had been transferred up, Mick and The Irishman made their way up the basement stairs to the ground floor with Mick taking the lead. Pat stayed with Jamie and the equipment and it was then Jamie noticed the automatic pistol stuffed down below Pat's belt in the small of his back.

Jamie looked quickly at the other two men who were now almost at the top of the stairs and saw that both had pistols in their hands and The Irishman still had the Armalite slung over his shoulder. All three men looked as if they knew how to use them and a wave of concern swept over him. Breaking open a safe was one thing, getting involved in a shootout with the R.U.C. was something else entirely.

'I thought you said this place was empty?' Jamie said casually as Mick and The Irishman disappeared through the door to the ground floor.

Pat looked at him steadily. 'It is,' he replied tersely.

'So why the guns?'

Pat laughed malevolently. 'The boys feel naked without them, that's all, don't fill yer pants son,' he said sarcastically.

'Fuck off,' Jamie replied, and Pat's laughter grew louder.

A patter of feet could be heard on the stairway and The Irishman appeared, out of breath. 'It's all clear,' he confirmed. 'Sean's watchin'…aw fuck,' he muttered, realising his mistake and stopping himself before getting more than a withering look from Pat. 'We're watchin' the front…it's all quiet.'

'Right, let's get the gear up there. The sooner ye get started the sooner we're out of here,' Pat ordered.

They moved the gear quickly up to the first floor and Jamie found the safe. It wasn't new, that was obvious at first glance, and closer inspection revealed a makers plate that gave a date of 1912. *Perfect*, Jamie smiled beneath his mask. *I'll be through this like a hot knife through butter*, he thought. The safe, a big brute, was fixed against the external wall in a back room facing out over the darkened yard below. Jamie set about fitting heavy blackout curtains over the windows while the others set up the equipment. Satisfied that the intense white light generated by the cutter wouldn't show outside, Jamie pulled on the vest, helmet and visor followed by the gauntlets and then advised the others to get out of the room. He adjusted the gas mix and ignited the cutter and a bright, white light filled the room.

He set to work immediately, cutting round the locking mechanism on the door of the safe. The work was hot and fumes quickly filled the room, forcing him to stop. He called for Pat and explained his problem, telling him he needed ventilation. They puzzled over how to achieve this and finally came up with a makeshift scheme that was workable but far from perfect. They opened the back window about nine inches and The Irishman kept the blackout curtains firmly in place while Mick opened and closed the room door repeatedly like a giant fan. It wasn't ideal but it was all they had and Jamie hoped that the fumes wouldn't be noticed by anyone using the lane at the rear. Recalling his driver's words from earlier that the park beyond was used for casual sexual encounters, he hoped the people using the lane would have other things on their minds.

Work resumed and the system worked reasonably effectively. Jamie made good progress and in just under two and a half hours from meeting with the three men, he completed the cut around the lock. It was just after ten o' clock. He turned off the gas and pulled off his helmet. With the noise of the cutter now silenced, Pat came into the room and looked at the giant safe with satisfaction. The room was swelteringly hot and Jamie was bathed in sweat.

Pat gave him an approving look. 'Finished?' he demanded.

'Hope so…it might need a wee bit more but I don't think so,' Jamie confirmed. 'Bring me the sledgehammer.'

Pat passed the instruction on to The Irishman who left the curtains and headed downstairs to the basement. He re-appeared a couple of minutes later with the sledgehammer and a crowbar. Jamie took the sledgehammer from him and hefted it in his hands, feeling its weight. 'Right, this will be noisy so we need something to deaden the sound,' he said. Pat handed him a thick file from a nearby desk with a questioning look in his eyes. 'Another couple of those will be fine,' Jamie confirmed, and Pat obliged, gathering up files and handing them over. 'Someone needs to hold them against the metal,' he continued. Pat nodded to The Irishman who reluctantly held the files where Jamie indicated. Jamie grinned at the man's apprehension. 'Don't worry, I won't miss,' he laughed.

He hefted the heavy hammer and crashed it against the centre of the files. There was a dull thud and the cut section, about 18" by 18" square, moved fractionally inwards. Jamie's second blow on the same spot produced the result he had been hoping for and the section broke free. Quickly swopping the sledgehammer for the crowbar, he slipped the end of it into the gap around the cut section and began levering it back and forth. Finally, he gripped the brass handle with both hands, feeling the residual heat from the cut through his gauntlets, and pulled the section free.

Pat let out a whoop of delight and slapped him on the back. 'Well done me auld son,' he chirped. 'Now get yerself down to the basement and leave the rest to us…ye don't need to know what's in there.'

Jamie nodded and trudged wearily out of the room and down the stairs. Everything had gone smoothly and he felt a degree of satisfaction with the job but the fact that he had cut into a safe used by the British Security Services did make him a little nervous. And he was right to be nervous.

He found some old wooden boxes in the basement and sat down, suddenly dog tired, and waited for the others. He was parched and the taste of burnt metal tormented his taste buds. He stretched and yawned. The work had been hot and tiring but not particularly difficult and he was pleased with the outcome. More to the point, Pat, the leader of the team, seemed to have mellowed towards him a little and some trust had been built up between them. Jamie rose up from his makeshift seat and peeled off the boiler suit, feeling the sheen of sweat on his arms and torso. With the boiler suit on top of his own clothes he was wearing too much but it prevented burns. He looked at the arms of the boiler suit and spotted numerous singe marks and small holes burned through the material. He was dying for a drink to clear his mouth but he could wait.

He heard a telephone ringing dully somewhere in the building. It stopped then rang again and it was then repeated for a third time. After that there was nothing until all hell broke loose. Suddenly, Jamie heard a rush of feet on the stairs and anxious voices shouting. Pat burst into the room beside him, his face set hard and his cheeks flushed beneath his mask.

'Get down into the tunnel, quickly. We'll be right behind ye. Go!' he instructed.

Jamie didn't wait or question him. There was no need; Pat's eyes told Jamie all he needed to know. Something had gone wrong, seriously wrong. He grabbed his boiler suit, scrambled to the manhole and dropped down into the tunnel, feeling the fetid water rise up his legs. Where now, he wondered? They had come into the tunnel from the basement of a building about 50 yards to the right but something told him to stay put. He could hear muffled shouting and things being moved about above him. There was a crackling noise, like fireworks, two, then three times, and then Pat dropped down into the tunnel beside him, followed quickly by The Irishman, his eyes blazing fiercely behind the slit of his mask.

Pat put a hand on Jamie's shoulder and turned him left, in the opposite direction from their entry point. 'Follow the tunnel about 200 yards and ye'll come to a ladder leading up to a manhole. We're going the other way, back the way we came. When ye hear gunfire, open up the manhole an' get out,' he ordered. 'Ye'll find yerself in a yard, just like the one ye came in through. Get out of yer gear, dump it somewhere, and wait there…someone will come for ye. Go with them and do exactly as they tell ye,' he continued urgently, as Mick dropped into the tunnel beside them.

'Surprise ready,' Mick reported and Pat gave Jamie a push.

'Go,' Pat shouted, handing Jamie a flashlight and holding out his hand for Jamie to shake. 'Good luck…and thanks.' Jamie pocketed the torch and took Pat's hand, shook it firmly and then started off down the tunnel. It was suddenly dark and he brought out the torch, pointing it down stream into the intense blackness of the tunnel. Two rats, grey and bloated, sitting on a ledge ahead of him, turned towards the light beam, startled, and slipped into the murky water, quickly disappearing from sight. Jamie gave an involuntary shudder. He had little fear of humans, but rats...they were another matter.

He pressed on, the foul water soaking through the cheap shoes and climbing up his legs. He kept the torch beam on the tunnel walls, preferring not to see what might be floating or swimming in the water, and followed the gentle curve of the tunnel. Behind him he could still hear muffled voices, growing fainter as he put more distance between himself and the others. Suddenly, the tunnel walls shook and there was a loud rumbling noise, like rolling thunder, and a blast of hot air billowed down the tunnel, causing him to drop the torch and almost knocking him off his feet. He leaned against the wall to regain his balance, totally disorientated now by the blackness around him. He felt panic rise from the pit of his stomach and fought to control it, breathing deeply on the fusty air. Finally looking down, he could just see the beam of the flashlight in the murky water and gave a sigh of relief.

Forgetting his distaste for what might be in the swirling water and his fear of the rats he bent down and scooped up the torch, shaking it dry. He had no idea how far he had come and there was still no sign of the ladder. He pressed on. The tunnel seemed to be turning to the right and he started to panic again, fearful that he might have missed the exit. He was about to turn back when the beam of the torch caught the metal of the ladder, a dull gleam of metal danced in the shaft of light and reflected onto the dark water below.

He reached out and caught hold of the rung immediately above him and started to climb. He had no idea how far below ground the tunnel was at this point and now he was climbing upwards in darkness. Climbing one handed had been difficult and dangerous and he had been forced to switch off the torch and slip it back into his pocket. He climbed on, slowly and carefully, until suddenly his hand reached the final rung. He raised himself as high as he could and brought out the torch once again.

Clinging on to the ladder with his left hand, he swung the torch beam around the enclosed space. He discovered he had been climbing up through a cylindrical structure and above him was a round metal manhole cover. He switched off the flashlight and pushed upwards with his hand on the cold metal but the cover refused to budge. He tried again but still the manhole remained stuck. Refusing to panic, Jamie climbed up another rung and used the side of the concrete tube for support, pushing upwards with his back against the circular slab of metal. There was a grating sound and the metal plate began to move. He lowered himself to his original position and used his hand once more. This time the metal lid rose up. Holding it open about an inch above ground level he listened for sounds of human activity. There was nothing other than the faint noise of traffic passing by on the other side of the buildings and music from the pubs. In the distance an owl hooted and a dog barked. He pushed higher and raised his head to peer out into the night.

He was in a yard, just as Pat had said, a high wall on three sides and the building itself towering up into the sky on the other. He couldn't see the door leading out to the alley or lane beyond but knew it would be there. Suddenly, away to his left in the direction he had come, there was a crackle of gunfire. Remembering Pat's words, he moved quickly, and heaving the manhole cover aside he clambered out into the night. The gunfire continued unabated while he removed his black outer clothes. His trousers were wet up to the middle of his calves and his shoes squelched when he walked. He bundled the black clothes together, wrapped them tightly inside the polo neck sweater and tied the bundle securely using the sweater's arms. He found a line of rubbish bins against the wall of the building and deposited the discarded garments in one of these, pushing the bundle to the bottom and covering it with the original waste.

A scraping sound caught disturbed him and he turned quickly, watching a shadow move against the back wall. The door leading to the lane was opening. He shrank back, pressing his body against the wall of the building, conscious that now out of the black clothing he would be spotted quickly. A shadowy figure came in through the opened door and Jamie prepared to defend himself. Was this the person coming to get him out or was it someone else? He crouched low, trying to make himself invisible behind the row of bins.

Roisin's voice, whispering urgently from the shadows, took him by surprise. What the hell was she doing here, he raged? He suddenly realised that he cared what happened to her, not a reaction he had expected. 'Dermott!' She whispered, keeping to his cover. 'Where are you? Oh God, Dermott, answer me.' He heard the anxiety in her tone and realised that she was as concerned for him as he was for her.

'Over here,' he called quietly, rising to his full height.

'Thank God,' she whispered with relief, 'I thought I was in the wrong place.' She ran to the sound of his voice and saw him emerge from the darkness. She thrust his jacket at him and then produced a bag containing his own shoes and dry socks.

He took them gratefully and sat on the nearest bin, changing out of the sodden black trainers and wet socks and into his own. He immediately felt better and the reality of Roisin's appearance hit him. 'What the fuck are you doin' here?' he demanded angrily, letting his emotion out.

'I'm gettin' you away,' Roisin fired back, just as irritably. 'Just keep quiet and come with me now!'

Jamie didn't argue. There would be time for talking later, when they were clear...if they got clear. He stuffed the shoes and wet socks into the rubbish bin with the rest of the discarded clothes and then felt Roisin take hold of him, leading him towards the gate.

A search had started around the building where the safe had been cracked and policemen were fanning out, searching the access lane and adjoining buildings. It wouldn't be long before they reached the yard Roisin and Jamie were in so they had to move. The alley was as dark as the yard and Roisin pulled him out, leading him away from the searchers. Time was the enemy now and they had to put as much distance as possible between them and the building before they were stopped. Being stopped, Roisin knew, was inevitable but she kept that from Jamie, unsure of how he would react. In a small recess, set into the wall about twenty five yards from the yard they had left, they passed a couple in the throes of passion, oblivious to everything around them. All Jamie could make out was the white of the guy's backside as it moved backwards and forwards to the accompaniment of syncopated breathing and soft moaning from the girl. So engrossed were they that they didn't miss a stroke as Roisin and Jamie ghosted past. Roisin smiled grimly...that was exactly what she and Jamie needed for their cover and she hoped there were more couples enjoying sex in the alley tonight, extra marital or otherwise.

They came to a junction with another alley leading off to the left and up to the lights of the main road. Roisin saw them first. Two R.U.C. men had entered the alley from the main road, moving cautiously, guns held out ahead of them. Reacting quickly, she grabbed hold of Jamie and pulled him to her, backing herself against the wall. She pressed her mouth to his ear. 'R.U.C., two of them, coming down the lane towards us,' she whispered urgently. 'Kiss me…even better, get your head down into my breasts,' she instructed, opening her coat and undoing the buttons of her blouse. 'And try to look as if you're enjoying it.'

It wasn't an onerous suggestion and Jamie complied without complaint but the rapid beating of his heart wasn't caused by contemplation of Roisin's breasts. He could hear the policemen now, their footsteps growing louder. Suddenly, a woman screamed from the alley that Jamie and Roisin had just left and a man's angry voice started shouting. Someone wasn't happy. More voices joined the ruckus, placatory to begin with, but growing irritated the longer the original man kept up his tirade. The two R.U.C. men coming down the lane increased their pace then slowed just as quickly as Roisin and Jamie came into view.

As the men closed on them Jamie realised Roisin had also pulled her skirt up over her thighs, exposing suspenders and a tiny triangle of white underwear and he was suddenly aroused. In fact, he was as hard as hell and he caught Roisin laughing nervously. 'Of all the times to get you randy,' she whispered. This wasn't the way she had hoped to have Jamie Raeburn, but it was a start.

The two policemen closed on them and a torch was shone in their faces. Jamie turned quickly, feigning shock. Roisin became indignant, screwing her eyes shut against the bright glare of the torch beam. 'What the feck!' she stormed. 'Can't a couple have a little bit of peace an' quiet in this city?'

The cops looked at her, one of them laughing harshly, his eyes alternating between her naked breasts, her thighs and the little white triangle of her knickers peeking out from beneath her raised skirt.

Roisin kept up her attack. 'It's not as if we're doin' anything wrong,' she ranted, 'we're only neckin.' She was playing an irate woman brilliantly.

The second cop laughed. 'Aye, so we see, but just leave lover boy's neck in his trousers and clear off out of here before we do ye'se both for indecency,' he threw back at her. His colleague was now scrutinising Jamie, his eyes hard and alert, taking in his clothes and then staring at him intimidatingly. Jamie stared back insolently, thinking this was what would be expected, and held his gaze. 'Before ye go,' the cop said softly. 'Let's have yer names and addresses…just in case we need to talk to ye'se again later.'

Roisin sighed and shook her head, giving the appearance of being exasperated by the request. 'It's always like this, Dermott,' she said, reminding him of the cover. For a girl who had been a bag of nerves in the taxi earlier she was handling herself well now, Jamie thought, cool as a cucumber in fact. 'I'm Roisin Kelly, I live in Glasgow…at 423 Dixon Avenue, Govanhill…an' I'm over here with my boyfriend visitin' my Auntie Molly,' she recited, keeping up the façade of annoyance. She carefully avoided giving Auntie Molly's address and, surprisingly, the policeman didn't ask. Instead, he noted down the Glasgow address and then turned to Jamie, pencil poised.

'Lynch,' Jamie said, 'Dermott,' his Glasgow accent as clear as day. '519 Roystonhill, Royston, Glasgow…Roisin's ma fiancée an', like she said, we're ower visitin' her Auntie. Is there anythin' else ye want tae know?' he added insolently.

The R.U.C. man glared at him then shook his head. 'No, that's all for now. Get out of our sight,' he said harshly, waving his pistol in the direction of the main road. Another two R.U.C. men had arrived and were enjoying the exchange as well as the sight of Roisin's ample breasts.

'What are youse two lookin' at?' Roisin shouted angrily, directing it at the two new arrivals, the younger of whom turned away, blushing. The others laughed at his discomfort. Roisin slipped her exposed breast back into her bra and pulled down her skirt, smoothing it primly over her thighs, before taking Jamie's hand and starting to lead him away. 'Come on Dermott, we can have some fun later back at the house,' she said suggestively, 'without an audience of dirty auld men.'

They had only taken a few steps when they were stopped in their tracks. 'Just a minute,' the older of the two new cops called out. 'How long have youse two been here?' he demanded.

They were frozen to the spot. Jamie's heart was racing and he could feel Roisin tense up but she was still in control. 'About five minutes before youse showed up, why?' she fired back brazenly.

'We're looking for some men.' Roisin felt Jamie twitch and gently squeezed his hand. 'Have youse two seen anyone suspicious?'

'Apart from you lot, we haven't seen anyone,' Roisin replied with a laugh. 'As ye could see, we had other things on our minds...until youse spoiled it.' She was letting the anger show again.

'Okay, okay,' the cop capitulated with a grin. 'Away ye go.'

They took his advice and sauntered off down the lane, laughing nervously. Another man and woman followed them, the couple who had been hard at it earlier when Jamie and Roisin had passed. They were young, the man about 19 with long curly hair and his girlfriend was maybe 17 or 18, a mousey little thing with thin legs and a flat chest. They both looked miserable. Jamie nudged Roisin and she turned to look at them. 'That's what happens when yer coitus gets interrupted an' ye have tae chuck it before the good bit,' he giggled and Roisin laughed with him, but their nerves were still frayed.

Once into the main road Roisin turned left and took Jamie back in the direction of the building he had left in a hurry. There was a red glow in the sky above it and that, together with the rumble he had heard, pointed Jamie to what had taken place. That would have been Mick's "surprise" he surmised. They passed two pubs, both now closed, getting closer to the noise and commotion. Jamie slowed, his eyes taking in the blackened shell of the building front and the flames billowing from the windows on the first floor where the safe had been located. A crowd had gathered to watch the firemen in action and the police had formed a cordon to prevent anyone getting too close.

'What the fuck happened?' Jamie whispered, gripping Roisin's arm tightly. She flashed him a "don't ask" look and pulled him away. They walked on in silence, Jamie now contemplating the mess he would be in if caught.

Roisin seemed to read his thoughts and gave him a reassuring hug. 'You're safe...I promise,' she said quietly, squeezing his arm. Jamie wanted to believe her but, for the first time in a long, long time, he was worried...not for himself, but about the consequences for Lucie if he was caught. They continued walking for about another quarter of a mile, past darkened pubs and shops, with Jamie ambling along as if shell-shocked. Abruptly, Roisin stopped outside a pub with lights on and music blaring. "The Happy Leprechaun" an enormous wall sign announced and a picture of a grinning little man with a straggly beard and dressed all in green confirmed it. But the doors were firmly shut.

'It's a lock in,' Roisin explained in response to Jamie's unasked question. 'It's well after eleven. The pubs here close at ten...but lock ins are tolerated by the police...they've got other things to worry about,' she smiled tellingly. She banged three times on the door and it opened about six inches and a bearded, wizened face not unlike the leprechaun in the picture, appeared in the gap. 'Let us in Sean, it's freezin' out here,' Roisin pleaded. The face behind the beard split into a wide grin and the door was opened wide to admit them.

'It's yerself, Roisin,' the old boy behind the door said quickly, giving her a lecherous look. Sean, giving a fair impression of the happy, if deviant, leprechaun himself, was about seventy years old but apparently still considered sharp enough to guard the door...and appreciate women. Not able to hold a pint without spilling it by the looks of his shirt and tie, Jamie noticed, but sharp enough to guard the door.

As they pushed through to the inner sanctum the heat hit them along with a wall of noise. The place was heaving and some guys were entertaining the customers with a selection of Irish Rebel songs. There wouldn't be any Orangemen in here tonight, Jamie mused, and the thought started him giggling uncontrollably. Roisin turned to him, a look of consternation on her face.

'What the feck are you giggling at?' she whispered angrily.

He pulled her close and whispered in her ear. 'I feel as if I've jumped out of the fryin' pan into the fire...I must be the only Protestant within half a mile.'

'Oh, it's *much* further than that Dermott. What's it worth for me to keep my mouth shut?' she teased, and then started to laugh with him, their nervous tension released. She pushed him through the crowd to the bar where another friendly face awaited, a pint of Guinness held out temptingly.

'Here ye go me auld son, I'm sure ye can do wi' this,' Liam Kelly greeted Jamie with a grin. 'As I said before, welcome to Free Belfast.'

Jamie accepted the drink gratefully and downed half of it in one long swallow. The metallic taste of burned steel was still in his mouth. He wiped his lips with the back of his hand then remembered his flight through the drain. 'Toilet?' he asked and saw Liam nod in the direction of the far corner of the pub. He set his pint down on the bar and headed off. 'I'll be back so get me another one of those,' he called over his shoulder.

Roisin hauled herself up onto a stool beside her cousin and started to tell him what had happened. She was still explaining when Jamie reappeared beside them.

'Feelin' better?' Liam asked, his eyebrows arched.

'Much,' Jamie replied with a grin. 'I just remembered where I'd been...and fishin' about in a sewer for a torch you've dropped isn't exactly hygienic.' He picked up his half-finished Guinness and noted another full glass beside it. 'Thanks,' he said, directing his words to Liam.

'Don't thank me, Roisin bought it for ye...she said something about ye needin' lead in yer pencil,' Liam laughed.

'I never did!' Roisin retorted, slapping him on the arm. 'Anyway, I happen to know there's plenty of lead in his pencil.' She started to laugh infectiously and soon all three were chortling together. When a degree of calm had returned, Jamie drank from his second pint and asked the question the other two were waiting for.

'What the fuck happened?' he asked quietly, conscious of the crowd around them. Liam looked around him, his expression blank, but Roisin was nervously checking the people nearest. Clearly, although it was a Nationalist pub, not everybody sang from the one hymn sheet.

'Not here, Jamie boy,' Liam whispered. 'We'll tell you everything later. Finish yer drink and we'll head for home...the van's not far from here.'

Jamie took the hint and finished his drink. Liam did a round of the pub, glad-handing, clasping people around the shoulder, slapping backs, whispering conspiratorially, sharing a joke here and a quiet word there. It became obvious to Jamie that the members of the Kelly family were important players in the Nationalist community, if not the I.R.A., he reasoned. Roisin took hold of Jamie's arm and fussed over him, letting the other customers see them together, but her eyes, though smiling, told Jamie to keep quiet until they were outside.

After what seemed an age, Liam finally extracted himself from the crowd and joined them at the door. Old Sean grinned his toothless grin and opened up, allowing them to step out into the cold of the night, taking the opportunity to have a good look down Roisin's cleavage. 'Thanks Sean,' Roisin smiled disarmingly and planted a kiss on the old man's cheek. If he's still got it in him he's probably got a hard on, Jamie smiled, suddenly remembering his own reaction to Roisin's charms in the alley earlier. But if anyone asked him tomorrow, or the next day or even next year, old Sean Murphy would swear that Roisin Kelly and her boyfriend, the bhoy from Glasgow, had been in The Happy Leprechaun pub all night…apart from a period of about half an hour when they had slipped out for a bit of nookie. Sean Murphy was sharp, as Jamie had already noted.

The three walked off down the street away from the bomb and fire ravaged building and the noise and commotion surrounding it, Roisin walking between the two men, each of them with an arm around her.

'So,' Jamie started as soon as they were clear. 'Back to my question…what the fuck happened?'

Liam looked at him with a weary expression. 'Pure bad luck, me auld son,' he started into the explanation. 'An off duty R.U.C. man went into the lane for a bit of extra marital activity, smelt the metal burning and saw the some smoke coming from the building and called it in.'

'But how did you know?' Jamie asked, interrupting the explanation.

'We listen in to the police radio frequency,' Liam explained. 'An' Roisin and meself were already back there in the pub, waiting for you to finish the job. When we got the warnin' we called through to you…and the bhoys set up a wee diversion.'

Jamie looked at him, taking it all in and recalling one of the telephones in the building ringing just before Pat told him to get out…two rings, followed by three rings, then it just kept ringing. 'An' the building?' he asked.

'That was the wee diversion,' Liam replied with a laugh. 'Don't worry, nobody was hurt. The bhoys set a wee bomb and exploded it before any of the R.U.C. managed to get inside. That stopped the fuckers dead in their tracks,' he continued, grinning now. 'And then, when the bhoys came out of the buildin' further down the street, shootin', it was like the gunfight at the O.K Coral.'

Jamie looked at him, seeing the unbridled excitement in his eyes, and then turned to Roisin. Her face was flushed and her eyes bright, dancing almost. They were both caught up in the excitement of it all, the adrenalin still pumping. He shook his head slowly. 'What the fuck are you people all about?' he said with a hint of amusement. 'Wee bombs and shootin'…you're fuckin mad, the lot of you.' Roisin and Liam turned on him as one, anger now in their expressions, but Jamie's cheeky grin defused them. 'Just get me home in one piece.'

*

Liam dropped them at "Aunty Molly's" house just after one o'clock. It was quiet, no lights on anywhere and the sky was angry, dark clouds flitting speedily across the moon. Rain was threatening again and it was cold. Jamie was shivering, but he put it down to reaction and all the excitement and drama of the evening. Liam wasn't staying and took off as soon as they were out of the van. They waited until the van turned the corner out into the main road then Roisin fished around in her handbag for her key.

A fire was still burning in the grate and the house was warm. There was no sound. Roisin's Auntie Molly had obviously gone to bed long before and Jamie felt uncomfortable wandering around her house unchecked. Roisin took him into the kitchen and watched him as he peeled off his leather jacket and hung it over a chair. A bottle of Bushmills Whiskey and two glasses sat on the kitchen table. 'Do you want a bath or a shower?' she asked, conscious of what he had been through. 'It'll heat you up, relax you.'

'One of those will heat me up and relax me too,' he said, nodding at the whiskey. 'A shower would be great later but I don't want to disturb your auntie,' he whispered.

Roisin laughed. 'You don't need to worry about our Molly,' she giggled. 'A bomb wouldn't waken her.'

Jamie drew her a sideways look. 'Not the best choice of words in the circumstances,' he said as she poured him a large glass of the golden liquid. He was suddenly dog tired and Roisin could see it. He finished the drink in one gulp, nodded, and headed for the stairs. 'Wash and sleep,' he mumbled as he left her and climbed wearily up the stairs.

Ten minutes later, washed and thoroughly warmed by the hot water and wrapped in a bath towel, Jamie slipped into the bedroom he had used earlier. The curtains were drawn and the big, double bed had been turned down for him. Dropping the towel at the side of the bed he slid, naked, between the sheets and pulled the covers up and over him.

He began to drift off to sleep almost immediately but Roisin's footsteps on the stairs kept him awake a little longer. A door opened and closed and then the sound of running water came to him as Roisin filled the bath. He tried once again to sleep but found that the events of the evening kept turning over in his head. Roisin's appearance in the yard, in particular, and her coolness throughout the confrontation with the police kept coming back to him. His own reaction to her troubled him, mostly because it had been unexpected. He had thought that his feelings for Lucie would put a brake on his ardour but that hadn't happened. Instead, the excitement of the moment had acted like an aphrodisiac. And Roisin had noticed; he knew *that* without any shadow of a doubt. That started him thinking about her again. She was one cool cookie, he told himself...not unlike Kate in many ways. There she was again...Kate, back in his mind...but wasn't she always there, he mused?

The water stopped running and he heard Roisin slip into the bath, listened to her splash the water and heard her singing softly, though the words were indistinct. After a while, he floated away into sleep and into dreams.

*

Roisin climbed from the bath and dried herself. She felt exhilarated; better than she had felt for a long time. She had soaked in the warm water, enjoyed the feel of the water against her body and thought of Jamie Raeburn. What was it about him that could make her feel like this? They were from different sides of the religious divide and she hardly knew him. In effect, they had simply been thrown together by circumstance...and he had someone else, she reminded herself. But when the R.U.C. men had come across them in the alley she had acted instinctively...acted as a lover would act, and he had reacted to her...*and boy, had he reacted*, she smiled with the memory.

Dried and wrapped in a bathrobe she started down the landing to her room, but she walked on past her door and found herself outside Jamie's room. She turned the door knob silently and pushed the door inwards, praying that it wouldn't squeak. It didn't. He lay in the middle of the big bed, flat on his back, his breathing low and steady and the bedcovers up to his chin. A bare arm and shoulder showed above the covers and she imagined him naked beneath the sheets. He moved and mumbled something in his sleep, turning towards her, and her heart stopped. She wanted him; wanted him more than she had wanted anyone over the last three years since...but she pushed the thought from her mind.

She was torn. She knew that this was hopeless but she couldn't pull herself away. If she went to him now how would he react? Would it be the way he had reacted in the alley or would he reject her? He turned again, his breathing rapid now, speaking in his sleep again. A name, she heard a name, but it was indistinct.

She couldn't say what drove her to do it. It just happened. One minute she was standing by the bedroom door, the next she was crossing the room, dropping her bathrobe and pulling back the bed covers. He was just as she expected he would be but she gasped as she saw the fresh scar across his abdomen, a long slash of red against the white of his skin. She climbed carefully onto the bed and sat astride his thighs looking down on him, feeling herself grow wet.

*

Jamie's dream was vivid. He was in an anonymous building with long corridors on different floors, each corridor having door after door set into its walls. He was running frantically down the corridor, opening the doors one after another, searching, but each room was empty, like prison cells without windows and bare whitewashed walls. He knew what he was looking for or, rather, who he was looking for. Kate had run into the building, willing him to follow her, and when he had she run from him, disappearing down the corridor, laughing and teasing as though wanting him to search for her. he opened door after door but there was no sign of her. He called her name and listened for the sound of her voice. He found her in the last room, waiting for him with her arms open, willing him to come to her and telling him that she still loved him. He fell into her arms, felt her skin against him, felt the tingle of her hair against his chest and her fingers grasp him, her tongue teasing him and then the heat of her mouth around him. He could smell the scent of her; the smell of soap mingled with freshly applied talcum powder.

He awoke then, groggily at first, with the realisation that senses such as touch and smell don't feature in dreams. Dreams are one dimensional. In the darkness of the curtained room he saw the figure bent over him, her dark hair falling to his stomach and brushing gently against his skin. He felt her fingers hold him firmly and the heat of her mouth as she took him. This had to be a dream...it had to be Kate. He closed his eyes, screwed them tightly shut, and then opened them again. 'Kate?' he whispered softly, hopefully.

Roisin raised her head from him, her fingers still curled round his erection, and looked into his eyes, her own wide and pleading. She said nothing. What could she say? She had wanted him and the craving for him, to have him, had driven her to this.

'Roisin?' he said quietly, his voice reflecting his astonishment.

'I'm sorry...I don't know why...I couldn't help myself,' she whispered, struggling to find words. 'Do you want me to go?' A small sob accompanied the question. She was still squatting astride his thighs and raised herself up, kneeling with her body straight and her breasts firmly thrust forward, anticipating his response. She looked down at him forlornly and saw a smile where she had expected anger. His arms stretched towards her and he gripped the back of her thighs. She felt him pull her gently towards him and her eyes opened wide in disbelief.

'No, don't go,' he murmured. 'Come here.' The pressure of his hands pulled her to him and she squatted down again, her legs spread over his chest. 'Closer,' he murmured.

Roisin felt the blood rush to her head. This hadn't been in her script, or even in her wildest fantasy. She eased forward, above him now, and watched his head move towards her. She felt his tongue on her and in her and moaned softly as he probed gently inside her. She gripped his hair in her fingers and rocked gently back and forth over him as his tongue excited her and her juices began to flow. She wanted to shout out, to scream, as the orgasm took hold of her. She shuddered with delight as the ecstasy of it crashed over her, and then she felt him move. Suddenly, their positions were reversed and he was above her, pinning her hands to the bed with his own. She felt the hardness of him between her thighs and then he was inside her, his body moving rhythmically in and out, faster and faster. She wanted him to come, wanted to feel the heat of him sear into her. She moved with him, taking him deeper, closing her thighs against him. His breathing was rapid, his breath filled her ear and then his mouth was on hers, locked in a kiss. She heard him moan, sensed his climax. 'Come,' she whispered urgently. 'Come, I want to feel it…pleeeease.'

She felt him shudder, pushing himself deep inside her as she clung to him, feeling herself climax for a second time with the force of his orgasm, their bodies writhing together like marionettes. His sperm spurted from him, filling her, and the sensation in each of them refused to die. Their mutual spasms seemed to go on forever until Jamie, finally drained, slumped on top of her. She could feel his heart race against her, taste the sweat on him as she kissed his shoulder, and feel the heat of his breath warm in her ear. She lay still beneath him, afraid to move for fear of breaking the spell. This was all that she had wanted. She had been thinking about it since their meeting but it had always been a hopeless dream…until now. They were silent, each wrapped in their own thoughts. What was there to say? They had needed each other; it was as simple as that. She felt him tense the muscles of his penis and a small tremor tripped through her. She responded in kind, tensing the muscles of her vulva around him and gripped him tightly.

On Monday morning, she told herself, she would walk away from him but tonight…and for the rest of this weekend, she would love him if he needed her.

*

When Jamie awoke on Saturday morning he was alone but he knew it hadn't been a dream. The evidence was all around him. He heard the sounds of domesticity from the rooms below and the voices of Roisin and her Auntie Molly, chattering happily. There was a lot of laughter. He rose and showered, dressed in clean denims and shirt and made his way downstairs.

'Well, well,' Roisin's aunt laughed as he entered the kitchen. 'Tired out, were you?' Jamie blushed slightly, unsure whether Roisin and he had disturbed her sleep with their lovemaking or not. Roisin was laughing happily. Hopefully, Auntie Molly had slept through it. Roisin had said a bomb wouldn't wake her but the noise they had been making had probably eclipsed even that.

He and Roisin spent most of the rest of the day wandering around Belfast. They did touristy things; visited historic buildings, churches, Queen's University, and had lunch in a small café in the city centre. Roisin was intent on keeping Jamie's cover intact. The explosion and the gunfight the night before were in all the papers but nothing was mentioned about the safe. It was unlikely that Jamie would be linked to the safe breaking but he and Roisin had been seen near the site and Roisin's family was steeped in intrigue. Accordingly, she stuck rigidly to Brendan's plan. Jamie wondered if what had taken place between them during the night was part of Brendan's plan as well. He doubted it.

They chatted a lot, comfortable with each other, and Roisin opened up a bit with him. He got a bit of family history and an insight into why they had followed the Republican path. Her grandfather had been a Wicklow man who had been involved in the 1916 uprising. He hadn't lived long afterwards, a British firing squad saw to that. Her grandmother had moved north taking the family to live with relatives in Belfast and when Partition finally came in 1923 they found themselves in the Six Counties. History, as it has a habit of doing, repeated itself. Her father had been in an Active Service Unit of the I.R.A. and had been killed when Roisin had been only six years old. She still had memories of him but like everything else they had faded with time. Her mother had struggled after that and died a couple of years later, a young woman with a broken heart. Auntie Molly stepped in then and Roisin had lived with her, her husband and all of her cousins until she had left for Glasgow two years earlier. She told him that she had been engaged but her fiancé had been killed three years before when she was twenty three. It had been an accident, she said, but her tone of voice and deep, reflective sadness suggested something darker. Following her fiancé's death she had found it difficult to settle in Belfast and had eventually moved to Glasgow to live with her brother Brendan and his wife. Now she was teaching in St. Thomas Aquinas Primary School in Govanhill and had a place of her own on the Southside. Jamie hoped that she would stay in Glasgow and have a life, a life that would be hard to have here. Something told him she deserved it.

When she had exhausted her own story she wanted to know all about him. She knew something of why he had come here, her brother had seen fit to enlighten her…more by way of a warning than anything else, but still she was intrigued. Jamie tried to avoid telling her too much but it was a battle he was bound to lose. She wheedled it out of him, bit by bit. She could give his mother lessons in the techniques of interrogation, he reflected at one point. He found himself telling Roisin about his life in Nottingham with Lucie and gave the Irish girl an abridged version of the events surrounding her abduction. Roisin listened interestedly but he could see that something else was piquing her curiosity.

When he got to the bit about the attack in Glasgow only days before which had left Jack in hospital, Roisin had gasped but now she knew where the new scar on his stomach originated. His concern for Jack and his quest to recover Lucie from the clutches of the gangster in Derby, confirmed Roisin's earlier belief that he had needed her last night every bit as much as she had needed him. His life, like hers, it appeared, was all fucked up. But strangely, after making love with him, she had felt a sense of release. The cross she had been bearing for so long had suddenly been lifted from her shoulders.

They returned to the house in Short Strand late in the afternoon and discovered it empty. A note on the kitchen table announced that Auntie Molly had gone to Bangor to visit one of her daughters, Roisin's cousin Mary, and wouldn't be back till late. The note went on to tell them that Liam had been in touch and he was staying with his girlfriend for the rest of the weekend. Auntie Molly finished with the words "Enjoy yourselves" and again Jamie wondered if she knew what had taken place the night before. If she did, it didn't seem to perturb her.

Roisin wasn't unhappy with this development. She would have Jamie all to herself and could play the housewife. There wasn't much to the housewife bit unless you counted providing him with conjugal rights but that suited her too. They made love, releasing themselves again and, as on the night before, their love making was intense. Roisin felt a little guilty, knowing now why he was here, and wondered if he too was experiencing remorse for what they had done…what they were doing. She had taken advantage of him…taken advantage of the situation he was in was probably a more accurate description, but she doubted if she could have taken advantage of him unless he had wanted her to. The rejection she had expected hadn't happened…it had been quite the opposite in fact. He had turned out to be attentive and loving, eager to satisfy her rather than simply settle for pleasing himself. Jamie Raeburn wasn't a "wham bam thank you ma'am" kind of boy, she reflected happily.

Roisin stayed with him again all that night and let him lie long on Sunday morning. She rose from the bed when she heard her aunt pottering about in the kitchen below. Jamie opened his eyes sleepily which, Roisin reasoned, was hardly surprising given what they had been up to for most of the night. He smiled ruefully at her and arched an eyebrow.

'I'm going to Mass with Auntie Molly,' she whispered. 'Go back to sleep.'

'Confession?' he asked with a laugh, his voice still husky.

'Aye, that too,' Roisin laughed with him. 'So I might be gone for a long time. I haven't been to Confession for ages…but then again, I haven't sinned much,' she giggled loudly. 'I've made up for it now though, haven't I?'

Jamie was laughing despite everything. 'You'd better say a prayer for me then, too,' he said and pulled the blanket back over his head.

*

Roisin knew she was losing him as they climbed the gangplank onto the Glasgow ferry. He was slipping back into the guise of the Jamie she had been with on the outward journey. He was still with her, but only just, and she knew his thoughts were drifting back to the girl in Nottingham, the girl he had risked so much for. And now he had what he needed…or at least, he would have soon after the ship docked at the Broomielaw tomorrow. She felt an indescribable sadness descend on her.

They stood at the stern as the ship left Belfast Lough, the lights of Belfast twinkling behind them and eventually fading, leaving only the darkness of the water and a bright moon turning the wake of the ship's propellers into a white iridescent trail leading all the way back to the port like a silver thread. Jamie was lost in thought.

'A penny for them,' Roisin said quietly, slipping her arm through his and laying her head against his arm.

'What?' he asked abruptly, his mind obviously somewhere else.

'Your thoughts,' she explained. 'A penny for them…that's what they say, isn't it?'

He looked down at her, admiring her dark red hair gleaming in the stern lights of the ship and the glow of her eyes set above her high cheekbones. She looked back questioningly, her eyes widening.

'Yes, that's what they say, but you don't want to know,' he replied, his voice so low she had to strain to hear him.

Roisin smiled. 'Kate, is it?' she asked with what she thought was a knowing smile on her face, but the tightness of his expression when he turned to face her told her she had misjudged.

'Kate?' he snapped, strain showing.

'Yes, Kate,' Roisin retorted, trying to keep it light. She said it with a laugh but she could tell by his tortured look that Kate, whoever she was, wasn't someone he took lightly. She kicked herself mentally.

Jamie was silent, his eyes gazing steadily out over the dark sea, following the silvery wake. 'It's Lucie,' he said eventually. 'I'm thinking about Lucie.'

'Then who's Kate?' Roisin asked automatically, wishing she had thought first, held her tongue and curbed her curiosity. But impetuosity had always been one of her biggest faults and keeping a rein on it had always been a problem...how else would she have ended up in his bed on Friday night, she smiled inwardly.

Jamie smiled grimly as he dragged his eyes back from the darkness of the sea and looked down at her. He was wrestling with some inner crisis and Roisin could see the battle in his dark, brooding eyes. 'I lost Kate a long time ago,' he said in a strangled voice. 'The question is, how do *you* know about her?'

Roisin didn't answer. It was her turn to be thoughtful. She looked out over the sea the same way Jamie had done moments before, wishing she had kept quiet. Clearly Kate, whoever she was, had been important to him...and still was, because she was still in his mind and, more than likely, she was still in his heart. 'You may have lost her,' she said gently. 'But she's still with you.'

Jamie gazed at her sceptically. 'What are you? A witch?' he asked. 'You'll be tellin' me next you read tealeaves.' The sting in his voice upset her but she laughed, breaking the tension that was building.

'It isn't magic...I'm not clairvoyant,' she said, laughing softly. 'It's much simpler than that...you talk in your sleep, my love.'

Jamie's eyebrows rose up a fraction as her words sank in. 'I talk in my sleep?' he repeated, laughing to cover his surprise.

'Yep,' she laughed. 'And...'

'And what?' he fired back at her before she had the chance to finish.

She sighed. 'When I came to you on Saturday morning you were dreaming. You said her name then. And just before you were properly awake, before you realised it was me in bed with you, you said her name again...you thought I was her.' She paused, looking at him tenderly, and then continued. 'The first time you came inside me you called me Kate.'

'Shit!' Jamie exclaimed quietly. 'I'm sorry, Roisin, honestly.'

Silence fell between them again. Who *was* this Kate, Roisin wondered, her curiosity devouring her? Whoever she was she had been really close to him, and she was close to him even now...though he seemed to be in denial about that. The quietness crept on until Roisin's curiosity finally got the better of her.

'So?' she pressed. 'Who's Kate?'

Jamie looked down at her, giving her a smile at last. She wasn't going to let it go, he could see that...like a dog with a rat. 'You don't give up, do you? It's a long story,' he said at last.

'That's alright, we've got all night,' she replied, giving his arm a squeeze.

They remained at the stern rail a while longer as Jamie debated with himself whether or not to let Roisin into his world. She had rescued him from the R.U.C. and they had shared some moments, something of themselves, with each other in the aftermath. He liked her. 'You remind me of her,' he said eventually, turning round to face her again. 'She's about your age, same confident manner – dominant and submissive at the same time – same impetuosity and the same brilliant, sparkling green eyes,' he said with a smile, a picture of Kate appearing in his mind's eye once again.

'So you like older women,' Roisin said, laughing as she said it.

'That's been said before,' he laughed again. 'The answer is that I like *some* older women...present company included.'

'What happened between you?' Roisin continued, serious again.

'She was married...still is, as far as I know,' he replied, sounding resigned to the fact, and Roisin guessed that he was about to tell her everything. She waited. 'Her man's an alkie...a drunk,' he continued. 'I met her when I was in hospital, just before Christmas last, after I'd been stabbed.'

'The scars on your back?' Roisin broke in automatically, having seen them on their first night together.

'The very same,' he smiled bitterly. 'Kate's a nurse...she worked in Intensive Care at the time and I was in there for a few days. We chatted, fell for each other, and started seeing each other...and it grew serious.'

'An affair,' Roisin commented quietly, her Catholic upbringing hinting at her being shocked by his disclosure.

Jamie almost laughed out loud at the incongruity of it. Apparently, it was alright for her to fuck him, but not alright for Kate because she was married. A strange take on morality, he thought, and was tempted to say something along those lines, but he curbed the urge and carried on. 'Aye, it started that way...but we really fell in love.' He paused again, becoming emotional, and Roisin waited. 'I was going to ask her to leave him, divorce him and marry me, but things started to go wrong.'

'Between you?' Roisin probed gently.

Jamie laughed softly. 'No. Our relationship, strangely enough, got stronger. Fate took a hand, I suppose. Her husband borrowed money from a loan shark, the man wanted it back, sent round his heavies to threaten him and managed to scare the life out of Kate. Her mother got involved then, told her to come home, put pressure on. She was left with no choice...it was them or me. They won.' He was staring vacantly out to sea again, oblivious to the cold that had now wrapped itself around them. He didn't tell her about saving Tom Maxwell's sorry arse, what was the point, he reasoned? 'I loved her. I really loved her,' he finished sadly.

'I think you still do,' Roisin responded knowingly, then changed tack. 'Come on, it's freezing out here...I'll buy you dinner.' She took his arm tightly and steered him away from the rail. 'And if you still want to talk, we'll talk.'

The ship docked on the Broomielaw at six thirty next morning. They had dined and Jamie had drunk a little too much. When they returned to their cabin, they lay together on Roisin's bunk, wrapped tightly in each other's arms simply for the comfort of being held by another human being. Both of them were engrossed in their own thoughts, preparing to return to their own versions of normality.

Over dinner they had spoken about what was to happen when the boat docked and Jamie knew he was returning with her to her flat in Dixon Avenue, just off Cathcart Road in Govanhill. There he would meet her brother. Roisin didn't say anything about the gun but Jamie suspected that was where he would receive it. He suspected too, rightly as it happened, that Roisin wasn't entirely happy with this arrangement. She wasn't entirely happy that she was taking him to her flat either, that bit she had spelled out to him, but her brother had told her that was what had to happen and no one, not even his sister, argued the point with Brendan Kelly.

Dixon Avenue sits in the "better off" part of Govanhill and runs from Cathcart Road at its eastern end along to Victoria Road on the west. Queens Park, one of Glasgow's big open urban green spaces sits to the south with the less salubrious areas of Govanhill to the north. The houses in Dixon Avenue reflect the different social standing of the two areas. On the Queens Park side of the street, the houses are substantial two storey terraces with gardens front and rear. On the other side, relatively new red sandstone four storey tenements dominate the skyline and the further north you travel, towards Alison Street and Calder Street, the older and less imposing the tenements become. Still, Jamie acknowledged, Govanhill was still one of the better areas of the city to live in.

The taxi dropped them outside Roisin's flat in one of the red sandstone buildings on the North side. Jamie waited as she paid the cabbie and together they trudged up the path to the close entrance, both of them showing signs of tiredness. As they entered the close Jamie noted the tiled walls and the spotless floor. He was impressed and thought back to his childhood days in the single-end in Townhead, with the toilet, commonly referred to as "the cludgie", sitting on the half landing and serving more than one family. He could remember his grandmother having to hide behind a chair in the kitchen to use a commode because her legs wouldn't take her as far as the toilet. Like night and day, he thought.

Roisin's flat was on the second floor and the climb up the stairs was laborious. It was relatively quiet, the only sound coming from a radio in one of the other apartments. Jamie could make out the voice of the presenter as a song ended and he recognised the channel as the Light Programme...light music to keep the proletariat happy, as his father used to say – a happy worker is a productive worker. Jamie's father could have given Joe Stalin lessons in real Communism.

As Roisin opened the flat door Jamie detected the acrid smell of cigarette smoke and guessed that Brendan Kelly was already there waiting for them. He wasn't disappointed. The big man was sitting in an easy chair next to the fireplace, his eyes watching them as they came into the room. Jamie looked around, taking in the furniture and the decor appreciatively. Roisin Kelly lived fairly comfortably, as you would expect of a teacher, and she had good taste.

Roisin dropped her bag at her feet and went over to her brother, a little irritably, and kissed him on the cheek. 'He did well,' she said, turning her eyes back to Jamie before addressing Brendan again. 'I'll leave you two to it...I need to have a shower and get ready for school.'

The big man smiled at her and gave her an affectionate pat on the cheek. 'I know he did,' he acknowledged. 'An' so did you, from what I hear,' he added with genuine appreciation. 'Away with ye an' get changed. We won't be long...we'll close the door behind us.' He leaned forward and pecked her on the cheek then ushered her out of the room.

As she passed Jamie she hesitated and then, impetuously, leaned towards him and kissed him quickly on the mouth. 'Take care of yourself, Jamie Raeburn,' she said with a sad smile, then headed off to the bathroom, pulling the living room door closed behind her.

Brendan Kelly watched the exchange with a humourless smile. 'I hope ye didn't take advantage of my little sister?' he said quietly as the sound of Roisin's footsteps faded down the hall.

Jamie looked him in the eye and tried to think of a snappy reply, given what *had* happened between him and Roisin, but thought better of it and settled for the simple truth instead. 'No, I didn't take advantage of your little sister,' he replied quietly, holding the older man's gaze.

Brendan Kelly's face broke into a wide grin. 'Relax,' he said. 'I know my sister...if anyone was takin' advantage of anyone, it would be her doin' the takin'.' He started to roll another cigarette and waved Jamie to the chair opposite him. Jamie produced his pack of Lucky Strikes and offered one but Brendan just shook his head. 'I prefer rollin' me own,' he said simply as he nimbly finished rolling the tobacco, licked the paper and sealed it. 'Ye can give me a light though.'

Jamie pulled a Lucky Strike from his pack and inserted it between his lips, took his lighter from his denims pocket and flicked the wheel, holding the flame over to the other man. They both drew heavily on their cigarettes and Jamie settled back in his chair. Brendan Kelly bent down and Jamie's eyes followed his movement, settling on a small parcel at Brendan's feet. It was the shape of a shoe box and was wrapped in plain brown paper. Brendan weighed the parcel in his hands, gazing at Jamie with his bright blue, penetrating eyes and Jamie stared back. He had been afraid of Brendan Kelly when they had met that first time only days ago but he had no fear of the man now and he sensed a mutual respect, even though he couldn't bring himself to like him.

Finally, Brendan held the package out towards him. 'Have you used a gun before?' he asked quietly.

Jamie took the package, unsure whether to open it or to wait until later, his eyes still locked on to those of the other man. 'Aye,' he said. 'I've done a bit of shootin',' he admitted, careful to avoid mentioning the Army Cadets. 'Mostly with a rifle though.'

Brendan Kelly nodded slowly. 'They both serve the same purpose,' he said coldly. 'But with a pistol ye have to get in close...can ye do that, son?'

Jamie bristled at the man's use of "son" but realised quickly that Brendan Kelly wasn't being patronising. 'If I have to,' he answered firmly, seeming to satisfying Brendan with that.

'Okay...in the box, a Walther PPK, ex German Police, and two boxes of 9mm, hollow point ammo. There's a silencer in there too. Open it.' Brendan waited as Jamie unwrapped the package, finding, as he had expected, a shoe box. He set the box on his knees, prised open the lid and picked up the Walther, still wrapped in oil cloth. He hefted it in his hand, testing the weight of it. It felt familiar. In the background he could hear Roisin in the shower, the soft hiss of the water and her voice, faint above the sound of the spray, singing a haunting Gaelic song. He wondered absently what the words of the song meant as he unwrapped the oil cloth to reveal the weapon. The gunmetal glinted in the light coming in through the window and it felt good in his hand.

'The safety catch is on the right,' Brendan resumed. 'There's a magazine already in...give it here,' he commanded, holding out his hand. Jamie handed it over. 'Ye change the magazine like this,' he said, demonstrating the movement and the magazine dropped into his hand. 'Just push a fresh one in till it locks...ye'll hear the click.' Brendan pushed the magazine back into place and Jamie heard the audible click as it locked. Brendan then went on to demonstrate how to load a magazine and then handed the gun back to Jamie. 'Wipe my prints off with the cloth,' he instructed and watched carefully as Jamie did so. 'Two final points, son...if yer in close it doesn't matter, but if yer shootin' from any distance over a few yards aim a wee bit low, the recoil will lift it a fraction. Second point...the ammo is hollow point and it's not a good idea to be caught with it. It's illegal,' he laughed, realising the absurdity of that statement given what Jamie was intending to do with it. 'Bein' caught with the gun will be bad enough but if yer found with hollow point ammo, ye'll be goin to gaol for a long, long time.'

'What's so special about it?' Jamie asked.

'It's designed to stop anythin' it hits...normal entry wound, but it takes a feckin great chunk of the body out with it when it exits...if it exits.'

'Like a dum-dum?' Jamie continued, and saw Kelly' eyes light up.

'Exactly like a dum-dum,' he replied appreciatively. The water of the shower stopped running and they heard Roisin leave the bathroom and pad along the hall to her bedroom. 'Wrap the gun up again…keep it in the box. The silencer just screws on.' Brendan paused and looked at Jamie shrewdly. 'And Roisin was singin' about a lover who goes off to war and doesn't come back, by the way,' he said with a cold smile. 'I hope it wasn't you she was singin' about.' He rose from his chair and held out his hand. Jamie rose and took it, feeling the strength of the man's grip. 'Finally,' Kelly said quietly, his voice again as cold as ice. 'If ye're caught and anythin', and I mean *anythin'*, comes back to me or the bhoys across the water…ye're a dead man.' His voice and eyes were cold and hard, both carrying equal amounts of the controlled menace that Jamie had sensed at their first meeting. Then suddenly, the eyes softened and Brendan reached into his inside jacket pocket and pulled out an envelope which he passed over.

'What's this?' Jamie asked, wary.

'Wages…ye told yer Mammy that ye were away workin', didn't ye?' Jamie nodded. 'Well, she'd expect ye to get paid, wouldn't she?' the big man said, clasping Jamie by the arm. 'There's forty quid in there…I'd slip about twenty five into my back pocket before I went home, if I were you,' he said with a smile as Jamie's eyes opened wide with surprise. 'Now, let's you an' me get out of here an' let my little sister get ready for work.'

Brendan Kelly ushered Jamie out of the flat with the box tucked tightly under Jamie's arm and called goodbye to Roisin as he pulled the door closed behind them. They stood together on the landing, Jamie feeling suddenly conspicuous. 'Wait here for two minutes,' Brendan instructed. 'Then get yerself home…an' good luck son, I think yer goin' to need it.'

Brendan Kelly trotted down the stairs, his footsteps fading as he reached the close mouth. Jamie heard the faint bang of a car door outside in the street, the roar of an exhaust, and the car pulled away from the close. He waited, listening carefully, but only the sound of the Light Programme coming from the unidentified apartment broke the stillness. It was time to go home.

Chapter 51

Jamie arrived home not long after his mother had left for work. He could still smell the residue of her morning cigarette lingering in the still air. The note, on a torn sheet of paper taken from a notebook and written in his mother's copperplate hand, was on the kitchen table, propped up prominently against a milk bottle; *Phone Jack's Mum, it's urgent. Sorry son, x*

He looked at it, unwilling to believe the unspoken message it contained. He read it again. It could only mean one thing and he was kidding himself if he thought otherwise. Replacing the torn sheet of paper on the table he walked into the living room towards the telephone. "Walked" is perhaps the wrong word; more accurately, he staggered, zombie like, all self-control gone. He knew what he was going to learn when he made the call and he didn't want to hear it. Until then, it was simply a nightmare, and you could waken up from a nightmare.

He lifted the handset and dialled, the number lodged at the front of his memory. It was Anne-Marie who answered on the fourth ring. 'Jamie,' she sobbed, recognising his voice. 'Oh Jamie, Jack's dead.'

He stood transfixed, his eyes blank, his mind in a vortex. This couldn't be happening, his brain screamed out at him, denying the truth. Jack had been recovering; the doctors had been hopeful, Teresa had said he was getting stronger, they had hoped he would regain consciousness on Friday and he had been going to visit him today and see his cheeky grin. 'When?' he asked, his voice a low monotone.

'Yesterday...yesterday afternoon. It was so sudden,' Anne-Marie sobbed fitfully. 'He regained consciousness on Friday, seemed strong, Teresa was so pleased.' There was a long pause as she tried to control her grief. 'Mammy and Da saw him on Friday night...he was able to talk for a while, and again on Saturday and I saw him on Saturday afternoon. He seemed stronger.' Another lengthy silence followed. Jamie couldn't speak. 'The hospital phoned yesterday morning...it was Mammy who took the call. Her face went white and she started to cry and then she was rushing about. They left for the Western right away...and they were there when...when Jack died.' The floodgates opened and it was a good few minutes before she was able to say anything else.

'Where are your Mammy and your Da now?' Jamie asked, forcing himself to speak.

'They've gone to see Father Daly, he was there yesterday when Jack left us, and after that they're going to the Undertakers. Mammy tried to get you, phoned and spoke to your mother...that was last night. Your mother said you were up in Aberdeen working but she expected you back later. Mammy waited up for your call.'

'I just got in,' he replied, his voice shaking. 'Christ Anne-Marie, tell me I'm dreaming this, tell me it's not true.'

'I wish I could, but it isn't a dream. That's how I felt when I heard. The whole family's devastated.'

'I'll be over in an hour,' Jamie said. 'If your Mammy gets back before I arrive tell her I'll be there as soon as possible.'

'Hurry Jamie, we need you here,' were the last words he heard as he hung up.

He gazed out of the living room window but saw nothing. His eyes were filled with tears and the self-recrimination was starting all over again; with a vengeance. Jack had died while he, the guy who caused it all, had been gallivanting over in Belfast, screwing Roisin Kelly and indulging in self-gratification...all to get a gun to kill a man. Was this God's way of paying him back? But why Jack, why not him? Guilt engulfed him and the tears came. He sat down, slumping into his father's favourite chair, and held his head in his hands, grief and guilt racking his body and his mind in equal measure.

It was some time before he was able to function again. Slowly, he began to recover from the shock of it all and anger began to replace the guilt and the grief. Kelman was behind all of it. He was the cause of everything that was bad in Jamie's life and Jamie was filled with a quiet determination to make him pay dearly for it. He rose up and went back into the kitchen, picking up the brown paper wrapped shoe box which he had left on the table. The weight of it was reassuring, somehow, and any lingering doubt that he had about his ability to use the gun had evaporated.

He climbed the stairs to his room, resolute now. Stashing the box beneath his bed with other personal items, he changed quickly, washed his face and called a taxi. He took out the envelope that Brendan Kelly had given him, removed ten pounds in one pound notes, and left the rest in the envelope in his top drawer. When he went south he'd leave most of it with his mother, just in case the unthinkable became the reality.

Fifty minutes after his conversation with Anne-Marie, Jamie stepped from the taxi in Saracen Street. He tossed his finished cigarette into the gutter and strode determinedly into the close, pushing himself up the flight of stone stairs to the second floor. The tiredness he had felt earlier had gone. He wondered if he would ever sleep again or at least before his business with Kelman was concluded.

Anne-Marie opened the door and threw herself into his arms, sobbing. He stroked her hair gently and escorted her back into the big living room. Everything was as he remembered it from his last visit after his release from Partick Police Station. That was only a week ago, he remembered suddenly, shocked. Anne-Marie went into the kitchen and he heard the gas stove being lit. He followed her, watching as she filled the kettle from the tap and placed it on the brightly burning ring. She looked over at him forlornly and asked the question that had been bouncing around in his head since he had spoken to her earlier. 'Why, Jamie?'

He shook his head sadly. 'I don't know. Maybe Father Daly's the man with the answer to that.' There was bitterness in his voice that Anne-Marie hadn't expected. 'It should have been me,' he said softly.

'You can't say that, Jamie,' she retorted quickly. 'You weren't to know it was going to happen.'

He thought about that. "Go home to Scotland...and watch your back", Tony Abrahams' had said to him. He should have seen it coming! The thought wasn't new. It was his fault. 'Yes I can, I should have expected it,' he replied glumly.

Anne-Marie gave him a strange, questioning look, as she tried to interpret his words. The arrival of her mother and father, contemporaneously with the boiling of the kettle, saved Jamie from more questions. Mr and Mrs Connelly smiled wanly as they saw him. There were hugs and handshakes and lots of tears but, fortunately for Jamie, no questions. What had happened had happened and no one, least of all the Connolly's, blamed him. There were things to arrange, people to notify, an announcement to be put into the newspaper. The funeral, Jamie learned, would take place on the following Tuesday, the 31 October, eight days away. The Undertakers, the Co-Op, had telephoned the police and, subject to the outcome of the Post Mortem examination, Jack's body would be released to the family and the funeral could proceed. 'You'll be with us, Jamie,' Jack's mother announced in a tone that brooked no argument. 'You're almost one of the family anyway…and Jack would want you with his Da and his brothers to carry him on his final journey.' She broke down then, momentarily, and dabbed her eyes with a handkerchief clutched tightly in her hand. She pulled herself together with an effort and looked sadly at him. 'Will you let the rest of the boys know?'

Jamie nodded and said he would call round the others later. Then, probably, they would all meet in the pub and drink to Jack's memory. There would be a lot of that this week. It was early afternoon when he took his leave, promising to contact the lads and to return later when all of the family would be together. The house in Knightswood was quiet, depressingly so, when he arrived home. The note lay on the table where he had left it. He picked it up and read it again then sat down and started to make his plans.

Conor said little when Jamie phoned him with the news. Death was something he had seen before. It was personal and he let Jamie deal with it in his own way, but at the same time he let him know that he was there for him if he needed help.

The call to Beeston was more traumatic. Jo cried. She hadn't known Jack long but she had liked him, even at one time had hopes that Jack and Julie might hit it off, but the vital spark that kindles true love hadn't been there. Julie wasn't around but she would be devastated, Jo said. Jamie didn't doubt it for a second but he knew that the news would also reinforce her desire to help him. And he needed her help now, more than ever. The call ended with the usual things that people say in circumstances like this, Jamie realised, but he hadn't taken them seriously in the past. Death had always been something remote before, something that happened to other people. His grandparents had died when he was young and he had little memory of them or of the grieving process that had gone on around him at the time. No one really close to him had died since…distant family, yes, but no one really close. He'd heard all the words and platitudes before but now they actually meant something.

He spent the next few hours telephoning round his and Jack's mates, all of whom knew Jack had been in hospital but, like Jamie, had been expecting him to make a full recovery. The reactions were varied but all were emotional; sorrow, sadness, grief, shock and, above all, anger. One by one Jamie ticked the lads off his cerebral list and by the end of his final call, to Vinnie, he felt mentally drained. He needed a drink but he fought the urge. One, he knew, would lead to two and two to three until he had drunk himself lifeless, and he had promised to return to see the Connolly family later. There would be time for succour in the bottom of a glass later…he had arranged to meet all of the boys in the Waldorf the following night and they would drink then to Jack's memory.

Julie called late in the afternoon. She had taken some time to gather herself together after her mother had broken the news but she was still in shock, sobbing intermittently. Jamie told her that the funeral was taking place on the following Tuesday and that it was his intention to come down south shortly after that, probably on Thursday second November. When her mind was working on the logistics of what Jamie needed Julie was able to switch off from her grief but it would come back when she was alone.

'I've found you a place in Normanton for four weeks,' she reported, giving him the address. 'I told the owner you were coming down to work at the Ratcliffe Power

Station but wanted to see if you could settle down here first so you only wanted the flat for a month. It's lying empty so the owner is quite happy though I think he's asking for a bit too much for rent…it's £13/10/00 for the month.'

'That's fine, Jules,' Jamie said enthusiastically, using her pet name. 'Tell him I want it from the beginning of November.'

'He'll want the rent in advance, is that alright?'

'Yeah, that's okay too. Do you have enough money to pay it or do you want me to send it to you?' Jamie asked, conscious that the cost might be onerous for her.

'It's alright. I'll pay it and get it when you come down on the second. You will be here, won't you?' she asked uncertainly.

'Oh, I'll be there, don't worry your pretty head about that,' he said grimly. 'Nobody knows what you've been doing?'

'Nobody,' she confirmed. 'I know how important it is Jamie. It seems so long since you left though it's just over a week. So much has happened.'

Jamie digested that. It did seem a long time, a lifetime, yet it was only ten days; ten days crammed with heartbreak and sadness, not to mention intrigue. A picture of Roisin Kelly flitted across his mind. Yes, there was Roisin too, he remembered guiltily. 'It will soon all be over,' he said softly. 'I'll call you next Wednesday and arrange to meet you for the key. Take care, Julie…and thanks.' Jamie heard her say goodbye and hung up, leaving her to her angst.

For Jamie, the next eight days passed in a daze. He felt lost and alone, as if part of him had died, and he spent a lot of time at the Connolly home. Mutual support worked and he managed to stay off the booze, something that had worried him. Other than on the Tuesday night after Jack's death, when he met the rest of the gang, he stayed dry. When he was at home his mother fussed around him solicitously, trying to ease his anguish whilst his father, the old soldier who had seen death up close, encouraged him to keep a stiff upper lip. But neither approach was particularly effective and Jamie found himself shutting off from them. Instead, he busied himself with his plans.

Conor called at the weekend to see how he was bearing up; at least that was what *he said* he was calling for. Jamie knew his reasons were deeper. Sure he was concerned, but his concern stretched way beyond the present. It came out eventually when Jamie suggested he say what he wanted to say rather than beat about the bush.

'I don't think you should go alone,' Conor had said at last. 'You need someone to watch your back.'

'And that someone should be you?' Jamie laughed rhetorically.

'Who else?'

There was a pause while Jamie figured out how to approach this. The American had helped enough and he didn't want him to have blood on his hands. 'I don't think it's a good idea, Conor,' he started. 'If this goes wrong it's better if it's only me who drops in it.'

Conor refused to accept that. 'I'm only here today because of you,' he argued, 'so I'm coming along whether you like it or not, kid.'

'Are all Americans as pig headed as you?' Jamie retorted.

'Not all, just the Irish Americans. It's the Celtic thing,' he laughed. 'You're not so different yourself.'

Jamie snorted. 'Okay, you win,' he conceded, 'but there are conditions.'

'I don't like conditions kid, but if that's what it takes, fair enough. Fire away.'

Jamie laughed hollowly again. 'There aren't many, but what there are you stick to. First, when I do it, I do it alone. I don't want you anywhere near. Second, if I tell you to leave and come back here because it's getting' too heavy, you go...and no arguments.'

'Woah, hold it,' Conor interrupted. 'If it's getting too heavy that's exactly when you'll need me.'

'I don't want you involved,' Jamie reiterated. 'I've already lost one close friend; I don't want to lose another. If I tell you to get out, you get out...but I promise I won't just use it as an excuse to dump you. Okay?'

'Okay,' Conor agreed reluctantly.

'Good,' Jamie came back, satisfied. 'I'm goin' down next Thursday, takin' the 'bike. It's probably better if we go separately.'

'Yeah, that sounds about right. I'll drive down at the weekend.'

Jamie thought about that and his face took on a look of horror. 'Just one thing about that, Conor, I want to be anonymous when I'm there so, for fuck sake, don't come in the Oldsmobile...everybody for a hundred miles will know we're there...anonymous it isn't!'

The American laughed. 'I'm not entirely stupid, kid...and you're forgetting my line of business. I'll drive down in Mary's Ford, can't get more anonymous than that now, can you?' They made arrangements to meet the following weekend, Jamie passing on the address given to him earlier by Julie, and Conor terminated the call, happy with the outcome. Jamie, on the other hand, still had misgivings, but only time would tell.

The evening before Jack's funeral, Jamie attended the Vigil with the family. The chapel was full and he was amazed at the emotion that Jack's death had created. Father Daly conducted the service, a sombre faced man with strong features and eyes that seemed to take in everything. A profound sadness filled the church. Funerals are meant to be a "Celebration of the Life of the Deceased" but to Jamie, there was damned little to be celebratory about. His friend's life had been cut short, without compunction, by men acting on behalf of a gangster sitting smugly in his office a couple of hundred miles away. Jamie would celebrate when that bastard was dead too.

He sat with the gang; Vinnie, Gerry, Tony and Jim...four of them when there should have been five, he thought disconsolately. He felt, rather than saw, Father Daly looking at him and turned towards the man, getting a reassuring smile in response. Jack's father and mother had been speaking with the priest off and on for most of the last week and Jamie had little doubt that his culpability and guilt had been discussed. The whole family had listened to his incessant self-reproach with a degree of disbelief; how could he blame himself for what happened, they said. But they didn't know what he knew.

After the service he retired to the Waldorf with the boys. It wasn't going to be a night for drinking but they all needed the company of each other. All of them now knew what had been behind the attack but were keeping it to themselves. Discussion centred on how to make the guilty party pay and all of them were for travelling south, mob handed, to resolve the issue. Jamie had a hard job persuading them that it would achieve nothing. Max Kelman had too many men for starters, and it would be almost impossible to get close to him. If they turned up as they suggested they would be noticed immediately and, when it was discovered they were from Glasgow, Kelman would be forewarned. No, the only way was a solo approach and Jamie let it be known he had something in mind. Reluctantly, they agreed to let him play it his way. It was Gerry Carroll who spoke for them all. 'You've got more reason to want this bastard dead than we have Jamie so we'll let you handle it. But, remember, if anything happens to you, or you need handers, we'll be there.'

Chapter 52

The funeral had been a trial but he had endured it. Father Daly had helped. Something about the man gave Jamie the strength to get through it...and now he had said his last goodbye. He stood up from the grave side and wiped his hands on a handkerchief. Teresa O'Brien gripped his hand tightly as he rose to his feet, both of them crying openly. They were alone, everyone else having left for the wake. The grave diggers huddled nearby, smoking, their cigarettes tucked inside the palms of their hands to keep them from the still falling rain. An almost leafless Rowan tree, the ubiquitous Mountain Ash, afforded the men minimal cover from the elements but, fortunately, at last the rain was easing.

Wrapping his arm around Teresa he guided her away from the graveside, nodding to the men as they passed. The men nodded back silently. Like the crows, they'd seen it all before.

'Right,' Jamie said with a cough as they reached the road, clearing the lump that still remained in his throat. 'The car will be back for us shortly, let's go to the wake...and I'll help you break the news,' he said gently, giving her a comforting squeeze.

Teresa smiled sadly in response. She was dreading it but she knew she had to face up to it eventually and, if Jamie was right, at least she would have someone else on her side. She looked at him affectionately. He had changed. Not in obvious ways, she reflected, but he was different somehow. He was still a caring person, the boy he had always been, and his reaction towards her over the last few minutes proved that; but he was quieter now, more thoughtful. It was as though he were carrying the weight of the world on his shoulders.

The limousine returned and took them to the wake. It stopped outside the Bowling Club and the driver waited patiently as they alighted. Jamie looked guiltily at the seat, soaked through, and apologised. The driver shrugged. 'You can't control the weather,' he said. Jamie dug some change from his pocket and handed it to the man who accepted it gratefully and pocketed it without looking at it, nodding appreciatively and tipping the skip of his hat.

Jamie escorted Teresa into the foyer of the club, taking her coat and hanging it up amongst the others. Anne-Marie appeared through the main door. She smiled sadly on seeing them, pleased that they were there but sad that it was in these circumstances. She kissed Teresa tenderly and held onto Jamie's arm.

'Where are your Mammy and Da?' Jamie asked quietly. 'I need to have a word with them before I head south again.' He didn't mention Teresa.

'They're in the committee room at the back of the hall with Father Daly,' Anne-Marie replied. 'When are you leaving?'

'A couple of days. There are things I need to do first...but I'll come and see you before I go, I promise.' Anne-Marie brightened a little at that. 'An' I'll see you this afternoon, after I talk to your Mammy.' Jamie took Teresa by the arm and steered her away into the hall. It was filled to capacity and food was set out on every table; the usual fare, sandwiches, sausage rolls, and cold meats. Jamie caught sight of the gang,

Gerry, Vinnie, Tony and Jim, all of them watching him closely. He nodded across and kept walking, taking Teresa to the most important meeting of her young life.

He felt her tremble and put his arm around her waist, pulling her closer. 'It'll be alright,' he whispered, 'don't worry.' She smiled tentatively in return and her trembling stopped. He knocked the Committee Room door and pushed it open.

Father Daly rose from his seat immediately, coming towards them with his hand outstretched and Jamie took it. The Priest looked quizzically at Teresa then ushered her to the chair he had just vacated and Jamie wondered if he had guessed why they were there. He smiled kindly at her and turned to Jamie. 'We were just talking about you,' he said. 'You don't have to bear any guilt for what happened, Jamie. Evil is all around us.'

Jamie listened but the words didn't help. Would the Priest say the same if he knew the circumstances, he wondered? He looked into the man's eyes and saw compassion there and that, at least, helped.

'I'm just leaving,' Father Daly continued, 'but if you need to talk, you know where to find me.' He patted Jamie on the arm, shook hands with Jacks parents and left to circulate around the other mourners and members of his flock.

Teresa looked apprehensively at Jamie now that the moment of truth had arrived. Clearly, she didn't know how to proceed and her fear of confronting the problem was returning. The last thing she needed now was rejection but Jamie was confident that wouldn't happen. He stood beside her, took her hand in his, and jumped in with both feet.

'Teresa needs your help,' he said, his eyes on Jack's mother who smiled and came towards them. She held out her hand and knelt down beside Teresa who had started to sob.

'It's alright, Teresa, it's alright,' she whispered softly. 'When is the baby due?'

Jamie's eyes opened wide in shock. Perhaps it was female intuition but even at that it was unbelievable. He looked across at Jack's father who appeared to be as stunned as he was. Teresa was sobbing uncontrollably now but Jamie thought it was more from relief than anything else. She looked at Jamie, acknowledging that he had been right in his judgement of the Connolly's, and put her arms round Jack's mother's neck.

'Thank you,' Jamie said, speaking for Teresa. 'No one else knows,' he continued. 'An' she needs help…she's scared.'

Jack's mother smiled wanly. 'You're a good boy, Jamie Raeburn, and you've got a big heart,' she said softly. 'Don't worry; we'll take care of everything. It's what Jack would have wanted, isn't it Da?' she continued, bringing Jack's father into the conversation. The older man joined them and wrapped his arms around both women and Jamie could have sworn there was a tear in his eye. Jamie began to edge towards the door but Jack's mother stopped him.

He turned to her as she rose from Teresa and came to him. 'Don't be a stranger to us, Jamie,' she said, hugging him. 'If you need anything, ask. You were like a brother to Jack and you're like another son to us.' There were tears in her eyes too. She wiped her hand across her face quickly. 'The others are waiting for you, on you go,' she said, releasing him. 'And thank them for coming.'

Jamie left them, closing the door gently behind him. He looked across at his friends and Vinnie rose to his feet, holding a whisky glass filled almost to the brim. Jamie made his way over to them and sat down heavily, accepting the glass.

'It's Laphroig,' Gerry said furtively. 'We sneaked it in fur ye… we didnae think this place wid huv it behind the bar and we thought ye'd need it.'

Jamie lifted the whisky to his mouth, drawing in the aroma of the heavy, peaty whisky through his nostrils, and sipped gratefully. 'To Jack Connelly,' he said aloud, raising his glass in a toast. 'The best mate we ever had.' He drank some more and smiled at Anne-Marie who smiled sadly back at him.

Chapter 53

Father Daly stood before his small congregation, his right hand making the sign of the cross over them and the words of the "Divine Praises" brought the Mass to its conclusion. *'Blessed be God. Blessed be His Holy Name. Blessed be Jesus Christ, true God and true Man. Blessed be the Name of Jesus. Blessed be His Most Sacred Heart. Blessed be His Most Precious Blood. Blessed be Jesus in the Most Holy Sacrament of the Altar. Blessed be the Holy Spirit, the Paraclete. Blessed be the great Mother of God, Mary most Holy. Blessed be her Holy and Immaculate Conception. Blessed be her Glorious Assumption. Blessed be the Name of Mary, Virgin and Mother. Blessed be St. Joseph, her most chaste spouse. Blessed be God in His Angels and in His Saints.'*

As he finished and his right hand rose to make the sign of the Cross, his eyes lifted over the subdued congregation to the rear of the chapel. The solitary figure had entered towards the end of the Mass and had slipped into the last pew but the Priest's efforts to identify the person had failed. The man, if it was a man, sat motionless, his head bowed, his coat buttoned tightly across his chest and a scarf covering his mouth and nose. *There's nothing unusual in that*, he thought. The nights were colder now and a nascent fog had been falling as the Evening Mass had started. He waited as his parishioners started to file away out into the night, many casting their eyes suspiciously towards the shadowy figure, before he made his way down the centre aisle.

The man hadn't moved and the Priest was about to ask him to leave. He felt uneasy as he moved closer to the man, sensing a deep foreboding surrounding him. Suddenly the man looked up and pulled back his scarf, revealing his features, and was instantly recognisable. Father Daly gave a subdued sigh of relief.

He walked past the pew and closed the big, double wooden doors, shutting out the darkness and the cold, then returned and slid into the pew beside his visitor. 'Well Jamie, you've come back,' he greeted softly. 'I wasn't sure if you would.'

Jamie regarded him with his doleful, dark eyes. 'Aye Father, I decided to take you up on your offer.'

'I'm glad,' the Priest answered. 'There are some things you can't keep to yourself…and killing someone isn't a subject you can talk freely about, is it? For someone like you, Jamie, guilt is a natural consequence of killing but, from what I hear, it was self-defence, wasn't it?'

Jamie turned to face him directly for the first time, his eyes cold and hard and the Priest understood that his problem had deeper roots. 'I don't feel guilty for that, Father – and in the same situation, I'd do it again. No, it's somethin' else.'

The priest returned Jamie's look and saw something there that he hadn't seen before; a cold determination tinged with an element of self-doubt. His assumption, correct as it happened, was that Jamie was wrestling with a greater problem now and vengeance played a part in it.

'You said I could talk to you…and that anythin' I tell you will stay just between us?' Father Daly nodded slowly, a feeling of apprehension growing inside him. Jamie continued. 'Does your God forgive people for doin' things they know are wrong but they do them because they have to…because they don't have a choice?'

The priest stood up and Jamie feared that perhaps he had gone too far. 'I think this conversation is going to last a while so we might as well be comfortable while we're having it,' he said lightly. 'Come with me. Father Mackenzie is out visiting parishioners this evening so we can talk in the house.' He moved away, slipping out of the pew and making his way back down the aisle towards the altar. Jamie heaved himself to his feet and followed.

At the altar, the priest began to extinguish the candles and Jamie detected the distinctive smell that follows the snuffing out of a candle. Like snuffing out a life, he reflected. The smell, fusing with the lingering scent of the incense in the Chapel, took Jamie back to the Funeral Mass of the day before.

The priest completed his task and turned to Jamie, taking him by the arm and leading him through a door set in the wall to the left of the altar and down a narrow, carpeted passageway into the priests' private quarters. Jamie found himself in a comfortable living room with two battered armchairs, one each side of a roaring coal fire. The chairs looked as if they had seen better days but they were still serviceable…and, apparently, comfortable. The walls of the room were lined with shelves from floor to ceiling, all stacked with books, mostly of a religious nature. In one corner there was a small dining table and four straight backed chairs. Papers were strewn about the table, hand written notes, scribbles, and an old King James Bible, its blue leather cover scuffed and marked and its gold lettering faded. An ashtray, almost overflowing with cigarette butts, sat precariously near the edge of the table and there was ash on the carpet.

'My sermon for Sunday,' the priest explained, seeing Jamie's eyes wander over the papers. 'You'll have to forgive the mess, Jamie. Mrs Thomson, our housekeeper – God bless her – won't be in until morning and she'll give us hell for getting the place into such a state…again.' He laughed, waving his arms to encompass the chaos. There was a moment's awkward silence before he continued. 'Sit down, Jamie, sit down,' he said, indicating the two armchairs next to the fire. 'They don't look it but they *are* comfortable. Father Mackenzie and I fall asleep in them regularly,' he grinned.'

It was oppressively hot in the room and Jamie, dressed as he was for a winter's night, was beginning to perspire heavily. 'Do you mind if I take off my coat, Father?' he asked.

Father Daly appeared lost in thought but snapped back to the present with Jamie's words, looking a little embarrassed. 'Of course Jamie, of course, what am I thinking…give it here.' He waited as Jamie unfastened the buttons and shrugged out of the coat. It was the same coat he had been wearing at the funeral, he noticed, and traces of mud still clung to its hem. He took it from Jamie and laid it carefully across one of the chairs around the table before making his way to a large, dark wood cabinet set against the wall.

The cabinet was fitted with a front lowering flap which Father Daly opened flamboyantly to reveal a fabulous array of bottles and Jamie identified a few bottles of Scotch whisky as well as Irish whiskey and Brandy. *They like their drink*, he thought to himself, *but then again, if you can't have sex, then drink is probably the best substitute.*

'If my memory serves me well, you were drinking whisky at the wake yesterday. Am I right?' Father Daly asked, interrupting Jamie's thoughts.

'Aye Father, I've been known to take a dram…sometimes too many drams,' he replied, watching as the priest half-filled two tumblers and carried them back to the fire, handing one to Jamie and sinking into the chair opposite.

'It's Glenmorangie,' he said, almost apologetically as he watched Jamie sniff it. 'I usually drink it as it comes. What about you, do you want anything in it?'

'No Father, it's fine as it is, thanks,' Jamie replied with a smile, taking his first sip. It wasn't a malt Jamie normally drank, preferring the heavier malts from Islay where his mother's family had originated, but it was pleasant on the palate.

They sat for a while in silence, sipping their whiskies, each of them gathering his thoughts. Jamie was contemplating the difficulty involved in explaining his dilemma and the Priest was wondering, uneasily, what was about to be disclosed to him. It was Jamie who broke the spell.

'I'm sorry about this Father. I've got the feelin' I'm goin' to land you in it with this.'

'I offered, Jamie…and I meant it. Priests often get "landed in it", as you put it,' he laughed.

'This thing is drivin' me crazy Father, an' it's not easy to talk about, especially with my family or people close to me.' He didn't mention Conor. The Priest nodded and waited for Jamie to continue. 'An' what I tell you won't go any further?' Jamie asked again.

'You have my word on that.'

There was another lengthy silence. Father Daly waited patiently, watching the conflicting emotions flitting across Jamie's face, each fighting for supremacy over him, and he began to wonder if Jamie would find the courage to disclose what it was that was troubling him.

Finally, Jamie reached a decision and the story flooded out. Father Daly sat in receptive silence, sipping his Glenmorangie and listening intently as Jamie recounted the events surrounding the initial disappearance of Lucie; his anxiety at the time; his search for her; being taken to Cranston Hall and finding her there; the threats and Lucie's final acceptance of Kelman's ultimatum, leading to Jamie's return to Glasgow. The final piece of the tragedy, the attack which resulted in Jack's death, lead the Priest to the inevitable conclusion that vengeance was going to be Jamie Raeburn's, and not The Lord's.

'I should have expected it,' Jamie said bitterly. 'Kelman had already had me beaten up…an' his boys weren't stoppin' at that; they would have killed me then but for Lucie an' some other people arrivin' on the scene.' He stopped and looked guiltily at the Priest. 'I should have seen it comin',' he repeated.

Jamie's guilt was rising to the surface once again but the Priest detected anger there too, bubbling away dangerously close. But anger at whom, Father Daly wondered, at himself or at this man Kelman? He waited, maintaining his silence, reluctant to interrupt Jamie's account. 'I'm the only one who can stop this once and for all, Father.'

Another silence ensued, broken this time by the Priest. 'How can you do that, Jamie? From what you've said, Lucie *can't* simply return to you…or even disappear with you, because of the threats to her family…and to you. So what can you do?' As the words left his mouth he knew the answer. 'Silly question!' he acknowledged. 'I can see now why you're here…I should have seen it earlier, shouldn't I?' he continued quietly.

Jamie gazed into the dying embers of the fire and finished off the last of his whisky. He turned eventually and gazed into the Priest's sad eyes. 'Aye Father, I can see you've guessed what I have to do.'

Father Daly rose from his chair, piled some more coal onto the fire, and took Jamie's glass. He said nothing, needing time to think. Walking slowly to the drinks cabinet he refilled their glasses and sank back into his chair. 'You want to know if killing this man...what's his name, Kelman?' He paused, waiting for Jamie's response. Jamie nodded but said nothing. 'You want to know if killing him is justifiable?'

'No Father, I don't think *anythin'* justifies killin' someone,' Jamie replied, surprising the Priest. 'I know that sounds crazy because I've been tryin' to convince myself that killin' Jack's murderer was justified...but maybe it's the intention part that's important. I killed that man because he had tried to kill Jack Connolly and because he was trying to kill me...I didn't intend to kill him, just stop him. But with Kelman, it's different; I *have* to kill him...I can't stop him if I don't. But what happens to me then?' He was rambling, his inner conflict throwing up argument and counter argument.

The priest regarded him reflectively. 'Do you believe in God, Jamie?' he asked softly.

Jamie took another sip of his whisky and contemplated his response. 'I'm not a Catholic, Father, you know that, but I was taken to church by my father and mother every Sunday when I was little and, as I grew older, I went on my own. I know the difference between right and wrong, good and evil, but do I believe in God? Honestly Father, I don't know. If there *is* a God, an all-powerful God as we're told there is, why does he allow things like this to happen?' It came out with a sob.

The priest smiled. 'Faith is a difficult, Jamie,' he conceded. 'Believing in the existence of an all-powerful being, without proof, almost seems absurd, doesn't it? But thousands of millions of people throughout the world believe in God...not just Catholics, but Buddhists, Hindus, Muslims.'

'Aye Father, but that's on the strength of what they've been *taught* to believe,' Jamie interrupted. 'Wasn't it Karl Marx who said that religion is the opium of the people?'

Father Daly looked at him in amazement. This was the last thing he had expected, a debate on the basis of religious belief and its use in controlling the masses. He smiled cautiously. 'Yes, Marx said that...or at least that's how it is paraphrased. What he actually said was "Religion is the sigh of the oppressed creature, the heart of a heartless world, and the soul of soulless conditions. It is the opium of the people". And he wasn't the first either; the Marquis de Sade came up with the same idea about a hundred years earlier...he described it as "this opium you feed your people"...and there have been others. But the fact remains, people believe.'

He paused, holding Jamie's look. The conversation was turning to the philosophical rather than the practical, not what he wanted. 'Let's get back to your immediate dilemma,' he continued, trying to regain control of the discussion. 'To kill, or not to kill? Can killing ever be justified? You've just said that nothing justifies killing another human being, yet men do it every day,' Father Daly continued. 'Most of them know that it is wrong, just as you do, but they do it none the less...and men like me...priests, ministers, rabbis, imams, we encourage them, and politicians incite them.' The Priest's voice was reflective, despondent, and Jamie felt compelled to listen. 'When I was younger, just after I finished my training to be a priest, I joined the Army.' Seeing the disbelief in Jamie's eyes he smiled sadly. 'It's hard to believe, I know, but I did…I was a padre, a "Sky Pilot" they called me, with the Argyll & Sutherland Highlanders. I went to Korea with them…as well as some other shitholes around the world,' he continued bitterly, his language shocking Jamie. 'I saw young men like you kill, and be killed, every day. I saw what it did to them; broken bodies and shattered minds…and I dished out absolution, like porridge for breakfast. Some of them could rationalise it to themselves…it was him or me, he was the enemy, he was a communist. Others couldn't justify it like that.' He paused and looked down into his glass. 'But they went out and they killed their fellow man, and they kept doing it, because politicians, and men like me, told them it was alright; it was justifiable, it was the fight of good over evil, the battle against Godlessness.' Jamie watched, enthralled, as the Priest's eyes drifted away, to places he had hoped he would never return to, even in conversation. He picked up the poker and stirred the fire then took another sip of his whisky. 'The situation those men were in isn't so different from yours, Jamie. They were fighting the good fight, struggling against an evil and oppressive enemy that they believed wanted to enslave them, because that is what they were told, and you believe that if you kill this man you will be ridding the world of an evil individual, a purveyor of drugs and prostitution, a racketeer…and the man who has, in essence, taken away your reason to live.' As he spoke, his eyes were unmoving, unblinking, locked on to Jamie's. The effect was almost hypnotic. 'And from what you've told me of this man, I have no reason to doubt it,' he finished.

'So, are you saying it's alright Father?' Jamie asked, astonished.

The priest laughed softly. 'No lad, I'm not saying it's alright. What I'm saying, in my priestly and somewhat convoluted way, is that I understand why you feel as you do, why you feel that you *have* to kill this man…and for many people, killing him would be justifiable.'

They sat in silence once more, sipping their drinks, watching the blue, green and yellow flames lick out of the fire as little pockets of gas trapped within the coal ignited. Father Daly pondered the words he had just said while Jamie wrestled with acceptance of them.

The priest looked at Jamie, seeing a lot of himself in the lad when he himself had been twenty one. Right and wrong were black and white, there was no in between, but as you grow older you realise that there is no black and white, only thousands of shades of grey. He decided to continue. 'Have you ever heard of the Roman God Janus?' he asked.

Jamie looked at him, trying to read what was behind the question, but failing. 'No Father,' he replied. 'I suppose he falls into the "graven image" category, eh?'

Father Daly laughed. 'You could say that…actually, it would be two graven images. Janus is the Roman God of time and transition, the keeper of the gates, and he's usually depicted with two faces, one looking back and one looking forward. He was an important God to the Romans…they even named the month of January after him.'

'Quite a guy,' Jamie interjected. 'But what does he have to do with my problem, Father?'

'Everything and nothing,' the Priest returned thoughtfully. He paused for an instant. 'Your quandary, as I see it Jamie, is this; if you do nothing, you lose everything, including your reason for living, to evil. If you do something, in this case kill the source of the evil, then you could end up losing your soul to evil. You don't want to end up becoming the man you kill. Tell me, how did you feel after when you discovered that the man who had attacked you and Jack Connolly was dead?'

'I felt numb; sick I suppose, but it passed quickly. I wasn't really thinking about him...I was thinking about Jack.'

'What about exhilaration, excitement? Did you get a kick out of it?'

Jamie looked askance at him. 'No, father, not at all.'

'Have you thought about that man since?' he continued and watched Jamie shake his head. 'That, at least, sets you apart from this Kelman creature, Jamie and I doubt if you'll ever be like him. But the course you seem set upon does appear to be the only one open to you. You can't simply go in and rescue the girl because he'll exact revenge on her family. And even if he doesn't do that, he'll search for you both and when he finds you, and he probably would find you...' He let the import of his words hang in the air for a heartbeat, and then continued. 'You can't threaten him; he's in too strong a position for that. In short, you only have two choices – either you do nothing, or you do what you've already made up your mind to do. And that's where Janus comes in. He's the God of Transition...and *you're* changing. What you do now and how you react to it later will determine what you become. As I said earlier, you don't want to become the man you kill.'

'But goin' back to my original question, Father,' Jamie responded quietly. 'Where will I stand with your God?'

Father Daly settled back in his chair, took another sip of whisky and looked at Jamie over the rim of his glass. 'Forget what your God or my God will think. Concentrate on yourself and what *you* think and do. If you go through with this and then spend your time looking back on what you've done it will destroy you...each time you look back you'll die a little. That's what I call the Janus Complex. Janus looks back in time *and* forward into the future, and both at the same time hence his two faces, but you can't do that.' He paused, watching Jamie wrestle with his words. 'If you were a Catholic, Jamie, and you came to me to confess this, telling me everything just as we've discussed it, then I'd grant you absolution. I would forgive you in the name of The Father...just as I've done in the past for countless other young men in Korea and Malaya...and Kenya,' he said dolefully. 'It seems to me your mind's made up, and while I should be trying to persuade you against following the course you've chosen, I can't.'

Jamie lifted his glass to his mouth and finished off his second dram. The two large whiskies and the heat in the room were having an effect on him but his mind was still clear. 'I have to do it, Father,' he said seriously. 'If I don't, I'll spend the rest of my life wishin' that I had.'

The sound of the outside door opening followed by a rush of cold air into the room heralded the return of Father Mackenzie and brought the discussion to a timely close. The priest rose and made his way over to the table, lifted Jamie's coat from the chair where he had left it and passed it to him. 'Don't worry Jamie, what we've spoken about won't leave these four walls,' he assured Jamie quietly. 'That's not to say that Father Mackenzie won't wheedle it out of me...but your secret will be safe with him too.'

Jamie held out his hand and the priest took it, shaking it firmly. 'Thank you Father,' he said gratefully. 'I know where I stand now.'

'I think you always did,' the Priest said in a kindly tone.

They passed Father Mackenzie in the passageway and the old priest gave them a questioning look but said nothing. 'Don't be a stranger here, Jamie. I'm here if you need to talk again,' Father Daly said as Jamie left him. He was gratified to see a smile of appreciation spread across Jamie's face.

Outside, the temperature had dropped and thick smog had settled over the city. Jamie disappeared quickly from view and the priest returned to his sitting room in need of another whisky. He was troubled but his conscience was clear. *Jamie Raeburn will do what he feels he must*, he reflected sombrely.

Jamie pulled his coat tightly around his body and walked carefully down the rapidly icing pathway to the main road. The smog swirled ominously around him, thickening by the second. It was what his mother would call a 'pea souper', and he could see the similarity. His breath exhaled in clouds of white mist which were quickly absorbed into the thicker, cloying, soot filled air. The silence was eerie. Every so often, as he neared a street lamp, a pale halo of light would appear above him only to be snuffed out within a few paces. There was no traffic. The buses had stopped and even the trams had given up. It was a long walk home but it didn't matter. He didn't mind. The walk would help him to work off the effects of the Glenmorangie before his drive south the next day. At last he felt he had everything clear in his mind and he knew exactly what he had to do...and he felt better than he had done for a very long time.

Chapter 54

Jamie set off for Derby early next morning. The smog had cleared during the night and a frost glistened on the grass and the hedgerows. He was dressed for the weather and suspected that it would grow colder as he climbed up over Beattock Summit and again when he moved further south through Cumbria. He was wearing his battered leather flying jacket and a pair of R.A.F. surplus fleece lined Bomber Crew trousers and boots. A leather flying helmet was fastened firmly under his chin and his goggles sat jauntily on his brow. Like Biggles on a bad day, he laughed to himself. The clothes restricted his movement but at least he would be warm. His mother had risen early to see him on his way, some inner sense telling her this trip was important to him.

The night before, returning late from his visit to Father Daly, Jamie had been surprised to find his father waiting for him. 'Be careful son,' his father had said and Jamie could read from his father's expression that he had deduced what was troubling him. 'Your mother's worried, and so am I.'

Jamie had looked at him lovingly. They'd had their differences in recent years but since Jamie had moved south their relationship had been solid. 'I will, don't worry,' he had responded. 'There's somethin' I have to do…an' I think that if you were in my shoes you would do the same. We're not so different, Dad.'

They had hugged for the first time in years and Jamie was sure he had seen tears in his father's eyes. 'I won't ask you what it is because I know you won't tell me, but whatever it is it has been eating away at you since you came home…and it's more than Jack's murder, isn't it?' his father had said softly.

'Yeah, it is, but what happened to Jack is part of it…and it wasn't Jack they were after.' He had seen the shock in his father's face as the words sank in. 'Just keep it to yourself, Mum doesn't need to know…an' I *will* be careful, I promise.

They had gone to bed then but Jamie felt an additional weight of guilt at having burdened his father with the truth, or at least part of it. But his father could handle it and, like most husbands, he surmised, he could keep the truth from his wife. He had to. And now his mother was showing him all her fears as well. What could he tell her? She knew something was seriously wrong because, like Teresa O'Brien, she had seen the dramatic change in him. His bubbly self-confidence had been replaced by a quiet resolve. He still smiled but sometimes his eyes, a barometer to his inner feelings, were cold. And she was worried.

She packed away sandwiches and something for him to drink and watched him load the panniers on the back of the Triumph. A cardboard box caught her attention, a box like a shoebox, and she noted the particular care he took with it. He caught her look and grinned but there was something in the grin that was forced and she knew then that there was something in the box he didn't want her to know about. She looked away sadly.

Jamie came to her, lumbering like a Sumo Wrestler, and wrapped her in his arms. 'I'll be careful,' he promised. 'I've already had this from Dad. I'll be back before you know it, so come on, give your wee boy a smile.' He kissed her affectionately on the cheek. 'I'll phone you regularly, just so you know I'm alright.'

She laughed at that. 'That will make a change,' she said, then grew serious again. 'I love you, you know.'

'Yes, I know you do, an' I love you too. Now get back inside before you freeze to death.' With a final kiss, Jamie mounted the Triumph, turned the ignition key and kicked the big 650cc engine into life. Mary Raeburn covered her ears in mock horror as she watched him manoeuvre the bike out through the gate and then, with a wave, he was gone, racing up onto Great Western Road and turning towards the city.

By 07.30 he had cleared Glasgow and was racing out through Lanarkshire on the A74, mindful of the frost still covering the grass verges. An accident on the road now would be the end of everything, particularly if the police became involved and the box with the Walther was discovered. He kept to a steady speed, increasing it gradually as the sun rose and warmed the road. By 09.10 he was passing Carlisle and was faced with a choice. He could go via the A66 through Penrith and Brough to Scotch Corner and then follow the A1 south through Yorkshire past Catterick and Wetherby into Nottinghamshire or he could take advantage of the recently opened M6 Motorway skirting Manchester and leaving at Stoke-On-Trent to cross the country on the A50. The weather was the deciding factor. By taking the former route he would be climbing higher across the Dales on the tortuous route to Scotch Corner. The new motorway would allow him to open up the bike and the A50 was a more direct road across country to Derby.

The M6, giving him the opportunity to open up the throttle on the Bonneville, won the battle and he flew along on the new surface at a steady 85mph. The big machine was performing beautifully, whisking him past lorries and cars as if they were standing still. He had telephoned Julie the night before and had arranged to meet her in Chellaston, just off the A50 to the south of Derby. Julie suggested a pub that did lunches, the Red Lion on the Derby Road, and he had readily agreed. Apart from anything else, it wasn't too far from the apartment she had rented for him in Normanton.

He arrived early at the Red Lion and dismounted from the bike, stretching his tired muscles. The scar across his stomach itched where the stitches were tight and he scratched cautiously to ease the irritation. A quick check on his watch told him he was about twenty minutes early for the rendezvous at mid-day but the pub looked inviting. He left the big bike in the car park where he could see it from the pub windows and ambled over to the entrance. The heat from inside hit him like a blast furnace as he opened the door and he quickly peeled off his helmet and loosened his jacket. A log fire was blazing furiously and a few customers were already gathered around it, sipping contentedly on their drinks. They looked at him disinterestedly as he entered and returned to their beers. Jamie breathed easily. He ordered a pint of bitter and sat near a window overlooking the car park where he could keep an eye on his bike.

Julie arrived at exactly mid-day. A car swung into the car park and he watched as she climbed from the passenger seat. He strained to see the driver and was rewarded with a full face view as the car swung round and left. The driver was a young woman that Jamie didn't recognise. Julie pushed open the door and spotted him right away, waving and coming to him with a broad smile. She kissed him as he rose to greet her. It was all perfectly normal, a young couple meeting for a quick lunch, the girl dressed in her nurse's uniform. It was all perfectly normal, except for the fact that it wasn't.

As Julie's lips brushed his cheek Jamie knew that something was wrong. The smile Julie wore was covering something else and Jamie was instantly on edge. 'What's wrong?' he asked, keeping his voice low and the smile fixed on his face.

'Word has been going around that you're dead,' she replied in a low tone. Jamie laughed bitterly. 'It's not funny, Jamie,' she continued, distressed. If Lucie hears that, God knows what she'll do. If she thinks you're dead...'

Jamie held up his hand, stopping her. 'Has she been out of Kelman's house?'

'No, not that I know of,' Julie replied, hesitantly. 'Why?'

'If she hasn't been out, how would she know?' Julie brightened, but she was still worried and Jamie could read the signs. 'The sooner I get this done, the better then,' he continued as they settled into their seats.

'What are you going to do? How are you going to do it?'

Jamie smiled coldly and took Julie's hand. 'It's better you don't know, Jules. You've done enough. If it goes wrong they'll come to you...'

'Who will? Kelman?'

'No sweetheart, the police, and it's important that you know nothing. All you've done is rent a flat for me, nothing more; you didn't know what I was going to do and, if you had done, you would have reported it...alright?'

'I'm scared, Jamie.'

'I know, but just trust me. If it goes wrong, you've had nothing to do with it.'

'And if it goes wrong, what happens to Lucie? What happens to you, I don't want you to end up like Jack?' She watched his face as she asked the questions and saw his tortured response.

'It won't go wrong,' he said emphatically. 'Come on, what do you want to drink?'

They ate lunch quietly. The words that flowed between them fell into the small talk category. Jamie slipped an envelope across the table as Julie handed over the keys to the flat. Julie lifted the envelope and dropped it into her handbag as Jamie pocketed the keys to the flat in Byron Street, Normanton, a couple of miles south of Derby City Centre.

'I bought you some food,' Julie said quietly. 'Some tins; milk, sugar, tea, coffee, butter...the essentials. Oh, and bread,' she added and Jamie smiled gratefully. Food wasn't something that had been on his mind. 'Tell me you're not doing this on your own,' Julie asked, still concerned.

'I'm not, don't worry. A friend is joining me tomorrow. I'll have someone watching my back.'

They left it at that. At two o'clock in the afternoon they left the pub and Julie accompanied him to the flat in Normanton before he took her back to Beeston. She clung to him throughout both journeys, her heart in her mouth, but the ride was exhilarating. She wondered if Lucie knew about him having the bike and whether she would cling to him the way she had. He dropped her in Beeston Town Centre and she kissed him tenderly on the cheek.

'Be careful,' she said as he left her, and saw his hand wave in response.

Chapter 55

Conor arrived two days later. As promised, he came in Mary's Ford Anglia and he complained incessantly about the cramped driving conditions presented by the little car. Jamie was pleased to see him. The two days he had spent on his own had proved difficult. He began to doubt his ability to see it through and his guilt around Jack's death and his brief affair with Roisin Kelly in Belfast had resurfaced.

Conor revived his spirit. He stood inside the hall looking at the sparse furnishings and the peeling paint and pulled a bottle of bourbon from his bag. 'I think we need a drink, kid,' he said with a broad smile. After an hour, and half a bottle of Jack Daniels, Conor hauled himself from his chair and started to unload the car. He brought in a suitcase and laid it on the floor in front of Jamie. 'That lot is for you kid,' he drawled as he disappeared out the door again.

When he returned, Jamie had already opened the case and was examining the contents. 'What the hell is this?' he asked, holding up what looked like a rubber body suit with a helmet like a balaclava, and rubber arms and legs.

'It's called a dry suit, kid,' Conor replied. 'Navy divers wear them. They're designed to keep the guys warm in cold water but for you it has a dual purpose. You'll be able to move about freely and your body will be completely camouflaged as well as warm.' The other items in the case were those which Jamie had asked Conor to bring with him; thin black cotton gloves, a black boiler suit, black shoes, a black ski mask and a black sweater. 'It's all there,' Conor said with a grin.

'Did you manage to get the mercury?'

'Oops, sorry kid, forgot about that, it's here,' he replied, patting his jacket. He removed a tiny bottle filled with the silvery liquid from his pocket and held it out. 'I kept it separate. What do you want it for?' he asked. He suspected he already knew the answer, and if he was right, there was more to Jamie than he had first thought.

'Thanks,' Jamie replied softly, taking hold of the tiny vial. 'I'm glad you're here…I've been suffering a bit. The mercury is for a little modification I want to do.'

Yeah, to the bullets, Conor mused, his suspicion confirmed, and immediately reappraised his opinion of Jamie. 'It's not good being on your own, kiddo. Your thoughts take over and there's no one to bounce them off. You'll be alright now.' Jamie smiled. Conor was the big brother he had never had. 'So, how's about you tell me the plan,' the American continued.

They settled down with another glass of Jack Daniels. 'I'm going to watch him for the next few days, maybe a week, find a weak spot.'

'And?'

'And then I'll kill him.'

*

The surveillance of Max Kelman took longer than Jamie or Conor had anticipated. The man was paranoid about his safety and was never without at least one bodyguard or, more usually, two. But eventually a pattern emerged. Every night, Kelman did the rounds of the "businesses" run by the gang, delivering bags to some and picking up bags at others. And every night he finished up at a Club on the

London Road, stayed there for half an hour to an hour, and then drove home to his father's pile out to the west of the city, arriving there between eleven o'clock and midnight. Jamie and Conor followed him on alternate nights, swapping between the Triumph and the little Ford. Each night, Kelman's car stopped outside the big gates leading to the driveway which in turn led to the house hidden behind the high wall and a screen of trees.

It was the eighth night before they sat down to discuss the options. They had just arrived back at the flat and Conor was frustrated. 'I've met some security conscious guys in my time,' Conor stated grimly. 'But this guy beats them all. He doesn't take chances…and I'm pretty sure his goons are carrying. I don't like it kid.'

'Like it or not, I have to do it Conor. I'm going for him at the gate.'

Conor smiled grimly and shook his head. 'We don't even know what's behind the gate. We need to know more. You could be walking into a death trap kid.'

'I don't think so,' Jamie replied thoughtfully. 'I've been in there, remember.'

'So what's behind the gate?'

'A long drive with trees on both sides and, in front of the house, a big expanse of lawn.'

'Guards? Cameras?' Conor asked.

'I wasn't looking for them,' Jamie admitted.

'So, like I said, you don't know what's behind that gate.'

'Then let's go and look. Get your coat,' Jamie said, grinning and rising to his feet.

Conor smiled and climbed wearily from his chair. 'Have you ever thought of making a career out of this, kiddo? You'd be good at it.'

They had used the Ford earlier so now they took the bike. Jamie retraced their journey from earlier and drove past the entrance to Cranston Hall, carrying on for about a quarter of a mile. Houses were few and far between and there was no traffic to speak of and the only living things interested in them were the cows filling the fields on both sides of the road. Jamie spotted a gate leading into a copse and slowed, looking over his shoulder to point it out to Conor who nodded agreement.

With the bike hidden off the road they began the short walk back to Cranston Hall. If anyone stopped them they would say they had taken a couple of girls home to Brailsford after a night out in Derby and then couldn't get a taxi back so they were walking. As a cover, it wouldn't hold up to serious scrutiny, but why should anyone doubt it? They hadn't done anything…yet.

They needn't have worried. The walk took them less than ten minutes and they met no one. They approached the big wrought iron gates cautiously but there was no sign of anyone watching the entrance. It was Conor who spotted the little keypad on the right hand gate support. 'Electric by the look of it,' he whispered, pointing the little pad out to Jamie. 'Punch in a code and the gate opens. One of the wonders of modern technology.' Jamie nodded, remembering his earlier visit here.

He went close to the gate and looked down the driveway beyond. Trees lined the road on both sides, just as he remembered, and it stretched away into the distance. A faint light shone through the trees and Jamie knew that it was coming from the house itself. It was a good three hundred yards away but what lay between, other than trees, he couldn't tell. Max Kelman's obsession with his safety made Jamie suspect that there might be further security measures in the grounds. But the house didn't belong to Max, it belonged to his old man and maybe *he* didn't expect anyone to be foolish enough to break in. Jamie turned his attention to his surroundings on this side of the gate. The main road was about ten yards back and the little access road was lined with shrubs and bushes, mainly overgrown rhododendron. He paced down towards the road on one side and back up the other, leaving Conor by the gates. Surprisingly, he found that no thought had been given to security here. First of all, the shrubs, particularly the rhododendrons, would provide excellent cover to conceal him and there were sufficient gaps in the tangled foliage to allow him to secret himself with ease. Secondly, there were no security lights anywhere to be seen and the location was in total darkness. When he was dressed in black he could stand next to the car and they wouldn't see him. He smiled to himself. 'Tomorrow night,' he whispered. Conor nodded silently.

The return journey to the bike was as uneventful as their walk to Cranston Hall twenty minutes earlier. They said nothing, both of them thinking about the "how" of it. Back in the flat, Conor brought out the Jack Daniels and poured two more generous tots. They drank it straight.

'A quick kill and out of there,' Conor said as he finished his drink and poured another. 'Before the goons can react. How are you intending getting there and back?' Jamie's smile told him that he had other ideas, probably ideas he, Conor, wouldn't like. 'Well?' he persisted.

Jamie's expression turned glacial, his normally warm brown eyes cold. 'I've got a score to settle, Conor. A quick shot in the head won't settle it for me. I want him to know it's me and I want him to experience fear…real fear.'

'Shit Jamie,' Conor retorted. 'That's too dangerous. Remember, there's at least one other guy in the car.'

'I remember,' Jamie replied coldly.

'Okay, okay,' Conor gave ground. 'So, back to my question; how are you getting there and back again?'

'I've thought about that too. After I dispose of his minders I'm taking him to a little place a few miles up the road.' Conor stared at him dumbfounded. 'And that's where I'm going to kill him…it's important to me but you don't need to know why. I'll leave the bike there, hidden, and you can drop me back at the house. 'When it's done, I'll burn my gear and head back here.'

Conor nodded slowly. Jamie had it all worked out. 'You're sure this is the way you want to do it?'

'I'm sure.'

Conor filled their glasses again and leaned back in his chair.

*

The night of Monday thirteenth November was cold and moonless with heavy cloud filling the sky. Jamie hid the Triumph about half a mile from Carr Wood and made his way back to the main road where Conor waited in the Ford. They had gone over Jamie's plan time and time again and Conor was *almost* confident that Jamie could see this thing through successfully.

Conor dropped Jamie at the end of the access road leading to the gates of the Kelman house. Jamie disappeared into the rhododendrons at the side of the road and Conor was impressed by his apparently natural ability when it came to camouflage. Had he not known Jamie was there he would never have spotted him, and Conor Whelan was a professional. Add to those qualities Jamie's skill with a gun and you had a formidable young man, he thought to himself. But all these talents would come to nothing if he couldn't pull the trigger. That was Conor's only doubt, but he suspected that the ability to do that was in Jamie's arsenal as well.

As Conor drove off in a cloud of exhaust smoke Jamie found a spot near the edge of the driveway, well hidden by tangled, overgrown rhododendron bushes, and settled down to wait. From the surveillance of Kelman over the last few days Jamie didn't expect him to arrive home before 11pm and it could be as late as one o'clock in the morning. It was now 10.42pm and growing colder but beneath the navy dry suit, the black overalls and the black ski mask, he was warm enough…for now.

As the time passed 11.30pm he began to feel the effects of the cold as the temperature dropped sharply. His hands, covered only by the thin, black cotton gloves, were numb and his fingers were stiff. He flexed them, trying to get the blood flowing again, and stamped his feet on the cold, hard ground. It was a quiet and the moonless night and that was perfect for what he was about to do. In the time he had been hidden there only one vehicle had passed on the main road, a lorry heading into Derby. In the distance a dog barked and an owl hooted somewhere nearby, but otherwise there was wall to wall silence.

Suddenly, the quiet was broken by the faint sound of a distant car engine, growing louder with every passing second, and then headlights swept around the bend in the main road and illuminated the verges and the shrubs. The car slowed and then swung into the driveway, coming to a halt in front of the big, double wrought iron gates. Jamie could hear music and laughter from the interior over the noise of the idling engine and a surge of adrenalin coursed through him. He was no more than three yards from the car.

He waited. There were three men in the car; Max Kelman was driving and he recognised the bulk of Tony Abrahams in the front passenger seat. The third man, made from the same mould as Abrahams, sat in the back. Jamie's next move would be determined by whichever of the men got out to open the gates. The only thing he was sure of was that it wouldn't be Kelman. The back passenger door opened and the noise from inside increased. Jamie emerged from his hiding place and drifted, wraith like, behind the vehicle, the Walther now held loosely in his right hand. The unknown man was heaving his heavy frame out of the car, cursing as the cold night air hit him. There was laughter from inside that Jamie recognised as coming from Abrahams.

The man was half in and half out of the car when Jamie struck. There were two quiet coughs from the Walther and the man's body was thrown back into the car, spraying the men in the front with blood, fine particles of bone, hair and brain tissue. He crumpled onto the bench seat like a broken puppet. Abrahams and Kelman turned as one, cursing loudly at their companion, unaware of the fate that had befallen him. Jamie followed the man's body into the car, moving quickly, the Walther centring on Abraham's forehead then swinging down in the direction of his heart. Abraham's mouth opened in shock and his hand scrabbled beneath his jacket for his weapon. The heavy butt of the Walther caught him sharply on the temple and he went out like a light.

In one fluid movement Jamie swung round and pressed the still warm silencer of the Walther against Kelman's forehead. Even in the bleak interior light Jamie could see the blood drain from the gangster's face. 'Reverse back to the main road,' Jamie ordered harshly, in a practiced Irish accent, and pulled the door closed behind him. 'Then head for Brailsford…nice and easy if ye don't want to end up like him,' he finished, nodding at the crumpled body of the dead man lying contorted beside him on the back seat.

Kelman, panicking, crunched the gears of the big car into reverse, causing it to jolt backwards and stalling the engine. Jamie lashed out, bringing the barrel of the gun down across the side of Kelman's face, ripping the flesh at his cheekbone and making him cry out in pain.

'Easy, I said,' Jamie hissed. 'If ye do that again yer brain will be decorating the dashboard and even yer own Mammy won't recognise ye,' he said coldly.

Kelman re-started the engine and manoeuvered the car carefully back out onto the main road then swung its nose in the direction of Brailsford. 'Where are we going?' His voice was shaking and higher pitched now and he stole a nervous glance at Jamie in the rearview mirror. What he saw there only served to heighten his fear. The figure behind him was dressed from head to toe in black and all Kelman could see of him was a slit of white skin and two dark, burning, hate filled eyes. *Who the fuck are you,* he thought, his fear increasing?

'Shut up and drive where I tell ye,' Jamie replied, 'Ye'll find out soon enough.' The evil laugh which accompanied his words turned Kelman's bones to jelly.

'If it's money you want I can get it,' Kelman persisted.

The tip of the silencer pressed hard against the base of his skull. 'I told ye to shut up,' Jamie warned. 'Open yer mouth again and I'll take one of yer ears off…and ye'll look like Van Gogh.' Jamie laughed frostily and Kelman lapsed into silence.

He drove along the deserted roads, his mind racing, trying to identify who could be behind this. Clearly, the job had been well planned and the man behind the mask was ruthless. *Whoever it is they don't give a shit about reputations*, he thought bitterly. But what was the Irish connection and why only one man? The questions kept tumbling into his brain but not the answers. He began to recognise landmarks along the road; isolated houses, country lanes. He'd brought people out this way before because it was out of the way, remote, and he suddenly realised that this was his captor's reasoning as well.

'We're going to Carr Wood,' Jamie told him, breaking into his thoughts. 'Ye've been there before, so ye won't get lost,' he added malevolently.

The words struck fear into Kelman. How much did these people know about him? He had kept his visits to Carr Wood from everyone…other than his victims and a couple of his men, he thought grimly, but they were all scared shitless and wouldn't open their mouths. How long had these people been watching him and how much did they know? More to the point, what did they want? The left turn which would take them onto the minor road leading to Carr Wood was approaching fast. He stole another look in the mirror at his antagonist who was sitting, relaxed, behind him, the Walther pointing unwaveringly at his head.

Jamie caught his fleeting glance in the mirror and smiled. He felt completely calm and totally in control. His earlier doubts about his ability to carry this out had evaporated the minute Kelman's car had pulled up at the gates. Killing the guy in the back seat wouldn't cause him any sleepless nights. What to do with Abrahams was another matter. He could have killed him back at the gates but something had stopped him.

Kelman had the heater on full blast and the car was hot, making the already nauseating smell emanating from the corpse beside Jamie even worse and blood and other body fluids had soaked into the upholstery. The man had also evacuated his bowels so a strong stomach was essential. The turn towards Carr Wood was coming up fast and Kelman hadn't begun to slow. Jamie suspected Kelman was going to try something. He leaned forward in his seat and rammed the pistol hard into the nape of Kelman's neck. 'I wouldn't if I were you,' he said casually. 'Hollow point ammunition does a lot of damage…an' even more when it's filled with a little mercury.'

Kelman's foot pressed hard on the brake and the big car slowed. Hollow point ammunition he knew about but what the fuck mercury did he could only guess. Fear originates in the imagination and now Kelman was truly afraid. Wrenching the steering wheel round he turned the Humber onto the narrow country road and Carr Wood appeared as a dark shape off to the right on the horizon ahead of them.

'Ye know where the track leads off the road,' Jamie said quietly, upping the man's anxiety again. 'And ye know where the clearing is...just stop when ye get there.'

'What the fuck do you want, Paddy?' Kelman shouted, his nerves jangling. 'I've told you, if it's money, I can get it for you.' Jamie ignored him and watched the entrance to the track coming up on the right. The gate was open, just as it had been when he left it earlier. He looked down at his watch, the luminous hands telling him it was just past midnight...the witching hour.

'You don't expect me to take the car up there do you?' Kelman asked, stopping the car in the middle of the road just before the entrance to the narrow track.

Jamie laughed coldly. 'Why not? Ye've done it before so one more time won't hurt ye.' His voice left no room for argument but Kelman tried none the less.

'And if I don't?'

'Then I'll kill ye right here and drive the fuckin' car up there meself,' Jamie laughed cruelly and raised the Walther. 'So what's it to be?'

The car moved forward slowly and turned onto the track as Jamie laughed mockingly. The headlights picked out the rutted path and the saplings bordering it, turning everything in the cone of light from the car's headlights a bright green. Ahead of them the clearing appeared and Jamie felt a sudden surge of disgust for Kelman. How many young girls had this bastard brought out here and raped, he wondered? How many were still here?

'Stop in the middle of the clearing,' he instructed, 'an' then switch off the engine.' He leaned forward and checked on Abrahams, keeping the Walther rammed into Kelman's neck. The big man still appeared to be out cold but he could be faking it. Even if he was still unconscious it wouldn't be long before he started to come round, Jamie reasoned. 'Take off yer belt,' he ordered, turning his attention back to Kelman.

'What?'

'Yer belt, take it off an' bind this guy's wrists with it,' Jamie instructed, waving the Walther in Abrahams' direction. 'And just so ye don't get any ideas, I know he's got a gun sitting snugly below his left armpit...so if you, or he for that matter, try to get yer hands on it ye'll both be dead before ye manage it. Now, bind his wrists, nice and tight.' He watched as Kelman wrapped the leather belt around Abrahams' wrists and tightened it. 'Tighter,' Jamie said quietly as Kelman started to knot it. The man sighed and pulled the ligature tighter. Satisfied, Jamie gave him instructions on how to finish the binding then ordered him out of the car but not before slipping his left hand round Abrahams' neck and withdrawing the bound man's pistol from its holster. He hefted it in his hand, feeling its weight to assess how many bullets were in the magazine, then tucked it into his overalls pocket and stepped out of the car behind Kelman. The clouds parted and the moon appeared momentarily, bathing the clearing in a pale white light.

'Why have you brought me here?' Kelman asked, his voice wavering. 'What the fuck do you want, Paddy?' he screamed hysterically.

'I want what you took from me,' Jamie replied, dropping the Irish accent. It didn't register with Kelman immediately but with Jamie's next sentence light began to dawn. 'An' I'm going to do to you what you thought you'd done to me.'

'Just who the fuck are you?' Kelman shouted, his voice shrill.

In one quick movement Jamie pulled the ski mask from his head and exposed his face to Kelman's stupefied eyes just before the clouds engulfed the moon again. 'It's you!' Kelman exclaimed in disbelief. 'It can't be…you're fuckin' dead,' he wailed. Jamie stared at him, a frosty smile playing around his mouth and eyes, and watched fear contort the gangster's face. Max Kelman now knew with certainty that he wouldn't be leaving Carr Wood alive unless he could get the better of his nemesis.

Jamie stood back from the car, the pistol held unwaveringly in his hand. 'No, you *thought* I was dead, but the guys you paid got the wrong man. I'm not goin' to make the same mistake.' He anticipated that Kelman himself might be armed so he kept the Walther aimed, unwaveringly, at the gangster's heart. This was the end game, the sole reason for his being here, with this scumbag, in this place, he reminded himself.

'There's cash in the boot,' Kelman shouted. 'Lots of cash…take it…I'll forget this ever happened.'

Jamie laughed coldly. 'Aye, and pigs might fly,' he retorted. 'I don't want your money, Kelman. You took someone from me and now I'm going to take her back. It's as simple as that.'

Kelman sagged. 'You can have the bitch, but killing me isn't going to end this,' he retorted. 'My old man will hunt you down.'

Jamie smiled, unperturbed by the threat. Kelman was clutching at straws and they both knew it. 'I don't think so,' he laughed, 'he'll be too busy watchin' his back and wonderin' who took you out.' He let Kelman digest that for a moment. 'Do you honestly think your old man will be able to finger me for this?' he continued, laughing again. 'If you do, you're a bigger prick than I took you for.'

'Just take the cash and disappear…take the girl with you,' Kelman pleaded.

Jamie shook his head slowly. Suddenly, the moon was back, edging out from behind the clouds and lighting up the clearing once more with its deathly pale glow. At last, Kelman was able to see Jamie's pitiless expression for the first time. Looking into Jamie's eyes was like looking into the Gates of Hell and for the first time in his worthless life Max Kelman knew true fear. His only chance of survival lay in the boot of the car. If he could persuade this Scotch bastard to let him open the boot for the money he might, just might, still have a chance.

'There's a fortune in the boot, Jock,' the gangster repeated, trying to entice Jamie with thoughts of riches. 'There's cash…and drugs. Let me show you,' he said, starting to walk hesitantly towards the back of the car and waiting for the crack of the pistol which would signal the end of his life. Not that he would hear it, he realised, because he would be dead before the sound came to him. But nothing happened. There was no shot. Gaining confidence, he kept walking, watching Jamie out of the corner of his eye. The Jock had fallen for it, he was sure, and he clutched at this glimmer of hope. He stopped behind the car, turning his back towards Jamie to hide his movements, and pressed the boot release button. There was a click, loud in the silence of the wood, as the boot lid sprung open and Kelman's heart soared. The stupid bastard had let him open the boot! He lifted the lid fully and slowly bent forward into the now gaping cavity. The sawn off shotgun was there, within easy reach, as was the Browning automatic pistol, both of them loaded. His fingers curled round the stock of the shotgun and his heart began to race.

'It's all here,' he called back loudly, trying to disguise the tell-tale click as he cocked the weapon. He had made it. The forefinger of his right hand curled round the triggers of both barrels and he started to swing round quickly.

'Don't even think about it,' Jamie said icily and Kelman froze, the sawn off shotgun still in his hands. 'You'll be dead before you can pull the trigger.'

Kelman dropped the shotgun and lifted his hands in the air, resigned to what was about to happen. All he had left to hurt Jamie Raeburn were words. 'She brought you here, didn't she,' he said, things now clear in his mind. 'Told you I raped her, did she? Is that it?' He turned fully round to see Jamie looking impassively at him. 'She's a liar,' he continued. 'She was just trying to cover her guilt. I didn't rape her…she wanted it; she fucking *enjoyed* it. We came back here a couple of weeks ago, just after you scurried off to Scotland, and we did it again for old times' sake.' He smiled cruelly, trying to unsettle Jamie in the vain hope of giving himself an opening. 'You're here under false pretences, Jock. She's been telling you porkies.'

The first bullet hit his right arm at the elbow, tearing away most of the joint. There was no pain at first, just numbing shock, and he looked at Jamie with surprise and shock which turned quickly to undisguised hatred. He looked up into Jamie's eyes and saw only cold determination and his lips were drawn back in a feral smile, wolf like. Kelman looked down at his arm; the forearm below the elbow was now connected to his upper arm by torn tendons, shattered bone and ripped flesh. Blood pumped from his severed arteries. The pain started and he began to scream.

'You can scream as loud as you like, no one can hear you,' Jamie said viciously. 'Remember those words?' Kelman stared at him, uncomprehendingly. 'Let me help you,' Jamie continued. 'That's what you told Lucie before you raped her here, you sadistic bastard.'

'It wasn't rape. She enjoyed it, I told you,' Kelman repeated, screaming as he finished.

'You raped her,' Jamie retorted. 'I know it and you know it…and if you were any sort of man you'd admit it, but you're not a man, you're just a fuckin' animal.' He raised the Walther again.

'My old man will hunt you down and rip your fucking heart out. You've got one last chance, get me to a hospital,' Kelman threatened, trying to keep the hysteria out of his voice, but all the while he sensed that the attempt was futile.

Jamie smiled and shook his head slowly as Kelman sagged against the edge of the boot, his life ebbing away. 'You don't need a hospital, you fucker, you need a priest' he said quietly, his finger tightening on the trigger of the Walther. 'An' as for your old man, he won't need to hunt me down because he's next.' He let Kelman absorb that, giving him just long enough for the import of it to register, before squeezing the trigger. The soft coughing sound came again and the bullet ripped into Kelman's abdomen, spreading on impact, releasing the mercury which tore through his stomach wall and ripped the other organs around it before exiting from his body through a wound the size of a clenched fist. Kelman was thrown backwards into the boot, his shrill scream cut off. His torso filled the boot cavity and his legs dangled loosely over the rim. Jamie walked slowly towards him. Amazingly, he found that Kelman was still alive…clinging to life by a thread.

Looking down on him, completely devoid of any emotion, Jamie saw resignation in the gangster's eyes. 'They say confession is good for the soul,' Jamie said with a smile. 'You've got a few seconds left to do that before you to bleed to death.'

'No-o,' Kelman wailed as pain racked him, the single word developing into a high pitched, piercing scream. It was an uncontrolled, un-natural sound, like a wild animal in pain rather than a man. Jamie's final 9mm bullet entered his head between his eyes and tore off the back of his skull on the way out, spraying bone, blood and cranial fluids around the interior of the car's boot.

Jamie stood still, drained of all emotion, the Walther hanging loosely in his hand. He felt nothing; no elation, no guilt, no shame. He had done what he had set out to do. Taking his time, he moved Kelman's inert body and examined what lay beneath. The still cocked shotgun lay below the gangster with the man's blood all over it. A Browning automatic lay beside it, the barrel and handgrip just protruding from beneath a zipped leather holdall.

Jamie pulled the bag from beneath Kelman's body and placed it on the ground before unzipping it. Inside, just as Kelman had said, there were bundles of banknotes; great wads of various denominations all held together with rubber bands. He had no idea how much money was there but clearly, judging by the number of bundles, there were hundreds of pounds, if not thousands. He straightened, leaving the bag on the ground, and then leaned back into the boot and removed the Browning which he slipped into his pocket beside Abrahams' gun. Kelman had no need of money or a gun where he was going, he smiled grimly.

There were more bags stacked at the back of the boot; some were filled with what Jamie was sure were blocks of marijuana and others with a brown powdery substance. "Brown sugar", he thought to himself; heroin. He had no need for the drugs and they would be good for the police to find when they eventually got here. The link back to Kelman senior would be established…two birds with one stone, he smiled grimly. But by the time they got to the old man he would be dead too.

Jamie stepped back and lifted Kelman's legs up, stuffing them into the boot and closing it with a thud. *Almost finished*, he told himself. He walked to the front of the car and saw Abrahams watching him from behind hooded eyes. Jamie opened the door and shook his head slowly. 'What the fuck am I goin' to do with you?' he said, more to himself than Abrahams. 'It's a pity you came round…I could have been gone. But something tells me you knew it was me from the outset.' Tony Abrahams' answering smile told him he was correct. 'Well, back to my dilemma…what am I goin' to do with you?'

Tony Abrahams remained silent. What will be, will be, he told himself.

'You tried to warn me when you took me back into Derby a few weeks ago…why?' Jamie asked.

Abrahams shrugged. 'I knew Max would try to have you topped…and I don't like the bastard,' Abrahams laughed coldly. 'I had a feeling you'd come back.'

Jamie laughed. 'If I leave you here the police will have you for the drugs and there won't be any incentive for you to tell them it was an Irish gang that did this, will there?' Again, Abrahams held his tongue. 'If I let you go you can deny having been with Kelman tonight…and you can walk away. If the cops come for me then I'll have to assume that you pointed them in my direction,' Jamie said and paused for a heartbeat. 'And then I'll have to come for you. You understand what I'm saying?'

'I won't talk.'

'No, I know you won't Tony,' Jamie responded softly, using his name for the first time and drawing him into the conspiracy. 'Now here's what you're goin' to do. I'm goin' to untie you and then I'm leavin'. You wait for half an hour and then you get out of here. Leave the drugs in the boot with Kelman…he's not a pretty sight anyway. Now, I want some info on the house. First, where is old man Kelman's bedroom? Secondly, where is Lucie Kent bein' held and, one final thing; what's the code for the gate at Cranston Hall?'

Tony Abrahams looked up at him in shock. 'You're joking, aren't you?' he laughed abruptly but Jamie detected a hint of fear behind it.

'Do I look like someone who jokes about this sort of thing Tony?' he fired back, his face expressionless.

'You're crazy! Why risk it? If you get caught the old man will know I gave you the gate code and I'll be a dead man.'

Jamie shook his head. 'It's a hard choice, Tony, I agree, but I'm sure ye can come up with a good story…tell him I knocked you out and dumped you on the way here. That way, the only person who could have given me the code would be Max, wouldn't it? And *he* can't deny it.' He paused again. 'I want that code Tony.'

'6442…6th April 1942, Max's date of birth,' Abrahams sighed, and then laughed wryly. 'The old man's bedroom is on the first floor, to the left at the top of the stair, and the girl is kept up on the third floor…with the others.'

'Others?' Jamie asked, intrigued.

'Yeah, others…an' that's why I don't like Max…he branched into providing girls for the London Sex Trade. Young kids…he picks them up, locks them up and sells them on. I don't like that. Call me old fashioned if you like.'

'You've got a conscience?' Jamie laughed disbelievingly.

'Laugh if you like…I tried to warn *you*, didn't I?' Jamie nodded. 'Don't get caught,' Abrahams said quietly.

Jamie patted him lightly on the cheek and started to undo the belt around the man's wrists. 'I won't. Now turn out your pockets,' he said as he undid the final strap binding him.

Abrahams didn't question the instruction and immediately started to bring things out of his pockets. As Jamie suspected, amongst other things, Abrahams was carrying a spare magazine for his automatic. 'I take it yer friend in the back has a spare too?' Jamie smiled expectantly.

'Yes, in his inside jacket pocket.'

Jamie opened the back passenger door and rummaged in the dead man's jacket, finding the clip quickly. He slipped it into his overalls beside the Beretta and pulled out Abrahams' pistol. Expertly, he ejected the magazine from the gun and removed the bullet in the chamber then tossed the weapon to Abrahams who caught it clumsily. 'You might need it in the future,' he laughed. 'Half an hour…and if anyone is waitin' for me at Cranston Hall you'd better have bullets in that before I come back for you.'

'No one will be waiting for you.'

'Good…I'm glad we understand each other. Nothing personal, Tony, but I hope I don't meet you again.'

'Mutual, I'm sure,' Abrahams said with a rueful grin and settled down to wait.

Jamie pulled the ski mask from his pocket and slipped it over his head. He nodded once to Abrahams and drifted away into the trees, disappearing quickly from sight. About ten minutes later Tony Abrahams heard the distant sound of a motorbike engine starting and then the noise faded as the machine headed off in the direction of Derby. Tony Abrahams was glad he wasn't at Cranston Hall tonight and even happier that he had tried to warn the Scotsman a few weeks back. That, he realised, had probably just saved his life.

*

Jamie rode steadily to Cranston Hall. He now had the code for the gate and was confident that even if the opening the gate set off some form of alarm in the house it would probably be assumed that it was Max returning. By the time the occupants worked out that it wasn't Max, he would be inside. His only worry, raised earlier in the evening by Conor, was dogs. When they had surveyed the gates the night before there had been no evidence of dogs in the grounds but that didn't mean there weren't any in the house itself. It was a chance he had to take.

He left the bike in the copse where he had left it the night before and made his way on foot to the gate. In the darkness he was virtually invisible and he made good time. It was 00.40 when he approached the gate and punched in the numbers. The electric hum started and the gate began to swing inwards. Jamie didn't wait. He squeezed through the gap as soon as it was wide enough and started to run up the long driveway towards the house. He was now in unknown territory although he had passed along the driveway before when had been brought to Kelman following Lucie's abduction. He hadn't paid too much attention to the surroundings at the time and regretted it now. But at least he had a clear recollection of the interior of the building. That would help.

He pounded along, pumping his legs as fast as he could to reach the house before suspicions were raised. He left the tree fringed part of the road and entered a flat area laid to lawn with flower beds arranged in ornamental sets, all now bare and empty. About twenty yards ahead stone steps led up to the main door. Taking the steps two at a time he came to a halt outside. A post lantern cast a soft glow over the entrance but there was no sign of life. He removed the keys he had taken from Kelman from his pocket. There were two keyholes, one a Yale and the other a mortise lock, but there were five keys on the key ring. He kicked himself mentally, berating himself for not asking Tony Abrahams which keys fitted which locks. Too late now, he cursed, so he would have to trust in fate.

There were three Yale type keys on the ring and he selected one. Gently, he tried to insert it into the lock but it was clear from the outset that it didn't fit. He chose another and repeated the operation. This time the key slid all the way in. He turned it and felt the lock snap open. Pushing gently he sighed with relief as the door swung silently inwards. There was no need to fiddle with the mortise. He waited silently on the doorstep, listening intently. There was no movement in the hall but a radio was playing quietly at the back of the house. He stepped into the brightly lit hall and closed the door. Ahead of him the main stairway, solid Italian marble, climbed majestically up to the first floor landing which stretched out on both sides. At each end of the landing another stairway curved upwards to the second floor. A crystal chandelier hung from the centre of the high ceiling, suspended above the stairwell. In any other circumstances he might have stopped to admire the surroundings but tonight he had other things on his mind. The interior of the hallway was just as he remembered it. On his earlier visit a man had appeared from a door in the far wall to the right hand side of the main stair and had taken him to a room off to the left where Max Kelman had been waiting.

The door to the right was a good starting point. It was late and he imagined Kelman Senior would be in bed but the guards on duty, if there were any, would be somewhere beyond that door. He walked quietly across the hall, the Walther held purposefully in his right hand. The house was still silent apart from the radio which he had now determined was coming from behind the door he was approaching.

At the door he paused and changed magazines. Five bullets used meant one bullet left so better to change now. That done, he turned the handle slowly and pushed the door open. The music was immediately louder and he smiled to himself. The noise would cover his entrance. Stepping into the room he took everything in with one searching look. There were two men, both seated at a table in the centre of the room and both in shirtsleeves, and shoulder holsters with pistols were fitted tightly below their left armpits. One had his back to the door, and to Jamie, and the other appeared to be asleep, his head resting on his arms on the table top. A coffee pot and two cups sat before them and the music was coming from a radio sitting on a wooden sideboard to the left of the door and within easy reach of Jamie's hand. He smiled coldly and slowly turned up the volume on the radio with his left hand, the Walther held steadily in his right. The guard with his back to the door turned slowly, a look of puzzlement on his face changing quickly to one of terror when he spied Jamie's black clad figure. He reacted as Jamie expected, reaching for his weapon and the Walther spat death. Two of the mercury filled hollow point bullets ripped into his body at point blank range, killing him instantly. He crashed back against the table, spilling the coffee pot and the cups and blood and coffee spread over the table top. The second guard, awakened by the commotion, was still half asleep when a bullet tore through his chest and sent him tumbling backwards. His chair toppled over with a loud crash.

Stealth was no longer possible, Jamie realised, the noise of those two killings would have awakened the rest of the household. There were voices from the floor above and the sound of running feet moving along the landing. Jamie slipped back through the door and into the hallway, pressing himself close to the stairwell. He counted the number of bullets used. That left three more bullets in this magazine. He felt for the other full magazines in his pocket and felt their bulk press reassuringly against his hand.

There were footsteps on the stair now and a voice was calling out names. Jamie stepped out from the wall, immediately visible to the man on the stairway, and stopped him in his tracks. A stupefied expression spread across his face and then he started to raise his weapon. But his reactions were slow...far too slow. The silenced Walther coughed once again and the bullet caught the man in the left shoulder, spinning him around with the impact. He looked down at the wound disbelievingly, as if the impossible had happened, then swung round to face Jamie. He was a young man, not much older than Jamie himself, his fair hair slicked back from his brow with Brylcreem and his eyes were narrow slits in a pock marked face. He was wearing a waistcoat and an open necked shirt above light grey slacks and the gun in his hand looked too big for him to handle. Jamie didn't wait to find out if the gun was too big or not. The Walther jerked in his hand again and the man went down, thrown backwards onto the stairs, and then slid down the light coloured Italian marble on his back all the way to the bottom, two smears of blood tracing his route.

The sound of a gunshot reverberated round the hall and Jamie felt a searing heat tear across his left arm. He spun quickly; searching for his new assailant he found him crouched behind the balustrade on the first floor. He raised the Walther and fired, the bullet this time crashing into the wooden balustrade and throwing sharp splinters across the landing. The man cried out and stood up, his face covered in blood, blinded by the flying fragments of wood. Jamie fired again and watched as he staggered across the landing and flipped over the balustrade, his body crashing to the floor a few feet from Jamie. Magazine empty, Jamie calculated coldly.

There was silence now other than the radio in the room behind him playing the silky tones of the "Ink Spots" crooning out that it was a lovely way to spend an evening and he laughed silently at the irony of it. Nothing was moving. A minute passed, then two, and Jamie stayed where he was, stock still, his back once more against the stairwell. How many more men could there be in the house, he wondered?

Suddenly, the stillness was broken by a man's voice, an older man, unused to being in this situation, with a voice that carried authority. 'Who are you and what do you want?' the man demanded.

'I want what Max Kelman stole from me,' Jamie shouted back, ejecting the spent magazine from the Walther and inserting a new one. The sound carried clearly even above the music. It was a night for appropriate music, Jamie thought absently as The Mamas and Papas told everyone listening that you can't trust Mondays. How true, he reflected.

'What the fuck are you talking about?' the man retorted angrily. 'Whatever it is you think was stolen you can take it up with Max. He'll be here soon…and then you'll be fucked, whoever you are. Two of us up here pinning you down and three coming through the door…you're a walking corpse.' The voice carried all the arrogance that Jamie expected from Kelman Senior. 'You think you can come into my house and get away with this, think again.'

Jamie laughed coldly. It was time to disabuse the old man of his notions. 'I've already taken it up with your boy,' he said coldly. 'And he won't be coming home…tonight or any other night, an' neither will the goons who were with him.'

There was another silence. Kelman Senior was weighing up his options. Footsteps scurried along the landing above Jamie and he guessed that someone was trying to position him or herself above him. If so, they would need to expose themselves above the balustrade to get a clear shot. Jamie waited, his eyes scanning the line of the landing. Suddenly, a head appeared, then shoulders. An arm swung down now, extended straight out with an automatic clutched tightly in the hand as the gunman searched for Jamie. Calmly, Jamie squeezed the trigger of the Walther and the gunman's head disappeared. The gun fell from his lifeless fingers and crashed to the marble floor with a loud bang.

'How many more men have you got in this doss house?' Jamie called out, needling the older man.

'Enough to take you,' Kelman Senior called back defiantly.

Jamie laughed again. 'I doubt it. I've already taken out four and add to that the two with Max.'

'You're a dead man,' Kelman Senior hissed.

Jamie's laugh in response had no humour in it. Rather it was cold and unequivocal. 'In case you've missed it, old man,' he rejoined. 'I'm holding an automatic and I know how to use it.' He paused, letting the older man stew a little. Nothing else was moving on the first landing but voices, female voices, were calling anxiously to one another on the floor above. Jamie realised that time was running out. He doubted that anyone in the house would even consider calling the police but he couldn't stay here forever. 'Get Lucie Kent and send her down here,' he shouted up to Kelman Senior. 'And you might just get out of this alive.'

There was a moment's hesitation before the older man responded. 'That's easier said than done,' he came back with an audible sigh. 'She's not here.'

Jamie laughed again. 'Don't lie to me, old man. Max told me she was here…as well as giving me all the information I needed to get in, so get her!' he shouted angrily.

There was silence now. No one and nothing moved and Jamie suddenly had a bad feeling.

'The girl's dead,' Cyril Kelman said, his voice barely audible.

'Liar!' Jamie screamed and threw himself forward onto the floor to give him a clear view and field of fire to the first and second floors. Kelman Senior was taken by surprise by the move and stood, immobile, at the top of the sweeping staircase. Jamie's gun arm was pointing directly at him and the man was shrewd enough to realise that any attempt to bring his own pistol to bear would be futile. 'Sit on the stair,' Jamie ordered.

Kelman Senior glared at him, his face turning purple with rage and the veins in his neck standing out as he fought to control himself. He remained standing, defying Jamie and challenging him.

The impasse was broken by the appearance of a woman at the top of the stair on the second floor. She was holding onto the bannister with one hand and her other hand was across her mouth, covering her shock. She would be around forty years of age, blonde hair swept back from her forehead and expensive taste in clothes. She was dressed in a silk dressing gown and filled it beautifully. She was too young to be Max Kelman's mother, Jamie guessed, but step-mother…maybe. Either that or she was Cyril Kelman's mistress, he assumed. One thing was certain, she was no pussy cat.

'Bring Lucie Kent to me,' Jamie called out to her but she stood motionless, staring down at Cyril. 'Bring her down,' he insisted.

The woman looked towards Kelman Senior who nodded his head. 'Tell him, Marissa,' the old man said with resignation.

'She's dead,' the woman said, her voice refined and steady and Jamie detected what he thought was sadness in it.

Everything was going wrong. He felt his control begin to slip. 'What the fuck have you done to her, you evil bastard?' he screamed at the older man, shaking with rage. The woman gasped, startled by his outburst, but Cyril Kelman simply stared at him from an expressionless face.

'I didn't do anything to her,' he replied, his voice strong again. 'She killed herself late this afternoon.'

Jamie stood motionless but his entire world was crashing around him. This was worse than anything he could have envisaged. From somewhere deep inside the understanding of what had happened came to him. Lucie had thought he was dead and had taken her life to join him. Rage took him over. He hated Kelman and everything about him and the old man standing there, unmoved by it all, was the epitome of that hate. The Walther kicked in his hand, once, a pause, and then twice more, the second and third shots coming almost as one. All control gone, he emptied the magazine into the already dead Kelman. The dull click on the empty chamber brought him back from the edge. He heard the woman scream and saw her fall to the landing and lie still.

Cyril Kelman had died where he stood. Jamie's first shot had caught him on the right forearm and he had been spun round by the impact; the spin was the death of him. Had he remained as he was, the second shot would have passed through his right shoulder, disabling him further, but now it entered the left side of his chest, bursting open on impact and tearing through his heart. The third bullet took him below the chin and sent him crashing against the pale lilac wall behind him before falling forward at the edge of the stairway. A broad swathe of bright red smeared the wall, set against a background spray of red spots of all sizes, like an expensive work of modern art. His torso lay precariously over the edge of the top stair and eventually his weight, and gravity, pulled him over. His body began to slide; gathering momentum as it careered downwards, striking the marble floor of the hall with a sickening thud. The man's head lay at a grotesque angle, his neck broken by the impact.

Jamie looked at him dispassionately. There was silence. The woman on the second landing began to stir. Jamie was suddenly conscious of pain in his left arm. He looked down at the floor and saw spots of blood gathering at his feet. He lifted his left hand and looked, almost uncomprehendingly, at the blood dripping from his fingers.

With a supreme effort he regained control. The woman on the landing had climbed unsteadily to her feet, still in shock, but soon hysteria would kick in. *You took too long to get here*, his brain screamed, *you've lost her, you've lost her*. His instinct for self-preservation took over. He had to get out, leave this place. The time to grieve would be later, not now. He backed towards the door.

With a final glance at the blonde woman he opened the door and slipped out into the night. He didn't run, just walked casually down the long drive to the gate, punched in the code and slipped through. He returned to his bike and took his change of clothes from the pannier, automatically following his original plan. He syphoned a small amount of petrol from the tank into a bottle he had brought with him for that purpose and walked further into the thicket. Satisfied he was out of sight he dug a hole in the soft pine needle strewn earth with one of the guns, stripped out of the black clothes and the U.S.Navy dry suit and dressed afresh. Working quickly now, he piled the clothes, shoes, socks and dry suit into the hole and poured the petrol over them. Standing back, he lit a match and tossed it onto the pile. It ignited with a loud whoosh and burned brightly. He stayed until every vestige of the clothes were reduced to ash and then returned to the Triumph. Surprisingly, everything remained silent. He had expected to hear the sound of sirens as police cars raced to Cranston Hall but there was nothing. He smiled grimly and kicked the starter. The Triumph came to life immediately, its roar reverberating around the little wood. Carefully, he guided it out onto the main road and rode back past Cranston Hall towards Derby and Normanton.

About a mile beyond the big Georgian house he came to a public telephone box in a small village. He stopped the bike, dismounted and stepped into the dimly lit box. If anyone had been watching they would have seen a young man making a call and chances are that they wouldn't recognise him later. But no one was watching. He picked up the handset and dialled 999.

The operator answered almost immediately. 'Emergency, which service please?' the woman's voice demanded with practiced urgency.

'Police and ambulance,' Jamie replied, his fake Ulster accent coming across clearly again. 'I've just passed a big house near Brailsford, Cranston Hall I think the sign said, and there were gunshots…a lot of them,' he said, and hung up before the operator could ask for more.

Chapter 56

Mary's Ford Anglia was parked in Byron Street, about 20 yards beyond the front door of the flat, when Jamie arrived. He parked the Triumph behind it, levering it up onto its stand with difficulty because of the wound to his left arm, and walked unsteadily to the door. As he expected, the door wasn't locked and he quickly let himself in.

The sound of the radio playing softly in the lounge came to him, the smooth voice of the night shift D.J. and then the distinctive voice of Dusty Springfield singing a sad song as he pushed open the lounge door and went in. Conor Whelan's long frame was stretched out on the settee and a bottle of Bushmills Whiskey sat on the coffee table, unopened, flanked by two large tumblers.

Conor looked up, arching his eyebrows, as Jamie entered the room and dropped the canvas bag beside the coffee table. A drip of blood splattered onto the flat surface of the table and Conor leapt to his feet, catching Jamie's swaying body and easing him onto the settee. 'What happened?'

'Flesh wound…I think,' Jamie said weakly. 'But it's over, finished…Lucie's dead.' His voice was hollow and it didn't sound like him. Tears came then, flooding from him, from a reservoir of grief overflowing from inside him, and Conor let him cry. What was there to say?

They sat there, together, Jamie seeming somehow frail now and the big American holding onto him, supporting him in every sense. Eventually, the tears abated but Jamie's face still showed the strain. He was grey; almost a deathly white, and his face was expressionless, his eyes vacant…as if staring at something or someone, and Conor feared that the traumatic events of the night had unhinged him.

With an effort, Conor finally managed to help him from his jacket and then tore away his shirt to reveal the wound. The bullet had furrowed its way across his forearm leaving a deep gouge in his flesh but it hadn't done any serious damage. Conor lowered him onto the settee and settled him there before making for his bedroom and returning with a U.S. Navy haversack from which he removed a selection of dressings and antiseptic creams. There were little glass pipettes of Morphine but Conor put these to the side. The pain Jamie was suffering wasn't physical and morphine wouldn't work…this pain could only heal with time.

'The wound isn't serious, kid,' he said softly while cleaning it gently. 'I can fix it…no need for hospitals and difficult questions. Just another war wound to add to your collection.' He laughed harshly as he said it but there was no humour in it. 'What happened?' he probed. His concern now was that, somehow, Lucie had been caught up in the carnage and killed in the action. Faced with a situation like that he doubted if *he* could cope, and Jamie would have no chance. He prayed to God that wasn't the case.

'She killed herself earlier today,' Jamie mumbled and lapsed back into silence.

Conor finished dressing Jamie's wound and studied his handiwork for a moment, then grasped the bottle of Bushmills and tore at the foil and the cork, throwing the latter angrily across the room. It wouldn't be needed again tonight anyway. He filled the glasses and held one out in front of Jamie. 'Drink this, kid,' he said softly. 'It won't make the pain go away but it'll help you to deal with it.'

Jamie took the glass and looked into it but his mind was still somewhere else. Conor settled onto the settee beside him and swallowed half a glassful of the whiskey. 'Drink it,' he repeated, taking Jamie's arm and lifting the glass to his lips.

Jamie drank. The whiskey burned its way down his throat and he could feel the heat of it warming him but for some reason he still felt cold. Not cold in the normal sense where the body shivers, a deeper cold, a cold beyond shivering, beyond feeling…glacial cold…the type that snuffs out life.

It was almost an hour, an anxious hour for Conor, before Jamie began to speak. It started with a broken sentence about Lucie, then two sentences, more coherent, and finally the story tumbled out. It was like an exorcism, Conor reflected, the evil being driven from Jamie's body but he knew it would take a while before it was exorcised from his psyche.

'How many?' Conor asked when Jamie described the action in Cranston Hall. He didn't have to explain the question; Jamie knew exactly what he meant.

'Seven,' he replied quietly, including Kelman an' one of his men before I came back to the house.

'Shit Jamie, Conor murmured quietly. 'That was a war, not an assassination.

Jamie smiled for the first time since returning to the flat earlier but still there was no warmth in it. He shook his head slowly. 'It wasn't a war Conor, it was a battle, the final battle, but it was a pyric victory…I had already lost the war.'

Conor regarded him questioningly but said nothing.

'Lucie was my Grail an' I've lost her. I was too late.'

'Are you sure she's dead?'.

Jamie's cold smile gave him his answer. 'I didn't believe the old man when he told me. I thought he was lying, trying to avoid letting her come to me…but the woman? She wasn't lying.'

'Woman?' Conor broke in, 'what woman?'

'Old man Kelman's wife, or his mistress…she appeared on the stairs behind him. I was screaming at him an' she stood there, looking down at us. Kelman saw her an' just said "tell him Marissa"…an' she did. I believed her, Conor; it was in her eyes. An' that's when I finally lost it…I don't remember shooting the old guy…but I know I did…I emptied the Walther into him.'

'And the woman? Christ Jamie, tell me you didn't kill the woman.'

'No, I didn't kill the woman…and I didn't kill Tony Abrahams either,' he added, almost as an afterthought.

'Abrahams, the guy you said tried to warn you when you left Nottingham?'

Jamie nodded in affirmation. 'That's the one. I left him in Carr Wood with a sore head…and a warnin'.'

'He knew it was you?' Conor rejoined anxiously.

'Aye, he knew it was me. He knew it was me the instant I got into the car at the gates. Don't worry, Conor, he won't talk…I gave him his life an' I gave him a way out of the mess that was about to swamp him. He won't talk.'

'I hope you're right Jamie. If you're not…' He let the implication hang there.

Jamie smiled coldly. 'I'm right. But I gave him a warnin', just in case…an' he already knew what I was capable of.'

'And what's in the bag?' Conor asked, changing tack.

'Money, lots of money,' Jamie replied disinterestedly. But what's money when I haven't got Lucie.

They finished the bottle of Bushmills and Jamie fell into a drink fuelled sleep. Conor laid him out on the settee and covered him with a quilt. The nightmare would start again when he awoke, Conor suspected, but for now he was at peace.

Morning came too soon. Conor wakened early. In truth, he had hardly slept, his mind turning over the events of the evening and the consequences for Jamie of Lucie's death. What the day would bring he dreaded to think.

He prepared breakfast and sat in the living room, sipping a strong black coffee and watching Jamie contorted on the couch. Jamie was surfacing slowly when the music of the Light Programme stopped, interrupted by the pips, and the 8 o'clock news came on the air. There were the usual introductions followed by bad news on the economy, the situation in the Middle East following the "Six Day War" and an outbreak of sectarian trouble in Northern Ireland. It was near the end of the broadcast when the newsreader moved on to the item that brought Jamie fully awake.

"*Police are investigating two multiple murders at Carr Wood and Cranston Hall in Derbyshire in the early hours of this morning, all apparently linked. A number of bodies were found in Cranston Hall following a fire there that ravaged the building, including that of Cyril Kelman, a notorious Midlands Gangster, who is believed to have died of gunshot wounds. Two more bodies, thought to be that of Max Kelman, Cyril Kelman's son, and an un-named associate, were found in Carr Wood a few miles from Cranston Hall. Police believe that there may be a link between these murders and the suicide of a young woman in Derby earlier yesterday. Police are also keen to speak to a man who called the emergency services in the early hours of this morning to report gun shots at Cranston Hall.*

Rail travel is expected to be disrupted next week when members of the train drivers union, ASLEF, stage a one day strike over pay and conditions…"

Jamie switched off the radio and turned to Conor, a perplexed look on his face.

'You didn't torch the place did you?' Conor demanded, concerned.

'No, of course I didn't,' Jamie retorted angrily. 'Accordin' to Tony Abrahams there were girls held there…on the top floor. Shit Conor, you know I wouldn't burn the place.'

Conor looked at him apologetically. 'Sorry kid, I spoke without thinking. I know you wouldn't.' You'd better get to a phone and call Julie. Find out where Lucie is.'

'But who would have done that…and why?' Jamie murmured, puzzled.

'It could have been accidental…or maybe somebody was covering their tracks. Are you sure Kelman was dead?'

Jamie smiled coldly. 'Oh, he was dead alright. Hollow point ammunition with a mercury fill doesn't just wound.'

Conor shuddered inside. He knew exactly what the bullets would do and it was highly unlikely, bordering on impossible, that the old Crime Boss was still alive. It was still a mystery to him as to how Jamie knew all about doctoring ammunition but that could wait. Right now, the priority was to find out how Lucie had died and try to discover what line the police were following. 'I think you should get to a phone and call Julie Bradley,' he suggested.

Jamie nodded and dragged himself up from the couch. His arm was stiff and painful but it was useable. He was still wearing his jeans from the night before but his shirt had been consigned to a bag of rubbish that Conor would dispose of later. He ran a hand over his face, feeling the roughness of stubble and his mouth was dry. Dehydration from too much whiskey, he realised. Pulling on a fresh shirt and tying up his shoes he made for the door.

Five minutes later he was slipping money into a public telephone in the next street. He dialled the Beeston number and sighed with relief when Julie herself answered the call. He pressed the button to connect the call and listened as the coins dropped into the coin box. His relief at hearing Julie's voice was short lived. Grief at Lucie's death radiated down the line to him as Julie spoke between bouts of sobbing but eventually, she began to talk coherently. 'Thank God you're alright,' she sobbed. 'Lucie's dead and I thought I'd lost both of you. What happened, Jamie? There was a fire. The police have been here.' She was starting to ramble again and Jamie heard Jo's voice in the background.

The two women's voices ebbed back and forth and then Jo came on the line. 'Where are you Jamie? The police are trying to contact you,' she said and the significance of her words sunk in.

If the police were trying to "contact him" and weren't "looking for him" then the chances were they hadn't linked him to the murders. But why would they be looking for him? He asked the question. 'Why do they want to contact me?'

'Because you're Lucie's husband,' Jo replied accusingly, 'and that makes you her next of kin.'

Jamie's first reaction was to apologise and he did. 'I'm sorry Jo, honestly. It was Lucie's idea to keep it a secret...she was afraid of what Kelman would do if he found out.'

'I know,' she replied softly. 'Julie told me. I just wish you had both been able to trust me...maybe things would have been different. As it is, they'll never be the same again.' She paused and a heavy silence followed. 'You didn't answer my question, where are you?'

Jamie thought about that. Julie had told her about the marriage but if Jo was asking where he was then Julie hadn't told her about Normanton and the fact that he had been there for over a week. Jo had said she wished that Lucie and he could have trusted her...could he trust her now? He had to. 'I'm in Normanton, Jo,' he said quietly.

He expected shock, a gasp of surprise, but he got neither. 'I sort of suspected you'd be close by,' she said in a whisper. 'It was you at Carr Wood and Cranston Hall, wasn't it?' His silence was enough of an answer. 'I told the police you were in Glasgow,' she continued. 'They'll be trying to contact you there. I told them that I didn't have number for you but I doubt if that will delay them long. What are you going to do?'

'I'll handle it Jo...I'll go and see them.'

'You can't do that Jamie,' she responded quickly. 'If you turn up now they'll suspect you were involved.'

'They won't if I've just arrived from Glasgow. Where have they taken Lucie?' He asked, his voice breaking for the first time.

'She's still in Derby City Hospital. They've probably still to carry out a medical examination for the Coroner and they'll then release her body to the undertakers. Do you want me to arrange things for you?' she asked gently. 'Her Dad is coming over from Germany but it really is up to you.'

He hadn't thought about that. He was her husband and it fell to him to arrange it all. He started to cry then and at that the pips interrupted the conversation. He struggled to find more money and pressed it into the slot just before the call was disconnected. 'Thanks Jo, I appreciate that. I'll talk to you later today after I've been to the police. If they contact you again tell them I called and I'm on my way down here. Will you do that?'

'Yes, I'll do that. Just be careful.'

'I will be,' he said and cut the connection. He stood there for a moment, clenching and unclenching his fists. *Get a grip*, he told himself angrily. He looked down at his watch. It was just coming up for 08.30 and his mother wouldn't have left home yet. He had to talk to her. Fishing more coins from his pocket he dialled the number. The phone rang a few times before an irritated Mary Raeburn picked up. 'Mum, it's me,' Jamie said quickly before his mother could start. Her voice brightened and Jamie surmised that the police hadn't been in touch. 'Listen Mum, I need you to do somethin' for me...an' you need to tell Dad too. You have to trust me.'

'What's happened?' his mother asked immediately.

'A lot,' he answered honestly but without the detail. 'The police will call asking for me. Something has happened to Lucie an' they want to talk to me.'

'Why? Do they think you've done something to her?'

Jamie smiled grimly at that. His mother was a gem. She didn't ask him if he had done something, she asked if the police *thought* he'd done something. 'No Mum, it isn't that, please trust me. They'll tell you that there's been an accident an' Lucie's dead an' that I need to get there.'

There was a loud gasp as the import of what he had said sunk in. 'Dead? Oh God...why Jamie, why do you need to get there?' she fired back at him, suspicion forming in her mind.

'Because Lucie an' I were married,' he replied simply. There was a second gasp. 'I'll explain everything to you later but not now, I don't have time Mum. When the police contact you tell them I left for Derby this mornin', please,' he pleaded, 'not last week.'

His mother was silent, taking everything in. She had known he was hiding something when he'd been home and now it was all coming out. But why did he need her to lie to the police? 'Alright,' she replied unhappily. 'But you've got a lot of explaining to do Jamie.'

'I know...and I will, I promise, he replied, but the truth of his situation was coming back to him again and the grief was killing him. His mother heard the sob in his voice. He had to tell her. 'Lucie killed herself,' he murmured.

'Oh my God Jamie, why? What drove her to do that?' His mother's voice broke with the shock of it.

'I think she thought *I* was dead,' he breathed quietly down the line. 'I'll know more when I talk to the police and I'll call you later tonight. Let Dad know the score...an' thanks Mum. I love you...an' I'm sorry.'

He returned quickly to the flat and relayed the news to Conor. The American listened quietly, his expression like stone. 'You think you can trust the Bradleys?' Conor asked at the end of Jamie's explanation of events.

'Yes, I'm sure of that,' he replied confidently.

'And your mother and father...you've landed them in a spot.'

'Yes, but that's parenthood, isn't it? They'll be alright...as long as I don't get caught.'

'Keep your nerve, kid. There's nothing to connect you to any of it so sort out your story and stick to it. Julie Bradley's the only weak link. She's the only one who knows what you were planning,' Conor said quietly...but he had forgotten about Tony Abrahams.

*

Jamie rode the Triumph into the parking area at Police Headquarters in Derby at ten minutes to mid-day. His movements and actions were those of a man who had just learned tragic news; he walked slowly, as though in a dream, sleepwalking, and anyone watching his arrival would see what they expected to see. It wasn't entirely an act. Throughout the morning his mind had been adjusting to the fact that he was alone; Lucie was gone from him…her smile, her laugh, the warmth of her body next to his each morning…all gone. His bloodshot eyes were circled by dark rings and he had cried, on and off, for most of the morning. Conor had left him alone. There were some things that no amount of friendship can assuage and grief is one of these. Grief, Conor knew well, was sometimes a road best travelled alone.

Jamie pushed through the swing doors and approached the desk. A bell on the counter had a sign saying "Ring for Attention" and he pressed down on it. A young woman appeared from behind a screen partition, a practiced smile of enquiry on her face. The man she saw before her, she would tell colleagues later, had been crying. He was haggard. When Jamie gave his name her attitude changed instantly and the smile became one of pity. She was young. She hadn't been hardened to the reality of life in the police yet, but that would come.

Quickly, she came round the counter to him and ushered him into the building, leaving him alone in a comfortably furnished room. It wasn't an interview room and Jamie assumed it was a room designed specifically for dealing with people in his situation…the recently bereaved. He doubted if a straight forward suicide…if there were such a thing, would warrant his being sought by the police in this way but the possible link to the Kelman murders made it inevitable, he supposed.

He was joined shortly afterwards by two men, faces grave and suitably sympathetic. They gave him their names and their ranks but Jamie was beyond caring. They thanked him for coming and gave him their condolences and Jamie smiled sadly in response. Their questions were gentle but searching, posed to him more like friendly chat than the interrogation it undoubtedly was; did he know Max Kelman? *No, not personally but I knew of him…who didn't?* Could he think of any reason why Lucie should kill herself? *No, they had been devoted to each other and they had been happy together.* Why had they decided to keep the news of their marriage from friends and family? Why had he returned to Glasgow, alone, weeks earlier? Why had he stayed in Glasgow so long…hadn't he been keen to return to his young wife? Did he know that Lucie hadn't been at work since his return to Glasgow?

He fielded all of their questions with the same forlorn tone and anguished expression and, at the end of the interview, asked them how Lucie had killed herself. He saw the look that passed between the two men and wondered who would break it to him and if the way she had chosen had been horrific. It was the older cop who dealt with it.

'I'm sorry Mr. Raeburn, I know this is all very painful for you. Your wife cut her wrists and the arteries in her thighs with a pair of scissors and she bled to death. She was a nurse so she no doubt knew how best to go about it. According to the doctor who pronounced her dead at the scene, death would have come quickly and relatively without pain.' As he said it he watched Jamie's face crumble and his tears come again.

Jamie was struggling to come to terms with all of it. There could only be one reason for her to do it and he needed to know if he was right in that. 'Did she say anything to anyone…leave a note?' he asked, his voice no louder than a whisper.

'She was in a shop…a dress shop. She asked the shop assistant for a sheet of paper and a pen to make some notes on what she was thinking of buying and it was when the shop girl was getting these for her that she took a pair of scissors from the shop counter. She took a selection of dresses into the fitting room and it was only after a lengthy period of time that the shop assistant became anxious. Apparently your wife had appeared depressed but the girl hadn't thought anything of it at the time. There was a note beside her body.' The policeman opened the file he had been carrying when he entered the room and withdrew the note. It was written in Lucie's hand writing. Jamie recognised it immediately, her delicate hand on a sheet of lined paper torn from a journal of some sort. The words jumped out at him. "You took away my only reason for living and now there is no point anymore." He felt the tears well up in his eyes again. He had been right all along. Lucie had though he was dead, killed by Kelman, and the last vestige of hope had been stripped from her. She had been coming to him. He thought of Max Kelman then, and of his father and the other men he had killed. All of them had been part of it and he had no regrets.

Chapter 57

December 4 1967 – Nottingham Road Cemetery, Derby

The cortege drove slowly and sedately along Nottingham Road, past the neat front lawns and regimented rows of suburban houses, and pulled off to the left, entering the cemetery through the arched tower of the chapel and on to the burial ground beyond. Jamie, his face drawn and his shoulders slumped, sat in the leading car with Lucie's father, her aunt and uncle and her two young cousins. He was numb. He felt that his life was over. Yes, he was still breathing, still thinking and feeling…but he was dead inside.

As he stood at the graveside watching the coffin being lowered, alone in the crowd, a vision of Lucie's face appeared before him, serene and tranquil, her lips and eyes smiling…so different from the cold lips he had kissed two weeks earlier in the morgue at Derby Central. Anger and rage filled him again, as it had done every day since then, and he clenched his fists, digging his nails into the palms of his hands until the pain brought him back to the moment. He ran over everything again in his mind. Like the rage and the anger, it filled him every day. It was difficult not to blame himself for her death; if he had been quicker getting back to her, if he hadn't left her in the first place, if, if, if…a tiny word with so much bearing on everything.

In the immediate days after Lucie's death he had drunk himself into oblivion, surfacing from his drink fuelled amnesia from time to time simply to top up again and forget. In the beginning he had been consumed with blind hatred for Max Kelman, but Max Kelman was dead and when that fact sunk in Jamie found he had no one left to hate but himself. And he had then to face his own demons…alone.

The police had spoken to him again. They had their suspicions, he knew that, but all of the evidence surrounding the killings of the Kelmans pointed to a well organised, professional, drugs related hit and Jamie Raeburn didn't fit that profile. Now he was simply a man who had lost his wife in grave circumstances. They hadn't been able to establish the link between Lucie's death and the murders at Cranston Hall and Carr Wood. Coincidence, they accepted eventually.

His mother had listened to his explanation and had cried, not for herself but for him. She and Jamie's father were here for the funeral, brought down by Conor and Mary Campbell but they, like Mary, had no idea of the secrets he bore.

The morning air was still and cool and the deep red coloured ball of winter sun had risen into the sky, following its time worn course across the heavens and warming everything in its path. Birds were singing and he tried to concentrate on the tiny winged creatures to escape the reality of what was happening around him. He listened intently, picking out three or four different calls and a wood pigeon's melancholy cooing prompted him to search the surrounding hedgerows and trees for the bird but, like happiness now, it eluded him.

He was sober today. Completely sober for the first time in almost two weeks…but for how long he would remain like that, God alone knew. It was strange, he thought, how peaceful everything was around here, how calm and serene, how *normal*, when for him normality was grief, turmoil and chaos.

Memories came flooding back to him; twelve months on a runaway rollercoaster, all of them flashing momentarily before his eyes just like at Jack's funeral and, just like at Jack's, each memory triggered another until the bogey hit the buffers on the day of Lucie's death. His head was spinning. The realisation that he would never see her again, or hold her, had sunk in but it was hard to accept. His tears fell freely and he felt a hand on his back, supporting him. Lucie's face was before him again, filling every cavity of his memory, but the serenity he had seen in her face before was now replaced by concern. Concern for whom, he wondered? For him? The man who had let her down? But he heard her voice in his mind telling him that she loved him and he smiled and closed his eyes. But when he opened them again she was gone, leaving him alone and lonely in this dark and desolate place.

The priest was saying the Benediction and Jamie felt the touch of hands on his arms. Twice in just over a month, he thought bitterly. At this rate, there would soon be no one left to love and bury. The single red rose he had been carrying now lay on top of the coffin, and with it the earth thrown in by the other mourners, but he couldn't remember dropping the rose there. The brief words on the brass plate glinted up at him and he remembered the scene a few weeks earlier at St. Kentigern's Cemetery as he stood in the rain reading Jack's coffin plate. This time was little different. "Lucie Marie Raeburn - 23 May 1949 – 13 November 1967". The headstone, which her father insisted would be erected, would say more. It would tell the world that Lucie had been the loving daughter of Lieutenant Colonel James Alexander Kent and the late Francine Lucienne Kent, and the loving wife of him, Jamie Raeburn…but it wouldn't tell why she had died, how she been taken from them…and no one outside of the small circle of close friends and relatives could ever know the truth of that. There was an empty void inside him and a deep sense of loss gnawing at his gut and filling his brain. Would he ever feel human again, he wondered?

'Come on, kid.' Conor's soft Irish-American voice broke into his solitude. 'They're waiting for you.'

Jamie looked around, finding himself standing alone at the edge of the grave, Lucie's grave. Conor stood a few feet behind him and the cars waited by the roadway about twenty yards away. Lucie's father, straight backed, erect, his face fixed in stone and showing no sign of the pain he, like Jamie, was now enduring, waited by the Bentley, holding the door open. His own father and mother were in the second Limousine, his mother watching him, concerned, and The Mason's Arms, a pub near the cemetery, was waiting. There he could share memories and reminisce with friends about Lucie's life. It was part of the closure process, someone had told him. There might be closure for them, he had thought at the time, but not for him. But now, he was holding everyone back from that.

Wiping his copious tears from his eyes with the back of his hand he stumbled from the graveside towards Conor and saw his friend reach out for him. He felt the strength of the man's arm around his shoulders and allowed himself to be guided across the grass, between the gravestones, to the waiting car. 'What next?' Jamie murmured quietly, turning his eyes heavenwards.

Conor looked at him uncertainly, a confused expression filling his handsome face as he searched for an answer. But his inability to answer Jamie's question didn't matter, it hadn't been directed at him. Only God knew the answer. God; The Almighty, The Creator…and finally, The Taker, *Only He* knew the answer. *He* knew all the answers…to all the questions, Jamie reflected grimly, but *He* keeps them to himself.

Everything came rushing back to him then; the things he had done…the good and the bad, the people he had met on the journey, everything he had learned and the love he had shared…all of it. He had changed. His "transition" had taken place, just as Father Daly had said it would, but what had he become? What was it he had said to Kate the night of their first date…in this city even the good guys have a wee bit of bad in them? But was he a good guy with a wee bit of bad in him or a bad guy with just a hint of good? The faces appeared again; Kate first. Where was *she* now, he wondered? Jack and Lucie…he knew where they were. 'What is your Great Plan, Big Man,' he asked bitterly? 'And do you have a plan for me?' He smiled but no one saw it. 'What next?' he repeated aloud, as he had done so often over the last twelve months…but there was still no answer.

Postscript

A year is a long time in anyone's life. People change; some beyond all recognition, some only superficially and some don't change at all. Jamie Raeburn changed, but given the events of the previous year, it was no more than those closest to him expected.

He struggled with life after Lucie's death and the killings of Max Kelman and the others, in what turned out to be a futile attempt to save his young wife, weighed heavily on him. Some had feared that he would go off the rails and, in the short time before Lucie's funeral, the evidence was there to suggest they may be right. He drank, and he drank, hiding himself in the bottom of a bottle like some recalcitrant genie, unwilling to listen to the advice of those who loved him and cared for him. His own self-hate and loathing were too strong then. But on the day of Lucie's interment, another transition took place. Life, he realised, brought responsibility and what he did next would impact, not just on him, but on people he loved and people who loved him. He began to rationalise his actions; he had tried to save his wife but it wasn't to be and, faced with the same circumstances in the future, he would do the same again. That part of him would never change but he began to look forward and didn't look back.

After Lucie's funeral he returned to Glasgow, but not for long. Glasgow too, he found, had changed as he had changed. He would say later that he had been searching for something there though what that something was he was never able to define. It seemed, however, that he found it.

Just before Christmas 1967 he visited the Connolly family. The pain of Jack's death was still with them but the rawness of the wound had been salved. He found that he was able to speak openly about the events that had led to Jack's death and for Jack's family it provided a reason for what had, until then, been a senseless and meaningless attack. There was no resentment at Jamie's part in it and from that he learned an important lesson. His statement that the man behind the murder was dead was accepted without the need for him to explain further though Jamie sensed that Jack's mother, more attuned to the subtlety of it, suspected that he had played some part in that.

When he left the family that day he found himself in Saracen Street and his steps followed an almost preordained path towards St. Gregory's. Christmas trees filled windows, their lights twinkling, and it was then, perhaps, that he finally accepted that his own life wasn't over and that he had a future. St. Gregory's too was bedecked in Christmas bunting to celebrate Advent and the choir was practicing for the forthcoming services when Jamie pushed his way in through the chapel doors. The draught caused some candles to dance and alerted the occupants. Father Daly, sitting alone at the front of the big church enjoying the perfectly pitched voices, turned to investigate the cause. Jamie was in shadow, as he had been that night a few months earlier, but the priest recognised him instantly. He rose from his place and came to him, his hand outstretched in welcome. They spent some hours together and drank some of Father Daly's Glenmorangie, and Jamie unburdened himself. He found it surprisingly easy and the more he spoke the less his burden seemed. Father Daly, if shocked, passed no comment on what Jamie had done or on the number of men who had met their end at his hand. The Priest knew instinctively that Jamie Raeburn was not a cold blooded psychopath. Jamie, from what they had discussed, was able to discern the difference between right and wrong and he had in him an innate sense of good, an inborn quality that ensured he would always try to do the right thing. They parted that night as friends and would remain so throughout the remainder of their days.

Returning to Beeston after Christmas 1967, Jamie started to follow the path that the Priest had envisaged for him. He visited France early in 1968, arriving unexpectedly in the small village of Cramant, which nestles in the vineyards of the Cote de Blancs to the south east of the great champagne producing town of Epernay. The Rochefauld family, Lucie's French relations, greeted him warmly and their feelings for him intensified with the news that he intended transferring Lucie's estate back to them. Lucie's death had left him as heir to an extensive estate, estimated conservatively at £350,000, but he neither wanted it nor, morally, did he think he had any right to it. In transferring it back to the Rochefauld family he cemented a lasting relationship with the family...closer than anyone else would know.

In any event, Jamie had no money problems. He still had the money he had taken from Max Kelman in Carr Wood. With the help and guidance of Conor Whelan he opened a number of different bank accounts, not all in his own name, and he used the money discretely. He also acquired a Safety Deposit Box in one of the banks, Lloyds in Nottingham, and there he kept the Walther and the ammunition he had "modified" for the killing of Kelman.

What he also did in the aftermath of the events of autumn 1967 surprised even him. Once he had accepted that life does go on and that he did have a future he decided to pursue a dream, one that had been reborn in him during his relationship with Kate Maxwell and nurtured by the love and encouragement of Lucie. Both had believed in him, and they had seen more in him than simply Jamie Raeburn the welder. They encouraged him to look beyond the immediate and had taught him that nothing in life is impossible if you truly believe in yourself.

He thought about what he *would* have done when younger if money had not been a problem for his family, but perhaps that too had been fate playing its hand, he reflected. If he had been able to follow his dream at that time then he would probably not have met either of the women who had grown to mean so much to him. But now? Now he owed it to himself and to both of them. He threw himself into study, encouraged all the while by Julie Bradley who had taken on the role of his conscience, his mentor and his friend. They grew close in the months after Lucie's death though their relationship was platonic and not carnal. There was never any prospect of that; Lucie had been too close to both for it to be a realistic prospect, but they were close and there was nothing that either of them would not do for the other, bound as they were in the events of November 1967.

Jamie returned to Glasgow and sat an entrance examination for Glasgow University in the summer of 1968, and he was successful. He was offered a place studying French and Russian and became an undergraduate in October of that year. But before that other changes had come about and these had prompted his return.

He had returned to Scotland from time to time and visited old friends. Teresa O'Brien married Gerry Carroll and Jack's little son now had a father to help bring him up, and a good father at that. Jack, sitting on his cloud and playing his harp would be pleased, Jamie thought, when he learned the news, just as he himself had been. Anne-Marie Connolly had grown up. No longer was she the little girl with pigtails and a childhood crush on Jamie Raeburn. She had a boyfriend now...actually, she had a string of boyfriends, but she still teased Jamie relentlessly when they met and there was still a spark of that childhood love alive in her.

Conor Whelan married Mary Campbell in Dunoon in July 1968 and asked Jamie to be his best man. It was a magnificent wedding with guests from Boston arriving in droves and the Dunoon hoteliers having a bonanza. Julie Bradley accompanied Jamie north, her first visit to Scotland, and she could see that the trip held bitter sweet memories for him. Jamie spent the weekend of the wedding in Mary Campbell's house, sleeping alone in the room that he and Kate had shared at the New Year celebrations more than eighteen months earlier, and he had found himself thinking of her again, more and more. *One day*, he promised himself.

Kate Maxwell reverted to her maiden name shortly after returning to Calverton at Easter 1967. Her marriage to Tom Maxwell was over long before that and Tom didn't contest the divorce action when Kate raised it. She was granted custody of Lauren though she was keen that the child should have contact with her father, Tom Maxwell, if he could overcome his addiction to alcohol. At first, the signs were good, but, after a promising start, Tom began the downward slide into his own personal hell. He disappeared in autumn 1967 and hasn't been heard from since. The baby, which Kate believed she was carrying when she left Glasgow, was born on 20th November 1967, a sturdy 8lbs and 12oz. A boy with a mop of brown hair, he was, she told everyone, the image of his father and, as he grew, that likeness grew with him, starting with his eyes. A deep, almost ebony, brown. She named him Jamie.

And what of the others? Carol Whyte moved away from Glasgow. Whether or not she was trying to find Jamie no one knew but many thought she was. She joined the Civil Service and moved to London and, by all accounts was making a career for herself in the Foreign Office.

Davie Miller, the telephone engineer from Edinburgh was still with Donna but he had given up travelling around the country installing equipment in telephone exchanges. He was now working with Donna's father selling insurance and making a success of it. He kept in touch with Jamie and still regaled people at parties with stories of his friend who could "turn a man's legs to jelly" with just one look from his eyes. Myth or fact, they invariably asked, but Davie simply smiled enigmatically.

Charlotte...Charley to her friends, and she still counted Jamie as one of those, married her airman. It wasn't a marriage made in heaven but they were making a go of it. Jamie met her by chance one day in Nottingham a few weeks before her wedding. She was with an older woman; her mother, Jamie had surmised, the resemblance between them being unmistakable. He had watched her for a while, keeping his distance as she had drifted around the shop examining the wares. When he finally approached her the change in her demeanour was as immediate as it was dramatic, a fact that wasn't missed by her mother. Charley's face lit up and she beamed happily at him, obviously more than pleased to see him again, and her loveliness shone out. This boy was dangerous, Charley's mother had quickly guessed, little knowing how accurate her assessment was. Jamie, too, read the signs and resolved to let her get on with her life as he hoped to get on with his.

The boys who had started out together in Beeston that sunny day in May 1967 were now scattered to the four winds. Michael (just call me Mick) had returned to Newcastle and lost touch. Terry Hughes, the big Scouser, was working at another Power Station in the south west near Bristol. He kept in touch religiously by letter and with the occasional visit back to the Bradley home in Beeston. Benny's "fingers and thumbs" got him into a bit of bother with an older, married lady of questionable provenance who found him "irresistible". Actually, the bother emanated more from the lady's husband rather than the lady herself. Benny, nimble as he was on his feet and hard with his punches, didn't fancy taking on a man almost a foot taller and about six stones heavier, and built, as Glaswegians would say, like a brick shithouse. He moved north, sharpish, and was now working on the oil rigs in the North Sea and living in Aberdeen. From word that filtered back to Jamie, he was working hard when he was off-shore and raising hell when he wasn't…and his fingers and thumbs were getting good use.

"Pat, Mick and The Irishman", the three men who accompanied Jamie on the safe cracking job in Belfast were never truly known to him. But, as the situation in Ulster changed for the worse and became more violent and extreme, so too did their activities. "Pat" went on to be a Brigade Commander in the Provisional I.R.A. and the other two remained with him throughout the Campaign that followed, both of them trusted lieutenants. Brendan Kelly, the man whose meeting with Conor Whelan in November 1966 inadvertently embroiled Jamie in the chain of events that followed, returned to Northern Ireland early in 1968. He had been called back to direct the Provisional I.R.A's. Security, but his career was cut short when he was arrested by British Special Branch officers in July 1968 and documents, taken from the safe breaking operation in Belfast in October 1967, were found in his possession. He would spend the next few years in Long Kesh Prison but rumours began to circulate that he had made a deal with his captors. Brendan denied it, of course, and no one will ever know the truth of it. Roisin Kelly returned to Belfast to stay with her Auntie Molly. After her brother was arrested and the rumours concerning his loyalty to "The Cause" started to do the rounds she became disillusioned. But her disillusionment led ultimately to her happiness when she met a man she fell in love with, a Protestant as it happened, and they moved to the United States, where they still live today, though Roisin returns home from time to time.

Jamie met Kate again in August 1968. It wasn't a chance meeting. Pestered by Julie Bradley to look for her he had thrown himself into the task with gusto. Using the only information he had; her married name, her maiden name and her family's home village of Calverton, he set out to find her. Using his charm he had approached the middle aged Post Mistress in the village one Saturday morning, spun his story of lost love and left a piece of paper with her giving his name, the address in Beeston and Jo Bradley's telephone number. The Post Mistress suggested he sample the delights of the local pub, The Red Lion, before returning to Beeston and a nod was as good as a wink to a blind man. Ten minutes later as he sat nursing a pint of bitter in the cool of the pub, Kate appeared, breathless and excited. She had come to him, throwing herself into his arms, and the eighteen months since they had been torn apart disappeared in a heartbeat. They talked. Jamie learned of her divorce and that she was staying with her parents. She was working in Nottingham General still doing the job she loved. Jamie, of course, already knew about Lauren but the news that Kate had borne him a son came as a bolt out of the blue. Anger had bubbled up inside him at first but Kate had cried as the story came out, clearly aware that having kept the news from him could now jeopardise their future. But Jamie's anger had quickly dissipated and he found himself filled with an overwhelming feeling of elation.

But he too had his secrets. Kate had listened quietly, saying nothing, as he told her about his marriage to Lucie and the circumstances of her death. She was less shocked by the news that Jamie had married than by the revelation that Lucie had died so young and in such circumstances. Her death raised many questions, Jamie knew that, and he wanted Kate to know everything that had happened. It was clear that they both wanted to be together so she should, after all, know the truth about the man she wanted to spend the rest of her life with. He tried, but Kate, with uncanny insight, had already seen the shadows gathering around him and stopped him. Jamie wondered at the time if she knew of Janus and of the consequences of looking back? 'I only need to know one thing,' she had said. 'Do you still love me and want me?'

'I never stopped,' he replied softly, and she knew that it was true.

They were married four weeks later. It was a small affair, attended by family and close friends only. Conor and Mary Whelan were there. Jamie returned the compliment and asked the big American to be his Best Man and Conor was delighted, and even more overjoyed that Kate and Jamie asked him and Mary to be God Parents to their young son. A small crowd gathered at the Church in Calverton to wish the happy couple good luck and traffic in the village Main Street was disrupted.

Everything was coming good at last for Jamie Raeburn. He didn't see the black Humber with the smoked glass windows or the two hard faced and suited men who watched the proceedings with interest from across the road. As Jamie stood on the steps of the Church with his arm around his bride, a visible shiver ran through him. Nerves or his sixth sense, he wondered briefly? Conor sensed the tension and looked at him uneasily, but Jamie returned his friend's worried look with a smile. 'Someone just walked over my grave,' he laughed, as the black Humber pulled away from the kerb and drove slowly out of the village.

Lightning Source UK Ltd.
Milton Keynes UK
UKOW01f2251271215

265414UK00009B/289/P